$3.00

DRAGON'S TEETH

DRAGON'S TEETH

Upton Sinclair

The Viking Press · New York

1942

In tragic times like these, an elderly author has nothing to give but words. This collection of words is dedicated to the men and women in many parts of the world who are giving their lives in the cause of freedom and human decency.

Autumn 1941

Contents

Book One:
The Morning Opes Her Golden Gates

Book Two: A Cloud That's Dragonish

Book Three:
Blow, Winds, and Crack Your Cheeks

Book Four: As on a Darkling Plain

Book Five: This Is the Way the World Ends

Book Six: Blood Hath Been Shed

BOOK ONE

The Morning
Opes Her Golden Gates

1

The Old Beginning

I

LANNY BUDD was the only occupant of a small-sized reception-room. He was seated in a well-padded armchair, and had every
reason to be comfortable, but did not appear so. He fidgeted a good
deal, and found occasions for looking at his watch; then he would
examine his fingernails, which needed no attention; he would look
for specks of lint on his tropical worsted trousers, from which he
had removed the last speck some time ago. He would look out of
the window, which gave on one of the fashionable avenues of the
city of Cannes; but he had already become familiar with the view,
and it did not change. He had a popular novel on his knee, and
every now and then would find that he could not interest himself
in the conversation of a set of smart society people.

Now and then one of several white-clad nurses would pass through
the room. Lanny had asked them so many questions that he was
ashamed to speak again. He knew that all husbands behave irration-
ally at this time; he had seen a group of them in a stage play, slightly
risqué but harmless. They all fidgeted and consulted their watches;
they all got up and walked about needlessly; they all bored the
nurses with futile questions. The nurses had stereotyped replies,
which, except for the language, were the same all over the world.
*"Oui, oui, monsieur. . . . Tout va bien. . . . Il faut laisser faire. . . .
Il faut du temps. . . . C'est la nature."*

Many times Lanny had heard that last statement in the Midi; it
was a formula which excused many things. He had heard it more
than once that afternoon, but it failed to satisfy him. He was in
rebellion against nature and her ways. He hadn't had much suf-

3

fering in his own life, and didn't want other people to suffer; he
thought that if he had been consulted he could have suggested
many improvements in the ways of this fantastic universe. The
business of having people grow old and pass off the scene, and new
ones having to be supplied! He knew persons who had carefully
trained and perfected themselves; they were beautiful to look at,
or possessed knowledge and skills, yet they had to die before long—
and, knowing that fact, must provide a new lot to take their places.

Lanny Budd belonged to the leisure classes. You could tell it by
a single glance at his smiling unlined face, his tanned skin with signs
of well-nourished blood in it, his precise little mustache, his brown hair
neatly trimmed and brushed, his suit properly tailored and freshly
pressed, his shirt and tie, shoes and socks, harmonizing in color and
of costly materials. It had been some time since he had seen any
bloodshed or experienced personal discomfort. His life had been
arranged to that end, and the same was true of his wife. But now
this damnable messy business, this long-drawn-out strain and suffering—good God, what were doctors and scientists for if they
couldn't devise something to take the place of this! It was like a vol-
canic eruption in a well-ordered and peaceful community; not much
better because you could foresee the event, going in advance to an
immaculate *hospice de la maternité* and engaging a room at so much
per week, an *accoucheur* at so much for the job.

A surgeon! A fellow with a lot of shiny steel instruments, prepared to assist nature in opening a woman up and getting a live
and kicking infant out of her! It had seemed incredible to Lanny
the first time he had heard about it, a youngster playing with the
fisherboys of this Mediterranean coast, helping them pull strange
creatures out of the sea and hearing them talk about the "facts of
life." It seemed exactly as incredible to him at this moment, when
he knew that it was going on in a room not far away, the victim his
beautiful young playmate whom he had come to love so deeply.
His too vivid imagination was occupied with the bloody details,
and he would clench his hands until the knuckles were white. His
protest against nature mounted to a clamor. He thought: "Any way

but this! Anything that's decent and sensible!" He addressed his ancient mother, asking why she hadn't stuck to the method of the egg, which seemed to work so well with birds and snakes and lizards and fishes? But these so-called "warm-blooded creatures," that had so much blood and spilled it so easily!

II

Lanny knew that Irma didn't share these feelings. Irma was a "sensible woman," not troubled with excess of imagination. She had said many times: "Don't worry. I'll be all right. It doesn't last forever." Everybody agreed that this young Juno was made for motherhood; she had ridden horseback, swum, played tennis, and had a vigorous body. She hadn't turned pale when she crossed the threshold of this hospital, or even when she heard the cries of another woman. Things always went all right with Irma Barnes, and she had told Lanny to go home and play the piano and forget her; but here he sat, and thought about the details which he had read in an encyclopedia article entitled "Obstetrics." From boyhood he had had the habit of looking up things in that dependable work; but, damn it all, the article gave an undue proportion of space to "breech presentations" and other variations from the normal, and Lanny might just as well have been in the delivery-room. He would have liked to go there, but that would have been considered an extreme variation from the normal in this land of rigid conventions.

So he sat in the little reception-room, and now and then the perspiration would start on his forehead, even though it was a cool spring day on the Riviera. He was glad that he had the room to himself; at times, when somebody came through, he would lower his eyes to his book and pretend to be absorbed. But if it was one of the nurses, he couldn't keep from stealing a glance, hoping that it was *the* nurse and *the* moment. The woman would smile; the conventions permitted her to smile at a handsome young gentleman, but did not permit her to go into obstetrical details. "*Tout va bien, monsieur. Soyez tranquille.*" In such places the wheel of life revolves on schedule; those who tend the machinery acquire a professional attitude, their phrases become standardized, and you have mass production of politeness as well as of babies.

III

Lanny Budd was summoned to the telephone. It was Pietro Corsatti, Italian-born American who represented a New York newspaper in Rome and was having a vacation on the Riviera. He had once done Lanny a favor, and now had been promised one in return. "Pete" was to have the news the moment it happened; but it refused to happen, and maybe wasn't going to happen. "I know how you feel," said the correspondent, sympathetically. "I've been through it."

"It's been four hours!" exclaimed the outraged young husband.

"It may be four more, and it may be twenty-four. Don't take it too hard. It's happened a lot of times." The well-known cynicism of the journalist.

Lanny returned to his seat, thinking about an Italian-American with a strong Brooklyn accent who had pushed his way to an important newspaper position, and had so many funny stories to tell about the *regime fascista* and its leaders, whom, oddly enough, he called "wops." One of his best stories was about how he had become the guide, philosopher, and friend of a New York "glamour girl" who had got herself engaged to a fascinating aristocrat in Rome and had then made the discovery that he was living with the ballerina of the opera and had no idea of giving her up. The American girl had broken down and wept in Pete's presence, asking him what to do, and he had told her: "Take a plane and fly straight to Lanny Budd, and ask him to marry you in spite of the fact that you are too rich!"

It is tough luck when a journalist cannot publish his best story. Pete hadn't been asked not to, but, all the same, he hadn't, so now Lanny was his friend for life, and would go out of his way to give him a break whenever he could. They talked as pals, and Lanny didn't mind telling what only a few of his friends knew, that Irma had done exactly what Pete had said, and she and Lanny had been married on the day she had found him in London. As the Brooklyn dialect had it, they had "gone right to it," and here was the result nine months later: Lanny sitting in a reception-room of an *hospice de la maternité*, awaiting the arrival of Sir Stork, the blessed event, the little bundle from heaven—he knew the phrases, because he and Irma had been in New York and had read the "tabs" and listened to "radio reporters" shooting out gossip and slang with the rapid-fire effect of a Budd machine gun.

Lanny had promised Pete a scoop; something not so difficult, because French newspapermen were not particularly active in the pursuit of the knightly stork; the story might be cabled back to Paris for the English language papers there. Lanny had hobnobbed with the correspondents so much that he could guess what Pete would send in his "cablese" and how it would appear dressed up by the re-write man in the sweet land of liberty. Doubtless Pete had already sent a "flash," and readers of that morning's newspapers were learning that Mrs. Lanny Budd, who was Irma Barnes, the glamour girl of last season, was in a private hospital in Cannes awaiting the blessed event.

The papers would supply the apposite details: that Irma was the only daughter of J. Paramount Barnes, recently deceased utilities magnate, who had left her the net sum of twenty-three million dollars; that her mother was one of the New York Vandringhams, and her uncle was Horace Vandringham, Wall Street manipulator cleaned out in the recent market collapse; that Irma's own fortune was said to have been cut in half, but she still owned a palatial estate on Long Island, to which she was expected to return. The papers would add that the expectant father was the son of Robert Budd of Budd Gunmakers Corporation of Newcastle, Connecticut; that his mother was the famous international beauty, widow of Marcel Detaze, the French painter whose work had created a sensation in New York last fall. Such details were eagerly read by a public which lived upon the doings of the rich, as the ancient Greeks had lived upon the affairs of the immortals who dwelt upon the snowy top of Mount Olympus.

IV

Lanny would have preferred that his child should be born outside the limelight, but he knew it wasn't possible; this stream of electrons, or waves, or whatever it was, would follow Irma on her travels—so long as she had the other half of her fortune. As a matter of fact the fortune wasn't really diminished, for everybody else had lost half of his or hers, so the proportions remained the same. Irma Barnes still enjoyed the status of royalty, and so did the fortunate young man whom she had chosen for her prince consort. In the days of the *ancien régime*, when a child was born to the queen of France it had been the long-established right of noblemen and ladies to satisfy themselves that it was a real heir to the throne and no fraud; no stork stories were accepted, but they witnessed with their own eyes the physical emergence of the infant dauphin. Into the chamber of Marie Antoinette they crowded in such swarms that the queen cried out that she was suffocating, and the king opened a window with his own hands. It wasn't quite that bad now with the queen of the Barnes estate, but it was a fact that the newspaper-reading and radio-listening public would have welcomed hourly bulletins as to what was going on in this *hospice de la maternité*.

But, damn it, even Lanny himself didn't know what was going on! What was the use of planning what to say to newspaper reporters about the heir or heiress apparent to the Barnes fortune, when it refused so persistently to make itself apparent, and for all the prince consort knew the surgeon might be engaged in a desperate struggle with a "cross-birth," or perhaps having to cut the infant to pieces, or perform a Caesarean section to save its life! Lanny dug his fingernails into the palms of his hands, and got up and began to pace the floor. Every time he turned toward the bell-button in the reception-room he had an impulse to press it. He was paying for service, and wasn't receiving it, and he was getting up steam to demand it. But just at that juncture a nurse came through the room, cast one of her conventional smiles upon him, and remarked: "*Soyez tranquille, monsieur. Tout va bien.*"

V

Lanny called his mother on the telephone. Beauty Budd had been through this adventure two and a half times—so she said—and spoke as one having authority. There wasn't a thing he could do, so why not come home and have something to eat, instead of worrying himself and getting in other people's way? This was the woman's job, and nobody in all creation was so superfluous as the husband. Lanny answered that he wasn't hungry, and he wasn't being allowed to bother anybody.

He went back to his seat in the reception-room, and thought about ladies. They were, as a rule, a highly individualistic lot; each on her own, and sharply aware of the faults of the others. He thought of those who made up his mother's set, and therefore had played a large part in his own life; he recalled the sly little digs he had heard them give one another, the lack of solidarity he had seen them display. They had been polite to Irma, but he was certain that behind her back, and behind his, they found it difficult to forgive her for being so favored of fortune. However, as her pregnancy had moved to its climax they had seemed to gather about her and become tender and considerate; they would have come and helped to fetch and carry, to hold her hands and pull against them in her spasms of pain, had it not been for the fact that there were professional women trained for these services.

Lanny thought about his mother, and her role in this drama, the stage entrance of another soul. Beauty had been an ideal mother-in-law so far. She had worked hard to make this marriage, for she believed in money; there was in her mind no smallest doubt of money's rightness, or of money's right to have its way. Had not her judgment been vindicated by the events of a dreadful Wall Street panic? Where would they all have been, what would have become of them, if it hadn't been for Irma's fortune? Who was there among Irma's friends who hadn't wanted help? Go ahead and pretend to be contemptuous of money if you pleased; indulge yourself in Pink talk, as Lanny did—but sooner or later it was proved that it is money which makes the mare go, and which feeds the mare, takes care of her shiny coat, and provides her with a warm and well-bedded stall.

Beauty Budd was going to become a grandmother. She pretended to be distressed at the idea; she made a *moue*, exclaiming that it would set the seal of doom upon her social career. Other handicaps you might evade by one device or another. You might fib about the number of your years, and have your face lifted, and fill your crow's-feet with skin enamel; but when you were a grandmother, when anyone could bring that charge publicly and you had to keep silent, that was the end of you as a charmer, a butterfly, a professional beauty.

But that was all mere spoofing. In reality Beauty was delighted at the idea of there being a little one to inherit the Barnes fortune and to be trained to make proper use of the prestige and power it conferred. That meant to be dignified and splendid, to be admired and courted, to be the prince or princess of that new kind of empire which the strong men of these days had created. Beauty's head was buzzing with romantic notions derived from the fairytales she had read as a child. She had brought these imaginings with her to Paris and merged them with the realities of splendid equipages, costly furs and jewels, titles and honors—and then the figure of a young Prince Charming, the son of a munitions manufacturer from her homeland. Beauty Budd's had been a Cinderella story, and it was now being carried further than the fairytales usually go. Grandma Cinderella!

VI

Lanny couldn't stand any more of this suspense, this premonition of impending calamity. He rang the bell and demanded to see the head nurse; yes, even he, the superfluous husband, had some rights in a crisis like this! The functionary made her appearance; grave, stiff with starch and authority, forbidding behind pincenez. In response to Lanny's demand she consented to depart from the established formula, that all was going well and that he should be tranquil. With professional exactitude she explained that in the female organism there are tissues which have to be stretched, passages which have to be widened—the head nurse made a gesture of the hands—and there is no way for this to be accomplished save the way of nature, the efforts of the woman in labor. The *accoucheur* would pay a visit in the course of the next hour or so, and he perhaps would be able to put monsieur's mind at rest.

Lanny was disturbed because this personage was not in attendance upon Irma now. The husband had assumed that when he agreed to the large fee requested, he was entitled to have the man sit by Irma's bedside and watch her, or at any rate be in the building, prepared for emergencies. But here the fellow had gone about other duties, or perhaps pleasures. He was an Englishman, and was probably having a round or two of golf; then he would have his shower, and his indispensable tea and conversation; after which he expected to stroll blandly in and look at Irma—and meanwhile whatever dreadful thing was happening might have gone so far as to be irremediable!

Lanny resumed his seat in the well-cushioned chair, and tried to read the popular novel, and wished he had brought something more constructive. The conversation of these fashionable characters was too much like that which was now going on in the casinos and tearooms and drawing-rooms of this playground of Europe. The financial collapse overseas hadn't sobered these people; they were still gossiping and chattering; and Lanny Budd was in rebellion against them, but didn't know what to do about it. Surely in the face of the awful thing that was happening in this *hospice*—knowing it to be their own fate through the ages—the women ought to be having some serious concern about life, and doing something to make it easier for others! They ought to be feeling for one another some of the pity which Lanny was feeling for Irma!

VII

The door to the street opened, and there entered a tall, vigorous-appearing American of thirty-five or so, having red hair and a cheerful smile: Lanny's one-time tutor and dependable friend, Jerry Pendleton from the state of Kansas, now proprietor of a tourist bureau in Cannes. Beauty had phoned to him: "Do go over there and stop his worrying." Jerry was the fellow for the job, because he had been through this himself, and had three sturdy youngsters and a cheerful little French wife as evidence that *la nature* wasn't altogether out of her wits. Jerry knew exactly how to kid his friend along and make him take it; he seated himself in the next chair and commanded: "Cheer up! This isn't the Meuse-Argonne!"

Yes, ex-Lieutenant Jerry Pendleton, who had enlisted and begun as a machine-gun expert, knew plenty about blood and suffering. Mostly he didn't talk about it; but once on a long motor ride, and again sitting out in the boat when the fish didn't happen to be biting, he had opened up and told a little of what he had seen. The worst of it was that the men who had suffered and died hadn't accomplished anything, so far as a survivor could see; France had been saved, but wasn't making much use of her victory, nor was any other nation. This battle that Irma was fighting in the other room was of a more profitable kind; she'd have a little something for her pains, and Lanny for his—so said the former doughboy, with a grin.

More than once Lanny had been glad to lean on this sturdy fellow. That dreadful time when Marcel Detaze had leaped from a stationary balloon in flames it had been Jerry who had driven Lanny and his mother up to the war zone and helped to bring the broken man home and nurse him back to life. So now when he chuckled and said: "You ain't seen nothin' yet," Lanny recognized the old doughboy spirit.

The tourist agent had troubles of his own at present. He mentioned how fast business was falling off, how many Americans hadn't come to the Riviera that season. Apparently the hard times were going to spread to Europe. Did Lanny think so? Lanny said he surely did, and told how he had argued the matter with his father. Maybe the money values which had been wiped out in Wall Street were just paper, as so many declared; but it was paper that you had been able to spend for anything you wanted, including steamship tickets and traveler's checks. Now you didn't have it, so you didn't spend it. Lanny and his wife could have named a score of people who had braved the snow and sleet of New York the past winter and were glad if they had the price of meal tickets.

Jerry said he'd been hard up more than once, and could stand it again. He'd have to let his office force go, and he and Cerise would do the work. Fortunately they had their meal tickets, for they still lived in the Pension Flavin, owned and run by the wife's mother and aunt. "You'll have to take me fishing some more and let me carry home the fish," said the ex-tutor; and Lanny replied: "Just as soon as I know Irma's all right, we'll make a date." The moment he said this his heart gave a jump. Was he ever going to know that Irma was all right? Suppose her heart was failing at this moment, and the nurses were frantically trying to restore it!

VIII

The surgeon arrived at last: a middle-aged Englishman, smooth-shaven, alert, and precise; his cheeks were rosy from a "workout" in the sunshine followed by a showerbath. He had talked with the head nurse over the telephone; everything was going excellently. Lanny could understand that a surgeon has to take his job serenely; he cannot suffer with all his patients; whatever others may do, he has to accept *la nature* and her ways. He said he would see Mrs. Budd and report.

Lanny and his friend resumed their discussion of depressions and their cause. Lanny had a head full of theories, derived from the Red and Pink papers he took. Jerry's reading was confined mostly to the *Saturday Evening Post* and the Paris edition of the New York *Tribune;* therefore he was puzzled, and couldn't figure out what had become of all the money that people had had early in October 1929, and where it had gone by the end of that month. Lanny explained the credit structure: one of those toy balloons, shining brightly in the sunshine, dancing merrily in the breeze, until someone sticks a pin into it. Jerry said: "By heck, I ought to study up on those things!"

The surgeon reappeared, as offensively cheerful as ever. Mrs.

Budd was a patient to be proud of; she was just the way a young woman ought to keep herself. The "bearing-down pains," as they were called, might continue for some little time yet. Meanwhile there was nothing to be done. Lanny was dismayed, but knew there was no use exhibiting his feelings; he too must maintain the professional manner. "I'll be within call," said the surgeon. "You might as well get it off your mind for a while." Lanny thanked him.

After the surgeon had gone, Jerry said: "When do we eat?" Lanny wanted to say that he couldn't eat, but he knew that Jerry was there for the purpose of making him change his mind. It was dinner-hour at the Pension Flavin, and Jerry recited a jingle to the effect that he knew a boarding-house not far away where they had ham and eggs three times a day. "Oh, how those boarders yell when they hear the dinner-bell!"—and so on. This was the sporting way to deal with the fact that your mother-in-law runs a medium-priced pension in the most fashionable of Riviera towns. Lanny knew also that he hadn't visited the Pendleton family for some time, and that, having won the biggest matrimonial sweepstakes, it was up to him to show that he didn't mean to "high-hat" his poor friends.

"All right," he said; "but I'll be glum company."

"The boarders know all about it," responded Jerry.

Indeed they did! Wherever the boarders came from and whatever they were, they knew about the Budd family and felt themselves members of it. For sixteen years Jerry Pendleton had been going fishing with Lanny Budd, and the boarders had eaten the fish. At the outset Jerry had been a boarder like themselves, but after he had driven the Boches out of France he had married the daughter of the pension. And then had come the time when another of the boarders had married Lanny's mother; from that time on, the boarders had all regarded themselves as Budds, and entitled to every scrap of gossip concerning the family.

IX

Driving back to the hospital, Lanny took the precaution to stop and purchase several magazines, French, English, and American.

He would equip himself for a siege, and if one subject failed to hold his attention he would try others. Arriving at the reception-room, he found that he was no longer alone; in one of the chairs sat a French gentleman, stoutish and prosperous, betraying in aspect and manner those symptoms which Lanny recognized.

The stranger's misery loved company, and he introduced himself as an *avocat* from a near-by town. It was his wife's first *accouchement*, and he was in a terrible state of fidgets and could hardly keep his seat; he wanted to bother the nurses with questions every time one entered the room. He seemed to Lanny absurdly naïve; he actually didn't know about the "bearing-down pains," that they were according to the arrangements of *la nature*, and that women didn't very often die of them. Speaking as a veteran of some ten hours, Lanny explained about the stretching of tissues, and comforted the stranger as best he could. Later on, seeing that his advice was without effect, Lanny became bored, and buried himself in the latest issue of the *New Statesman*.

He would have liked very much to inquire whether there had been any change in the status of his wife; but the egregious emotionalism of Monsieur Fouchard reminded him that the Budds were stern Anglo-Saxons and should behave accordingly. He resolutely fixed his attention upon an article dealing with the final reparations settlement of the World War, now more than eleven years in the past, and the probable effects of that settlement upon the various nations involved. This was a subject of interest to a young man who had been born in Switzerland of American parents and had lived chunks of his life in France, Germany, England, and "the States." His many friends in these countries belonged to the ruling classes and took political and economic developments as their personal affairs.

The surgeon was a long time in returning, and Lanny began once more to feel himself a defrauded client. He forgot that there are telephones, whereby an obstetrician can keep informed as to his patient while reading the latest medical journal at home or playing a game of billiards at his club. When the Englishman at last appeared, he informed the anxious husband that the time for action was approaching, and that Mrs. Budd would soon be taken to the delivery-room. After that Lanny found it impossible to interest himself in what *L'Illustration* had to report about the prospects for the spring Salons—important though this subject was to one who earned his living by buying or selling works of art on commission.

There was no use trying to be Anglo-Saxon any longer. Better give up and admit the hegemony of mother nature. Lanny put down his magazine and watched Monsieur Fouchard pacing the floor of the reception-room, and when Monsieur Fouchard sat down and lighted a cigarette, Lanny got up and did the pacing. Meanwhile they talked. The Frenchman told about his wife; she was only nineteen, her charms were extraordinary, and Monsieur Fouchard spared no details in describing them. He wanted to tell the whole story of their courtship and marriage, and was grateful to a stranger for listening.

Lanny didn't tell so much; nor was it necessary. Monsieur Fouchard had heard the surgeon call him by name, and was aware who this elegant young American must be. He had read about Irma Barnes, and began to talk as if he were an old friend of the family, indeed as if he were about to take charge of Irma's convalescence and the nursing of her infant. Lanny, who had grown up in France, knew that it wasn't worth while to take offense; much better to be human. They would set up a sort of temporary association, a League of Husbands in Labor. Others might be joining them before the night was over.

X

The *accoucheuse* of Madame Fouchard arrived, a Frenchwoman; she succeeded in persuading the husband that it would be a long time before the blessed event could take place, so that gentleman bade his fellow league-member a sentimental farewell. Lanny answered a call from his mother and reported on the situation; after pacing the floor some more, he sat down and tried to put his mind upon an account of a visit to the hanging monasteries of Greece. He had seen them as a boy, but now wouldn't have cared if all the monks had been hanged along with the monasteries. He simply couldn't believe that a normal delivery could take so long a time. He rang the bell and had a session with the night head nurse, only to find that she had learned the formulas. "*Tout va bien, monsieur. Soyez tranquille.*"

Lanny was really glad when the door opened and a lady was escorted in, obviously in that condition in which ladies enter such places. With her came a French gentleman with a dark brown silky beard; Lanny recognized him as a piano-teacher well known in Cannes. The lady was turned over to the nurse's care, and the gentleman became at once a member of Lanny's league. Inasmuch as Lanny was a pianist himself, and had a brother-in-law who was a violin virtuoso, the two might have talked a lot of shop; but no, they preferred to tell each other how long they had been married, and how old their wives were, and how they felt and how their wives felt. This confrontation with nature in the raw had reduced them to the lowest common denominator of humanity. Art, science, and culture no longer existed; only bodies, blood, and babies.

Lanny would listen for a while, and then he would cease to hear what the bearded Frenchman was saying. Lanny was walking up and down the floor of the reception-room, with beads of perspiration standing out upon his forehead. Oh, God, this surely couldn't be right! Something dreadful must be happening in that delivery-room, some of those things which the encyclopedia told about: a failure of the mother's heart, the breaking of the "waters," or one of those irregular presentations which occur in varying percentages of cases. Manifestly, if the *accoucheur* had encountered trouble, he wouldn't come running out to tell the expectant father; he'd be busy, and so would the nurses. Only when it was all over would anyone break the tragic news; and then Lanny would never be able to forgive himself.

A serious defect in the practical arrangements of this *hospice de la misère!* There ought to be some system, a telephone in the delivery-room, a bulletin board, a set of signals! It is a problem which calls for collective solution; the opening of a paternity hospital, a place for expectant fathers, where they may receive proper care! Nurses will have some time for them. Attendants will consider their feel-ings, and give them information—perhaps lectures on the subject of obstetrics, especially prepared for sensitive minds, with the ab-normalities omitted or played down. There will be soft music, per-haps motion pictures; above all there will be news, plenty of it, prompt and dependable. Perhaps a place like a broker's office, where a "Translux" gives the market figures on a screen.

Every time Lanny came near the wall with the bell-button he wanted to press it and demand exact information as to the condition of his beloved wife. Every time the French music-teacher asked him a question it was harder to conceal the fact that he wasn't lis-tening. A damnable thing! Put the blame wherever you chose, on nature or on human incompetence, the fact remained that this wife whom he loved so tenderly, with so much pity, must be in agony, she must be completely exhausted. Something ought to be done! Here it was getting on toward midnight—Lanny looked at his wristwatch and saw that three minutes had passed since he had looked the last time; it was only twenty-two minutes to eleven— but that was bad enough—some thirteen hours since the labor pains had begun, and they had told him it was time to leave her to her fate. Damn it——

XI

A door of the room opened, and there was a nurse. Lanny took one glance, and saw that she was different from any nurse he had seen thus far. She was smiling, yes, actually beaming with smiles. "*Oh, monsieur!*" she exclaimed. "*C'est une fille! Une très belle fille! Si charmante!*" She made a gesture, indicating the size of a female prodigy. Lanny found himself going suddenly dizzy, and reached for a chair.

"*Et madame?*" he cried.

"*Madame est si brave! Elle est magnifique! Tout va bien.*" The formula again. Lanny poured out questions, and satisfied himself that Irma was going to survive. She was exhausted, but that was to be expected. There were details to be attended to; in half an hour or so it should be possible for monsieur to see both mother and daughter. "*Tout de suite! Soyez tranquille!*"

The teacher of piano had Lanny Budd by the hand and was shaking it vigorously. For some time after the American had resumed his seat the other was still pouring out congratulations. "*Merci, merci*," Lanny said mechanically, meanwhile thinking: "A girl! Beauty will be disappointed." But he himself had no complaint. He had been a ladies' man from childhood, seeing his father only at long intervals, cared for by his mother and by women servants. There had been his mother's women friends, then his half-sister and his stepmother in New England, then a new half-sister at Bienvenu, then a succession of his sweethearts, and last of all his wife. He had got something from them all, and would find a daughter no end of fun. It was all right.

Lanny got up, excused himself from the French gentleman, and went to the telephone. He called his mother and told her the news. Yes, he said, he was delighted, or would be when he got over being woozy. No, he wouldn't forget the various cablegrams: one to his father in Connecticut, one to Irma's mother on Long Island, one to his half-sister Bess in Berlin. Beauty would do the telephoning to various friends in the neighborhood—trust her not to miss those thrills! Lanny would include his friend Rick in England and his friend Kurt in Germany; he had the messages written, save for filling in the word "girl."

He carried out his promise to Pietro Corsatti. It was still early in New York; the story would make the night edition of the morning papers, that which was read by café society, whose darling Irma Barnes had been. After receiving Pete's congratulations, Lanny went back for others which the French gentleman had thought up. Astonishing how suddenly the black clouds had lifted from the sky of a young husband's life, how less murderous the ways of mother nature appeared! It became possible to chat with a piano-teacher about the technique he employed; to tell one's own experiences with the Leschetizsky method, and later with the Breithaupt; to explain the forearm rotary motion, and illustrate it on the arm of one's chair. Lanny found himself tapping out the opening theme of

Liszt's symphonic poem, *From the Cradle to the Grave*. But he stopped with the first part.

XII

The cheerful nurse came again, and escorted the successful father down a passage to a large expanse of plate-glass looking into a room with tiny white metal cribs. Visitors were not permitted inside, but a nurse with a white mask over her mouth and nose brought to the other side of the glass a bundle in a blanket and laid back the folds, exposing to Lanny's gaze a brick-red object which might have been a great bloated crinkled caterpillar, only it had appendages, and a large round ball at the top with a face which would have been human if it hadn't been elfish. There was a mouth with lips busily sucking on nothing, and a pair of large eyes which didn't move; however, the nurse at Lanny's side assured him that they had been tested with a light, and they worked. He was assured that this was his baby; to prove it there was a tiny necklace with a metal tag; monsieur and madame might rest assured that they would not carry home the baby of an *avocat*, nor yet that of a teacher of piano technique.

The bloated red caterpillar was folded up in the blanket again, and Lanny was escorted to Irma's room. She lay in a white hospital bed, her head sunk back in a pillow, her eyes closed. How pale she looked, how different from the rich brunette beauty he had left that morning! Now her dark hair was disordered—apparently they hadn't wished to disturb her even that much. Lanny tiptoed into the room, and she opened her eyes slowly, as if with an effort; when he recognized him she gave him a feeble smile.

"How are you, Irma?"

"I'll be all right," she whispered. "Tired, awfully tired."

The nurse had told him not to talk to her. He said: "It's a lovely baby."

"I'm glad. Don't worry. I'll rest, and get better."

Lanny felt a choking in his throat; it was pitiful, the price that women had to pay! But he knew he musn't trouble her with his superfluous emotions. A nurse came with a little wine, which she took through a tube. There was a sedative in it, and she would sleep. He took her hand, which lay limp upon the coverlet, and kissed it gently. "Thank you, dear. I love you." That was enough.

Outside in the passage was the surgeon, all cleaned up and ready for the outside world. His professional manner was second nature. Everything was as it should be; never a better patient, a more perfect delivery. A few hours' sleep, a little nourishment, and Mr. Budd would be surprised by the change in his wife. A lovely sturdy infant, well over nine pounds—that had caused the delay. "Sorry you had such a long wait; no help for that. Do you read the Bible, Mr. Budd? 'A woman when she is in travail hath sorrow, because her hour is come: but as soon as she is delivered of the child, she remembereth no more the anguish, for joy that a man is born into the world.' In this case it's a woman, but we're no longer in ancient Judea, and the women are bossing the show. In my country and yours they have the vote, and they own more than half the property, I'm told; it's their world, and what they are going to do with it we men have to wait and find out. Good night, Mr. Budd."

"Good night," said Lanny. He owed the man thirty thousand francs, which sounded like a thumping price, but the franc was low. Lanny didn't begrudge it. He thought: "I'd have offered a hundred thousand an hour ago!"

2

Those Friends Thou Hast

I

THE house on the Bienvenu estate in which Irma and Lanny were living was called the Cottage, but was nearly as large as the villa and uniform in style, built around a central patio, or court; the walls were of pink stucco with window shutters of pale blue, and a red-tiled roof over its single story. It looked out over the ever-changing Golfe Juan, and beyond to the mountains behind which the sun went down. The house was only three years old, but already the banana plants in the patio were up to the eaves, and the bougain-villaea vines were crawling over the tiles. Early April was the love-liest time of the year, and the patio was a little paradise, with blos-soms of every hue exulting in the floods of sunshine. The young mother might lie on a chaise-longue in sun or shade, and read in a New York paper about March weather, with icy gales wrecking the seashore cottages and piling small boats up on beaches.

In the most exquisite of silk-lined bassinets lay the most precious of female infants, with a veil to protect her from over-curious insects. Near by sat a trained nurse, a mature and conscientious Church of England woman. She had two nursemaids under her orders, which were based on the latest discoveries in the physiology and psychology of infants. There was to be no coddling, no kissing, no rocking to sleep of this mite of royalty; there was to be no guesswork and no blundering in its care; no hostile germs were to steal past the barricades which surrounded it, and anyone who showed the least trace of a cold was banished from the premises. Guests and even relatives had to obey the orders of the all-knowing Miss Severne; she was armed with authority to defy even grandmothers. As for Irma, she had agreed to make the supreme sacrifice; every four hours the precious bundle was to be brought for her nursing, and she was to be on hand, no matter what temptations the world of fashion might put in her way. Back to Rousseau!

There had been family councils and international negotiations concerning a name for this multimillionaire heiress. Many claims had been entered, and if they had all been granted, the little one would have been loaded down after the fashion of European royalty. Manifestly, it wouldn't do to give her the name Beauty; that was something that had to be earned—and suppose she failed to meet the test? Beauty's real name, Mabel, she didn't like—so that was out. Irma's own claims she renounced in favor of her mother, to whom it would mean so much. Irma was going to live most of her life in Europe, because that was what Lanny wanted; so should they not give a pining dowager in a Long Island palace whatever solace she could derive from having her name carried on? The Barnes clan also was entitled to consideration, having furnished the money. "Frances Barnes Budd" was a name not hard to say; but never, never was it to be "Fanny"! The Queen Mother of Shore Acres was helpless to understand how her once lovely name was being put to such base uses in these modern days.

II

Irma was reclining in the patio, enjoying the delight of holding the naked mite in her arms while it absorbed the sunshine of the Midi for a measured three minutes. Lanny came in, saying: "Uncle Jesse is over at the villa. Do you want to meet him?"

"Do you think I should?"

"You surely don't have to if you don't feel like it."

"Won't his feelings be hurt?"

"He's used to that." Lanny said it with a grin.

Irma had heard no little talk about this "Red sheep" of her mother-in-law's family. At first her curiosity hadn't been aroused, for she didn't take political questions to heart, and while she had no doubt that Communists were dreadful people, still, if that was what Jesse Blackless believed, he had to say it. Threats to the social order had never been real to Irma—at least not up to the time of the panic. During that convulsion she had heard many strange ideas discussed, and had begun to wonder about them. Now she said: "If you and your mother see him, I ought to see him too."

"Don't let him corrupt you," replied the husband, grinning again. He got fun out of arguing with his Red uncle, and used him for teasing other people.

Lanny went over to the villa and came back with a tall, odd-looking man, having an almost entirely bald head fairly baked by the sun—for he went about most of the time without a hat. He was dressed carelessly, as became a painter, with sandals, white duck trousers, and a shirt open at the throat. His face had many wrinkles, which he increased when he smiled in his peculiar twisted way; he was given to that kind of humor which consists in saying something different from what you mean, and which assumes understanding on the part of other people which they do not always possess. Jesse Blackless was ill-satisfied with the world in which he lived, and found his pleasure in reducing it to absurdity.

"Well, so this is Irma!" he said, looking down at her. She had covered up her bosom with the orange-colored peignoir of Chinese silk which she was wearing. Her vivid brunette color, which had come back quickly, should have pleased a painter; but Uncle Jesse painted only street urchins and poor beggar folk and workingmen with signs of hard toil on them.

"And this is the baby!" he said, peering into the well-shaded bassinet. He didn't offer any forbidden intimacies, but instead remarked: "Watch out for her—she'd be worth a lot to kidnapers." A sufficiently horrid idea.

The visitor seated himself in a canvas chair and stretched his long legs. His glance wandered from the young wife to the young husband and back again, and he said: "You made a lucky choice, Irma. A lot of people have tried to ruin him, but they haven't succeeded."

It was the first time Lanny had ever known his Red uncle to

pay anybody a compliment, and he valued it accordingly. Irma thanked the speaker, adding that she was sure his judgment was good.

"I know," declared the painter, "because I tried to ruin him myself."

"Have you given up hope?"

"There'd be no use in trying now, since he's married to you. I am a believer in economic determinism."

Lanny explained: "Uncle Jesse thinks he believes that everybody's behavior is conditioned by the state of his pocketbook. But he's a living refutation of his own theory. If he followed his pocketbook, he'd be painting portraits of the idle rich here on this coast, whereas he's probably been meeting with a group of revolutionary conspirators somewhere in the slums of Cannes."

"I'm a freak," said Uncle Jesse. "Nature produces only a few of these, and any statement of social causes has to be based upon the behavior of the mass."

So this pair took to arguing. Irma listened, but most of her thoughts were occupied with the personality of the man. What was he really like? Was he as bitter and harsh as he sounded, or was this only a mask with which he covered his feelings? What was it that had hurt him and made him so out of humor with his own kind of people?

III

The discussion lasted quite a while. They both seemed to enjoy it, even though they said sarcastic things, each about the other. The French word for abuse is "*injures*," which also means injuries, but no hard saying appeared to injure either of these men. Apparently they had heard it all before. Lanny's favorite remark was that his uncle was a phonograph; he put on a record and it ground out the old dependable tune. There was one called "dialectical materialism" and another called "proletarian dictatorship"—long words which meant nothing to Irma. "He wants to take my money and divide it up among the poor," she thought. "How far would it go, and how long would it take them to get rid of it?" She had heard her father say this, and it sounded convincing.

They talked a great deal about what was happening in Russia. Irma had been a child of nine at the time of the revolution, but she had heard about it since, and here on the Riviera she had met Russians who had escaped from the dreadful Bolsheviks, sometimes with nothing but what they had on. You would be told that the handsome and distinguished-looking head waiter in a café was a former Russian baron; that a night-club dancer was the daughter of a one-time landowner. Did Uncle Jesse want things like that to happen in France and the United States? Irma tried to tell herself that he didn't really mean it; but no, he was a determined man, and there often came a grim look on his face; you could imagine him willing to shoot people who stood in his way. Irma knew that the Paris police had "detained" him a couple of times, and that he had defied them. Apparently he was ready to pay whatever price his revolution cost.

Presently he revealed the fact that he was taking steps to become a citizen of France. He had lived in the country for thirty-five years without ever bothering; but now it appeared that "the party" wanted him to run for the Chamber of Deputies. He had made himself a reputation as an orator. Said Lanny: "They want him to put on his phonograph records for all France."

Irma, who was money-conscious, thought at once: "He's come to get us to put up for his campaign." Lanny didn't have much money since his father had got caught in the slump. Irma resolved: "I won't help him. I don't approve of it." She had discovered the power of her money during the Wall Street crisis, and was learning to enjoy it.

But then another point of view occurred to her. Maybe it would be a distinguished thing to have a relative in the Chamber, even if he was a Communist! She wasn't sure about this, and wished she knew more about political affairs. Now and then she had that thought about various branches of knowledge, and would resolve to find out; but then she would forget because it was too much trouble. Just now they had told her that she musn't get excited about anything, because excitement would spoil her milk. A nuisance, turning yourself into a cow! But it was pleasant enough here in the sunshine, being entertained with novel ideas.

Lanny apparently agreed with his uncle that what the Russians were doing was important—for them. The dispute was over the question whether the same thing was going to happen in France and England and America. Lanny maintained that these countries, being "democracies," could bring about the changes peaceably. That was his way; he didn't want to hurt anybody, but to discuss ideas politely and let the best ideas win. However, Uncle Jesse kept insisting that Lanny and his Socialist friends were aiding the capitalists by fooling the workers, luring them with false hopes, keeping them contented with a political system which the capitalists had bought and paid for. Lanny, on the other hand, argued that it was the Reds who were betraying the workers, frightening the middle classes by violent threats and driving them into the camp of the reactionaries.

So it went, and the young wife listened without getting excited. Marriage was a strange adventure; you let yourself in for a lot of things you couldn't have foreseen. These two most eccentric families, the Budds and the Blacklesses! Irma's own family consisted of Wall Street people. They bought and sold securities and made fortunes or lost them, and that seemed a conventional and respectable kind of life; but now she had been taken to a household full of Reds and Pinks of all shades, and spiritualist mediums and religious healers, munitions makers and Jewish *Schieber*, musicians and painters and art dealers—you never knew when you opened your eyes in the morning what strange new creatures you were going to encounter before night. Even Lanny, who was so dear and sweet, and with whom Irma had entered into the closest of all intimacies, even he became suddenly a stranger when he got stirred up and began pouring out his schemes for making the world over—schemes which clearly involved his giving up his own property, and Irma's giving up hers, and wiping out the hereditary rights of the long-awaited and closely guarded Frances Barnes Budd!

IV

Uncle Jesse stayed to lunch, then went his way; and after the nap which the doctor had prescribed for the nursing mother, Irma enjoyed the society of her stepfather-in-law—if there is a name for this odd relationship. Mr. Parsifal Dingle, Beauty's new husband, came over from the villa to call on the baby. Irma knew him well, for they had spent the past summer on a yacht; he was a religious mystic, and certainly restful after the Reds and the Pinks. He never argued, and as a rule didn't talk unless you began a conversation; he was interested in things going on in his own soul, and while he was glad to tell about them, you had to ask. He would sit by the bassinet and gaze at the infant, and there would come a blissful look on his round cherubic face; you would think there were two infants, and that their souls must be completely in tune.

The man of God would close his eyes, and be silent for a while, and Irma wouldn't interrupt him, knowing that he was giving little Frances a "treatment." It was a sort of prayer with which he filled his mind, and he was quite sure that it affected the mind of the little one. Irma wasn't sure, but she knew it couldn't do any harm, for there was nothing except good in the mind of this gentle healer. He seemed a bit uncanny while sitting with Madame Zyszynski, the Polish medium, in one of her trances; conversing in the most matter-of-fact way with the alleged Indian spirit. "Tecumseh," as he called himself, was whimsical and self-willed, and would tell something or refuse to tell, according to whether or not you were respectful to him and whether or not the sun was shining in the spirit world. Gradually Irma had got used to it all, for the spirits didn't do any harm, and quite certainly Mr. Dingle didn't; on the contrary, if you felt sick he would cure you. He had cured several members of the Bienvenu household, and it might be extremely convenient in an emergency.

Such were Irma's reflections during the visits. She would ask him questions and let him talk, and it would be like going to church. Irma found it agreeable to talk about loving everybody, and thought that it might do some people a lot of good; they showed the need of it in their conversation, the traces they revealed of envy, hatred, malice, and all uncharitableness. Mr. Dingle wanted to change the world, just as much as any Bolshevik, but he had begun with himself, and that seemed to Irma a fine idea; it didn't threaten the Barnes fortune or the future of its heiress. The healer would read his mystical books, and magazines of what he called "New Thought," and then he would wander about the garden, looking at the flowers and the birds, and perhaps giving them a treatment—for they too had life in them and were products of love. Bienvenu appeared to contain everything that Mr. Dingle needed, and he rarely went off the estate unless someone invited him.

The strangest whim of fate, that the worldly Beauty Budd should have chosen this man of God to accompany her on the downhill of life! All her friends laughed over it, and were bored to death with her efforts to use the language of "spirituality." Certainly it hadn't kept her from working like the devil to land the season's greatest "catch" for her son; nor did it keep her from exulting brazenly in her triumph. Beauty's religious talk no more than Lanny's Socialist talk was causing them to take steps to distribute any large share of Irma's unearned increment. On the contrary, they had stopped giving elaborate parties at Bienvenu, which was hard on everybody on the Cap d'Antibes—the tradesmen, the servants, the musicians, the *couturiers*, all who catered to the rich. It was hard on the society folk, who had been so scared by the panic and the talk of hard times on the way. Surely somebody ought to set an example of courage and enterprise—and who could have done it better than a glamour girl with a whole bank-vault full of "blue chip" stocks and bonds? What was going to become of smart society if its prime favorites began turning their estates into dairy farms and themselves into stud cattle?

V

There came a telegram from Berlin: "Yacht due at Cannes we are leaving by train tonight engage hotel accommodations. Bess."

Of course Lanny wouldn't follow those last instructions. When friends are taking you for a cruise and paying all your expenses for several months, you don't let them go to a hotel even for a couple of days. There was the Lodge, a third house on the estate; it had been vacant all winter, and now would be opened and freshly aired and dusted. Irma's secretary, Miss Featherstone, had been established as a sort of female major-domo and took charge of such operations. The expected guests would have their meals with Irma and Lanny, and "Feathers" would consult with the cook and see to the ordering of supplies. Everything would run as smoothly as water down a mill-race; Irma would continue to lie in the sunshine, read magazines, listen to Lanny play the piano, and nurse Baby Frances when one of the maids brought her.

Lanny telephoned his old friend Emily Chattersworth, who took care of the cultural activities of this part of the Riviera. Her drawing-room was much larger than any at Bienvenu, and people were used to coming there whenever a celebrity was available. Hansi Robin always played for her, and the fashionable folk who cared for music and the musical folk who were socially acceptable would be invited to Sept Chênes for a treat. Emily would send Hansi a check, and he would endorse it over to be used for the workers' educational project which was Lanny's special hobby.

Just before sundown of that day Lanny and Irma sat on the loggia of their home, which looked out over the Golfe Juan, and watched the trim white *Bessie Budd* glide into the harbor of Cannes. They knew her a long way off, for she had been their home during the previous summer, and Lanny had taken two other cruises in her. With a pair of field-glasses they could recognize Captain Moeller, who had had a chance to marry them but had funked it. They could almost imagine they heard his large Prussian voice when it was time to slow down for passing the breakwater.

Next morning but one, Lanny drove into the city, with his little half-sister Marceline at his side and Irma's chauffeur following with another car. The long blue express rolled in and delivered five of their closest friends, plus a secretary and a nursemaid in a uniform and cap with blue streamers, carrying an infant in arms. It was on account of this last that the cruise was being taken so early in the year; the two lactant mothers would combine their dairy farms, put them on shipboard, and transport them to delightful places of this great inland sea, famed in story.

Just prior to the World War, Lanny Budd, a small boy traveling on a train, had met a Jewish salesman of electrical gadgets; they had liked each other, and the stranger had given Lanny his card. This small object had lain in a bureau drawer; and if, later on, Lanny hadn't happened to be rummaging in that drawer, how much would have been different in his life! He wouldn't have written to Johannes Robin, and Johannes wouldn't have come to call on him in Paris, and met Lanny's father, and with the father's money become one of the richest men in Germany. Lanny's half-sister wouldn't have met Hansi Robin, and shocked her family by marrying a Jewish musician. The yacht wouldn't have been called the *Bessie Budd*, and wouldn't have taken Lanny and his family on three cruises, and been the means of Lanny and Irma's getting married in a hurry. They mightn't have got married at all, and there wouldn't have been any honeymoon cruise to New York, or any Baby Frances, or any floating dairy farm! In short, if that business card, "*Johannes Robin, Agent, Maatschappij voor Elec-trische Specialiteiten, Rotterdam*," had stayed covered up by Lanny Budd's neckties and handkerchiefs most of Lanny's life would have been missing!

VI

Two happy members of the prosperous classes welcoming five of their intimate friends on the platform of a railroad station. Everybody there knew who the Budds were, and knew that when they hugged and kissed people, and laughed and chatted with them gaily, the people must be wealthy and famous like themselves. A pleasant thing to have friends whom you can love and appreciate, and who will love and appreciate you. Pleasant also to have villas and motor-cars and yachts; but many people do not have them, and do not have many dear friends. They know themselves to be dull and undistinguished, and feel themselves to be lonely; they stand and watch

with a sad envy the behavior of the fortunate classes on those few
occasions when they condescend to manifest their feelings in public.

Johannes Robin was the perfect picture of a man who has known
how to make use of his opportunities in this world. His black over-
coat of the finest cloth lined with silk; his black Homburg hat; his
neatly trimmed little black mustache and imperial; his fine leather
traveling-bags with many labels; his manner of quiet self-possession;
his voice that seemed to be caressing you—everything about him
was exactly right. He had sought the best of both body and mind
and knew how to present it to the rest of the world. You would
never hear him say: "Look at what I, Johannes Robin, have achieved!"
No, he would say: "What an extraordinary civilization, in which a
child who sat on the mud floor of a hut in a ghetto and recited ancient Hebrew texts while scratching his flea-bites has been able in
forty years to make so much money!" He would add: "I'm not
sure that I'm making the best use of it. What do you think?" That
flattered you subtly.

As for Mama Robin, there wasn't much you could do for her in
the way of elegance. You could employ the most skillful *couturier*
and give him *carte blanche* as to price, but Leah, wife of Jascha
Rabinowich, would remain a Yiddishe mother, now a grandmother;
a bit dumpier every year, and with no improvement in her accent,
whether it was Dutch or German or English she was speaking. All
she had was kindness and devotion, and if that wasn't enough you
would move on to some other part of the room.

The modern practice of easy divorces and remarriages makes complications for genealogists. Lanny had grown tired of explaining
about his two half-sisters, and had taken to calling them sisters, and
letting people figure it out. The name of Marceline Detaze made it
plain that she was the daughter of the painter who had been killed
in the last months of the war; also it was possible to guess that Bessie
Budd Robin was the daughter of Lanny's father in New England.
On that stern and rock-bound coast her ancestors had won a hard
and honest living; so Bess was tall and her features were thin and
had conscientiousness written all over them. Her straight brown
hair was bobbed, and she wore the simplest clothes which the style-

makers would allow to come into the shops. She was twenty-two and had been married four years, but had put off having children because of her determination to play accompaniments for Hansi in exactly the way he wanted them.

Very touching to see how she watched every step he took, and managed him exactly as her mother at home managed a household. She carried his violin case and wouldn't let him pick up a suitcase; those delicate yet powerful fingers must be devoted to the stopping of violin strings or the drawing of a bow. Hansi was a piece of tone-producing machinery; when they went on tour he was bundled up and delivered on a platform, and then bundled up and carried to a hotel and put to bed. Hansi's face of a young Jewish saint, Hansi's soulful dark eyes, Hansi's dream of loveliness embodied in sound, drove the ladies quite beside themselves; they listened with hands clasped together, they rushed to the platform and would have thrown themselves at his feet, to say nothing of his head. But there was that erect and watchful-eyed granddaughter of the Puritans, with a formula which she said as often as it was called for: "I do everything for my husband that he requires—absolutely *everything!*"

The other members of the party were Freddi Robin's wife, and her baby boy, a month older than little Frances. Freddi was at the University of Berlin, hoping to get a degree in economics. Rahel, a serious, gentle girl, contributed a mezzo-soprano voice to the choir of the yacht; also she led in singing choruses. With two pianos, a violin, a clarinet, and Mr. Dingle's mouth-organ, they could sail the Mediterranean in safety, being able to drown out the voices of any sirens who might still be sitting on its rocky shores.

VII

If music be the food of love, play on! They were gathered in Lanny's studio at Bienvenu, which had been built for Marcel and in which he had done his best work as a painter. There were several of his works on the walls, and a hundred or so stored in a back room. The piano was the big one which Lanny had purchased for Kurt Meissner and which he had used for seven years before going back to Germany. The studio was lined with bookcases containing the library of Lanny's great-great-uncle. Here were all sorts of memories of the dead, and hopes of the living, with cabinets of music-scores in which both kinds of human treasures had been embodied and preserved. Hansi and Bess were playing Tchaikovsky's great concerto, which meant so much to them. Hansi had rendered it at his debut in Carnegie Hall, with Bess and her parents in the audience; a critical occasion for the anxious young lovers.

Next evening they went over to Sept Chênes to meet a distinguished company, most of the fashionable people who had not yet left the Côte d'Azur. The whole family went, including Irma and Rahel. Since it was only a fifteen-minute drive from Bienvenu, the young nursing mothers might have three hours and a half of music and social life; but they mustn't get excited. The two of them heartened each other, making bovine life a bit more tolerable. The feat they were performing was considered picturesque, a harmless eccentricity about which the ladies gossiped; the older ones mentioned it to their husbands, but the younger ones kept quiet, not wishing to put any notions into anybody's head. No Rousseau in our family, thank you!

Hansi and Bess played Lalo's *Symphonie Espagnole*, a composition which audiences welcome and which has to be in the repertoire of every virtuoso: a melancholy and moving *andante* over which the ladies may sigh; a *scherzando* to which young hearts may dance over flower-strewn meadows. It was no holiday for Bess, who wasn't sure if she was good enough for this fastidious company; but she got through it all right and received her share of compliments. Lanny, who knew the music well, permitted his eyes to roam over the audience, and wondered what they were making of it, behind the well-constructed masks they wore. What to them was the meaning of these flights of genius, these incessant calls to the human spirit, these unremitting incitements to ecstasy? Whose feet were swift enough to trip among these meadows? Whose spring was high enough to leap upon these mountain-tops? Who wept for these dying worlds? Who marched in these triumphal processions, celebrating the birth of new epochs?

The thirty-year-old Lanny Budd had come to understand his world, and no longer cherished any illusions concerning the ladies and gentlemen at a *soirée musicale*. Large, well-padded matrons who had been playing bridge all afternoon, and had spent so many hours choosing the fabrics, the jeweled slippers, the necklaces, brooches, and tiaras which made up their splendid ensemble—what fairy feet did they have, even in imagination? What tears did they shed for the lost hopes of mankind? There was Beauty's friend, Madame de Sarcé, with two marriageable daughters and an adored only son who had squandered their fortune in the gambling-palaces. Lanny doubted if any one of the family was thinking about music.

And these gentlemen, with their black coats and snowy shirt-fronts in which their valets had helped to array them—what tumults of exultation thrilled their souls tonight? They had all dined well, and more than one looked drowsy. Others fixed their eyes upon the smooth bare backs of the ladies in front of them. Close to the musicians sat Graf Hohenstauffen, monocled German financier, wearing a pleased smile all through the surging *finale;* Lanny had heard him tell Johannes Robin that he had just come from a broker's office where he had got the closing New York prices. In this April of 1930 there was a phenomenon under way which was being called "the little bull market"; things were picking up again, and the speculators were full of enthusiasms. Was the Graf converting Hansi's frenzied runs on the violin into movements of stocks and bonds?

However, there might be somebody who understood, some lonely heart that hid its griefs and lived in secret inner happiness. Someone who sat silent and abstracted after the performance, too shy to approach the players and thank them; who would go out with fresh hopes for a world in which such loveliness had been embodied in sound. In any case, Hansi and Bess had done their duty by their hostess, a white-haired *grande dame* who would always seem wonderful to them because it was in her château near Paris that they had met and been revealed each to the other.

VIII

It was considered a social triumph, but it was not sufficient for young people tinged with all the hues between pink and scarlet. In the Old Town of Cannes, down near the harbor, dwelt members of depressed classes, among whom Lanny had been going for years, teaching his ideas in a strange, non-religious Sunday school, helping with his money to found a center of what was called "workers' education." He had made many friends here, and had done all he could to break down the social barriers. As a result, the waiter in some fashionable café would say: *"Bon soir*, Comrade Lanny!" When he got out of his car to enter the Casino, or the Cercle Nautique, or some other smart place, he would be delayed by little street urchins running up to shake hands or even to throw their arms about him.

What would these people feel if they knew that the famous violinist who was Lanny's brother-in-law had come to town and given a recital for the rich but had neglected the poor? Unthinkable to go sailing off in a luxurious pleasure yacht without even greeting the class-conscious workers! Lanny's Socialist friend Raoul Palma, who conducted the school, had been notified of the expected visit, and had engaged a suitable hall and printed leaflets for the little street urchins to distribute. When Hansi Robin played in concert halls the rich paid as much as a hundred francs to hear him, but the workers would hear him for fifty centimes, less than a cent and a half in American money. From the point of view of Hansi's business manager it was terrible; but Hansi was a rich man's son and must be allowed to have his eccentricities. Wherever he went, the word would spread, and working-class leaders would come and beg his help. He was young and strong, and wanted to practice anyway, so why not do it on a platform for this most appreciative kind of audience?

Perhaps it was because they knew he was a "comrade," and read into his music things which were not there. Anyhow, they made a demonstration out of it, they took him to their hearts, they flew with him upon the wings of song to that happy land of the future where all men would be brothers and poverty and war only an evil memory. Hansi played no elaborate composition for them, he performed no technical feats; he played simple, soul-warming music: the *adagio* from one of the Bach solo sonatas, followed by Scriabin's *Prelude*, gently solemn, with very lovely double-stopping. Then he added bright and gay things: Percy Grainger's arrangement of *Molly on the Shore*, and when they begged for more he led them into a riot with Bazzini's *Goblins' Dance*. Those goblins squeaked and squealed, they gibbered and chattered; people had never dreamed that such weird sounds could come out of a violin or anything else, and they could hardly contain their laughter and applause until the goblins had fled to their caverns or wherever they go when they have worn themselves out with dancing.

When it was late, and time to quit, Bess struck the opening chords of the *Internationale*. It is the work of a Frenchman, and, pink or scarlet or whatever shade in between, everybody in that crowded hall seemed to know the words; it was as if a charge of electricity had passed through the chairs on which they sat. They leaped to their feet and burst into singing, and you could no longer hear the violin. "Arise, ye prisoners of starvation; arise, ye wretched of the earth!" The workers crowded about the platform, and if Hansi had let them they would have carried him, and Lanny, and Bess too, out to their car, and perhaps have hauled the car all the way to the Cap d'Antibes.

IX

The trim white *Bessie Budd* crept slowly beyond the breakwater of Cannes and through the Golfe Juan, passing that group of buildings with the red-tiled roofs which had been Lanny Budd's home since his earliest memory. Now for several months the yacht was to be his home. It carried five members and a small fraction of the Robin family—if that be the way to count an infant—and four members and two fractions of the Budd family: Lanny, his wife, and their baby; Beauty, her husband, and her daughter. This was the twelve-year-old Marceline's first yacht trip, and with her came the devoted English governess, Miss Addington; also Miss Severne, to look after

Baby Frances, with one of the nursemaids assisting. Finally there was Madame Zyszynski and, it was hoped, Tecumseh with his troop of spirits, requiring no cabin-space.

A windless morning, the sea quite still, and the shore quite close. The course was eastward, and the Riviera glided past them like an endless panorama. Lanny, to whom it was as familiar as his own garden, stood by the rail and pointed out the landmarks to his friends. A most agreeable way of studying both geography and history! Amusing to take the glasses and pick out the places where he had played tennis, danced, and dined. Presently there was Monte Carlo, a little town crowded onto a rock. Lanny pointed out the hotel of Zaharoff, the munitions king, and said: "It's the time when he sits out in the sunshine on those seats." They searched, but didn't see any old gentleman with a white imperial! Presently it was Menton, and Lanny said: "The villa of Blasco Ibáñez." He had died recently, an exile from the tyranny in Spain. Yes, it was history, several thousand years of it along this shore.

Then came Italy; the border town where a young Socialist had been put out of the country for trying to protest against the murder of Matteotti. Then San Remo, where Lanny had attended the first international conference after the peace of Versailles. Much earlier, when Lanny had been fourteen, he had motored all the way down to Naples, in company with a manufacturer of soap from Reubens, Indiana. Lanny would always feel that he knew the Middle Western United States through the stories of Ezra Hackabury, who had carried little sample cakes of Bluebird Soap wherever he traveled over Europe, giving them away to beggar children, who liked their smell but not their taste. Carrara with its marbles had reminded Ezra of the new postoffice in his home town, and when he saw the leaning tower of Pisa he had remarked that he could build one of steel that would lean further, but what good would it do?

A strange coincidence: while Lanny was sitting on the deck telling stories to the Robin family, Lanny's mother and her husband had gone to the cabin of Madame Zyszynski to find out whether Tecumseh, the Indian "control," had kept his promise and followed her to the yacht. The Polish woman went into her trance, and right away there came the powerful voice supposed to be Iroquois, but having a Polish accent. Tecumseh said that a man was standing by his side who gave the name of Ezra, and the other name began with H, but his voice was feeble and Tecumseh couldn't get it; it made him think of a butcher. No, the man said that he cleaned people, not animals. He knew Lanny and he knew Italy. Ask Lanny if he remembered—what was it?—something about smells in the Bay of Naples and about a man who raised angleworms. Mr. Dingle, doing the questioning, asked what that meant, but Tecumseh declared that the spirit had faded away.

So there was one of those incidents which cause the psychical researchers to prepare long reports. Beauty thought of Ezra Hackabury right away, but she didn't know that Lanny was up on the deck telling the Robins about him, nor did she know how the Bluebird Soap man had cited the smells of the Naples waterfront as proof that romance and charm in Italy were mostly fraudulent. But Lanny remembered well, and also that the gentleman from Indiana had told him about the strange occupation of raising angleworms and planting them in the soil to keep it porous.

What were you going to make out of such an episode? Was Mr. Hackabury really there? Was he dead? Lanny hadn't heard from him for years. He sat down and wrote a letter, to be mailed at Genoa, not mentioning anything about spirits, but saying that he was on his way to Naples, planning to retrace the cruise of the yacht *Bluebird*, and did his old friend remember the drive they had taken and the smells of the bay? And how was the man who raised angleworms making out? Lanny added: "Let me know how you are, for my mother and I often talk about your many kindnesses to us." He hoped that, if Ezra Hackabury was dead, some member of his family might be moved to reply.

X

They went ashore at Genoa, to inspect that very ancient city. They had in Lanny a cicerone who had wandered about the streets during several weeks of the Genoa Conference. A spice of excite-

ment was added by the fact that he wouldn't be allowed to enter
the country if he were identified. But local officers would hardly
know about that old-time misadventure, or cross-question fashionable people coming ashore from a private yacht; they could hardly
check every tourist by the records of the Fascist *militi* in Rome.

No question was raised. Italy was a poor country, and visitors
brought much-needed foreign exchange; the richer they were, the
more welcome—a rule that holds good in most parts of the world.
They engaged three cars and were driven about the town, which
is crowded between mountains and sea, and since it cannot float on
the latter is forced to climb the former. Ancient tall buildings
jammed close together; churches having façades with stripes of
white and black marble, and inside them monotonous paintings of
sorrowful Italian women with infants in their arms. Before the
shrines were wax images of parts of the body which had been
miraculously healed, displays not usually seen outside of hospitals.
Mr. Dingle might have been interested, but he had a deep-seated
prejudice against the Catholic system, which he called idolatrous.
Mr. Hackabury had had the same idea.

Lanny showed them the old Palazzo di San Giorgio, where the
conference had been held, a dingy and depressing place, in keeping
with the results of the assemblage. Lloyd George had made the
most inspiring promises of peace and prosperity to the representatives of twenty-nine nations; after which, behind the scenes, the
leaders had spent six weeks wrangling over what oil concessions
the Russians were to make to what nations. Lanny's father had been
here, trying to get a share; it had been his first fiasco, and the beginning of a chain of them for all parties concerned. Instead of peace
the nations had got more armaments and more debts. Instead of
prosperity had come a financial collapse in Wall Street, and all
were trembling lest it spread to the rest of the world.

XI

All this wasn't the most cheerful line of conversation for a sight-
seeing jaunt; so Lanny talked about some of the journalists and

writers whom he had met at this conference, and forbore to refer
to the tragic episode which had cut short his stay in Genoa. But
later, when Irma and Rahel had gone back to the yacht, he went
for a stroll with Hansi and Bess, and they talked about the Italian
Syndicalist leader who had set them to thinking on the subject of
social justice. The young Robins looked upon Barbara Pugliese as
a heroine and working-class martyr, cherishing her memory as the
Italians cherish that virgin mother whose picture they never grow
tired of painting. But the Fascist terror had wiped out every trace
of Barbara's organization, and to have revealed sympathy for her
would have exposed an Italian to exile and torture on those barren
Mediterranean islands which Mussolini used as concentration camps.

When you talked about things like this you lost interest in ancient
buildings and endlessly multiplied Madonnas. You didn't want to
eat any of the food of this town, or pay it any foreign exchange;
you wanted to shake its polluted dust from your feet. But the older
people were here to entertain themselves with sight-seeing; so, take
a walk, climb the narrow streets up into the hills where the flowers
of springtime were thick and the air blew from the sea. These gifts
of nature were here before the coming of the miserable Fascist braggart, and would remain long after he had become a stench in the
nostrils of history. Try not to hate his strutting Blackshirts with their
shiny boots, and pistols and daggers in their belts; think of them as
misguided children, destined some day to pay with their blood for
their swagger and bluster. "Father, forgive them, for they know not
what they do!"

And when you come down from the heights and get on board the
yacht again, keep your thoughts to your own little group, and say
nothing to your elders, who have grown up in a different world.
You cannot convert them; you can only worry them and spoil their
holiday. Play your music, read your books, think your own thoughts,
and never let yourselves be drawn into an argument! Not an altogether satisfactory way of life, but the only one possible in times
when the world is changing so fast that parents and children may be
a thousand years apart in their ideas and ideals.

3

And Their Adoption Tried

I

THE trim white *Bessie Budd* was among the Isles of Greece, where burning Sappho loved and sung, and where Lanny at the age of fourteen had fished and swum and climbed hills and gazed upon the ruins of ancient temples. The yacht stole through the Gulf of Corinth and made fast to a pier in the harbor of the Piraeus, now somewhat improved; the guests were motored to the city of Athens, and ascended the hill of the Acropolis on little donkeys which had not been improved in any way. They gazed at the most famous of all ruins, and Lanny told them about Isadora Duncan dancing here, and how she had explained to the shocked police that it was her way of praying.

The *Bessie Budd* anchored in the Channel of Atalante, and the experienced Lanny let down fishing-lines and brought up odd-appearing creatures which had not changed in sixteen years, and perhaps not in sixteen million. The guests were rowed ashore at several towns, and drank over-sweet coffee out of copper pots with long handles, and gazed at the strange spectacle of tall men wearing accordion-pleated and starched white skirts like those of ballet-dancers. They climbed the hills surmounted by ancient temples, and tried to talk in sign language to shepherds having shelters of brush built into little cones.

History had been made in these waters between Lanny's visits. German submarines had lurked here, British and French craft had hunted them, and a bitter duel of intrigue had been carried on over the part which Greece was to play. The Allies had landed an army at Salonika, and the *Bessie Budd* now followed in the wake of their

transports; her guests were driven about in a dusty old city of narrow crooked streets and great numbers of mosques with towering
minarets. The more active members of the party wandered over the
hills where the armies of Alexander had marched to the conquest of
Persia; through which the Slavs had come in the seventh century,
followed by Bulgars, Saracens, Gauls, Venetians, Turks.

There are people who have a sense of the past; they are stirred by
the thought of it, and by the presence of its relics; there are others
who have very little of this sense, and would rather play a game of
bridge than climb a hill to see where a battle was fought or a goddess
was worshiped. Lanny discovered that his wife was among these
latter. She was interested in the stories he told the company, but only
mildly, and while he and Hansi were studying the fragments of a
fallen column, Irma would be watching the baby lambs gamboling
among the spring flowers. "Oh, how charming!" Observing one of
them beginning to nuzzle its mother, she would look at her wristwatch and say: "Don't forget that we have to be back on board in
an hour." Lanny would return to the world of now, and resume the
delights of child study which he had begun long ago with Marceline.

II

When you live day and night on a yacht, in close contact with
your fellow-guests, there isn't much they can hide from you. It was
Lanny's fourth cruise with a Jewish man of money, but still he did
not tire of studying a subtle and complex personality. Johannes
Robin was not merely an individual; he was a race and a culture, a
religion and a history of a large part of human society for several
thousand years. To understand him fully was a problem not merely
in psychology, but in business and finance, in literature and language,
ethnology, archaeology—a list of subjects about which Lanny was
curious.

This man of many affairs could be tender-hearted as a child, and
again could state flatly that he was not in business for his health.
He could be frank to the point of dubious taste, or he could be

devious as any of the diplomats whom Lanny had watched at a dozen international conferences. He would drive a hard bargain, and then turn around and spend a fortune upon hospitality to that same person. He was bold, yet he was haunted by fears. He ardently desired the approval of his fellows, yet he would study them and pass judgments indicating that their opinion was not worth so very much. Finally, with his keen mind he observed these conflicts in himself, and to Lanny, whom he trusted, he would blurt them out in disconcerting fashion.

They were sitting on deck after the others had gone to bed; a still night, and the yacht gliding through the water with scarcely a sound. Suddenly the host remarked: "Do you know what this show costs every hour?"

"I never tried to estimate," said the guest, taken aback.

"You wouldn't, because you've always had money. I figured it up last night—about a hundred dollars every hour of the day or night. It cost me several hours' sleep to realize it."

There was a pause. Lanny didn't know what to say.

"It's a weakness; I suppose it's racial. I can't get over the fear of spending so much!"

"Why do you do it, then?"

"I force myself to be rational. What good is money if you hoard it? My children don't want it, and their children won't know how to use it; and, anyhow, it mayn't last. I assume that I give my friends some pleasure, and I don't do any harm that I can think of. Can you?"

"No," replied the other.

"Of course I shouldn't mention it," said the host, "but you like to understand people."

"We'd all be happier if we did," replied Lanny. "I, too, am conscious of weaknesses. If I happened to be in your position, I would be trying to make up my mind whether I had a right to own a yacht."

III

Lanny went to bed thinking about this "racial" peculiarity. When he had first met Johannes Robin, the salesman had been traveling over Europe with two heavy suitcases full of electric curling-irons and toasters, and a "spiel" about promoting international trade and the spread of civilization. During the war he had made money buying magnetos and such things to be sold in Germany. Then he had gone in with Robbie Budd and bought left-over supplies of the American army. He had sold marks and bought shares in German industry, and now he was sometimes referred to as a "king" of this and that. Doubtless all kings, underneath their crowns and inside their royal robes, were hesitant and worried mortals, craving affection and tormented by fears of poison and daggers, of demons and gods, or, in these modern times, of financial collapses and revolutions.

Jascha Rabinowich had changed his name but had remained a Jew; which meant that he was race-conscious; he was kept that way by contempt and persecution. Part of the time he blustered and part of the time he cringed, but he tried to hide both moods. What he wanted was to be a man like other men, and to be judged according to his merits. But he had had to flee from a pogrom in Russia, and he lived in Germany knowing that great numbers of people despised and hated him; he knew that even in America, which he considered the most enlightened of countries, the people in the slums would call him a "sheeny" and a Christ-killer, while the "best" people would exclude him from their country clubs.

He talked about all this with Lanny, who had fought hard for his sister's right to marry Hansi. People accused the Jews of loving money abnormally. "We are traders," said Johannes. "We have been traders for a couple of thousand years, because we have been driven from our land. We have had to hide in whatever holes we could find in one of these Mediterranean ports, and subsist by buying something at a low price and selling it at a higher price. The penalty of failure being death has sharpened our wits. In a port it often happens that we buy from a person we shall never see again, and sell to some other person under the same conditions; they do not worry much about our welfare, nor we about theirs. That may be a limitation in our morality, but it is easy to understand."

Lanny admitted that he understood it, and his host continued:

"My ancestors were master-traders all the way from Smyrna to Gibraltar while yours were barbarians in the dark northern forests, killing the aurochs with clubs and spears. Naturally our view of life was different from yours. But when you take to commerce, the differences disappear quickly. I have heard that in your ancestral state of Connecticut the Yankee does not have his feelings hurt when you call him slick. You have heard, perhaps, of David Harum, who traded horses."

"I have heard also of Potash and Perlmutter," said Lanny, with a smile.

"It is the same here, all around the shores of this ancient sea which once was the civilized world. The Greeks are considered skillful traders; take Zaharoff, for example. The Turks are not easy to deceive, and I am told that the Armenians can get the better of any race in the world. Always, of course, I am referring to the professional traders, those who live or die by it. The peasant is a different proposition; the primary producer is the predestined victim, whether he is in Connecticut buying wooden nutmegs or in Anatolia receiving coins made of base metal which he will not be clever enough to pass on."

IV

Lanny sat with Madame Zyszynski, but the results he obtained were not of the best. Tecumseh, the noble redskin, was suspicious and inclined to be crotchety; he took offense when one did not accept his word, and Lanny had made the mistake of being too honest. The way to get results was to be like Parsifal Dingle, who welcomed the spirits quite simply as his friends, chatting with them and the "control" in an amiable matter-of-fact way. Apparently it was with the spirits as with healing: except ye be converted, and become as little children! . . .

What Tecumseh would do was to send messages to Lanny through

Parsifal. He would say: "Tell that smart young man that Marcel was here, and that he is painting spirit pictures, much more wonderful than anything he ever did on earth—but they will never be sold at auctions." Lanny wanted to know if Marcel objected to having his works sold; but for a long time the painter ignored his question. Then one day Tecumseh said, rather grudgingly, that it didn't really matter to Marcel; everything was sold in Lanny's world, and it was no use keeping beautiful things in a storeroom. This sounded as if the spirit world was acquiring a "pinkish" tinge.

Madame gave several séances every day. She had done it while she was earning her living on Sixth Avenue, and insisted that it didn't hurt her. She would accommodate anyone who was interested, and presently she was delving into the past of the Rabinowich family, telling about those members who had "passed over." It was a bit unsatisfactory, for there were many members of that family, and Jascha had lost track of them; he said that he never heard from them except when someone needed money for some worthy purpose, and all purposes were worthy. He said that the way to check on the identity of any member of his family in the spirit world would be that he was asking for money to be given to a son or daughter, a nephew or niece still on earth!

But there had been indeed an Uncle Nahum, who had peddled goods in Russian-Polish villages, and had been clubbed to death by the Black Hundreds. The realistic details of this event sounded convincing to Mama Robin, who had witnessed such an incident as a child and still had nightmares now and then as a result. Then it was Jascha's own father talking to him; when he mentioned that his beard had turned white faster on one side than on the other, and how he had kept his money hidden under a loose brick in the hearth, Lanny saw his urbane host look startled. Johannes said afterward that he had thought all this must be a fraud of some sort, but now he didn't know what to think. It was really unthinkable.

So it went on, all over the pleasure vessel. The gray-bearded and heavy-minded Captain Moeller condescended to try the experiment, and found himself in conversation with his eldest son, who had been a junior officer on a U-boat, and told how it felt to be suffocated at the bottom of the sea. Baby Frances's nursemaid, a girl with a Cockney accent who had got a few scraps of education at a "council school," learned to sit for long periods talking with her father, a Tommy who had been killed on the Somme, and who told her all about his early life, the name of the pub where he had made bets on horse races, and where his name was still chalked up on a board, along with that of other dead soldiers of the neighborhood.

How did Madame Zyszynski get such things? You could say that she sneaked about in the yacht and caught scraps of conversation, and perhaps rummaged about in people's cabins. But it just happened that she didn't. She was a rather dull old woman who had been first a servant and then the wife of the butler to a Warsaw merchant. She suffered from varicose veins and dropsy in its early stages. She understood foreign languages with difficulty and didn't bother to listen most of the time, but preferred to sit in her own cabin playing endless games of solitaire. When she read, it was the pictures in some cheap magazine, and the strange things she did in her trances really didn't interest her overmuch; she would answer your questions as best she could, but hardly ever asked any of you. She declared again and again that she did these things because she was poor and had to earn her living. She insisted, furthermore, that she had never heard the voice of Tecumseh, and knew about him only what her many clients had told her.

But what a different creature was this Indian chieftain! He was not the Tecumseh of history, he said, but an Iroquois of the same name. His tribe had been all but wiped out by smallpox. Now he ruled a tribe of spirits, and amused himself at the expense of his former enemies, the whites. He was alert, masterful, witty, shrewd— and if there was anything he didn't know, he would tell you to come back tomorrow and perhaps he would have it for you. But you had to be polite. You had to treat him as a social equal, and the best way to get along was to be a humble petitioner. "Please, Tecumseh, see if you can do me this great favor!"

V

What did it all mean? Was this really the spirit of an American aborigine dead more than two hundred years? Lanny didn't think so. After reading a number of books and pondering over it for months, he had decided that Tecumseh was a genius; something of the sort which had worked in William Shakespeare, producing a host of characters which the world accepted as more real than living people. In the case of the poet, this genius had been hitched up with his conscious mind, so that the poet knew what it was doing and could put the characters into plays and sell them to managers. But the genius in Madame Zyszynski wasn't hitched up; it stayed hidden in her unconscious and worked there on its own; a wild genius, so to speak, a subterranean one. What, old mole, work'st i' the earth so fast!

This energy played at being an Indian; also it gathered facts from the minds of various persons and wove stories out of them. It dipped into the subconscious mind of Lanny Budd and collected his memories and made them into the spirit of Marcel Detaze, painting pictures on the Cap d'Antibes or looking at ruins in ancient Greece. It dipped into the mind of Jascha Rabinowich and created the spirits of his relatives. Like children finding old costumes in a trunk, putting them on and making up stories about people they have heard of or read of in books—people alive or dead! Every child knows that you have to pretend that it's true, otherwise it's no fun, the imagination doesn't work. If you put on a bearskin, get down on your hands and knees and growl. If you put on the headdress of an Indian chieftain, stalk about the room and command the other children in a deep stern voice—even if it has a Polish accent!

All this seemed to indicate that there was some sort of universal pool of mindstuff, an ocean in which Lanny's thoughts and Madame Zyszynski's and other people's merged and flowed together. Figure yourself as a bubble floating on the surface of an ocean; the sun shines on you and you have very lovely colors; other bubbles float near, and you come together and form a cluster of bubbles—the guests of the yacht *Bessie Budd*, for example. One by one the bubbles break, and their substance returns to the ocean, and in due course becomes the substance of new bubbles.

This theory obliged you to believe that a medium had the power to dip into this mind substance and get facts to which the medium did not have access in any normal way. Was it easier to believe that than to believe that the spirits of dead persons were sending communications to the living? Lanny found it so; for he had lived long enough to watch the human mind develop along with the body and to decay along with it. In some strange way the two seemed to be bound together and to share the same fate. But don't fool yourself into thinking that you knew what the nature of that union was; how a thought could make a muscle move, or how a chemical change in the body could produce cheerful or depressed thoughts. Those questions were going to take wiser men than Lanny Budd to answer them; he kept wishing that people would stop robbing and killing one another and settle down to this task of finding out what they really were.

VI

The hundred-dollar-an-hour cruise was continued eastward, and presently they were approaching the Peninsula of Gallipoli, where so many Englishmen had paid with their lives for the blundering of their superiors. Great ships had gone down, and the beaches had been piled with mangled bodies. Among the many wounded had been the father of Lanny's *amie*, Rosemary Codwilliger, Countess of Sandhaven. He had "passed over" not long ago, and Lanny wondered, did his spirit haunt this place? He asked Tecumseh about it, and it wasn't long before Colonel Codwilliger was "manifesting"; but unfortunately Lanny hadn't known him very well, and must write to Rosemary in the Argentine to find out if the statements were correct.

They passed through the Dardanelles on a gusty, rainy afternoon, and the shores looked much like any other shores veiled in mist. Lanny and Bess walked for a while on deck, and then went into the saloon and played the Schubert four-hand piano sonata. Then Lanny came out again, for somewhere ahead was the Island of Prinkipo which had been so much in his thoughts at the Peace Conference eleven years before. It had been chosen as the place for a meeting with the Bolsheviks, in President Wilson's effort to patch up a truce with them. The elder statesmen had found it difficult to believe there existed a place with such a musical-comedy name.

It might as well have been a musical-comedy performance—such was Lanny's bitter reflection. The statesmen didn't go to Prinkipo, and when later they met the Russians at Genoa they didn't settle anything. They went home to get ready for another war—Lanny was one of those pessimistic persons who were sure it was on the way. He told people so, and they would shrug their shoulders. What could they do about it? What could anybody do? *C'est la nature!*

Perhaps it was the rain which caused these melancholy thoughts; perhaps the spirits of those tens of thousands of dead Englishmen and Turks; or perhaps of the dogs of Constantinople, which during the war had been gathered up and turned loose on this musical-comedy island to starve and devour one another. Under the religion of the country it was not permitted to kill them, so let them eat one another! The Prophet, born among a nomadic people, had loved the dog and praised it as the guardian of the tent; he had endeavored to protect it, but had not been able to foresee great cities with swarms of starveling curs and a dénouement of cannibalism.

The southern hills of this Sea of Marmora had been the scene of events about which Lanny had heard his father talking with Zaharoff. The munitions king had financed the invasion of Turkey by his fellow-Greeks, spending half his fortune on it, so he had said— though of course you didn't have to assume that everything he said was true. Anyhow, the Greeks had been routed and hosts of them driven into the sea, after which the victorious Turkish army had appeared before the British fortifications and the guns of the fleet. This critical situation had brought about the fall of the Lloyd George government and thus played hob with the plans of Robbie Budd for getting oil concessions. Robbie was one of those men who use governments, his own and others', threatening wars and some-times waging them; while Lanny was an amiable playboy who traveled about on a hundred-dollar-an-hour yacht, making beautiful music, reading books of history and psychic research, and being troubled in his conscience about the way the world was going. He asked his friends very earnestly what ought to be done. Some thought they knew; but the trouble was, their opinions differed so greatly.

VII

The company went ashore in the crowded city, which had once been the capital of the Moslem world, and now was known as Istanbul. They got cars, as usual, and were driven about to see the sights. They visited the great cathedral of St. Sophia, and in the seraglio of the late sultan they inspected the harem, in which now and then a faithless wife had been strangled with a cord, tied in a sack, and set afloat in the Bosporus. They strolled through the bazaars, where traders of various races labored diligently to sell them souvenirs, from Bergama rugs to "feelthy postcards." Through the crowded street came a fire-engine with a great clangor; a modern one, painted a brilliant red—but Lanny saw in imagination the young Zaharoff riding the machine, busy with schemes to collect for his services. Were they still called *tulumbadschi?* And did they still charge to put out your fire—or to let it burn, as you preferred?

The unresting *Bessie Budd* stole northward along the coast of the immensely deep Black Sea, called by the ancient Greeks "friendly to strangers." The Soviet Union was in the middle of the Five-Year Plan, and miracles were confidently expected. The travelers' goal was Odessa, a city with a great outdoor stairway which they had seen in a motion picture. Their passports had been visaed and everything arranged in advance; they had only to make themselves known to Intourist, and they would have automobiles and guides and hotels to the limit of their supply of *valuta*.

"I have seen the future and it works." So Lincoln Steffens had said to Lanny Budd. Stef had had the eyes of faith, and so had Hansi and Bess and Rahel. When they looked at buildings much in need of repair and people wearing sneakers and patched sweaters, they said: "Wait till the new factories get going." They told the girl guides that they were "comrades," and they were taken off to inspect the latest styles in day nurseries and communal kitchens. They were motored into the country to visit a co-operative farm; when Hansi was asked about his occupation at home, he admitted that he was a violinist, and the people rushed to provide an instrument. All work on the place stopped while he stood on the front porch and played *Old Folks at Home* and *Kathleen Mavourneen* and Achron's *Hebrew Melody*. It was heart-warming; but would it help get tractors and reapers into condition for the harvest soon to be due?

VIII

Irma went on some of these expeditions, and listened politely to the enthusiasms of her friends; but to Mama Robin she confessed that she found "the future" most depressing. Mama shrugged her shoulders and said: "What would you expect? It's Russia." She had learned about it as a child, and didn't believe it could ever be changed. In the days of the Tsar people had been so unhappy they had got drunk and crawled away into some hole to sleep. The Bolsheviks had tried to stop the making of liquor, but the peasants had made it and smuggled it into the towns—"just like in America," said Mama. She would have preferred not to have these painful old memories revived.

Odessa had changed hands several times during the revolution and civil war. It had been bombarded by the French fleet, and many of its houses destroyed. One of the sights of the city was the Square of the Victims, where thousands of slain revolutionists had been buried in a common grave, under a great pyramid of stones. The young people went to it as to a shrine, while their elders sought entertainment without success. The young ones insisted upon visiting some of the many sanatoriums, which are built near bodies of water formed by silted-up river mouths. These too were shrines, because they were occupied by invalided workers. That was the way it was going to be in the future; those who produced the wealth would enjoy it! "They shall not build, and another inhabit; they shall not plant, and another eat." Thus the ancient Hebrew prophet, and it sounded so Red that in Canada a clergyman had

been indicted by the grand jury for quoting it. Hansi and Rahel
had the blood of these ancient prophets in their veins, and Bess had
been taught that their utterances were the word of God, so this
new religion came easily to them. It promised to save the workers,
and Lanny hoped it would have better success than Mohammed had
had in his efforts to help the watch-dogs of the tents.

Lanny was in his usual position, between the two sets of extremists. During this Russian visit he served as a sort of liaison officer
to the Robin family. Johannes didn't dare to discuss Communism
with any of his young people, for he had found that by doing so
he injured his standing; he talked with Lanny, hoping that something could be done to tone them down. In the opinion of the man
of money, this Bolshevik experiment was surviving on what little
fat it had accumulated during the old regime. People could go on
living in houses so long as they stood up, and they could wear old
clothes for decades if they had no sense of shame—look about you!
But the making of new things was something else again. Of course,
they could hire foreign experts and have factories built, and call it
a Five-Year Plan—but who was going to do any real work if he
could put it off on somebody else? And how could any business
enterprise be run by politicians? "You don't know them," said
Johannes, grimly. "In Germany I have had to."

"It's an experiment," Lanny admitted. "Too bad it had to be
tried in such a backward country."

"All I can say," replied the man of affairs, "is I'm hoping it
doesn't have to be tried in any country where I live!"

IX

This was a situation which had been developing in the Robin
family for many years, ever since Barbara Pugliese and Jesse Blackless had explained the ideals of proletarian revolution to the young
Robins in Lanny's home: an intellectual vaccination which had
taken with unexpected virulence. Lanny had watched with both
curiosity and concern the later unfoldment of events. He knew

how Papa and Mama Robin adored their two boys, centering all their hopes upon them. Papa made money in order that Hansi and Freddi might be free from the humiliations and cares of poverty. Papa and Mama watched their darlings with solicitude, consulting each other as to their every mood and wish. Hansi wanted to play the fiddle; very well, he should be a great musician, with the best teachers, everything to make smooth his path. Freddi wished to be a scholar, a learned person; very well, Papa would pay for everything, and give up his natural desire to have the help of one of his sons in his own business.

It had seemed not surprising that young people should be set afire with hopes of justice for the poor, and the ending of oppression and war. Every Jew in the world knows that his ancient prophets proclaimed such a millennium, the coming of such a Messiah. If Hansi and Freddi were excessive in their fervor, well, that was to be expected at their age. As they grew older, they would acquire discretion and learn what was possible in these days. The good mother and the hard-driving father waited for this, but waited in vain. Here was Hansi twenty-five, and his brother only two years younger, and instead of calming down they appeared to be acquiring a mature determination, with a set of theories or dogmas or whatever you chose to call them, serving as a sort of backbone for their dreams.

To the Jewish couple out of the ghetto the marriage of Hansi to Robbie Budd's daughter had appeared a great triumph, but in the course of time they had discovered there was a cloud to this silver lining. Bess had caught the Red contagion from Hansi, and brought to the ancient Jewish idealism a practicality which Johannes recognized as Yankee, a sternness derived from her ancestral Puritanism. Bess was the reddest of them all, and the most uncompromising. Her expression would be full of pity and tenderness, but it was all for those whom she chose to regard as the victims of social injustice. For those others who held them down and garnered the fruits of their toil she had a dedicated antagonism; when she talked about capitalism and its crimes her face became set, and you knew her for the daughter of one of Cromwell's Ironsides.

Lanny understood that in the depths of his soul Johannes quailed before this daughter-in-law. He tried to placate her with soft words, he tried to bribe her with exactly the right motor-car, a piano of the most exquisite tone, yachting-trips to the most romantic places of the seven seas, and not a single person on board who would oppose her ideas; only the members of her own two families and their attendants. "Look!" the poor man of millions seemed to be saying. "Here is Rahel with a baby who has to be nursed, and here is the lovely baby of your adored brother; here is this ship of dreams which exists for the happiness of all of you. It will go wherever you wish, and the service will be perfect; you can even break the rules of discipline at sea, you and Hansi can go into the forecastle and play music for the crew, or invite them up into the saloon once a week and play for them—in spite of the horror of an old martinet trained in the merchant marine of Germany. Anything, anything on earth, provided you will be gracious, and forgive me for being a millionaire, and not despise me because I have wrung my fortune out of the toil and sweat of the wage-slaves!"

This program of appeasement had worked for four years, for the reason that Bess had laid hold of the job of becoming a pianist. She had concentrated her Puritan fanaticism upon acquiring muscular power and co-ordination, in combining force with delicacy, so that the sounds she produced would not ruin the fine nuances, the exquisite variations of tone, which her more highly trained husband was achieving. But Johannes knew in his soul that this task wasn't going to hold her forever; some day she and Hansi both would consider themselves musicians—and they meant to be Red musicians, to play for Red audiences and earn money for the Red cause. They would make for themselves the same sort of reputation that Isadora Duncan had made by waving red scarves at her audiences and dancing the *Marseillaise*. They would plunge into the hell of the class struggle, which everyone could see growing hotter day by day all over Europe.

X

Besides Mama, the only person to whom Johannes Robin unbos-omed himself of these anxieties was Lanny Budd, who had always been so wise beyond his years, a confidant at the age of fourteen, a counselor and guide at the age of nineteen. Lanny had brought Johannes together with his father, and listened to their schemes, and knew many of the ins and outs of their tradings. He knew that Johannes had been selling Budd machine guns to Nazi agents, to be used in the open warfare these people carried on with the Commu-nists in the streets of Berlin. Johannes had asked Lanny never to mention this to the boys, and Lanny had obliged him. What would they do if they found it out? They might refuse to live any longer in the Berlin palace, or to travel in the hundred-dollar-an-hour yacht. Bess might even refuse to let it carry her name. Thus Jascha Rabinowich, standing in front of his private wailing wall. *Oi, oi!*

He was in the position only too familiar to the members of his race through two thousand years of the Diaspora: surrounded by enemies, and having to play them one against another, to placate them by subtle arts. Johannes had risen to power by his shrewd-ness as a speculator, knowing whom to pay for inside information and how to separate the true from the false. Having made huge sums out of the collapse of the mark, he had bought up concerns which were on the verge of bankruptcy. To hold them and keep them going meant, in these days of governmental interference with business, some sort of alliance with politicians; it meant paying them money which was close to blackmail and became ever closer as time passed. It meant not merely knowing the men who were in power, but guessing who might be in power next week, and mak-ing some sort of deal with them.

So it came about that Johannes was helping to maintain the coa-lition government of the Republic and at the same time supporting several of the ambitious Nazis; for, under the strain of impending national bankruptcy, who could tell what might happen? Knowing that his children were in touch with the Reds, and continually being importuned for money—who wasn't, that had money?—Johannes

would give them generous sums, knowing that they would pass
these on to be used for their "cause." Yet another form of insurance! But do not let any of these groups know that you are giving
to the others, for they are in a deadly three-cornered war, each
against the other two.

All this meant anxious days and sleepless nights. And Mama, from
whom nothing could be hidden, would argue: "What is it for?
Why do we need so much money?" It was hard for her to understand that you must get more in order to protect what you had.
She and the children would join in efforts to get Papa away from
it all. For the past three summers they had lured him into a yachting-
trip. This year they had started earlier, on account of the two young
mothers, and they were hoping to keep him away all summer.

But it appeared that troubles were piling up in Berlin: business
troubles, political troubles. Johannes was receiving batches of mail
at the different ports, and he would shut himself up with his secretary and dictate long telegrams. That was one of his complaints
concerning the Soviet Union: letters might be opened, and telegrams were uncertain; you paid for them but couldn't be sure they
would arrive. Everything was in the hands of bureaucrats, and you
were wound up in miles of red tape—God pity the poor people who
had to get a living in such a world. Johannes, man of swift decisions, plowman of his own field, builder of his own road, couldn't
stand Odessa, and asked them to give up seeing the beautiful Sochi.
"There are just as grand palaces near Istanbul, and the long-distance
telephone works!"

XI

The *Bessie Budd* returned in her own wake, and in Istanbul its
owner received more telegrams which worried him. The yacht had
to wait until he sent answers and received more answers, and in the
end he announced that he couldn't possibly go on. There was serious trouble involving one of the banks he controlled. Decisions had
to be made which couldn't be left to subordinates. He had made a
mistake to come away in such unsettled times!—the Wall Street

crash had shaken all Europe, and little by little the cracks were revealing themselves. Johannes had to beg his guests to excuse him. He took a plane for Vienna, and from there to Berlin.

It had come to be that way now; there were planes every day between all the great capitals of Europe. You stepped in, hardly knew that you were flying, and in a few hours stepped out and went about your affairs. Not the slightest danger; but it tormented Mama to think of Jascha up there amid thunder and lightning, and so many things to bump into when you came down. They waited in Istanbul until a telegram arrived, saying that the traveler was safe in his own palace and that Freddi was well and happy, and sent love to all.

It was too late to visit the coast of Africa—the rains had come, and it was hot, and there would be mosquitoes. They made themselves contented on the yacht, and did not bother to go ashore. The dairy farm prospered; the ample refrigerators provided the two young mothers with fresh foods, and they in turn provided for the infants. The grandmothers hovered over the scene in such a flutter of excitement as made you think of humming-birds' wings. Really, it appeared as if there had never been two babies in the world before and never would be again. Grandmothers, mothers, babies, and attendants formed a closed corporation, a secret society, an organization of, by, and for women.

It was a machine that ran as by clockwork, and the balance wheel was the grave Miss Severne. She had been employed to manage only Baby Frances; but she was so highly educated, so perfectly equipped, that she overawed the Robins; she was the voice of modern science, speaking the last word as to the phenomena of infancy. Equally important, she had the English manner, she was Britannia which rules the waves and most of the shores; she was authority, and the lesser breeds without the law decided to come in. What one grandmother was forbidden to do was obviously bad form for the other to do; what little Frances's nursemaid was ordered to do was obviously desirable for little Johannes's nursemaid to do. So in the end Jerusalem placed itself under the British flag; Rahel made Miss Severne a present now and then, and she ran the whole enterprise.

Every morning Marceline was in Miss Addington's cabin, reciting her lessons. Mr. Dingle was in his cabin thinking his new thoughts and saying his old prayers. Madame Zyszynski was in hers, playing solitaire, or perhaps giving a "sitting." That left Hansi, Bess, and Lanny in the saloon, the first two working out their interpretation of some great violin classic, and Lanny listening critically while they played a single passage many times, trying the effect of this and that. Just what did Beethoven mean by the repetition of this rhythmic pattern? Here he had written *sforzando*, but he often wrote that when he meant *tenuto*, an expressive accent, the sound to be broadened—but be careful, it is a trick which becomes a bad habit, a meretricious device. They would discuss back and forth, but always in the end they deferred to Hansi; he was the one who had the gift, he was the genius who lived music in his soul. Sometimes the spirit caught them, they became not three souls but one, and it was an hour of glory.

These young people could never be bored on the longest yachting-cruise. They took their art with them, a storehouse of loveliness, a complex of ingenuities, a treasure-chest of delights which you could never empty. Lanny had stabbed away at the piano all his life, but now he discovered that he had been skimming over the surface of a deep ocean. Now he analyzed scientifically what before he had enjoyed emotionally. Hansi Robin had had a thorough German training, and had read learned books on harmony, acoustics, the history of music. He studied the personalities of composers, and he tried to present these to his audiences; he did not try to turn Mozart into Beethoven, or Gluck into Liszt. He would practice the most difficult Paganini or Wieniawski stuff, but wouldn't play it in public unless he could find a soul in it. Finger gymnastics were for your own use.

XII

Every afternoon, if the weather was right, the vessel would come to a halt, and the guests, all but Mama Robin, would emerge on the deck in bathing-suits; the gangway would be let down over the side, and they would troop down and plunge into the water. A

sailor stood by with a life-belt attached to a rope, in case of accident; they were all good swimmers, but the efficient Captain Moeller
took no chances and was always on watch himself. When they had
played themselves tired, they would climb up, and the yacht would
resume her course. The piano on little rubber wheels would be
rolled out from the saloon, and Hansi and Bess would give an al-
fresco concert; Rahel would sing, and perhaps lead them all in a
chorus. Twilight would fall, "the dusk of centuries and of song."

There was only one trouble on this cruise so far as concerned
Lanny, and that was the game of bridge. Beauty and Irma had to
play; not for money, but for points, for something to do. These
ladies knew how to read, in the sense that they knew the meaning
of the signs on paper, but neither knew how to lose herself in a
book or apply herself to the mastering of its contents. They grew
sleepy when they tried it; they wanted other people to tell them
what was in books; and Irma at least had always been able to pay
for the service. Now she had married a poor man, and understood
it to mean that he was to keep her company. In the world of Irma
Barnes the nursery rhyme had been turned about, and every Jill
must have her Jack.

Lanny didn't really mind playing bridge—only there were so
many more interesting things to do. He wanted to continue child
study with the two specimens he had on board. He wanted to read
history about the places he visited, so that a town would be where
a great mind had functioned or a martyr had died. But Beauty and
Irma were willing to bid five no trumps while the yacht was passing the scene of the battle of Salamis. They would both think it
inconsiderate of Lanny if he refused to make a fourth hand because
he wanted to write up his notes of the last séance with Madame
Zyszynski. Lanny thought it was important to keep proper records,
and index them, so that the statements of Tecumseh on one occasion could be compared with those on another. He had the books
of Osty and Geley, scientists who had patiently delved into these
phenomena and tried to evolve theories to explain them. This seemed
much more important than whether Culbertson was right in his
rules about the total honor-trick-content requirement of hands.

Irma had persuaded Rahel to prepare herself for life in the *beau monde*, and Lanny had helped to teach her. Then he had given the same sort of help to Marceline, who was going to be thirteen in a short while, and already was the most perfect little society lady you could imagine. Even on board a yacht she spent much time in front of the mirror, studying her charms and keeping them at their apex; surely she ought to be preparing to defend herself against those harpies with signaling-systems who would soon be trying to deprive her of her pocket-money. After she had been taught, Lanny could plead that he wasn't needed any more, and go back to the study of Liszt's four-hand piano compositions with Bess: the *Concerto Pathétique*, a marvel of brilliant color, turning two pianos into an orchestra; the *Don Juan Fantaisie*, most delightful of showpieces— Hansi came in while they were playing it, and said they really ought to give it on a concert stage. A memorable moment for two humble amateurs.

XIII

The *Bessie Budd* came to rest in the harbor of Cannes, and the company returned to Bienvenu for a few days. Beauty wished to renew her wardrobe—one gets so tired of wearing the same things. Lanny wished to renew the stock of music-scores—one's auditors get tired of hearing the same compositions. Also, there were stacks of magazines which had been coming in, and letters with news of one's friends. Lanny opened one from his father, and exclaimed: "Robbie's coming to Paris! He's due there now!"

"Oh, dear!" said the wife. She knew what was coming next.

"I really ought to see him, Irma. It's been eight months."

"It's been exactly as long since I've seen my mother."

"Surely if your mother were in Paris, I'd be offering to take you."

"It'll be so dreadfully lonesome on the yacht, Lanny!"

"I'll take a plane and join you at Lisbon in three or four days. You know Robbie's been in a crisis and I ought to find out how he's getting along."

Irma gave up, but not without inner revolt. She was going through such a trying ordeal, and people ought to do everything to make it easier for her. A violent change from being the glamour girl of Broadway, the observed of all observers, the darling of the columnists and target of the spotlights—and now to be in exile, almost in jail for all these months! Would anybody ever appreciate it? Would Baby appreciate it? Irma's observation of children suggested that Baby probably would not.

She thought of taking a couple of cars and transporting her half of the lactation apparatus up to Paris. But no, it would upset all the arrangements of the admirable Miss Severne; Baby might pick up a germ in the streets of a crowded city; it was so much safer out at sea, where the air was loaded with a stuff called ozone. And there was Rahel, with whom Irma had agreed to stick it out; knowing it would be hard, she had wanted to tie herself down, and had made a bargain.

"Another thing," Lanny said; "Zoltan Kertezsi should be in Paris and might help me to sell a picture or two."

"Oh, dear!" exclaimed the wife. "Do you still want to fool with that business?"

"A little cash would come in handy to both Beauty and me."

"I don't think it's kind of you, Lanny. There's no sense in your bothering to make money when I have it. If you have any time to sell, do please let me buy it!"

They had talked about this many times. Since Robbie couldn't afford to send Beauty her thousand dollars a month, Irma insisted upon putting it up. She wanted the life of Bienvenu to go on exactly as before. The cost was nothing to her, and she liked the people around her to be happy. She would send money to Lanny's account in Cannes, and then she didn't want anybody to talk or think about the subject. That her husband might actually enjoy earning a few thousand dollars by selling Marcel's paintings, or those of old masters, was something hard for her to make real to herself. It was harder still for Lanny to explain that he sometimes wanted to do other things than entertain an adored young wife!

4

I Can Call Spirits

FROM the windows of the Hotel Crillon Lanny Budd had looked out upon quite a lot of history: the World War beginning, with soldiers bivouacked in the Place de la Concorde; the war in progress, with enemy planes overhead and anti-aircraft firing; after the armistice, with a great park of captured German cannon, and May Day mobs being sabered by cuirassiers. In the hotel had lived and worked a couple of hundred American peace-makers, all of them kind to a very young secretary-translator and willing to assist with his education. The only trouble was, they differed so greatly among themselves that Lanny's mind had reached a state of confusion from which it had not yet recovered.

Now the hotel had been restored to the system of private enterprise in which Robbie Budd so ardently believed and which he was pleased to patronize regardless of cost. In view of his reduced circumstances, he might well have gone to a less expensive place, but that would have been to admit defeat and to declass himself. No, he was still European representative of Budd Gunmakers, still looking for big deals and certain that Europe was going to need American weapons before long. Keep your chin up, and make a joke out of the fact that you have lost five or six million dollars. Everybody knows that you had to be somebody to have that happen to you.

Here he was, comfortably ensconced in his suite, with a spare room for Lanny; his whisky and soda and ice early in the morning, his little portable typewriter and papers spread out on another table. He was in his middle fifties, but looked younger than he had in New York under the strain of the panic. He had got back his ruddy complexion and well-nourished appearance; a little bit portly, but still vigorous and ready to tackle the world. Already he was in the midst of affairs; there was a Rumanian purchasing-commission in town, and a couple of Soviet agents—Robbie grinned as he said that he was becoming quite chummy with the "comrades"; he knew how to "talk their language," thanks to Lanny's help. He meant, not that he could speak Russian, but that he could speak Red.

Lanny told the news about the Dingles and the Robins, and Robbie in turn reported on the family in Newcastle. Amazing the way the head of the Budd tribe was holding on; at the age of eighty-three he insisted upon knowing every detail of the company's affairs; he sat in his study and ran the business by telephone. Esther, Lanny's stepmother, was well. "I really think she's happier since the crash," said the husband. He didn't add: "I have kept my promise to stay out of the market." Lanny knew he didn't break promises.

They talked about Wall Street, about that "little bull market" which had everybody so stirred up, a mixture of hope and fear currently known as the "jitters." When the *Bessie Budd* was setting out, the market had been booming, and Robbie in a letter had repeated his old formula: "Don't sell America short." Now stocks were slipping again, business going to pot, unemployment spreading; but Robbie had to keep up his courage, all America had to hold itself up by its bootstraps. The most popular song of the moment announced: "Happy days are here again."

II

They discussed Johannes Robin and his affairs, in which Robbie was deeply interested. He was going to Berlin on this trip: a subtle change in the relationship of the two associates, for in the old days it had been Johannes who came to Paris to see Robbie. The Jewish trader was on top; he hadn't lost any part of his fortune, and wasn't going to. He would never make Robbie Budd's mistake of being too optimistic about this world, for he had made most of his money by expecting trouble. Now he had sent a message, by Lanny, that he was going to help Robbie to come back; but it would have to be by the same judicious pessimism.

"He's a good sort," said Robbie, English-fashion. He knew, of course, that his old associate couldn't very well drop him, even if he had wished to, because Hansi and Bess had made them relatives. Moreover, Johannes was one of those Jews who desire to associate with gentiles and are willing to pay liberally for it.

Having had long talks with the financier on board the yacht, Lanny could tell what was in his mind. He considered that Germany was approaching the end of her rope; she couldn't make any more reparations payments, even if she wished. Taxation had about reached its limits, foreign credit was drying up, and Johannes couldn't see any chance of Germany's escaping another bout of inflation. The government was incompetent, also very costly to deal with; that, of course, was a money-man's polite way of intimating that it was corrupt and that he was helping to keep it so. Elections were scheduled for the end of the summer, and there would be a bitter campaign; sooner or later the various factions would fall to fighting, and that wouldn't help the financial situation any. Johannes was trimming his sails and getting ready for rough weather. He was taking some of his investments out of the country. Those he kept in Germany were mostly in industries which produced goods for export.

Lanny made a brief report upon the younger Robins, and the present condition of their political diseases. Fate had played a strange prank upon the business association known as "Robin and Robbie." The Robin half had got somewhat the worst of it, having two Reds and two Pinks, whereas Robbie had only one Red and one Pink, and didn't see either very often. The Robin half was considerate and never referred to the fact that the infection had come from the Robbie side. Johannes knew how his associate hated and despised Jesse Blackless, the man who had talked revolution to Lanny, and then to Hansi and Freddi, seducing these sensitive, idealistic minds away from their fathers.

Robbie wanted to know about Irma, and how she and Lanny

were making out. Very important, that; the father had found out last October what a convenient thing it was to have the Barnes fortune back of you. He hoped that Lanny wasn't going to fail to make a success of it. Lanny reported that he and Irma were getting along as well as most young couples he had known; better than some. Irma wanted a lot, and most of the things he was interested in didn't mean much to her, but they were in love with each other, and they found the baby a source of satisfaction. Robbie said you never got everything you wanted out of a marriage, but you could put up with a lot when it included a thumping big fortune. Lanny knew that wasn't the noblest view to take of the holy bonds of matrimony, but all he said was: "Don't worry. We'll make out."

III

One of Robbie's purposes was to see Zaharoff. The New England-Arabian Oil Company had managed to survive the panic, but Robbie and his associates at home needed cash and must find a buyer for their shares. Doubtless the old spider knew all about their plight, but Robbie would put up a bold front. As usual, he asked if his son would like to go along, and as usual the son wouldn't have missed it for anything. He had never given up the hope that somehow he might be able to help his father in his dealings with the retired munitions king of Europe.

Robbie phoned the old man's home, and learned that he was at his country estate, the Château de Balincourt in Seine-et-Oise, close to Paris. Robbie sent a telegram, and received an appointment for the next afternoon; he ordered a car through the hotel, and they were motored to the place, which had once belonged to King Leopold of Belgium. Now there was a new kind of kings in Europe, and one of them was this ex-fireman of Constantinople. A lodge-keeper swung back the gates for them, and they rolled down a tree-lined drive and were received at the door by an East Indian servant in native costume. All the servants were Hindus; an aged king wanted silence and secrecy, and one way was to have attend-

ants who understood only a few simple commands. One of Zaharoff's married daughters lived with him, and no one came save by
appointment.

The visitors were escorted into a drawing-room decorated in the
lavish French fashion. On the walls were paintings, and Lanny had
been invited to see them, so now he took the occasion. But it didn't
last long, for the owner came in. His heavy shoulders seemed a bit
more bowed than when Lanny had watched him, in his undershirt,
burning his private papers in the drawing-room of his Paris house
and setting fire to the chimney in the process. Now he wore an
embroidered purple smoking-jacket, and his white mustache and
imperial were neatly trimmed. He had become almost entirely bald.

"*Eh, bien, mon garçon?*" he said to Lanny.

Being at the beginning of his thirties, Lanny felt quite grown up,
but understood that this might not impress one who was at the
beginning of his eighties. "I was looking at your paintings," he
remarked. "You have a fine Ingres."

"Yes; but I have looked at it for so many years."

"Paintings should be like old friends, Sir Basil."

"Most of my old friends are gone, and the younger ones are busy
with their affairs. They tell me you have been making your fortune."

It was an allusion to Irma, and not exactly a delicate one; but
Lanny knew that this old man was money-conscious. The duquesa,
his companion, had tried tactfully to cure him of the defect, but
without succeeding. Lanny was not surprised when Zaharoff added:
"You will no longer have to be a picture-dealer, *hein?*"

He smiled and answered: "I get a lot of fun out of it."

The old man's remark was noted by Robbie, who had said on the
way out that if Zaharoff knew that Lanny had the Barnes fortune
behind him, he might expect to pay a higher price for the shares of
the New England-Arabian Oil Company!

They seated themselves, and tea was served; for Robbie it was
scotch and soda. The two men discussed the state of business in
Europe and America, and Lanny listened attentively, as he had
always done. One who found pleasure in buying and selling old
masters could learn from the technique being here revealed. The

Knight Commander of the Bath of England and Grand Officer of the Légion d'Honneur of France was the very soul of courtesy, of suavity in manner; a bit deprecating, as if he were saying: "I am a very old man, and it would not be fair to take advantage of me." His soft voice caressed you and his smile wooed you, but at the same time his blue eyes watched you warily.

He was known as "the mystery man of Europe," and doubtless there had been mysteries enough about what he was doing in the political and financial worlds; but so far as his character was concerned, Lanny no longer found any mystery. An aged plutocrat had fought his way up in the world by many deeds of which he now did not enjoy the contemplation. He had intrigued and threatened, bribed and cajoled, made promises and broken them; by tireless scheming and pushing he had acquired the mastery of those great establishments which the various countries of Europe needed in order to wage their wars of power. But all the time he had remained in his soul a Greek peasant living among cruel oppressing Turks. He had been afraid of a thousand things: of his own memories, of the men he had thwarted and ruined, of slanderers, blackmailers, assassins, Reds—and, above all, of what he had helped to make Europe. A man who wanted to sell munitions, who wanted all the nations of the earth to spend their incomes upon munitions, but who didn't want any munitions shot off—at least not anywhere within his own hearing! Unaccountably the shooting continued, Europe seemed to be going from bad to worse, and Zaharoff's conversation revealed that he trusted nobody in power and had very little hope of anything.

A bitter, sad old man, he felt his powers waning, and had hidden himself away from dangers. He would soon be gone; and did he worry about where he was going? Or was it about what was going to become of his possessions? He mourned his beloved Spanish duquesa of the many names. Did he contemplate the possibility of being reunited to her? Lanny had something to say to him on that subject, but must wait until the two traders had got through with their duel of wits.

IV

It was Robbie Budd who had sought this interview, and he who would have to say what he had come for. Zaharoff, while waiting, would be gravely interested in what Robbie had to tell about the state of Wall Street and the great American financial world. The visitor was optimistic, sure that the clouds would soon blow over. Lanny knew that his father really believed that, but would Zaharoff believe that he believed it? No, the Greek would think that Robbie, having something to sell, was playing the optimist. Zaharoff, the prospective buyer, was a pessimist.

At last Robbie saw fit to get down to business. He explained that his father was very old, and the cares of the Budd enterprise might soon be on Robbie's shoulders. Budd's was largely out of munitions; it was making everything from needles to freight elevators. Robbie would no longer be in a position to travel—in short, he and his friends were looking for someone to take the New England-Arabian shares off their hands at a reasonable figure.

There it was; and Zaharoff's pessimism assumed the hues of the nethermost stage of Dante's inferno. The world was in a most horrible state; the Arabians were on the point of declaring a jihad and wiping out every European on their vast desolate hot peninsula; Zaharoff himself was a feeble old man, his doctors had given him final warning, he must avoid every sort of responsibility and strain —in short, he couldn't buy anything, and didn't have the cash anyhow.

A flat turn-down; but Lanny had heard a Levantine trader talk, and knew that Zaharoff's real purpose and desire would not be revealed until the last minute, when his two guests had their hats in their hands, perhaps when they were outside the front door. Meanwhile they mustn't show that they knew this; they mustn't betray disappointment; they must go on chatting, as if it didn't really mean very much to them, as if Robbie Budd had crossed the ocean to have one more look at Zaharoff's blue eyes, or perhaps at his very fine Ingres.

It was time for Lanny to mention the paintings, which he had been invited to inspect. He asked if he might stroll about the room, and the Knight Commander and Grand Officer rose from his seat and strolled with him, pointing out various details. Lanny said: "You know I am interested in the value of paintings, that being my business." The remark gave no offense; quite the contrary. The old man told the prices, which he had at his fingertips: a hundred thousand francs for this Fragonard, a hundred and fifty thousand for that David. "Before-the-war francs," he added.

They went into the great library, a magnificent room with a balcony all around it, having heavy bronze railings. Then they inspected the dining-room, in which was a startling Goya, the portrait of an abnormally tall and thin Spanish gentleman wearing brilliant-colored silks with much lace and jewelry. "An ancestor of my wife," remarked the old man. "She didn't care for it much; she found it cynical."

An opening which Lanny had been waiting for. "By the way, Sir Basil, here is something which might interest you. Have you ever tried any experiments with mediums?"

"Spiritualist mediums, you mean? Why do you ask?"

"Because of something strange which has been happening in our family. My stepfather interested my mother in the subject, and in New York they found a Polish woman with whom they held séances, and she gave them such convincing results that we brought her to the Riviera with us, and she has become a sort of member of our family."

"You think she brings you messages from—" The old man stopped, as if hesitating to say "the dead."

"We get innumerable messages from what claim to be spirits, and they tell us things which astonish us, because we cannot see how this old and poorly educated Polish woman can possibly have had any means of finding them out."

"There is a vast system of fraud of that sort, I have been told," said the cautious Greek.

"I know, Sir Basil; and if this were an alert-minded woman, I might think it possible. But she is dull and quite unenterprising. How could she possibly have known that the duquesa was fond of tulips, and the names of the varieties she showed me?"

"*What?*" exclaimed the host.

"She mentioned the names Bybloem and Bizarre, and spoke of Turkestan, though she didn't get it as the name of a tulip. She even gave me a very good description of the garden of your town house, and the number fifty-three. She was trying to get Avenue Hoche, but could only get the H."

Lanny had never before seen this cautious old man reveal such emotion. Evidently a secret spring had been touched. "Sit down," he said, and they took three of the dining-room chairs. "Is this really true, Lanny?"

"Indeed it is. I have the records of a hundred or more sittings."

"This concerns me deeply, because of late years I have had very strange feelings, as if my wife was in the room and trying to communicate with me. I have told myself that it could only be the product of my own grief and loneliness. I don't need to tell you how I felt about her."

"No, Sir Basil, I have always understood; the little I saw of her was enough to convince me that she was a lovely person."

"Six years have passed, and my sorrow has never diminished. Tell me—where is this Polish woman?" When Lanny explained about the yacht, he wanted to know: "Do you suppose it would be possible for me to have a séance with her?"

"It could be arranged some time, without doubt. We should be deeply interested in the results."

V

For half an hour or more the rich but unhappy old man sat asking questions about Madame Zyszynski and her procedure. Lanny explained the curious obligation of pretending to believe in an Iroquois Indian chieftain who spoke with a Polish accent. No easy matter for an intellectual person to take such a thing seriously; but Lanny told about a lady who had been his *amie* for many years

prior to her death; she had sent him messages, including little details such as two lovers remember, but which would have no meaning for others: the red-and-white-striped jacket of the servant who
attended them in the inn where they had spent their first night, the
pear and apricot trees against the walls of the lady's garden. Such
things might have come out of Lanny's subconscious mind, but
even so, it was a curious experience to have somebody dig them up.

"I would like very much to try the experiment," said Zaharoff.
"When do you think it could be arranged?"

"I will have to consult my mother and my stepfather. The yacht
is on the way from Cannes to Bremen, and the plan is to go from
there to America and return in the autumn. If you go to Monte
Carlo next winter, we could bring Madame over to you."

"That is a long time to wait. Would it not be possible for me to
bring her here for at least a trial? Perhaps the yacht may be stopping
in the Channel?"

"We expect to stop on the English coast, perhaps at Portsmouth
or Dover."

"If so, I would gladly send someone to England to bring her to
me. I would expect to pay her, you understand."

"There is no need of that. We are taking care of her, and she is
satisfied, so it would be better not to raise the question."

"This might mean a great deal to me, Lanny. If I thought that
I was in contact with my wife, and that I had some chance of seeing her again, it would give me more happiness than anything I can
think of." There was a pause, as if a retired munitions king needed
a violent effort to voice such feelings. "I have met no one in any
way approaching her. You have heard, perhaps, that I waited thirty-
four years to marry her, and then she was spared to me barely
eighteen months."

Lanny knew that Zaharoff and the duquesa had been living together during all those thirty-four years; but this was not to be
mentioned. A young free lance could mention casually that he had
had an *amie*, but the richest man in Europe had to look out for
chantage and scandal-mongers—especially when the lady's insane
husband had been a cousin to the King of Spain!

"If you want to make a convincing test," continued Lanny, "it would be better not to let Madame Zyszynski know whom she is to meet. She rarely asks questions, either before or after a sitting. She will say: 'Did you get good results?' and if you tell her: 'Very good,' she is satisfied. I should advise meeting her in some hotel room, with nothing to give her any clue."

"Listen, my boy," said the old man, with more eagerness than Lanny had ever seen him display in the sixteen years of their acquaintance, "if you will make it possible for me to see this woman in the next few days, I will come to any place on the French coast that you name."

"In that case I think I can promise to arrange it. I am to fly and join the yacht at Lisbon, and as soon as I can set a date, I will telegraph you. In the meantime, say nothing, and my father and I will be the only persons in the secret. I will tell my mother that I have a friend who wants to make a private test; and to Madame I won't say even that."

VI

To this long conversation Robbie Budd had listened in silence. He didn't believe in a hereafter, but he believed in giving the old spider, the old gray wolf, the old devil, whatever would entertain him and put him under obligations to the Budd family. When they rose to leave, Zaharoff turned to him and said: "About those shares: would you like me to see if some of my old-time associates would be interested in them?"

"Certainly, Sir Basil."

"If you will send me the necessary data concerning the company——"

"I have the whole set-up with me." Robbie pointed to his brief-case. "I have thirty-five thousand shares at my disposal."

"Are you prepared to put a price on them?"

"We are asking a hundred and twenty dollars a share. That represents exactly the amount of the investment."

"But you have had generous profits, have you not?"

"Not excessive, in view of the period of time and the work that I have put in on it."

"People are glad to get back the half of their investment these days, Mr. Budd."

"Surely not in oil, Sir Basil."

"Well, leave the documents with me, and I'll see what I can do and let you hear in the next few days."

They took their leave; and in their car returning to Paris, Robbie said: "Son, that was an inspiration! How did you think of it?"

"Well, it happened, and I thought he'd want to know."

"That business about the tulips really happened?"

"Of course."

"It was certainly most convenient. If that woman can convince him that the duquesa is sending him messages, there's nothing he won't do. We may get our price."

Lanny well knew that his father wasn't very sensitive when he was on the trail of a business deal; but then, neither is a spider, a wolf, or a devil. "I hope you do," he said.

"He means to buy the shares himself," continued Robbie. "It will take a lot of bargaining. Don't let him see too much of the woman until he pays up."

"The more he sees, the more he may want," countered the son.

"Yes, but suppose he buys her away from you entirely?"

"That's a chance we have to take, I suppose."

"My guess is he won't be able to believe that the thing is on the level. If he gets results, he'll be sure you told the woman in advance."

"Well," said the young idealist, "he'll be punishing his own sins. Goethe has a saying that all guilt avenges itself upon earth."

But Robbie wasn't any more interested in spirituality than he was in spirits. "If I can swing this deal, I'll be able to pay off the notes that I gave you and Beauty and Marceline."

"You don't have to worry about those notes, Robbie. We aren't suffering."

"All the same, it's not pleasant to know that I took the money which you had got by selling Marcel's paintings."

"If it hadn't been for you," said the young philosopher, "I

wouldn't have been here, Beauty would have married some third-rate painter in Montmartre, and Marceline wouldn't have been traveling about in a private yacht. I have pointed that out to them."

"All the same," said Robbie, "I came over here to sell those shares. Let's get as much of the old rascal's money as we can."

Lanny had made jokes about the firm of "R and R." In the days when his mother and Bess had been trying to find him a wife, there had been a firm of "B and B." Now he said: "We'll have a 'Z and Z.' "

VII

Back in Paris Lanny might have sat in at a conference and learned about the rearmament plans of the Rumanian government; but he had an engagement with Zoltan Kertezsi to visit the Salon and discuss the state of the picture market. The blond Hungarian was one of those happy people who never look a day older; always he had just discovered something new and exciting in the art world, always he wanted to tell you about it with a swift flow of words, and always his rebellious hair and fair mustache seemed to be sharing in his gestures. There wasn't anything first rate in the Salon, he reported, but there was a young Russian genius, Alexander Jacovleff, being shown at one of the galleries; a truly great draftsman, and Lanny must come and have a look right away. Also, Zoltan had come upon a discovery, a set of Blake water-color drawings which had been found in an old box in a manor-house in Surrey; they were genuine, and still fresh in color; nobody else on earth could have done such angels and devils; doubtless they had been colored by Blake's wife, but that was true of many Blakes. They ought to fetch at least a thousand pounds apiece——

Immediately Lanny began running over in his mind the names of persons who might be interested in such a treasure trove. It wasn't only because Zoltan would pay him half the commission; it was because it was a game that he had learned to play. No use for Irma to object, no use to think that the money she deposited to his account would ever bring him the same thrills as he got from putting through a deal.

"We shan't be able to get what we used to," said the friend. "You'd be astonished the way prices are being cut."

No matter; the pictures were just as beautiful, and if you kept your tastes simple, you could live and enjoy them. But the dealers who had loaded themselves up were going to have trouble paying their high rents; and the poor devils who did the painting would wander around with their canvases under their arms, and set them up in the windows of tobacco-shops and every sort of place, coming back two or three times a day and gazing at them wistfully, hoping that this might cause some passer-by to stop and take an interest.

Paris in the springtime was lovely, as always, and the two friends strolled along, feasting their eyes upon the chestnut blossoms and their olfactories upon the scents of flowerbeds. Zoltan was near fifty, but he acted and talked as young as his friend; he was full of plans to travel here and there, to see this and that. He was always meeting some delightful new person, discovering some new art treasure. Happy indeed is the man with whom business and pleasure are thus combined! A thousand old masters had made life easy for him, by producing works over which he could rave and feel proud when he secured one for some customer.

There were always wealthy persons on the hunt for famous works of art; and Zoltan would caution his Pink friend not to be too contemptuous in his attitude toward such persons. Many were ignorant and pretentious, but others were genuine art lovers who could be helped and encouraged; and that was not only good business, it was a public service, for many of these collections would come to museums in the end. Zoltan didn't know much about economics, and didn't bother his head with Lanny's revolutionary talk; he said that, no matter what happened, the paintings would survive, and people would want to see them, and there would be occupation for the man who had cultivated his tastes and could tell the rare and precious from the cheap and common.

VIII

Lanny rented a car and motored Zoltan out to have lunch with
Emily Chattersworth at her estate, Les Forêts, where she spent the
greater part of each year, a very grand place of which Lanny had
memories from childhood. On this lawn under the great beech-
trees he had listened to Anatole France exposing the scandals of the
kings and queens of old-time France. In this drawing-room he had
played the piano for Isadora Duncan, and had been invited to elope
with her. Here also he had played accompaniments for Hansi, the
day when Hansi and Bess had met and fallen irrevocably in love.

The white-haired châtelaine wanted to hear the news of all the
families. She was interested in the story of Zaharoff and the duquesa,
whom she had known. Emily had had a séance with Madame Zyszynski, but hadn't got any significant results; it must be because she
was hostile to the idea, and had frightened the spirits! She preferred
to ask Zoltan's opinion of the Salon, which she had visited. Having
a couple of paintings which no longer appealed to her taste, she
showed them to the expert and heard his estimate of what they might
bring. She told him not to hurry; she had lost a lot of money, as
everybody else had, but apparently it was only a paper loss, for the
stocks were still paying dividends. Lanny advised her not to count
on that.

A young Pink wouldn't come to Paris without calling at the office
of *Le Populaire* and exchanging ideas with Jean Longuet and Léon
Blum. Lanny knew what they thought, because he read their paper,
but they would want to hear how the workers' education movement was going in the Midi, and what the son of an American industrialist had seen in the Soviet Union. From a luncheon with Longuet,
Lanny strolled to look at picture exhibitions, and then climbed the
Butte de Montmartre to the unpretentious apartment where Jesse
Blackless was in the midst of composing a manifesto to be published
in *L'Humanité*, denouncing Longuet and his paper as agents and
tools of capitalist reaction. When Jesse learned that his nephew had
been to Odessa he began to ply him with questions, eager for every
crumb of reassurance as to the progress of the Five-Year Plan.

Jesse lived here with his companion, a Communist newspaper employee. Theirs was a hard-working life with few pleasures; Jesse had no time to paint, he said; the reactionaries were getting ready to shut down upon the organized workers and put them out of business. The next elections in France might be the last to be held under the Republic. Lanny's Red uncle lived under the shadow of impending class war; his life was consecrated to hating the capitalist system and teaching others to share that feeling.

He was going into this campaign to fight both capitalists and Socialists. Lanny thought it was a tragedy that the labor groups couldn't get together to oppose enemies so much stronger than themselves. But there couldn't be collaboration between those who thought the change might be brought about by parliamentary action and those who thought that it would have to be done by force. When you used the last phrase to Jesse Blackless, he would insist that it was the capitalists who would use force, and that the attitude of the workers was purely defensive; they would be attacked, their organizations overthrown—the whole pattern had been revealed in Italy.

Lanny would answer: "That is just quibbling. The Communists take an attitude which makes force inevitable. If you start to draw a gun on a man, he knows that his life depends upon his drawing first."

Could capitalism be changed gradually? Could the job be done by voting some politicians out of office and voting others in? Lanny had come upon a quotation of Karl Marx, admitting that a gradual change might be brought about in the Anglo-Saxon countries, which had had parliamentary institutions for a long time. Most Reds didn't know that their master had said that, and wouldn't believe it when you told them; it seemed to give the whole Bolshevik case away. Jesse said that quoting Marx was like quoting the Bible: you could find anything you wanted.

They went on arguing, saying little that they hadn't said before. Presently Françoise came in, and they stopped, because she didn't share the carefree American sense of humor, and would get irritated with Lanny. He told her the good things about the Soviet Union;

and soon came Suzette, her young sister, married to one of the murderous taxi drivers of Paris. Uncle Jesse said this *garçon* had the right solution of the social problem: to run over all the bourgeois, while using Suzette to increase the Red population. They had a second baby.

The women set to work to prepare supper, and Lanny excused himself and walked back to the Crillon to meet his father. When Robbie asked: "What have you been doing?" he answered: "Looking at pictures." It was the truth and nothing but the truth—yet not the whole truth!

IX

One other duty: a visit to the Château de Bruyne. Lanny had promised Marie on her deathbed that he would never forget her two boys. There wasn't much that he could do for them, but they were friendly fellows and glad to tell him of their doings. He phoned to the father, who came and motored him out. Denis de Bruyne, though somewhat over seventy, was vigorous; his hair had become white, and his dark, sad eyes and pale aristocratic features made him a person of distinction. He was glad to see Lanny because of the memories they shared.

On the way they talked politics, and it was curious to note how the same world could appear so different to two different men. Denis de Bruyne, capitalist on a modest scale, owner of a fleet of taxicabs and employer of Suzette's husband—though he didn't know it—agreed with Jesse Blackless that the Communists were strong in Paris and other industrial centers and that they meant to use force if they could get enough of it. Denis's conception of statesmanship was to draw the gun first. He was a Nationalist, and was going to put up money to keep Jesse and his sort from getting power. Lanny listened, and this was agreeable to an entrepreneur who was so certain of his own position.

Denis de Bruyne was worried about the state of his country, which was in a bad way financially, having counted upon German reparations and been cheated out of most of her expectations. A French Nationalist blamed the British business men and statesmen; Britain was no true ally of France, but a rival; Britain used Germany to keep France from growing strong. Why did American business men further this policy, helping Germany to get on her feet, which meant making her a danger to France? Foreign investors had lent Germany close to five billion dollars since the end of the war: why did they take such risks?

Lanny replied: "Well, if they hadn't, how would Germany have paid France any reparations at all?"

"She would have paid if she had been made to," replied Denis. He didn't say how, and Lanny knew better than to pin him down. The men who governed France hadn't learned much by their invasion of the Ruhr and its failure; they still thought that you could produce goods by force, that you could get money with bayonets. It was useless to argue with them; their fear of Germany was an obsession. And maybe they were right—how could Lanny be sure? Certainly there were plenty of men in Germany who believed in force and meant to use it if they could get enough of it. Lanny had met them also.

Denis wanted to know what was going to be the effect of the Wall Street collapse upon French affairs. The season was beginning, and many of the fashionable folk were not here. Would the tourists fail to show up this summer? A question of urgency to the owner of a fleet of taxicabs! Lanny said he was afraid that Paris would have to do what New York had done—draw in its belt. When Denis asked what Robbie thought about the prospects, Lanny reported his father's optimism, and Denis was pleased, having more respect for Robbie's judgment than for Lanny's.

The Château de Bruyne was no great showplace like Balincourt and Les Forêts, but a simple country home of red stone; its title was a tribute to its age, and the respect of the countryside for an old family. It had been one of Lanny's homes, off and on, for some six years. The servants knew him, the old dog knew him, he felt that even the fruit trees knew him. Denis, *fils*, had got himself a wife of the right sort, and she was here, learning the duties of a châtelaine; they had a baby boy, so the two young fathers could make jokes about a possible future union of the families. Charlot, the younger brother, was studying to be an engineer, which meant that he might travel to far parts of the earth; incidentally, he was interested in politics, belonging to one of the groups of aggressive French patriots. Lanny didn't say much about his own ideas—he never had, for it had been his privilege to be the lover of Denis's wife, but not the corrupter of his sons. All that he could hope for was to moderate their vehemence by talking about toleration and open-mindedness.

The two young men—one was twenty-four and the other a year younger—looked up to Lanny as to an abnormally wise and brilliant person. They knew about his marriage, and thought it a coronation. In this opinion their mother would have joined, for she had had a Frenchwoman's thorough-going respect for property. The French, along with most other Europeans, were fond of saying that the Americans worshiped the dollar; a remark upon which Zoltan Kertezsi had commented in a pithy sentence: "The Americans worship the dollar and the French worship the sou."

5

From the Vasty Deep

I

LANNY rejoined the *Bessie Budd* at Lisbon, and they sailed again and put in at the yacht basin of Cowes. Awaiting them was a letter from Johannes, saying that he was tied up in some bad business, so no use hurrying to Bremen; also a letter from Rick, begging them to come to The Reaches for a few days; he and his wife hadn't seen them for a whole year. Lanny consulted Mama, and then "shot a wire" to Rick, inviting him to bring his wife and their oldest boy for a short cruise.

Friendship is a delightful thing when you have had the good judgment to choose the right friends. Eric Vivian Pomeroy-Nielson had come in the course of the years to be the most congenial of Lanny's friends. It could be doubted whether the younger man would have had the courage to stick to so many unorthodox ideas if it hadn't been for Rick's support. The baronet's son watched everything that went on in the world, analyzed the various tendencies, and set forth his understanding of them in newspaper articles which Lanny would clip and send to persons with whom he got into arguments. Not that he ever converted anybody, but he kept his cause alive.

Rick was only about a year and a half the elder, but Lanny was in the habit of deferring to him, which pleased Rick's wife and didn't altogether displease Rick. Whenever the Englishman wrote another play, Lanny was sure it was bound to make the long-awaited "hit." When it didn't, there was always a reason: that Rick persisted in dealing with social problems from a point of view unpopular with those who bought the best seats in theaters. The young playwright was fortunate in having parents who believed in him and gave him and his family a home while he wrote the truth as he saw it.

Nearly thirteen years had passed since a very young English flier had crashed in battle, and been found with a gashed forehead and a broken and badly infected knee. In the course of time he had learned to live with his lameness. He could go bathing from the special landing-place which Lanny had had made for him at Bienvenu; and now the carpenter of the *Bessie Budd* bolted two handles onto the landing-stage of the yacht's gangway, so that a man with good stout arms could lift himself out of the water without any help. He would unstrap his leg-brace, slide in, and enjoy himself just as if humanity had never been cursed with a World War.

II

Nina was her usual kind and lovely self, and as for Little Alfy— he had to be called that on account of his grandfather the baronet, but it hardly fitted him any more, for he had grown tall and leggy for his almost thirteen years. He had dark hair and eyes like his

father's, and was, as you might have expected, extremely precocious; he knew a little about all the various political movements,
also the art movements, and would use their patter in a fashion which
made it hard for you to keep from smiling. He had thin, sensitive
features and was serious-minded, which made him the predestined
victim of Marceline Detaze, the little flirt, the little minx. Marceline
didn't know anything about politics, but she knew some of the arts,
including that of coquetry. Half French and half American, she also
had been brought up among older people, but of a different sort.
From the former Baroness de la Tourette, the hardware lady from
Cincinnati, she had learned the trick of saying outrageous things
with a perfectly solemn face and then bursting into laughter at a
sober lad's look of bewilderment. Apparently Alfy never would
learn about it.

The families had planned a match for these two by cable as soon
as they had appeared on the scene. The parents made jokes about it,
in the free and easy modern manner, and the children had taken up
the practice. "I'll never marry you if you don't learn to dance better," Marceline would announce. Alfy, peeved, would respond:
"You don't have to marry me if you don't want to." He would
never have the least idea what was coming next. One time her feelings would be hurt, and the next time she would be relieved of a
great burden; but whichever it was, it would turn out to be teasing,
and Alfy would be like a man pursuing a will-o'-the-wisp on a dark
night.

There had been dancing in Marceline's home ever since she was
old enough to toddle about. So-called "society" dancing, Dalcroze
dancing, Isadora Duncan dancing, Provençal peasant dancing, English and American country dancing—every sort that a child could
pick up. Some kind of music going most of the time, and a phonograph and a radio so that she could make it to order. On the yacht,
as soon as her lessons were finished, she would come running to
where Hansi and Bess were practicing; she would listen for a minute
to get the swing of it, then her feet would start moving and she
would be dancing all over the saloon. She would hold out her hands
to Lanny, and they would begin improvising; they had learned to

read each other's signals, and once more, as in the old Dalcroze days, you saw music made visible.

No wonder Marceline could dance rings all around a lad who knew only that somnambulistic walking in time to jazz thumping which prevailed in fashionable society. Alfy would try his best, but look and feel like a young giraffe caught in an earthquake. "Loosen up, loosen up!" she would cry, and he would kick up his heels and toes in a most un-English manner. The girl would give him just enough encouragement to keep him going, but never enough to let him doubt who was going to call the tune in their household.

Lanny would see them sitting apart from the others while music was being played in the evening. Sometimes they would be holding hands, and he would guess that they were working out their problem in their own way. He recalled the days when he had paid his first visit to The Reaches, and had sat on the bank of the River Thames, listening to Kurt Meissner playing the slow movement of Mozart's D-minor concerto. How miraculous life had seemed to him, with one arm about Rosemary Codwilliger, pronounced Culliver, shivering with delight and dreaming of a marvelous future. Nothing had worked out as he had planned it; he reflected upon life, and how seldom it gives us what we expect. The young people come along, and clamor so loudly for their share, and have so little idea of the pain that awaits them. One's heart aches at the knowledge, but one cannot tell them; they have to have their own way and pay their own penalties.

III

The *Bessie Budd* cruised in waters frequented by vessels of every size, from ocean liners down to tiny sailboats. One more did not matter, provided you kept a lookout and blew your whistle now and then. They went up into the Irish Sea; the weather was kind, one day of blue sky succeeded another, and the air resounded with music and the tapping of feet upon the deck. Hansi and Bess practiced diligently, Beauty and Irma played bridge with Nina and Rahel, while Lanny and Rick sat apart and discussed everything that had happened to them during the past year.

Lanny had visited the great manufacturing-plant of his forefathers, and had been received as a prince consort in the Newcastle Country Club and in Irma's imitation French château on Long Island. Rick, meanwhile, had written a play about a young married couple who were divided over the issue of violence in the class struggle. Rick had written several plays about young people tormented by some aspect of this struggle. In the present opus the talk of his young idealist sounded much like that of Lanny Budd, while the ultra-Red wife might have had a private yacht named after her. Rick apologized for this, saying that a dramatist had to use such material as came to his hand. Lanny said that doubtless there were plenty of futile and bewildered persons like himself, but not many determined, hard-fighting rebels like Bess among the parasitic classes.

Rick had talked with editors and journalists in London, with statesmen, writers, and all sorts of people in his father's home. He knew about the upsurge of the Nazi movement in the harassed Fatherland. Not long ago he had had a letter from Kurt, who was always hoping to explain his country to the outside world; he sent newspaper clippings and pamphlets. The Germans, frantic with a sense of persecution, were tireless propagandists, and would preach to whoever might be persuaded to listen. But you rarely heard one of them set forth both sides of the case or admit the slightest wrong on his country's side.

They were put ashore in a small Irish harbor, and the young people took a ride in a jaunting car, while the ladies dickered with sharp-witted peasant women for quantities of hand-embroidered linen. They were put ashore in Wales, where the mountains did not seem imposing to one who had lived so close to the Alps. They visited the Isle of Man, and Lanny recalled a long novel which he had thought was tremendous in his boyhood, but which he now guessed to be no great shakes. They put into Liverpool, where they had arranged to receive mail, and among other things was a telegram from Robbie, who was back in Paris. "Sale concluded at eighty-three better than expected thanks to you sailing tomorrow good luck to the ghosts."

At his father's request Lanny had put off making the promised date with Zaharoff. Now he mailed a note, saying that the yacht was due on the French coast in a few days and he would wire an appointment. The *Bessie Budd* idled her way south again, and returned the Pomeroy-Nielsons to Cowes, from which place Lanny sent a wire to the Château de Balincourt, saying that he would bring his friend to a hotel in Dieppe on the following afternoon. He had explained to Mama Robin that he wished to meet a friend there, and she was pleased to oblige him. His mother and his stepfather were told that he desired to make a test with Madame, and to name no names until after it was over. As for the Polish woman, she was used to being bundled here and there for demonstrations of her strange gift.

IV

Dieppe is a thousand-year-old town with a church, a castle, and other sights for tourists; also it is a popular watering-place with a casino, so Lanny didn't have to think that he was inconveniencing his friends. The yacht was laid alongside a pier, and at the proper time he called a taxi and took his charge to the hotel. He had received an unsigned telegram informing him that "Monsieur Jean" would be awaiting him; at the desk he asked for this gentleman, and was escorted to the suite in which Zaharoff sat waiting, alone.

A comfortable chaise-longue had been provided for the medium and an armchair for each of the men. Since the old one had been thoroughly instructed, no talk was necessary. Lanny introduced him by the fictitious name, and he responded: "*Bon jour*," and no more. Lanny said: "*Asseyez-vous, Madame*," and not another word was spoken. The retired munitions king was inconspicuously dressed, and one who was not familiar with his photograph might have taken him for a retired business man, a college professor or doctor.

The woman began to shudder and moan; then she became still, and was in her trance. There was a long wait; Lanny, who kept telling himself that these phenomena were "telepathy," concentrated his mind upon the personality of María del Pilar Antonia Angela Patrocino Simón de Muguiro y Berute, Duquesa de Marqueni y Villafranca de los Caballeros. It was a personality which failed to live up to the magnificent-sounding names; a rather small, dark lady, very quiet, reserved, but kind. She had fitted the needs of an extremely exacting man of affairs; guarded him, cared for him, loved him, and, if gossip was correct, borne him two daughters. Anyhow, he had adored her, and shown his pride in the restrained fashion which circumstances imposed upon him. For more than thirty-five years they had been inseparable, and a million memories of her must be buried in the old man's subconscious mind. Would the medium be able to tap them? If so, it might be embarrassing, and perhaps it would have been more tactful of Lanny to offer to withdraw. But Zaharoff had placed a chair, possibly with the idea that the younger man's help might be needed for the guiding of the experiment.

Suddenly came the massive voice of the Iroquois chieftain, speaking English, as always. "Hello, Lanny. So you are trying to bowl me out!" It certainly wasn't an Iroquois phrase, nor did it seem exactly Polish.

Said Lanny, very solemnly: "Tecumseh, I have brought a gentleman who is deeply sincere in his attitude to you."

"But he does not believe in me!"

"He is fully prepared to believe in you, if you will give him cause; and he will be glad to believe."

"He is afraid to believe!" declared the voice, with great emphasis. There was a pause; and then: "You are not a Frenchman."

"I have tried to be," said Zaharoff. Lanny had told him to answer every question promptly and truly, but to say no more than necessary.

"But you were not born in France. I see dark people about you, and they speak a strange language which I do not understand. It will not be easy for me to do anything for you. Many spirits come; you have known many people, and they do not love you; it is easy to see it in their faces. I do not know what is the matter; many of them talk at once and I cannot get the words."

V

From where Lanny sat he could watch the face of Madame, and saw that it was disturbed, as always when Tecumseh was making a special effort to hear or to understand. By turning his eyes the observer could watch the face of the old munitions king, which showed strained attention. On the arm of Lanny's chair was a notebook, in which he was setting down as much as he could of what was spoken.

Suddenly the control exclaimed: "There is a man here who is trying to talk; to you, not to me. He is a very thin old man with a white beard. He says, in very bad English, he was not always like that, he had a black beard when he knew you. His name is like Hyphen; also he has another name, Tidy; no, it is one name, very long; is it Hyphen-tidies? A Greek name, he says, Hiphentides. Do you know that name?"

"No," said Zaharoff.

"He says you lie. Why do you come here if you mean to lie?"

"I do not recall him."

"He says you robbed him. What is it he is talking about? He keeps saying gall; you have gall; many sackfuls of gall. Is it a joke he is making?"

"It must be." Zaharoff spoke with quiet decisiveness. Of all the persons Lanny knew, he was the most completely self-possessed.

"He says it is no joke. Gall is something that is sold. A hundred and sixty-nine sacks of gall. Also gum, many cases of gum. You were an agent." Tecumseh began to speak as if he were the spirit, something which he did only when the communications came clearly. "You took my goods and pledged them for yourself. Do you deny it?"

"Of course I do."

"You did not deny it in the London court. You pleaded guilty. You were in prison—what is it?—the 'Old' something, Old Basin? It was more than fifty years ago, and I do not remember."

"Old Bailey?" ventured Lanny.

"That is it—Old Bailey. I was in Constantinople, and I trusted you. You said you did not know it was wrong; but they were my goods and you got the money——"

The voice died away; it had become querulous, as of an old man complaining of something long forgotten. If it wasn't real it was certainly well invented.

VI

Lanny stole a glance at the living old man, and it seemed to him there was a faint dew of perspiration on his forehead. From what Robbie had told him he was prepared to believe that the Knight Commander of the Bath and Grand Officer of the Legion of Honor had many recollections which he would not wish to have dragged into the light of day.

Said Tecumseh, after a pause: "I keep hearing the name Mugla. What is Mugla?"

"It is the village where I was born."

"Is that in Greece?"

"It is in Turkey."

"But you are not a Turk."

"My parents were Greeks."

"Somebody keeps calling you Zack. Then I hear Ryas. Is your name Ryas?"

"Zacharias is one of my names."

"There is a man here who says he is your uncle. Anthony; no, not that. I don't know these Greek names."

"I had an Uncle Antoniades."

"He says: 'Do you wish to talk to me?'"

"I do not especially wish it."

"He says: 'Ha, ha!' He does not like you either. You were in business with him, too. It was not so good. You made up wonderful stories about it. Do you write stories, or something like that?"

"I am not a writer."

"But you tell stories. All the spirits laugh when Uncle Antoniades says that. You have become rich and important and you tell stories about the old days. They tell stories about you. Do you wish to hear them?"

"That is not what I came for."

"There is a big strong man with a white beard; it looks like your own, only more of it. He gives the name Max. He speaks good English—no, he says it is not good, it is Yankee. Do you know the Yankee Max?"

"I don't recognize him."

"He says he is Maxim. You were in business with him, too."

"I knew a Maxim."

"You bought him out. He made millions, but you made tens of millions. There was no stopping you. Maxim says he did not believe in the future life, but he warns you, it is a mistake; you will be happier if you change all that materialism. Do you know what he means?"

"It does not sound like him."

"I have put off the old man. I was a strapping fellow. I could lick anybody in the Maine woods. I could lick anybody in Canada, and I did. I licked you once, you old snollygoster. Does that sound more like me?"

"Yes, I recognize that."

"I once wrote the emperor's name with bullets on a target. You haven't forgotten that, surely!"

"I remember it."

"All right, then, wake up, and figure out how you will behave in a better world. You cannot solve your problems as you used to do, putting your fingers in your ears."

A moment's pause. "He went away laughing," said Tecumseh. "He is a wild fellow. When he ate soup it ran down his beard; and it was the same with icecream. You do not like such manners; you are a quiet person, Zacharias—and yet I hear loud noises going on all around you. It is very strange! What are you?"

VII

The old Greek made no reply, and the voice of the control sank to a murmur, as if he was asking the spirits about this mystery. For quite a while Lanny couldn't make out a word, and he took the occasion to perfect his notes. Once or twice he glanced at the munitions king, who did not return the glance, but sat staring before him as if he were an image of stone.

"What is this noise I keep hearing?" burst out the Indian, suddenly. "And why are these spirits in such an uproar? A rattling and banging, and many people yelling, as if they were frightened. What is it that you do, Zacharias?"

Sir Basil did not speak.

"Why don't you answer me?"

"Cannot the spirits tell you?"

"It is easier when you answer my questions. Don't you like what these people are saying? It is not my fault if they hate you. Did you cheat them? Or did you hurt them?"

"Some thought that I did."

"What I keep hearing is guns. That is it! Were you a soldier? Did you fight in battles?"

"I made munitions."

"Ah, that is it; and so many people died. That is why they are screaming at you. I have never seen so many; never in the days when I commanded a tribe of the Six Nations, and the palefaces came against us. They had better guns and more of them, and my people died, they died screaming and cursing the invaders of our land. So men died screaming and cursing Zacharias the Greek. Do you run and hide from them? They come crowding after you, as if it was the first time they ever could get at you. They stretch out their hands trying to reach you. Do you feel them touching you?"

"No," said Zaharoff. For the first time Lanny thought there was a trace of quavering in his voice. Another quick glance revealed distinct drops of sweat on his forehead.

"It is like a battle going on—it gives me a headache, with all the smoke and noise. I see shells bursting away off, and men are falling out of the sky. No, no, keep back, he can't hear you, and there is no use yelling at me. Let somebody speak for you all. Any one of you. Come forward, you man, you with the ragged flag. What is it you want to say? No, not *you!* I don't want to talk to a man with the top of his head blown off. What sense can come out of only half a head? Keep your bloody hands off me—I don't care who you are. What's that? Oh, I see. All right, tell him. . . . I am the Unknown Soldier. I am the man they have buried by the Arc de Triomphe. They keep the undying flame burning for me, and they come and lay wreaths on my tomb. You came once and laid a wreath, did you not? Answer me!"

"I did." The munitions king's voice was hardly audible.

"I saw you. I see all who come to the tomb. I want to tell them to go away and stop the next war. I want to tell them something else that will not please them. Do you know my name?"

"Nobody knows your name."

"My name is Mordecai Izak. I am a Jew. Their Unknown Soldier is a Jew, and that would worry them very much. Are you a Jew?"

"I have been called that, but it is not so."

"I understand, brother. Many of us have had to do it."

There was a pause, and then Tecumseh was speaking. "They are all laughing. They tell me not to mind if you do not speak the truth. You are a very important man, they say. They push forward a little old woman. I cannot make out her name; it sounds like Haje —is that a woman's name? She says that she is the mother of your son. Is that possible?"

"It might be."

"She says that your name was Sahar. You changed it in Russia. It was a place called Vilkomir, a long, long time ago. She says your son is living; he is a very poor fellow. She says you have grand-children, but you do not wish to know it. Does that mean anything to you?"

"Possibly."

"The wounded men crowd her away. They do not let her talk. They are shouting again: 'There is blood on your money! You have a great deal of money, and there is a curse upon it. You murdered a man when you were young, but that is nothing, you have murdered all of us. We are waiting for you in the spirit world. We are the avengers—we, the men without faces, without bowels! Some day you will come to us——' "

The voice of Tecumseh had become shrill; and suddenly the aged Greek started to his feet. Two steps brought him to Lanny's side, and he said: "Give me the book." The younger man, taken aback, handed over his notebook; Zaharoff grabbed it and hastened, almost running, to the door, and went out, slamming it behind him.

VIII

That was the end of the séance. Not another word was spoken, but the medium began to moan pitiably. Lanny was prepared for trouble, because any sort of abrupt action always had a bad effect on her; it was something about which he had warned Zaharoff. Now she was seized by a sort of light convulsion, and sputum began to drip from her lips. Lanny ran and got a towel and wiped it away; he was frightened for a while, but gradually the moaning died, and after a space the woman opened her eyes.

"Oh, what is the matter?" she asked; and then, seeing the empty chair: "Where is the old gentleman?"

"He went away."

"He should not have done that. Something went wrong; I feel so bad."

"I am sorry, Madame. He was frightened."

"Did he hear something bad?"

"Very bad indeed."

"Somebody is dead?"

Lanny thought that was an easy way out. "Yes," he said. "He was not prepared for it and did not want to show his feelings."

"It is terribly bad for me. Tecumseh will be angry."

"I think he will understand, Madame."

"It made me so weak; and my head aches."

"I am sorry. I will call for a little wine, if you like."

"Please do."

Lanny ordered some wine and biscuits. She would not eat, but she sipped the wine, and after a while he helped her downstairs and into a taxi. He was interested to note that even under these rather sensational circumstances the woman did not press him with questions. It was her own feelings that she was concerned about. People should not treat her that way; they should be more considerate.

He helped her on board the yacht, and Baby Johannes's nurse-maid, who had become her friend, helped her into bed. Beauty and the others were out seeing the sights of Dieppe, so Lanny went to his own cabin to write up his notes a second time before his memories grew cold.

A really striking experience! He couldn't judge about all the details—for example, the hundred and sixty-nine sacks of gall—but Zaharoff's behavior was proof of the general accuracy of the revelations. The young observer was clinging to his theory that these details had come out of the subconscious mind of Zacharias Basileos Zaharoff, formerly Sahar, who had given several names, several birthplaces and birthdates, according to his convenience at the moment. But what a subconscious mind for a man to carry about with him! Were those the things he thought about when he woke up in the small hours of the morning and couldn't get to sleep again? How much money would it take to compensate a man for having such memories and such feelings?

IX

Lanny could not forget that his own father was a manufacturer and salesman of munitions, and that he had bribed and deceived and had documents stolen in order to promote various deals. Did Robbie have a subconscious mind like that? Certainly he showed few signs of it. His cheeks were rosy, he was sleeping well (so he reported), and he seemed to have his zest for life. But was that all bluff? Was he holding himself up by his bootstraps? Lanny remembered how quickly and how angrily Robbie would leap to the defense of the munitions industry whenever he heard it attacked. That wasn't the sign of a mind perfectly at ease.

Lanny had learned his father's formulas in earliest childhood. Budd Gunmakers Corporation was one of the bulwarks of American national security, and what it did was a great patriotic service. To say that it worked for profit was the vilest demagogy, because it put the profits back into the business—that had been the family tradition for nearly a hundred years. To blame them for selling munitions to other countries in times of peace was mere nonsense, for you couldn't make munitions without skilled labor and you couldn't have such labor unless you gave it work to do and paid it wages to live. The government wouldn't order any large supplies in times of peace, but it expected to have a completely equipped plant running and ready to serve it in case of need. What could you do but follow the example of all other merchants and sell your goods whenever and wherever you could find customers?

There was a basic difference between Zacharias Basileos Zaharoff and Robbie Budd. Robbie really considered himself a patriot, and no doubt that is an excellent thing for a subconscious mind. On the other hand, Lanny had heard the old Greek say that he was a citizen of every country where he owned property. Did he want to enable each of his countries to fight his other countries? No, for Lanny had heard him, early in the year 1914, expressing his dread of war, in language which had surprised and puzzled a very young idealist. Robbie had joked about his attitude, saying that the old spider, the old wolf, the old devil wanted to sell munitions but didn't want them used.

But they had been used, and Zaharoff had had to live and see them used—and evidently that had been bad for his subconscious mind! Zaharoff had attended the Armistice Day ceremonies and laid a wreath on the tomb of the Unknown Soldier. He had thought about that soldier, and now Lanny knew what he had thought! Had he guessed that the national hero of France might be a Jew? Or was it that the national hero really had been a Jew? Was Zaharoff himself a Jew, or part Jew? Lanny didn't know, and wasn't especially interested. There were few people in Europe who didn't have Jewish blood, even those who despised the outcast race. For two thousand years the Jews had been scattered over the old Continent like thistledown in the wind; and the most carefully tended family trees don't always show what pollen has fallen upon them.

X

Lanny thought: What is the old man going to make of this? He can hardly believe that I planted it on him; that I knew about his uncle Antoniades! No, he will know that the thing must be genuine, and when he cools off he will realize that he wasn't quite a gentleman. Maybe he'll want to beg Tecumseh's pardon and have another try for the duquesa.

Lanny decided that this would be interesting; so he sat down and wrote a note to be mailed in Dieppe:

My dear Sir Basil:
   I am truly sorry that the séance turned out to be so disturbing. I want to assure you that I am not telling anyone about it. I have seen many inaccuracies appear at sittings, and I have no interest in spreading them. You may count upon me in this.

Also he wrote a note to Rick, as follows:

   I wish you would see if you can find someone to do a job of research for me; that is, go through the records of Old Bailey prison during the 1870's and see if there is an entry of a prisoner by the name of Sahar, or Zahar, or Zaharoff. I enclose check for ten pounds to start it off, and if you will let me know the cost from time to time, I'll send more. Please say nothing about this, except to the dependable person you employ.

It wasn't going to be so easy to keep quiet about that afternoon's events. Beauty's curiosity had been aroused, and Irma's also. Fortunately Lanny had time to get over his own excitement, and to let Madame get over her bad feelings. He told his family that he had tried an experiment with someone who was interested, but the tests had not been conclusive, there were certain matters which had to be looked up, and then a second test might be made; he would tell them all about it later on. This was far from satisfactory, but he stuck to it, and pretty soon there were other séances, and other matters to talk about. Every now and then Beauty or Irma would say: "By the way, whatever became of that Dieppe affair?" Lanny would answer: "It hasn't been settled yet."

From Zaharoff he received no reply.

XI

The trim white *Bessie Budd* steamed away—or, to be exact, was propelled by crude oil, burning in a Diesel engine. At Bremerhaven the owner and his younger son were waiting, both proud and happy—the latter especially so, because he was a father and his fatherhood was new and shiny. How Freddi adored that gentle, sweet wife, and how he shivered with delight while gazing upon the mite of life which they had created! Nearly three months had passed since he had seen them both, and a newborn infant changes a lot in that time. The other Robins, including Bess and the nurse-maid, stood by when Freddi came aboard, sharing his happiness, of which he made quite a show, not being an Anglo-Saxon.

They all had a right to share, because this lovely infant was a prize exhibit of their dairy farm, so carefully supervised. Both father and grandfather had to certify themselves free of all diseases before they came on board, and there were to be no contaminating kisses, no demoralizing pettings, pokings, or ticklings. Wash your hands before you permit an infant to clutch your finger, for you can observe that the first thing he does is to convey your collected germs to his mouth.

Freddi had worked tremendously hard all year, and had got him-self the coveted title of doctor. He was a handsome fellow, not quite so tall as his brother, but having the same large dark eyes and serious expression. He lacked Hansi's drive—he was never going to be a famous man, only an earnest student and teacher, a devoted husband and father. Not so Red as Hansi and Bess, but nearer to Lanny's shade; he still had hopes of the German Social-Democrats, in spite of the timidity and lack of competence they were dis-playing. Freddi had said that he was studying bourgeois economics in order to be able to teach the workers what was wrong with it. Already he and a couple of his young friends had set up a night school along the lines of Lanny's project in the Midi. A non-party affair, both the Socialists and the Communists took potshots at it, greatly to Freddi's disappointment. The workers were being lined up for class war, and there was no room for stragglers between the trenches.

Johannes had bad news for them. Business conditions in Germany were such that it was impossible for him to set out across the Atlantic. He wanted them to go without him, and the rest of the

Robin family were willing to do this because of the promises they had made. But the Budds knew that the purpose for which the yacht existed was to get Papa away from business cares, and they knew that the Robins would have a hard time enjoying themselves without him. Beauty talked it over with Lanny and his wife, and they agreed not to accept such a sacrifice. Irma would be sorry to miss seeing her mother, but, after all, it was easier to transport one stout queen mother across the ocean than to put a whole establishment ashore on Long Island. Irma said she really didn't have much pleasure in any sort of social life when she had to keep within four-hour time limits and have Miss Severne look grim if she came in hot and tired from any sort of exercise. Irma's smart young friends would all laugh at her and make jokes about cows. So it was better to stay on the yacht, where no explanations or apologies had to be made and where Rahel backed you up by her good example. "Jewish women seem to be much more maternal," said Irma. "Or is it because she is German?"

XII

It was decided that the *Bessie Budd* would loaf about in the North Sea and its adjoining waters so as to come back quickly and take its owner aboard whenever he was free. There would be regattas during the summer, and concerts and theaters in near-by cities and towns; art galleries to be visited—yes, one could think of worse ways of spending two or three months than on a luxury yacht based on Bremerhaven. The ship's library included Heine's *Nordseebilder*, also musical settings of some of these poems. Rahel would sing, Freddi would tootle, Hansi would scrape and scratch, Lanny and his sister would rumble and thump, Marceline would caper and prance, and Irma and Beauty and Johannes would raid the orchestra for a fourth hand at bridge.

The *Bessie Budd* steamed, or was propelled, to Copenhagen, where the party inspected the royal palace and attended a performance at the royal theater—the latter being comfortably within the young mothers' time limit. Lanny studied the sculptures in the Thorvaldsen museum. Many interesting works of man to be seen, but not many of nature in these low, flat islands and inlets, once the haunt of fishermen and pirates. Having loaded themselves up with culture, they returned Johannes to Bremerhaven, and then set out behind the Frisian islands, visiting Norderney, where a hundred years previously an unhappy Jewish poet had written immortal verses. *Sei mir gegrüsst, du ewiges Meer!*

Back to port, where the owner of the yacht joined them again, bringing with him a large packet of mail. Included was a letter from Rick to Lanny, as follows:

> With regard to your request concerning the Old Bailey, these records are not available, so I had a search made of the criminal reports in the *Times*. Under the date of January 13, 1873, appears an entry numbered 61: "Zacharoff, Zacharia Basilius, agent pledging goods intrusted to him for sale." In the *Times* of January 17 appears a column headed "Criminal Court," beginning as follows: "Zacharia Basilius Zacharoff, 22, was indicted for that he, being an agent intrusted by one Manuel Hiphentides of Constantinople, merchant, for the purpose of sale with possession, among other goods, 25 cases of gum and 169 sacks of gall of the value together of £1000, did unlawfully and without any authority from his principal, for his own use make a deposit of the said goods as and by way of pledge."

Rick's letter gave a summary of the entire account, including the statement: "Subsequently, by advice of his counsel, the prisoner withdrew his plea of 'Not Guilty' and entered a plea of 'Guilty.'" Rick added: "This is interesting, and I am wondering what use you intend making of it. Let me add: Why don't your spirits give you things like this? If they would do so, I would begin to take them seriously!"

BOOK TWO

A Cloud That's Dragonish

6

Deutschland Erwache!

I

THE autumn storms begin early on the North Sea, and judging from his text the poet Heine had stayed to witness them. The storm rages and whips the waves, and the waves, foaming with fury and leaping, tower up, and the white water mountains surge with life, and the little ship mounts upon them, hasty-diligent, and suddenly plunges down into black wide-gaping abysses of flood. O sea! Mother of beauty, arise from the foam! Grandmother of love, spare mine!

But when you are running a floating dairy farm you cannot take chances of your stock's becoming seasick; you must put them on dry land before the equinoctial season and learn about storms from the pages of a book. Hansi and Bess had a concert tour, Freddi was going to apply the economic knowledge he had gained, and Lanny wanted to examine some pictures which might come on the market. Lanny, his wife, his mother, and her husband were urged to confer distinction and charm upon an oversized Berlin palace. "What else did I buy it for?" argued the proprietor.

To Lanny the young wife said privately: "Do you think it is a good thing for us to be associating with Jews all the time?"

The husband smiled. "You can meet anybody you want in that house. I assure you they will come."

"Maybe so; but won't they think there must be something wrong with us?"

"I assure you, my dear, they all know exactly what you are worth."

"Lanny, that's a horrid view to take of people!"

103

"You can save yourself a lot of unhappiness by taking my word about Europe. I have lived here most of my life." Lanny might have added: "Remember Ettore!" But he rarely permitted himself to mention the dashing Italian duca with whom she had once fancied herself in love.

"But, Lanny, we have been living off the Robins for nearly five months! Am I never going to spend any of my own money?"

"If your conscience worries you, give Freddi a good check for his new school. Nothing will please Johannes more."

"But if he wants that done, why doesn't he do it himself?"

"I think he may be afraid to; it would make too many enemies. But if you do it, he will have an alibi."

"Is he really that much of a coward, Lanny?"

The young husband chuckled. "Again I tell you, take my word about Europe!"

II

The German-Jewish money-lord had several of his guest-suites opened up, dusted, aired, and supplied with fresh flowers. He would have had them redecorated if there had been time. The one assigned to Irma and Lanny had a drawing-room with a piano in it; also a bedroom, dressing-room, and bath for each. Each dressing-room had a clothes closet which was almost a room and would hold all the imitations of Paris costumes which the *couturiers* of Berlin might persuade Irma to purchase. She didn't have gold bathroom fixtures and Lanny didn't have silver—one had to go to America for styles such as that; but they had drawings by Boucher and Fragonard, Watteau and Lancret on their walls, and Lanny knew these were genuine, for he and Zoltan had purchased them and divided a ten per cent commission. Irma found that rather embarrassing, but Lanny said: "It was what enabled me to dress properly while I was courting you!"

Next door to their suite was one for the baby and the dependable Miss Severne. Feathers had been telegraphed for, and was on hand to take charge of Irma's affairs: writing her letters, paying her bills, keeping track of her appointments. Johannes had provided an

English-speaking maid, ready to serve her from the moment of her arrival; indeed, he would have ordered a baby giraffe from the Hagenbeck zoo if he had thought that would have added to her happiness.

Feathers had only to telephone to the steward's office downstairs and a car would be at the door in a minute or two. There were theaters, operas, concerts, and cabaret entertainments for every sort of taste, high or low. The palace was in the fashionable district, convenient to everything, so the two young mothers had no trouble in keeping their schedules; lying back in the cushions of a limousine, they had time to recover from any excitement and thus avoid displeasing the head nurse. Their babies, being so well cared for, rarely cried at night, and, anyhow, that was the night nurse's affair. In the early morning hours this nurse would steal into Irma's bedroom, bringing Baby Frances for her first meal, and Irma would suckle her while still half asleep. Oh, yes, modern science can make life pleasant for those fortunate ones who have the price! Fond dreamers talk about making it that way for everybody, but the daughter of a utilities magnate would repeat an ancient question: "Who will do the dirty work?" She never found out who would, but she knew quite certainly who wouldn't.

Each member of the visiting party had his or her own idea of happiness. Miss Severne inquired concerning the English church in Berlin, and there she met persons near enough to her social station so that she could be happy in their company. Mr. Dingle discovered a New Thought group with a lecturer from America, and thus was able to supply himself with the magazines he had been missing. It is a fortunate circumstance about Christian Science and New Thought publications, that dealing with eternal truths they never get out of date. The only trouble is that, saying the same things, they are apt to become monotonous. Undeterred by this, Mr. Dingle began escorting Madame to a spiritualist church; they knew only a few words of the German language, but the spirits were international, and there were always living persons willing to help two foreigners.

III

The great city of Berlin, capital of the shattered Prussian dream. Triumphal arches, huge marble statues of Hohenzollern heroes, palaces of old-time princes and new-time money-lords; sumptuous hotels, banks that were temples of Mammon, department stores filled with every sort of luxury goods—and wandering about the streets, hiding in stone caves and cellars, or camping out in tents in vacant spaces, uncounted hordes of hungry, ill-clothed, fear-driven, and hate-crazed human beings. Out of a population of four million it might be doubted if there were half a million really contented. There was no street where you could escape the sight of pinched and haggard faces; none without beggars, in spite of the law; none where a well-dressed man could avoid the importunities of women and half-grown children, male or female, seeking to sell their bodies for the price of a meal.

Shut your eyes to these sights and your mind to these thoughts. The city was proud and splendid, lighted at night like the Great White Way in New York. The shop windows were filled with displays of elegance, and there were swarms of people gazing, and some buying. Tell yourself that the stories of distress were exaggerated; that the flesh of boys and girls had been for sale in Nineveh and Baghdad, and was now for sale in London and New York, though perhaps they used a bit more Anglo-Saxon hypocrisy. Prostitution has been the curse of great cities ever since they began; swarms of people come piling into them, lured by the hope of easy wealth, or driven from the land by economic forces which men have never learned to control.

This was something about which Freddi Robin should have been able to speak, he being now a duly certified Herr Doktor in the science of economics. He reported that the great university had left it still a mystery to students. The proper academic procedure was to accumulate masses of facts, but to consider explanations only historically. You learned that the three-stage pattern of primitive economic progress as taught by Friedrich List had been abandoned after the criticisms of anthropologists, and that Roscher's theory of national economics as a historical category had been replaced by the new historical school of Schmoller. It was all right for you to know that in ancient Rome the great estates, the latifundia, had been worked with slave labor, thus driving independent farmers to the city and herding them into ramshackle five-story tenements which often burned down. But if in the class you pointed out that similar tendencies were apparent in Berlin, you would be looked at askance by a professor whose future depended upon his avoidance of political controversy.

To be sure, they were supposed to enjoy academic freedom in Germany, and you might listen to a Catholic professor in one lecture hall and to a Socialist in the next; but when it came to promotions, somebody had to decide, and you could hardly expect the authorities to give preference to men whose teachings fostered that proletarian discontent which was threatening to rend the country apart. At any rate, that is the way Freddi Robin reported the situation in the great University of Berlin.

IV

The Budds arrived a week or so before the national elections in September 1930. The city was in an uproar, with posters and placards everywhere, hundreds of meetings each night, parades with bands and banners, crowds shouting and often fighting. The tension was beyond anything that Lanny had ever witnessed; under the pressure of the economic collapse events in Germany were coming to a crisis, and everybody was being compelled to take sides.

The young people wanted to see these sights. Hansi and Bess must attend a big Communist gathering the very night of their arrival, and the others went along out of curiosity. The great hall in the Moabit district was draped with red streamers and banners having the hammer and sickle in black. Also there were red carnations or rosettes in people's buttonholes. The crowd was almost entirely proletarian: pitiful pinched faces of women, haggard grim faces of men; clothing dingy, generally clean but so patched that

the original cloth was a matter of uncertainty; many a man had had
no new suit since the war.

The speakers raved and shouted, and worked the crowd into a
frenzy; the singing made you think of an army marching into battle. A quartet sang chants with hammering rhythms, the repetition
of simple words, like lessons repeated by children in school. Lanny
translated for his wife: "Be ready to take over! Be ready to take
over!"

Irma had learned a lot about this subject during her sojourn in
these two strange families; she had listened to Uncle Jesse, and to
Hansi and Bess arguing with Lanny, and now and then with Hansi's
father. They didn't want to kill anybody—not unless somebody
resisted. All they wanted was to reproduce in Germany what they
had done in Russia; to confiscate the property of the rich and reduce them to their own slum level. Johannes had smiled and said
they would make a museum out of his palace, and that would be
all right with him, he would buy another in London, and then one
in New York, and then one in Tahiti—by which time Russia would
have restored capitalism, and he would return to that region and
make his fortune all over again.

The financier made a joke of it, but it was no joke at this *Versammlung*. Not one single laugh in a whole evening; the nearest to
it was mocking jeers, hardly to be distinguished from cries of rage.
This was what they called the "proletariat," the creatures of the
slums, threatening to burst out, overcome the police, and raid the
homes of those whom they called "exploiters." The speakers were
seeking election to the Reichstag, where they would pour out the
same kind of tirades. Irma looked about her uneasily, and was glad
she had had the sense not to wear any of her jewels to this place.
It wasn't safe anyhow, for the National Socialists often raided the
crowds coming out from Red meetings, and there were fights and
sometimes shootings.

V

The Social-Democrats also were holding great meetings. They
were by far the largest party in the Republic, but had never had an

outright majority, either of votes or of representation; therefore they had not been able to have their way. If they had, would they have known what to do? Would they have dared trying to bring Socialism to the Fatherland? Hansi and Bess declared that they were paralyzed by their notions of legality; it was a party of office-holders, of bureaucrats warming swivel-chairs and thinking how to keep their jobs and salaries. They continued to call themselves Socialist and to repeat the party shibboleths, but that was simply bait for the voters. How to get Socialism they had no idea, and they didn't consider it necessary to find out.

Lanny, yearning after the orderly methods of democracy, considered that it was up to him to help this party. In days past he had brought letters of introduction from Longuet, and now he went to renew old acquaintanceships, and to prove his sincerity by making a contribution to the party's campaign chest. He took his family to one of the mass meetings, and certainly, if there was any tired-ness or deadness, it didn't show on this public occasion. The hall was packed to the doors, banners and streamers were everywhere, and when the party's favorite orators made their appearance volumes of cheering rolled to the roof and back. These men didn't rave and threaten as the Communists did; they discussed the practical problems confronting the German workers, and denounced both groups of extremists for leading the people astray with false promises. It was a dignified meeting, and Irma felt more comfortable; there didn't seem to be anything to start a fight about.

On their way home the young people discussed what they had heard. Bess, who used the same phonograph records as Uncle Jesse, said that the party was old—a grandfather party—so it had the machinery for getting out the crowds. "But," she added, "those municipal councilors repeating their formulas make one think of stout, well-fed parrots dressed up in frock-coats."

"The Communists don't have any formulas, of course!" countered Lanny, not without a touch of malice. These two loved each other, but couldn't discuss politics without fighting.

Bess was referring to officials who had reported on their efforts to increase the city's milk supply and reduce its price. Lanny had found the Socialists discussing the same subject in New York; it was no unimportant matter to the women of the poor. "Of course it's dull and prosy," he admitted; "not so exciting as calling for the revolution next week——"

"I know," broke in the sister; "but while you're discussing milk prices, the Nazis are getting arms caches and making their plans to bring about the counter-revolution next week."

"And the reactionary princes conspiring with them, and the great capitalists putting up money to pay for the arms!" Thus Hansi, stepping onto dangerous ground, since his father was one of those capitalists. How much longer was that secret going to be kept in the Robin family?

VI

Lanny wanted to hear all sides; he wanted to know what the Nazis were doing and saying, if only so as to send Rick an account of it. Among his acquaintances in Berlin was Heinrich Jung, blue-eyed "Aryan" enthusiast from Upper Silesia. Heinrich had spent three years training himself to succeed his father as head forester of Graf Stubendorf's domain; but now all that had been set aside, and Heinrich was an official of the National Socialist German Workingmen's Party, high up in what they called the Hitler Youth. For seven or eight years he had been mailing propaganda to Lanny Budd in Bienvenu, having never given up hope that a pure-blooded "Aryan" would feel the pull of his racial ties.

Lanny called him on the telephone, and Heinrich was delighted and begged him to come to party headquarters. The visitor didn't consider it necessary to mention the fact that he was staying in the home of one of the most notorious of Jewish *Schieber*. It wouldn't really have mattered, for such eccentricities in an American didn't mean what they would have meant in a German. A German traveler had described America as "the land of unlimited possibilities," and rich, successful persons from that fabulous region walked the common earth of Europe as demigods. Even the Führer himself was in awe of them, having heard the report that they had not run away from the mighty German army. A bright feather in the cap of a young party official if he should bring in such a convert to the new religion of blood and soil.

The blue-eyed and fair-haired young Prussian had matured greatly in the three or four years since Lanny had seen him. He had his private office in the great Nazi building, and was surrounded by the appurtenances of power: files and charts, a telephone on his desk, and a buzzer to summon his subordinates. He wore the uniform of the Sturmabteilung, those party soldiers whose marching and drum-beating were by now among the familiar sights in German cities: brown shirt and trousers with black stripes, shiny black boots, red armband with the swastika in black. Handsome, smart, snappy—and keep out of their way, for they mean business. *Die Strasse frei den braunen Bataillonen!*

Heinrich stopped only long enough to ask after Lanny's wife and baby, about whom he had heard from Kurt. Then he began pouring out the story of the miracles which had been achieved by the N.S.D.A.P.—the initials of the party's German name—since those old days when a student of forestry had revealed it as a tiny shoot just pushing its head through the wintry soil. "Tall oaks from little acorns grow!" said Heinrich; having written it as an English copybook exercise in school.

A ladder was provided and Lanny was taken up to the topmost branches of that ever-spreading oak tree. The Hitler Youth constituted the branches where the abundant new growth was burgeoning; for this part of the tree all the rest existed. The future Germany must be taught to march and to fight, to sing songs of glory, hymns to the new Fatherland it was going to build. It must be well fed and trained, sound of wind and limb; it must know the Nazi creed, and swear its oath of loyalty to what was called the *Führerprinzip*, the faith that the individual exists for the state, and that the state is guided by one inspired leader. No matter from what sort of homes the young people came, the Nazis would make them all the same: perfect party members, obedient because it is a joy to obey, because the future belongs to those who are strong, confident, and united.

Lanny had seen this principle working in the soul of one sturdy young "Aryan," and now he discovered him as a machine engaged in turning out thousands of other specimens exactly like himself. A machine for making machines! On the wall was a map showing where the branch offices of this youth-machine were situated— and they weren't only in Germany, but in every city on earth where Germans lived. There were charts and diagrams, for in this land things are done scientifically, including Hitler propaganda. *"Deutschland Erwache!"* said a placard on Heinrich's wall. The Führer was a great deviser of slogans; he would retire to a secret place and there ponder and weigh many hundreds which came to his mind, and when he chose one, it would appear on posters and be shouted at meetings in every hamlet of the land. "Germany, Awake!"

VII

Lanny was touched by the pride with which the young official revealed and explained the complex organization he had helped to build; its various departments and subdivisions, each having an official endowed with one of those elaborate titles which Germans so dearly love. The head of the great machine was, of course, the one and only Adolf, *Partei- und oberster S.A. Führer, Vorsitzender der N.S.D.A.P.* Under him were adjutants and Secretariat and Chief of Staff, the *Reichsjugendführer* (who was Heinrich's superior) and his Staff Director, the Subdirectors of half a dozen different staffs, the Business Manager, the Secretary, the Presidium, the Reich Directorate.

Also there was a Political Organization, or rather two, P.O. 1 and P.O. 2—they had two of everything, except of the Führer. It made you dizzy merely to hear about all these obligations and responsibilities: the Foreign Division, Economic Policy Division, Race and Culture Division, Internal Political Division, Legal Division, Engineering-Technical Division, Labor Service Division; the Reich Propaganda Leaders Number 1 and Number 2, the Leaders of the Reich Inspection 1 and 2; the Investigation and Adjustment Committee—what a whopper of a title had been assigned to them: *Untersuchungs- und Schlichtungsausschuss*, or USCHLA! But don't smile over it, for Heinrich Jung explains that the party is preparing to take over the destinies of the Fatherland, to say nothing of many decadent nations of Europe and elsewhere, and all this machinery and even more will be needed; the Gymnastics and Sports Committee, the Bureau Leader for the Press, the *Zentralparteiverlag*, the *Personalamt*, and much more.

Heinrich was responsible for the affairs of one department of the Hitler Youth, with twenty-one geographic sections throughout Germany. They maintained a school for future Nazi leaders, and published three monthlies and a semi-monthly. There were divisions dealing with press, culture, propaganda, defense-sport—they were learning not merely to fight the Young Communists, but to make a sport of it! Also there were the junior organizations, the *Deutsches Jungvolk* and the *Bund Deutscher Mädel*, and a *Studentenbund*, and a Women's League, and so on apparently without end. The polite Lanny Budd was glad in his heart that it was election time and that so many subordinates were waiting to receive orders from this overzealous expounder.

VIII

One thing a young party official would not fail to do for an old friend: to take him to the mighty *Versammlung* in the Sportpalast which was to climax the Nazi campaign. Here the Führer himself would make his final appeal to the German voters; and it would be like nothing ever seen in the world before. For several months this marvelous man had been rushing all over the land making speeches, many hundreds of them; traveling by airplane, or in his fast Mercédès car, wearing the tan raincoat in which Lanny had seen him in the old days; possibly not the same coat, but the same simple, devoted, inspired, and inspiring leader whose mission it was to revive Germany and then the whole world. *Heute gehört uns Deutschland und morgen die ganze Welt!*

Heinrich explained that seats would be difficult to obtain; there would be a line of people waiting at the doors of the Sportpalast from early morning to be sure of getting good places. There would of course be reserved seats for important persons, and Lanny accepted four tickets. He knew that none of the Robins would attend a Nazi meeting—it really wouldn't be safe, for someone might spit in their faces, or beat them if they failed to give the Nazi salute and shout *"Heil Hitler!"* Bess loathed the movement and its creed, and her curiosity had been fully satisfied by watching the Stormtroopers on the march and by occasional glances at their newspapers.

Well in advance of eight o'clock Lanny and his wife and Beauty and her husband were in their seats. Bands playing, literature-sellers busy, and armed squads keeping watch all over the enormous arena —Communists keep out! A display of banners and streamers with all the familiar slogans: "Down with Versailles!" "Freedom and Bread!" "Germany, Awake!" "An End to Reparations!" "Common Wealth before Private Wealth!" "Break the Bonds of Interest Slavery!" These last were the "radical" slogans, carried down from the old days; Robbie had said they were practically the same as those of the "money cranks" in the United States, the old-time Populists and Greenbackers; they appealed to the debtor classes, the small farmers, the little business men who felt themselves being squeezed by the big trusts. This Hitler movement was a revolt of the lower middle classes, whose savings had been wiped out by the inflation and who saw themselves being reduced to the status of proletarians.

To Irma they seemed much nicer-looking people than those she had seen at the other two meetings. The black-and-silver uniforms of the Schutzstaffel, who acted as ushers and guards, were new and quite elegant; these young men showed alertness and efficiency. Twenty or thirty thousand people singing with fervor were impressive, and Irma didn't know that the songs were full of hatred for Frenchmen and Poles. She knew that the Nazis hated the Jews, and this she deplored. She had learned to be very fond of one Jewish family, but she feared there must be something wrong with the others—so many people said it. In any case, the Germans had to decide about their own country.

Singing and speech-making went on for an hour or so; then came a roll of drums and a blast of trumpets in the main entrance, and all the men and women in the huge place leaped to their feet. *Der Führer kommt!* A regiment of Stormtroopers in solemn march, carrying flags with spearpoints or bayonets at the tips of the poles. The bands playing the magnificent open chords to which the gods march across the rainbow bridge into Valhalla at the close of *Das Rheingold*. Then the party leaders, military and magnificent, marching in the form of a hollow square, protecting their one and only leader. Someone with a sense of drama has planned all this; someone who has learned from Wagner how to combine music, scenery, and action so as to symbolize the fundamental aspirations of the human soul, to make real to the common man his own inmost longing.

Who was that genius? Everyone in the hall, with the possible exception of a few Lanny Budds, believed that it was the little man who marched in the center of that guard of honor; the simple man with the old tan raincoat, the one whom honors could not spoil, the one consecrated to the service of the Fatherland; one born of the common people, son of an obscure Austrian customs official; a corporal of the World War wounded and gassed; an obscure workingman, a dreamer of a mighty dream, of Germany freed and restored to her place among the nations, or perhaps above them.

He wore no hat, and his dark hair, long and brushed to one side, fell now and then across his pale forehead and had to be swept away. No fashion here, a plain man, just like you and me; one whose hand you can shake, who smiles in a friendly way at those who greet him. A storm of cheering arises, the *Heils* become like raindrops falling in a cloudburst—so many that you cannot hear the individual ones, the sounds become a union like the National Socialist German Workingmen's Party.

Lanny has never attended an old-fashioned American revival meeting, but his friend Jerry Pendleton from Kansas has told him about one, and here is another. Has someone from the American South or Middle West come over and taught these arts of stirring the souls of primitive people, of letting them take part in what is being done to them? Or is it something that rises out of the primitive soul in every part of the world? The speakers on this platform ask questions, and twenty thousand throats shout the answers. Only they do not shout: "Glory Hallelujah!" and "Bless the Lord!"; theirs are secular cries: "Down with Versailles!" *"Juda verrecke!"* and *"Deutschland erwache!"*

IX

Seven years since Lanny watched Charlie Chaplin come out upon the stage of a great beerhall in Munich; and here he is again, the same foolish little dark mustache, the same shy manner, humble, deprecating. But now he is stouter, he gets better food. Now, also, there are a score of spotlights centered upon him, telling everybody that appearances are deceptive, and that this is a special One. Banners and symbols, slogans and rituals, hopes and resolves, all have come out of his soul; he is the Messiah, the One appointed and sent to save the Fatherland in its hour of greatest trial.

He begins to speak, and Lanny knows every tone. Quiet at first, and the vast hall as still as the universe must have been before God created it. But soon the man of visions begins to warm up to his theme. The slogans which he has taught to all Germany work upon himself as upon others; they dominate his entire being; they are sparks from a white-hot flame which burns day and night within him. The flame of "Adi's" hatred of his miserable and thwarted life! Hatred of his father, the dumb petty bureaucrat who wanted to make his son like himself and wouldn't let him become an artist; hatred of the critics and dealers who wouldn't recognize his pitiful attempts at painting; hatred of the bums and wastrels in the flop-houses who wouldn't listen to his inspired ravings; hatred of the Russians and the French and the British and the Americans who wouldn't let an obscure corporal win his war; hatred of Marxists who betrayed Germany by a stab in the back; hatred of the Jews who made money out of her misery; hatred of all who now stood in the way of her destiny, who opposed Adi's party which was to save her from humiliation. All these hatreds had flamed forth from one thwarted soul and had set fire to the tinder-box which Germany had become—and here it was, blazing, blazing!

The Führer possessed no gleam of humor, no trace of charm. He was an uneducated man, and spoke with an Austrian country accent, not always grammatically. His voice was hoarse from a thousand speeches, but he forced it without mercy. He raved and shrieked; he waved his arms, he shook his clenched fists in the face of Germany's enemies. Perspiration poured from his pasty and rather lumpy countenance; his heavy hair fell down over his eyes and had to be flung back.

Lanny knew every gesture, every word. Adi hadn't learned a thing, hadn't changed a thing in seven years; he had merely said the same things a million times. His two-part book which Lanny had read with mingled dismay and laughter had become the bible of a new religion. Millions of copies had been sold, and extracts from it and reiterations of it had been printed in who could guess how many pamphlets, leaflets, and newspapers? Certainly well up in the billions; for some of the Nazi newspapers had circulations of hundreds of thousands every day, and in the course of years that mounts up. Heinrich told Lanny that they had held nearly thirty-five thousand meetings in Germany during the present campaign and quantities of literature had been sold at every one of them. Lanny, listening and watching the frenzied throng, remembered some lines from his poetry anthology, lines which had sounded melodious and exciting, but which he hadn't understood when he had read them as a boy:

> One man with a dream, at pleasure,
>   Shall go forth and conquer a crown;
> And three with a new song's measure
>   Can trample an empire down.

X

There had been an election to the Reichstag less than two and a half years before, and at that election the Social-Democrats had polled more than nine million votes, the Communists more than three million, and the Nazis less than one million. The two last-named parties had been active since then, and everyone agreed that conditions favored the extremists. The business collapse in America had made farm products unsalable there, and this had caused an immediate reaction in Germany; the peasants had their year's harvest to sell at a heavy loss. As for the workers, there were four million unemployed, and fear in the hearts of all the rest. These groups were sure to vote for a change—but of what sort?

Impossible to spend a week in a nation so wrought up and not come to share the excitement. It became a sort of sporting proposition; you chose sides and made bets to back yourself. After the fashion of humans, you believed what you hoped. Lanny became sure that the cautious, phlegmatic German people would prefer the carefully thought-out program of the Socialists and give them an actual majority so that they could put it into effect. But Johannes Robin, who thrived on pessimism, expected the worst—by which he meant that the Communists would come out on top. Red Berlin would become scarlet, or crimson, or whatever is the most glaring of shades.

The results astounded them all—save possibly Heinrich Jung and his party comrades. The Social-Democrats lost more than half a million votes; the Communists gained more than a million and a quarter; while the Nazis increased their vote from eight hundred thousand to nearly six and a half million: a gain of seven hundred per cent in twenty-eight months! The score in millions stood roughly, Social-Democrats eight and a half, Nazis six and a half, and Communists four and a half.

The news hit the rest of the world like a high-explosive shell. The statesmen of the one-time Allied lands who were so certain that they had Germany bound in chains; the international bankers who had lent her five billion dollars; the negotiators who, early in this year of 1930, had secured her signature to the Young Plan, whereby she bound herself to pay reparations over a period of fifty-eight years—all these now suddenly discovered that they had driven six and a half million of their victims crazy! War gains were to be confiscated, trusts nationalized, department stores communalized, speculation in land prevented, and usurers and profiteers to suffer the death penalty! Such was the Nazi program for the inside of

Germany; while for the outside, the Versailles treaty was to be denounced, the Young Plan abrogated, and Germany was to go to war, if need be, in order to set her free from the "Jewish-dominated plutocracies" of France, Britain, and America!

Lanny's host was unpleasantly surprised by these returns, but, after thinking matters over, he decided not to worry too much. He said that no soup is ever eaten as hot as it is cooked. He said that the wild talk of the Nazis was perhaps the only way to get votes just now. He had his private sources of information, and knew that the responsible leaders were embarrassed by the recklessness of their young followers. If you studied the Nazi program carefully you would see that it was full of all sorts of "jokers" and escape clauses. The campaign orators of Berlin had been promising the rabble "confiscation without compensation" of the great estates of the Junkers; but meanwhile, in East Prussia, they had got the support of the Junkers by pointing to the wording of the program: the land to be confiscated must be "socially necessary." And how easy to decide that the land of your friends and supporters didn't come within that category!

But all the same Johannes decided to move some more funds to Amsterdam and London, and to consult Robbie Budd about making more investments in America. Hundreds of other German capitalists took similar steps; and of course the Nazis found it out, and their press began to cry that these "traitor plutocrats" should be punished by the death penalty.

XI

The rich did not give up their pleasures on account of elections, nor yet of election results. The fashionable dressmakers, the milliners, the jewelers came clamoring for appointments with the famous Frau Lanny Budd, *geborene* Irma Barnes. They displayed their choicest wares, and skilled workers sat up all night and labored with flying fingers to meet her whims. When she was properly arrayed she sallied forth, and the contents of her trunks which Feathers had brought from Juan were placed at the disposal of the elder Frau Budd, who dived into them with cries of delight, for they had barely been worn at all and had cost more than anything she had ever been able to afford in her life. A few alterations, to allow for *embonpoint* attributable to the too rich fare of the yacht, and a blond and blooming Beauty was ready to stand before kings—whether of steel, coal, or chemicals, potash, potatoes, or *Rentenmarks*.

She did not feel humiliated to play second fiddle in the family, for after all she was a grandmother; also, she had not forgotten the lesson of the Wall Street collapse. Let Irma go on paying the family bills and nursing the family infant, and her mother-in-law would do everything in the power of a highly skilled social intriguer to promote her fortunes, put her in a good light, see that she met the right people and made the right impressions. Beauty would even write to Irma's mother and urge her to come to Berlin and help in this task; there must never be any rivalry or jealousy between them; on the contrary, they must be partners in the duty of seeing that Irma got everything to which her elegance, charm, and social position—Beauty didn't say wealth—entitled her.

Lanny, of course, had to play up to this role; he had asked for it, and now couldn't back out. He had to let the tailors come and measure him for new clothes, and stand patiently while they made a perfect fit. No matter how bored he was, no matter how much he would have preferred trying some of Hindemith's new compositions! His mother scolded him, and taught his wife to scold him; such is the sad fate of kind-hearted men. When he and Irma were invited to a dinner-party by the Prinz Ilsaburg zu Schwarzadler or to a ball at the palace of the Baron von Friedrichsbrunn, it would have been unthinkable to deprive Irma of such honors and a scandal to let some other man escort her.

It wasn't exactly a scandal for Johannes Robin to escort the elder Frau Budd, for it was known that he had a wife who was ill-adapted to a fashionable career. Beauty, on the other hand, had taken such care of her charms that you couldn't guess her years; she was a gorgeous pink rose, now fully unfolded. Fashionable society was mistaken in its assumptions concerning her host and her-

self, for both this strangely assorted pair were happy with their re-
spective spouses, and both spouses preferred staying at home—Mama
Robin to watch over the two infants whom she adored equally, and
Parsifal Dingle to read his New Thought publications and say those
prayers which he was firmly assured were influencing the souls of
all the persons he knew, keeping them free from envy, hatred, malice,
and all uncharitableness. Parsifal himself had so little of these worldly
defects that he didn't even know that it was a humiliation to have
his wife referred to as the elder Frau Budd.

The Jew who had been born in a hut with a mud floor in the
realm of the Tsar was proud to escort the Budd ladies about *die
grosse Welt* of Berlin. He told them so with a frankness touched
with humor and untouched with servility. He said that when he was
with them his blood was pure and his fortune untainted. He said
that many a newly arrived *Schieber* was paying millions of marks
for social introductions which he, the cunning one, was getting
practically free. He could say such things, not merely because Bess
and Hansi had made their families one, but because he knew that
Robbie Budd needed Johannes in a business way as much as Johannes needed Robbie's ladies in a social way. A fair deal, and all parties
concerned understood it.

So the former Jascha Rabinowich of Lodz gave a grand reception
and ball in honor of the two Damen Budd. Decorations were
planned, a list of guests carefully studied, and the chefs labored for
a week preparing fantastical foods; the reception-rooms of the
marble palace which looked like a railway station came suddenly
to resemble a movie director's dream of Bali or Brazil. Anyhow, it
was a colossal event, and Johannes said that the magnates who came
wouldn't be exclusively his own business associates, the statesmen
wouldn't be exclusively those who had got campaign funds from
him, and the members of the aristocracy wouldn't be exclusively
those who owed him money. "Moreover," added the shrewd observer, "they will bring their wives and daughters."

XII

Lanny Budd, in his best bib and tucker, wandering about in this dazzling assemblage, helping to do the honors, helping to make people feel at home; dancing with any overgrown Prussian *Backfisch* who appeared to be suffering from neglect; steering the servitors of food toward any dowager whose stomach capacity hadn't been entirely met. Dowagers with large pink bosoms, no shoulder-straps, and perfectly incredible naked backs; servitors in pink-and-green uniforms with gold buttons, white silk gloves and stockings, and pumps having rosettes. Lanny has dutifully studied the list of important personages, so that he will know whom he is greeting and commit no *faux pas*. He has helped to educate his wife, so that she can live up to the majesty of her fortune. Never think that a social career is for an idler!

"Do you know General Graf Stubendorf?" inquires one of the enormous elderly Valkyries.

"I have never had the honor," replies the American. "But I have visited Seine Hochgeboren's home on many occasions."

"Indeed?" says Seine Hochgeboren. He is tall and stiff as a ramrod, with sharp, deeply lined features, gray hair not more than a quarter of an inch in length, a very bright new uniform with orders and decorations which he has earned during four years of never-to-be-forgotten war.

Lanny explains: "I have been for most of my life a friend of Kurt Meissner."

"Indeed?" replies the General Graf. "We consider him a great musician, and are proud of him at Stubendorf."

"I have spent many Christmases at the Meissner home," continues the young American. "I had the pleasure of listening to you address your people each year; also I heard your honored father, before the war."

"Indeed?" says Seine Hochgeboren, again. "I cannot live there any longer, but I go back two or three times a year, out of loyalty to my people." The gray-haired warrior is conveying to a former foe: "I cannot bear to live in my ancestral home because it has become a part of Poland, and is governed by persons whom I consider almost subhuman. You and your armies did it, by meddling without warrant in the affairs of Germany and snatching her hard-won victory from her grasp. Then you went off and left us to be plundered by the rapacious French and the shopkeeping British."

It is not a subject to be explored, so Lanny says some polite words of no special significance and passes on, reflecting: "If Johannes thinks he is winning that gentleman, he is surely fooling himself!"

XIII

But Lanny was making a mistake, as he discovered later in the evening. The stiff aristocrat approached him and spoke again, in a more cordial tone. "Mr. Budd, I have been realizing, I remember you in Stubendorf. Also I have heard Meissner speak of you."

"Herr Meissner has treated me as if I were another of his sons," replied Lanny, modestly.

"*Ein braver Mensch*," said Seine Hochgeboren. "His sons have rendered admirable service." He went on to speak of the family of his Comptroller-General, upon whose capability and integrity he depended as had his father before him. While hearing this formal speech, Lanny guessed what must have happened. The dowager Valkyrie had reminded the General Graf that this was the lucky young *Taugenichts* who had married the fabulously wealthy heiress. Not, as Seine Hochgeboren had supposed, some young snipe trying to make himself important by claiming intimacy with one of a nobleman's employees!

So here was a great aristocrat manifesting condescension, *noblesse oblige*. He knew all about Mr. Budd, oh, of course! "Kurt Meissner composed much of his music in your home, I have heard." He didn't add: "Kurt Meissner was your mother's lover for many years, I have heard." He talked about Kurt's compositions and showed that he really knew about them; *echt deutsche Musik* which could be praised without reserve. A young Franco-American who had built a studio for a musical genius to work in could meet on equal terms a Junker who had furnished a cottage for the genius to raise his family in.

Presently it came out that Lanny had served as a secretary-translator on the staff of the American Commission to Negotiate Peace. "I should be interested to talk to you about those Paris days," remarked the officer. "You might be able to explain some points about the American attitude which have always been a mystery to me."

"I should be pleased to do my best," said Lanny, politely. "You must realize that your beautiful *Schloss* made a great impression upon a small boy, and your father and yourself appeared to me as very grand personalities."

Seine Hochgeboren smiled graciously. He hadn't the slightest doubt that his father had been a grand personality, or that he was one now. "Are you planning to come to Stubendorf this Christmas?" he inquired.

"Kurt has been inviting us," was the reply. "I am not sure if we can arrange it."

"I would be happy if you and your wife would visit the *Schloss* as my guests," said the General Graf.

"Thank you very much," replied the younger man. "I should have to ask the Meissners to give us up."

"I think they would do so," the other suggested, dryly.

"I will let you know a little later. I must consult my wife." Another peculiarity of Americans—they consulted their wives instead of telling them! But of course when the wife was as rich as this one —what was her name?

XIV

They watched that valuable wife, dancing with a handsome young attaché of the American embassy staff. She was more than ever the young brunette Juno; some skilled *couturier* must have had the thought, for he had made her a gown of white silk chiffon with a hint of ancient Greece in it. For jewels she wore only her double rope of pearls; a fortune such as hers was beyond any quantity of stones to symbolize, and had better be left to the newspapers to proclaim. She danced with stately grace, smiled gently, and never chattered; yes, a young goddess, and an ornament to any *Schieber's* ballroom.

When the party was over, Lanny escorted her upstairs. She had promised to have no more than two glasses of champagne, and had kept her word, but was not a little excited by the presence of so many distinguished persons, all of whom had costumes, manners, and modes of speech calculated to impress the daughter of a one-time Wall Street errand-boy. She and her husband talked about this one and that while the maid helped her off with her gown. After she had rested for the required fifteen minutes, the baby was brought in for a nursing; quite a bundle now, nearly eight months old, and full of kicks and squirms and gurgles. She never needed any invitation, but took hold promptly, and while she worked away, Lanny told the mother about the invitation to Stubendorf. He had talked a lot about the "Christmas-card castle" with its snow-covered roofs gleaming in the early morning sunshine, and had made it seem as romantic to Irma as it had to him seventeen years ago.

"Shall we go?" she asked.

"If you would enjoy it."

"I think it would be ducky!" Then, after some reflection: "You and I really make a pretty good social team, don't we, Lanny!"

7

I Have Seen Tempests

I

THE results of the election had set Heinrich Jung in a seat of authority. He called Lanny on the telephone and poured out his exultation. There was no party but the N.S.D.A.P., and Heinrich was its prophet! Therefore, would Lanny come to his home some evening and meet his wife and one of his friends? Lanny said he would be happy to do so; he had just received a letter from Rick, saying that the German vote had made a great impression in England, and if Lanny would send a bunch of literature and some of his own notes as to the state of mind of the country, Rick could write an article for one of the weeklies. Lanny wanted to help his friend, and thought the English people ought to understand what the new movement signified. This, of course, was right down Heinrich's alley; he volunteered to assemble a load of literature—and even to have the article written and save Rick the bother!

Lanny left his wife in a comfortable family bridge game while he drove out to the suburbs toward Potsdam, where the young official lived in a modest cottage. Heinrich had chosen himself a proper *deutsches Mädel* with eyes as blue as his own, and according to the Nazi-Nordic principles they had set to work to increase the ruling race. They proudly showed two blond darlings asleep in their cribs, and one glance at Ilsa Jung was enough to inform Lanny that another would soon be added. There was a peculiarity of the Nazi doctrine which Lanny had observed already among the Italian Fascists. Out of one side of their mouths they said that the nation had to expand in order to have room for its growing population, while out of the other side they said that their population must be increased in order that they might be able to expand. In the land of Mussolini this need was known as *sacro egoismo*, and Lanny had tried in vain to puzzle out why a quality which was considered so offensive in an individual should become holy when exhibited by a group. He hoped that a day might come when nations would be gentlemen.

Heinrich had invited to meet his guest a sports director of one of the youth groups in Berlin. Hugo Behr was his name, and he was another exemplar of the Nordic ideal—which oddly enough a great many of the party leaders were not. There was a joke going the rounds among Berlin's smart intellectuals that the ideal "Aryan" was required to be as blond as Hitler, as tall as Goebbels, as slender as Göring, and so on, as far as your malicious memory would carry you. But Hugo had smooth rosy cheeks and wavy golden hair, and doubtless when in a gym costume presented a figure like that of a young Hermes. He had until recently been an ardent Social-Democrat, a worker in the youth movement in that party; not only could he tell all its scandals, but he knew how to present National Socialism as the only true and real Socialism, by which the German workers were to win freedom for themselves and later for the workers of the world.

The human mind is a strange thing. Both this pair had read *Mein Kampf* as their holy book, and had picked out what they wanted from it. They knew that Lanny had also read the book, and assumed that he would have picked out the same things. But Lanny had noted other passages, in which the Führer had made it clear that he hadn't the slightest interest in giving freedom to the workers of other nations or races, but on the contrary was determined to put them all to work for the benefit of the master race. "Aryan" was merely a fancy word for German—and for other persons of education and social position who were willing to join with the Nazis and help them to seize power.

However, Lanny wasn't there to convert two Nazi officials. He permitted Hugo Behr to speak to him as one comrade to another, and now and then he made notes of something which might be of interest to the reading public of Britain. Hugo was newer in the movement than Heinrich, and more naïve; he had swallowed the original Nazi program, hook, line, and sinker; that was the creed, and when you had quoted it, you had settled the point at issue. Lanny Budd, cynical worldling, product of several decadent cultures, wanted to say: "How can Hitler be getting funds from von Papen and the other Junkers if he really means to break up the great landed estates of Prussia? How can he be getting funds from Fritz Thyssen and the other steel kings if he means to socialize big industry?" But what good would it do? Hugo doubtless thought that all the party funds came from the pfennigs of the workers; that banners and brassards, brown shirts and shiny boots, automatic pistols and Budd machine guns were purchased with the profits of literature sales! Heinrich, perhaps, knew better, but wouldn't admit it, and Lanny wasn't free to name the sources of his own information. Better simply to listen, and make careful notes, and let Rick write an article entitled: "England, Awake!"

II

Right after the elections came a trial in Berlin of three officers charged with having made Nazi propaganda in the army. It attracted a great deal of public attention, and Adolf Hitler appeared as a witness and delivered one of his characteristic tirades, declaring that when his party took power the "November criminals," meaning the men who had established the Republic, would be judged by a people's tribunal. "Heads will roll in the sand," he said. Such language shocked the civilized German people, and Johannes Robin took it as a proof of what he had been saying to Lanny, that all you had to do was to give this fellow rope enough and he would hang himself. There was a demand from many quarters that Hitler be tried for treason; but probably the government was of the same opinion as Johannes. Why hang a man who was so ready to hang himself? The three officers were dismissed from the army, and Adi went on making his propaganda—in the army as everywhere else.

Lanny invited Hauptmann Emil Meissner to lunch with him, and they talked about these problems. Kurt's eldest brother, a World War veteran, had the younger's pale blue eyes and close-cropped straw-colored hair, but not his ardent temperament; he agreed with Lanny that Kurt had been led astray, and that the Führer was a dangerous fanatic. Emil was loyal to the existing government; he said that would always be the attitude of the army, and was the obligation of every officer, no matter how much he might disapprove the policies of the politicians in control.

"Would you obey the Nazis if they should take power?" inquired the American.

Emil shut his eyes for a moment, as if to hide the painful reaction which such a question caused in him. "I don't think it is necessary to contemplate that," he said.

Lanny replied: "The present election has made me do it." But he didn't press the point.

Emil placed his faith in Germany's symbol of loyalty, Feldmarschall and now Präsident Paul Ludwig Hans Anton von Beneckendorff und von Hindenburg. The old commander had won the battle of Tannenberg, the one complete victory the Germans had gained, with the result that the people had idolized him all through the rest of the war. In every town they had set up huge wooden statues of him, and it had been the supreme act of patriotism to buy nails and drive them into this statue, the money going to the German Red Cross. The Hindenburg line had been another name for national security, and now the Hindenburg presidency was the same. But the stern old titan was now eighty-three years old, and his wits were growing dim; it was hard for him to concentrate upon complex matters. The politicians swarmed about him, they pulled him this way and that, and it was painful to him and tragic to those who saw it.

Emil Meissner had been on the old field marshal's staff during part of the war, and knew his present plight; but Emil was reserved in the presence of a foreigner, especially one who consorted with Jews and had a sister and a brother-in-law whose redness was notorious. On the other hand, an officer of the Reichswehr owed no love to Adolf Hitler, and reported that the President refused to recognize this upstart even as an Austrian, but persisted in referring to him as "the Bohemian corporal," and using the name of his father, which was Schicklgruber, a plebeian and humiliating name. *Der alte Herr* had steadily refused to meet Corporal Schicklgruber, because he talked too much, and in the army it was customary for a non-commissioned officer to wait for his superior to speak first.

Emil expressed his ideas concerning the disorders which prevailed in the cities of the Republic, amounting to a civil war between the two sets of extremists. The Reds had begun it, without doubt, and the Brownshirts were the answer they had got; but Emil called it an atrocious thing that anybody should be permitted to organize a private army as Hitler had done. Hardly a night passed that the rival groups didn't clash in the streets, and Emil longed for a courageous Chancellor who would order the Reichswehr to disarm both sides. The Nazi Führer pretended to deplore what his followers did, but of course that was nonsense; every speech he made was an incitement to more violence—like that insane talk about heads rolling in the sand.

So far two cultivated and modern men could agree over their coffee-cups. But Emil went on to reveal that he was a German like the others. He said that fundamentally the situation was due to the Allies and their monstrous treaty of Versailles; Germany had been stripped of everything by the reparations demands, deprived of her ships, colonies, and trade—and no people ever would starve gladly. Lanny had done his share of protesting against Versailles, and had argued for helping Germany to get on her feet again; but somehow, when he listened to Germans, he found himself shifting to the other side and wishing to remind them that they had lost the war. After all, it hadn't been a game of ping-pong, and somebody had to pay for it. Also, Germany had had her program of what she meant to do if she had won; she had revealed it clearly in the terms she had forced upon Russia at Brest-Litovsk. Also, there had been a Franco-Prussian War, and Germany had taken Alsace-Lorraine; there had been Frederick the Great and the partition of Poland; there had been a whole string of Prussian conquests—but you had better not mention them if you wanted to have friends in the Fatherland!

III

Three evenings a week Freddi and Rahel went to the school which they helped to support. Freddi taught a class in the history of economic theory and Rahel taught one in singing, both subjects important for German workers. Lanny went along more than once, and when the students old and young discovered that he lived in France and had helped with a school there, they wanted to hear about conditions in that country and what the workers were thinking and doing. Discussions arose, and Lanny discovered that the disciplined and orderly working people of Germany were not so different from the independent and free-spoken bunch in the Midi. The same problems vexed them, the same splits turned every discussion into a miniature war.

Could the workers "take over" by peaceable processes? You could tell the answer by the very words in which the speaker put the question. If he said "by parliamentary action," he was some sort of Socialist; if he said "by electing politicians," he was some sort of Communist. The former had the prestige of the greatest party of the Fatherland behind him, and quoted Marx, Bebel, and Kautsky. His opponent in the controversy took the Soviet Union for his model, and quoted Marx, Lenin, and Stalin. Between the two extremes were those who followed the recently exiled Trotsky, or the martyred Karl Liebknecht and "Red Rosa" Luxemburg. There were various "splinter groups" that Lanny hadn't heard of; indeed, it appeared that the nearer the rebel workers came to danger, the more they fought among themselves. Lanny compared them to people on a sinking ship trying to throw one another overboard.

At the school the "Sozis" were in a majority; and Lanny would explain to them his amiable idea that all groups ought to unite against the threat of National Socialism. Since he was a stranger, and Freddi's brother-in-law, they would be patient and explain that nobody could co-operate with the Communists, because they

wouldn't let you. Nobody talked more about co-operating than
the Communists, but when you tried it you found that what they
meant was undermining your organization and poisoning the minds
of your followers, the process known as "boring from within."
Any Socialist you talked to was ready with a score of illustrations—
and also with citations from Lenin, to prove that it was no accident, but a policy.

Members of the Social-Democratic party went even further;
they charged that the Communists were co-operating with the
Nazis against the coalition government in which the Social-
Democrats were participating. That too was a policy; the Bolsheviks
believed in making chaos, because they hoped to profit from it;
chaos had given them their chance to seize power in Russia, and
the fact that it hadn't in Italy did not cause them to revise the
theory. It was easy for them to co-operate with Nazis, because both
believed in force, in dictatorship; the one great danger that the
friends of peaceful change confronted was a deal, more or less
open, between the second and third largest parties of Germany.
To Lanny that seemed a sort of nightmare—not the idea that it
might happen, but the fact that the Socialists should have got themselves into such a state of hatred of another working-class party
that they were willing to believe such a deal might be made. Once
more he had to sink back into the role of listener, keep his thoughts
to himself, and not tell Hansi and Bess what the friends of Freddi
and Rahel were teaching in their school.

IV

Once a week the institution gave a reception; the Left intellectuals came, and drank coffee and ate great quantities of *Leberwurst*
and *Schweizerkäse* sandwiches, and discussed the policies of the
school and the events of the time. Then indeed the forces of chaos
and old night were released. Lanny decided that every Berlin
intellectual was a new political party, and every two Berlin intellectuals were a political conflict. Some of them wore long hair
because it looked picturesque, and others because they didn't own

a pair of scissors. Some came because they wanted an audience, and others because it was a chance to get a meal. But whatever their reason, nothing could keep them quiet, and nothing could get them to agree. Lanny had always thought that loud voices and vehement gestures marked the Latin races, but now he decided that it wasn't a matter of race at all, but of economic determinism. The nearer a country came to a crisis, the more noise its intellectuals made in drawing-rooms!

Lanny made the mistake of taking his wife to one of these gatherings, and she didn't enjoy it. In the first place, most of the arguing was done in German, which is rarely a very pleasant-sounding language unless it has been written by Heine; it appears to the outsider to involve a great deal of coughing, spitting, and rumbling in the back of the throat. Of course there were many who were able to speak English of a sort, and were willing to try it on Lanny's wife; but they wished to talk about personalities, events, and doctrines which were for the most part strange to her. Irma's great forte in social life was serenity, and somehow this wasn't the place to show it off.

She commented on this to her husband, who said: "You must understand that most of these people are having a hard time keeping alive. Many of them don't get enough to eat, and that is disturbing to one's peace of mind."

He went on to explain what was called the "intellectual proletariat": a mass of persons who had acquired education at heavy cost of both mind and body, but who now found no market for what they had to offer to the world. They made a rather miserable livelihood by hack-writing, or teaching—whatever odd jobs they could pick up. Naturally they were discontented, and felt themselves in sympathy with the dispossessed workers.

"But why don't they go and get regular jobs, Lanny?"

"What sort of jobs, dear? Digging ditches, or clerking in a store, or waiting on table?"

"Anything, I should think, so long as they can earn an honest living."

"Many of them have to do it, but it's not so easy as it sounds.

There are four million unemployed in Germany right now, and a job usually goes to somebody who has been trained for that kind of work."

Thus patiently Lanny would explain matters, as if to a child. The trouble was, he had to explain it many times, for Irma appeared reluctant to believe it. He was trying to persuade her that the time was cruelly out of joint, whereas she had been brought up to believe that everything was for the best in the best of all possible worlds. If people didn't get jobs and keep them, it must be because there was something wrong with those people; they didn't really want to work; they wanted to criticize and sneer at others who had been successful, who had worked hard, as Irma's father had done. He had left her secure. Who could blame her for wanting to stay that way, and resenting people who pulled her about, clamored in her ears, upset her mind with arguments?

It wasn't that she was hard of heart, not at all. Some pitiful beggar would come up to her on the street, and tears would start into her eyes, and she would want to give him the contents of her well-filled purse. But that was charity, and she learned that Lanny's friends all spurned this; they wanted a thing they called "justice." They required you to agree that the social system was fundamentally wrong, and that most of what Irma's parents and teachers and friends had taught her was false. They demanded that the world be turned upside down and that they, the rebels, be put in charge of making it over. Irma decided that she didn't trust either their capacity or their motives. She watched them, and announced her decision to her too credulous husband: "They are jealous, and want what we've got, and if we gave it to them they wouldn't even say thank you!"

"Maybe so," replied the husband, who had suffered not a few disillusionments himself. "It's no use expecting human beings to be better than they are. Some are true idealists, like Hansi and Freddi."

"Yes, but they work; they would succeed in any world. But those politicians, and intellectuals who want to be politicians but don't know how——"

Lanny laughed; he saw that she was beginning to use her own

head. "What you have to do," he cautioned, "is to consider principles and not individuals. We want a system that will give everybody a chance at honest and constructive labor, and then see that nobody lives without working."

V

The daughter of J. Paramount Barnes was forced to admit that there was something wrong, because her dividends were beginning to fall off. In the spring she had been hearing about the little bull market, which had sounded fine; but during the summer and fall had come a series of slumps, no less than four, one after another. Nobody understood these events, nobody could predict them. You would hear people say: "The bottom has been reached now; things are bound to take a turn." They would bet their money on it—and then, next day or next week, stocks would be tumbling and everybody terrified.

There came a letter from Irma's uncle Joseph, one of the trustees who managed her estate. He warned her about what was happening, and explained matters as well as he could; during the past year her blue-chip stocks had lost another thirty points, below the lowest mark of the great panic when she had been in New York. It appeared to be a vicious circle: the slump caused fear, and fear caused another slump. The elections in Germany had had a bad reaction in Wall Street; everybody decided there wouldn't be any more reparations payments. Mr. Joseph Barnes added that there hadn't really been any for a long time, and perhaps never had been, since the Germans first borrowed in Wall Street whatever they wished to pay. Irma didn't understand this very well, but gave the letter to Lanny, who explained it to her—of course from his Pink point of view.

One thing Uncle Joseph made plain: Irma must be careful how she spent money! Her answer was obvious: she had been living on the Robins for half a year, and when she went back to Bienvenu they would resume that ridiculously simple life. You just couldn't spend money when you lived in a small villa; you had no place to put things, and no way to entertain on a large scale. Lanny and his mother had lived on thirteen hundred dollars a month, whereas Irma had been accustomed to spend fifty times that. So she had no trouble in assuring her conscientious uncle that she would give heed to his advice. Her mother had decided not to come to Europe that winter; she was busy cutting down the expenses of the Long Island estate. Lanny read the letter and experienced the normal feelings of a man who learns that his mother-in-law is not coming to visit him.

VI

Heinrich Jung called Lanny on the telephone. "Would you like to meet the Führer?" he inquired.

"Oh, my gosh!" exclaimed Lanny, taken aback. "He wouldn't be interested in me."

"He says he would."

"What did you tell him about me?"

"I said that you were an old friend, and the patron of Kurt Meissner."

Lanny thought for a moment. "Did you tell him that I don't agree with his ideas?"

"Of course. Do you suppose he's only interested in meeting people who agree with him?"

Lanny had supposed something of the sort, but he was too polite to answer directly. Instead he asked: "Did you say that I might become a convert?"

"I said it might be worth while to try."

"But really, Heinrich, it isn't."

"You might take a chance, if he's willing."

Lanny laughed. "Of course he's an interesting man, and I'll enjoy meeting him."

"All right, come ahead."

"You're sure it won't injure your standing?"

"My standing? I went three times to visit him while he was a prisoner in the Landsberg fortress, and he is a man who never forgets a friend."

"All right, then, when shall we go?"

"The sooner the better. He's in Berlin now, but he jumps about a lot."

"You set the time."

"Are you free this afternoon?"

"I can get free."

Heinrich called again, saying that the appointment was for four o'clock, and he would be waiting for Lanny in front of the head-quarters at three-thirty. When he was in the car and had given the address, he began, with some signs of hesitation: "You know, American manners are not quite the same as German. The Führer, of course, understands that you are an American——"

"I hope he won't expect me to say '*Heil Hitler!*' "

"Oh, no, of course not. You will shake hands with him."

"Shall I address him as '*Er*'?" Lanny had read a recent announcement of the introduction of this custom, previously reserved for royalty. It meant speaking in the third person.

"That will not be expected of a foreigner. But it is better if one doesn't contradict him. You know that he is under heavy pressure these days——"

"I understand." From many sources Lanny had heard that Adi was a highly excitable person; some even called him psychopathic.

"I don't mean that you have to agree with him," the other hastened to add. "It's all right if you just listen. He is very kind about explaining his ideas to people."

"Sure thing." Lanny kept a perfectly straight face. "I have read *Mein Kampf*, and this will be a sort of postscript. Five years have passed, and a lot has happened."

"Isn't it marvelous how much has come true!" exclaimed the faithful young "Aryan."

VII

The Partei- und oberster S.A. Führer, Vorsitzender der N.S.D.A.P., lived in one of those elegant apartment houses having a uniformed doorkeeper. The Führer was a vegetarian, and an abstainer from alcohol and tobacco, but not an ascetic as to interior decoration; on the contrary, he thought himself an artist and enjoyed fixing up his surroundings. With the money of Fritz Thyssen and other magnates he had bought a palace in Munich and made it over into a showplace, the Nazi Braune Haus; also for the apartment in Berlin he had got modernistic furniture of the utmost elegance. He lived with a married couple to take care of him, South Germans and friends of his earlier days. They had two children, and Adi was playing some sort of parlor game with them when the visitors were brought in. He kept the little ones for a while, talking to them and about them part of the time; his fondness for children was his better side, and Lanny would have been pleased if he had not had to see any other.

The Führer wore a plain business suit, and presented the aspect of a simple, unassuming person. He shook hands with his Franco-American guest, patted Heinrich on the back, and called for fruit juice and cookies for all of them. He asked Lanny about his boyhood on the Riviera, and the children listened with open eyes to stories about hauling the seine and bringing in cuttlefish and small sharks; about digging in one's garden and finding ancient Roman coins; about the "little Septentrion child" who had danced and pleased in the arena of Antibes a couple of thousand years ago. Adi Schicklgruber's own childhood had been unhappy and he didn't talk about it.

Presently he asked where Lanny had met Kurt Meissner, and the visitor told about the Dalcroze school at Hellerau. His host took this as a manifestation of German culture, and Lanny forbore to mention that Jaques-Dalcroze was a Swiss of French descent. It was true that the school had been built and endowed by a German patron. Said Hitler: "That kind of thing will be the glory of our National Socialist administration; there will be such an outburst of artistic and musical genius as will astound the world." Lanny noted that in all the conversation he took it for granted that the N.S.D.A.P. would soon be in control of Germany; he never said "if," he said "when"—and this was one of the subjects on which the visitor was surely not going to contradict him.

They talked about Kurt and his music, which was pure "Aryan," so the Führer declared; nothing meretricious, no corrupt foreign influences; life in France for so many years had apparently not affected the composer in the slightest. Lanny explained that Kurt had kept almost entirely to himself, and had seldom gone out unless one dragged him. He told about his life at Bienvenu, and the Führer agreed that it was the ideal way for an artist. "It is the sort of life I would have chosen; but, alas, I was born under a different star." Lanny had heard that he believed in astrology, and hoped he wouldn't get onto that subject.

VIII

What the Führer of all the Nazis planned was for this elegant and extremely wealthy young foreigner to go out to the world as a convert to the National Socialist ideas. To that end he laid himself out to be charming, for which he had no small endowment. He had evidently inquired as to Lanny's point of view, for everything he said was subtly directed to meeting that. Lanny was a Socialist, and Hitler, too, was a Socialist, the only true, practical kind of Socialist. Out of the chaos of competitive capitalism a new order was about to arise; an order that would endure, because it would be founded upon real understanding and guided by scientists. Not the evil, degenerate Socialism of the Marxists, which repudiated all that was most precious in human beings; not a Socialism poisoned with the delusion of internationalism, but one founded upon recognition of the great racial qualities which alone made such a task conceivable.

Patiently and kindly the Führer explained that his ideas of race were not German in the narrow sense. Lanny, too, was an "Aryan," and so were the cultured classes in America; theirs was a truly "Aryan" civilization, and so was the British. "I want nothing in the world so much as understanding and peace between my country and Britain, and I think there has been no tragedy in modern times so great as the war they fought. Why can we not understand one another and get together in friendship for our common task?

The world is big enough, and it is full of mongrel tribes whom we dare not permit to gain power, because they are incapable of making any intelligent use of it."

Hitler talked for a while about these mongrels. He felt quite safe in telling a young Franco-American what he thought about the Japanese, a sort of hairless yellow monkeys. Then he came to the Russians, who were by nature lazy, incompetent, and bloodthirsty, and had fallen into the hands of gutter-rats and degenerates. He talked about the French, and was careful of what he said; he wanted no enmity between France and Germany; they could make a treaty of peace that would last for a thousand years, if only the French would give up their imbecile idea of encircling Germany and keeping her ringed with foes. "It is the Polish alliance and the Little Entente which keep enmity between our peoples; for we do not intend to let those peoples go on ruling Germans, and we have an iron determination to right the wrongs which were committed at Versailles. You must know something about that, Mr. Budd, for you have been to Stubendorf, and doubtless have seen with your own eyes what it means for Germans to be governed by Poles."

Lanny answered: "I was one of many Americans at the Peace Conference who pleaded against that mistake."

So the Führer warmed to his visitor. "The shallow-minded call my attitude imperialism; but that is an abuse of language. It is not imperialism to recognize the plain evidence of history that certain peoples have the capacity to build a culture while others are lacking in it entirely. It is not imperialism to say that a vigorous and great-souled people like the Germans shall not be surrounded and penned in by jealous and greedy rivals. It is not imperialism to say that these little children shall not suffer all their lives the deprivations which they have suffered so far."

The speaker was running his hand over the closely cropped blond head of the little boy. "This *Bübchen* was born in the year of the great shame, that wicked Versailles *Diktat*. You can see that he is thin and undersized, because of the starvation blockade. But I have told him that his children will be as sturdy as his father was, because I intend to deliver the Fatherland from the possibility of

blockades—and I shall not worry if my enemies call me an imperialist. I have written that every man becomes an imperialist when he
begets a child, for he obligates himself to see to it that that child
has the means of life provided."

Lanny, a Socialist not untainted with internationalism, could have
thought of many things to answer; but he had no desire to spoil
this most amiable of interviews. So long as a tiger was willing to
purr, Lanny was pleased to study tigers. He might have been influenced by the many gracious words which had been spoken to him,
if it had not been for having read *Mein Kampf*. How could the
author of that book imagine that he could claim, for example, to
have no enmity against France? Or had he changed his mind in
five years? Apparently not, for he had formed a publishing-house
which was selling his bible to all the loyal followers of the National
Socialist German Workingmen's Party, and at the price of twelve
marks per copy somebody was making a fortune.

IX

Lanny thought: "I am taking a lot of a busy man's time." But
he knew that when you are calling on royalty you do not leave
until you are dismissed; and perhaps it would be the same here.
The children had been sent away, it being their suppertime; but
still the Führer went on talking. Heinrich Jung sat leaning forward
with an aspect of strained attention, and there was nothing for
Lanny to do but follow his example.

The Führer retold the wrongs which had been done to his country; and as he went on he became more and more aroused, his voice
swelled and he became the orator. Lanny remembered having read
somewhere of Queen Victoria's complaining about her audiences
with Gladstone: "He treats me as if I were a public meeting."
Lanny found it somewhat embarrassing to be shouted at from a
distance of six feet. He thought: "Good Lord, with this much
energy the man could address all Germany!" But apparently Adolf
Hitler had enough energy for all Germany and for a foreign visitor
also; it was for him to decide how much to expend, and for the

visitor to sit and gaze at him like a fascinated rabbit at a hissing snake.

Lanny had seen this same thing happen at several meetings. The Führer took fire from his own phrases; he was moved to action by his own eloquence. Now, now was the moment to overthrow these enemies of the Fatherland, to punish them for their crimes. Heads will roll in the sand! The orator forgot all about being sweet and reasonable for the benefit of a member of two of these enemy nations. Perhaps he thought that Lanny, having heard the whole story of Versailles, of reparations and starvation blockade and Ruhr invasion and Polish alliance and all the rest, must now be completely a convert. Away with the pretense that the Führer of the Nazis did not hate the French for their avarice, the British for their arrogance, the Americans for their upstart pretensions, the Bolsheviks for being bloodthirsty monsters, the Jews for being the spawn of hell. In short, he became that man of frenzy whom Lanny and Rick had first heard in the Bürgerbräukeller in Munich seven years ago. Lanny had said: "One must admit that he is sincere," and Rick had replied: "So are most lunatics."

How long this would have continued no one could say. The housekeeper opened the door and said: "*Verzeihung, mein Führer. Herr Strasser.*" Behind her came, without delay, a large man in S.A. uniform. He had large, rather coarse features, a somewhat bulbous nose, a drooping mouth with deep lines at the sides. According to the practice with which Lanny was familiar he should have halted in the doorway, clicked his heels, given the Nazi salute, and said: "*Heil Hitler!*" Instead he came forward, remarking in a nonchalant way: "*Grüss Gott, Adolf.*" This meant that he was an old friend, and also that he came from Bavaria.

The visitors were greatly startled by the Führer's response, delivered with the force of a blow: "You have not been conducting yourself as a friend, and therefore you have not been summoned as a friend!" The speaker rose to his feet and, pointing an accusing finger at the new arrival, went on: "Learn once for all, I have had enough of your insubordination! You continue at your peril!" It set the big man back on his heels, and his large mouth dropped open.

Would the Führer of the Nazis have attacked his subordinate in that abrupt and violent way if he had not already got steamed up? Impossible to say; but the astonishment and dismay of Herr Strasser were apparent. He opened his mouth as if to ask what was the matter, but then he closed it again, for he got no chance. Hitler was launched upon a tirade; he rushed at the man—not to strike him, but to thrust the accusing finger within a couple of inches of the big nose and shriek:

"Your intrigues are known! Your insolence is resented! Your public utterances are incitements to treason, and if you do not mend your ways you will be driven out. Go and join your brother's *Schwarze Front*, and the other disguised Communists and scoundrels! I—I, Adolf Hitler, am the Führer of the N.S.D.A.P., and it is for me to determine policies. I will not have opposition, I will not have argument, I will have obedience. We are in the midst of a war, and I demand loyalty, I demand discipline. *Zucht! Zucht! Zucht!*" It is one of those many German words which require a clearing of the throat, and the unfortunate Strasser flinched as if from a rain of small particles of moisture.

"Adolf, who has been telling you stories about me?" He forced the sentence in while the Führer caught his breath.

"I make it my business to know what is going on in my movement. Do you imagine that you can go about expressing contempt for my policies without word of it coming to me?"

"Somebody has been lying, Adolf. I have said only what I have said to you: that now is the time for action, and that our foes desire nothing but delay, so that they can weaken us by their intrigues——"

"They weaken us because of arrogance and self-will in my own party officials; because these presumptuous ones dare to set themselves up as authorities and thinkers. *I* think for the National Socialists, *I*—and I have ordered you to hold your tongue—*Maul halten*—and obey my orders, follow my policies and not your own stupid notions. Your brother has turned himself into a criminal and an outlaw because of that same arrogance——"

"Leave Otto out of it, Adolf. You know that I have broken with him. I do not see him and have no dealings with him."

"*Ich geb' 'n Dreck d'rum!*" cried Adolf; he spoke that kind of German. Talking to a Bavarian, he added: "*Das ist mir Sau-wurscht!*"

He rushed on: "You stay in the party and carry on Otto's agitation in favor of discarded policies. I am the captain of this ship, and it is not for the crew to tell me what to do, but to do what I tell them. Once more, I demand unity in the face of our foes. Understand me, I command it! I speak as your Führer!"

Lanny thought he had never seen a man so beside himself with excitement. Adolf Hitler's face had become purple, he danced about as he talked, and every word was emphasized as with a hammer blow of his finger. Lanny thought the two men would surely fight; but no, presently he saw that the other was going to take it. Perhaps he had seen the same thing happen before, and had learned to deal with it. He stopped arguing, stopped trying to protest; he simply stood there and let his Führer rave, let the storm blow itself out— if it ever would blow itself out. Would the ocean ever be the same after such a hurricane?

X

Lanny had learned much about the internal affairs of the Nazi party from the conversation of Kurt and Heinrich. Also, during the summer he had been getting the German papers, and these had been full of a furious party conflict over the question of the old program, which Hitler had been paring down until now there was nothing left of it. Here in North Germany many of the Nazis took the "Socialist" part of their label seriously; they insisted upon talking about the communizing of department stores, the confiscation of landed estates, the ending of interest slavery, common wealth before private wealth, and so on. It had caused a regular civil war in the party earlier in the year. The two Strasser brothers, Gregor and Otto, had fought for the old program and had been beaten.

Gregor had submitted, but Otto had quit the party and organized a revolutionary group of his own, which the Hitlerites called the "Black Front" and which they were fighting with bludgeons and revolvers, just as they fought the Communists. Later on, immediately before the elections, there had been another attempt at internal revolution; the rebels had seized the offices of the Berlin party paper, *Der Angriff*, holding it by force of arms and publishing the paper for three days. A tremendous scandal, and one which the enemies of the movement had not failed to exploit.

So here was Gregor Strasser, Reich Organization Leader Number 1. A lieutenant in the World War, he had become an apothecary, but had given up his business in order to oppose the Reds and then to help Adi prepare for the Beerhall Putsch. He was perhaps the most competent organizer the party had, and had come to Berlin and built the Sturmabteilung by his efforts. Hitler, distrusting him as too far to the left, had formed a new personal guard, the Schutzstaffel, or S.S. So there were two rival armies inside the Nazi party of all Germany; which was going to prevail?

Lanny wondered, had Hitler really lost his temper or was this merely a policy? Was this the way Germans enforced obedience— the drill-sergeant technique? Apparently it was working, for the big man's bull voice dropped low; he stood meekly and took his licking like a schoolboy ordered to let down his pants. Lanny wondered also: why did the Führer permit a foreigner to witness such a demonstration? Did he think it would impress an American? Did he love power so much that it pleased him to exhibit it in the presence of strangers? Or did he feel so secure in his mastery that he didn't care what anybody thought of him? This last appeared to be in character with his procedure of putting his whole defiant program into a book and selling it to anybody in the world who had twelve marks.

Lanny listened again to the whole story of *Mein Kampf*. He learned that Adolf Hitler meant to outwit the world, but in his own good time and in his own way. He meant to suppress his land program to please the Junkers and his industrial program to please the steel kings, and so get their money and use it to buy arms for his S.A. and his S.S. He meant to promise everything to everybody and so get their votes—everybody except the *abscheulichen Bolschewisten* and the *verfluchten Juden*. He meant to get power and take office, and nobody was going to block him from his goal. If any *Dummkopf* tried it he would crush him like a louse, and he told him so.

When Strasser ventured to point out that Dr. Joseph Goebbels, the Führer's favorite propagandist, had said that he was developing a "legality complex," the Führer replied that he would deal with "Juppchen" at his own convenience; he was dealing now with Gregor Strasser, and telling him that he was not to utter another word of criticism of his Führer's policies, but to devote his energies to putting down the Reds and teaching discipline to his organization, which lacked it so shamefully. Adolf Hitler would do his own dickering with the politicians, playing them one against another, worming his way closer and closer to the chancellorship which was his goal—and in due course he would show them all, and his own friends would be ashamed of their blindness and presumption in having doubted their inspired leader.

So Lanny received a demonstration of what it meant to be a master of men. Perhaps that was what the Führer intended; for not until he had received the submission of his Reich Organization Leader Number 1 and had dismissed him did he turn again to his guest. "Well, Mr. Budd," he said, "you see what it takes to put people to work for a cause. Wouldn't you like to come and help me?"

Said Lanny: "I am afraid I am without any competence for such a task." If there was a trace of dryness in his tone the Führer missed it, for he smiled amiably, and seemed to be of the opinion that he had done a very good afternoon's work.

Long afterward Lanny learned from Kurt Meissner what the Führer thought about that meeting. He said that young Mr. Budd was a perfect type of the American privileged classes: good-looking, easy-going, and perfectly worthless. It would be a very simple task to cause that nation to split itself to pieces, and the National Socialist movement would take it in charge.

8

To Give and to Share

I

IN THE month of December Irma and Rahel completed the tremendous feat they had undertaken; having kept the pact they had made with each other and with their families, they were now physically and morally free. The condition of two lusty infants appeared to indicate that Rousseau and Lanny had been right. Little by little the greedy sucklings learned to take the milk of real cows instead of imitation ones; they acquired a taste for fruit juices and for prune pulp with the skins carefully removed. At last the young mothers could go to a bridge party without having to leave in the middle of it.

Marceline with her governess had returned to Juan at the end of the yacht cruise, and her mother had promised to join her for Christmas. Farewells were said to the Robin family, and Beauty and her husband went by train, taking the baby, Miss Severne, the nursemaid, and Madame. The General Graf Stubendorf's invitation to Lanny and Irma had been renewed, and Kurt had written that they should by all means accept; not only would it be more pleasant for Irma at the Schloss, but it would advantage the Meissners to have an old friend return as a guest of Seine Hochgeboren. Lanny noted this with interest and explained it to his wife; what would have been snobbery in America was loyalty in Silesia. The armies of Napoleon having never reached that land, the feudal system still prevailed and rank was a reality.

Stubendorf being in Poland, the train had to stop, and luggage and passports to be examined. The village itself was German, and only the poorer part of the peasantry was Polish. This made a situation full of tension, and no German thought of it as anything but a truce. What the Poles thought, Lanny didn't know, for he couldn't talk with them. In Berlin he had shown his wife a comic paper and a cartoon portraying Poland as an enormous fat hog, being ridden by a French army officer who was twisting the creature's tail to make it gallop and waving a saber to show why he was in a hurry. Not exactly the Christmas spirit!

Irma Barnes Budd explored the feudal system, and found it not so different from the South Shore of Long Island. She was met at the train by a limousine, which would have happened at home. A five-story castle didn't awe her, for she had been living in one that was taller and twice as broad. The lady who welcomed her was certainly no taller or broader than Mrs. Fanny Barnes, and couldn't be more proud of her blood. The principal differences were, first, that the sons and daughters of this Prussian family worked harder than any young people Irma had ever known; and, second, there were uniforms and ceremonies expressive of rank and station. Irma gave close attention to these, and her husband wondered if she was planning to introduce them into the New World.

Visiting his father's home in Connecticut, Lanny had discovered that being married to a great heiress had raised his social status; and now he observed the same phenomenon here. Persons who through the years had paid no particular attention to him suddenly recognized that he was a man of brilliant parts; even the Meissner family, whom he had known and loved since he was a small boy, appeared to be seized with awe. Whereas formerly he had shared a bed in Kurt's small room, he was now lodged in a sumptuous suite in the castle; the retainers and tenants all took off their hats to him, and he no longer had to hear the *gräflichen* ideas explained second-hand by Herr Meissner, but got them from the horse's mouth, as the saying is.

It was unfortunate that the ideas no longer impressed him as they did in the earlier years. The General Graf was a typical Junker, active in the Nationalist party; his policies were limited by the interests of his class. He did not let himself be influenced by the fact that his estate was now in Poland; that was a temporary matter, soon to be remedied. He supported a tariff on foodstuffs so that the German people would pay higher prices to landowners. He wanted his coal mined, but he didn't want to pay the miners enough so that they could buy his food. He wanted steel and chemicals and other products of industry, which required swarms of workers, but he blamed them for trying to have a say as to the conditions of their lives, or indeed whether they should live at all.

II

Fortunately it wasn't necessary to spend much time discussing politics. There was a great deal of company, with music, dancing, and feasting. If the country products couldn't be sold at a profit they might as well be eaten at home, so everyone did his best, and it was astounding how they succeeded. Modern ideas of dietetics, like Napoleon, hadn't penetrated the feudalism of Upper Silesia. It was the same regimen which had startled Lanny as a boy: a preliminary breakfast with *Dresdener Christstollen*, a sort of bun with raisins inside and sugar on top; then at half-past ten the "fork breakfast," when several kinds of meat were eaten—but without interfering with anybody's appetite for lunch. An afternoon tea, only it was coffee, and then an enormous dinner of eight or ten courses, served with the utmost formality by footmen in satin uniforms. Finally, after cards, or music and dancing, it was unthinkable that one should go to bed on an empty stomach. That meant six meals a day, and it produced vigorous and sturdy young men, but when they came to middle age they had necks like bulls' and cheeks like pelicans' and eyes almost closed by fat in the lids.

One discovery Lanny made very quickly: this was the life for which his wife had been created. Nobody shouted at her, nobody confused her mind with strange ideas; everybody treated her as a person of distinction. and found her charming, even brilliant. A world in which serenity and poise counted; a world which didn't have to be changed! The Gräfin became a second mother to her, and she was invited to visit so many distinguished families, she might have been carried through the entire winter without spending any of her money. One aspect of the feudal system appeared to be that most of its ruling members were bored on their estates, and eager for visitors, provided they were of proper station. They all had bursting larders, with a host of servants trained to put meals on tables. Do come and enjoy your share!

III

What Lanny really wanted was to spend the time with his boyhood chum. Kurt now lived with his own family in a stone cottage on the outskirts of the village of Stubendorf, all of which belonged to Seine Hochgeboren. Lanny met for the first time Kurt's gentle and devoted young wife, and three little blond "Aryans" produced according to the Schicklgruber prescription. Irma went along on the first visit as a matter of courtesy, and also of curiosity, for she had heard how this wonderful *Komponist* had been Beauty Budd's lover for some eight years; also, she had heard enough about Kurt's adventures in Paris during the Peace Conference to make him a romantic figure.

Kurt hadn't changed much in the four years since Lanny had seen him. The war had aged him prematurely, but from then on he seemed to stay the same: a grave and rather silent man, who chose to speak to the world through his art. He worshiped the classic German composers, especially the "three B's." Each of these had written a few four-hand piano compositions, and in the course of the years others of their works had been arranged in this form, so now there were more than a hundred such available. Lanny had ordered a complete collection from one of the dealers in Berlin; not often can one make a Christmas present which will give so much pleasure to a friend! The two of them wanted to sit right down and not get up even for meals. Irma couldn't see how it was possible for human fingers to stand the strain of so much pounding; she couldn't see how human ears could take in so many notes. She had to remind them of an engagement at the Schloss; whereupon Kurt leaped up at once, for Seine Hochgeboren must not be kept waiting, even for Bach, Beethoven, and Brahms.

In return for his pension and his home it was Kurt's duty to play for his patron, and to assemble, rehearse, and conduct a small orchestra for special occasions such as this Christmas visit. He did this with scrupulous fidelity, as the young Haydn had done for the great Prince Esterhazy of Vienna. It wasn't an onerous job, for of late years Seine Hochgeboren came only rarely. To his people living under the Poles he made a formal address, full of Christmas cheer, but also of quiet unbending faith that God would somehow restore them to their Fatherland. *Deutsche Treue und Ehre* acquired a special meaning when used by those living in exile.

That was what the National Socialist movement meant to Kurt Meissner. He and his young wife listened with eager attention while Lanny told about his meeting with Adolf Hitler; then Herr Meissner asked to have the story told to his family, and later on the lord of the Schloss wanted his friends to hear it. They questioned the visitor closely as to just what Adi's program now was; and of course Lanny knew what was in their minds. Had the Führer of the Nazis really dropped that crazy Socialist stuff with which he had set out on his career? Could he be depended upon as a bulwark against Bolshevism, a terror so real to the people on Germany's eastern border? Would he let the landowners alone and devote himself to rearming the country, and forcing the Allies to permit the return of Stubendorf and the other lost provinces, the Corridor and the colonies? If the Germans in exile could be sure of these things, they might be willing to support him, or at any rate not oppose him actively.

IV

Kurt had composed a symphony, which he called *Das Vaterland*. He and his adoring wife had copied out the parts for an orchestra of twenty pieces, and Kurt had engaged musicians from the near-by towns, of course at the Graf's expense. They had been thoroughly drilled, and now played the new work before a distinguished company on Christmas night. This was the high point of Lanny's visit, and indeed of his stay in Germany. In his boyhood he had taken

Kurt Meissner as his model of all things noble and inspiring; he had predicted for him a shining future, and felt justified when he saw all the *hochgeboren Herrschaften* of Kurt's own district assembled to do him honor.

During the composer's time in Bienvenu his work had been full of bitterness and revolt, but since he had come home he had apparently managed to find courage and hope. He didn't write program music, and Lanny didn't ask what the new work was supposed to signify; indeed, he would rather not be told, for the military character of much of the music suggested it was meant for the Nazis. It pictured the coming of a deliverer, it portrayed the German people arising and marching to their world destiny; at its climax, they could no longer keep in march tempo, but broke into dancing; great throngs of them went exulting into the future, endless companies of young men and maidens, of that heroic and patriotic sort that Heinrich Jung and Hugo Behr were training.

The music didn't actually say that, and every listener was free to make up his own story. Lanny chose to include youths and maidens of all lands in that mighty dancing procession. He remembered how they had felt at Hellerau, in the happy days before the war had poisoned the minds of the peoples. Then internationalism had not been a *Schimpfwort*, and it had been possible to listen to Schubert's C-major symphony and imagine a triumphal procession shared by Jews and Russians, by young men and maidens from Asia and even from Africa.

Irma was much impressed by the welcome this music received. She decided that Kurt must be a great man, and that Beauty should be proud of having had such a lover, and of having saved him from a French firing-squad. She decided that it was a distinguished thing to have a private orchestra, and asked her husband if it wouldn't be fun to have one at Bienvenu. They must be on the lookout for a young genius to promote.

Lanny knew that his wife was casting around in her mind for some sort of career, some way to spend her money that would win his approval as well as that of their friends. She had timidly broached the idea of becoming a *salonnière*, like Emily. He had felt compelled to point out that this was a difficult thing to do, for it was better to have no salon at all than to have a second-rate one, and the eminent persons who frequent such assemblages expect the hostess not merely to have read their books but to have understood them. It isn't enough to admire them extravagantly—indeed they rather look down on you unless you can find something wrong with their work.

Now Lanny had to mention that musical geniuses are apt to be erratic, and often it is safer to know them through their works. One cannot advertise for one as for a butler or a chef; and suppose they got drunk, or took up with the parlor-maid? Lanny said that a consecrated artist such as Kurt Meissner would be hard to find. Irma remarked: "I suppose they wouldn't be anywhere but in Germany, where everybody works so hard!"

V

Among the guests they had met at the Schloss was an uncle of their host, the Graf Oldenburg of Vienna. The Meissners had told them that this bald-headed old Silenus was in financial trouble; he always would be, it having been so planned by the statesmen at Paris, who had cut the Austro-Hungarian Empire into small fragments and left a city of nearly two million people with very little hinterland to support it. The Graf was a gentleman of the old school who had learned to dance to the waltzes of the elder Strauss and was still hearing them in his fancy. He invited Irma and Lanny to visit him, and mentioned tactfully that he had a number of fine paintings. Since it was on their way home, Lanny said: "Let's stop and have a look."

It was a grand marble palace on the Ringstrasse, and the reception of the American visitors was in good style, even though the staff of servants had been cut, owing to an outrageous law just passed by the city administration—a graduated tax according to the number of your servants, and twice as high for men as for women! But a Socialist government had to find some way to keep going. Here was a city with great manufacturing power and nowhere to export its goods. All the little states surrounding it had put up tariff barriers, and all efforts at a customs union came to naught. Such an agreement with Germany seemed the most obvious thing in the world, but everybody knew that France would take it as an act of war.

An ideal situation from the point of view of a young art expert with American dollars in the bank! The elderly aristocrat, his host, was being hounded by his creditors, and responded promptly when Lanny invited him to put a price on a small-sized Jan van Eyck representing the Queen of Heaven in the very gorgeous robes which she perhaps was now wearing, but had assuredly never seen during her sojourn on earth.

Among Irma's acquaintances on Long Island was the heiress of a food-packing industry; and since people will eat, even when they do nothing else, Brenda Spratt's dividends were still coming in. She had appeared fascinated by Lanny's accounts of old masters in Europe and his dealings in them; so now he sent her a cablegram informing her that she could obtain a unique art treasure in exchange for four hundred and eighty thousand cans of spaghetti with tomato sauce at the wholesale price of three dollars per case of forty-eight cans. Lanny didn't cable all that, of course—it was merely his way of teasing Irma about the Long Island plutocracy. Next day he had a reply informing him at what bank he could call for the money. A genuine triumph of the soul of man over the body, of the immortal part over the mortal; and incidentally it would provide Lanny Budd with pocket-money for the winter. He invited his wife to state whether her father had ever done a better day's business at the age of thirty-one.

The over-taxed swells of Vienna came running to meet the American heiress and to tell her brilliant young husband what old masters they had available. Irma might have danced till dawn every night, and Lanny might have made a respectable fortune, transferring culture to the land of his fathers. But what he preferred was meeting Socialist writers and party leaders and hearing their stories of suffering and struggle in this city which was like a head without a body. The workers were overwhelmingly Socialist, while the peasants of the country dis·icts were Catholic and reactionary. To add to the confusion, the Hitlerites were carrying on a tremendous drive, telling the country yokels and the city hooligans that all their troubles were due to Jewish profiteers.

The municipal government, in spite of near-bankruptcy, was going bravely ahead with a program of rehousing and other public services. This was the thing of which Lanny had been dreaming, the socialization of industry by peaceful and orderly methods, and he became excited about it and wished to spend his time traveling about looking at blocks of workers' homes and talking to the people who lived in them. Amiable and well-bred people, going to bed early to save light and fuel, and working hard at the task of making democracy a success. Their earnings were pitifully small, and when Lanny heard stories of infant mortality and child malnutrition and milk prices held up by profiteers, it rather spoiled his enjoyment of stately banquets in mansions with historic names. Irma said: "You won't let yourself have any fun, so we might as well go on home."

VI

It wasn't much better at Bienvenu, as the young wife was soon to learn. The world had become bound together with ties invisible but none the less powerful, so that when the price of corn and hogs dropped in Nebraska the price of flowers dropped on the Cap d'Antibes. Lanny explained the phenomenon: the men who speculated in corn and hogs in Chicago no longer gave their wives the money to buy imported perfumes, so the leading industry of the Cap went broke. Leese, who ran Bienvenu, was besieged by nieces and nephews and cousins begging to be taken onto the Budd staff. There was a swarm of them already, twice as many as would have been employed for the same tasks on Long Island; but in the Midi they had learned how to divide the work, and nobody ever died from overexertion. Now there were new ones added, and it was a delicate problem, because it was Irma's money and she was entitled to have a say. What she said was that servants oughtn't to be permitted to bother their employers with the hard-luck stories of their relatives. Which meant that Irma still had a lot to learn about life in France!

The tourists didn't come, and the "season" was slow—so slow that it began to stop before it got started. The hotelkeepers were frightened, the merchants of luxury goods were threatened with ruin, and of course the poor paid for it. Lanny knew, because he went on helping with that Socialist Sunday school, where he heard stories which spoiled his appetite and his enjoyment of music, and troubled his wife because she knew what was in his thoughts—that she oughtn't to spend money on clothes and parties while so many children weren't getting enough to eat.

But what could you do about it? You had to pay your servants, or at any rate feed them, and it was demoralizing if you didn't give them work to do. Moreover, how could you keep up the prices of foods except by buying some? Irma's father and uncles had fixed it firmly in her mind that the way to make prosperity was to spend; but Lanny seemed to have the idea that you ought to buy cheap foods and give them to the poor. Wouldn't that demoralize the poor and make parasites of them? Irma thought she saw it happening to a bunch of "comrades" on the Riviera who practically lived on the Budd bounty, and rarely said "Thank you." And besides, what was to become of the people who raised the more expensive foods? Were they going to have to eat them?

Life is a compromise. On Sunday evening Lanny would go down into the Old Town of Cannes and explain the wastes of the competitive system to a group of thirty or forty proletarians: French and Provençal, Ligurian and Corsican, Catalan and even one Algerian. On Monday evening he would take his wife and mother to Sept Chênes and play accompaniments for a singer from the Paris opera at one of Emily's soirées. On Tuesday he would spend the day helping to get ready for a dinner-dance at Bienvenu, with a colored jazz band, Venetian lanterns with electric lights all over the lawns, and the most fashionable and titled people coming to do honor to the daughter of J. Paramount Barnes. Yes, there were still some who had money and would not fail in their economic duty! People who had seen the storm coming and put their fortune into bonds; people who owned strategic industries, such as the putting up of canned spaghetti for the use of millions who lived in tiny apartments in cities and had never learned how to make tomato sauce!

VII

Robbie Budd came visiting that winter. He had some kind of queer deal on; he was meeting with a former German U-boat commander who had entered the service of a Chinese mandarin, and this latter had been ousted and now wanted Budd machine guns so as to get back. He had got the support of some bankers in French Indo-China, but they didn't want to buy French munitions, for fear of publicity—a shady affair all round, but Robbie explained with a grin that one had to pick up money where one could these days. No chance to sell any of the products of peace in Europe now!

He told the same stories of hard times which his son had heard in Berlin and Vienna. There were breadlines in all the American cities, and on street corners one saw men, and some women, stamping their feet and holding out apples in their half-frozen hands. The price of apples having slumped, this was a way to get rid of them; a nickel apiece, Mister, and won't you help a poor guy get a cup of coffee? There was no way to count the unemployed, but everybody agreed that the number was increasing and the situation was terrible. Robbie thanked God for the Great Engineer whom he had helped to elect President; that harassed man was standing firm as a rock, insisting that Congress should balance the budget. If it was done, business would pick up in the end. It always had and always must.

Robbie had paid off one-half of the notes which he had given to Lanny, Beauty, and Marceline as security for the money turned over to him during the Wall Street panic. He had invested a hundred and fifty thousand dollars for the three of them in United States government bonds, and now tried to persuade them to shift it to stocks. They discussed the matter for an hour or so, sitting in front of a blazing fire of cypress wood in the drawing-room of the home. Beauty wavered, but Lanny said "No," and said it again and again.

"Look where steel is now!" exclaimed the father.

"But," argued the younger man, "you said exactly the same thing when you were here last time. You were sure it couldn't go lower."

He took his father on a tour of the civilized world. Where was there a nation that had money to buy American steel? Britain, France, Germany—all could make more than they could market, and the smaller nations were kept going only by the fears of their creditors. Here was Robbie, himself a steel man, reduced to selling to Chinese mandarins and South American revolutionists! Russia wanted steel desperately, but had to learn to make it for herself because she had no foreign exchange and nobody would trust her. "And you talk about steel 'coming back'!" exclaimed the son.

Robbie couldn't answer, but neither could he change. He knew that Lanny got his ideas out of his Pink and Red papers—which he kept in his own study, so as not to offend the eyesight of his relatives and friends. All these papers had a vested interest in calamity; but they couldn't be right, for if so, what would become of Robbie's world? He said: "Have it your way; but mark what I tell you, if only Hoover can hold out against inflationary tendencies, we'll be seeing such a boom as never was in the world before."

VIII

Lanny returned to the delights of child study. Truly a marvelous thing to watch a tiny organism unfolding, in such perfect order and according to schedule. They had a book which told them what to expect, and it was an event when Baby Frances spoke her first word two full weeks ahead of time, and a still greater thrill when she made her first effort to get up on her feet. All, both friends and servants, agreed that they had never seen a lovelier female infant, and Lanny, with his imaginative temperament, fell to speculating as to what might become of her. She would grow up to be a fine young woman like her mother. Would it be possible to teach her more than her mother knew? Probably not; she would have too much money. Or would she? Was there any chance of a benevolent revolution on the Viennese model, compelling her to do some useful work?

He had the same thought concerning his half-sister, who was ripening early in the warm sunshine of the Midi and in the pleasure-seeking of its fashionable society. Marceline was going to be a beauty like her mother; and how could she fail to know it? From earliest childhood she had been made familiar with beauty-creating and beauty-displaying paraphernalia: beauty lotions, beauty creams, beauty powders and paints, all put up in such beautiful receptacles that you couldn't bear to throw them away; clothing designed to reveal beauty, mirrors in which it was to be studied, conversation concerning the effects of it upon the male for whom it was created. Self-consciousness, sex-consciousness were the very breath of being of this young creature, paused on tiptoe with excitement, knowing by instinct that she was approaching the critical period of her life.

The prim Miss Addington was troubled about her charge, but Beauty, who had been that way herself, took it more easily. Lanny, too, had been precocious at that age, and so could understand her. He would try to teach her wisdom, to moderate her worldly desires. He would talk about her father, endeavoring to make him effective as an influence in her life. The pictures made him a living presence, but unfortunately Marceline did not know him as a poor painter on the Cap, working in a pair of stained corduroy trousers and an old blue cap. She knew him as a man of *renommée*, a source of income and a subject of speculation; his example confirmed her conviction that beauty and fame were one. To receive the attentions of other persons was what she enjoyed. Important persons, if possible—but anyone was better than no one!

IX

Amid this oddly assorted family Parsifal Dingle went on living his quietist life. He had the firm faith that it was impermissible to argue with people; the only thing was to set an example, and be certain that in due course it would have its effect. He took no part in any controversy, and never offered an opinion unless it was asked for. He sought nothing for himself, because, he said, everything was within him. He went here and there about the place, a friend of the flowers and the birds and the dogs. He read a great deal, and often closed his eyes; you wouldn't know whether he was praying or asleep. He was kind to everybody, and treated rich and poor the same; the servants revered him, having become certain that he was some kind of saint. His fame spread, and he would be asked to come and heal this person and that. The doctors resented this, and so did the clergy of the vicinity; it was unsanctioned, a grave violation of the proprieties.

At least an hour every day Mr. Dingle spent with Madame Zyszynski, and often Beauty was with him. The spirits possessed the minds of this pair, and the influence of the other world spread through the little community. Beauty began asking the spirits' advice, and taking it in all sorts of matters. They told her that these were dangerous times, and to be careful of her money. The spirit of Marcel told her this, and so did the spirit of the Reverend Blackless—so he referred to himself. Beauty had never taken his advice while he was living, but assumed he would be ultra-wise in the beyond. As economy was what Lanny wanted her to practice, he felt indebted to the shades. Being a talkative person, Beauty told her friends about her "guides," and Bienvenu acquired a queerer reputation than it had ever had, even when it was a haunt of painters, munitions buyers, and extra-marital couples.

Lanny would try his luck with a séance now and then. The character of his spirit life underwent a change; Marie receded into the background and her place was taken by Marcel and Great-Great-Uncle Eli Budd. These two friends of his boyhood told him much about themselves, and held high converse with each other in the limbo where they dwelt; just so had Lanny imagined them after their death, and it confirmed his idea that he was getting an ingenious reconstruction of the contents of his own mind. Now and then would appear some fact which he hadn't known before; but he argued that he might have heard it and forgotten it. He had had many intimate talks with both his former relatives, and surely couldn't remember every detail.

His theory was confirmed by the fact that he received a cordial letter from Mr. Ezra Hackabury, who was trying to keep out of bankruptcy in the town of Reubens, Indiana. Terrible times, he reported; but he hoped people would still have to have kitchen soap. The question was being answered in monthly sales reports, and meanwhile Mr. Hackabury pitched horseshoes behind the barn, as in the old days, and wondered if Lanny had kept up his skill in this art. When Lanny wrote what the spirits had said, the soapman replied that it was with him as it had been with Mark Twain: the report of his death was exaggerated. In the course of a year and a half of intercourse with Tecumseh, Lanny had recorded several cases of the chieftain's failure to distinguish between the living and the dead, and Lanny drew from this fact the conclusion which satisfied his own mind—at the same time overlooking a number of other facts which didn't. In this behavior he had the example of many leading men of science.

X

So passed a pleasant period in the well-cushioned limousine in which Lanny Budd was rolling through life. He was unhappy about the sufferings of the world, but not so unhappy that he couldn't eat the excellent meals which the servants of both the villa and the Cottage prepared; not so unhappy that he couldn't read the manuscripts which Rick sent him, and the first draft of a *Silesian Suite* which Kurt submitted. He taught his Pink class, and argued with the young Reds who came to bait him—and at the same time to borrow money when they got into trouble. He spent his own funds, and some of Irma's, playing patron to the social discontent of the Midi; but Irma didn't mind especially, because she had the money, and had the instinctive feeling that the more the family was dependent upon her, the more agreeable they would make themselves. Who eats my bread, he sings my song!

A surprising incident. One afternoon Lanny was in his studio, playing that very grand piano which he had bought for Kurt, but which was beginning to show the effects of a decade of sea air. A sunshiny afternoon of spring; Lanny had the doors and windows open, and was filling the surrounding atmosphere with the strains of Rubinstein's *Waltz Caprice*. The telephone rang, for they now had phones in all the buildings on the estate; to Irma it had seemed ridiculous to have to send a servant every time she wished to invite

Beauty over to the Cottage for lunch, or when she wanted to tell Lanny to come swimming. Now a servant was calling from the villa, reporting that there was an elderly gentleman who said his name was "Monsieur Jean." Lanny wasn't usually slow, but this time he had to have the name repeated. Suddenly he remembered the town of Dieppe.

The Knight Commander of the Bath and Grand Officer of the Legion of Honor had held off for the better part of a year, until Lanny had given up the idea of hearing from him. It seemed hard to believe, for Zaharoff was bound to know that he had got something real at that séance—and how could he bear not to get more? At last he had decided to give way, and characteristically he wasn't taking half-measures; he had come in person, the first time he had ever thus honored the Budd family. He honored very few persons in that manner.

"Monsieur Jean" was alone. He had seated himself on the edge of a straight chair, as if he wasn't sure that he would be welcomed; he had kept his walking-stick, and was leaning on it with both hands folded over it. The cold blue eyes met Lanny's. Was Lanny mistaken in thinking that there was an anxious look on the face of the old spider, the old wolf, the old devil? Anyhow, the younger man greeted his caller with cordiality, and the latter said quickly: "For a long time I have known that I owed you an apology."

"Don't bother about it, Monsieur Jean," said the younger man. He used that name because some servant might overhear. "I realized that you were upset. Several times in these séances I have been told things which didn't happen to be true, and which would have been embarrassing if there had been others present." Nothing could have been more tactful.

"I should have written to you," continued the other. "But I put it off, thinking you might come to see me."

"I had no way of knowing what your wishes would be." To himself Lanny added: "You were trying other mediums, to see if you could get what you want!"

"I decided that the proper thing to do was to make my apologies in person. I will make them to the medium, if she is still with you."

"She is." Lanny would wait, and make the old man ask for what he wanted.

"Do you suppose it would be possible for me to see her again?"

"You mean, to try another séance?"

"I would esteem it a great favor."

"I can't answer for her, Monsieur Jean. As I explained at the time, it causes her distress if anything goes wrong. She was very much upset."

"I realize that. I am thoroughly prepared now, and can give you my word that nothing of the sort will happen again. Whatever comes, I will 'take it,' as you Americans say."

"Perhaps," suggested Lanny, "you might prefer to sit with her alone?"

"If she will trust me, that would be better. You may tell her that I will pay her generously."

"I would beg you not to mention that. We have a financial arrangement with her, and her time is ours."

"Surely it would be proper for me to pay a portion of the cost?"

"There is no need to raise the question. The amount is small—and you may not get the results you want."

"If I should get them, and if I might see her now and then, you will surely let me make some financial arrangement?"

"We can talk about that by and by. First, I will see if I can persuade her to give you another sitting."

"You have not told her about me?"

"I haven't told anybody. You remember I wrote you that that was my intention."

"You have been very kind, Lanny, and I shall never forget it."

XI

It wasn't an easy matter to persuade Madame Zyszynski. She was still angry with "that rude old gentleman." What he had done to her was unforgivable. But Lanny told her that the rude old gentleman had been extremely unhappy, and something had come from Tecumseh which had broken him down; it had taken him nearly a year to get over it. But now he was penitent, and had given his word, and Lanny felt sure he would keep it. Madame was used to trusting Lanny—she was a lonely old woman, and had adopted him as her son in her imagination. Now she said she would give Monsieur Jean another chance to behave, but first Lanny must explain to him the physical shock which he had caused her, that she had been ill and depressed for days, and so on. Tecumseh would doubtless be extremely angry, and would scold the sitter without the least regard to his dignity.

Lanny dutifully went back and delivered these messages; and the armament king of Europe solemnly agreed to humble his pride before the chieftain of the Iroquois. Lanny said: "I don't know what he really is, but he acts like a personage, and you have to treat him that way. You have given him offense, and you will have to pretend that you are petitioning for pardon." Lanny said it with a smile, but the Knight Commander and Grand Officer was serious; he replied that if it would get him a message from the source desired he would submit to torture from real Indians.

So Lanny took him down to his studio, and showed him some of Marcel's paintings on the walls—though he probably didn't have much mind for art just then. The medium came in, and said: "*Bon jour, monsieur*." Zaharoff answered: "*Bon jour, madame*," and they seated themselves in the two chairs which Lanny had moved into place for them. He waited until he saw the woman going into her trance successfully; then he went out, closing the studio door behind him.

Beauty and Irma had been in to Cannes for shopping. They came back; and of course it would no longer be possible to keep the secret from them. No need to, anyhow, for the matter would doubtless be settled this time; the duquesa would "come through," or Zaharoff would give up. Lanny took them into his mother's room and told them who had attended Madame's séance in Dieppe. Both the ladies were excited, for Zaharoff was the same kind of royalty as Irma, and sovereigns do not often meet their social equals. "Oh, do you think he'll stay for dinner?" inquired Beauty.

Anyhow, the ladies would dress; but not too much, for Monsieur

Jean wouldn't be dressed. Lanny explained the reason for the name. Then he walked up and down on the loggia in front of the villa, watching the sun set behind the dark mountains across the Golfe Juan. Many times he had watched it, as far back as his memory went. He had seen war come, and vessels burning and sinking in that blue expanse of water. He had watched the tangled fates of human beings woven on these grounds; love and hate, jealousy and greed, suffering and fear; he had seen people dancing, laughing and chatting, and more than once crying. Marcel had sat here with his burned-off face, meeting his friends in the protecting darkness. Here, too, Kurt had played his music, Rick had outlined his plays, and Robbie had negotiated big munitions· deals. Now Lanny walked, waiting to hear if the spirit of a noble Spanish lady was going to speak to her Greek husband through the personality of an American redskin, dead a couple of centuries and using the vocal cords of a Polish peasant woman who had been a servant in the home of a Warsaw merchant. One thing you could say about life, it provided you with variety!

XII

The old man came up from the studio alone, walking with his head thrust forward, as he always did, as if smelling his way. Lanny went to meet him, and he said, with unwonted intensity: "My boy, this is really a disturbing thing!"

"You got some results?"

"I got what certainly seemed results. Tell me, are you convinced of this woman's honesty?"

"We are all convinced of that."

"How long have you known her?"

"For some eighteen months."

"You think she is really in a trance when she pretends to be?"

"She would have to be a skilled actress if that were not true; we have watched her closely, and we don't think she is intelligent enough to fool us."

"You are sure she doesn't know who I am?"

"I can't imagine how she could have found out. No one but my father knew about the matter, and you know that my father is not a loose talker. When you wrote me the appointment, I took the precaution to tear up your letter and throw it into the sea."

"Lanny, it was just as if my wife was sitting in the next room, sending me messages. You can understand how important this is to me."

"It is important to all of us, for we all get communications like that."

"She reminded me of things from my childhood, and from hers; things we both knew but which nobody else knows—at least, not that I can think of."

They went inside, for it grows chilly on the Riviera the moment the sun is down. The old man wanted to know all that Lanny thought about these phenomena, the most mysterious which confront the modern thinker. When Lanny told him of the books of Geley and Osty, Zaharoff took out his notebook and jotted down the names; also the two great volumes of Pierre Janet—he promised to study them all. His education had been neglected, but now he would try to find out about the subconscious mind and its powers, so different from those of a munitions king! He had missed a great deal, and was only beginning to be aware of it when life was ebbing.

The ladies came in: two most elegant ladies, about whom he had heard; concerning Irma nothing but good. He was extraordinarily courteous; he hoped for a favor from them, and asked it as a humble petitioner: would they graciously permit Madame Zyszynski to visit him in Monte Carlo if he would send his car for her and send her back? Beauty said: "Why, certainly. That is, of course, if Madame is willing, and I am sure she will be."

"We got along all right this time," said Zaharoff. And Lanny, not untrained in observation, perceived that the old spider, likewise not untrained, was watching for some hint of the fact that Beauty knew of the earlier fiasco. Since Beauty didn't know what had happened on that occasion, it was easy for her to appear innocent. Not that it would have been difficult, anyhow!

Lanny went down to the studio for the purpose of consulting Madame and found her pleased with the old gentleman's new humility. She said she would be willing to visit his hotel, and Lanny went back and made a date. Zaharoff excused himself from dinner, saying that he ate very little and that his mind was full of the things he had heard.

He went out to his car and was driven away. Beauty said to Irma: "That poor old man! He has so much money, yet he can't get the one thing in the world he wants!" After saying it, the mother-in-law wondered if it mightn't sound a wee bit tactless!

9

Land Where My Fathers Died

I

IRMA had promised her mother to visit Long Island that summer and exhibit the new heiress of the Barnes and Vandringham clans. Johannes Robin had said that they would make it another yachting-trip, but now he wrote sorrowfully that it was impossible for him to leave Berlin; financial conditions were becoming desperate, and he would have to be on hand every day and perhaps every hour. With a princely gesture he offered the Budd family the yacht with all expenses paid, but perhaps he knew that they would not accept such a favor.

Irma said: "We might rent it from him." They talked about the idea for a while, but they knew the young Robins wouldn't come, they would feel it their duty to stick by their mother and father. Freddi would prefer to carry on the school, for workers don't have vacations—when they stop work, their pay stops, and this was happening to great numbers of them. Hansi and Bess were helping by playing at low-priced concerts in large halls for the people. A violinist doesn't promote his reputation by that kind of thing, but he helps his conscience.

There were plenty of persons who would have been pleased to be offered a free yachting-trip, but Irma admitted that it might be a bore to be with a small group for so long a time; better to be foot-loose, and free to change friends as well as places. The efficient Bureau International de Voyage, which now consisted of Mr. and Mrs. Jerry Pendleton and nobody else, was happy to supply them with information concerning steamers from Marseille to New York. There were sumptuous Mediterranean cruises on which one could book for the return trip; there were steamers making so-called de luxe tours around the world, coming by way of the Suez Canal and Gibraltar to New York. De luxe was what Irma Barnes desired, and it was pleasant to learn that the choicest suites of these floating hotels were vacant on account of hard times. Irma chose the best for herself and Lanny, and a near-by one for Miss Severne, the nurse-maid, and the baby; also a second-class passage for her maid, and for the demoted Feathers, whose duty it now was to run all the errands and accept all humiliations.

Early in May the party embarked, and Lanny found himself returned suddenly into that café society from which he had fled a year and a half ago. Ten to twelve million dollars had been expended to provide a sea-going replica of the Great White Way, and by expertly contrived advertising exactly the right sort of crowd had been lured on board. This floating hotel included a swimming-pool deep enough for high diving, a game room, a gymnasium with instructors, a squash court, a playground for children, an arcade with beauty parlors and luxury shops, several bars and barber-shops used mainly by ladies, a jazz band and a small orchestra, a motion-picture theater, and a grill room where you could order anything you wanted if you became hungry in between the elaborate regular meals. Here were people one had met at first nights on Broadway, in the swanky night clubs and the Park Avenue penthouses. A sprinkling of sight-seers and curiosity-seekers from the "sticks," which meant any place west of Seventh Avenue; people who had "made their pile" in hogs or copper and put it into bonds, and wished to get away from the troubles of their world. They had expected the depression to be over by the time they got back, but they had miscalculated.

Before the vessel docked at Marseille word had got about that Irma Barnes and her husband were coming on board; so there was a crowd lined up by the rail to spot them and watch them. Once upon a time it had been rude to stare, but that time was gone with the daisies. Several old friends rushed up to greet Irma, and to be introduced to the lucky young prince consort; so right away the pair were plunged into the midst of events: supper parties, bridge parties, dancing, sports of one sort or another. So much gossip to hear and to impart, so many new people to meet and play with! Everybody's cabin was loaded with souvenirs; everybody had stories of places visited. But on the whole it had been rather a bore, you know; they would be glad to get back home, where you could play golf and ride and motor, and get rid of the people who bored you.

II

Living under the feudal system, Irma had found herself impressed by the idea of being exclusive; but here she was back in the easy-going world which was much less trouble and much more fun. All sorts of people wanted to know her, and how was she to find out who they were or what they wanted? It might be an expert thief, trying to find out what jewels she wore and where she kept them; it might be a blackmailer on the watch for something he could put to use; there was a good chance of its being a cardsharp, for swarms of them preyed upon the passengers of ocean liners. Irma and a New York acquaintance played against a couple of ladies with manners and costumes beyond criticism; quite probably the pair had some means of signaling other than the bids which were a part of the game and which everybody studied and argued about. They proposed a dollar a point for stakes, and Irma didn't mind; she didn't mind especially when she found that her side was a couple of thousand dollars in the hole at the end of an afternoon. Her partner broke down and wept, saying she didn't have the money, so Irma paid for both, and didn't like it when Lanny insisted that all three women were probably in cahoots.

Also there was the question of liquor. The young people were drinking all the time, and how they managed to carry it was a problem. Lanny said: "Why not choose some friends who know something to talk about?" But those were older persons, and Irma could only listen. Presently along would come some of her own set and carry her off to a gaily decorated bar; or they would order drinks while they were playing shuffleboard on deck. Lanny could no longer say: "You have the health of our baby to think of." He was put in the unpleasant position of the sober man at a feast; he was a wet blanket, a sorehead, a grouch. Irma didn't say these things, but others said them behind her back, and looked them; you had either to play the game or antagonize people. Lanny decided that he would be glad when his wife was under the sheltering wing of Fanny Barnes, who had the right to scold her daughter and exercised it.

Among the conveniences on board this movable city was a broker's office where you could get quotations and gamble in your favorite stocks; also a daily newspaper which reported what was happening in Wall Street and the rest of the world. Shortly before the vessel reached New York it was learned that the troubles in Vienna had come to a climax; there was a failure of the Creditanstalt, biggest bank in the city. Next day the panic was spreading to Germany. Lanny heard people say: "All right. It's time they had some troubles." But others understood that if Germany couldn't pay reparations, Britain and France would soon be unable to pay their debts to the United States. These financial difficulties traveled like waves of sound; they met some obstruction and came rolling back. The world had become a vast sounding-board, filled with clashing echoes hurled this way and that. Impossible to guess what was coming next!

III

The Statue of Liberty stood, erect and dignified, holding her torch immovable; in bright sunlight she appeared quite sober. Lanny wondered: was she "on the wagon," or did she, like so many of his acquaintances in café society, never get drunk until night? It was still the time of Prohibition, and you couldn't buy anything on the ship after she had passed the three-mile limit; but everybody knew that as soon as you stepped ashore you could get whatever you wanted.

Fanny Barnes, accompanied by her brother Horace, was waiting on the pier for the first sight of the most precious of all babies. When gangplanks were lowered and the family procession came down, she took the soft warm bundle in her arms, and Lanny saw the first tears he had ever seen in what he had thought were hard, worldly eyes. She refused to put the bundle down, but carried it off to the waiting car and sat there, breaking every rule which Miss Severne had laid down for the hygienic and psychological protection of infants. Lanny saw the Englishwoman watching with disapproval; he feared that a first-class row was pending, for the head nurse had explained many times that she was a professional person and considered that her services were superfluous if her advice was disregarded.

They left Feathers to attend to the customs formalities and to bring Irma's maid and the nursemaid and the bags in another car. The family drove away in state, with Miss Severne in front with the chauffeur, so that she wouldn't be so aware of a grandmother coddling and cuddling a fourteen-month-old child, poking a finger at her and talking nonsense. That went on all the way across Fourteenth Street, and through the slums of New York's East Side, over a great bridge, and on the new speedway. Lanny recognized what a serious action he had committed in keeping the precious creature in Europe—and what a fight he was going to have to get her back there!

Plenty of news to talk about: family affairs, business affairs, and all their friends who had got married, or died, or been born. Presently Uncle Horace Vandringham was telling Lanny about stocks. They were down again—very bad news from Germany, and rumors that the trouble might spread to Britain. The one-time market manipulator gave it as his opinion that prices had just about reached bottom; the very same words that Robbie Budd had said: "Look where steel is now!" Uncle Horace had written Irma, begging her to put up a little money, so that he might get back into the game; he would go fifty-fifty with her—it was a crime to waste the expert knowledge which he had spent a lifetime in acquiring. Irma had said no, and had told her husband that she would continue to say it and not let herself be bothered with importunities.

IV

Life at Shore Acres was taken up where it had been left off. The question of Baby Frances was settled quickly, for the head nurse came to Irma, who had employed her; she didn't say that Irma had been raised wrong, or that grandmothers were *passées*, but simply that modern science had made new discoveries and that she had been trained to put them into practice. Irma couldn't dream of losing that most conscientious of persons, so she laid down the law to her mother, who took it with surprising meekness. Likewise, Uncle Horace made only the feeblest of tentatives in the direction of Wall Street. Lanny perceived that they had had family consultations; the haughty Fanny was going to be the ideal mother-in-law, her brother was going to make himself agreeable at all costs, and everybody in the house was to do the same—in the hope that a prince consort might be persuaded to settle down in his palace and enjoy that state of life to which it had pleased God to call him.

All that Lanny and his royal spouse had to do was to be happy, and they had the most expensive toys in the world to play with. The estate had been created for that purpose, and thousands of skilled workers had applied their labor and hundreds of technicians had applied their brains to its perfection. If the young couple wanted to ride there were horses, if they wanted to drive there were cars, if they wanted to go out on the water there were sailboats and launches. There were two swimming-pools, one indoors and one out, besides the whole Atlantic Ocean. There were servants to wait upon them and clean up after them; there were pensioners and courtiers to flatter and entertain them. The world had been so contrived that it was extremely difficult for the pair to do any sort of useful thing.

Playmates came in swarms: boys and girls of Irma's set who were "lousy with money"—their own phrase. Irma had romped and danced with them from childhood, and now they were in their twenties, but lived and felt and thought as if still in their teens. The depression had hit many of them, and a few had had to drop out, but most were still keeping up the pace. They drove fast cars, and thought nothing of dining in one place and dancing fifty miles away; they would come racing home at dawn—one of them would be assigned to drive and would make it a point of honor not to get drunk. The boys had been to college and the girls to finishing-schools, where they had acquired fashionable manners, but no ideas that troubled them. Their conversation was that of a secret society: they had their own slang and private jokes, so that if you didn't "belong," you had to ask what they were talking about.

It was evident to all that Irma had picked up an odd fish, but they were willing enough to adopt him; all he had to do was to take them as they were, do what they did, and not try to force any ideas upon them. He found it interesting for a while; the country was at its springtime best, the estates of Long Island were elaborate and some of them elegant, and anybody who is young and healthy enjoys tennis and swimming and eating good food. But Lanny would pick up the newspaper and read about troubles all over the world; he would go into the swarming city where millions had no chance to play and not even enough to eat; he would look at the apple-sellers, and the breadlines of haggard, fear-driven men—many with clothes still retaining traces of decency. Millions wandering over the land seeking in vain for work; families being driven from their farms because they couldn't pay the taxes. Lanny wasn't content to read the regular newspapers, but had to seek out the Pink and Red ones, and then tell his wealthy friends what he had found there. Not many would believe him, and not one had any idea what to do about it.

Nobody seemed to have such ideas. The ruling classes of the various nations watched the breakdown of their economy like spectators in the neighborhood of a volcano, seeing fiery lava pour out of the crater and dense clouds of ashes roll down the slopes, engulfing vineyards and fields and cottages. So it had been when the younger Pliny had stood near Mt. Vesuvius some nineteen hundred years back, and had written to the historian Tacitus about his experience:

"I looked behind me; gross darkness pressed upon our rear, and came rolling over the land after us like a torrent. We had scarce sat down, when darkness overspread us, not like that of a moonless or cloudy night, but of a room when it is shut up, and the lamp put out. You could hear the shrieks of women, the crying of children, and the shouts of men; some were seeking their children, others their parents, others their wives or husbands, and only distinguishing them by their voices; one lamenting his own fate, another that of his family; some praying to die, from the very fear of dying; many lifting their hands to the gods; but the great part imagining that there were no gods left anywhere, and that the last and eternal night was come upon the world."

V

By way of the automobile ferry from Long Island to New London, Connecticut, Lanny drove his wife to his father's home, and they spent a week with the family. The town of Newcastle had been hard hit by the depression: the arms plant was shut down entirely; the hardware and elevator and other plants were running only three days a week. The workers were living on their savings if they had any; they were mortgaging their homes, and losing their cars and radio sets because they couldn't meet installment payments. There were a couple of thousand families entirely destitute, and most of them were Budd workers, so it was a strain upon the consciences and pocketbooks of all members of the ruling family. Esther was working harder than even during the World War; she was chairman of the finance committee of the town's soup kitchens and children's aid, and went about among the women's clubs and churches telling harrowing stories and making the women weep, so that private charity might not break down entirely.

That was a crucial issue, as her husband told her. If America was forced to adopt the British system of the dole, it would be the end of individual initiative and private enterprise. Robbie seemed to his son like the anchor-man of a tug-of-war team, his heels dug into the ground, his teeth set, the veins standing out purple in his forehead with the effort he was making to keep his country from moving the wrong way. Robbie had been down to Washington to see President Hoover, his hero and the captain of his team. The Great Engineer was literally besieged; all the forces of disorder and destruction—so he considered them and so did Robbie—were trying to pry him from his stand that the budget must be balanced, the value of the dollar maintained, and business allowed to "come back" in due and regular course.

The cities and the counties, nearing the end of their resources, were clamoring for Federal aid; the returned soldiers had organized to demand a bonus for the services they had rendered overseas while the business men at home were filling their pocketbooks. So the agitators charged, frothing at the mouth, and they had forced their bill through Congress over the President's veto. Poor Herbert went on making speeches about the American system of "rugged individualism"; it was heartening to him to have a solid business man, one who had been an oil man like himself, come in and tell him that he was saving civilization.

Esther, of course, had to believe her husband; she told all the club ladies and church ladies that they were saving civilization, and they put in their dimes or their dollars, and gathered together and knitted sweaters or cooked and served hot soup. But every slump in Wall Street threw more men out of work in Newcastle, and the ladies were at their wit's end. When Irma wrote a check for five thousand dollars for the children, tears of gratitude ran down the cheeks of Lanny's stepmother. He had given her great sorrow in years past, but now his credit rating was triple-A. Even his Pinkness had been made respectable by the crimson hues of Bess, concerning whom the mother inquired with deepest anxiety.

The Newcastle Country Club was giving a costume dance for charity. You paid twenty-five dollars for a ticket, and if you weren't there you were nobody. Irma and Lanny had to drive to a near-by city, since everybody who knew how to sew in Newcastle was already at work on costumes. But it was all right, for that city likewise had its smokeless factory chimneys. Several women worked day and night, and as a result the visiting pair appeared as a very grand Beatrice and Benedick in red-and-purple velvet with gold linings. A delightful occasion, and when it was over, Irma and Lanny presented the costumes to the country club's dramatics committee, for Irma said that if you folded them and carried them in the car they'd be full of creases and not fit to use again.

VI

Not much fun visiting a factory town in times like these. But it was the Budd town, and in prosperous days everybody had been cordial to the young couple and their friends, even the Jewish ones. So now it was necessary to stay, and give sympathy and a little help, and have receptions held in their honor, and shake hands and chat with innumerable Budds—not even Lanny could remember them all, and had to "bone up" as if it were for a college examination. Also they played golf and tennis at the country club, and swam and went sailing in delightful June weather. The countryside put on a show of wild roses, and all nature told them not to worry too much, that life was going on.

Also they had to pay a visit to the president of Budd Gunmakers. The old man had told Lanny that he would probably never see him again; but here he was, still holding on, still running the company by telephone. His hands shook so that it was painful to watch; his cheeks hung in flaps so that he seemed to have twice as much yellow skin as was needed to cover his shrinking form; but he was the same grim Puritan, and still questioned Lanny to make sure he had not forgotten his Bible texts. He had heard about Baby Frances, of course, and said he had carried out his promise to put her in his will, though he didn't know if he really had any property any more, or if Budd stocks would be worth the paper. He pinned the pair down on whether they were going to have another try for a son, and Irma told him they were leaving it to the Lord; this wasn't so, but Lanny didn't contradict her, and afterward she said it would have been a shame to worry that old man so close to the grave.

Everybody knew that he couldn't hold on much longer, and there was an underground war going on for control of the company; a painful struggle between Robbie and his oldest brother Lawford, that silent, morose man who was in charge of production, and whom Lanny and Irma saw only when they attended the First Congregational Church. The old grandfather had not said whom he wished to have succeed him, and of course nobody liked to ask him. For some time Lawford had been seeking out the directors and presenting his side of the case, which involved telling them of the blunders which Robbie had committed—or what Lawford considered blunders. Naturally, this made it necessary for Robbie to defend himself, and it was an ugly situation. Robbie thought he had the whip hand so far. His father had renewed his contract as European sales representative for another five years, so if Lawford got the presidency they'd have to pay a pretty price to buy Robbie out.

VII

The business situation in Germany went from bad to worse. Robbie received a letter from Johannes, saying that it looked like the end of everything. Foreign loans were no more, and Germany couldn't go on without them. Johannes was taking more money out of the country, and asking Robbie's help in investing it. Robbie told his son in strict confidence—not even Irma was allowed to know —that President Hoover had prepared a declaration of a moratorium on international debts; he was still hesitating about this grave step; would it help or would it cause more alarm? The French, who had not been consulted, would probably be furious.

The declaration was issued soon after the young couple had returned to Shore Acres, and the French were furious, but the Germans were not much helped. In the middle of July the great Danat Bank failed in Berlin, and there was terror such as Lanny had witnessed in New York. Chancellor Brüning went to Paris to beg for help, and Premier Laval refused it; France was now the strongest

European power financially, and was sitting on her heap of gold, lending it only for the arming of Poland and her other eastern allies —which were blackmailing her without mercy. Britain had made the mistake of trying to buttress German finances, and now her own were shaky as a result. "We're not that sort of fools," wrote young Denis de Bruyne to Lanny, who replied: "If you let the German Republic fall and you get Hitler, will that help you?" Young Denis did not reply.

Such were the problems faced by the statesmen while two darlings of fortune were having fun all over the northeastern states. Invitations would come, and they would order their bags packed, step into their car in the morning, drive several hours or perhaps all day, and step out onto an estate in Bar Harbor or Newport, the Berkshires or the Ramapo Hills, the Adirondacks or the Thousand Islands. Wherever it was, there would be a palace—even though it was called a "cottage" or a "camp." The way you knew a "camp" was that it was built of "slabs," and you wore sport clothes and didn't dress for dinner; but the meal would be just as elaborate, for nobody stayed anywhere without sending a staff of servants ahead and having all modern conveniences, including a dependable bootlegger. Radios and phonographs provided music for dancing, and if you didn't have the right number for games, you called people on the long-distance telephone and they motored a hundred miles or more, and when they arrived they bragged about their speed. Once more Lanny thought of the English poet Clough, and his song attributed to the devil in one of his many incarnations: "How pleasant it is to have money, heigh ho! How pleasant it is to have money!"

These young people still had it, though the streams were drying up. The worst of the embarrassments of a depression, as it presented itself to the daughter of J. Paramount Barnes, was that so many of her friends kept getting into trouble and telling her about it. A truly excruciating situation: in the midst of a bridge game at Tuxedo Park the hostess received a telephone call from her broker in New York, and came in white-faced, saying that unless she could raise fifty thousand dollars in cash by next morning she was "sunk." Not everybody had that much money in the bank, and especially not in times when rumors were spreading about this bank and that. Irma saw the eyes of the hostess fixed upon her, and was most uncomfortable, because she couldn't remedy the depression all by herself and had to draw the line somewhere.

Yes, it wasn't all fun having so much money. You didn't want to shut yourself up in yourself and become hard-hearted and indifferent to others' suffering; but you found yourself surrounded by people who wanted what you had and didn't always deserve it, people who had never learned to do anything useful and who found themselves helpless as children in a crisis. Of course they ought to go to work, but what could they do? All the jobs appeared to be filled by persons who knew how to do them; right now there were said to be six, or eight, or ten million people looking for jobs and not finding any. Moreover, Lanny and Irma didn't seem to be exactly the right persons to be giving that sort of advice!

VIII

The first of July was a time for dividends, and many of the biggest and most important corporations "passed" them. This gave a shock to Wall Street, and to those who lived by it; Irma's income was cut still more, and the shrinkage seemed likely to continue. The news from abroad was as bad as possible. Rick, who knew what was going on behind the scenes, wrote it to his friend. The German Chancellor was in London, begging for funds, but nobody dared help him any further; France was obdurate, because the Germans had committed the crime of attempting to set up a customs union with Austria. But how could either of these countries survive if they couldn't trade?

All Lanny's life it had been his habit to sit and listen to older people talking about the state of the world. Now he knew more about it than most of the people he met, even the older ones. While Irma played bridge, or table tennis with her young friends who had acquired amazing skill at that fast game, Lanny would be telling the president of one of the great Wall Street banks just why he had blundered in advising his clients to purchase the bonds of Fascist

Italy, or trying to convince one of the richest old ladies of America
that she wasn't really helping to fight Bolshevism when she gave
money for the activities of the Nazis in the United States. Such a
charming, cultivated young German had been introduced to her,
and had explained this holy crusade to preserve Western civilization
from the menace of Asiatic barbarism!

It was a highly complicated world for a devout Episcopalian and
member of the D.A.R. to be groping about in. A great banking
fortune gave her enormous power, and she desired earnestly to use
it wisely. Lanny told her the various radical planks of the Nazi program, and the old lady was struck with dismay. He told her how
Hitler had been dropping these planks one by one, and she took
heart again. But he assured her that Hitler didn't mean the dropping
any more than he had meant the planks; what he wanted was to get
power, and then he would do whatever was necessary to keep it and
increase it. Lanny found it impossible to make this attitude real to
gentle, well-bred, conscientious American ladies; it was just too
awful. When you persisted in talking about it, you only succeeded
in persuading them that there must be something wrong with your
cynical self.

IX

Lanny just couldn't live with these overstuffed classes all the time;
he became homesick for his Reds and Pinks, and went into the hot,
teeming city and paid another visit to the Rand School of Social
Science. He told them what he had been doing for workers' education on the Riviera, and made a contribution to their expenses. The
word spread quickly that here was the bearer of a Fortunatus purse,
and everybody who had a cause—there appeared to be hundreds of
them—began writing him letters or sending him mimeographed or
printed appeals for funds. The world was so full of troubles, and
there were so few who cared!

Also he sent in a subscription to the *New Leader*, and got a weekly
dose of the horrors of the capitalist system, which had developed
such marvelous powers of production and was unable to use them;

which left millions to starve while a few parasites fattened themselves in luxury. This paper would lie on the table in his room, and Irma would see the prominent headlines and say: "Oh, dear! Are you still reading that stuff?" It irritated her to be referred to as a parasite and to have Lanny say: "But that's what we are," and go on to prove it.

Several of the workers' groups and labor unions had summer camps where their members could spend a vacation. Lanny went to have a look at one of them, having the idea that he ought to know the workers at first hand. But he made the mistake of taking his wife along, which spoiled matters. Irma did her best, but she didn't know how to unbend. The place was crowded, and mostly they were Jews; their dress was informal and their manners hearty; they were having a good time in their own way, and didn't mind if it was different from her way; they didn't look up to royalty, and didn't enjoy being looked at as a zoo. In short, as an effort to bridge the social chasm the visit was a flop.

On the same South Shore of Long Island with the Barnes estate is the resort known as Coney Island. Lanny had heard about it but had never seen it, and Irma had only vague memories from a time in childhood when her father had taken her. On a hot Sunday afternoon the perverse idea occurred to one of their smart crowd: "Let's go and see Coney!" It really was a spectacle, they insisted; the world's premier slumming-tour—unless you went to Shanghai or Bombay on one of those de luxe cruises.

Two motor-carloads of them drove to the resort, which is a long spit of land. It was hard to find a place to park, and they had to walk a couple of miles; but they were young, and were out for fun. There must have been a million people at the resort, and most of them crowded onto the wide stretch of beach; it was barely possible to move about for the swarms of people lying or sitting in the sand, sweltering in the blazing sunshine. If you wanted to know the elementary facts about the human animal, here was the place to see exactly how fat they were, or how skinny, how hairy, how bowlegged, how stoop-shouldered, how generally different from the standards established by Praxiteles. You could discover also how they stank, what raucous noises they made, what a variety of ill-odored foods they ate, and how utterly graceless and superfluous they were.

To the fastidious Lanny Budd the worst thing of all was their emptiness of mind. They had come for a holiday, and wanted to be entertained, and there was a seemingly endless avenue of devices contrived for the purpose. For prices from a dime up you could be lifted on huge revolving wheels, or whirled around sitting on brightly painted giraffes and zebras; you could ride in tiny cars which bumped into one another, you could walk in dark tunnels which were a perpetual earthquake, or in bright ones where sudden breezes whipped up the women's skirts and made them scream; you could be frightened by ghosts and monsters—in short, you could have a thousand fantastic things done to you, all expressive of the fact that you were an animal and not a being with a mind; you could be humiliated and made ridiculous, but rarely indeed on Coney Island could you be uplifted or inspired or taught any use-ful thing. Lanny took this nightmare place as an embodiment of all the degradations which capitalism inflicted upon the swarming mil-lions of its victims. Anything to keep them from thinking.

Thus a young Pink; and he got himself into a red-hot argument with a carload of his young companions, who had drawn their own conclusions from this immersion in carnality. Irma, who monopo-lized a half-mile of ocean front, was disgusted that anyone should be content to squat upon ten or a dozen square feet of it. Her child-hood playmate, Babs Lorimer, whose father had once had a "cor-ner" in wheat, drew political conclusions from the spectacle and wondered how anybody could conceive of the masses' having any-thing to say about the running of government. "Noodles" Win-throp—his name was Newton—whose widowed mother collected a small fraction of a cent from everyone who rode to Coney Island on a street railway, looked at the problem biologically, and said he couldn't imagine how such hordes of ugly creatures had survived, or why they desired to. Yet look at the babies they had!

X

With the members of Irma's immediate family Lanny found that he was getting along surprisingly well. The domineering Fanny Barnes was set in her opinions, but for the most part these had to do with questions of manners and taste and family position; she didn't give much thought to politics and economics. Pride was her leading motive; she lived in the faith that her Protestant Episcopal God had assigned to her family a specially precious strain of blood. She had the firm conviction that bearers of this blood couldn't do anything seriously wrong, and she found ways to persuade herself that they hadn't. She had made up her mind to make the best of this son-in-law whom fate had assigned to her, and presently she was finding excuses for him. Did someone call him a Socialist? Well, he had been reared in Europe, where such ideas didn't mean what they did in America. Hadn't some distinguished Englishman —Fanny couldn't recall who it was—declared: "We are all Socialists now"?

For Lanny as a prince consort there was really quite a lot to be said. His manners were distinguished and his conversation even more so. He didn't get drunk, and he had to be urged to spend his wife's money. The uncertainty about his mother's marriage ceremony hadn't broken into the newspapers, and he was received by his father's very old family. So the large and majestic Queen Mother of Shore Acres set out to butter him with flattery and get from him the two things she ardently desired: first, that he should help Irma to produce a grandson to be named Vandringham; and second, that they should leave Baby Frances at Shore Acres to be reared in the Vandringham tradition.

Uncle Horace, that pachyderm of a man who moved with such astonishing energy, proved to be an equally complaisant relative. He had a sense of humor, with more than a trace of mischief in it. He was amused to hear Lanny "razz" the American plutocracy, and especially those representatives of it who came to the Barnes estate. The fact that he himself had been knocked down and out had diminished his admiration for the system and increased his

pleasure in seeing others "get theirs." He chuckled at Lanny's Pinkish jokes, and took the role of an elderly courtier "playing up" to
a newly crowned king. Did he hope that Lanny might some day
persuade Irma to let him have another fling in the market? Or was
he merely making sure of holding onto the comfortable pension
which she allowed him? Anyhow, he was good company.

XI

The echoes of calamity came rolling from Germany to England.
Trade was falling off, factories closing, unemployment increasing;
doubts were spreading as to the soundness of the pound sterling,
for a century the standard of value for all the world; investors were
taking refuge in the dollar, the Dutch florin, the Swiss franc. Rick
told about the situation in his country; boldness was needed, he
said—a capital levy, a move to socialize credit; but no political party
had the courage or the vision. The Tories clamored to balance the
budget at any cost, to cut the dole, and the pay of the school-
teachers, even of the navy. It was the same story as Hoover with
his "rugged individualism." Anything to save the gold standard and
the power of the creditor class.

At the beginning of September the labor government fell. An
amazing series of events—the labor Prime Minister, Ramsay Mac-
Donald, and several of his colleagues in the old Cabinet went over
to the Tories and formed what he called a "National" government
to carry out the anti-labor program. It had happened before in
Socialist history, but never quite so dramatically, so openly; Rick,
writing about it for one of the leftist papers, said that those who
betrayed the hopes of the toiling masses usually managed to veil
their sell-out with decorous phrases, they didn't come out on the
public highway to strip themselves of their old work-clothes and
put on the livery of their masters.

Rick was a philosopher, and tried to understand the actions of
men. He said that the ruling classes couldn't supply their own quota
of ability, but were forced continually to invade the other classes
for brains. It had become the function of the Socialist movement

to train and equip lightning-change artists of politics, men who understood the workers and how to fool them with glittering promises and then climb to power upon their shoulders. In Italy it had been Mussolini, who had learned his trade editing the principal Socialist paper of the country. In France no fewer than four premiers had begun their careers as ardent revolutionaries; the newest of them was Pierre Laval, an innkeeper's son who had driven a one-horse omnibus for his father, and while driving had read Socialist literature and learned how to get himself elected mayor of his town.

For what had these men sold out their party and their cause? For cash? That played a part, of course; a premier or prime minister got considerably more than a Socialist editor, and learned to live on a more generous scale. But more important yet was power: the opportunity to expand the personality, to impress the world, to be pictured and reported in the newspapers, to hold the reins and guide the national omnibus. A thousand flatterers gather round the statesman, to persuade him that he is indispensable to the country's welfare, that danger lies just ahead, and that he alone can ride in the whirlwind and direct the storm.

Rick sent his friend a bunch of clippings, showing how the man who had once lost his seat in the House of Commons for his convictions had now become the hero and darling of those who had unseated him. The entire capitalist press had rallied behind him, praising his action as the greatest of public services. "He will find that he is their prisoner," wrote Rick. "He can do nothing but what they permit; he can have no career except by serving them."

Rick mailed this letter; but before the steamer reached New York, the cables brought word that the prisoner of the Tories had failed. Britain was off the gold standard, and the pound sterling had lost about twenty per cent of its value! It happened to be the twenty-first of September, a notable day in Wall Street history, for it marked two years from the high point of the big bull market. In those two years American securities had lost sixty per cent of their value; and now came this staggering news, causing another drop! "Look where steel is *now!*" said Lanny Budd to his father over the telephone.

XII

In the midst of this world chaos Pierre Laval, innkeeper's son, paid a visit to Germany to see what could be done for that frantic government. The boy driver had grown up into a short, stocky man with black hair always awry, with somber, rather piratical features and a thick black mustache. He had made a lot of money, a tremendous aid to a political career. Of his Socialist days he kept one souvenir: he always wore the little four-in-hand wash ties which had been the fashion in his youth, and had been cheap because he could wash them himself. In France it was well for a statesman to retain some proletarian eccentricity; that he sold out his convictions mattered less, for the people had become so cynical about public men that they hoped only to find the least dishonest.

With Laval traveled Aristide Briand, his Foreign Minister, another innkeeper's son and another Socialist who had changed his mind. He had been a member of twenty-one cabinets—which had required not a little flexibility. But he had labored with genuine conviction to make peace between France and Germany. Now he was an old man, bowed and gray; the glorious organ voice was broken and the strong heart was soon to break. He was still pleading for peace, but he was the prisoner of Laval; and anyhow it was too late. Ancient hatreds and fears had prevailed, and now Germany was in a desperate plight, and France in a worse one, but couldn't realize it.

A curious whim of history: Briand meeting with Hindenburg! The washerwoman's child and the East Prussian aristocrat; old-time enemies, now both nearing their graves; each thinking about his country's safety, and helpless to secure it. *Der alte Herr* talking about the menace of revolution in Germany; not the respectable kind which would put the Kaiser's sons on the throne, but a dangerous gutter-revolution, an upsurge of the *Lumpenproletariat*, led by the one-time odd-job man, the painter of picture postcards, the "Bohemian corporal" named Schicklgruber. Briand demanding the dropping of the Austro-German customs-union project, while Hindenburg pleaded for a chance for his country to sell goods.

Briand denouncing the Stahlhelm and the new pocket-battleships, while Hindenburg complained that France was not keeping her promise to disarm. Hindenburg begging for loans, while Briand explained that France had to keep her gold reserve as the last bulwark of financial security in Europe. No, there wasn't much chance of their getting together; the only one who could hope to profit by the visit was the aforesaid "Bohemian corporal," whose papers were raving alike at the French visitors and at the German politicians who licked their boots to no purpose.

Adolf Hitler Schicklgruber wouldn't attack Hindenburg, for Hindenburg was a monument, a tradition, a living legend. The Nazi press would concentrate its venom upon the Chancellor, a Catholic and leader of the Center party, guilty of the crime of signing the Young Plan which sought to keep Germany in slavery until the year 1988. Now Hoover had granted a moratorium, but there was no moratorium for Brüning, no let-up in the furious Nazi campaign.

Lanny Budd knew about it, because Heinrich Jung had got his address, presumably from Kurt, and continued to keep him supplied with literature. There was no one at Shore Acres who could read it but Lanny himself; however, one didn't need to know German, one had only to look at the headlines to know that it was sensational, and at the cartoons to know that it was a propaganda of cruel and murderous hate. Cartoons of Jews as monsters with swollen noses and bellies, of John Bull as a fat banker sucking the blood of German children, of Marianne as a devouring harpy, of the Russian bear with a knife in his teeth and a bomb in each paw, of Uncle Sam as a lean and sneering Shylock. Better to throw such stuff into the trash-basket without taking off the wrappers.

But that wouldn't keep the evil flood from engulfing Germany, it wouldn't keep millions of young people from absorbing a psychopath's view of the world. Lanny Budd, approaching his thirty-second birthday, wondered if the time hadn't come to stop playing and find some job to do. But he kept putting it off, because jobs were so scarce, and if you took one, you deprived somebody else of it—someone who needed it much more than you!

10

Conscience Doth Make Cowards

I

OCTOBER and early November are the top of the year in the North Atlantic states. There is plenty of sunshine, and the air is clear and bracing. A growing child can toddle about on lawns and romp with dogs, carefully watched by a dependable head nurse. A young mother and father can enjoy motoring and golf, or going into the city to attend art shows and theatrical first nights. Irma had been taken to the museums as a child, but her memories of them were vague. Now she would go with an expert of whom she was proud, and would put her mind on it and try to learn what it was all about, so as not to have to sit with her mouth shut while he and his intellectual friends voiced their ideas.

This pleasant time of year was chosen by Pierre Laval for a visit to Washington, but it wasn't because of the climate. The Premier of France came because there were now only two entirely solvent great nations in the world, and these two ought to understand and support each other. Germany had got several billion dollars from America, but had to have more, and France didn't want her to get them until she agreed to do what France demanded. The innkeeper's son was received with cordiality; excellent dinners were prepared for him, and nobody brought up against him his early Socialistic opinions. Robbie Budd reported that what Laval wanted was for the President to do nothing; to which Robbie's flippant son replied: "That ought to suit Herbert Hoover right down to the ground."

A few days later came the general elections in Britain. Ramsay MacDonald appealed to the country for support, and with all the great newspapers assuring the voters that the nation had barely escaped collapse, Ramsay's new National government polled slightly less than half the vote and, under the peculiarities of the electoral system, carried slightly more than eight-ninths of the constituencies. Rick wrote that Ramsay had set the Labor party back a matter of twenty-one years.

Robbie Budd didn't worry about that, of course; he was certain that the rocks had been passed and that a long stretch of clear water lay before the ship of state. Robbie's friend Herbert had told him so, and who would know better than the Great Engineer? Surely not the editors of Pink and Red weekly papers! But Lanny perversely went on reading these papers, and presently was pointing out to his father that the British devaluation of the pound was giving them a twenty per cent advantage over American manufacturers in every one of the world's markets. Odd as it might seem, Robbie hadn't seen that; but he found it out by cable, for the Budd plant had a big hardware contract canceled in Buenos Aires. One of Robbie's scouts reported that the order had gone to Birmingham; and wasn't Robbie hopping!

II

Mr. and Mrs. Lanny Budd took passage on a German steamer to Marseille; a spick-and-span, most elegant steamer, brand-new, as all German vessels had to be, since the old ones had been confiscated under the treaty of Versailles. One of the unforeseen consequences of having compelled the Germans to begin life all over again! Britain and France didn't like it that their former foe and ever-present rival should have the two fanciest ocean liners, the blue-ribbon holders of the transatlantic service; also the two most modern warships—they were called pocket-battleships, because they weren't allowed to weigh more than ten thousand tons each, but the Germans had shown that they could get pretty nearly everything into that limit.

This upstart nation was upstarting again, and outdistancing everybody else. The Germans filled the air with outcries against persecutions and humiliations, but they had gone right ahead borrowing money and putting it into new industrial plant, the most modern, most efficient, so that they could undersell all competitors. You might not like Germans, but if you wanted to cross the ocean, you liked a new and shiny boat with officers and stewards in new uniforms, and the cleanest and best table-service. They were so polite, and at the same time so determined; Lanny was interested in talking with them and speculating as to what made them so admirable as individuals and so dangerous as a race.

Right now, of course, they were in trouble, like everybody else. They had the industrial plant, but couldn't find customers; they had the steamships, but it was hard to get passengers! The other peoples blamed fate or Providence, economic law, the capitalist system, the gold standard, the war, the Reds—but Germans everywhere blamed but one thing, the Versailles *Diktat* and the reparations it had imposed. Every German was firmly set in the conviction that the Allies were deliberately keeping the Fatherland from getting on its feet again, and that all their trouble was a direct consequence of this. Lanny would point out that now there was a moratorium on all their debts, not only reparations but post-war borrowings, so it ought to be possible for them to recover soon. But he never knew that argument to have the slightest effect; there was a national persecution complex which operated subconsciously, as in an individual.

Since there were so few passengers, Lanny had a week in which to study the ship and those who manned it. Knowing Germany so well, he had a passport to their hearts. He could tell the officers that he had been a guest of General Graf Stubendorf; he could tell the stewards that he had talked with Adolf Hitler; he could tell the crew that he was a brother-in-law of Hansi Robin. The vessel was a miniature nation, with representatives of all the various groups in about the right proportions. Some of the officers had formerly served in the German navy, and some of those who tended the engines had rebelled against them and made the Socialist revolution. In between were the middle classes—stewards, barbers, clerks, radio men, petty officers—all of whom worked obsequiously for tips but would work harder for love if you whispered: "*Heil Hitler!*"—even though you said it in jest.

Irma couldn't understand Lanny's being interested to talk to such people, and for so long a time. He explained that it was a sociological inquiry; if Rick had been along he would have written an article: "The Floating Fatherland." It was a question of the whole future of Germany. How deeply was the propaganda of Dr. Joseph Goebbels taking effect? What were the oilers thinking? What did the scullerymen talk about before they dropped into their bunks? There were dyed-in-the-wool Reds, of course, who followed the Moscow line and were not to be swerved; but others had become convinced that Hitler was a genuine friend of the people and would help them to get shorter hours and a living wage. Arguments were going on day and night, an unceasing war of words all over the ship. Which way was the balance swinging?

Important also was what Capain Rundgasse said. As the physician has a bedside manner, so the captain of a passenger liner has what might be called a steamer-chairside manner. He talked with two wealthy and fashionable young Americans, saying that he could understand why they were worried by the political aspect of his country; but really there was no need for concern. Fundamentally all Germans were German, just as all Englishmen were English, and when it was a question of the welfare and safety of the Fatherland all would become as one. That applied to the deluded Socialists, and even to the Communists—all but a few criminal leaders. It applied to the National Socialists especially. If Adolf Hitler were to become Chancellor tomorrow, he would show himself a good German, just like any other, and all good Germans would support him and obey the laws of their country.

III

Bienvenu seemed small and rather dowdy when one came to it from Shore Acres. But it was home, and there were loving hearts here. Beauty had spent a quiet but contented summer, or so she said. That most unlikely of marriages was turning out one of the best; she couldn't say enough about the goodness and kindness of Parsifal Dingle—that is, not enough to satisfy herself, although she easily satisfied her friends. She was trying her best to become spiritual-minded, and also she had the devil of *embonpoint* to combat. She consoled herself with the idea that when you were well padded, you didn't develop wrinkles. She was certainly a blooming Beauty.

Madame Zyszynski had been two or three times to visit Zaharoff at Monte Carlo; then he had gone north to the Château de Balincourt, and had written to ask if Beauty would do him the great favor of letting Madame come for a while. She had spent the month of August there, and had been well treated, and impressed by the grandeur of the place, but rather lonely, with those strange Hindu servants to whom she couldn't talk. When she was leaving, the old gentleman had presented her with a diamond solitaire ring which must have cost twenty or thirty thousand francs. She was proud of it, but afraid to wear it and afraid it might be stolen, so she had asked Beauty to put it away in her safe-deposit box.

Lanny took up the subject of child study again. He would have liked to find out if Baby Frances would discover the art of the dance for herself; but this was not possible, because Marceline was there, dancing all over the place, and nothing could keep her from taking a tiny toddler by the hands and teaching her to caper and jump. Every day the baby grew stronger, and before that winter was over there was a pair of dancers, and if the phonograph or the piano wasn't handy, Marceline would sing little tunes and sometimes make up words about Baby and herself.

Sophie and her husband would come over for bridge with Beauty and Irma; so Lanny was left free to catch up on his reading or to run over to Cannes to his workers'-education project. The workers hadn't had any vacation, but were right where he had left them. Intellectually they had gained; nearly all could now make speeches, and as a rule they made them on the subject of Socialism *versus* Communism. While they all hated Fascism, they didn't hate it enough to make them willing to get together to oppose it. They were glad to hear Lanny tell about the wonderland of New York; many had got it mixed up with Utopia, and were surprised to hear that it was not being spared by the breakdown of capitalism. Bread-

lines and apple-selling on the streets of that city of plutocrats—
sapristi!

<h1 style="text-align:center">IV</h1>

Another season on the Riviera: from the point of view of the
hotelkeepers the worst since the war, but for people who had
money and liked quiet the pleasantest ever. The fortunate few had
the esplanade and the beaches to themselves; the sunshine was just
as bright, the sea as blue, and the flowers of the Cap as exquisite.
Food was abundant and low in price, labor plentiful and willing—
in short, Providence had fixed everything up for you.

When Irma and Beauty Budd emerged from the hands of *mo-
distes* and *friseurs,* all ready for a party, they were very fancy
showpieces; Lanny was proud to escort them and to see the attention they attracted. He kept himself clad according to their standards, did the honors as he had been taught, and for a while was
happy as a young man *à la mode.* His wife was deeply impressed
by Emily Chattersworth, that serene and gracious hostess, and was
taking her as a model. Irma would remark: "If we had a larger
house, we could entertain as Emily does." She would try experiments, inviting this eminent person and that, and when they came
she would say to her husband: "I believe you and I could have a
salon if we went about it seriously."

Lanny came to recognize that she was considering this as a career. Emily was growing feeble, and couldn't go on forever; there
would have to be someone to take her place, to bring the fashionable French and the fashionable Americans together and let them
meet intellectuals, writers and musicians and statesmen who had
made names for themselves in the proper dignified way. As a rule
such persons didn't have the money or time to entertain, nor were
their wives up to it; if you rendered that free service, it made you
"somebody" in your own right.

Lanny had said, rather disconcertingly, that she didn't know
enough for the job; since which time Irma had been on watch. She
had met a number of celebrities, and studied each one, thinking:
"Could I handle you? What is it you want?" They seemed to like

good food and wine, like other people; they appreciated a fine
house and liked to come into it and sun themselves. Certainly they
liked beautiful women—these were the suns! Irma's dressing-room
in the Cottage was rather small, but it contained a pier-glass mirror,
and she knew that what she saw there was all right. She knew that
her manner of reserve impressed people; it gave her a certain air of
mystery, and caused them to imagine things about her which
weren't really there. The problem was to keep them from finding
out!

Each of the great men had his "line," something he did better
than anybody else. Lanny assumed that you had to read his book,
listen to his speeches, or whatever it was; but Irma made up her
mind that this was her husband's naïveté. *He* would have had to,
but a woman didn't. A woman observed that a man wanted to talk
about himself, and a woman who was good at listening to that
was good enough for anything. She had to express admiration, but
not too extravagantly; that was a mistake the gushy woman made,
and the man decided that she was a fool. But the still, deep woman,
the Mona Lisa woman, the one who said in a dignified way: "I have
wanted very much to know about that—please tell me more," she
was the one who warmed a celebrity's heart.

The problem, Irma decided, was not to get them to talk, but to
get them to stop! The function of a *salonnière* was to apportion
the time, to watch the audience and perceive when it wanted a
change and bring about the change so tactfully that nobody noticed it. Irma watched the technique of her hostess, and began asking questions; and this was by no means displeasing to Emily, for
she too was not above being flattered and liked the idea of taking
on an understudy. She showed Irma her address-book, full of secret
marks which only her confidential secretary understood. Some
meant good things and some bad.

V

Lanny perceived that this developing interest in a salon was based
upon a study of his own peculiarities. He had always loved Emily

and enjoyed her affairs, having been admitted to them even as a boy, because he had such good manners. What Irma failed to note was that Lanny was changing: the things which had satisfied him as a boy didn't necessarily do so when he had passed his thirty-second birthday, and when the capitalist system had passed its apogee. He would come home from one of Emily's soirées and open up a bunch of mail which was like a Sophoclean chorus lamenting the doom of the House of Oedipus. The front page of a newspaper was a record of calamities freshly befallen, while the editorial page was a betrayal of fears of others to come.

For years the orthodox thinkers of France had congratulated that country upon its immunity from depressions. Thanks to the French Revolution, the agriculture of the country was in the hands of peasant proprietors; also the industry was diversified, not concentrated and specialized like that of Germany, Britain, and America. France had already devalued her money, one step at a time; she possessed a great store of gold, and so had escaped that hurricane which had thrown Britain off the gold standard, followed by a dozen other countries in a row.

But now it appeared that the orthodox thinkers had been wishful. Hard times were hitting France; unemployment was spreading, the rich sending their money abroad, the poor hiding what they could get in their mattresses or under the oldest olive tree in the field. Suffering and fear everywhere—so if you were a young idealist with a tender heart, how could you be happy? Especially if your doctrines persuaded you that you had no right to the money you were spending! If you persisted in keeping company with revolutionists and malcontents who were only too ready to support your notions—and to draw the obvious conclusion that, since your money didn't belong to you, it must belong to them! As a rule they asked you to give it for the "cause," and many were sincere and would really spend it for the printing of literature or the rental of meeting-places. That justified them in their own eyes and in yours, but hardly in the eyes of the conservative-minded ladies and gentlemen whom your wife expected to invite to a salon!

Some five years had passed since Lanny had begun helping work-

ers' education in the Midi, and that was time enough for a generation of students to have passed through his hands and give him some
idea of what he was accomplishing. Was he helping to train genuine
leaders of the working class? Or was he preparing some careerist
who would sell out the movement for a premiership? Sometimes
Lanny was encouraged and sometimes depressed. That is the fate of
every teacher, but Lanny had no one of experience to tell him so.

Bright lads and girls revealed themselves in the various classes,
and became the objects of his affection and his hopes. He found
that, being children of the Midi, they all wanted to learn to be
orators. Many acquired the tricks of eloquence before they had got
any solid foundation, and when you tried to restrain them and
failed, you decided that you had spoiled a good mechanic. Many
were swept off their feet by the Communists, who for some reason
were the most energetic, the most persistent among proletarian agitators; also they had a system of thought wearing the aspect and
using the language of science, and thus being impressive to young
minds. Lanny Budd, talking law and order, peaceable persuasion,
gradual evolution, found himself pigeon-holed as *vieux jeu*, or in
American a "back number." "Naturally," said the young Reds,
"you feel that way because you have money. You can wait. But
what have we got?"

This was true enough to trouble Lanny's mind continually. He
watched his own influence upon his proletarian friends and wondered, was he really doing them good? Or were the preachers of
class struggle right, and the social chasm too wide for any bridge-
builder? What community of feeling or taste could survive between the exquisite who lived in Bienvenu and the roustabout's son
who lived in the cellar of a tenement in the Old Town of Cannes?
Was it not possible that in coming to the school well dressed, and
speaking the best French, Lanny was setting up ideals and standards
which were as apt to corrupt as to stimulate?

His friends at the school saw him driving his fancy car, they saw
him with his proud young wife; for though she came rarely, they
knew her by sight and still more by reputation. And what would
that do to youths at the age of susceptibility? Would it teach them

to be loyal to some working-class girl, some humble, poorly dressed comrade in their movement? Or would it fill them with dreams of rising to the heaven where the elegant rich ladies were kept? Lanny, surveying his alluring spouse, knew that there was in all the world no stronger bait for the soul and mind of a man. He had taken that bait more than once in his life; also he knew something about the four Socialists who had become premiers of France, and knew that in every case it had been the hand of some elegant siren which had drawn him out of the path of loyalty and into that of betrayal.

VI

There stood unused on the Bienvenu estate a comfortable dwelling, the Lodge, which Lanny had built for Nina and Rick. He begged them to come and occupy it this season; he had some important ideas he wanted to discuss. But Rick said the pater had been hit too hard by the slump, which seemed to have been aimed at landowners all over the world. Lanny replied with a check to cover the cost of the tickets; it had been earned by the sale of one of Marcel's pictures, and there were a hundred more in the storeroom. Also, Lanny explained, the vegetable garden at Bienvenu had been enlarged, so as to give some of Leese's cousins a chance to earn their keep. Come and help to eat the stuff!

Mother and father and the three children came; and after they had got settled, Lanny revealed what he had in mind: to get some more money out of the picture business (perhaps Irma would want to put some in) to found a weekly paper, with Rick as editor. They would try to wake up the intellectuals and work for some kind of co-operative system in Europe before it was too late. Lanny said he didn't know enough to edit a paper himself, but would be what in America was called an "angel."

Rick said that was a large order, and did his friend realize what he was letting himself in for? The commercial magazine field was pretty crowded, and a propaganda paper never paid expenses, but cost like sin. Lanny said: "Well, I've spent my share on sin, and I might try something else for a change."

"One can't publish a paper in a place like Cannes," declared Rick. "Where would you go?"

"I've wondered if it mightn't be possible to bring out a paper in London, and at the same time in Paris in French?"

"You mean with the same contents?"

"Well, practically the same."

"I should say that might be done if the paper were general and abstract. If you expect to deal with current events, you'd find the interests and tastes of the two peoples too far apart."

"The purpose would be to bring them together, Rick. If they read the same things, they might learn to understand each other."

"Yes, but you're trying to force them to read what they don't want. The paper would seem foreign to both sides; your enemies would call it that and make it appear still more so."

"I don't say it would be easy," replied the young idealist. "What makes it hard is exactly what makes it important."

"I don't dispute the need," Rick said. "But it would cost a pile of money. A paper has to come out regularly, and if you have a deficit, it goes on and on."

"Would you be interested in it as a job?" persisted the other.

"I'd have to think it over. I've come down here with a mind full of a play."

That was the real trouble, as it turned out. There was no use imagining that anybody could edit a paper as a sideline; it was a full-time job for several men, and Rick would have to give up his life's ambition, which was to become a dramatist. He had had just enough success to keep him going. That, too, was an important task: to force modern social problems into the theater, to break down the taboo which put the label of propaganda upon any effort to portray that class struggle which was the basic fact of the modern world. Rick had tried it eight or ten times, and said that if he had put an equal amount of energy and ability into portraying the sexual entanglements of the idle rich, he could have joined that envied group and had plenty of entanglements. But he was always thinking of some wonderful new idea which no audience would be able to resist; he had one now, and so the Franco-British weekly would have to wait until the potential editor had relieved his mind.

Lanny said: "If it's a good play, maybe Irma and I will back it." He always included his wife, out of politeness, and the same motive would cause her to come along.

"That costs money, too," was Rick's reply. "But at least, if the play falls flat, you don't have to produce it again the next week and the week after."

VII

Zaharoff was back at his hotel in Monte, and would send his car for Madame Zyszynski, and write notes expressing his gratitude to the family. He said he wished there were something he could do in return; and apparently he meant it, for when Robbie Budd came into possession of a block of New England-Arabian stock, he came to see the old man, who bought the stock at Robbie's own price. It wasn't a large amount, but Lanny said it was a sign that the duquesa really was "coming through."

Beauty was devoured by curiosity about these séances, and questioned Madame every time she came back; but the medium stuck to her story that she had no idea of what happened when she was in her trance. Evidently Tecumseh was behaving well, for when she came out she would find the sitter gracious and considerate. She always had tea with the maid of Sir Basil's married daughter, and sometimes the great man himself asked questions about her life and ideas. Evidently he was reading along the lines of spiritualism, but he never said a word about himself, nor did he mention the duquesa's name.

Beauty thought it was poor taste for a borrower to keep the owner so entirely in the dark; and perhaps the idea occurred to Sir Basil, for he called Lanny on the telephone and asked if he could spare time to run over and see him. Lanny offered to drive Madame on the next trip, and Zaharoff said all right; Lanny might attend the séance if it would interest him. That was certainly an advance, and could only mean that Zaharoff had managed to make friends with the Iroquois chieftain and his spirit band.

"All flesh is grass, and all the goodliness thereof is as the flower of the field." So Lanny's stern grandfather had quoted, at the time when Lanny was making a scandal in Newcastle by falling in love with a young actress. The playboy thought of it now as he sat and watched this man who might be as old as Grandfather Samuel. His suave manners were a mask and his soul a bundle of fears. He had fought so hard for wealth and power, and now he sat and watched infirmity creeping over him and everything slipping out of his grasp. "Then I looked on all the works that my hands had wrought, and on the labor that I had labored to do: and, behold, all was vanity and vexation of spirit, and there was no profit under the sun."

Secretiveness was the breath of the munitions king's being. For nearly a year he had had Tecumseh and the spirits to himself, and if he had told anyone what was happening it hadn't come to Lanny's ears. But he couldn't hold out indefinitely, because his soul was racked with uncertainties. Was it really the duquesa who was sending him messages? Or was it merely a fantasy, a cruel hoax of somebody or something unknown? Lanny had attended many séances, and was continually studying the subject. The old man had to know what he made of it.

The sitting itself was rather commonplace. Evidently the munitions king and the spirit of his dead wife had become established on a firm domestic basis. She came right away, as she would have done if he had called her from the next room. She didn't have much to talk about—which probably would have been the case if her "grass" had not withered and blown away. The only difference was that Zaharoff would have known the "grass" for what it was; but this imitation grass, this mirage, this painting on a fog—what was it? She assured him that she loved him—of which he had never had any doubt. She assured him that she was happy—she had said it many times, and it was good news if it was she.

As to the conditions of her existence she was vague, as the spirits generally are. They explain that it is difficult for mortal minds to comprehend their mode of being; and that is a possibility, but also it may be an evasion. The duquesa had given evidence of her reality, but now she seemed to wish that he should take it as settled; that made her happier—and of course he sought to make her happy.

But afterward he tormented himself with doubts. Should he torment her with them?

She greeted Lanny and talked to him. She had come to him first, with messages to her husband, and now she thanked him for delivering them. It was exactly as if they had been together in the garden of the Paris mansion. She reminded him of it, and of the snow-white poodles shaved to resemble lions. She had escorted him into the library, and he, a courteous youth, had understood that she might have no more time for him, and had volunteered to make himself happy with a magazine. Did he remember what it was? She said: *La Vie Parisienne*, and he remembered. He darted a glance at Zaharoff, and thought he saw the old white imperial trembling. "Tell him that that is correct," insisted the Spanish duquesa with a Polish accent. "He worries so much, *pauvre chéri*."

The spirit talked about the unusually wet weather, and about the depression; she said that both would end soon. Such troubles did not affect her, except as they affected those she loved. She knew everything that was happening to them; apparently she knew whatever she wanted to know. Lanny asked her politely, could she bring them some fact about the affairs of her ancient family which her husband had never known, but which he might verify by research; something that was in an old document, or hidden in a secret vault in a castle; preferably something she hadn't known during her own lifetime, so that it couldn't have been in the subconscious mind of either of them?

"Oh, that subconscious mind!" laughed the Spanish lady. "It is a name that you make yourself unhappy with. What is mind when it isn't conscious? Have you ever known such a thing?"

"No," said Lanny, "because then it would be conscious. But what is it that acts like a subconscious mind?"

"Perhaps it is God," was the reply; and Lanny wondered: had he brought with him some fragment of the subconscious mind of Parsifal Dingle, and injected it into the subconscious mind which called itself María del Pilar Antonia Angela Patrocino Simón de Muguiro y Berute, Duquesa de Marqueni y Villafranca de los Caballeros?

VIII

When the séance was over, the maid invited Madame into another room to have tea; and Sir Basil had tea and a long talk with Lanny. He wanted to know what the younger man had learned and what he now believed. Lanny, watching the aging and anxious face, knew exactly what was wanted. Zaharoff wasn't an eager scientist, loving truth for truth's sake; he was a man tottering on the edge of the grave, wanting to believe that when he departed this earth he was going to join the woman who had meant so much to him. And what was Lanny, a scientist or a friend?

He could say, quite honestly, that he didn't know; that he wavered, sometimes one way, sometimes the other. Then he could go on to waver in the right direction. Certainly it had seemed to be the duquesa speaking: not the voice, but the mind, the personality, something which one never touches, never sees, but which one comes to infer, which manifests itself by various modes of communication. The duquesa speaking over a telephone, for example, and the line in rather bad condition!

Zaharoff was pleased. He said he had been reading the books. "Telepathy?" he said. "It seems to me just a word they have invented to save having to think. What is this telepathy? How would it work? It cannot be material vibrations, because distance makes no difference to it. You have to suppose that one mind can dip into another mind at will and get anything it wants. And is that easier to credit than survival of the personality?"

Said Lanny: "It is reasonable to think that there might be a core of the consciousness which survives for a time, just as the skeleton survives the body." But he saw that this wasn't a pleasing image to the old gentleman, and hastened to add: "Maybe time isn't a fundamental reality; maybe everything which has ever existed still exists in some form beyond our reach or understanding. We have no idea what reality may be, or our own relationship to it. Maybe we make immortality for ourselves by desiring it. Bernard Shaw says that birds grew wings because they desired and needed to fly."

The Knight Commander and Grand Officer had never heard of *Back to Methuselah*, and Lanny told him about that metabiological panorama. They talked about abstruse subjects until they were like Milton's fallen angels, in wand'ring mazes lost; also until Lanny remembered that he had to take his wife to a dinner-party. He left the old gentleman in a much happier frame of mind, but he felt a little guilty, thinking: "I hope Robbie doesn't have any more stocks to sell him!"

IX

Lanny found his wife dressing, and while he was doing the same she told him some news. "Uncle Jesse was here."

"Indeed?" replied Lanny. "Who saw him?"

"Beauty was in town. I had quite a talk with him."

"What's he doing?"

"He's absorbed in his election campaign."

"How could he spare the time to come here?"

"He came on business. He wants you to sell some of his paintings."

"Oh, my God, Irma! I can't sell those things, and he knows it."

"Aren't they good enough?"

"They're all right in a way; but they're quite undistinguished—there must be a thousand painters in Paris doing as well."

"Don't they manage to sell their work?"

"Sometimes they do; but I can't recommend art unless I know it has special merit."

"They seemed to me quite charming, and I should think a lot of other people would like them."

"You mean he brought some with him?"

"A whole taxicab-load. We had quite a show, all afternoon; that, and the Comintern, and that—what is it?—diagrammatical?—"

"Dialectical materialism?"

"He says he could make a Communist out of me if it wasn't for my money. So he tried to get some of it away from me."

"He asked you for money?"

"He may be a bad painter, dear, but he's a very good salesman."

"You mean you bought some of those things?"

"Two."

"For the love of Mike! What did you pay?"

"Ten thousand francs apiece."

"But, Irma, that's preposterous! He never got half that for a painting in all his life."

"Well, it made him happy. He's your mother's brother, and I like to keep peace in the family."

"Really, darling, you don't have to do things like that. Beauty won't like it a bit."

"It's much easier to say yes than no," replied Irma, watching in the mirror of her dressing-table while her maid put the last touches to her coiffure. "Uncle Jesse's not a bad sort, you know."

"Where are the paintings?" asked the husband.

"I put them in the closet for the present. Don't delay now, or we'll be late."

"Let me have just a glance."

"I didn't buy them for art," insisted the other; "but I do like them, and maybe I'll hang them in this room if they won't hurt your feelings."

Lanny got out the canvases and set them up against two chairs. They were the regular product which Jesse Blackless turned out at the rate of one every fortnight whenever he chose. One was a little gamin, and the other an old peddler of charcoal; both sentimental, because Uncle Jesse really loved these poor people and imagined things about them which fitted in with his theories. Irma didn't have such feelings, but Lanny had taught her that she ought to, and doubtless she was trying. "Are they really so bad?" she asked.

"They aren't any bargain," he answered.

"It's only eight hundred dollars, and he says he's broke on account of putting everything into the campaign. You know, Lanny, it might not be such a bad thing to have your uncle a member of the Chamber."

"But such a member, Irma! He'll make himself an international scandal. I ought to have mentioned to you that he's gone into a working-class district and is running against a Socialist."

"Well," said the young wife, amiably, "I'll help the Socialist, too, if you wish it."

"You'll take two horses, and hitch one to the front of your cart and one to the back, and drive them as hard as you can in opposite directions."

Irma wasn't usually witty; but now she thought of Shore Acres, and said: "You know how it is, I've been paying men right along to exercise my horses."

X

Alfred Pomeroy-Nielson the younger was at school in England; he came to Bienvenu for the Easter vacation, and he and Marceline took up their life at the point where they had dropped it on board the *Bessie Budd*, a year and a half ago. Meanwhile they had been getting ready for each other, and at the same time making important discoveries about themselves.

The daughter of Marcel Detaze and Beauty Budd, not quite fourteen, was at that point "where the brook and river meet, womanhood and childhood fleet." Like the diving-champion on the end of a springboard, with every muscle taut, the body poised in the moment of swaying forward, so she presented herself above the swimming-pool of fashion, pleasure, and so many kinds of glory. She had gazed into it as a fascinated spectator and now was getting ready to plunge—much sooner than any member of her family knew or desired. That was her secret; that was the meaning of the fluttering heart, the flushed cheeks, the manner of excitement—she couldn't wait to begin to live!

Marceline loved her mother, she adored her handsome and fashionable half-brother, she looked with awe upon the blooming Juno who had come recently into her life, surrounded by a golden aura, talked about by everybody, pictured in the newspapers—in short, a queen of plutocracy, that *monde* which Marceline had been taught to consider *beau, grand, haut, chic, snob, élégant, et d'élite.* She was going to show herself off in it, and no use trying to change her mind. Men were beginning to look at her, and she was not failing to notice that or to know what it meant. Hadn't it been in the conversation of all the smart ladies since she had begun to understand the meaning of words? Those ladies were growing old, they were on the way out—and Marceline was coming, it was her turn!

And now this English lad, of almost the same age as herself, and destined, in the family conversation, to become her life partner. Maybe so, but first there were a few problems to be settled; first it was necessary to determine who would be the boss in that family. Alfy was serious, like his father; extremely conscientious, more reticent than seemed natural in one so young, and tormented by a secret pride. Marceline, on the other hand, was impulsive, exuberant, talkative, and just as proud in her own way. Each of these temperaments was in secret awe of the other; the natural strangeness of a youth to a maid and of a maid to a youth accentuated their differences and offended their self-esteem. Was he scorning her when he was silent? Was she teasing him when she laughed? Exasperation was increased by arrogance on both sides.

It is the English custom, when two boys fall to pommeling each other, to form a ring and let them fight it out. Now it appeared to be the same with the sex-war. Rick said: "They'd better settle it now than later." He gave advice only when it was asked, and poor Alfy was proud even with his father. It was up to a man to handle his own women!

Marceline, on the other hand, fled to her mother and had weeping-fits. Beauty tried to explain to her the peculiar English temperament, which makes itself appear cold but really isn't. The short vacation was passing, and Beauty advised her daughter to make it up quickly; but Marceline exclaimed: "I think they are horrid people, and if he won't have better manners I don't want to have anything more to do with him." The French and the English had been fighting ever since the year 1066.

XI

Oddly enough, it was the man from Iowa who served as international mediator. Parsifal Dingle never meddled in anybody's affairs, but talked about the love of God, and perhaps it was a coincidence that he talked most eloquently when he knew that two persons were at odds. God was all and God was love; God was alive and God was here; God knew what we were doing and saying and thinking, and when what we did was not right, we were deliberately cutting ourselves off from Him and destroying our own happiness. That was the spiritual law; God didn't have to punish us, we punished ourselves; and if we humbled ourselves before Him, we exalted ourselves before one another. So on through a series of mystical statements which came like a message from a much better world.

All this would have been familiar doctrine to the forebears of either of these young people. Perhaps ideas have to be forgotten in order to become real again; anyhow, to both Marceline and Alfy this strange gentleman was the originator or discoverer of awe-inspiring doctrines. A rosy-cheeked, cherubic gentleman with graying hair and the accent of the prairies. Once when he wanted to bathe his hands on board the sailboat he had used what he called a "wawsh-dish," which Alfy thought was the funniest combination of words he had ever heard.

But apparently God didn't object to the Iowa accent, for God came to him and told him what to do. And when you thought of God, not somewhere up in the sky on a throne, but living in your heart, a part of yourself in some incomprehensible way, then suddenly it seemed silly to be quarreling with somebody who was a friend of the family, even if not your future spouse! Better to forget about it—at least to the extent of a game of tennis.

Beauty thought how very convenient, having a spiritual healer in the family! She thought: "I am an unworthy woman, and I must try to be like him and love everybody, and value them for their best qualities. I really ought to go to Lanny's school, and meet some of those poor people, and try to find in them what he finds." She would think these thoughts while putting on a costly evening-gown which

Irma had given her after two or three wearings; she would be escorted to a party at the home of the former Baroness de la Tourette, and would listen to gossip about a circus-rider who had married an elderly millionaire and was cutting a swath on this Coast of Pleasure. The ladies would tear her reputation to shreds, and Beauty would enjoy their cruel cleverness and forget all about the fact that God was listening to every word.

A complicated world, so very hard to be good in!

BOOK THREE

Blow, Winds,
and Crack Your Cheeks

11

'Tis Woman's Whole Existence

I

THE betrayal of the British labor movement had entered like a white-hot iron into the flesh of Eric Vivian Pomeroy-Nielson. He had brooded over it and analyzed its causes; he had filled his soul with images of it; and the result was to be a drama called *The Dress-Suit Bribe*. No literary title, dignified and impartial, but a fighting title, a propaganda title.

The central figure was a miner's son who had escaped from the pits by becoming a secretary of his union. He had a wife who had been a schoolteacher, somewhat above him in station. They had no children, because the labor movement was to be their child. At the opening of the play he was a newly elected member of Parliament. There were characters and episodes recalling his early days of fervor and idealism, but now we saw him absorbed in the not very edifying details of party politics, the maneuvers for power, the payment of past obligations in the hope of incurring more.

The leisure-class woman in the story had no doubt been modeled on Rosemary, Countess of Sandhaven, Lanny's old flame; one of those women touched by the feminist movement who did not permit themselves to love deeply because it would interfere with their independence, their enjoyment of prominence and applause. She was a political woman who liked to wield power; she set out to seduce a labor leader, not because she wanted to further the interests of her Tory group, but because she enjoyed playing with a man and subjecting him to her will. She tried to teach him what she called common sense, not merely about love, but about politics and all the affairs of the world they lived in. She didn't mind breaking the heart

211

of a wife whom she considered an inferior and superfluous person; if in the process she broke up a labor union, that was an incidental gain.

It was a "fat" part for an actress, and at Lanny's suggestion Rick had endowed the woman with an American mother; a common enough phenomenon in London society, this would make the role possible for Phyllis Gracyn. Lanny's old friend and playmate had been starred in two plays which had "flopped" on Broadway through no fault of her own; so she was in a humble frame of mind, and when Lanny wrote her about Rick's play she cabled at once, begging to be allowed to see the script. The part had been written for her— even to allowing for traces of an American accent.

Lanny had become excited about the play, and had talked out every scene with his friend, both before and after it was put down on paper. Irma and Beauty read it, and Emily and Sophie, and of course Rick's wife; these ladies consulted together, and contributed suggestions as to how members of the *grand* and *beau* and *haut monde* felt and behaved. So the play became a sort of family affair, and there was small chance of anything's being wrong with its atmosphere and local color. After Emily had read the entire script, she offered to put in five thousand dollars on the same terms as the rest of them, and Sophie, the ex-baroness, was not to be outdone.

The play would be costly to produce, on account of the money atmosphere. If you want actors to look like workingmen or labor leaders, you can hire them cheaply, but if you want one who can play the Chancellor of the Exchequer, you have to dip into your own. Rick, who by now had considerable experience, estimated the total at thirty thousand dollars, and the figure sounded familiar to Lanny, because that had been the cost of Gracyn's first production, the sum for which she had thrown him over. Now he would take a turn at being the "angel"; a higher, celestial kind, for whom she wouldn't have to act anywhere but on the stage.

II

The play was finished early in April, and the family went north, with Alfy returning to school. Lanny and Irma motored the mother and father as far as Paris, starting several days ahead; for Zoltan Kertezsi was there, and they wanted to see the spring Salon through his expert eyes; also there were plays to be seen, of interest to professionals such as they were about to become. As it happened, France was in the midst of a furious election campaign, and when you had an uncle running for the Chamber of Deputies, you were interested to see the show. Hansi and Bess had consented to come and give a concert for the benefit of his campaign, so it would be a sort of family reunion.

The Hungarian art expert was his usual serene and kindly self. He had just come back from a trip to the Middle West, where, strange as it might seem, there were still millionaires who enjoyed incomes and wanted to buy what they called "art paintings." Lanny had provided Zoltan with photographs of the Detazes which were still in the storeroom, and three had been sold, at prices which would help toward the production of *The Dress-Suit Bribe*. Irma insisted upon putting up a share of the money, not because she knew anything about plays, but because she loved Lanny and wanted him to have his heart's desires.

She took the same tolerant attitude toward political meetings. If Lanny wanted to go, she would accompany him, and try to understand the French language shouted in wildly excited tones. Jesse Blackless was running as candidate in one of those industrial suburbs which surrounded Paris with a wide Red band. Under the French law you didn't have to be a resident of your district but had to be a property-owner, so the Red candidate had purchased the cheapest vacant lot he could find. He had been carefully cultivating the constituency, speaking to groups of workers every night for months on end, attending committee meetings, even calling upon the voters in their homes—all for the satisfaction of ousting a Socialist incumbent who had departed from the "Moscow line." Irma didn't understand these technicalities, but she couldn't help being thrilled to find this newly acquired uncle the center of attention on a platform, delivering a fervid oration which drove the crowd to frenzies of delight. Also she couldn't fail to be moved by the sight of Hansi Robin playing for the workers of a foreign land and being received as a comrade and brother. If only they hadn't been such terrible-looking people!

III

All this put Lanny in a peculiar position. He attended his uncle's *réunion*, but didn't want him to win and told him so. Afterward they repaired with a group of their friends to a café where they had supper and argued and wrangled until the small hours of the morning. A noisy place, crowded and full of tobacco smoke; Irma had been taken to such haunts in Berlin, London, and New York, so she knew that this was how the intelligentsia lived. It was supposed to be "bohemian," and certainly it was different; she could never complain that her marriage had failed to provide her with adventures.

By the side of the millionairess sat a blond young Russian, speaking to her in English, which made things easier; he had just come out of the Soviet Union, that place about which she had heard so many terrible stories. He told her about the Five-Year Plan, which was nearing completion. Already every part of its program had been overfulfilled; the great collective farms were sowing this spring more grain than ever before in Russian history; it meant a complete new era in the annals of mankind. The young stranger was quietly confident, and Irma shivered, confronting the doom of the world in which she had been brought up. From the attitude of the others she gathered that he was an important person, an agent of the Comintern, perhaps sent to see that the campaign followed the correct party line; perhaps he was the bearer of some of that "Moscow gold" about which one heard so much talk!

Across the table sat Hansi and Bess; and presently they were telling the Comintern man details about the situation in Germany. Elections to the diets of the various states had just been held, and the parties of the two extremes had made tremendous gains; the middle classes were being wiped out, and with them the middle-class point of view. Hansi said that the battle for the streets of the German cities, which had been waged for the last two or three years, was going against the Communists; their foes had the money and the arms. Hansi had witnessed a battle in broad daylight in Berlin. A squad of Stormtroopers had been marching with their *Hakenkreuz* banners and a fife and drum, and passing a co-operative store they had hurled stones through the windows; the men inside had rushed out and there had been a general clubbing and stabbing. The Jewish violinist hadn't stayed to see the outcome. "I don't suppose I ought to use my hands to beat people," he said, spreading them out apologetically.

"Poor Hansi!" thought Irma. He and Freddi were unhappy, having discovered how their father was dealing with all sides in this German civil war. The Nazis were using Budd machine guns in killing the workers, and how could that have come about without the firm of "R & R" knowing about it? The boys hadn't quarreled with their father—they couldn't bear to—but their peace of mind was gone and they were wondering how they could go on living in that home.

Also Irma thought: "Poor Lanny!" She saw her husband buffeted between the warring factions. The Reds were polite to him in this crowd because he was Jesse's nephew, and also because he was paying for the supper, a duty he invariably assumed. He seemed to feel that he had to justify himself for being alive: a person who didn't enjoy fighting, and couldn't make up his mind even to hate wholeheartedly.

Yet he couldn't keep out of arguments. When the Communist candidate for the Chamber of Deputies put on his phonograph record and remarked that the Social-Democrats were a greater barrier to progress than the Fascists, Lanny replied: "If you keep on asking for it, Uncle Jesse, you may have the Fascists to deal with."

Said the phonograph: "Whether they mean to or not, they will help to smash the capitalist system."

"Go and tell that to Mussolini!" jeered Lanny. "You've had ten years to deal with him, and how far have you got?"

"He knows that he's near the end of his rope."

"But we're talking about capitalism! Have you studied the dividend reports of Fiat and Ansaldo?"

So they sparred, back and forth; and Irma thought: "Oh, dear, how I dislike the intelligentsia!"

But she couldn't help being impressed when the elections came off, and Zhess Block-léss, as the voters called him, showed up at the top of the poll in his district. On the following Sunday came a run-off election, in which the two highest candidates, who happened to be the Red and the Pink, fought it out between them. Uncle Jesse came to Irma secretly to beg for funds, and she gave him two thousand francs, which cost her seventy-nine dollars. As it happened, the Socialist candidate was a friend of Jean Longuet, and went to Lanny and got twice as much; but even so, Zhess Block-léss came out several hundred votes ahead, and Lanny had the distinction of having an uncle who was a member of the Chamber of Deputies of the French Republic. Many a young man had made his fortune from such a connection, but all Lanny could expect was a few more *additions*—that is to say, accounts for food and wine consumed by parties in restaurants.

IV

The Pomeroy-Nielsons had gone to London, where Rick was engaging a stage director and a business manager. The Budds and the Robins went for a visit to Les Forêts, where Emily Chattersworth had just arrived. Hansi and Bess played for her; and later, while Bess and Lanny practiced piano duets, Irma sought out the hostess to ask her advice about the problems of a Pink husband and a Red uncle-in-law.

Mrs. Chattersworth had always been open-minded in the matter of politics; she had allowed her friends and guests to believe and say what they chose, and as a *salonnière* had been content to steer the conversation away from quarrels. Now, she said, the world appeared to be changing; ever since the war it had been becoming more difficult for gentlemen—yes, and ladies, too—to keep their political discussions within the limits of courtesy. It seemed to have begun with the Russian Revolution, which had been such an impolite affair. "You have to be either for it or against it," remarked Emily; "and whichever you are, you cannot tolerate anyone's being on the other side."

Said Irma: "The trouble with Lanny is that he's willing to tolerate anybody, and so he's continually being imposed upon."

"I watched him as a little boy," replied her friend. "It seemed very sweet, his curiosity about people and his efforts to understand them. But like any virtue, it can be carried to extremes."

Lanny's ears would have burned if he could have heard those two women taking him to pieces and trying to put him together according to their preferences. The wise and kind Emily, who had been responsible for his marriage, wanted to make it and keep it a success, and she invited the young people to stay for a while so that she might probe into the problem. Caution and tact were necessary, she pointed out to the young wife, for men are headstrong creatures and do not take kindly to being manipulated and maneuvered. Lanny's toleration for Reds and Pinks was rooted in his sympathy for suffering, and Irma would love him less if that were taken out of his disposition.

"I don't mind his giving money away," said Irma. "If only he didn't have to meet such dreadful people—and so many of them!"

"He's interested in ideas; and apparently they come nowadays from the lower strata. You and I mayn't like it, but it's a fact that they are crashing the gates. Perhaps it's wiser to let in a few at a time."

Irma was willing to take any amount of trouble to understand her husband and to keep him entertained; she was trying to acquire ideas, but she wanted them to be safe, having to do with music and art and books and plays, and not politics and the overthrowing of the capitalist system. "What he calls the capitalist system," was the way she phrased it, as if it were a tactical error to admit that such a thing existed. "I've made sure that he'll never be interested in my friends in New York," she explained. "But he seems to be impressed by the kind of people he meets at your affairs, and if you'll show me how, I'll do what I can to cultivate them—before it's too late. I mean, if he goes much further with his Socialists and Communists, the right sort of people won't want to have anything to do with him."

"I doubt if that will happen," said Emily, smiling. "They'll tolerate him on your account. Also, they make allowances for Americans— we're supposed to be an eccentric people, and the French find us entertaining, much as Lanny finds his Reds and Pinks."

V

The husband wasn't told of this conversation, or others of the kind which followed; but he became aware, not for the first time in his life, of female arms placed about him, exerting a gentle pressure in one direction and away from another. Not female elbows poked into his ribs, but soft, entwining arms; a feeling of warmth, and perhaps a contact of lips, or whispered words of cajolement: darling, and dear, and intimate pet names which would look silly in print and sound so from any but a chosen person. Never: "Let's not go there, dear," but instead: "Let's go here, dear." And always the "here" had to do with music or pictures, books or plays, and not with the overthrow of the so-called, alleged, or hypothetical capitalist system.

Under Emily's guidance Irma decided that she had made a mistake in discouraging Lanny's efforts as an art expert. To be sure, it seemed silly to try to make more money when she had so much, but the prejudices of men had to be respected; they just don't like to take money from women, and they make it a matter of prestige to earn at least their pocket-money. Irma decided that Zoltan Kertezsi was an excellent influence in her husband's life. So far she had looked upon him as a kind of higher servant, but now decided to cultivate him as a friend.

"Let's stay in Paris a while, dear," she proposed. "I really want to understand about pictures, and it's such a pleasure to have Zoltan's advice."

Lanny, of course, was touched by this act of submission. They went to exhibitions, of which there appeared to be no end in Paris.

Also, there were private homes having collections, and Zoltan possessed the magic keys that opened doors to him and his guests. Pretty soon Irma discovered that she could enjoy looking at beautiful creations. She paid attention and tried to understand the points which Zoltan explained: the curves of mountains or the shape of trees which made a balanced design in a landscape; the contrasting colors of an interior; the way figures had been placed and lines arranged so as to lead the eye to one central feature. Yes, it was interesting, and if this was what Lanny liked, his wife would like it, too. Marriage was a lottery, she had heard, and you had to make the best of what you had drawn.

VI

"Zaharoff's house on the Avenue Hoche contains some gay and bright Bouchers," remarked Lanny. "He's not apt to be there, but the servants know me, so no doubt we can get in."

The three of them called at the white-stone mansion with the glass-covered window-boxes full of flowers. The tottery old butler was still on duty, and the beautiful portraits still hung in the drawing-room where Sir Basil had burned his private papers and set fire to his chimney. The butler reported that his master was at the château and seldom came to town now; but no one knew when he might come, and he continued the custom which had prevailed ever since Lanny had known him, of having a full-course dinner prepared every evening, enough for himself and several guests. If after a certain hour he had not arrived, the servants ate what they wanted and gave the rest to worthy poor. The duquesa's *by bloemen* and *bizarres* still bloomed in her garden, fifteen springtimes after she had shown them to Lanny. "They have their own kind of immortality," she had said; and these words had been repeated to him by an old Polish woman in a Mother Hubbard wrapper, then living in a tenement room on Sixth Avenue, New York, with the elevated railroad trains roaring past the windows.

There were old masters worth seeing at Balincourt, and Lanny telephoned and made an appointment to bring his wife and his friend. He motored them out on a day of delightful sunshine, and the Knight Commander and Grand Officer received the party with every evidence of cordiality. He had discovered that Lanny's wife was kind, and any lonely old man appreciates the attentions of a beautiful young woman. He showed them his David and his Fragonard, his Goya, his Ingres, and his Corots. These also had their kind of immortality, a magical power to awaken life in the souls of those who looked at them. Zaharoff had told Lanny that he was tired of them, but now it appeared that the fires of the young people's appreciation warmed up the dead ashes of his own.

The Hungarian expert never failed to have something worth while to say about a painting, and Zaharoff didn't fail to recognize that what he said was right; they talked about prices, which were of interest to them both, and important to Zoltan—one never knew what might come of such a contact. Lanny said: "This is the man who has taught me most of what I know about art." Zoltan, flushing with pleasure, replied: "This from the stepson of Marcel Detaze!"

They talked about that painter, of whom Zaharoff had heard. He asked questions, and in his mind the seed of an idea fell and began to germinate. Perhaps this was a way to get more of Madame Zyszynski's time! Buy a Detaze!

Tea was served on the terrace in front of the château. A beautiful view of formal gardens and distant forest, and when Lanny commented on it, Zaharoff said: "My wife chose this place and I bought it from King Leopold of Belgium."

He didn't go any further, but Lanny knew the story, and on the drive back to Paris entertained his passengers with the scabrous details. The King of the Belgians, a tall, magnificent personage wearing a great square-cut white beard, had been wont to roam the highways and byways of Paris in search of likely pieces of female flesh. The sixty-five-year-old monarch had chanced upon the sixteen-year-old sister of one of the famous *demi-mondaines* of the city and had sent a procuress to buy her; he had taken her to live in Hungary for a while, had fallen madly in love with her and brought her back to Paris, and purchased this splendid château for her home. He hadn't been content with it, but had insisted upon remodeling a great part, tearing out the ceiling of his lady's bedroom and making it two stories tall, like a church. The four windows facing the bed had draperies which had cost twenty thousand francs; the coverlet of English point lace had cost a hundred and ten thousand—the pre-war kind of francs! Her bathroom was of massive porphyry and her tub of silver; in the basement was a swimming-pool of gold mosaic. Lanny, who had never had a bath here, wondered if the very proper Duquesa Marqueni had retained these Byzantine splendors.

VII

Another of the homes which the trio visited was the town house of the Duc de Belleaumont, a member of the old French nobility who had married a cattle-king's daughter from the Argentine and so was able to live in the state of his forefathers. The palace stood on a corner near the Parc Monceau, and had an impressive white marble exterior and about thirty rooms, many of them spacious. It was decorated with that splendor which the French have cultivated through centuries. Every piece of furniture, every tapestry and statue and vase was worthy of separate study. A crystal cross set with sixteenth-century gold-enamel reliquaries, an inlaid Louis Seize writing cabinet, a set of translucent azure ginger jars from ancient China—such things moved Zoltan Kertezsi to raptures. The total effect was somewhat like a museum, but this does not trouble anyone in France, and has been known to occur on Long Island, too.

The family was away, and the furniture was under dust-covers, but Zoltan knew the caretaker, who, being sure of a generous tip, exhibited anything in which they expressed interest. The idea occurred to Irma that the depression might have affected the market for Argentine beef, and she inquired whether the place could be rented; the reply was that Madame should consult the agent of M. le Duc. Irma did so, and learned that a properly accredited family might lease the residence for the sum of a million francs per year.

"Why, Lanny, that's nothing!" exclaimed Irma. "Less than forty thousand dollars."

"But what on earth would you do with it?"

"Wouldn't you like to live in Paris and be able to entertain your friends?"

"But you've got one white elephant on your hands already!"

"Be sensible, darling, and face the facts. You don't like Shore Acres, or the people who come to it. You want to live in France."

"But I've never asked for a palace!"

"You want your friends about you, and you want to do things for them. All your life you've taken it for granted that somebody will do the entertaining, and you enjoy the benefits. You're delighted to go to Sept Chênes and meet intellectual and cultivated people. You hear famous musicians, you hear poets read their work —and apparently you think that kind of pleasure grows on trees, you don't even have to pick the fruit, it comes already cut up in little cubes and served on ice! Hasn't it occurred to you that Emily's health is failing? And some day you won't have your mother, or Sophie, or Margy—you'll be dependent on what your wife has learned."

He saw that she had thought it all out, and he guessed that she had consulted the other ladies. Naturally, they would approve, because it would provide good fun for them. "You'll be taking a heavy load on your shoulders," he objected, feebly.

"It won't be so easy in a foreign country; but I'll get help, and I'll learn. It will be my job, just as it has been Emily's."

"What will you do with Shore Acres?"

"Let's try this place for a year. If we like it, perhaps we can buy it, and sell Shore Acres; or if mother wants to go on living there, she can cut down on the staff. If this depression goes on, they'll be glad to work for their keep, and that'll be fair."

"But suppose your income goes on dropping, Irma!"

"If the world comes to an end, how can anybody say what he'll do! Anyhow, it can't do us any harm to have a lot of friends."

VIII

It was a compromise she was proposing; she would live in France, as he desired, but she would live according to her standards. In order to stop her, he would have to say a flat no, and he didn't have the right to say that. It was her money, and all the world knew it.

There was nothing very novel to Lanny Budd in the idea of living in Paris. He had spent a winter here during the Peace Conference, and another during the period of his *vie à trois* with Marie de Bruyne. Paris offered every kind of art and entertainment, and it was centrally situated; roads and cars had been so improved that you could reach London or Geneva or Amsterdam in a few hours. They could step into their car in the morning and be in Bienvenu by nightfall. "Really, it'll be about the same as commuting," said Irma.

What astonished him was the zest with which she set to work, and the speed with which she put the job through. She was the daughter of J. Paramount Barnes, and all her life she had been used to hearing decisions made and orders given. As soon as Lanny gave his consent she seated herself at the telephone and put in a call for Jerry Pendleton in Cannes. "How's business?" she asked, and when the familiar cheery voice informed her that it was dead and buried, she asked if he would like to have a job. He answered that he would jump for it, and she said: "Jump for the night express, and don't miss your hold."

"But darling!" objected Lanny. "He doesn't know anything about running a palace!"

"He's honest, he's lived in France for fifteen years, and employed some help. It won't take him long to learn the ropes."

When the red-headed ex-lieutenant from Kansas arrived, she put it up to him. He would become steward, or perhaps *Contrôleur-Général*, like Herr Meissner in Stubendorf. "Put on lots of side," she advised, "and be taken at your own valuation." He would engage a first-class major domo and a butler who would know what was done and what wasn't. He would be paid enough so that he could have his own car, and run down to see his family now and then.

Jerry Pendleton had once undertaken to tutor Lanny Budd without any preparation, and now he was taking another such chance. No time even to read a book on the duties of a *Contrôleur-Général!* Go right to work; for the "season" was soon to begin, and Irma wanted what she wanted when she wanted it. The elaborate inventory of the contents of the palace was made and checked and signed on every page; the lease was signed, the money paid, and the keys delivered. Emily's butler had a brother who was also in the profession, and knew everything there was to know about Paris society. Also he knew servants, enough for an emergency staff, and they came and took off the dust-covers and got things ready with American speed.

Irma and her prince consort and her *Contrôleur-Général* moved into their new home, and it was but a few hours before the newspapers had got word of it, and the doorbell was ringing and the flashlight bulbs of the photographers exploding. Lanny saw that his wife was once more getting her money's worth; they were back in café society, with the spotlight centered upon them. Paris was going to have a new hostess, a famous one. The marble steps of the palace were worn by the feet of chauffeurs and lackeys leaving calling cards with distinguished names on them, and the side entrance bell was ringing to announce the presence of *bijoutiers* and *couturiers* and *marchands de modes*.

Irma said: "Your mother must come and help us." So Lanny wrote at once, and that old war-mare said "Ha, ha!" and scented the battle afar off. It would have been a mortal affront to invite one mother-in-law and not the other, so Irma sent a cablegram to Shore Acres, and that older and more experienced charger dropped all her plans and took the first steamer. Even Emily came to town for a few days, bringing her calling lists with the secret symbols. Feathers sat by her side with a stenographer's notebook, collecting pearls of information which dropped from the lips of the most esteemed of Franco-American hostesses.

In short, Lanny Budd found himself in the midst of a social whirlwind; and it would have been cruelly unkind of him not to like it. Once more the ladies were in charge of his life, and what they considered proper was what he did. He listened to their talk and he met the people they brought for him to meet; if he wanted to play the piano it had to be done at odd moments between social engagements; while, as for sitting down in a splendid library and burying himself in a book—well, it was just too selfish, too solitary, too inconsiderate of all those persons who wanted to pay their attentions to the lessee of so much magnificence.

IX

The election results had given a tremendous jolt to the conservative elements in France. The party of Jesse Blackless had gained only two seats, but the party of Léon Blum had gained seventeen, while the "Radicals" had gained forty-eight. To be sure that word didn't mean what it meant in the United States; it was the party of the peasants and the small business men, but it was expected to combine with the Socialists, and France would have a government of the left, badly tainted with pacifism, and likely to make dangerous concessions to the Germans. The groups which had been governing France, the representatives of big industry and finance capital, popularly known as the *mur d'argent*, the "wall of money," were in a state of great alarm.

One of Lanny's duties in Paris was to keep in touch with his ex-family, the de Bruynes. Having now a suitable home of his own, he invited them to dinner and they came, father, two sons, and the young wife of Denis *fils*. Irma hadn't met them before, but had heard a lot about them, and felt herself being fascinatingly French when she welcomed the family of her husband's former mistress. They, for their part, appeared to take it as a matter of course, which made it still more French. They were people of high culture and agreeable manners, so Irma was pleased to assist in carrying out the death-bed promises which Lanny had made to the woman who had done so much to prepare him to be a good and satisfactory husband.

They talked about politics and the state of the world. That was what this splendid home was for; so that Lanny wouldn't have to meet his friends in crowded cafés, where they were jostled and could hardly hear one another's voices, but might sit in comfort and express themselves with leisure and dignity. It was Irma's hope that the things said would take on something of the tone of the surroundings; and certainly this appeared to be true with the de Bruynes, who were Nationalists, all four of them, and in a state of great concern as to the trend of the country and its position in the world.

Said the proprietor of a great fleet of taxicabs, speaking with some hesitation to a hostess from overseas: "I am afraid that the people of your country do not have a clear realization of the position in which they have placed my country."

"Do feel at liberty to speak freely, Monsieur," replied Irma, in her most formal French.

"There is a natural barrier which alone can preserve this land from the invasion of barbarians, and that is the River Rhein. It was our intention to hold and fortify it, but your President Veelson"—so they called him, ending with their sharp nasal "n"—"your President Veelson forced us back from that boundary, onto ground which is almost indefensible, no matter how hard we may try with our Maginot line. We made that concession because of your President's pledge of a protective agreement against Germany; but your Congress ignored that agreement, and so today we stand wellnigh defenseless. Now your President Oovay has declared a moratorium on reparations, so that chapter is at an end—and we have received almost nothing."

Lanny wanted to say: "You received twenty-five billions of francs under the Dawes plan, and the products have glutted the world markets." But he had learned in Denis's home that it was futile to argue with him, and it would be no less so in the palace of the Duc de Belleaumont, one of Denis's financial associates.

"You do not feel that there is any possibility of trusting the German Republic?" inquired Irma, trying hard to perfect her political education.

"When one says Germany today, Madame, one means Prussia; and to these people good faith is a word of mockery. For such men as Thyssen and Hugenberg, and for the Jewish money-lenders, the name 'Republic' is a form of camouflage. I speak frankly, because it is all in the family, as it were."

"Assuredly," said the hostess.

"Every concession that we make is met by further demands. We have withdrawn from the Rheinland, and no longer have any hold upon them, so they smile up their sleeves and go on with their re-arming. They waited, as you have seen, until after our elections, so as not to alarm us; then, seeing the victory of the left, they over-throw their Catholic Chancellor, and we see a Cabinet of the Barons, as it is so well named. If there is a less trustworthy man in all Europe than Franz von Papen, I would not know where to seek him."

Irma perceived that you might invite a French Nationalist to the most magnificent of homes and serve him the best of dinners, but you would not thereby make him entirely happy. Practicing her new role of *salonnière*, she brought the young people into the con-versation; but this succeeded no better, for it turned out that Char-lot, the young engineer, had joined the Croix de Feu, one of the patriotic organizations which did not propose to surrender *la patrie* either to the Reds or to the Prussians. The Croix de Feu used the technique of banners and uniforms and marching and singing as did the Fascists of Italy and the Nazis of Germany; but Lanny said: "I'm afraid, Charlot, you won't get so far, because you don't make so many promises to the workers."

"They tell the people falsehoods," said the young Frenchman, haughtily; "but we are men of honor."

"Ah, yes," sighed his old friend; "but how far does that go in politics?"

"In this corrupt republic, no distance at all; but we have set out to make France a home for men who mean what they say."

Lanny spoke no more. It made him sad to see his two foster sons —they were supposed to be something like that—going the road of Fascism; but there was nothing he could do about it. He knew that their mother had shared these tendencies. They were French pa-triots, and he couldn't make them internationalists, or what he called "good Europeans."

X

Having had such a dose of reaction, he had to have one of hope. He said to Irma: "I really ought to call on Léon Blum, and perhaps take him out to lunch. Would you care to come along?"

"But Lanny," she exclaimed, "what is this house for?"

"I didn't suppose you'd want to have him here."

"But dear, what kind of home will it be if you can't bring your friends?"

He saw that she was determined to be fair. He guessed that she had talked the matter out with the wise Emily, and was following the latter's program. If one's husband must have vices, let him have them at home, where they may be toned down .and kept within limits. After all, Léon Blum was the leader of the second largest political party in France; he was a scholar and a poet, and had once had a fortune. In the old days, as a young aesthete, he had been a frequenter of Emily's salon; now he had exchanged Marcel Proust for Karl Marx, but he remained a gentleman and a brilliant mind. Surely one might invite him to lunch, and even to dinner—if the company was carefully chosen. Emily herself would come; and Lanny knew from this that the matter had been discussed.

He took the good the gods had provided him. The Socialist leader sat in the same chair which Denis de Bruyne had filled, and maybe he felt some evil vibrations, for he spoke very sadly. In the midst of infinite corruption he was trying to believe in honesty; in the midst of wholesale cruelty he was trying to believe in kindness. The profit system, the blind competitive struggle for raw materials and markets, was wrecking civilization. No one nation could change this by itself; all must help, but someone must begin, and the voice of truth must be heard everywhere. Léon Blum spoke tirelessly in the Chamber, he wrote daily editorials for *Le Populaire*, he traveled here and there, pleading and explaining. He would do it at the luncheon table of a friend, and then stop and apologize, smiling and saying that politics ruined one's manners as well as one's character.

He was a tall slender man with the long slim hands of an artist; a thin, sensitive face, an abundant mustache which made him a joy to the caricaturists of the French press. He had been through campaigns of incredible bitterness; for to the partisans of the French right it was adding insult to injury when their foes put up a Jew as their spokesman. It made the whole movement of the workers a part of the international Jewish conspiracy, and lent venom to all Fascist attacks upon France. "Perhaps, after all, it is a mistake that I try to serve the cause," said the statesman.

He was ill content with the showing which his party had made at the polls. A gain of seventeen was not enough to save the day. He said that immediate and bold action was required if Europe was to be spared the horrors of another war. He said that the German Republic could not survive without generous help from France. He said that the "Cabinet of the Barons" was a natural answer to the cabinet of the bigot, Poincaré, and to that of the cheat, Laval. Blum was standing for real disarmament of all the nations, including France, and he had been willing to split his party rather than to yield on that issue. Said Irma, after the luncheon: "We won't ever invite him and the de Bruynes at the same time!"

XI

From the time her decision was taken to rent the palace, Irma's mind was occupied with the problem of a party which *tout Paris* would attend; a sort of housewarming—Lanny said that a building of that size, made of white marble, would require a lot of cordiality to affect its temperature. His wife wanted to think of something original. Parties were so much alike. People ate your food and drank your wine, often too much of it; they danced, or listened to a singer they had heard many times at the opera and been bored by. Lanny quoted an old saying: "Gabble, gobble, git."

Irma insisted that *tout Paris* would expect something streamlined and shiny from America. Couldn't they think of something? The husband tried various suggestions: a performing elephant from the circus, a troop of Arabian acrobats he had seen in a cabaret—their black hair was two feet long and when they did several somersaults in one leap they brought down the house. "Don't be silly, dear," said the wife.

He thought of an idea to end all ideas. "Offer a prize of a hundred thousand francs for the most original suggestion for a party. That will start them talking as nothing ever did." He meant it for burlesque, but to his amusement Irma was interested; she talked about it, speculating as to what sort of suggestions she would get, and so on; she wasn't satisfied until she had asked Emily, and been assured that it might be a good idea for Chicago, but not for Paris. Even after Irma dropped it, she had a hankering, and said: "I believe my father would have done it. He didn't let people frighten him away from things."

It would have to be a conventional soirée. The young Robins would come and play—a distinguished thing to furnish the talent from your own family, and have it the best. Fortunately the Paris newspapers did not report Communist doings—unless it was a riot or something—therefore few persons knew that Hansi had assisted in electing Zhess Block-léss to the Chamber of Deputies. (Already that body had met, and the new member, refusing to be intimidated by the splendid surroundings, had put on his old phonograph record, this time with a loud-speaker attachment, so that his threats against the *mur d'argent* had been heard as far as Tunisia and Tahiti, French Indo-China and Guiana.)

Lanny was fascinated to observe his young wife functioning in the role which she had chosen for herself. She was not yet twenty-four, but she was a queen, and had found out how queens conduct themselves. No worry, no strain, no sense of uncertainty. Being an American, she could without sacrifice of dignity ask the chef or the butler how things were done in France; then she would say whether or not they were going to be done that way in her home. She spoke with quiet decision, and the servants learned quickly to respect her; even the new *Contrôleur-Général* was impressed, and said to Lanny: "By heck, she's a whiz!"

When the great day arrived, she didn't get excited, like many hostesses, and wear herself out so that she couldn't enjoy her own triumph; no chain smoking of cigarettes, no coffee or nips of brandy to keep her going. Nor did she put responsibilities off on her mother or mother-in-law; that would be a bad precedent. She said: "This is my home, and I want to learn to run it." She had thought everything out, and had lists prepared; she summoned the servitors before her and checked off what had been done and gave them their final instructions. She had learned to judge them in two or three weeks. Jerry was a "brick," and anything he undertook was just as good as done. Ambroise, the butler, was conscientious, but had to be flattered; Simone, the housekeeper, was fidgety and lacking in authority; Feathers had always been a fool and would get rattled in any emergency. Having checked everything, Irma took a long nap in the afternoon.

At about nine in the evening the shiny limousines began rolling up before the palace, and a stream of immaculate guests ascended the white marble stairs, covered with a wide strip of red velvet carpet. It was the cream of that international society which made its headquarters in the world's center of fashion. Many of them had met Irma in New York or on the Riviera, in Berlin, London, Vienna, or Rome. Others were strangers, invited because of their position; they came because of curiosity as to a much-talked-about heiress. They would see what sort of show she put on, and were prepared to lift an eyebrow and whisper behind a fan over the slightest wrong detail.

But there wasn't much to quarrel with. The young Juno was good to look at, and the best artists had been put to work on her. The prevailing fashions favored her; they had gone back to natural lines, with high waists. The décolletage for backs was lower; in fact, where the back of the dress might have been there was nothing but Irma; but it was enough. Her dark brown hair was in masses of curls, and that looked young and wholesome. Her gown of pale blue silk chiffon appeared simple, but had cost a lot, and the same was true of her long rope of pearls.

The daughter of the utilities king was naturally kind; she liked people, and made them feel it. She did the honors with no visible coaching. She had taken the trouble to learn who people were, and if she had met them before, she remembered where, and had something friendly to say. If they were strangers, she assumed that they were welcoming her to Paris and thanked them for their courtesy. At her side stood a good-looking young fellow, *bon garçon*, son of his father—Budd Gunmakers, you know, quite a concern in America. In the background was a phalanx of older women: the two mothers, large and splendid, and Mrs. Chattersworth, whom everyone knew. In short, *tout comme il faut*, viewed by *tout le monde*.

XII

A modest-appearing young Jewish violinist came forward, and with his wife accompanying him played César Franck's violin sonata; French music, written in Paris by a humble organist and teacher who had lived obscurely among them until an omnibus had killed him; now they honored him, and applauded his interpreter. As an encore Hansi played Hubay's *Hejre Katy*, fiery and passionate; when they applauded again, he smiled and bowed, but did not play any more. His sister-in-law, Rahel Robin, whom nobody had ever heard of, came to the piano, and with Lanny Budd accompanying and her husband playing a clarinet obbligato, sang a couple of Provençal peasant songs which she herself had arranged. She had a pleasing voice, and it was a sort of homelike family affair; you wondered if they were showing themselves off, or if they were saving money.

Certainly they hadn't saved on the food and drink, and that is important at any party. In the ball-room a smart colored band played jazz, and in the other rooms the young wife and the young husband moved here and there, chatting with this one and that. Madame Hellstein, of the international banking-house, with her daughter Olivie, now Madame de Broussailles; Lanny had told his wife: "I might have married her, if Rosemary hadn't written me a note at the critical moment!" So, naturally, Irma was interested to look her over. A lovely daughter of Jerusalem—but she was growing stout! "These Jewish women all do," thought Irma.

And then one of Zaharoff's married daughters, who also had looked upon the son of Budd as a *parti*. And old M. Faure, rich importer of wines and olive-oil who had bought paintings of nude ladies from Zoltan. A traveling maharajah who bought ladies—but from another dealer! A Russian grand duke in exile; a crown prince from one of the Scandinavian lands; a couple of literary lions, so that you wouldn't appear to be snobbish. Lanny had been a dear and hadn't asked for any Reds or Pinks; they wouldn't appreciate the honor, he said.

Irma wasn't clever; but that is a quality for the "outs," whereas she was among the "ins." She was serene and gracious, and as she moved among this elegant company little shivers of happiness ran over her and she thought: "I am getting away with it; it is truly *distingué*"—this being one of the first French words she had learned. Lanny, thirty-two and world weary, thought: "How hard they all try to keep up a front and to be what they pretend!" He thought: "All the world's a stage, and all the men and women merely players"—these being among the first words of Shakespeare he had learned.

He knew much more about these players than his wife did. He had been hearing stories from his father and his business friends, from his mother and her smart friends, from his Red uncle, from Blum and Longuet and other Pinks. This lawyer for the Comité des Forges who had all the secrets of *la haute finance* hidden in his skull; this financier, paymaster for the big banks, who had half the members of the Radical party on his list; this publisher who had taken the Tsar's gold before the war and now was a director of Skoda and Schneider-Creusot! Who would envy these men their stage roles? The whole show was tolerable to the players only because of the things they didn't know, or which they thrust into the back of their minds. Lanny Budd, treading the boards, playing acceptably his part as prince consort, enjoyed it with one-half his mind, while the other half wondered: how many of his guests could bear to dance if they knew what would be happening to them ten years from now?

12

Pleasure at the Helm

I

*T*HE *Dress-Suit Bribe* was in rehearsal in London, and if Lanny could have had his own way, he would have been there to watch every moment. But Irma had her new white elephant on her hands, and had to get some use of it; several weeks would have to pass before she would feel justified in going away and leaving its staff of servants idle. Meanwhile, she must invite people to come, at any hour from noon to midnight. Supposedly she was doing it because she wanted to see them, but the real reason was that she wanted them to see her. And having offered them hospitality, she was under obligation to accept theirs; she would be forever on the go, attending social affairs or getting ready for future affairs.

Always she wanted company; and Lanny went along, because it had been his life's custom to do what he didn't want to do rather than to see a loved one disappointed and vexed. His wife was attaining her uttermost desire, she was standing on the apex of the social pyramid; and what could it mean to her to climb down and go off to London to watch a dozen actors and actresses rehearsing all day on an empty stage, the women in blouses and the men with their coats off on a hot day? The fact that one of these women was Phyllis Gracyn didn't increase her interest, and Lanny mustn't let it increase his too much!

He persuaded the young Robins to stay for a while; he much preferred their company to that of the fashionable folk. They would play music every morning, and at odd times when social duties permitted. Nothing was allowed to interfere with Hansi's violin practice; it was his task to master one great concert piece after another—which meant that he had to fix in his head hundreds of thousands of notes, together with his own precise way of rendering each one. Nobody who lived near him could keep from being touched by his extraordinary conscientiousness. Lanny wished he might have had some such purpose in his own life, instead of growing up an idler and waster. Too late now, of course; he was hopelessly spoiled!

II

Sitting in the fine library of the Duc de Belleaumont, filled with the stored culture of France, Lanny had a heart-to-heart talk with his half-sister, from whom he had been drifting apart in recent years. She was one who had expected great things of him, and had been disappointed. It wasn't necessary that he should agree with her, she insisted; it was only necessary that he should make up his mind about anything, and stick to it. Lanny thought that he had made up his mind as to one thing: that the Communist program, applied to the nations which had parliamentary institutions, was a tactical blunder. But it would be a waste of time to open up this subject to Bess.

She had something else she wanted to talk about: the unhappiness which was eating like a cancer into the souls of the members of the Robin family. They had become divided into three camps; each husband agreeing with his own wife, but with none of the other members of the family; each couple having to avoid mentioning any political or economic problem in the presence of the others. With affairs developing as they now were in Germany, that meant about every subject except music, art, and old-time books. Johannes read the *Börsenzeitung*, Hansi and Bess read the *Rote Fahne*, while Freddi and Rahel read *Vorwärts;* each couple hated the very sight of the other papers and wouldn't believe a word that was in them. Poor Mama, who read no newspaper and had only the vaguest idea what the controversy was about, had to serve as a sort of liaison officer among her loved ones.

There was nothing so unusual about this. Lanny had lived in disagreement with his own father for the greater part of his life; only it happened that they both had a sense of humor, and took it out in "joshing" each other. Jesse Blackless had left home because he couldn't agree with his father; now he never discussed politics with his sister, and always ended up in a wrangle with his nephew. The majority of radicals would tell you the same sort of stories; it was a part of the process of change in the world. The young outgrew their parents—or it might happen that leftist parents found themselves with conservative-minded children. "That will be my fate," opined the playboy.

In the Robin family the problem was made harder because all the young people took life so seriously; they couldn't pass things off with teasing remarks. To all four of them it seemed obvious that their father had enough money and to spare, and why in the name of Karl Marx couldn't he quit and get out of the filthy mess of business plus politics in which he wallowed? Just so the person who has never gambled cannot understand why the habitué hangs on, hell-bent upon making up his night's losses; the teetotaler cannot understand the perversity which compels the addict to demand one more nip. To Johannes Robin the day was a blank unless he made some money in it. To see a chance of profit and grab it was an automatic reflex; and besides, if you had money you had enemies trying to get it away from you, and you needed more of it in order to be really safe. Also you got allies and associates; you incurred obligations to them, and when a crisis came they expected you to play a certain part, and if you didn't you were a shirker. You were no more free to quit than a general is free to resign in the midst of a campaign.

The tragedy is that people have lovable qualities and objectionable ones, impossible to separate. Also, you have grown up with them, and have become attached to them; you may be under a debt of gratitude, impossible to repay. If the young Robins were to lay down the law: "Either you quit playing at *Gross Kapital* in Germany, or we move out of your palace and sail no more in your yacht"—they might have had their way. But how much would have been left of Johannes Robin? Where would they have taken him, and what would they have done with him? Lanny had put such pressure on his father in the matter of playing the stock market, and had got away with it. But in the case of Johannes it was much more; he would have had to give up everything he was doing, every connection, associate, and interest except his children and their affairs. Said Lanny to Bess: "Suppose he happened to dislike music, and thought the violin was immoral—what would you and Hansi do about it?"

"But nobody could think that, Lanny!"

"Plenty of our Puritan forefathers thought it; I've a suspicion that Grandfather thinks it right now. Very certainly he thinks it would be immoral to keep business men from making money, or to take away what they have made."

So Lanny, the compromiser, trying to soothe the young people, and persuade them that they could go on eating their food in the Berlin palace without being choked. Including himself, here were five persons condemned to dwell in marble halls—and outside were five millions, yes, five hundred millions, looking upon them as the most to be envied of all mortals! Five dwellers begging to be kicked out of their marble halls, and for some strange reason unable to persuade the envious millions to act! More than a century ago a poet, himself a child of privilege, had called upon them to rise like lions after slumber in unvanquishable number; but still the many slept and the few ruled, and the chains which were like dew retained the weight of lead!

III

The dowager queen of Vandringham-Barnes had gone down to Juan in order to be with the heir apparent. A dreadful thing had happened in America, something that sent a shudder of horror through every grandmother, mother and daughter of privilege in the civilized world. In the peaceful countryside of New Jersey a criminal or gang of them had brought a ladder and climbed into the home of the flyer Lindbergh and his millionaire wife, and had carried off the nineteen-month baby of this happy young couple. Ransom notes had been received and offers made to pay, but apparently the kidnapers had taken fright, and the body of the slain infant was found in a near-by wood. It happened that this ghastly discovery fell in the same week that the President of the French republic was shot down by an assassin who called himself a "Russian Fascist." The papers were full of the details and pictures of both these tragedies. A violent and dreadful world to be living in, and the rich and mighty ones shuddered and lost their sleep.

For a full generation Robbie Budd's irregular family had lived on the ample estate of Bienvenu and the idea of danger had rarely crossed their minds, even in wartime. But now it was hard to think about anything else, especially for the ladies. Fanny Barnes imagined kidnapers crouching behind every bush, and whenever the wind made the shutters creak, which happened frequently on the Côte d'Azur, she sat up and reached out to the baby's bed, which had been moved to her own room. Unthinkable to go on living in a one-story building, with windows open, protected only by screens which could be cut with a pocket-knife. Fanny wanted to take her tiny namesake to Shore Acres and keep her in a fifth-story room, beyond reach of any ladders. But Beauty said: "What about fire?" The two grandmothers were close to their first quarrel.

Lanny cabled his father, inquiring about Bub Smith, most dependable of bodyguards and confidential agents. He was working for the company in Newcastle, but could be spared, and Robbie sent him by the first steamer. So every night the grounds of Bienvenu would be patrolled by an ex-cowboy from Texas who could throw a silver dollar into the air and hit it with a Budd automatic. Bub had been all over France, doing one or another kind of secret work for the head salesman of Budd Gunmakers, so he knew the language of the people. He hired a couple of ex-poilus to serve as daytime guards, and from that time on the precious mite of life which was to inherit the Barnes fortune was seldom out of sight of an armed man. Lanny wasn't sure if it was a good idea, for of course all the Cap knew what these men were there for, and it served as much to advertise the baby as to protect her. But no use telling that to the ladies!

Bub came by way of Paris, so as to consult with Lanny and Irma.

He had always been a pal of Robbie's son, and now they had a confidential talk, in the course of which Bub revealed the fact that he had become a Socialist. A great surprise to the younger man, for Bub's jobs had been among the most hardboiled, and Bub himself, with his broken nose and cold steely eyes, didn't bear the appearance of an idealist. But he had really read the papers and the books and knew what he was talking about, and of course that was gratifying to the young employer. The man went down to the Cap and began attending the Socialist Sunday school in his free time, becoming quite a pal of the devoted young Spaniard, Raoul Palma.

That went on for a year or more before Lanny discovered what it was all about. The bright idea had sprung in the head of Robbie Budd—to whom anarchists, Communists, and kidnapers were all birds of a feather. Robbie had told Bub that this would be a quick and easy way to get in touch with the underworld of the Midi; so before stepping onto the steamer, Bub had got himself a load of Red literature, and all the way across had been boning up as if for a college entrance examination. He had "passed" with Lanny, and then with Raoul and the other comrades, who naturally had no suspicions of anybody coming from Bienvenu. It was somewhat awkward, because Bub was also maintaining relations with the French police; but Lanny didn't know just what to do about it. It was one more consequence of trying to live in the camps of two rival armies getting ready for battle.

IV

Hearing and thinking so much about the Lindbergh case had had an effect upon Irma's maternal impulses; she decided that she couldn't do any more traveling without having at least a glimpse of Baby. She proposed that they hop into the car and run down to Bienvenu—the weather was hot there, and they could have a swim, also. The young Robins hadn't seen Baby for more than a year; so come along! Hansi had been motored to Paris by Bess, in her car; now the couples "hopped" into two cars, and that evening were in Bienvenu, with Irma standing by the bedside of her sleeping darling, making little moaning sounds of rapture and hardly able to keep from waking the child.

The next two days she had a debauch of mother emotions, crowding everything into a short time. She didn't want anybody else to touch the baby; she washed her, dressed her, fed her, played with her, walked with her, talked to her, exclaimed over every baby word she managed to utter. It must have been bewildering to a twenty-seven-month child, this sudden irruption into her well-ordered life; but she took it serenely, and Miss Severne permitted some rules to be suspended for a brief period.

Lanny had another talk with Bub Smith, keeper of the queen's treasure and sudden convert to the cause of social justice. Bub reported on his experiences at the school, and expressed his appreciation of the work being done there; a group of genuine idealists, he said, and it was a source of hope for the future. Lanny found it a source of hope that an ex-cowboy and company guard should have seen the light and acknowledged his solidarity with the workers.

Also Bub told about conditions in Newcastle, where some kind of social change seemed impossible to postpone. There wasn't enough activity in those great mills to pay for the taxes and upkeep, and there was actual hunger among the workers. The people had mortgaged their homes, sold their cars, pawned their belongings; families had moved together to save rent; half a dozen people lived on the earnings of a single employed person. So many New Englanders were proud and wouldn't ask for charity; they just withdrew into a corner and starved. Impossible not to be moved by such distress, or to realize that something must be done to get that great manufacturing plant to work again.

Bub Smith had always been close to Robbie Budd, and so this change of mind appeared important. There was no secret about it, the man declared; he had told Mr. Robert how he felt, and Mr. Robert had said it would make no difference. Lanny thought that, too, was important; for some fifteen years or so he had been hoping that his father would see the light, and now apparently it was beginning to dawn. In a letter to Robbie he expressed his gratification; and Robbie must have had a smile!

V

The young people had their promised swim, diving off the rocks into that warm blue Mediterranean water. Afterward they sat on the shore and Bub lugged a couple of heavy boxes from the car, one containing Budd automatics and other weapons, the other containing several hundred rounds of ammunition. Bub had brought a liberal supply from Newcastle, enough to stave off a siege by all the bandits in France. He said the family ought to keep in practice, for they never knew when there might be an uprising of the Fascists or Nazis, and "we comrades" would be the first victims. He was shocked to learn that neither Hansi nor Freddi had ever fired a gun in his life, and hadn't thought of the possible need. The ex-guard wanted to know, suppose their revolution went wrong and the other side appeared to be coming out on top?

He showed them what he would propose to do about it. He threw a corked bottle far out into the water, then popped off the cork with one shot from an army service revolver. He threw out a block of wood and fired eight shots from a Budd .32 automatic, all in one quick whir, and not one of the shots struck the water; Bub admitted that that took a lot of practice, because the block jumped with every hit, and you had to know how far it would jump in a very small fraction of a second. He did it again to show them that it was no accident. He couldn't do it a third time, because the block of wood had so much lead in it that it sank.

Lanny couldn't perform stunts like that, but he was good enough to hit any Nazi, Bub said. All the targets were either Nazis or Fascists, for the guard had made up his mind that trouble was coming and no good fooling yourself. He wanted Hansi to learn to shoot, but Hansi said he would never use his bowing hand for such a nerve-shattering performance. Bess would have to protect him; she had learned to shoot when a child, and proved that she had not forgotten. Then it was Freddi's turn, and he tried it, but had a hard time keeping his eyes open when he pulled the trigger. The consequences of this pulling upon a Budd automatic were really quite alarming, and to a gentle-souled idealist it didn't help matters to imagine a member of the National Socialist German Workingmen's Party in the line of the sights.

Lanny, who had been used to guns all his life, had no idea of the effect of these performances upon two timid shepherd boys out of ancient Judea. Hansi declared that his music didn't sound right for a week afterward; while as for the younger brother, the experiment had produced a kind of moral convulsion in his soul. To be sure, he had seen guns being carried in Berlin and elsewhere by soldiers, policemen, S.S.'s and S.A.'s; but he had never held one in his hand, and had never realized the instantaneous shattering effect of an automatic. Calling the targets a portion of the human anatomy had been a joke to an ex-cowboy, but Freddi's imagination had been filled with images of mangled bodies, and he kept talking about it for some time afterward. "Lanny, do you really believe we are going to see another war? Do you think you can live through it?"

Freddi even talked to Fanny Barnes about the problem, wondering if it mightn't be possible to organize some sort of society to teach children the ideal of kindness, in opposition to the dreadful cruelty that was now being taught in Germany. The stately Queen Mother was touched by a young Jew's moral passion, but she feared that her many duties at home would leave her no time to organize a children's peace group in New York. And besides, wasn't Germany the country where it needed to be done?

VI

Fanny set up a great complaint concerning the heat at Bienvenu; she became exhausted and had to lie down and fan herself and have iced drinks brought to her. But Beauty Budd, that old Riviera hand, smiled behind her *embonpoint*, knowing well that this was one more effort—and she hoped the last—to carry Baby Frances away. Beauty took pleasure in pointing out the great numbers of brown and healthy babies on the beaches and the streets of Juan; she pointed to Lanny and Marceline as proof that members of the less tough classes could be raised here successfully. Baby herself had developed no rashes or "summer complaints," but on the contrary rollicked in the sunshine and splashed in the water, slept long hours, ate everything she could get hold of, and met with no worse calamity than having a toe nipped by a crab.

So the disappointed Queen Mother let her bags be packed and stowed in the trunk of Lanny's car, and herself and maid stowed in the back seat, from which she would do as much driving as her polite son-in-law would permit. On the evening of the following day they delivered her safely in London, and obtained for her a third-row seat on the aisle for the opening performance of *The Dress-Suit Bribe*, a play of which she wholly disapproved and did not hesitate to say so. Next day when most of the London critics agreed with her, she pointed out that fact to the author, who, being thirty-four years of age, ought to have sowed his literary wild oats and begun to realize the responsibilities he owed to his class which had built the mighty British Empire. The daughter of the Vandringhams and daughter-in-law of the Barneses was as Tory as the worst "diehard" in the House of Lords, and when she encountered a propagandist of subversion she wanted to say, in the words of another famous queen: "Off with her head!"—or with "his."

But not all the audience agreed with her point of view. The house divided horizontally; from the stalls came frozen silence and from the galleries storms of applause. The critics divided in the same way; those with a pinkish tinge hailed the play as an authentic picture of the part which fashionable society was playing in politics, an indictment of that variety of corruption peculiar to Britain, where privileges which would have to be paid for in cash in France or with office in America, go as a matter of hereditary right or of social prestige. In any case it was power adding to itself, "strength aiding still the strong."

It was the kind of play which is automatically labeled propaganda and therefore cannot be art. But it was written from inside

knowledge of the things which were going on in British public life
and it told the people what they needed to know. From the first
night the theater became a battleground, the high-priced seats were
only half filled but the cheap ones were packed, and Rick said:
"It's a question whether we can pay the rent for two or three
weeks, until it has a chance to take hold."

Lanny replied: "We'll pay, if I have to go and auction off some
pictures." No easy matter raising money with hard times spreading
all over the world; but he telephoned all the fashionable people
he knew, begging them to see the play, and he cajoled Margy,
Dowager Lady Eversham-Watson, to have a musicale and pay the
Robin family a couple of hundred pounds to come and perform:
the money to go for the play. Irma "chipped in," even though
in her heart she didn't like the play. As for Hansi, he wrote to his
father, who put five hundred pounds to his son's credit with his
London bankers—a cheap and easy way to buy peace in his family,
and to demonstrate once again how pleasant it is to have money,
heigh ho!

In one way or another they kept the play going. Gracyn, to
whom it gave such a "fat" part, offered to postpone taking her
salary for two weeks. Lanny wrote articles for the labor papers,
pointing out what the production meant to the workers, and so
they continued to attend and cheer. The affair grew into a scandal,
which forced the privileged classes to talk about it, and then to
want to know what they were talking about. In the end it turned
out that Eric Vivian Pomeroy-Nielson had a "hit"—something he
had been aiming at for more than ten years. He insisted on paying
back all his friends, and after that he paid off some of the mort-
gages of "the Pater," who had been staking him for a long time.
The main thing was that Rick had managed to say something to
the British people, and had won a name so that he would be able
to say more.

VII

The Robins were begging the Budds to take a little run into
Germany. Yachting time was at hand, and they had persuaded

Papa to put the *Bessie Budd* into commission again; they wanted so much to get him away from the worries of business—and who could do it so well as the wonderful Lanny Budd and his equally wonderful wife? Lanny might even be able to persuade him to retire for good; or perhaps to take a long cruise around the world, where he couldn't be reached by friends or foes.

Germany was in the midst of a hot election campaign. A new Reichstag was being chosen; the "Cabinet of the Barons," otherwise known as the "Monocle Cabinet," was asking for popular support. Elections were always interesting to Lanny, and the young people urged him to come and see. But Irma had another maternal seizure; she said "Let's run down to Juan again, and come back for a cruise at the end of the campaign." Lanny said: "Any way you want it."

So the party broke up. Fanny took a steamer to New York, the Robins took the ferry to Flushing, and the Budds took one to Calais. They sent a telegram to the palace in Paris, and dinner was ready when they arrived. Irma observed: "It's nice to have your own place; much nicer than going to a hotel." Lanny saw that she wished to justify herself for having spent all that money, so he admitted that it was "nicer." Jerry was there, and with a lot of checks ready for her to sign; he wanted her to go over the accounts, but she was sure they were all right, and she signed without looking. The three went to a cabaret show, very gay, with music and dancing and a scarcity of costumes; some of it made Irma blush, but she was trying to acquire the cosmopolitan tone.

The following evening they were at Bienvenu again. Baby was bigger and brighter; she knew more words; she remembered what you had taught her. She was growing a mind! "Oh, Lanny, come see this, come see that!" Lanny would have been glad to settle down to child study, and to swimming and target-shooting with Bub, and talking to the workers at the school; but they had made a date with the Robins; and also there came a letter from Pietro Corsatti, who was at Lausanne, reporting the conference for his paper. He said: "A great show! How come you're missing it?"

At this time there were two of Europe's international talk-fests being held on the same Swiss lake. For many years such gatherings had been Lanny's favorite form of diversion; he had attended a dozen, and had met all the interesting people, the statesmen and writers, the reformers and cranks. Irma had never been to one, but had heard him tell about them, and always in glowing terms. Now he proposed: "Let's stop off on our way to Berlin."

"O.K. by me!" said Irma.

VIII

They followed the course of the River Rhone, every stage of which had some memory of Marie de Bruyne: the hotels where she and Lanny had stopped, the scenery they had admired, the history they had recalled. But Lanny judged it better for Irma to have her own memories, unscented by the perfume of any other woman. They climbed into the region of pine-trees and wound through rocky gorges where the air was still and clear. Many bridges and a great dam, and it was Lake Leman, with Geneva, home of the League of Nations, an institution which for a few years had been the hope of mankind, but now appeared to have fallen victim to a mysterious illness. Since the beginning of the year a great Conference on Arms Limitation, with six hundred delegates from thirteen nations, had been meeting here, and was to continue for a year longer; each nation in turn would bring forward a plea to limit the sort of weapon which it didn't have or didn't need, and then the other nations would show what was wrong with that plan.

Farther up the lake was Lausanne, where the premiers and foreign ministers were gathered to debate the ancient question of reparations. Lanny Budd greeted his friend Pete and other journalists whom he had been meeting off and on since the great peace conference thirteen summers ago. They remembered him and were glad to see him; they knew about his gold-embossed wife and her palace in Paris; they knew about Rick and his play. Here was another show, and a fashionable young couple was taken right behind the scenes.

Lausanne is built on a mountainside, with each street at a different level. The French had a hotel at the top, the British one at the bottom, and the other nations in between; the diplomats ascended or descended to have their wrangles in one another's suites, and the newspapermen wore themselves thin chasing the various controversies up hill and down. Such, at any rate, was Corsatti's description. The statesmen were trying to keep their doings secret, and Pete declared that when one saw you he dived into his hole like a woodchuck. Your only chance was to catch one of them in swimming.

It was good clean fun, if you were a spectator who liked to hear gossip and ferret out mysteries, or a devil-may-care journalist with an expense account which you padded freely. The food was of the best, the climate delightful, the scenery ditto, with Mont Blanc right at your back door—or so it seemed in the dustless Alpine air. You would be unhappy only if you thought about the millions of mankind whose destiny was being gambled with by politicians. The gaming-table was a powder-keg as big as all the Alps, and the players had no thought but to keep their own country on top, their own class on top within their country, and their own selves on top within their class.

IX

The statesmen had to drop the Young Plan, by which Germany had been bound to pay twenty-five billion dollars in reparations. But France couldn't give up the hope of getting something; so now with incessant wrangling they were adopting a plan whereby at the end of three years Germany was to give bonds for three billion marks. But most observers agreed that this was pure futility; Germany was borrowing, not paying. Germany was saying to the bankers of the United States: "We have five billions of your money, and if you don't save us you will lose it all!" The people of Germany were saying: "If you don't feed us we shall vote for Hitler, or worse yet for Thälmann, the Bolshevik." The statesmen of Germany were saying: "We are terrified about what will happen"—and who could say whether they were really terrified or only pretending? Who could trust anybody in power, anywhere in all the world?

Robbie Budd had told his son a story, which he said all business men knew. A leather merchant went to his banker to get his notes renewed and the banker refused to comply with the request. The leather merchant told his troubles and pleaded hard; at last he asked: "Were you ever in the leather business?" When the banker replied: "No," the other said: "Well, you're in it now." And that, opined Pietro Corsatti, was the position of the investing public of the United States; they were in the leather business in Germany, in the steel and coal and electrical and chemical businesses, to say nothing of the road-building business and the swimming-pool business. Nor was it enough to renew the notes; it was necessary to put up working capital to keep these businesses from falling into ruins and their workers from turning Red!

Irma knew that this was the "great world" in which her career was to be carried on, so she listened to the gossip and learned all she could about the eminent actors in the diplomatic drama. Lanny had met several of the under-secretaries, and these realized that the wealthy young couple were entitled to be introduced to the "higher ups." Irma was told that next winter would probably see more negotiations in Paris, and it was her intention that these important personages should find her home a place for relaxation and perhaps for private conferences. Emily herself couldn't have done better.

Lanny observed his wife "falling for" the British ruling class. Many Americans did this; it was a definite disease, known as "Anglomania." Upper-class Englishmen were tall and good-looking, quiet and soft-spoken, cordial to their friends and reserved to others; Irma thought that was the right way to be. There was Lord Wickthorpe, whom Lanny had once met on a tally-ho coach driving to Ascot; they had both been youngsters, but now Wickthorpe was a grave diplomat, carrying a brief-case full of responsibility— or so he looked, and so Irma imagined him, though Lanny, who had been behind many scenes, assured her that the sons of great families didn't as a rule do much hard work. Wickthorpe was divinely handsome, with a tiny light brown mustache, and Irma said: "How do you suppose such a man could remain a bachelor?"

"I don't know," said the husband. "Margy can probably tell you. Maybe he couldn't get the girl he wanted."

"I should think any girl would have a hard time refusing what he has."

"It can happen," replied Lanny. "Maybe they quarrel, or something goes wrong. Even the rich can't always get what they want." Lanny's old "Pink" idea!

X

The assembled statesmen signed a new treaty of Lausanne, in which they agreed to do a number of things, now that it was too late. Having signed and sealed, they went their various ways, and Irma and Lanny motored out of Switzerland by way of Basle, and before dinner-time were in Stuttgart. A bitterly fought election campaign had covered the billboards with slogans and battle-cries of the various parties. Lanny, who got hold of a newspaper as soon as he arrived anywhere, read the announcement of a giant *Versammlung* of the Nazis to be held that evening, the principal speaker being that Reich Organization Leader Number One who had received such a dressing-down from his Führer in Lanny's presence some twenty months ago. Lanny remarked: "I'd like to hear what he's saying now."

"Oh, dear!" exclaimed Irma. "Such a bore!" But she didn't want to be left in a hotel room alone, so she said: "Let's not stay too late."

During those twenty months a Franco-American playboy had been skipping over the world with the agility conferred by railroads and motor-cars, airplanes, steamships, and private yachts. He had been over most of western Europe, England, and New England. He had read books on many subjects, he had played thousands of musical compositions, looked at as many paintings, been to many theaters, danced in many ball-rooms, and swum in many seas; he had chatted with his friends and played with his baby, eaten the choicest of foods, drunk the best wines, and enjoyed the love of a beautiful and fashionable wife. In short, he had had the most delightful sort of life that the average man could imagine.

But meantime the people of Germany had been living an utterly different life; doing hard and monotonous labor for long hours at low wages; finding the cost of necessities creeping upward and insecurity increasing, so that no man could be sure that he and his family were going to have their next day's bread. The causes of this state of affairs were complex and hopelessly obscure to the average man, but there was a group which undertook to make them simple and plain to the dullest. During the aforementioned twenty months the customs official's son from Austria, Adi Schicklgruber, had been skipping about even more than Lanny Budd, using the same facilities of railroad trains and motor-cars and airplanes. But he hadn't been seeking pleasure; he had been living the life of an ascetic, vegetarian, and teetotaler, devoting his fanatical energies to the task of convincing the German masses that their troubles were due to the Versailles *Diktat*, to the envious foreigners who were strangling the Fatherland, to the filthy and degraded Jews, and to their allies the international bankers and international Reds.

Say the very simplest and most obvious things, say them as often as possible, and put into the saying all the screaming passion which one human voice can carry—that was Adolf Hitler's technique. He had been applying it for thirteen years, ever since the accursed treaty had been signed, and now he was at the climax of his efforts. He and his lieutenants were holding hundreds of meetings every night, all over Germany, and it was like one meeting; the same speech, whether it was a newspaper print or cartoon or signboard or phonograph record. No matter whether it was true or not—for Adi meant literally his maxim that the bigger the falsehood, the easier to get it believed; people would say you wouldn't dare make up a thing like that. Imagine the worst possible about your enemies and then swear that you knew it, you had seen it, it was God's truth and you were ready to stake your life upon it—shout this, bellow this, over and over, day after day, night after night. If one person states it, it is nonsense, but if ten thousand join in it becomes an indictment, and when ten million join in it becomes history. The

Jews kill Christian children and use their blood as a part of their religious ritual! You refuse to believe it? But it is a well-known fact; it is called "ritual murder." The Jews are in a conspiracy to destroy Christian civilization and rule the whole world. It has all been completely exposed in the *Protocols of the Elders of Zion;* the party has printed these, the Führer has guaranteed their authenticity, the great American millionaire Henry Ford has circulated them all over America. Everybody there knows that the charges are true, the whole world knows it—save only the Jew-lovers, the Jew-kissers, the filthy Jew-hirelings. *Nieder mit den Juden!*

XI

So here was another huge mass meeting, such crowds that you could hardly get in, and two rich Americans having to climb to distant seats in a gallery. But it was all right, for there were loudspeakers, a wonderful device whereby one small figure on a platform could have the voice of a score of giants, while a dissenter became a pigmy, uttering a squeak like a mouse. The radio was a still more marvelous invention; that feeble little "crystal set" with earphones which Robbie Budd had brought to Bienvenu ten years ago had become the most dominating of psychological forces, whereby one man could indoctrinate a hundred million. Learned technicians of the mind had evolved methods of awakening curiosity, so that the millions would listen; and no matter how much anyone disagreed, he was powerless to answer back. The dream of every dictator was to get exclusive control of that colossal instrument, so that never again in all history would it be possible to answer back. Then what you said would become the truth and the only truth—no matter how false it might have been previously! He who could get and hold the radio became God.

Once more Lanny observed the application of the art of moving the mass mind. Adolf Hitler taught that the masses did not think with their brains but with their blood; that is to say, they did not reason but were driven by instincts. The most basic instinct was the desire to survive and the fear of not surviving; therefore Adolf

Hitler told them that their enemies desired to destroy them and that he alone could and would save them; he told them that they were the *Herrenvolk*, the master race, designed by nature to survive and to rule all other races of the earth. The second basic instinct was hunger, and they had suffered it, and he promised them that under his leadership Germany would break into the storehouses of the world's plenty; the Fatherland would have *Lebensraum*, the space in which to expand and grow. The third basic instinct is sex, and he told them that they were destined to populate the earth, and that every pure-blooded Aryan *Mädchen* was the predestined mother of blond heroes; that was what she was created for, and no permission was needed for her to begin; a wise Fatherland would provide for her care and give all honor to her and her offspring.

All these instincts added up into pride and victory over the foes of Germany. "*Sieg Heil!*" they shouted; and the party had invented an elaborate ritual to embody these concepts and to thrill the dullest soul. At the futile Beerhall Putsch which Lanny had witnessed in Munich there had been carried banners, and these banners had been riddled with bullets and stained with the blood of martyrs; that made them holy, and Adolf Hitler had carried them all over Germany, and upon public platforms had performed the ceremony of touching the new banners with the old; that made all the Nazi banners holy, and worthy of being stained with the blood of martyrs. So now when they were carried all hearts beat high, and all good party members longed for a chance to become martyrs and have a new *Horst Wessel Lied* sung about them. Shrill trumpets proclaimed the entry of these banners, drums beat and fifes shrilled and a bodyguard of heroes marched into the hall with faces solemn and grim.

To the speakers' platform ascended large, heavy Gregor Strasser; not humbled and browbeaten as Lanny had last seen him, but bursting with assurance of power. He was one of the original party leaders, and had helped Adolf to keep alive in the early days. He had believed in the early program with all its promises for the overthrow of the rich and the setting up of the disinherited. Did he believe in them still, when he knew that the Führer no longer meant them? You could never have guessed it from listening to his speech, for he seemed to have but one rule: to think of everything that ten thousand Württembergers could possibly want, and promise it to them, to be delivered on the day when they would elect the candidates of the N.S.D.A.P.

Lanny said: "That's surely the way to get out the vote!"

Irma, who didn't understand what the orator was promising, and had to judge by gestures and tones, remarked: "It is surprising how much like Uncle Jesse he sounds."

"Don't let either of them hear that!" chuckled the husband.

XII

It was a political campaign of frenzied hate, close to civil war. Troops of armed men marched, glaring at other troops when they passed, and ready to fly at the others' throats; in the working class districts they did so, and bystanders had to flee for their lives. The conservatives, who called themselves Democrats and Nationalists, had their *Stahlhelm* and their *Kampfring*, the Nazis had their S.S.'s and S.A.'s, the Sozis had their *Reichsbanner*, and the Communists their *Rotfront*, although the last named were forbidden to wear uniforms. The posters and cartoons, the flags and banners, all had symbols and slogans expressive of hatred of other people, whether Germans of the wrong class, or Russians, French, Czechs, Poles, or Jews. Impossible to understand so many kinds of hatreds or the reasons for them. Irma said: "It's horrible, Lanny. Let's not have any more to do with it."

She had met charming people in Berlin, and now Johannes gave her a reception, and they all came; when they found that she didn't like politics they said they didn't blame her, and talked about the music festivals, the art exhibitions, the coming yacht regattas. The Jewish money-lord tried to keep friendly with everybody, and he knew that many who would not ordinarily darken his door were willing to come when a celebrated American heiress was his guest. According to his custom, he did not try to hide this, but on the contrary made a point of mentioning it and thanking her. She knew that this Jewish family had risen in the world with the help of the Budds; but so long as they showed a proper gratitude and didn't develop a case of "swelled head," it was all right for the help to continue.

German big business men came, and their wives, still bigger as a rule. German aristocrats came, tall, stiff gentlemen wearing monocles, and their *Damen* who seemed built for the stage of Bayreuth. All had long titles, and left off none of the *vons* and *zus;* Irma had trouble in telling Herr vons from Herr Barons, Herr Grafen from Erlauchts, and Erlauchts from Durchlauchts.

Graf Stubendorf came, reported on affairs at home, and cordially renewed his invitation for next Christmas, or for the shooting season earlier. The new Chancellor came; tall and thin-faced, the smartest of diplomats and most elegant of Catholic aristocrats, he lived entangled in a net of intrigue of his own weaving. A son of the Russian ghetto might have been overwhelmed by the honor of such a presence, but Johannes took it as the payment of a debt. The gentlemen of the fashionable Herren Klub hadn't been able to raise enough money to save their party, so the Chancellor had had to come to the Jew for help.

Irma found him charming, and told her husband, who remarked: "There is no greater rascal in all Europe. Franz von Papen was put out of the United States before we entered the war because he was financing explosions in munitions plants."

"Oh, darling!" she exclaimed. "You say such horrid things! You can't really know that!"

Said the young Pink: "He didn't have sense enough to burn his check-stubs, and the British captured his ship on the way home and published all the data."

13

Even to the Edge of Doom

I

THE cruise of the *Bessie Budd* began. Not a long cruise, never more than a week at a time in these disturbed days. They stopped to fish and swim, and they sent out upon the North Sea breezes a great deal of romantic and delightful music. The seamen and the fishermen who glided by in the night must have been moved to wonder, and perhaps some young Heine among them took flight upon the wings of imagination. Far on the Scottish rock-coast, where the little gray castle towers above the raging sea, there, at the high-arched window, stands a beautiful frail woman, tender-pellucid and marble-pale, and she plays the harp and sings, and the wind sweeps through her long tresses and carries her dark song over the wide storming sea.

Resting from such flights of fancy the solicitous Lanny Budd had quiet talks with his host, hoping by gentle and tactful intervention to lessen the strain of that family conflict which had been revealed to him. Johannes explained, in much the same words that Robbie Budd had used when Lanny was a small boy, that the business man did not think merely of the money he was making or might make; he acquired responsibilities to thousands of investors, not all of them greedy idlers, but many aged persons, widows, and orphans having no means of support but their shares of stock; also to workingmen whose families starved unless the weekly pay envelopes were filled. It was a libel upon business administrators to suppose that they had no sense of duties owed to other people, even though most of these people were strangers.

"Moreover," said Johannes, "when a man has spent his life learn-

255

ing to pursue a certain kind of activity, it is no easy matter to
persuade him to drop it at the height of his powers. Difficulties,
yes; but he has expected them, and takes them as a challenge, he
enjoys coping with them and showing that he can master them. To
give up and run away from them is an act of cowardice which
would undermine his moral foundations; he would have no use for
himself thereafter, but would spend his time brooding, like an admiral who veered about and deserted his fleet.

"My children have their own moral code," continued the money
master, "and they have the task of convincing me that it applies
to my case. They wish to build a new and better world, and I would
be glad if they could succeed, and if I saw any hope of success
I would join them. I ask for their plans, and they offer me vague
dreams, in which as a man of affairs I see no practicality. It is like
the end of *Das Rheingold:* there is Valhalla, very beautiful, but only
a rainbow bridge on which to get to it, and while the gods may
be able to walk on a rainbow, my investors and working people
cannot. My children assure me that a firmer bridge will be constructed, and when I ask for the names of the engineers, they offer
me party leaders and propagandists, speechmakers who cannot
even agree among themselves; if it were not for what they call
the capitalist police they would fall to fighting among themselves
and we should have civil war instead of Utopia. How can my
two boys expect me to agree with them until they have at least
managed to agree between themselves?"

Lanny was sad to have no answer to this question. He had already
put it to his sister, and she could say only that she and her husband
were right, while Freddi and Rahel were wrong. No use putting
the question to the other pair, for their answer would be the same.
Neither couple was going to give way—any more than Lanny
himself was going to give up his conviction that it was the program of the Communists which had caused the development of
Fascism and Nazism—or at any rate had made possible its spread
in Italy and Germany. Only in the Scandinavian and Anglo-Saxon
lands, where democratic institutions were firmly rooted, had neither
Reds nor anti-Reds been able to make headway.

II

So there wasn't any chance of persuading Johannes Robin to retire to a monastery or even to a private yacht right now. He didn't pretend to know what was going to happen in Germany, but he knew that these were stormy times and that he, the admiral, would stand by his fighting fleet. He would protect his properties and keep his factories running; and if, in order to get contracts and concessions it was necessary to make a present to some powerful politician, Johannes would bargain shrewdly and pay no more than he had to. That had been the way of the world since governments had first been invented, and a Jewish trader, an exile barely tolerated in a strange land, had to be satisfied with looking out for his own. His sons felt more at home in Germany and dreamed of trying to change it; but for the child of the ghetto it was enough that he obeyed the law. "Not very noble," he admitted, sadly; "but when the nobler ones come to me for help, they get it."

The world was in a bad way and getting worse. Banks were failing all over the United States, and unemployment increasing steadily. A presidential election was due in November, and the political parties had held their conventions and made their nominations; the Republicans had endorsed the Great Engineer and all that he had done, while the Democrats nominated the Governor of New York, Franklin Roosevelt by name. Johannes asked if Lanny knew anything about this man, and Lanny said no; but when the yacht picked up some mail, there was Robbie's weekly letter, a cross between a business man's report and one of the lamentations of Jeremiah. Robbie said that the Democratic candidate was a man wholly without business experience, and moreover an invalid, his legs shriveled by infantile paralysis. Surely these times called for one at least physically sound; the presidency was a man-killing job, and this Roosevelt, if elected, couldn't survive it for a year. But he wasn't going to be elected, for Robbie and his friends were pulling off their coats, to say nothing of opening their purses.

"I suppose Robbie will be asking you for a contribution!" chuckled the irreverent son, and the other replied: "I have many

interests in America." Lanny recalled the remark he had once heard
Zaharoff make: "I am a citizen of every country where I have
investments."

III

They discussed conditions in Germany, living on borrowed capital and sliding deeper and deeper into the pit. The existing government had no popular support, but was run by the Herren Klub,
an organization of big business men, aristocrats, and "office generals," having some twenty branches throughout Germany. Its two
most active politicians were Chancellor von Papen and General von
Schleicher, and they were supposed to be colleagues, but neither
could trust the other out of his sight. Now Papen was in office, and
Schleicher was trading secretly with the Nazis for their support
to turn him out. Nobody could trust anybody, except the eighty-
five-year-old monument of the Junkerdom, General von Hindenburg. Poor *alte Herr*, when the burdens of state were dumped upon
him he could only answer: *"Ich will meine Ruhe haben!"*—I must
have my rest.

Johannes judged it certain that the Nazis would make heavy
gains at the coming elections, but he refused to worry about this.
He had several of them on his payroll, but what he counted upon
most was the fact that Hitler had gone to Düsseldorf and had a
long session with Thyssen and other magnates of the Ruhr. They
wanted the Red labor unions put down, and Hitler had satisfied
them that he was ready to do the job. You might fool one or two
of those tough steel-men, but not many; they knew politicians, and
dealt with one crop after another; it was part of the game of conducting industry in a world full of parliaments and parties. A
nuisance, but you learned to judge men and saw to it that none
got into power who couldn't be trusted. The same thing applied to
the great landlords of Prussia; they wanted above all things a bulwark against Bolshevism, and were willing to pay a heavy price
for that service. These two powers, the industrialists of the west and
the landed gentry of the east, had governed Germany since the
days of Bismarck and would go on doing so.

"But aren't you afraid of Hitler's anti-Semitism?" asked Lanny.

"*Herrgott!*" exclaimed the owner of the *Bessie Budd*. "I was brought up in the midst of pogroms, and what could I do then? It is said that there once lived a Jew called Jesus, and other Jews had him executed by the Romans; such things happened ten thousand times, no doubt; but because of this one time my poor people have to be spat upon and clubbed and stabbed to death. What can any of us do, except to pray that it will not break out in the street where we live?"

"But they threaten it wholesale, Johannes!"

"It is a means of getting power in a world where people are distracted and must have some one to blame. I can only hope that if ever the Nazis come into office they will have real problems to deal with, so that the spotlight will be turned away from my unfortunate people."

IV

Irma had voted to keep out of German political affairs, but that couldn't be arranged entirely. There was the workers' school, in which Freddi was so deeply interested, and which had been more or less modeled upon Lanny's own project. When they came back to Berlin Lanny's wife played bridge while he went with Freddi and Rahel to a reception at which he met the teachers and friends of the enterprise, heard its problems discussed, and told them how things were going in the Midi.

In his way of thinking Lanny was nearer to these young Socialists than to any other group; yet what a variety of opinion there was among them, and how difficult to get them together on any program of action! A few days before the election the von Papen government had effected a *coup d'état* in the state of Prussia, which includes Berlin; the premier and the principal officials, all Social-Democrats, were turned out of office and threatened with arrest if they attempted to resist—which they did so feebly that it amounted to submission. As a result, the Socialists were buzzing like a swarm of bees whose hive has been upset; but alas, they appeared to be bees which had lost their stingers! The Communists had proposed a general strike of the workers and called upon the Socialists to co-operate with them; but how could anybody co-operate with Communists? They would take advantage of an uprising to seize the reins themselves; they would turn upon their allies as they had done with Kerensky in Russia. The Socialists were more in fear of the Communists than of the reactionaries; they were afraid of acting like Communists, of looking like Communists, of being called Communists.

So the Cabinet of the Barons seized control of the Berlin police and all the other powers of the local government. How different it had been twelve years ago during the "Kapp Putsch"! Then the workers hadn't waited for their leaders, they had known instantly what to do—drop their tools and come into the streets and show their power. But now, apparently, they had lost interest in the Republic. What good had it done them these twelve years? It couldn't prevent hard times and unemployment, it couldn't even make promises any more! It was so chained by its own notions of legality that it couldn't resist the illegality of others.

Lanny listened to the discussions of these Berlin intellectuals. They came from all classes, brought together by community of ideas. They had the keenest realization of danger to the cause of freedom and social justice. They all wanted to do something; but first they had to agree what to do, and apparently they couldn't; they talked and argued until they were exhausted. Lanny wondered, is this a disease which afflicts all intellectuals? Is it a paralysis which accompanies the life of the mind? If so, then it must be that the thinkers will be forever subject to the men of brute force, and Plato's dream of a state ruled by philosophers will remain forever vain.

Lanny thought: "Somebody ought to lead them!" He wanted to say: "My God, it may be settled this very night. Your republic will be dead! Let's go now, and call the workers out!" But then he thought: "What sort of a figure would I cut, taking charge of a German revolution? I, an American!" He settled back and listened to more arguments, and thought: "I'm like all the others. I'm an intellectual, too! I happen to own some guns, and know how to use them—but I wouldn't!"

V

There was a teacher of art at the school, by name Trudi Schultz, very young, herself a student at an art school, but two or three evenings a week she came to impart what she knew to the workers, most of them older than herself. She was married to a young commercial artist who worked on a small salary for an advertising concern and hated it. Both Trudi and Ludi Schultz were that perfect Aryan type which Adolf Hitler lauded but conspicuously was not; the girl had wavy fair hair, clear blue candid eyes, and sensitive features which gave an impression of frankness and sincerity. Lanny watched her making sketches on a blackboard for her class, and it seemed to him that she had an extraordinary gift of line; she drew something, then wiped it out casually, and he hated to see it go.

She was pleased by his interest and invited him to come and see her work. So, on another evening while Irma played bridge, Lanny drove Freddi and Rahel to a working class quarter of the city where the young couple lived in a small apartment. Lanny inspected a mass of crayon drawings and a few water-colors, and became interested in what he believed was a real talent. This girl drew what she saw in Berlin; but she colored it with her personality. Like Jesse Blackless she loved the workers and regarded the rich with moral disapprobation; that made her work "propaganda," and hard to sell. But Lanny thought it ought to appeal to the Socialist press and offered to take some with him and show it to Léon Blum and Jean Longuet. Of course the Schultzes were much excited—for they had heard about Lanny's having selected old masters for the palace of Johannes Robin, and looked upon the wealthy young American as a power in the art world.

Lanny, for his part, was happy to meet vital personalities in the workers' movement. More and more he was coming to think of art as a weapon in the social struggle, and here were young people who shared his point of view and understood instantly what he said.

He had traveled to many far places, while they knew only Berlin and its suburbs and the countryside where they sometimes had walking trips; yet they had managed to get the same meaning out of life. More and more the modern world was becoming one; mass production was standardizing material things, while the class struggle was shaping the minds and souls of workers and masters. Lanny had watched Fascism spread from Italy to Germany, changing its name and the color of its shirts, but very little else; he heard exactly the same arguments about it here in Berlin as in Paris, the Midi, and the Rand School of Social Science in New York.

These five young people, so much alike in their standards and desires, talked out of their hearts in a way that Lanny had not had a chance to do for some time. All of them were tormented by fears of what was coming in Europe, and groping to determine their own duty in the presence of a rising storm of reaction. What were the causes of the dreadful paralysis which seemed to have fallen upon the workers' movement of the world?

Trudi Schultz, artist-idealist, thought that it was a failure of moral forces. She had been brought up in a Marxist household, but was in a state of discontent with some of the dogmas she had formerly taken as gospel; she had observed that dialectical material-ism didn't keep people from quarreling, from being jealous, vindic-tive, and narrow-minded. Socialists talked comradeship, but too often they failed in the practice of it, and Trudi had decided that more than class consciousness was needed to weld human beings into a social unity.

Freddi Robin, who had a scholar's learning in these matters, ven-tured the opinion that the identification of Social-Democracy with philosophic materialism was purely accidental, due to the fact that both had originated in nineteenth-century Germany. There was no basic connection between the two, and now that modern science had moved away from the old dogmatic notion of a physical atom as the building material of all existence, it was time for the Socialists to find themselves a philosophy which justified creative effort and moral purpose.

The eager girl student was glad to hear someone say that, in the long philosophical terms which made it sound right to a German. She said that she had observed this error working in everyday life. Men who preached that matter and force were the bases of life, the sole reality, were tempted to apply this dogma in their own lives; when they got a little power they thought about keeping it, and forgot their solidarity with the humble toilers. People had to believe in moral force, they had to let love count in the world, they had to be willing to make sacrifices of their own comfort, their own jobs and salaries, yes, even their lives, if need be. It was lack of that living spirit of brotherhood and solidarity which had made it possible for Otto Braun, Social-Democratic Premier of the Prussian state, and Karl Severing, Minister of the Interior, to bow to the threats of monocled aristocrats, and slink off to their villas without making the least effort to rouse the people to defend their republic and the liberties it guaranteed them.

Lanny thought: "Here, at last, is a German who understands what freedom means!"

VI

On a Sunday, the last day of July, more than thirty-seven million citizens of the German Republic, both men and women, went to the polls and registered their choice for deputies to represent them in the Reichstag. As compared with the elections of two years previously, the Socialists lost some six hundred thousand votes, the Communists gained as many, while the Nazis increased their vote from six and a half million to fourteen million. They elected two hundred and thirty deputies out of a total of six hundred and eight—outnumbering the Socialists and Communists, even if combined, which they wouldn't. So from then on it became impossible for anyone to govern Germany without Adolf Hitler's consent.

There began a long series of intrigues and pulling of wires behind the scenes. Johannes would report events to Lanny, and also to Lanny's father, who had come over for a conference with his associate and went for a short cruise on the *Bessie Budd*. The politicians of the right, who had polled less than five per cent of the vote, nevertheless hung on to power, trying to persuade Hitler to come into their cabinet, so that they might flatter him and smooth him down as had been done with MacDonald in England. They would offer him this post and that; they would try to win his followers away from him—and Adi would summon the waverers to his presence and scream at them hysterically. When he couldn't get his way he would threaten suicide, and his followers never knew whether he meant it or not.

A great event in Berlin life when the haughty old Field Marshal consented to receive the "Bohemian corporal." Hitler was driven to the Wilhelmstrasse, with crowds cheering him on the way. He had lunch with von Papen, the Chancellor whose post he was demanding, and when he was escorted into the presence of Hindenburg he was so nervous that he stumbled over a rug; he started one of his orations, just like Gladstone before Queen Victoria, and had to be stopped by his old commander. Hindenburg told him that he would not turn over the chancellorship to a man whose followers practiced terrorism and systematic violations of the law; he thought the vice-chancellorship was enough for such a man. But Hitler refused it, demanding full power. The aged Junker stormed, but the ex-corporal had been brought up on that, and all he would reply was: "Opposition to the last ditch." Said Hindenburg: *"Ich will meine Ruhe haben!"*

There began a new wave of terrorism; attacks upon Reds of all shades by the Nazi Stormtroopers in and out of uniform. Irma heard about it and began begging Lanny to cease his visits among these people; she tried to enlist Robbie's help, and when that failed she wanted to leave Berlin. What was this obscure tropism which drove her husband to the companionship of persons who at the least wanted to get his money from him, and frequently were conspiring to involve him in dangerous intrigues? What had they ever done for him? What could he possibly owe them?

Lanny insisted that he had to hear all sides. He invited Emil Meissner to lunch—not in the Robin home, for Emil wouldn't come there. Kurt's oldest brother was now a colonel, and Lanny wanted to know what a Prussian officer thought about the political deadlock. Emil said it was deplorable, and agreed with Lanny that the Nazis were wholly unfitted to govern Germany. He said that if von Papen had been a really strong man he would never have permitted that election to be held; if the Field Marshal had been the man of the old days he would have taken the reins in his hands and governed the country until the economic crisis had passed and the people could settle into a normal state of mind.

"But wouldn't that mean the end of the Republic?" asked Lanny.

"Republics come and go, but nations endure," said Oberst Meissner.

VII

Heinrich Jung called up, bursting with pride over the triumph of his party. He offered to tell Lanny the inside story, and Lanny said: "But I am consorting with your enemies." The other laughed and replied: "Then you can tell *me* the inside story!" He seemed to take the view that Lanny, an American, was above the battle. Was it that a young Nazi craved the admiration of a foreigner? Was there in his secret heart some pleasure in free discussion, the expression of unbiased opinion which he did not get from his party press? Or was it that Lanny was so rich, and looked like a figure out of a Hollywood movie?

The Jung family had been increased again. "More Junkers," said Lanny, with what seemed a pun to him. Heinrich's salary had been increased and he had moved into a larger home. He had invited Hugo Behr, and the three of them sat for a couple of hours sipping light beer and settling the destiny of Germany and its neighbors. Lanny was interested to observe that there were disagreements among Nazi intellectuals, as elsewhere; the two names of Hitler's party covered widely different and inconsistent points of view. Heinrich was the National and Hugo was the Socialist, and while they agreed in worship of the Führer and in the certainty that he could do no wrong, they differed as to the party's immediate policies as well as its ultimate goal. It seemed to the visitor that the split had widened greatly since he had last met the pair. Hugo, the convert from Marxism, had brought over with him the attitude of workingclass consciousness and the program of socialization; whereas Heinrich, son of one of Graf Stubendorf's employees, had the mentality of a Prussian state servant to whom *Ordnung und Zucht* were the breath of being.

Lanny thought there was drama in this, and that it might pay an English playwright to come to Berlin and study what was going on. He had suggested the idea to Rick, who hadn't thought the Nazi movement important enough; but maybe the recent vote would change his mind! Anyhow, Lanny was interested to listen to two young zealots, setting out to make the world over in the image of their inspired leader; it pleased him to take a mental crowbar and insert it in the crack between their minds and make it wider and deeper. Just how deep would it go before they became aware of it themselves?

Lanny couldn't tell them what he knew. He couldn't say to Hugo: "Your Führer is in the thick of negotiations with Thyssen, and Krupp von Bohlen, and Karl von Siemens, and others of the greediest industrialists of your country. He is making fresh promises of conservatism and legality. He will do anything to get power, and anything to keep it. You and your friends are just so many pawns that he moves here and there and will sacrifice when his game requires it." No, for they would ask: "How do you know this?" And he couldn't reply: "Fritz Thyssen told my father yesterday." They would assume that he had got the stories from Johannes Robin, a Jew, which would mean to them two things: first, that the stories were lies, and second, that some Nazi patriots ought to visit the Robin palace by night and smash all its windows and paint *Juda verrecke!* on its front door.

No, among Catholics one did not question the purity of the Holy Virgin, and among Nazis one didn't question the honor of the Führer. When he said in his book that he would have no honor, he meant as regards his foes; but for his *Parteigenossen* he was a loving shepherd, to be followed after the manner of sheep. All that Lanny could do was to ask impersonal questions. "How can the Führer get commercial credits, if Germany defaults in payments on her bonds? I don't mean reparations, but the bonds of private investors." Hugo Behr, naïve young Socialist, didn't even know that there were such bonds. Lanny said: "I have several of them in a safe-deposit box in Newcastle, Connecticut. I bought them because I wanted to help your Socialist republic."

"It is a bourgeois fraud!" said the ex-Marxist; and that settled all Lanny's claims.

VIII

Kurt had written, begging Irma and Lanny to come for a visit. Lanny had never been to Stubendorf except at Christmas time, and he thought it would be pleasant to see the country in midsummer. They drove with a speed greater than the wind over the splendid level roads of Prussia, past fields where gangs of Polish immigrant women labored on the potato crops. The roads were lined with well-tended fruit trees, and Irma said: "We couldn't do that in America. People would steal all the fruit." She had never seen vast fields so perfectly cultivated: every inch of ground put to use, no such thing as a weed existing, and forests with trees planted in rows like orchards. She renewed her admiration for the German *Volk*.

They stayed at the Schloss, even though the Graf was not at home. Kurt had a new "Junker," and so had his brother's family and his sister's. Herr Meissner was feeble, but able to talk politics; he renewed his complaints of corruption and incompetence of the Polish government under which he was forced to live. Just now there was wrangling over religious questions; the old problem of the relations of church and state was being fought over with bitterness inherited through six centuries or more. There were Polish Lutherans and German Lutherans who couldn't and wouldn't say the Lord's prayer together. There were Polish Catholics trying to polonize German Catholics. There was the Volhynian Russian church, and the Uniat church which was half-way between Russian Orthodox and Roman Catholic—they accepted the Pope, but their priests married and had large families. Superimposed upon all this was a new Polish ecclesiastical system, which subjected all the churches to the government. Herr Meissner, soon to depart from this earth, found the making of a proper exit as complicated a problem as had ever confronted him while staying on.

Lanny had been looking forward to having a frank talk with his old chum. He wanted to tell Kurt what he had learned about the Nazi political machine, and make one last effort to get him out of it. But he realized that it would be a waste of effort. Kurt was in a state of exultation over the election results, for which he had been hoping for ten years and working for five. He considered that Germany was being redeemed, and he was composing a *Victory March* to end all marches. Lanny decided sadly that it was better to play piano duets and consider politics as beneath the notice of inspired musicians.

He and Irma had intended to return to Berlin for another cruise; but there came a telegram from Miss Severne, who was under strict orders to report the slightest sign of indisposition on the part of her charge. She reported a digestive disturbance and a temperature of 101; that didn't mean much in a child, and the nurse was sure it wasn't serious, but Irma fell into a panic right away—she was a neglectful and selfish mother who had run away from her responsibilities, amusing herself all over Europe. She wanted to take a plane; but Lanny said: "By the time you get to an airport and arrange for one we can be half way home. You spell me and we'll drive straight through."

So they did, and reached Juan in a little over two days—not so bad considering the mountains in Austria and Italy. Twice on the way they stopped to telephone, and when they arrived they found that the fire was all out. Was it the magic of Parsifal Dingle, or just the natural tendency of very young children to get over a fever as quickly as they get it? There was no way to know; suffice it that Lanny's stepfather had done his best, and Miss Severne had done hers, and Baby Frances was well—and ready to take full advantage of a reformed and penitent mother! Irma was so happy to prattle and dance and play with her darling that she couldn't understand how she had ever wanted to be fashionable.

IX

They settled down to domestic life. In the evening Sophie and her husband would come over to play bridge with Irma and Beauty. Marceline had begun attending a private school, where fashionable young ladies didn't learn very much but were watched and kept out of mischief. That left Lanny free to read the magazines which had accumulated in his absence, and to play the music that took his fancy; also to attend the workers' school and tell them what he had learned in England and Germany, and advise them how to avoid the misfortunes which had befallen their comrades in these countries.

The only trouble was, the data appeared so complicated and the conclusions so uncertain. "MacDonaldism" appeared to indicate the futility of "gradualness" and legality; the moment you mentioned it, up popped some young Red to say: "You see what happens when the workers put their trust in parliaments!" When you mentioned Hitler, right away a wrangle started as to what had caused him. Was he an agent of German heavy industry, and a proof that capitalism would not submit peaceably to any form of limitation upon its rule? Or were the Nazis a product of the fears which Bolshevism had inspired in the *Kleinbürgertum*—the small business men, the petty officials, the white collar workers who had no unions and couldn't protect their status?

You could take either side of this debate, produce a mass of facts to prove your case, and come out feeling certain that you had won. The uncomfortable person was the one like Lanny, who wanted the whole truth, and could see that there was some of it on both sides. Nobody could look at an issue of a Nazi newspaper without seeing that they were exploiting the fear of Red Russia to the limit; on the other hand, who could look at Hitler's Braune Haus with its costly equipment, or see the Stormtroopers marching with their shiny new uniforms and weapons—and not know that this movement was being financed by big money of some sort. *Gross Kapital* was afraid of Russia, just as the white collar workers were; but *Gross Kapital* was exploiting all the workers, and these two groups couldn't agree on any domestic policies. Sooner or later the Nazis would have to make up their minds which master they meant to serve.

There lay the drama of present day events in Germany, and Lanny strove to explain it to the French workers and to such of their leaders as he met. Hitler sat in his study in Berlin, or in Munich, or in the retreat which he had bought for himself in the mountains, and the Nazi chieftains came to him and argued and pulled him this way and that; he thought it over, and chose whatever course seemed to him to open the way to power. He was as slippery as an eel, and as quick to move, and nobody could say what he was going to do until he had done it. The one thing you could say for sure was that National Socialism was power without conscience; you might call it the culmination of capitalism, or a degenerate form of Bolshevism—names didn't matter, so long as you understood that it was counter-revolution.

The important question was, whether this same development was to be expected in every country. Was the depression going to wipe out the middle classes and drive them into the arms of demagogues? Were the workers being driven to revolt, and would their attempts be met by the overthrow of parliaments? Were the Communists right in their seemingly crazy idea that Fascism was a necessary stage in the breakdown of capitalism?

Apparently the question was up for answer in the land which Lanny and Irma called theirs. The ex-service men who had gone overseas to fight for their country had come back to find the jobs and the money in the hands of others. Now they were unemployed, many of them starving, and they gathered in Washington demanding relief; some brought their destitute families and swarmed upon the steps of the Capitol or camped in vacant lots beside the Potomac. The Great Engineer fell into a panic and could think of nothing to do but turn the army loose on them, kill four, and burn the tents and pitiful belongings of all. The "bonus men" were driven out, a helpless rabble, no one caring where they went, so long as they stopped bothering politicians occupied with getting re-elected.

To Lanny this appeared the same thing as the Cabinet of the

Barons, seizing control of Prussia and ruling Germany with only a few votes in the Reichstag. It was Poincairé occupying the Ruhr for the benefit of the Comité des Forges; it was Zaharoff sending an army into Turkey to get oil concessions. It was the same type of men all over the world. They tried to grab one another's coal and steel and oil and gold; yet, the moment they were threatened by their wage slaves anywhere, they got together to fight against the common peril. Do it with the army, do it with gangsters, do it with the workers' own leaders, buying them or seducing them with titles, honors, and applause!

Lanny could see that clearly; and it is a pleasure to the mind to discover unity in the midst of variety. But then the thought would come to him: "My father is one of these men, and so are his father and his brothers. My sister's father-in-law is one, and so was my wife's father, and all the men of her family." That spoiled the pleasure in Lanny's mind.

X

Two or three weeks passed, and ambition began to stir once more in the soul of Irma Barnes Budd. There was that splendid palace in Paris, for which she was paying over eighty thousand francs rent per month, and nearly as much for upkeep, whether she used it or not. Now it was autumn, one of the delightful seasons in la Ville Lumière. The *beau monde* came back from the mountains and the sea, and there were the autumn Salons, and operas and concerts and all the things that Lanny loved; there were balls and parties, an automobile show and other displays of luxury. The young couple set out in their car, and Sophie and her husband in theirs, and Beauty and her husband in hers. Mr. Dingle didn't mind wherever she took him, for, strange as it might seem, God was in Paris, and there were people there who knew Him, even in the midst of the rout of pleasure-seeking.

Margy, Dowager Lady Eversham-Watson, came from London, bringing Nina and Rick for a short holiday. Rick was a celebrity now, and the hostesses were after him. Also General Graf Stuben-dorf was invited, in return for his hospitality, and to Lanny's surprise he accepted. Others of the fashionable Berliners came, and it was hands across the Rhein again—but Lanny was no longer naïve, and couldn't persuade himself that this was going to keep the peace among the great European powers. The Conference on Arms Limitation was still arguing at Geneva, and facing complete breakdown. The statesmen and fashionable folk, even the army men, would wine and dine one another and be the best of friends; but they would go on piling up weapons and intriguing, each against all the others—until one day an *alerte* would be sounded, and you would see them all scurrying back to their own side of the river, or mountains, or whatever the boundary line might be.

It didn't take Irma long to become the accomplished hostess. With Emily Chattersworth and the other ladies coaching her, she played her part with dignity and success; everybody liked her, and the most fastidious denizens of St. Germain, *le gratin*, could find no fault in her. She wasn't presuming to attempt a salon—that would take time, and perhaps might grow as it were by accident. Meanwhile she gave elegant entertainments with no sign of skimping, at a time when all but a few were forced to that least pardonable of improprieties.

For three years the business prophets had been telling the world that the slump was only temporary, that prosperity was just around the corner. But apparently it was a round house. Apparently some devil had got into the economic structure and was undermining it. In Wall Street, at the culmination of a furious political campaign, there was a new wave of bank failures; dividends seemed to have stopped, and now interest on bonds was stopping. Irma's income for the third quarter of the year had fallen to less than a hundred thousand dollars. She said to her husband: "We'll have a splurge for the rest of this lease and then go back and crawl into our storm-cellar."

He answered: "All right," and let it go at that. He knew that he couldn't change Irma's idea that she was helping to preserve the social order by distributing money among domestic servants, wine merchants, florists, dressmakers, and all the train that came to the side-door of this palace—as they had come in the days of Marie

Antoinette a hundred and fifty years ago. It hadn't succeeded in saving feudalism, and Lanny doubted if it was going to save capitalism; but there was no use upsetting anybody ahead of time!

Lanny worried because his life was too easy; he had worried about that for years—but how could he make it hard? Even the harsh and bitter Jesse Blackless, *député de la république française,* couldn't forget the fact that he owed his election to Irma's contributions, and that sooner or later he would have to be elected again. Even Jean Longuet, man of letters as well as Socialist editor, didn't presume to question the judgment of a wealthy young American who brought him some drawings by a German art student. He said he would be delighted to use them, and Trudi Schultz was made happy by a modest honorarium from *Le Populaire.* She had no idea that the money came out of a contribution which Lanny had made to the war-chest of that party organ.

XI

Hitler's program of "opposition to the last ditch" had forced the dissolution of the Reichstag, and a new election campaign was going on. It was hard on Adolf, for he couldn't get the money which such an effort required, and when the election took place, early in November, it was found that he had lost nearly two million votes in three months. Johannes Robin was greatly relieved, and wrote that it was the turning of the tide; he felt justified in his faith in the German people, who couldn't be persuaded to entrust their affairs to a mentally disordered person. Johannes said that the Führer's conduct since the setback showed that he couldn't control himself and ought to be in an institution of some sort.

Two days after the German elections came those in the United States. Robbie Budd had his faith in the American people, and he clung to it up to 7:00 p.m. on the Tuesday after the first Monday of November 1932, but then it was completely and irremediably shattered. The Great Engineer, Robbie's friend and idol, went down in ignominious defeat, and "that man Roosevelt" carried all the states but six. One that he failed to carry was Robbie's home state, and a rock-ribbed Republican could thank God for that small atom of self-respect left to him! Adi Hitler might be a mental case, but he had the wisdom of Jove compared with Roosevelt as Robbie saw him; a candidate who had gone on a joy-ride about the country, promising everything to everybody—completely incompatible things such as the balancing of the budget and a program of government expansion which would run the public debt up to figures of the sort used by astronomers.

Both Robbie and Johannes made it a practice to send Lanny carbon copies of their letters containing comments on public affairs. For the first time since the World War the Jewish trader was the optimist. He repeated his favorite culinary formula, that no soup is ever eaten as hot as it is cooked. He offered to prove his faith in the land of the pilgrims' pride by letting Robbie buy more Budd shares for him; but Robbie wrote in the strictest confidence—typing the letter himself—that Budd's might soon be closing down entirely; only Hoover's wise and merciful Reconstruction Finance Corporation had kept it from having to default on its bonds.

Under the American system, four months had to elapse between Roosevelt's election and his taking of power. Robbie thought that would be a breathing-spell, but it proved to be one of paralysis; nothing could be done, and each side blamed the other. Herbert was sure that Franklin wanted to see the country go to wreck in order that he might have the glory of saving it. Anyhow, there it was, wave after wave of bank failures, and people hiding their money in mattresses, business men buying gold because of the expected inflation, and people in Europe who had shipped their money to America now calling it back. Seventeen million workers were said to be without jobs—a world record!

XII

Meanwhile the deadlock in Germany continued. The Socialists had lost another big chunk of votes to the Communists, and they hated each other more than ever. Hitler had another interview with Hindenburg, and demanded the chancellorship, but didn't get it.

The Nazi extremists were infuriated by Hitler's "legality complex," and clamored for him to seize power. There was another violent quarrel between the Führer and his Reich Organization Leader Number One, Gregor Strasser; the former threatened suicide again, and the latter threatened to resign from the party and set up a new one of his own.

Strasser began intriguing with the gentlemen of the Herren Klub, who were ready to make a deal with anybody who could deliver votes. General von Schleicher wanted to supplant von Papen, who was supposed to be his friend and ally; he had the bright idea of a cabinet which would combine the extreme Junkers with the extreme Nazis—they could browbeat Hitler, because his party was bankrupt, his paymasters had drawn the purse-strings, and he himself was in a state of distraction. Schleicher and Strasser combined would threaten another dissolution of the Reichstag and another election, with the certainty that without money the Nazi vote would be cut in half. Such was the X-ray picture of German politics which Johannes Robin sent to his trusted friends; he didn't say in so many words that both the conspirators had come to him for funds, but he said that he hadn't got the above information at second hand.

This deal apparently went through. When the members of the Budd family drove to Bienvenu to spend Christmas, the "office general" was Chancellor of the German Republic, Gregor Strasser had broken with Hitler and was being talked of for a cabinet post, and Hitler had been browbeaten into consenting to an adjournment of the Reichstag until January.

From Connecticut and from Long Island came Christmas letters in which you could see that the writers had labored hard to think of something cheerful to say. Irma, reading them, said to her husband: "Maybe we'd better close up the palace and save money, so that we can take care of my mother and your father if we have to."

"Bless your heart!" replied the prince consort. "You've hired that white elephant until April, so you might as well ride him that long."

"But suppose they get really stuck, Lanny!"

"Robbie isn't playing the market, and I don't suppose your mother is, so they can't be broke entirely."

Irma thought for a while, then remarked: "You know, Lanny, it's really wonderful the way you've turned out to be right about business affairs. All the important people have been wrong, while you've hit the nail on the head."

Said the young Pink: "It's worth going through a depression to hear that from one's wife!"

14

The Stormy Winds Do Blow

I

BACK in Paris during the month of January Lanny would receive every morning a copy of the Berlin *Vorwärts*, twenty-four hours late; he would find on the front page details of the political situation, displayed under scare headlines and accompanied by editorial exhortations. All from the Socialist point of view, of course; but Lanny could check it by taking a stroll up the Butte de Montmartre and hearing the comments of his deputy-uncle, based on the reading of *L'Humanité*, the paper which Jaurès had founded but which now was in the hands of the Communists. This paper also had its Berlin news, set off with scare headlines and editorial exhortations. Because *L'Humanité* got its stories by wire, Lanny would sometimes swallow the antidote ahead of the poison.

"You see!" the Red uncle would exclaim. "The Social-Democrats haven't a single constructive proposal. They only denounce what we propose!"

"But you do some denouncing also, Uncle Jesse."

"The workers know our program; and every time there's an

election, the Socialist bureaucrats lose half a million or a million votes, and we gain them."

"But suppose there aren't any more elections, Uncle Jesse. Suppose Hitler takes power!"

"He can't do any harm to our monolithic party. We have educated and disciplined our members and they will stand firm."

"But suppose he outlaws your organization!"

"You can't destroy a party that has several hundred thousand members, and has polled four or five million votes."

"Don't make the mistake of underestimating your enemy."

"Well, if necessary we'll go underground. It has happened before, and you may be sure that we have made plans—in France as well as in Germany."

"I hope you're not mistaken, Uncle Jesse." Lanny said it and meant it. He argued against the Communists, but was only half-hearted about it, because after all, they were a workers' party, and nobody could be sure they mightn't be needed. The first Five Year Plan of the Soviet Union had been completed with success, and all the Reds were exulting over it; the Pinks couldn't fail to be impressed, and many wavered and wondered if maybe the Russian way might be the only way. Anyhow, they had a right to be heard; Lanny did what he could to persuade both sides to stop quarreling, and he set them an example by refusing to let them quarrel with him.

II

Any time he was in doubt about what was really happening in Germany he had only to write to Johannes Robin. A letter from the Jewish money-master was like a gust of wind blowing away a fog and revealing the landscape. It disclosed the German nation traveling upon a perilous path, with yawning abysses on every side, earthquakes shaking the rocks loose and volcanoes hurling out clouds of fiery ashes. Assuredly neither of the Plinys, uncle or nephew, had confronted more terrifying natural phenomena than did the Weimar Republic at the beginning of this year 1933.

The ceaselessly aggressive Nazis were waging daily and nightly battles with the Communists all over the country. And meantime the two ruling groups, the industrialists of the west and the landlords of the east, were concentrating their attention upon getting higher tariffs to protect their interests; one hundred per cent wasn't enough in these days of failing markets. The workers, who wanted lower prices for goods and for food, had refused time after time to vote for candidates of these groups; but with less than five per cent of the votes, the reactionary politicians still clung to power, playing one faction against another, using cajolements mixed with threats.

Chancellor von Schleicher had begun wooing the labor unions, calling himself the "social general," and pointing out to the moderates among Socialists and Catholics how much worse things would be if either set of extremists came in. By such blandishments he lost favor with the paymasters of the Ruhr, who wanted the labor unions broken and were listening to the siren song of Hitler, promising this service. Also there was the problem of *Osthilfe*, a scandal hanging over the heads of the landed aristocrats of East Prussia. Huge public funds had been voted to save the farmers from ruin, but the owners of the big estates, the powerful aristocrats, had managed to get most of the money, and they had used it for other purposes than land improvements. Now hardly a day passed that the Socialist and Communist press didn't print charges and demand investigations.

Papen and Schleicher still pretended to be friends, while scheming to cut each other's throats. Schleicher had ousted Papen by a deal with the Nazis, and two could play at that game. Papen, the "gentleman jockey," was the most tireless of wirepullers. A pale blond aristocrat with a thin, lined face wearing a perpetual smile, he went from one secret meeting to another telling a different story to everybody—but all of them carefully calculated to injure his rival.

"Papen has had a meeting with Hitler at the home of Thyssen's friend, Baron von Schroeder," wrote Johannes, and Lanny didn't need to ask what that meant. "I am told that Papen and Hugenberg have got together;"—that, too, was not obscure. Hugenberg, the "silver fox," had come to one of the Robin soirées; a big man with a walrus mustache, brutal but clever; leader of the Pan-German group and owner of the most powerful propaganda machine in the world, practically all of the big capitalist newspapers of Germany, plus U.F.A., the film monopoly. "Papen is raising funds for Hitler among the industrialists," wrote Johannes. "I hear that the Führer has more than two million marks in notes which he cannot meet. It is a question whether he will go crazy before he becomes chancellor!"

III

The Nazis held one of their tremendous meetings in the Sportpalast, and Hitler delivered one of his inspired tirades, promising peace, order, and restoration of self respect to the German people. The conservative newspapers in Paris published his promises and half believed them; they were far more afraid of the Reds than of the Nazis, and Lanny found that Denis de Bruyne was inclined to look upon Hitler as a model for French politicians. Even Lanny himself began hesitating; he was so anxious to be sure that he was right. Hitler was calling upon Almighty God to give him courage and strength to save the German people and right the wrongs of Versailles. Lanny, who had protested so energetically against those wrongs, now wondered if it mightn't be possible for Hitler to scare France and Britain into making the necessary concessions, and then to settle down and govern the country in the interest of those millions of oppressed "little people" for whom he spoke so eloquently.

The son of Robbie Budd and husband of Irma Barnes might waver, but the German workers didn't. A hundred thousand of them met in the Berlin Lustgarten, clamoring for the defense of the Republic against its traitor enemies. "Something is going to pop," wrote Johannes, American fashion. "*Der alte Herr* is terrified at the prospect of having the *Osthilfe* affair discussed in the Reichstag. Schleicher is considering with the labor unions the idea of refusing to resign and holding on with their backing. I am told that the Catholics have assented, but the Socialists are afraid it wouldn't be legal. What do you think?" Lanny knew that his old friend was teasing him, and didn't offer any opinion on German constitutional law.

Johannes didn't say what he himself was doing in this crisis, but Lanny guessed that he was following his program of keeping friendly with all sides. Certainly he possessed an extraordinary knowledge of the intrigues. Now and then Lanny would call him on the long distance telephone, a plaything of the very rich, and Johannes would speak a sort of camouflage. He would say: "My friend Fränzchen wants to be top dog, but so does his friend the publisher, and their schemes will probably fall through because they can't agree." Lanny understood that this meant Papen and Hugenberg; and when Johannes added: "They may harness up the Wild Man and get together to drive him," Lanny had no trouble guessing about that. Presently Johannes said: "They are telling the Old Gent that the General is plotting a *coup d'état* against him." It was like reading a blood and thunder novel in instalments, and having to wait for the next issue. Would the rescue party arrive in time?

IV

On the thirtieth of January the news went out to a startled world that President von Hindenburg had appointed Adolf Hitler Chancellor of the German Republic. Even the Nazis were taken by surprise; they hadn't been invited to the intrigues, and couldn't imagine by what magic it had been brought about that their Führer's enemies suddenly put him into office. Franz von Papen was Vice-Chancellor, and Hugenberg was in the Cabinet; in all there were nine reactionaries against three Nazis, and what could that mean? The newspapers outside Germany were certain that it meant the surrender of Hitler; he was going to be controlled, he was going to be another Ramsay MacDonald. They chose not to heed the proclamation which the Führer himself issued, telling his followers that the struggle was only beginning. But the Stormtroopers heeded, and turned out, exultant, parading with torchlights through Unter den Linden; seven hundred thousand persons marched past the Chancellery, with Hindenburg greeting them from one window and Hitler from another. The Communist call for a general strike went unheeded.

So it had come: the thing which Lanny had been fearing for the past three or four years. The Nazis had got Germany! Most of his friends had thought it unlikely; and now that it had happened, they preferred to believe that it hadn't. Hitler wasn't really in power, they said, and could last but a week or two. The German people had too much sense, the governing classes were too able and well trained; they would tone the fanatic down, and the soup would be eaten cool.

But Adolf Hitler had got, and Adolf Hitler would keep, the power which was most important to him—that of propaganda. He was executive head of the German government, and whatever manifesto he chose to issue took the front page of all the newspapers. Hermann Göring was Prussian Minister of the Interior and could say to the world over the radio: "Bread and work for our countrymen, freedom and honor for the nation!" Dwarfish little Jupp Goebbels, President of the Propaganda Committee of the Party, found himself Minister of Propaganda and Popular Enlightenment of the German Republic. The Nazi movement had been made out of propaganda, and now it would cover Germany·like an explosion.

Hitler refused to make any concessions to the other parties, and thus forced Hindenburg to dissolve the Reichstag and order a new election. This meant that for a month the country would be in the turmoil of a campaign. But what a different campaign! No trouble about lack of funds, because Hitler had the funds of the nation, and his tirades were state documents. Goebbels could say anything he pleased about his enemies and suppress their replies. Göring, having control of the Berlin police, could throw his political opponents into jail and nobody could even find out where they were. These were the things of which Adi Schicklgruber had been dreaming ever since the end of the World War; and where else but in the Arabian Nights had it happened that a man awoke and found such dreams come true?

V

Lanny Budd lived externally the life of a young man of fashion. He accompanied his wife to various functions, and when she entertained he played the host with dignity. Having been married nearly four years, he was entitled to enjoy mild flirtations with various charming ladies of society; they expected it, and his good looks and conversation gave him reason to expect success. But instead, he would pick out some diplomat or man of affairs and disappear into the library to discuss the problems of Europe. These gentlemen were impressed by a young man's wide range of knowledge, but they thought he was unduly anxious concerning this new movement of Nazism; they had learned what a French revolution was, and a Russian one, but had difficulty in recognizing a revolution that happened in small instalments and under ingenious camouflage. Hardly a man of wealth and importance in France who didn't accept Nazism as a business man's answer to Bolshevism. When they read in the papers that Communists were being shot pretty freely throughout Germany, they shrugged their French shoulders and said: "*Eh, bien?* Do the Reds complain of illegality?"

Lanny ran up a large telephone bill calling his friends in Berlin. It was his one form of dissipation, and Irma learned to share it; she would take the wire when he got through and ask Rahel about the baby, or Mama about anything—for Mama's Yiddish-English was as delightful as a vaudeville turn. Lanny was worried about the safety of his friends, but Johannes said: "*Nu, nu!* Don't bother your head. I have assurances that I cannot tell you about. I wear the Tarnhelm."

He would retail the latest smart trick of those Nazis, whose cleverness and efficiency he couldn't help admiring. "No, they will not outlaw the Communist party, because if they did, the vote would go to the Sozis, and there would be the same old deadlock in the Reichstag. But if they let the Communist deputies be elected, and then exclude them from their seats, the Nazis may have a majority of what is left! What is it that you say about skinning a cat? There are nine ways of doing it?"

How long would a Jew, even the richest, be allowed to tell the inmost secrets of the Führer over the telephone to Paris? Lanny wondered about that, and he wondered about the magic cap which Johannes thought he was wearing. Might he not be fooling himself, like so many other persons who put their trust in political adventurers? Who was there among the Nazi powers who had any respect for a Jew, or would keep faith with one for a moment after it suited his purpose? To go to a rich *Schieber* to beg money for a struggling outcast party was one thing; but to pay the debt when you had got the powers of the state into your hands—that was something else again, as the Jews said in New York.

Lanny worried especially about Hansi, who was not merely of the hated race, but of the hated party, and had proclaimed it from public platforms. The Nazi press had made note of him; they had called him a tenth-rate fiddler who couldn't even play in tune. Would they permit him to go on playing out of tune at Red meetings? The Stormtroopers were now turned loose to wreak their will upon the Reds, and how long would it be before some ardent young patriot would take it into his head to stop this Jewish swine from profaning German music?

Lanny wrote, begging Hansi to come to Paris. He wrote to Bess, who admitted that she was afraid; but she was a granddaughter of the Puritans, who hadn't run away from the Indians. She pointed out that she and her husband had helped to make Communists in Berlin, and now to desert them in the hour of trial wouldn't be exactly heroic, would it? Lanny argued that a great artist was a special kind of being, different from a fighting man and not to be held to the military code. Lanny wrote to Mama, telling her that it was her business to take charge of the family in a time like this. But it wasn't so easy to manage Red children as it had been in the days of Moses and the Ten Commandments.

However, there was still a Providence overseeing human affairs. At this moment it came about that a certain Italian diva, popular in Paris, was struck by a taxicab. The kind Providence didn't let her be seriously hurt, just a couple of ribs broken, enough to put her out of the diva business for a while. The news appeared in the papers while Lanny and Irma were at Bienvenu, having run down to see the baby and to attend one of Emily's social functions. Lanny recalled that the diva was scheduled with one of the Paris symphony orchestras; she would have to be replaced, and Lanny asked Emily to get busy on the long distance telephone. She knew the conductor of this orchestra, and suggested Hansi Robin to replace the damaged singer; Mrs. Chattersworth being a well-known patron of the arts, it was natural that she should offer to contribute to the funds of the symphony society an amount equal to the fee which Hansi Robin would expect to receive.

The bargain was struck, and Lanny got to work on Hansi at some twenty francs per minute, to persuade him that German music ought to be promoted in France; that every such performance was a service to world culture, also to the Jewish race, now so much in need of international sympathy. After the Paris appearance, Emily would have a soirée at Sept Chênes, and other engagements would help to make the trip worth while.

"All right," replied the violinist, anxious to cut short the expenditure of francs. "I'm scheduled to give a concert at Cologne, and that is half way."

Lanny said: "For God's sake, keep off the streets at night, and don't go out alone!"

VI

Lanny missed his inside news about Germany, because the government forbade the publication of *Vorwärts* for three days, as a punishment for having published a campaign appeal of the Social-Democratic Party. Communist meetings were forbidden throughout the whole nation, and many Communist and Socialist papers were permanently suspended. "In ten years there will be no Marxism in Germany," proclaimed the Führer. All over Prussia Göring was replacing police chiefs with Nazis, and the Stormtroopers were now attending political meetings in force, stopping those in which the government was criticized. Next, all meetings of the Centrists, the Catholic party, were banned; the Catholic paper, *Germania*, of which Papen was the principal stockholder, was suppressed, and then *Rote Fahne*, the Communist paper of Berlin. These events were reported in *L'Humanité* under the biggest of headlines, and Uncle Jesse denounced them furiously in the Chamber of Deputies; but that didn't appear to have much effect upon Hitler.

What the Nazis were determined to do was to win those elections on the fifth of March. If they could get a majority in the Reichstag, they would be masters of the country; the Nationalists and aristocrats would be expelled from the cabinet and the revolution would be complete. Papen, Hugenberg, and their backers knew it well, and were in a state of distress, according to Johannes's reports. A curious state of affairs—the gentlemen of the Herren Klub defending the Reds, because they knew that Hitler was using the Red bogy to frighten the people into voting for him! Goebbels was demanding the head of the Berlin police chief because he wouldn't produce evidence of treasonable actions on the part of the Communists. "The history of Germany is becoming a melodrama," wrote the Jewish financier. "In times to come people will refuse to believe it."

He was now beginning to be worried about the possibility of attacks upon his boys; those gentle, idealistic boys who had been playing with fire without realizing how hot it could get. Being now twenty-eight and twenty-six respectively, they ought to have had some sense. Johannes didn't say it was Lanny's half-sister who led them into the worst extremes, but Lanny knew the father thought this, and not without reason. Anyhow, he had got a trusted bodyguard in the palace—a well-established and indubitable Aryan bodyguard. Freddi's school had been closed; such a simple operation—a group of Stormtroopers appeared one evening and ordered the people out. Nothing you could do, for they had arms and appeared eager to use them. Everybody went, not even being allowed to get their hats and coats in February. The building was closed, and all the papers had been carted away in a truck.

The Nazis wouldn't find any treason in those documents; only receipted bills, and examination papers in Marxist theory. But maybe that was treason now! Or maybe the Nazis would prepare other documents and put them into the files. Orders to the students to blow up Nazi headquarters, or perhaps the Chancellery? Such forgeries had been prepared more than once, and not alone in Germany. Hadn't an election been won in Britain on the basis of an alleged "Zinoviev letter"?

The headquarters of the Communist Party of Germany was in Karl Liebknecht Haus, and that was the place where treason was to be sought. The police had seized the documents, and two days later Herr Goebbels's press service gave details about "catacombs" and "underground vaults," a secret and illegal organization functioning in the basement of the building, and so on. Johannes reported an embittered conflict in the Cabinet over these too obvious forgeries; they were considered beneath the dignity of the German government—but perhaps the German government wasn't going to be so dignified from now on! The Jewish financier couldn't conceal his amusement over the discomfiture of the "gentleman jockey," the "silver fox," and the rest of the Junker crew. They had made this bed of roses, and discovered too late how full of thorns it was.

The thing that worried Lanny was the possibility that some Nazi agent might produce letters proving that Hansi Robin had been carrying dynamite in his violin case, or Freddi in his clarinet case. They must have had spies in the school, and known everything that both boys had been doing and saying. Lanny said: "Johannes, why don't you and the whole family come visit us for a while?"

"Maybe we'll all take a yachting trip," replied the man of money, with a chuckle. "When the weather gets a little better."

"The weather is going to get worse," insisted the Paris end of the line.

VII

Lanny talked this problem over with his wife. She couldn't very well refuse hospitality to Johannes, from whom she had accepted so much. But she didn't like the atmosphere which the young Robins brought with them, and she thought them a bad influence for her husband. She argued that the danger couldn't really be so great as Lanny feared. "If the Nazis are anxious to get votes, they won't do anything to important persons, especially those known abroad."

Lanny replied: "The party is full of criminals and degenerates, and they are drunk with the sense of power."

He couldn't stop worrying about it, and when the day for Hansi's coming drew near, he said to Irma: "How would you like to motor to Cologne and bring them out with us?"

"What could we do, Lanny?"

"There's safety in numbers; and then, too, Americans have a certain amount of prestige in Germany."

It wasn't a pleasant time for motoring, the end of February, but they had heat in their car, and with fur coats they would be all right unless there happened to be a heavy storm. Irma liked adventure; one of the reasons she and Lanny got along so well was that whenever one suggested hopping into a car the other always said: "O.K." No important engagement stood in the way of this trip, and they allowed themselves an extra day on chance of bad weather.

Old Boreas was kind, and they rolled down the valley of the Meuse, by which the Germans had made their entry into France some eighteen and a half years ago. Lanny told his wife the story of Sophie Timmons, Baroness de la Tourette, who had been caught in the rush of the armies and had got away in a peasant's cart pulled by a spavined old horse.

They reached Cologne late that evening, and spent the next day looking at a grand cathedral, and at paintings in a near-by Gothic museum. Hansi and Bess arrived on the afternoon train, and thereafter they stayed in their hotel suite, doing nothing to attract attention to a member of the accursed race. Among the music-lovers Hansi would be all right, for these were "good Europeans," who for a couple of centuries had been building up a tradition of internationalism. A large percentage of Europe's favorite musicians had been Jews, and there would have been gaps in concert programs if their works had been omitted.

Was the audience trying to say this by the storms of applause with which they greeted the performance of Mendelssohn's gracious concerto by a young Jewish virtuoso? Did Hansi have such a message in his mind when he played Bruch's *Kol Nidrei* as one of his encores? When the audience leaped to its feet and shouted, "Bravo!" were they really meaning to say: "We are not Nazis! We shall never be Nazis!" Lanny chose to believe this, and was heartened; he was sure that many of the adoring Rheinlanders had a purpose in waiting at the stage door and escorting the four young people to their car. But out in the dark street, with a cold rain falling, doubts began to assail him, and he wondered if the amiable Rhinelanders had guns for their protection.

However, no Nazi cars followed, and no Stormtroopers were waiting at the Hotel Monopol. Next morning they drove to the border, and nobody searched Hansi's two violin cases for dynamite. They went through the routine performance of declaring what money they were taking out of the country, and were then passed over to the Belgian customs men. Lanny remembered the day when he had been ordered out of Italy, and with what relief he had seen French uniforms and heard French voices. Eight years had passed, and Benito, the "Blessed Little Pouter Pigeon," was still haughtily declaring that his successor had not yet been born. Now his feat was being duplicated in another and far more powerful land, and rumors had it that he was giving advice. In how many more countries would Lanny Budd see that pattern followed? How many more transformations would it undergo? Would the Japanese conquerors of Manchuria adopt some new-colored shirts or kimonos? Or would it be the Croix de Feu in France? Or Mosley's group in England? And if so, to what part of the world would the lovers of freedom move?

VIII

The tall slender figure of Hansi Robin stood before the audience in the symphony hall; an audience of fastidious Parisians whose greeting was reserved. In the front row sat Lanny, Irma, and Bess, greatly excited. Hansi's appearance was grave and his bows dignified; he knew that this performance was an important one, but was not too nervous, having learned by now what he could do. The conductor was a Frenchman who had given a long life to the service of the art he loved; his hair had grown white, and what was left of it stood out as a fringe under his shiny bald pate. He tapped upon the edge of his stand and raised his baton; there came four beats of the kettledrum, followed by a few notes of a timid marching song; then four more beats, and more notes. It was Beethoven's violin concerto.

Hansi stood waiting, with his instrument in the crook of his arm and his bow at his side; the introduction is elaborate, and not even by a movement of his eyes would he distract anyone's attention from the sounds. Lanny Budd, in the front row with his wife and Bess, knew every note of this composition, and had played a piano transcription of the orchestral part for Hansi at Les Forêts, on that fateful day seven years ago when Bess had first met the shepherd boy out of ancient Judea and fallen under his spell. That was one reason why Hansi made a specialty of this concerto; love infused his rendition, as love has a way of doing with whatever it touches.

The march acquired the firm tread of Beethoven; the orchestra thundered, and Lanny wanted to say: "Careful, Maestro. He didn't have so many instruments!" But the conductor's expressive hands signed for gentleness as Hansi's bow touched the strings. The song floated forth, gay yet tender, gentle yet strong—those high qualities which the soul of Beethoven possessed and which the soul of Hansi honored. The fiddle sang and the orchestra made comments upon it; various instruments took up the melody, while Hansi wove embroidery about it, danced around it, over and under it, leaping, skipping, flying in feats of gay acrobatics. A concerto is a device to exhibit the possibilities of a musical instrument; but at its best it may also illustrate the possibilities of the human spirit, its joys and griefs, toils and triumphs, glories and grandeurs. Men and women plod through their daily routine, they become tired and insensitive, skeptical or worse; then comes a master spirit and flings open the gates of their being, and they realize how much they have been missing in their lives.

For more than twenty years this sensitive young Jew had consecrated himself to one special skill; he had made himself a slave to some pieces of wood, strips of pig's intestine, and hairs from a horse's tail. With such unlikely agencies Beethoven and Hansi contrived to express the richness, elegance, and variety of life. They took you into the workshop of the universe, where its miracles are planned and executed; the original mass-production process which turns out the myriad leaves of trees and the petals of flowers, the wings of insects and birds, the patterns of snow crystals and solar systems. Beethoven and Hansi revealed the operation of that machinery from which color and delicacy, power and splendor are poured forth in unceasing floods.

Lanny had made so many puns upon the name of his brother-in-law that he had ceased to think of them as such. There was nothing in the physical aspect of Hansi to suggest the robin, but when you listened to his music you remembered that the robin's wings are marvels of lightness and grace, and that every feather is a separate triumph. The robin's heart is strong, and he flies without stopping, on and on, to lands beyond the seas. He flies high into the upper registers, among the harmonic notes, where sensations are keener than any known upon earth. The swift runs of Hansi's violin were the swooping and darting of all the birds; the long trills were the fluttering of the humming-bird's wings, purple, green, and gold in the sunlight, hovering, seeming motionless; each moment you expect it to dart away, but there it remains, an enchantment.

IX

Hansi was playing the elaborate cadenza. No other sound in the auditorium; the men of the orchestra sat as if they were images, and the audience the same. Up and down the scale rushed the flying notes; up like the wind through the pine trees on a mountain-side, down like cascades of water, flashing rainbows in the sunshine. Beethoven had performed the feat of weaving his two themes in counterpoint, and Hansi performed the feat of playing trills with two of his fingers and a melody with the other two. Only a musician could know how many years of labor it takes to train nerves and muscles for such "double-stopping," but everyone could know that it was beautiful and at the same time that it was wild.

The second movement is a prayer, and grief is mixed with its longing; so Hansi could tell those things which burdened his spirit. He could say that the world was a hard and cruel place, and that his poor people were in agony. "Born to sorrow—born to sorrow," moaned the wood-winds, and Hansi's violin notes hovered over them, murmuring pity. But one does not weep long with Beethoven; he turns pain into beauty, and it would be hard to find in all his treasury a single work in which he leaves you in despair. There comes a rush of courage and determination, and the theme of grief turns into a dance. The composer of this concerto, humiliated and enraged because the soldiers of Napoleon had seized his beloved Vienna, went out into the woods alone and reminded himself that world conquerors come and go, but love and joy live on in the hearts of men.

"Oh, come, be merry, oh, come be jolly, come one, come all and dance with me!" Lanny amused himself by finding words for musical themes. This dance went over flower-strewn meadows; breezes swept ahead of it, and the creatures of nature joined the gay procession, birds fluttering in the air, rabbits and other delightful things scampering on the ground. Hand in hand came young people in flowing garments. "Oh, youths and maidens, oh, youths and maidens, come laugh, and sing, and dance with me!" It was the Isadora rout that Lanny would always carry in his memory. When the storm of the orchestra drowned out Hansi's fiddle, the listener was leaping to a mountain-top and from it to the next.

Others must have been having the same sort of adventure, for when the last note sounded they started to their feet and tried to tell the artist about it. Lanny saw that his brother-in-law had won a triumph. Such a sweet, gentle fellow he was, flushed from his exertions, but even thinner than usual, showing the strain under which he was living. People seemed to realize that here was one who was not going to be spoiled by adulation. He wasn't going to enjoy himself and his own glory, he would never become blasé and bored; he would go on loving his art and serving it. Nobody in that hall failed to know that he was a Jew, and that this was a time of anguish for his people. Such anti-Semitism as there was in Paris was not among the art-lovers, and to shout "Bravo!" at this young virtuoso was to declare yourself for the cause of freedom and human decency.

Lanny thought about the great composer, friend of mankind and champion of the oppressed. His concerto had been played badly in his own lifetime, and what a revelation it would have been to him to hear it rendered by a soloist and a conductor, neither having a score. But then Lanny thought: "What would Beethoven think if he could see what is happening in the land of his birth?" So the dreams of art fled, and painful reality took their place. Lanny thought: "The German soul has been captured by Hitler! What can he give it but his own madness and distraction? What can he make of it but an image of his distorted self?"

X

Hansi always wanted to be taken straight home after a performance; he was exhausted, and didn't care for sitting around in cafés. He entered the palace and was about to go to his room, when the telephone rang; Berlin calling, and Hansi said: "That will be Papa, wanting to know how the concert went."

He was right, and told his father that everything had gone well. Johannes didn't ask for particulars; instead he had tidings to impart. "The Reichstag building is burning."

"*Herrgott!*" exclaimed the son, and turned and repeated the words to the others.

"The Nazis are saying that the Communists set fire to it."

"But, Papa, that is crazy!"

"I must not talk about it. You will find the news in the papers, and do your own guessing. The building has been burning for a couple of hours, and they say that men were seen running through it with torches."

"It is a plot!" exclaimed Hansi.

"I cannot say; but I am glad that you are not here. You must stay where you are for the present. It is a terrible thing."

So Hansi did not go to bed for a long while. They sat and talked, and Lanny, who had friends on *Le Populaire*, called up that paper to get further details. It was believed that the great building was gutted, and the government was charging that it had been deliberately fired by emissaries of the Red International.

All four of the young people were familiar with that elaborate specimen of the Bismarck style of architecture, and could picture the scenes, both there and elsewhere in the city. "It is a frame-up," said Bess. "Communists are not terrorists." Lanny agreed with her, and Irma, whatever she thought, kept it to herself. It was inevitable that every Communist would call it a plot, and every Nazi would be equally certain of the opposite.

"Really, it is too obvious!" argued Hansi. "The elections less than six days away, and those scoundrels desperate for some means of discrediting us!"

"The workers will not be fooled!" insisted Bess. "Our party is monolithic."

Lanny thought: "The old phonograph record!" But he said: "It's a terrible thing, as Papa says. They will be raiding Communist headquarters all over Germany tonight. Be glad that you have a good alibi."

But neither of the musicians smiled at this idea. In their souls they were taking the blows which they knew must be falling upon their party comrades.

XI

What happened in the Reichstag building on that night of February 27 would be a subject of controversy inside and outside of Germany for years to come; but there could be no doubt about what happened elsewhere. Even while the four young people were talking in Paris, the leader of the Berlin S.A., Count Helldorf, was giving orders for the arrest of prominent Communists and Socialists.

The list of victims had been prepared in advance, and warrants, each with a photograph of the victim in question. The Count knew that the Marxists were the criminals, he said; and Göring announced that the demented Dutchman who was found in the building with matches and fire-lighters had a Communist party membership card on him. The statement turned out to be untrue, but it served for the moment.

Next day Hitler persuaded Hindenburg to sign a decree "for the safeguarding of the state from the Communist menace," and after that the Nazis had everything their own way. The prisons were filled with suspects, and the setting up of concentration camps began with a rush. The Prussian government, of which Göring was the head, issued a statement concerning the documents found in the raid on Karl Liebknecht Haus three days before the fire. The Communists had been plotting to burn down public buildings throughout Germany, and to start civil war and revolution on the Russian model; looting had been planned to begin right after the fire and terrorist acts were to be committed against persons and property. The publication of these documents was promised, but no one ever saw them, and the story was dropped as soon as it had served its purpose—which was to justify the abolishing of civil liberties throughout what had been the German Republic.

XII

As the evidence began to filter into the newspapers of Britain and France, the young Reds and Pinks spent many an hour trying to make up their minds about one of the great "frame-ups" of history. What brain had conceived it? What hand had carried it out? For the former role their suspicions centered upon a German World War aviator who had fled to Sweden, where he had become a dope addict and had been in a psychopathic institution. Hermann Göring was a great hulk of a man, absurdly vain, with a fondness for gaudy uniforms which was to make him the butt of Berlin wits; he was also a man of immense energy, brutal and unscrupulous, the perfect type of those freebooters who had ravaged the borders of the German empire in medieval times, had given themselves titles, and now had huge white marble statues of themselves in the Siegesallée, known to the Berlin wits as "the Cemetery of Art."

Hermann Göring had got his titles: Minister without Portfolio, Federal Commissioner for Air Transport, Prussian Minister of the Interior. They carried the same grants of power as in the old free-booting days, but unfortunately they were subject to elections; on the following Sunday the proletariat might go to the polls and strip Hermann of his glories—and this would be extremely annoying to a man of aristocratic tastes, a friend of the former Crown Prince and of Thyssen. As it happened, the man of action was in position to act, for his official residence was connected with the Reichstag building by a long underground passage; also he had at his command a well-trained army, eager to execute any command he might give. What did a building amount to, in comparison with the future of the N.S.D.A.P.?

The man whom the Nazis were finally to convict of the crime was a feeble-minded Dutchman who had been expelled from the Communist party of that country and had been a tramp all over Europe. The police maintained that at his original examination he had told a detailed story of setting fire to the curtains of the restaurant with matches and fire-lighters. But the restaurant wasn't the only room that burned; there had been a heavy explosion in the session chamber, and that vast place had become a mass of flames and explosive gases. The head of the Berlin fire department had observed trains of gasoline on the floors of the building. Immediately after the fire he announced that the police had carted away a truck-load of unburned incendiary materials from the scene of the fire; and immediately after making this announcement he was dismissed from his post.

Such were the details which the young radicals abroad put together and published in their papers. But the papers which might have spread such news in Germany had all been suppressed; their editors were in prison and many were being subjected to cruel tortures. A sickening thing to know that your comrades, idealists whom you had trusted and followed, were being pounded with rubber hose, danced upon with spiked boots, having their kidneys kicked loose and their testicles crushed. Still more terrible to know that civil rights were being murdered in one of the world's most highly developed nations; that the homeland of Goethe and Bach was in the hands of men who were capable of planning and perpetrating such atrocities.

XIII

The fire had the intended effect of throwing all Germany into a panic of fear. Not merely the Nazis, but Papen and Hugenberg were denouncing the Red conspirators over the radio. All the new techniques of propaganda were set at work to convince the voters that the Fatherland stood in deadly peril of a Communist revolution. Friday was proclaimed the "Day of the Awakening Nation." The Nazis marched with torchlights, and on the mountain-tops and on high towers in the cities great bonfires burned—fires of liberation, they were called. "O Lord, make us free!" prayed Hitler over the radio, and loud-speakers spread his words in every market-square in every town.

On Sunday the people voted, and the Nazi vote increased from nearly twelve million to more than seventeen million. But the Communists lost only about a million, and the Socialists practically none. The Catholics actually gained, in spite of all the suppressions; so it appeared that the German people were not so easy to stampede after all. The Nazis still didn't have a majority of the Reichstag deputies, so they couldn't form a government without the support and approval of the aristocrats. What was going to come out of that?

The answer was that Adi Hitler was going to have his way. He was going right on, day after day, pushing to his goal, and nobody was going to stop him. Objections would be raised in the Cabinet, and he would do what he had done in party conferences—argue, storm, plead, denounce, and threaten. He would make it impossible for anyone else to be heard, raise such a disturbance as could not be withstood, prove that he could outlast any opposition, that his frenzy was uncontrollable, his will irrepressible. But behind this seeming madness would be a watchful eye and a shrewd, calculating brain. Adi would know exactly what he was doing and how far he could go; if the opposition became too strong, he would give way, he would make promises—and then next day it would be discovered that his followers were going right ahead doing what he wanted done, and he would be saying that he couldn't control them. If it was something serious, like the Reichstag fire, he would know nothing about it, he would be completely taken aback, astounded, horrified; but it would be too late—the building would be burned, the victim would be dead, the die would be cast.

For more than a decade he had been training his followers to these tactics. They must be a band of desperadoes, stopping at nothing to get their way. Nothing on earth or in heaven was sacred except their cause; nothing was wrong that helped their cause and nothing was right that delayed it for a single hour. Individually and collectively they must be the most energetic and capable of criminals, also the most shameless and determined liars. They must be able to say anything, with the most bland and innocent expression, and if they were caught they must admit nothing, but turn the charge against the other fellow; he was the liar, he was the crook, he alone was capable of every wrongdoing. Adolf Hitler had never admitted anything to anybody; he had never told a lie in his life, had never committed any improper action; he was a consecrated soul, who lived and was ready to die for one single cause, the triumph of National Socialism and the liberation of the German *Volk*.

For ten years he had been organizing two private armies of young men, several hundred thousand fanatics imbued with that spirit: the Sturm Abteilung, or Storm Division, and the Schutz Staffel, or Defense Formation. They were the men who were going to carry out his will, and by now they knew it so well that they could act while he was eating, resting, sleeping—even while he was telling the world that he didn't want them to do what they were doing. Even if he told them to stop they would go right ahead to crush the last foe of National Socialism inside the Fatherland, and make the streets free to the brown battalions—the promise of that *Horst Wessel Lied* which Hitler had taught them to sing.

XIV

A dreadful series of events to watch; and the fact that you were physically safe from them wasn't enough for persons with any sensitiveness of soul. Hansi and Bess couldn't eat, they couldn't sleep, they couldn't think about anything except what was happening to their friends and associates at home. The Stormtroopers came when they pleased and did what they pleased; the police had orders to co-operate with them. They came to people's homes at night and took them away, and nothing more was heard of them. But gradually, through secret channels, word began to leak out concerning the dreadful happenings in the cellars of the Nazi headquarters in the Hedemannstrasse, in the Columbus-Haus, and in the old military prison in the General-Papen-Strasse.

Papa wrote brief notes, carefully guarded; he said: "Don't worry about us, we have friends." But Hansi and Bess knew a hundred people to worry about, and they read all the papers they could get and tried to put this item of news together with that and guess about the fate of their "monolithic party." They wrote anxious letters and then worried because no replies came. What had become of this leader and of that? Surely some must have escaped, and it didn't take long to get from Berlin to Paris.

Very difficult to practice music under such circumstances. What did the turn of a phrase matter, when madmen were loose in one's homeland, when a great civilization was being strangled. But the young couple had made engagements and had to keep them. They had to let Lanny and Irma drive them to Juan, dress themselves properly, and go to Emily's villa and play a program, not too mournful. When an encore was called for, Hansi played one of his favorites, Achron's *Jewish Prayer*, and he put two thousand years of weeping and wailing into it; it was quite wonderful, and the fashionable audience was deeply moved. The tears ran down Hansi's own cheeks, and he would have liked to say: "It is my people, weeping now in Germany."

But no, he couldn't say anything, it wouldn't have been good form; art must remain inside its ivory tower, and not descend onto that darkling plain where ignorant armies clash by night. Elegantly gowned ladies with sensitive souls enjoy mournful tones from the G-string of a fiddle, but do not care to weep over a bunch of Jews being beaten and kicked in the underground dungeons of old castles and prisons on the other side of the eastern border.

15

Die Strasse Frei

I

HANSI and Bess didn't return to Germany. Papa and Mama forbade them to come, and Lanny forbade them to go; Robbie Budd cabled, forbidding Bess; and more important yet, Adolf Hitler forbade them both. He did it by hunting down and jailing all prominent Communists, and making it plain that they could no longer exert any influence or accomplish any purpose in Germany. The policy of *Schrecklichkeit*, made famous during the World War, hadn't worked on the outside world, but could surely be made to work inside the Fatherland.

There was the Lodge at Bienvenu, and the young couple settled down in it. Beauty felt exactly as Irma did, she didn't want Reds about her, or want her home to have such an atmosphere; but she, too, had been a guest on the *Bessie Budd* and at the Berlin home, and couldn't fail to make a return; nor could she fail in kindness to Robbie's daughter. A compromise was worked out without ever a word being said about it; Hansi and Bess didn't invite their Red friends to the estate, but met them in Juan or Cannes. That helped a little, but not entirely, for the young couple couldn't help bringing their troubles home with them in their thoughts and aspect.

It was the same thing Lanny had witnessed ten years ago, when Mussolini had seized power. Swarms of refugees fled from the terror, and naturally it wasn't long before they found out where Hansi and Bess were staying. The young couple were supposed to be rich, and, compared to the status of most Communists, they were. They could hardly say no to anybody—for what did the word "comrade" mean if not to open your heart and your purse in a time of agony such as this? Papa would send money; they didn't tell him what it was for—since it was to be assumed that letters both going and coming were liable to be opened; but Papa could guess, and no price was too high to keep his darlings from coming back into danger.

But he couldn't send enough; not the purse of Fortunatus, not the touch of Midas, would suffice for the needs of all the Hitler victims, from this time on for years beyond any man's guessing. Either you must have the hide of a rhinoceros, or you would have heartache for your portion. Fate would devise new ways to make you suffer—every day, every hour, if you would permit it. The most pitiful victims, the most tragic stories: people who had been tortured until they were physical and mental wrecks; people whose husbands or wives, sweethearts, children, parents, or what not, were being tortured, or might be tomorrow. People who had fled, leaving everything, and had not the price of a meal; people begging for railroad fare to bring this or that imperiled person out of the clutches of the fiends.

Hansi and Bess were having their own meals, with one of Leese's relatives to work for them, and presently this girl began to report that they weren't having enough to eat; they had given their last franc to some hungry comrade, and were even taking out of the house food which they had obtained on credit. Beauty would invite them over to a meal, and they would come; because, after all, you can't play music if you don't eat, and it wouldn't do for Hansi to faint in the middle of concerts which they were giving for the benefit of refugees. Beauty broke down and wept, and Bess wept, and they had a grand emotional spree; but there wasn't a word they could say to each other, literally not a word, without getting into an argument.

Beauty wanted to say: "My God, girl, don't you know about Europe? I've lived here more years than I like to tell, and I can't remember the time when there weren't people fleeing from oppression somewhere. Even before the war, it was revolutionists from Russia, and Jews, and people from the Balkans, and from Spain, and from Armenia—I forget most of the places. Do you think you can solve all the problems of the world?"

Bess wanted to reply: "It is your bourgeois mind." But you can't say that to your hostess, so she would content herself with the statement: "These are my comrades and this is my cause."

II

Lanny and Irma went back to Paris, and it was the same there. The refugees had Lanny's address—the first arrivals got it from Uncle Jesse, and the rest from one another. It was an extremely fashionable address, and it was incomprehensible to any comrade in distress that a person who lived, even temporarily, in the palace of the Duc de Belleaumont could fail to be rolling in wealth, and be in position to help him, and all his comrades, and his sisters and his cousins and his aunts back in the homeland, and bring them all to Paris and put them up in one of the guest suites of the palace—or at least pay for the rent of a garret. It was a situation trying to the tempers and to the moral sense of many unfortunate persons. Not all of them were saints, by any means, and hunger is a powerful force, driving people to all sorts of expedients. There were Reds who were not above exaggerating their distress; there were common beggars and cheats who would pretend to be Reds, or anything whatever in order to get a handout. As time went on such problems would grow worse, because parasites increase and multiply like all other creatures, and are automatically driven to perfect the arts by which they survive.

Lanny had been through this and had learned costly and painful lessons from the refugees of Fascism; but now it was worse, because Hitler was taking Mussolini's arts and applying them with German thoroughness. Also, Lanny's own position was worse because he had a rich wife, and no refugee could be made to understand how, if he lived with her, he couldn't get money from her. He must be getting it, because look at his car, and how he dressed, and the places he went to! Was he a genuine sympathizer, or just a playboy seeking thrills? If the latter, then surely he was a fair mark; you could figure that if you didn't get his money, the tailors and restaurateurs and what not would get it; so keep after him and don't be troubled by false modesty.

Irma, like Beauty, had a "bourgeois mind," and wanted to say the things which bourgeois ladies say. But she had discovered by now what hurt her husband's feelings and what, if persisted in, made him angry. They had so many ways of being happy together, and she did so desire to avoid quarreling, as so many other young couples were doing. She would repress her ideas on the subject of the class struggle, and try by various devices to keep her weak-minded partner out of the way of temptation. The servants were told that when dubious-looking strangers called, they were to say that Monsieur Budd was not at home, and that they didn't know when he would return. Irma would invent subtle schemes to keep him occupied and out of the company of Red deputies and Pink editors.

But Lanny wasn't altogether without understanding of subtleties. He had been brought up with bourgeois ladies, and knew their minds, and just when they were engaged in manipulating him, and what for. He tried to play fair about it, and not give too much of Irma's money to the refugees, and not so much of his own that he would be caught without funds. This meant that he, too, had to do a lot of dodging and making of excuses to the unfortunates; and then he would feel ashamed of himself, and more sick at heart than

ever, because the world wasn't what he wanted it to be, **nor was**
he the noble and generous soul he would have preferred to believe
himself.

III

In spite of the best efforts in the world, Lanny found it impossible to keep out of arguments with the people he met. Political and
economic affairs kept forcing themselves upon him. People who
came to the house wanted to talk about what was happening in
Germany, and to know what he thought—or perhaps they already
knew, and were moved to challenge him. Nobody had been better
trained in drawing-room manners than Beauty Budd's son, but in
these times even French urbanity would fail; people couldn't listen
to ideas which they considered outrageous without giving some
signs of disapproval. Gone were the old days when it was a gossip
tidbit that Mr. Irma Barnes was a Pink and that his wife was upset
about it; now it was a serious matter, and quite insufferable.

"I thought you said you were not a Communist," remarked
Madame de Cloisson, the banker's wife, with acid in her tone.

"I am not, Madame. I am only defending those fundamental liberties which have been the glory of the French Republic."

"Liberties which the Communists repudiate, I am told!"

"Even so, Madame, we do not wish to make ourselves like them,
or to surrender what we hold dear."

"That sounds very well, but it means that you are doing exactly
what they would wish to have done."

That was all, but it was enough. Madame de Cloisson was a
grande dame, and her influence might mean success or failure to
an American woman with social ambitions. Irma didn't hear this
passage at arms, but some kind friend was at pains to tell her about
it, and she knew that it might cancel the efforts she had been making during the past year. But still she didn't say anything; she
wanted to be fair, and she knew that Lanny had been fair—he had
told her about his eccentricities before he asked for her, and she
had taken him on his own terms. It was her hard luck that she

hadn't realized what it would mean to have a husband dyed a
shade of Pink so deep that the bourgeois mind couldn't tell it from
scarlet.

IV

The new Reichstag was summoned promptly. It met in Potsdam,
home of the old glories of Prussia, and Hitler applied his genius
to the invention of ceremonies to express his patriotic intentions
and to arouse the hopes of the German *Volk*. All the land burst
out with flags—the new *Hakenkreuz* flag, which the Cabinet had
decreed should replace that of the dying Republic. Once more the
beacons blazed on the hilltops, and there were torchlight parades
of all the Nazi organizations, and of students and children. Hitler
laid a wreath on the tomb of his dead comrades. Hindenburg opened
the Reichstag, and the ceremonies were broadcast to all the schools.
The "Bohemian corporal" delivered one of his inspired addresses,
in which he told his former Field Marshal that by making him
Chancellor he had "consummated the marriage between the symbols of ancient glory and of young might."

Hitler wanted two things: to get the mastery of Germany, and
to be let alone by the outside world while he was doing it. When
the Reichstag began its regular sessions, in the Kroll Opera House in
Berlin, he delivered a carefully prepared address in which he declared that it was the Communists who had fired the Reichstag
building, and that their treason was to be "blotted out with barbaric
ruthlessness." He told the rich that "capital serves business, and
business the people"; that there was to be "strongest support of
private initiative and the recognition of property." The rich could
have asked no more. To the German peasants he promised "rescue,"
and to the army of the unemployed "restoration to the productive
process."

To enable him to carry out this program he asked for a grant of
power in a trickily worded measure which he called a "law for the
lifting of want from the people and empire." The purpose of the
law was to permit the present Cabinet, and the present Cabinet

alone, to make laws and spend money without consulting the Reichstag; but it didn't say that; it merely repealed by number those articles in the Constitution which reserved these crucial powers to the Reichstag. The new grant was to come to an end in four years, and sooner if any other Cabinet came into office. Nobody but Adolf was ever to be the Führer of Germany!

This device was in accord with the new Chancellor's "legality complex"; he would get the tools of power into his hands by what the great mass of the people would accept as due process of law. His speech in support of the measure was shrewdly contrived to meet the prejudices of all the different parties, except the Communists, who had been barred from their seats, and the Socialists, who were soon to share that fate. A mob of armed Nazis stood outside the building, shouting their demands that the act be passed, and it carried by a vote of 441 to 94, the dissenters being Socialists. Then Göring, President of the Reichstag, declared the session adjourned, and so a great people lost their liberties while rejoicing over gaining them.

V

During this period there were excitements in the United States as well as in Germany. Crises and failures became epidemic; in one state after another it was necessary for the governor to decree a closing of all the banks. Robbie Budd wrote that it was because the people of the country couldn't contemplate the prospect of having their affairs managed by a Democrat. When the new President was inaugurated—which fell upon the day before the Hitler elections—his first action was to order the closing of all the banks in the United States—which to Robbie was about the same thing as the ending of the world. His letter on the subject was so pessimistic that his son was moved to send him a cablegram: "Cheer up you will still eat."

Really it wasn't as bad as everybody had expected. People took it as a joke; the richest man in the country might happen to have only a few dimes in his pocket, and that was all he had, and his friends thought it was funny, and he had to laugh, too. But every-body trusted him, and took his checks, so he could have whatever he wanted, the same as before. Robbie didn't miss a meal, nor did any other Budd. Meanwhile they listened to a magnificent radio voice telling them with calm confidence that the new government was going to act, and act quickly, and that all the problems of the country were going to be solved. The New Deal was getting under way.

The first step was to join Britain and the other nations off the gold standard. To Robbie it meant inflation, and that his country was going to see what Germany had seen. The next thing was to sort out the banks, and decide which were sound and in position to open with government backing. The effect of that was to move Wall Street to Washington; the government became the center of power, and the bankers came hurrying with their lawyers and their brief-cases. A harum-scarum sort of affair, in which all sorts of blunders were made; America was going to be a land of absurdities for many years, and the Robbie Budds would have endless oppor-tunities to ridicule and denounce. But business would begin to pick up and people would begin to eat again—and not just the Budds.

Lanny didn't have any trouble, for the French banks weren't closed, and he had money to spare for his refugees. If Irma's income stayed in hock they could go back to Bienvenu—the cyclone cellar, she called it. She had never had to earn any money in her life, so it was easy for her to take her husband's debonair attitude to it. If she lost hers, everybody else would lose theirs, and you wouldn't have any sense of inferiority. Really, it was rather exciting, and the younger generation took it as a sporting proposition. Irma would swing between that attitude and her dream of an august and dis-tinguished salon; when Lanny pointed out to her the inconsistency of the two attitudes she was content to laugh.

VI

Rick came over to spend a few days with them; he was no longer so poor that he had to worry about a trip to Paris, and it was his business to meet all sorts of people and watch what was going on. A lame ex-aviator who would some day become a baronet, and who meanwhile had made a hit as a playwright, was a romantic figure, even though he was extreme in his talk. The ladies were pleased with him, and Irma discovered that she had what she might call a home-made lion; she would tell the smartest people how Lanny had been Rick's boyhood chum, had taken him to conferences all over Europe and helped to plan and even revise his plays; also how she, Irma, had helped to finance *The Dress-Suit Bribe*, and was not merely getting her money back but a considerable profit. It was the first investment that had been her very own, and she could be excused for being proud of it, and for boasting about it to her mother and her several uncles.

Irma decided more and more that she liked the English attitude to life. Englishmen felt intensely, as you soon found out, but they were content to state their position quietly, and even to understate it; they didn't raise their voices like so many Americans, or gesticulate like the French, or bluster like the Germans. They had been in the business of governing for a long time, and rather took it for granted; but at the same time they were willing to consider the other fellow's point of view, and to work out some sort of compromise. Especially did that seem to be the case with continental affairs, where they were trying so hard to mediate between the French and the Germans. Denis de Bruyne said: "*Vraiment*, how generous they can be when they are disposing of French interests!"

The Conference on Arms Limitation was still in session at Geneva, still wrangling, exposing the unwillingness of any nation to trust any other, or to concede what might be to a rival nation's advantage. Rick, the Socialist, said: "There isn't enough trade to go round, and they can't agree how to divide it." Jesse Blackless, the Communist, said: "They are castaways on a raft, and the food is giving out; they know that somebody has to be eaten, and who will consent to be the first?"

There was a lot of private conferring between the British and the French, and British officials were continually coming and going in Paris. Rick brought several of them to the palace for tea and for

dancing, and this was the sort of thing for which Irma had wanted
the palace; she felt that she was getting her money's worth—though
of course she didn't use any such crude phrase. Among those who
came was that Lord Wickthorpe whom she had met in Geneva
last year. He had a post of some responsibility, and talked among
insiders, as he counted Rick and the Budds. Irma listened attentively, because, as a hostess, she had to say something and wanted
it to be right. Afterward she talked with Lanny, getting him to
explain what she hadn't understood. Incidentally she remarked: "I
wish you could take a balanced view of things, the way Wickthorpe
does."

"Darling," he answered, "Wickthorpe is a member of the British
aristocracy, and is here to fight for the Empire. He's got pretty
much of everything he wants, so naturally he can take things easy."

"Haven't you got what you want, Lanny?"

"Not by a darn sight! I want a better life for masses of people
who aren't in the British Empire, and for many in the Empire whom
Wickthorpe leaves out of his calculations."

"But, Lanny, you heard him say: 'We're all Socialists now.' "

"I know, dear; it's a formula. But they write their definition of
the word, and it means that Wickthorpe will do the governing, and
decide what the workers are to get. The slum-dwellers in the East
End will go on paying tribute to the landlords, and the ryots in
India and the niggers in South Africa will be sweated to make
luxury for British bondholders."

"Oh, dear!" exclaimed the would-be *salonnière*. "Who will want
to come to see us if you talk like that?"

VII

Lanny was interested in the point of view of these official persons, and sat in the splendid library of his wife's rented home and
listened to Rick discussing the Nazi movement with Wickthorpe
and his secretary, Reggie Catledge, who was also his cousin. It was
a point of view in no way novel to Lanny, his father having explained it when he was a very small boy. The governing classes of

Britain made it a fixed policy never to permit one nation to become strong enough to dominate the Continent; regardless of which nation it might be, they would set themselves the task of raising some rival as a counterweight.

Wickthorpe disliked the Nazis and what they were doing, but he didn't rave at them; he just said they were a set of bounders. He took it for granted that their fantastic promises had been made as a means of getting power. "Just politics," he said, and refused to be disturbed by the possibility that the bounders might mean what they said. The two Englishmen listened with interest to what Lanny had to tell about his meeting with Hitler, and asked him some questions, but at the end they were of the same opinion still.

"We've had so many wild men in our public life," said his lordship. "You and I are too young to remember how old John Burns used to rave in his speeches at Trafalgar Square, but my parents got up slumming parties to go and listen. Long afterward you could meet the old boy in the New Reform Club and hear him talk about it—in fact you could hardly get him to talk about anything else."

"He was a very strict teetotaler, but his face was as red as a turkey-cock's wattles," added Catledge.

"Hitler doesn't drink, either," said Lanny; but the others didn't appear to attach any importance to that.

They went on to point out to Rick that the French imperialists were arrogant, and their diplomats had made a lot of trouble in Syria, Iraq, and other places. French bankers had a great store of gold, and made use of it in ways inconvenient to their rivals. Wickthorpe didn't say that Hitler would serve to keep the French occupied, but his arguments made plain the general idea that you couldn't entrust any one set of foreigners with too much power. It was even possible to guess that he wasn't too heartbroken over what had happened in Wall Street during the past four years; because a large part of Britain's prosperity depended upon her service as clearinghouse for international transactions, and it had been highly embarrassing to have the dollar prove more stable than the pound.

Wickthorpe and his cousin had it comfortably figured out what was to be Hitler's role in world affairs. Assuming that he was able to continue in power, he was going to fight Russia. He was the logical one to do this, because of his geographical position; for Britain this factor made it almost impossible. Lanny wanted to ask: "Why does anybody have to fight Russia?"—but he was afraid that would be an improper question.

Here sat this tall young lord, smooth-skinned, pink-cheeked, with his fair hair and little toy mustache; perfectly groomed, perfectly at ease; one couldn't say perfectly educated, for there were many important things about which he knew nothing—science, for example, and the economics of reality as opposed to those of classical theory. He knew ancient Greek and Roman civilization, and Hebrew theology made over by the Church of England; he had recent world affairs at his fingertips. He possessed perfect poise, charm of manner, and skill in keeping to himself those thoughts which particular persons had no right to share. He was sure that he was a gentleman and a Christian, yet he took it for granted that it was his duty to labor and plan to bring about one of the most cruel and bloody of wars.

"You know, you might do quite a spot of trade with the Soviet Union," suggested Lanny, mildly. "They have the raw materials and you have the machines."

"Yes, Budd, but one can't think merely about business; there are moral factors."

"But might not the Reds be toned down and acquire a sense of responsibility, just as well as the Nazis?"

"We can't trust the blighters."

"I'm told that they meet their bills regularly. The Chase National gets along with them quite well."

"I don't mean financially, I mean politically. They would start breaking into the Balkans, or India, or China; their agents are trying to stir up revolution all the time."

Lanny persisted. "Have you thought of the possibility that if you won't trade with them, the Nazis may? Their economies supplement each other."

"But their ideologies are at opposite poles!"

"They seem to be; but you yourself say how ideologies change when men get power. It seems to me that Stalin and Hitler are self-made men, and might be able to understand each other. Suppose one day Stalin should say to Hitler, or Hitler tc Stalin: 'See here, old top, the British have got it fixed up for us to ruin ourselves fighting. Why should we oblige them?' "

"I admit that would be a pretty bad day," said young Lord Wickthorpe. He said it with a smile, not taking it seriously. When Rick pinned him down to it, he gave yet another reason why it was impossible to consider a large-scale deal with the Soviet Union—the effect it would have upon politics at home. "It would set up the Reds, and it might bring labor back into power."

Said Rick to Lanny, when they were alone: "Class is more than country!"

VIII

The Nazi program of repression of the Jews was being carried out step by step, which was going to be the Nazi fashion. Civil servants of Jewish blood were being turned out of their jobs and good Aryans of the right party affiliations put in their place. Jewish lawyers were forbidden to practice in the courts. "Jew signs" were being pasted or painted on places of business which belonged to the despised race. Beatings and terrorism were being secretly encouraged, for the purpose of driving the Jews out and depriving them of jobs and property. When such incidents were mentioned in the press they would be blamed upon "persons unknown masquerading as Stormtroopers."

But refugees escaping to the outside world would report the truth, and there was a ferment of indignation among the Jews of all countries; they and their sympathizers held meetings of protest, and a movement was started to boycott trade with Germany. The reaction in the Fatherland was immediate, and Johannes wrote about it—very significantly he wrote only to Lanny, never to his son, and mailed the letters unsigned and with no mark to identify them. It had been made a prison offense to give information to foreigners, and in his letters Johannes addressed Lanny as a German, and warned him not to tell anyone in Paris!

The boycott was worrying the business men of the country, and at the same time enraging the party leaders, and it was a question which point of view would prevail. Jupp Goebbels was calling for a boycott of Jewish businesses in Germany, and the result was a panic on the stock exchange—for some of the principal enterprises of the Fatherland were Jewish-owned, including the big department stores of Berlin. These were the concerns which the original party program had promised to "socialize," and now the ardent young S.A.'s and S.S.'s were on tiptoe to go in and do the job.

The Cabinet was having one of its customary rows over the question, so Johannes explained. The business magnates who had financed Hitler's rise were coming down on him; how could they pay taxes, how could the government be financed, if rowdies were to be turned loose to wreck business both at home and abroad? The result of this tug-of-war was a curious and rather comical compromise; the boycott which the party fanatics had announced to begin on the first day of April was to be carried on, but it was to continue for only one business day of eight hours; then Germany would wait for three days, to see if there was a proper response from the foreign agents and Jewish vampires who had been so shamelessly lying about the Fatherland. If they showed repentance and abandoned their insolent threats, then Germany would in turn permit the Jewish businesses to continue in peace; otherwise they would be sternly punished, perhaps exterminated, and the blame would rest upon the Jewish vampires abroad.

This boycott was the idea of Dr. Goebbels—the Führer himself being busy with the reorganizing of the various state governments. On the evening before the event the crippled little dwarf with the huge wide mouth spoke to his party comrades at a meeting in a hall of the West End, and all over Germany the Stormtroopers listened over the radio. The orator called for a demonstration of "iron discipline"; there must be no violence, but all Jewish establishments would be picketed, and no German man or woman would enter such a place.

The day was made into a Nazi holiday. The Jews stayed at home, and the Brownshirts marched through all the cities and towns of the Fatherland, singing their song to the effect that Jewish blood must spurt from the knife. They posted "Jew signs" wherever there was a merchant who couldn't prove that he had four Aryan grand-parents. They did the same for doctors and hospitals, using a poster consisting of a circular blob of yellow on a black background, the recognized sign of quarantine throughout Europe; thus they told the world that a Jewish doctor was as bad as the smallpox or scarlet fever, typhus or leprosy he attempted to cure.

These orders were followed pretty well in the fashionable districts, but in poorer neighborhoods and the smaller towns the ardent Stormtroopers pasted signs on the foreheads of shoppers in Jewish stores, and they stripped and beat a woman who insisted on entering. That evening there was a giant meeting in the Tempelhof Airdrome, and Goebbels exulted in the demonstration which had been given to the world. The insolent foreigners would be awed and brought to their knees, he declared; and since most of the newspapers had by now been confiscated, the people could either believe that or believe nothing. The foreigners, of course, laughed; they knew that they weren't awed, and the mass meetings and distribution of boycott leaflets went on. But the Nazi leaders chose to declare otherwise, and next day there was a washing of windows throughout Germany, and "business as usual" became the motto for both Aryans and non-Aryans.

IX

There were curious outgrowths of this anti-Semitic frenzy. An "Association of German National Jews" was formed, and issued a manifesto saying that the Jews were being fairly treated and there was no truth in the stories of atrocities; some leading Jews signed this, and the name of Johannes Robin was among them. Perhaps he really believed it, who could say? He had to read German newspapers, like everybody else; those foreign papers which reported the atrocities were banned. Perhaps he considered that the outside boy-cotts would really do more harm than good, and that the six hundred thousand native Jews in the Fatherland were not in position to offer resistance to a hundred times as many Germans. The Jews had survived through the centuries by bending like the willow instead of standing like the oak. Johannes didn't mention the subject in his letters, either signed or unsigned. Was he a little ashamed of what he did?

It seemed to an American that a man could hardly be happy living under such conditions. Lanny wrote a carefully guarded letter to the effect that Hansi was giving important concerts and Irma various social events; they would be delighted to have the family present. Johannes replied that some business matters kept him from leaving just now; he bade them not to worry about the new decrees forbidding anyone to leave Germany without special passports, for he could get them for himself and family whenever he wished. He added that Germany was their home and they all loved the German people. That was the right sort of letter for a Jew, and maybe the statements were true, with a few qualifications.

The Nazis had learned a lesson from the boycott, even though they would never admit it. The brass band stage of persecution was at an end, and they set to work to achieve their purpose quietly. The weeding out of Jews, and of those married to Jews, went on rapidly. No Jew could teach in any school or university in Germany; no Jewish lawyer could practice; no Jew could hold any official post, down to the smallest clerkship. This meant tens of thousands of positions for the rank and file Nazis, and was a way of keeping promises to them, much easier than socializing industry or breaking up the great landed estates.

The unemployed intellectuals found work carrying on genealogical researches for the millions of persons who desired to establish their ancestry. An extraordinary development—there were persons who had an Aryan mother and a Jewish father, or an Aryan grandmother and a Jewish grandfather, who instituted researches as to the morals of their female ancestors, and established themselves as Aryans by proving themselves to be bastards! Before long the Nazis discovered that there were some Jews who were useful, so there was officially established a caste of "honorary Aryans." Truly it seemed that a great people had gone mad; but it is a fact well known to alienists that you cannot convince a madman of his own condition, and only make him madder by trying.

By one means or another it was conveyed to leading Jews that they had better resign from directorships of corporations, and from executive positions which were desired by the nephews or cousins of some Nazi official. Frequently the methods used were such that the Jew committed suicide; and while these events were not reported in the press, word about them spread by underground channels. That was the way with the terror; people disappeared, and rumors started, and sometimes the rumors became worse than the reality. Old prisons and state institutions, old army barracks which had stood empty since the Versailles treaty, were turned into concentration camps and rapidly filled with men and women; motor trucks brought new loads daily, until the total came near to a hundred thousand.

Lanny wrote again to say what a mistake his friends were making not to come and witness Hansi's musical and Irma's social triumphs. This time Johannes's reply was that his business cares were beginning to wear on him, and that his physicians advised a sea trip. He was getting the *Bessie Budd* ready for another cruise, this time a real one; he wanted Hansi and Bess to meet him at one of the northern French ports, and he hoped that the Budds would come along—the whole family, Lanny and Irma, Mr. and Mrs. Dingle, Marceline and Baby Frances, with as many governesses and nurses as they pleased. As before, the cruise would be to whatever part of the world the Budd family preferred; Johannes suggested crossing the Atlantic again and visiting Newcastle and Long Island; then, in the autumn, they might go down to the West Indies, and perhaps through the Panama Canal to California, and if they wished, to Honolulu and Japan, Bali, Java, India, Persia—all the romantic and scenic and historic places they could think of. A university under Diesel power!

X

This made it necessary for Irma to come to a decision which she had postponed to the last moment. Was she going to take the palace for another year? She had got used to it, and had a competent staff well trained; also she was established as a hostess, and it seemed a shame to lose all this momentum. But, on the other hand, money was growing scarcer and scarcer. The dreadful depression—Lanny had shown her the calculations of an economist that it had cost the United States half a dozen times the cost of the World War. Thanks to the Reconstruction Finance Corporation, interest payments on industrial bonds were being met, but many of Irma's "blue chip" stocks were paying no dividends, and she was telling her friends that she was living on chocolate, biscuits, and Coca-Cola—meaning not that these were her diet, but her dividends.

She had Shore Acres on her hands with its enormous overhead; she had had to cut down on her mother, and the mother in turn had notified all the help that they might stay on and work for their keep, but there would be no more salaries. Even so, the food bill was large, and the taxes exorbitant—when were taxes not? Mrs. Barnes's letters conveyed to her daughter a sense of near destitution.

"You don't really care very much for this palace, do you, Lanny?" So asked the distressed one, lying in the pink satin splendor of the bed in which Madame de Maintenon was reputed to have entertained the Sun King.

"You know, dear, I don't undertake to tell you how to spend your money."

"But I'm asking you."

"You know without asking. If you spend more money than you have, you're poor, no matter what the amount is."

"Do you think if we come back to Paris after the depression, I'll be able to start as a hostess again?"

"It depends entirely upon how much of your money you have managed to hold on to."

"Oh, Lanny, you're horrid!" exclaimed the hostess.

"You asked for it," he chuckled.

Nearly a year had passed since the Queen Mother had seen her grandchild, and that was something to be taken into consideration. Her satisfaction would be boundless; and it would be a pleasure to meet all those New York friends and hear the gossip. Lanny could stand it if it wasn't for too long. And what a relief to Uncle Joseph Barnes, trustee and manager of the Barnes estate, to know that his charge wouldn't be drawing any checks for a year!

"Lanny, do you suppose that Johannes can really afford to take care of us all that time?"

"He could go alone if he preferred," replied the son of Budd's. "As a matter of fact, I suspect the rascal has more money now than ever before in his life. He makes it going and coming; whether times are good or bad; whether the market goes up or down."

"How does he manage it, Lanny?"

"He's watching all the time, and he keeps his money where he can shift it quickly. He's a bull in good times and a bear in bad."

"It's really quite wonderful," said Irma. "Do you suppose we could learn to do things that way?"

"Nothing would please him more than to teach us; but the trouble is you have to put your mind on it and keep it there."

"I suppose it *would* get to be a bore," admitted Irma, stretching her lovely arms and yawning in the pink satin couch of the Grand Monarque's official mistress.

XI

The young couple ran down to Juan, and Irma and Beauty held a sort of mothers' conference on the problems of their future. Beauty was keen on yachting trips; she found them a distinguished mode of travel; she had learned her geography and history that way, and Irma might do the same. But the important thing was the safety they afforded. Beauty didn't care how much Red and Pink talk her young people indulged in, provided that outside Reds and Pinks couldn't get at them, to borrow their money, get them to start schools or papers or what not, and involve them in fights with Fascists and police. Carry them off to sea and keep them—and perhaps find some lovely tropical island where they could settle down and live in peace and harmony until the cycle of revolutions and counter-revolutions had been completed! Let the yacht serve as a supply ship to bring the latest musical compositions and whatever else they had read of; but no Communist or Socialist agitators, no Fascists or Nazis marching, shouting, brandishing guns and daggers! "Do you suppose they have mosquitoes in the South Seas?" inquired the soft pink Beauty Budd.

She persuaded Irma that this was the way to keep her temperamental husband happy and safe. Paris was a frightfully dangerous place right now; look at the way Jesse was carrying on, rushing about from one meeting to another, making hysterical speeches, calling the Nazis all the bad names in the French language! A copy of *L'Humanité* came every day to Bienvenu, and Beauty would look into it sometimes, thinking that it was her duty to keep track of her brother's doings; it made her quail, for she knew what fury it would arouse in the Hitlerites, and she knew how many rich and important persons in France sympathized with them. The Croix de Feu, the Jeunesse Française and other groups were preparing to meet force with force; the great banks and other vested interests would surely not permit their power to be destroyed without a fight, and it would be far more bloody and terrible than what had happened in Germany. "Let's get away from it," pleaded Beauty. "Stay until the storm blows over, and we can judge whether it's safe to return."

Irma was persuaded, and they sat down and composed between them a letter to Nina, tactfully contrived to be read by Rick without giving him offense. There wasn't any danger in England—at least, none that Rick would admit—and the word "escapist" was one of his strongest terms of contempt. To Rick the cruise was presented as an ideal opportunity to concentrate upon the writing of a new play. On Nina's part it would be an act of friendship to come and make a fourth hand at bridge. To Alfy it would offer lessons in geography and history, plus a chance to fight out his temperamental differences with Marceline. If the parents didn't want to take the youngster from school so early, he could cross to New York by steamer and spend the summer with the party.

They read this letter to Lanny, who said it was all right, but he could do better as concerned his chum. Lanny was cooking up in his head a marvelous scheme. He was guessing the psychology of a Jewish money-master who had just witnessed the seizing of his country by a bunch of gangsters. It was bound to have made a dent in his mind, and dispose him to realize that he and the other capitalists were living and operating inside the crater of a volcano. Lanny was planning to lay a subtle and well-disguised siege to one of the wealthiest of Jews, to persuade him that some form of social change was inevitable, and to get his help to bring it about in orderly fashion. It was the plan which Lanny had already discussed with Rick, to start a weekly paper of free discussion, not pledged to any party or doctrine, but to the general tendency towards co-operative industry conducted under the democratic process.

"We can have him to ourselves for several months, maybe for a year; and if we can persuade him to back us, we can do the job on a big scale and make a real go of it. Won't you come and help? You can answer his questions so much better than I, and I believe you could put it through."

This was a greater temptation than any Utopian dreamer could resist. Rick said, "All right," and Lanny telegraphed the decision to Johannes. He was tempted to repeat the quotation from Tennyson's *Ulysses* which he had used a few years ago on a similar occasion—"My purpose holds to sail beyond the sunset and the baths of all the western stars, until I die." But he reminded himself that the Fatherland was now Hitlerland, and a sense of humor has never been a prominent German characteristic. What might not a Nazi party censor make out of eight or ten lines of English blank verse telegraphed from the French Riviera!

BOOK FOUR

As on a Darkling Plain

16

Root of All Evil

I

A WORLD conqueror had appeared in modern times. Alexander, Caesar, Attila, Genghis Khan, Napoleon—another such as these, appearing in the age of electricity, of rotary presses and radio, when nine men out of ten would have said it was impossible. A world conqueror has to be a man of few ideas, and those fixed; a peculiar combination of exactly the right qualities, both good and bad—iron determination, irresistible energy, and no scruples of any sort. He has to know what he wants, and permit no obstacle to stand in the way of his getting it. He has to understand the minds of other men, both foes and friends, and what greeds, fears, hates, jealousies will move them to action. He must understand the mass mind, the ideals or delusions which sway it; he must be enough of a fanatic to talk their language, though not enough to be controlled by it. He must believe in nothing but his own destiny, the glorified image of himself on the screen of history; whole races of mankind made over in his own image and according to his will. To accomplish that purpose he must be liar, thief, and murderer upon a world-wide scale; he must be ready without hesitation to commit every crime his own interest commands, whether upon individuals or nations. He must pave the highway for his legions with the bones of his enemies, he must float his battleships upon oceans of human blood, he must compose his songs of glory out of the groans and curses of mankind.

The singular advantage enjoyed by Adolf Hitler was that his own people believed what he said, while other peoples couldn't and wouldn't. The attitude of the outside world to him was that of the farmer who stared at a giraffe in the circus and exclaimed: "There ain't no sich animal!" The more Adolf told the world what he was and what he meant to do, the more the world smiled incredulously. There were men like that in every lunatic asylum; the type was so familiar that any psychiatrist could diagnose it from a single paragraph of a speech or a single page of a book. Sensible men said: "*Nut!*" and went on about their affairs, leaving Adolf to conquer the world. Here and there a man of social insight cried out warnings of what was going on; but these, too, were a well-known type and the psychiatrists had names for them.

Adolf Hitler got the mastery of the National Socialist Party because of his combination of qualities; because he was the most fanatical, the most determined, the most tireless, and at the same time the shrewdest, the most unscrupulous, the most deadly. From the beginning men had revolted against his authority, and while he was weak he had wheedled and cajoled them and when he became strong he had crushed them. There had been split after split in his movement, and he had gone after the leaders of the factions without ruth; even before he had got the authority of government in his hands, his fanatical Stormtroopers had been beating and sometimes murdering the opponents of this new dark religion of *Blut und Boden*, blood and soil. Work with Adolf Hitler and you would rise to power in the world; oppose him, and your brains would be spattered on the pavement, or you would be shot in the back and left unburied in a dark wood.

Hermann Göring, aviator and army officer, man of wealth, of luxurious tastes and insatiable vanities, hated and despised Joseph Goebbels, the blabbing journalist, the club-footed little dwarf with the venom-spitting tongue; and these sentiments were cordially reciprocated. Jupp would have thrown vitriol into Hermann's face, Hermann would have shot Jupp on sight—if either had dared. But the Führer needed Hermann as a master executive and Jupp as a master propagandist, and he put them into harness and drove them as a team. The same thing was true of hundreds of men in that party of madness and hate: World War victims, depression victims, psychopaths, drug addicts, perverts, criminals—they all needed Adolf a little more than Adolf needed them, and he welded them into something more powerful than themselves. Hardly one who wasn't sure that he was a greater man than Adolf, and better fitted to lead the party; in the old days many had patronized him, and in their hearts they still did so; but he had won out over them, because of the combination of qualities. He was the one who had persuaded the masses to trust him, and he was the one who could lead the N.S.D.A.P. and all its members and officials upon the road to conquest.

II

Adolf Hitler had watched Lenin, he now was watching Stalin and Mussolini, and had learned from them all. In June of the year 1924, when Lanny Budd had been in Rome, Benito Mussolini had been Premier of Italy for more than twenty months, but the Socialists were still publishing papers with several times as many readers as Mussolini's papers, and there was still freedom of speech in the Italian parliament and elsewhere; there was still an opposition party, there were labor unions and co-operatives and other means of resistance to the will of the Fascists. It had taken the murderer of Matteotti another year and more to accomplish his purpose of crushing opposition and making himself master of the Italian nation.

But Adolf's time-table was different from that. Adolf had a job to do in the outside world, and had no idea of dawdling for three years before beginning it. He knew how to wait, but would never wait an hour longer than necessary, and would be his own judge of the timing; he would startle the world, and even his own followers, by the suddenness and speed of his moves.

First, always first, the psychological preparation. Was he going to wipe out the rights of German labor, to destroy a movement which the workers had been patiently building for nearly a century? Obviously, then, the first step was to come to labor with outstretched hands, to enfold it in a brotherly clasp while it was stabbed in the back; to set it upon a throne where it could be safely and surely riddled with machine gun bullets.

Europe's labor day was the First of May, and everywhere over the continent the workers paraded, they held enormous meetings, picnics and sports, they sang songs and listened to speeches from their leaders, they heartened and inspired themselves for the three hundred and sixty-four hard days. So now, several weeks in advance, it was announced that the Hitler government was going to take over the First of May and make it the "Day of National Labor." This was a government of "true Socialism"; it was the friend of labor, it *was* labor, and no longer could there be a class struggle or any conflict of interest. The revolution having been accomplished, the workers would celebrate their conquest and the new and splendid future which lay before them. All these golden, glowing words —and all the power of press and radio to carry the message to every corner of the Fatherland. Also, of course, the power of the police and the private Nazi armies to terrify and crush anyone who might try to voice any other idea.

"Oh, Lanny, you should come to see it!" wrote Heinrich Jung, ecstatically. "It will be something the like of which has not been seen in the world before. All our youth forces will assemble in the Lustgarten in the morning and President Hindenburg himself will address us. In the afternoon there will be costume parades of every craft and trade, even every great factory in Germany. All will gather in the Tempelhof Airfield, and the decorations will exceed anything you could imagine. The rich are paying for them by buying tickets so as to sit near the Führer. Of course He will speak, and afterwards there will be fireworks like a battle—three hundred meters of silver rain! I beg you and your wife to come as my guests—you will always be glad that you witnessed these historic scenes. . . . P.S. I am sending you some literature about our wonderful new labor program. You cannot have any doubts after this."

Lanny wrote, acknowledging the letter and expressing his regrets. It cost nothing to keep in touch with this ardent young official, and the literature he sent might some day be useful to Rick. Lanny was quite sure that he wouldn't care to enter Germany so long as Adolf Hitler remained its Chancellor.

III

The celebration came off, with all the splendor which Heinrich had promised. Everything was the biggest and most elaborate ever known, and even the hardboiled foreign correspondents were awestricken; they sent out word that something new was being born into the world. On the enormous airfield three hundred thousand persons had assembled by noon, to sit on the ground and await ceremonies which did not begin until eight in the evening. By that time there were a million or a million and a half in the crowd, believed to be the greatest number ever gathered in one place. Hitler and Hindenburg drove side by side, the first time that had happened. They passed along Friedrichstrasse, packed to the curb with shouting masses, and hung with streamers reading: "For German Socialism," and "Honor the Worker." In front of the speaker's platform stood the new Chancellor, looking over a vast sea of faces. He stood under the spotlight, giving the Nazi salute over and over, and when at last he spoke, the amplifiers carried his voice to every part of the airfield, and wireless and cables carried it over the world.

The new Chancellor's message was that "the German people must learn to know one another again." The divisions within Germany had been invented "by human madness," and could be remedied "by human wisdom." Hitler ordained that from now on the First of May should be a day of universal giving of hands, and that its motto was to be: "Honor work and have respect for the worker." He told the Germans what they wanted most of all to hear: "You are not a second-rate nation, but are strong if you wish to be strong." He became devout, and prayed: "O Lord, help Thou our fight for liberty!"

Nothing could have been more eloquent, nothing nobler. Did Adi wink to his journalist and say: "Well, Juppchen, we got away with it," or some German equivalent for that slang? At any rate, on the following morning the labor unions of Germany, representing four million workers and having annual incomes of nearly two hundred million marks, were wiped out at one single stroke. The agents of the job were so-called "action committees" of the Shop-

Cell Organization, the Nazi group which had carried on their propaganda in the unions. Armed gangs appeared at the headquarters of
all the unions, arrested officials and threw them into concentration
camps. Their funds were confiscated, their newspapers suppressed,
their editors jailed, their banks closed; and there was no resistance.
The Socialists had insisted upon waiting until the Nazis did something "illegal"; and here it was.

"What can we do?" wrote Freddi to Lanny, in an unsigned
letter written on a typewriter—for such a letter might well have cost
him his life. "Our friends hold little meetings in their homes, but
they have no arms, and the rank and file are demoralized by the
cowardice of their leaders. The rumor is that the co-operatives are
to be confiscated also. There is to be a new organization called the
'German Labor Front,' to be directed by Robert Ley, the drunken
braggart who ordered these raids. I suppose the papers in Paris will
have published his manifesto, in which he says: 'No, workers, your
institutions are sacred and inviolable to us National Socialists.' Can
anyone imagine such hypocrisy? Have words lost all meaning?

"Do not answer this letter and write us nothing but harmless
things, for our mail is pretty certain to be watched. We have to
ask our relatives abroad not to attend any political meetings for the
present. The reason for this is clear."

An agonizing thing to Hansi and Bess, to have to sit with folded
hands while this horror was going on. But the Nazis had made plain
that they were going to revive the ancient barbarian custom of punishing innocent members of a family in order to intimidate the
guilty ones. A man doesn't make quite such a good anti-Nazi fighter
when he knows that he may be causing his wife and children, his
parents, his brothers and sisters, to be thrown into concentration
camps and tortured. Hansi had no choice but to cancel engagements
he had made to play at concerts for the benefit of refugees.

"Wait at least until the family is out of Germany," pleaded
Beauty; and the young Reds asked their consciences: "What then?"
Did they have the right to go off on a pleasure yacht while friends
and comrades were suffering agonies? On the other hand, what
about Papa's need of rest? The sense of family solidarity is strong

among the Jews. "Honor thy father and thy mother: that thy days may be long upon the land which the Lord thy God giveth thee." The Lord in His wisdom had seen fit to take away the land, but the commandment still stood, and Hansi thought of his father, who had given him the best of everything in the world, and now would surely get no rest if his oldest son should declare war upon the Nazis. Also, there was the mother, who had lived for her family and hardly had a thought of any other happiness. Was she to be kept in terror from this time on?

"What do you think, Lanny?" asked the son of ancient Judea who wanted to be artist and reformer at the same time. Lanny was moved to reveal to him the scheme which was cooking in his mind for the entrapment of Johannes and the harnessing of his money. Hansi was greatly pleased; this would put his conscience at rest and he could go on with his violin studies. But Bess, the tough-minded one, remarked: "It'll be just one more liberal magazine."

"You can have a Red section, and put in your comments," replied Lanny, with a grin.

"It would break up the family," declared the granddaughter of the Puritans.

I V

Johannes wrote that he had got passports for his party, and set the date for the yacht to arrive at Calais. Thence they would proceed to Ramsgate, run up to London for a few days, and perhaps visit the Pomeroy-Nielsons—for this was going to be a pleasure trip, with time to do anything that took anybody's fancy. "We have all earned a vacation," said the letter. Lanny reflected that this might apply to Johannes Robin—but did it apply to Mr. Irma Barnes?

He wrote in answer: "Emily Chattersworth has arrived at Les Forêts, and Hansi is to give her a concert with a very fine program. Why don't you and the family come at once and have a few days in Paris? We are extremely anxious to see you. The spring Salon is the most interesting I have seen in years. Zoltan is here and will sell you some fine pictures. Zaharoff is at Balincourt, and Madame is out there with him; I will take you and you can have a séance, and perhaps meet once more the spirits of your deceased uncles. There are other pleasures I might suggest, and other reasons I might give why we are so very impatient to see you."

Johannes replied, with a smile between the lines: "Your invitation is appreciated, but please explain to the spirits of my uncles that I still have important matters which must be cleared up. I am rendering services to some influential persons, and this will be to the advantage of all of us." Very cryptic, but Lanny could guess that Johannes was selling something, perhaps parting with control of a great enterprise, and couldn't let go of a few million marks. The spirits of his uncles would understand this.

"Do not believe everything that the foreign press is publishing about Germany," wrote the master of caution. "Important social changes are taking place here, and the spirit of the people, except for certain small groups, is remarkable." Studying that sentence you could see that its words had been carefully selected, and there were several interpretations to be put upon them. Lanny knew his old friend's mind, and not a few of his connections. The bankrupted landlords to whom he had loaned money, the grasping steel and coal lords with whom he had allied himself, were still carrying on their struggle for the mastery of Germany; they were working inside the Nazi party, and its factional strife was partly of their making. Lanny made note of the fact that the raids on the labor unions had been made by Robert Ley and his own gangs. Had the "drunken braggart" by any chance "jumped the gun" on his party comrades? If so, one might suspect that the steel hand of Thyssen had been at work behind the scenes. Who could figure how many billions of marks it would mean to the chairman of the Ruhr trust to be rid of the hated unions and safe against strikes from this day forth?

Robbie Budd wrote about this situation, important to him. He said: "There is a bitter fight going on for control of the industry in Germany. There are two groups, both powerful politically. It is Thyssen and Krupp vs. the Otto Wolff group. The latter is part Jewish, and the present set-up is not so good for them. Johannes believes he has friends in both camps, and I hope he is not fooling himself. He is sailing a small ship in a stormy sea."

Robbie also gave another item of news: "Father is failing and I fear you may not find him here when you arrive. It is no definite disease, just the slow breakdown of old age, very sad to witness. It means heavy responsibilities for me; a situation which I prefer not to write about, but will tell you when I see you. Write the old gentleman and assure him of your appreciation of his kindness to you; he tries to keep his hold on all the family as well as on the business. He forgets what I told him yesterday, but remembers clearly what happened long ago. That is hard on me, because I caused him a great deal of unhappiness in those days, whereas of late he had been learning to take me for what I am and make the best of it. I try not to grieve about him, because he has had more out of life than most men, and fate neither lets us live forever nor have our way entirely while we are here."

V

Adolf Hitler was the man who was having his own way, more than any who had lived in modern times. He was going ahead to get the mastery of everything in Germany, government, institutions, even cultural and social life. Every organization which stood in his way he proceeded to break, one after another, with such speed and ruthlessness that it left the opposition dizzy. The Nationalist party, which had fondly imagined it could control him, found itself helpless. Papen, Vice-Chancellor, was reduced to a figurehead; Göring took his place in control of the Prussian state. Hugenberg had several of his papers suppressed, and when he threatened to resign from the Cabinet, no one appeared to care. One by one the Nationalist members were forced out and Nazis replaced them. Subordinates were arrested, charged with defalcation or what not— the Minister of Information was in position to charge anybody with anything, and it was dangerous to answer.

On the tenth day of May there were ceremonies throughout Germany which riveted the attention of the civilized world. Quantities of books were collected from the great library of Berlin University, including most of the worthwhile books which had been written during the past hundred years: everything that touched even remotely upon political, social, or sexual problems. Some forty thousand volumes were heaped into a pile in the square between the University and the Opera House and drenched with gasoline. The students paraded, wearing their bright society caps and singing patriotic and Nazi songs. They solemnly lighted the pyre and a crowd stood in a drizzling rain·to watch it burn. Thus modern thought was symbolically destroyed in the Fatherland, and a nation which had stood at the forefront of the intellectual life would learn to do its thinking with its "blood."

On that same tenth of May the schools of Germany were ordered to begin teaching the Nazi doctrines of "race." On that day the government confiscated all the funds belonging to the Socialist party and turned them over to the new Nazi-controlled unions. On that day Chancellor Hitler spoke to a Labor Congress, telling it that his own humble origin and upbringing fitted him to understand the needs of the workers and attend to them. On that day the correspondent of the· *New York Times* was forbidden to cable news of the suicide of the daughter of Scheidemann, the Socialist leader, and of a woman tennis champion who had brought honor to Germany but who objected to the process of "co-ordinating" German sport with Nazi propaganda. Finally, on that day there was a parade of a hundred thousand persons down Broadway in New York, protesting against the treatment of German Jews.

VI

The members of the Budd family in Bienvenu and in Paris were packing and getting ready for a year's absence from home. What should they take and what leave behind? Everything that was going on board the yacht had to be marked for the cabins or the hold. What was to be sent from Paris to Bienvenu was left in charge of Jerry Pendleton, who would see to its packing and unpacking. The ex-tutor and ex-lieutenant had saved most of his year's salary, and would go back to the *pension* and wait for the tourists to return. Madame Zyszynski was to be loaned for a year to the munitions king—for the spirits of the Budds and Dingles appeared to have said their say, whereas the Duquesa Marqueni was still going strong. Bub Smith was to escort the priceless little Frances to the yacht and see her safely on board; then he would take a steamer and return to his job in Newcastle, until such time as the baby should arrive in the land of the gangsters and the home of the kidnapers.

The expedition from Bienvenu arrived in Paris by train: Hansi and Bess; Beauty and her husband; Marceline and her governess—the former nearly sixteen, an elegant young lady, but she would be made to study every day on the yacht, and if there was anything Miss Addington didn't know, she would look it up in the encyclopedia, or the all-knowing Lanny would tell it to her. Frances was now three years old, and her entourage was made up of Miss Severne, a nurse, and the ex-cowboy from Texas. These ten persons arrived in the morning, and there was fuss and clamor, because they all wanted this or that before they got onto a yacht, and it seemed that so many bags and boxes had never before been heaped up in the entrance hall of a palace.

In the evening the expedition entrained for Calais; four more of them now: Irma and her husband, her maid and her Feathers—who, as Irma said over and over, was a fool, but a good one, doing all the errands, the shopping, and telephoning; keeping the accounts and getting hopelessly mixed up in them; taking her scoldings with tears, and promising to reform and doing her best, poor soul, but not having it in her, since she had been brought up as a lady, and thought about her own ego more than she could ever think about her job.

There were now twice as many boxes and bags, and twice as much fuss, but carried on in low tones, because Irma was strict about having the dignity of the family preserved. It was a conspicuous family, and there were reporters at the station to see them off and to ask about their proposed trip. Millions of people would read about their doings and get vicarious thrills; millions would admire them and millions would envy them, but only a small handful would love them—such appeared to be the way of the world.

VII

Next morning the party emerged on the station platform of the ancient seaport and bathing resort. They waited while Lanny got busy on the telephone and ascertained that the yacht had not yet been reported. They were loaded into taxis and taken to the Hotel du Commerce et Excelsior, where the mountain of luggage was stacked in a room and Feathers set to watch over it. A glorious spring day, and the family set out to find a point of vantage from which they could watch the approach of the trim white *Bessie Budd*. Irma and Lanny had a memory of this spectacle, never to be forgotten: the day at Ramsgate when they had been trying to get married in a hurry, and the yacht and its gay-spirited owner had provided them with a way of escape from the dominion of the Archbishop of Canterbury.

Now the yacht was going to transport them to Utopia, or to some tropical isle with an ivory tower on it—any place in the world where there were no Nazis yelling and parading and singing songs about Jewish blood spurting from the knife. Oil-burning vessels make no smudges of smoke on the horizon, so they must look for a dim speck that grew gradually larger. Many such appeared from the east, but when they got larger they were something else. So the party went to lunch, fourteen at one long table, and it was quite a job getting them settled and all their orders taken and correctly distributed. Belonging to the important classes as they did, neither they nor their servants must do anything to attract attention to themselves in public, and this was impressed on a member of the family even at the age of three. Hush, hush, Baby!

They sat on the esplanade and watched all afternoon. Some of them took a swim, some looked at the sights of the town—the four-hundred-year-old bastion, the citadel, the church of Notre Dame with a painting by Rubens. They bought postcards and mailed them to various friends. Every now and then they would inspect the harbor again, but still there was no trim white *Bessie Budd*. Again they had tables put together in the restaurant, and the fourteen had supper; they went out and watched till dark—but still no sign of the yacht.

They were beginning to be worried. Johannes had set a definite hour for leaving Bremerhaven, and he was a precise man who did everything on time and had his employees do the same. If anything unforeseen had turned up he would surely have telegraphed or telephoned. He had specified in his last letter what hotel they should go to, so that he would know where to look for them. They had sailed so often with him that they knew how many hours it would take to reach Calais, and it had been planned for the yacht to arrive simultaneously with the train from Paris. She was now twelve hours overdue.

Something must have happened, and they spent time discussing possibilities. Private yachts which are properly cared for do not have machinery trouble in calm weather, nor do they butt into the Frisian islands on the way from Germany to France. They travel as safely by night as by day; but of course some fisherman's boat or other obstruction might conceivably have got in the way. "Tire trouble!" said Lanny, the motorist.

VIII

When it was bedtime and still no word, he went to the telephone and put in a call for the yacht *Bessie Budd* at Bremerhaven—that being the quickest way to find out if she had taken her departure. Hansi and Bess sat with him, and after the usual delays he heard a guttural voice saying in German: "*Dieselmotorjacht Bessie Budd.*"

"*Wer spricht?*" inquired Lanny.

"*Pressmann.*"

"*Wer ist Pressmann?*"

"*Reichsbetriebszellenabteilung Gruppenführerstellvertreter.*" The Germans carry such titles proudly and say them rapidly.

"What are you doing on board the yacht?"

"*Auskunft untersagt*," replied the voice. Information forbidden!

"But the yacht was supposed to sail yesterday!"

"*Auskunft untersagt.*"

"*Aber, bitte——*"

"*Leider, nicht erlaubt*"—and that was all. "Sorry, not permitted!" The receiver clicked, and Lanny, aghast, listened on a dead wire.

"My God!" he exclaimed. "Can the Nazis have seized the *Bessie Budd?*" Hansi went white and Bess dug her nails into the palms of her hands. "Why would they do that!" she exclaimed.

"I don't know," answered Lanny, "unless one of them wanted a yacht."

"They have arrested Papa!" whispered Hansi. He looked as if he was about to keel over, and Bess caught him by the shoulders. "Oh, Hansi! Poor Hansi!" It was characteristic that she thought of him. He was the one who would suffer most!

It was as if a bolt of lightning had fallen from the sky and blasted their plans, turned their pleasures into a nightmare of suffering. Utter ruin, doom without escape—that was the way it appeared, and none could think of anything to say to comfort the others. More than thirty-six hours had passed since the scheduled sailing, and was it conceivable that Johannes would have delayed that length of time to get word to his friends? If any member of the family was at liberty, would that person have failed to communicate?

Just one other possibility: they might have been "tipped off" and have made their escape. They might be on their way out of Germany; or they might be hiding somewhere, not daring to wire. In the latter case they would use the method which they had already resorted to, of an unsigned letter. If such a letter was on the way it was to be expected in the morning.

"I'll try Berlin," said Lanny. Anything to break that dreadful spell of inaction! He put in a call for the Robin palace, and when he got the connection, an unfamiliar voice answered. Lanny asked if Johannes Robin was there, and the stranger tried to find out who was calling; when Lanny gave his name, the other started to put him through a questioning as to his reasons for calling. When Lanny insisted upon knowing to whom he was talking, the speaker abruptly hung up. And that again could mean only one thing: the Nazis had seized the palace!

"I must go and help Papa!" exclaimed Hansi, and started up as if to run to the station right away, or perhaps to the airplane field if there was one. Lanny and Bess caught him at the same moment. "Sit down," commanded the brother-in-law, "and be sensible. There's not a thing you can do in Germany but get yourself killed."

"I certainly must try, Lanny."

"You certainly must *not!* There's nobody they would better like to get hold of."

"I will go under another name."

"With false passports? You who have played on so many concert stages? Our enemies have brains, Hansi, and we have to show that we have some, too."

"He is right," put in Bess. "Whatever is to be done, I'm the one to do it."

Lanny turned upon her. "They know you almost as well as Hansi, and they will be looking for you."

"They won't dare do anything to an American."

"They've been doing it pretty freely. And besides, you're not an American, you're the wife of a German citizen, and that makes you one." All four of the Robins had made themselves citizens of the Weimar Republic, because they believed in it and planned to live their lives there. "So that's out," declared Lanny. "You both have to give me your word of honor not to enter Germany, and not to come anywhere near the border, where they might kidnap you. Then Irma and I will go in and see what we can find out."

"Oh, *will* you do it, Lanny?" Hansi looked at his brother-in-law with the grateful eyes of a dog.

"I promise for myself. I'm guessing that Irma will go along, but of course I'll have to ask her."

IX

Irma was in her room resting, and he went to her alone. He couldn't be sure how she would take this appalling news, and he wanted to give her a chance to make up her mind before it was revealed to anybody else. Irma was no reformer and no saint; she was a young woman who had always had her own way and had taken it for granted that the world existed to give it to her. Now fate was dealing her a nasty blow.

She sat staring at her husband in consternation; she really couldn't bring herself to realize that such a thing could happen in this comfortable civilized world, created for her and her kind. "Lanny, they *can't* do that!"

"They do what they see fit, dear."

"But it ruins our cruise! It leaves us stranded!"

"They probably have our friends in prison somewhere; and they may be beating and abusing them."

"Lanny, how perfectly unspeakable!"

"Yes, but that won't stop it. We have to figure out some way to save them."

"What can we do?"

"I don't know yet. I'll have to go to Berlin and see what has happened."

"Lanny, you *can't* go into that dreadful country!"

"I can't refuse, dear. Don't forget, we have been Johannes's guests; we were going to be his guests another whole year. How could we throw him down?"

She didn't know what to say; she could only sit staring at him. She had never thought that life could play such a trick upon her and her chosen playmate. It was outrageous, insane! Lanny saw her lips trembling; he had never seen her that way before, and perhaps she had never been that way before.

For that matter, he didn't like it any too well himself. But it was as if fate had got him by the collar, and he knew he couldn't pull loose. "Get yourself together, darling," he said. "Remember, Johannes is Hansi's father, and Hansi is my sister's husband. I can't let them see that I'm yellow."

"But Lanny, what on earth can you do? Those Nazis control everything in Germany."

"We know some influential people there, and I'll ask their advice.

The first thing, of course, is to find out what has happened, and why."

"Lanny, you'll be in frightful danger!"

"Not too great, I think. The high-ups don't want any scandals involving foreigners, I feel sure."

"What do you expect me to do? Go with you?"

"Well, it's not a holiday. You might prefer to go to Bienvenu with Baby. You could have your mother come; or you could take Baby and visit her."

"I wouldn't have a moment's peace, thinking you might be in trouble. I haven't the least idea what I could do, but I think I ought to be with you."

"I have no doubt there'll be ways to help. The fact that you have money impresses the Germans—and that includes the Nazis."

"Oh, Lanny, it's a horrid nuisance and a disappointment! I thought we were going to have such fun!"

"Yes, dear, but don't let Hansi or Bess hear you say that. Remember what it means to them."

"They should have thought of this long ago. But they wouldn't let anybody tell them. Now they see the results of their behavior— and we are expected to pay for it!"

"Dear, there's no reason to suppose that they have been the cause of the trouble."

"There must be some reason why Johannes is picked on, and not other rich Jews. The fact that one of his sons is a Communist and the other a Socialist certainly must have made him enemies."

Lanny couldn't deny that this was so; but he said: "Please don't mention it now, while Hansi and Bess are half beside themselves with grief. Let's go and get their family out, and then we'll be in position to talk to them straight."

"Yes, but you *won't!*" said Irma, grimly. She would go with him into the lion's den, but she wouldn't pretend that she liked it! And when it was over, she would do the talking herself.

X

The adult members of the family had no sleep that night. The six sat in conference, going over and over what meager data they had, trying to anticipate the future and to plan their moves. A distressing thing, to have their happiness for a year upset, and to be "stranded" here in Calais; but they were well-bred persons and concealed their annoyance. Beauty couldn't bear letting her darling go into danger, and for a while insisted that she must go along and put her social powers to work. But Lanny argued no—he wasn't in the least worried for himself, and in a few days the yacht might be freed and their plans resumed. Let the family stay here for a few days, and serve as a clearing house for communicating with their friends in the outside world. If the worst proved true, and a long siege was to be expected, Marceline and Frances could be taken back to Juan, and the Dingles and Hansi Robins could go to Paris—or perhaps Emily would shelter them at Sept Chênes.

Lanny got Jerry Pendleton on the phone in the middle of the night. Jerry was still in Paris, having bills to pay and other matters to settle. The plan had been for him to drive his car home, and the chauffeur to drive the Mercédès, the car of Irma and Lanny. But now Lanny ordered Jerry to remain in Paris, and the chauffeur to leave at once for Calais; with fast driving he could arrive before noon, and Lanny and Irma would take the car and set out for Berlin. They were going alone, since neither the chauffeur, Bub Smith, nor Feathers was any good for Germany, not knowing the language. "If you were worth your keep you would have learned it," said Irma to the secretary, taking out her irritation on this unfortunate soul.

Lanny sent cables to his father and to Rick, telling them what had happened. He guessed that in times such as these a foreign journalist might prove a powerful person, more so than an industrialist or an heiress. Lanny saw himself in a campaign to arouse the civilized world on behalf of a Jewish *Schieber* and his family. His head was boiling with letters and telegrams, manifestoes and appeals. Robbie would arouse the businessmen, Uncle Jesse the Communists, Longuet and Blum the Socialists, Hansi and Bess the musical world, Zoltan the art lovers, Parsifal the religious, Beauty and Emily and Sophie and Margy the fashionable, Rick the English press, Corsatti the American—what a clamor there would be when they all got going!

Taking a leaf from his father's notebook, Lanny arranged a code so that he could communicate with his mother confidentially. His letters and telegrams would be addressed to Mrs. Dingle, that being an inconspicuous name. Papa Robin would be "money" and Mama "corsets"—she wore them. Freddi would be "clarinet," and Rahel "mezzo." Lanny said it was to be assumed that all letters and telegrams addressed to him might be read by the Nazis, and all phone calls listened to; later he might arrange a secret way of communication, but nothing of the sort could come to the Hotel Adlon. If he had anything private to impart, he would type it on his little portable machine and mail it without signature in some out-of-the-way part of Berlin. Beauty would open all mail that came addressed to Lanny, and forward nothing that was compromising. All signed letters, both going and coming, would contain phrases expressing admiration for the achievements of National Socialism.

"Don't be surprised if you hear that they have converted me," said the playboy turned serious.

"Don't go too far," warned his mother. "You could never fool Kurt, and he's bound to hear about it."

"I can let him convert me, little by little."

Beauty shook her lovely blond head. She had done no little deceiving in her own time, and had no faith in Lanny's ability along that line. "Kurt will know exactly what you're there for," she declared. "Your best chance is to put it to him frankly. You saved his life in Paris, and you have a right to ask his help now."

"Kurt is a Nazi," said Lanny. "He will help no one but his party."

Irma listened to this conversation, and thought: "This can't be real; this is a melodrama!" She was frightened, but at the same time began to experience strange thrills. She wondered: "Could I pretend to be a Nazi? Could I fool them?" Her mind went on even bolder flights. "Could I be a vamp, like those I've seen on the screen? How would I set about it? And what would I find out?"

XI

They got the morning newspapers. Hard to imagine a millionaire's yacht and palace being seized, and no word of it getting to the outside world; but the rules were being changed in Naziland, and you didn't know what was possible until you saw it. They searched the French papers and found much news from Germany, having to do with the Conference on Arms Limitation at Geneva, and Germany's threats to withdraw from it. Hitler had unexpectedly summoned the Reichstag to meet, and the correspondents assumed that it was to give him a platform from which to address the world. All France was agog to know what he was going to say, and apparently that left the papers no space for the troubles of a Jewish *Schieber*.

The next chance was the mail. A letter mailed in Bremerhaven or Berlin on the day before yesterday might have arrived yesterday afternoon or it might not, but surely it would arrive this morning. Hansi was waiting downstairs at the hotel office; he couldn't think about anything else, not even Lanny's plans. He came rushing into the room, out of breath from running and from anxiety. "A letter in Mama's handwriting!" He handed it to Lanny, to whom it was addressed; his own sense of propriety had not permitted him to open it.

The letter had been scrawled in haste on a scrap of paper and mailed in a plain cheap envelope. Lanny tore it open, and his eyes took it in at a glance. He hated to read such words aloud, but there were five persons waiting in suspense. The letter was in German, and he translated it:

"Oh, Lanny, the Nazis have seized the boat. They have arrested Papa. They would not tell us a word what they will do. They will arrest us if we go near them, but they will not arrest you. We are going to Berlin. We will try to stay there and wait for you. Come to the Adlon, and put it in the papers, we will watch there. We are so frightened. Dear Lanny, do not fail poor Papa. What will they do to him? I am alone. I made the children go. They must not find us all together. God help us all. Mama."

So there it was! Those poor souls traveling separately, and doomed to spend their days and nights in terror for themselves and grief for what might be happening to the father of the family! Hansi broke down and cried like a child, and Beauty did the same. Bess sat twisting her hands together. The others found it difficult to speak.

Somebody had to take command of that situation, and Lanny thought it was up to him. "At least we know the worst," he said, "and we have something to act on. As soon as the car comes, Irma and I will drive to Berlin, not stopping for anything."

"Don't you think you ought to fly?" broke in Bess.

"It will make only a few hours' difference, and we shall need the car; it's the right sort, and will impress the Nazis. This job is not going to be one of a few hours, I'm afraid."

"But think what they may be doing to him, Lanny!"

"I've been thinking about it a lot, and I doubt if they'll do him serious harm. It must be money they're after, and the job will be one of bargaining."

"He's a Jew, Lanny."

"I know; but he has a great many friends at home and abroad, and the Nazis know it, and I don't believe they want any needless scandals. It's up to Irma and me to serve as mediators, as friends to both sides; to meet the right people and find out what it's going to cost."

"You'll be exhausted when you arrive," objected Beauty, struggling with tears. She wanted him to take the chauffeur.

"No," said Lanny. "We'll take turns sleeping on the back seat, and all we'll need when we get there is a bath, a shave for me and some make-up for Irma. If we drive ourselves we can talk freely, without fear of spies, and I wouldn't want to trust any servant, whether German or French. That goes for all the time we're in Naziland."

XII

There was a phone call for Lanny: Jerry Pendleton calling from Paris, to report that a letter from Germany had arrived. It bore no sender's name, but Jerry had guessed that it might have some bearing on the situation. Lanny told him to open and read it. It proved to be an unsigned letter from Freddi, who had reached Berlin. He wrote in English, telling the same news, but adding that he and his wife were in hiding; they were not free to give the address, and were not sure how long they could stay. If Lanny would come to the Adlon, they would hear of it and arrange to meet him.

To Jerry, Lanny said: "My family is coming to Paris at once. Do what you can to help them. I am telling them to trust you completely. You are to trust nobody but them."

"I get you."

"You are still *Contrôleur-Général*, and your salary goes on. Whatever expenses you incur will be refunded. Has the chauffeur left?"

"He left at four this morning. He thinks he can make it by ten."

"All right, thanks."

Lanny reported all this to the family, and his mother said: "You ought to get some sleep before you start driving."

"I have too many things on my mind," he replied. "You go and sleep, Irma, and you can do the first spell of driving."

Irma liked this new husband who seemed to know exactly what to do and spoke with so much decisiveness. She had once had a father like that. Incidentally, she was extremely tired, and glad to get away from demonstrative Jewish grief. Lanny said "Sleep," and she was a healthy young animal, to whom it came easily. She had been half-hypnotized watching Parsifal Dingle, who would sit for a long time in a chair with his eyes closed; if you didn't know him well you would think he was asleep, but he was meditating. Was he asking God to save Johannes Robin? Was he asking God to soften the hearts of the Nazis? God could do such things, no doubt; but it was hard to think out the problem, because, why had God made the Nazis in the beginning? If you said that the devil had made them, why had God made the devil?

There was no longer any reason for anyone's remaining in Calais, so Feathers went to buy tickets for Paris and arrange to have the mountain of luggage transported. Meanwhile Hansi and Bess and Lanny discussed the best way of getting Papa's misfortune made known to the outside world. That would be an important means of help—perhaps the most important of all. Lanny's first impulse was to call up the office of *Le Populaire;* but he checked himself, realizing that if he was going to turn into a Nazi sympathizer, he oughtn't to be furnishing explosive news items to a Socialist paper. Besides, this was not a Socialist or Communist story; it had to do with a leading financier and belonged in the bourgeois press; it ought to come from the victim's son, a distinguished person in his own right. Hansi and his wife should go to the Hotel Crillon, and there summon the newspaper men, both French and foreign, and tell them the news, and appeal for world sympathy. Lanny had met several of the American correspondents in Paris, and now he gave Hansi their names.

"The Nazis lie freely," said the budding intriguer, "and they compel you to do the same. Don't mention the rest of your family, and if the reporters ask, say that you have not heard from them and have no idea where they are. Say that you got your information by telephoning to the yacht and to the palace. Put the burden of responsibility off on *Reichsbetriebszellenabteilung Gruppenführerstellvertreter* Pressmann, and let his *Hauptgruppenführer* take him down into the cellar and shoot him for it. Don't ever drop a hint that you are getting information from your family, or from Irma or me. Make that clear to Jerry also. We must learn to watch our step from this moment on, because the Nazis want one thing and we want another, and if they win, we lose!"

17

Will You Walk into My Parlor?

I

MR. and Mrs. Lanning Prescott Budd of Juan-les-Pins, France, registered themselves at the Hotel Adlon, on Unter den Linden. That is where the rich Americans stop, and this richest of young couples were installed in a suite appropriate to their state. Every luxury was put at their command. Attendants took their car and serviced it promptly and faithfully; a maid and a valet came to unpack their things and to carry off their clothes and press them; a bellboy brought iced drinks and copies of various morning newspapers. Lanny sat down at once and made certain that these contained no mention of a confiscated palace and yacht. There might be ever so much clamor in the outside world, but the German people would know only what their new masters considered proper for them. It was the seventeenth of May, and the headlines were devoted to the speech which the Führer was to deliver to the Reichstag at three o'clock that afternoon, dealing with the Geneva Conference on Arms Limitation and the attitude of the German government to its proposals.

The telephone rang: a reporter requesting the honor of an interview with Mr. and Mrs. Budd. Lanny had wondered how it was going to be in this new world. Would money still make one a personage? Apparently it would. Tourist traffic, so vital to the German economy, had fallen off to a mere trickle as a result of the Jew-baiting, and the insulting of foreigners who had failed to give the Nazi salute on the proper occasions. The papers must make the most of what few visitors came to them.

Every large newspaper has a "morgue," in Germany called the

346

Archiv, from which one can ascertain without delay what has been published concerning any person. The reporter who receives an assignment of consequence consults this file before he sets out. So here was a smart young representative of the recently "co-ordinated" *Zeitung am Mittag,* fully informed as to the new arrivals, and asking the customary questions, beginning with: "What do you think of our country?"

Lanny said that they had motored to Berlin in twenty-four hours, so their impressions were fleeting. They had been struck by the order and neatness they had seen along the way. They were non-political persons, and had no opinions concerning National Socialism, but they were open-minded, and glad to be shown. Lanny winced as he spoke, thinking of his Socialist friends who would read this. When the reporter asked if the outside world believed the stories of atrocities and persecutions in Germany, Lanny said he supposed that some did and some did not, according to their predilections—*ihre Gesinnung,* he said. He and his wife had come to renew old friendships, and also to make purchases of old masters for American collectors.

All this would put him right with the Nazi world, and enable him to stay without exciting suspicion. Nothing was said about a Jewish brother-in-law or the brother-in-law's *Schieber* father, either by this reporter or by others who followed. They were made welcome and treated to cigars and drinks by two friendly and informal darlings of fortune. Delightful people, the Americans, and the Germans admired them greatly, went to see their movies, adopted their slang, their sports, their drinks, their gadgets and fashions.

II

It was Lanny's immediate duty to report himself to the Polizeiwache. He submitted the passports of himself and wife, and stated his business as art expert and his race as Aryan. Then he went back to the hotel, where he found a telegram from his mother in Paris: "Robbie reports grandfather died last night impossible Robbie come now he is cabling embassy concerning you advises you report there immediately."

So the old Puritan armorer was gone! Lanny had thought of him for so long as going that the news brought no shock. He had to keep his mind on his Berlin job, and without delay he wrote notes to Seine Hochgeboren the General Graf Stubendorf, to Oberst Emil Meissner, and to Heinrich Jung. Irma, at his suggestion, wrote to several of the ladies of prominence whom she had met. No Jews, no *Schieberfrauen*, but the socially untainted!

By that time the afternoon papers were on the street, making known Lanny's arrival, and he had reason to expect a telephone call. It came, and he heard a voice saying: "I understand that you are interested in the paintings of Alexander Jacovleff." Lanny replied without hesitation that he was greatly interested, and the voice informed him: "There is some of his work at the Dubasset Galleries which you should see."

"Very well," said Lanny. "Should I come at once?"

"If you please."

He had agreed with Irma that hotel rooms might have ears; so all he said to her was: "Come." She looked at him, and he nodded. Without another word she got up and slipped on a freshly pressed spring costume. Lanny ordered his car, and in a short time they were safe from prying ears. "Yes, it's Freddi," he said.

The art dealer's place was on Friedrichstrasse, only a short way from the Adlon. Lanny drove slowly by, and there was a tall, dark young Jew strolling. The Mercédès slowed up at the curb and he stepped in; they went on down the street, and around several corners, until they were certain that no car was following.

"Oh, I am so glad to see you!" Freddi's voice broke and he buried his face in his hands and began to weep. "Oh, thank you, Lanny! Thank you, Irma!" He knew he oughtn't to behave like that, but evidently he had been under a heartbreaking strain.

"Forget it, kid," said the "Aryan." He had to drive, and keep watch in the mirror of the car. "Tell us—have you heard from Papa?"

"Not a word."

"Has anything been published?"

"Nothing."

"You have no idea where he's been taken?"

"No idea. We dare not go to the authorities, you know."

"Are Mama and Rahel and the baby all right?"

"They were when I left them."

"You're not staying together?"

"We're afraid of attracting attention. Mama is staying with one of our old servants. Rahel and the baby with her father's family."

"And you?"

"I slept in the Tiergarten last night."

"Oh, Freddi!" It was Irma's cry of dismay.

"It was all right—not cold."

"You don't know anyone who would shelter you?"

"Plenty of people—but I might get them into trouble as well as myself. The fact that a Jew appears in a new place may suggest that he's wanted—and you can't imagine the way it is, there are spies everywhere—servants, house-wardens, all sorts of people seeking to curry favor with the Nazis. I couldn't afford to let them catch me before I had a talk with you."

"Nor afterward," said Lanny. "We're going to get all of you out of the country. It might be wiser for you and the others to go at once—because it's plain that you can't do anything to help Papa."

"We couldn't go even if we were willing," replied the unhappy young man. "Papa had our exit permits, and now the Nazis have them."

He told briefly what had happened. The family with several servants had gone to Bremerhaven by the night train and to the yacht by taxis. Just as they reached the dock a group of Brownshirts stopped them and told Papa that he was under arrest. Papa asked, very politely, if he might know why, and the leader of the troop spat directly in his face and called him a Jew-pig. They pushed him into a car and took him away, leaving the others standing aghast. They didn't dare go on board the yacht, but wandered along the docks, carrying their bags. They talked it over and decided that they could do no good to Papa by getting themselves arrested. Both Freddi and Rahel were liable to be sent to concentration camps on account of their Socialist activities; so they decided to travel separately to Berlin and stay in hiding until they could get word to their friends.

III

Freddi said: "I had only a little money when I was going on board the yacht, and I had to pay my fare back here."

Lanny took out his billfold and wanted to give him a large sum, but he said no, it might be stolen, or, if he was arrested, the Nazis would get it; better a little bit at a time. He started to say that Papa would make it all good, but Lanny told him not to be silly; whatever he needed was his.

"Where are you going to stay?" asked Irma, and he said he would join the crowd in *die Palme*, a refuge for the shelterless; it would be pretty bad, but it wouldn't hurt him, and no one would pay any attention to him there, no one would call him a Jew-pig. He hoped the wait wouldn't be too long.

Lanny had to tell him it might be quite a while. His activities would be in the higher circles, and things did not move rapidly there; you had to apply the social arts. Freddi said: "I hope poor Papa can stand it."

"He will be sure that we are doing our best," replied Lanny; "so at least he will have hope."

The American didn't go into detail concerning his plans, because he feared that Freddi might be tempted to impart some of it to his wife or his mother; then, too, there was the fearful possibility that the Nazis might drag something out of him by torture—and he surely wouldn't tell what he didn't know. Lanny said: "You can always write or call me at the hotel and make an appointment to show me some art."

They contrived a private code. Pictures by Bouguereau would mean that everything was all right, whereas Goya would mean danger. Lanny said: "Think of something to say about a painting that will convey whatever you have in mind." He didn't ask the addresses of the other members of the family, knowing that in case of need they, too, could write him or phone him about paintings. Freddi advised that they should meet as seldom as possible, because an expensive automobile driven by foreigners was a conspicuous object, and persons who got into it or out of it might be watched.

They stopped for a while on a quiet residence street and talked. Freddi's mind was absorbed by the subject of concentration camps; he had heard so many horrible stories, some of which he couldn't repeat in Irma's presence. He said: "Oh, suppose they are doing such things to Papa!" Later he said: "Have you thought what you would do if you had to stand such things?"

Lanny had to answer no, he hadn't thought much about it. "I suppose one stands what one has to."

Freddi persisted: "I can't help thinking about it all the time. No Jew can help it now. They mean it to break your spirit; to wreck you for the rest of your life. And you have to set your spirit against theirs. You have to refuse to be broken."

"It can be done," said Lanny, but rather weakly. He didn't want to think of it, at least not while Irma was there. Irma was afraid enough already. But the Jewish lad had two thousand years of it in his blood.

"Do you believe in the soul, Lanny? I mean, something in us that is greater than ourselves? I have had to think a lot about it. When they take you down into the cellar, all alone, with nobody to help you—you have no party, no comrades—it's just what you have in yourself. What I decided is, you have to learn to pray."

"That's what Parsifal has been trying to tell us."

"I know, and I think he is right. He's the one they couldn't conquer. I'm sorry I didn't talk more about it with him while I had the chance."

"You'll have more chances," said Lanny, with determination.

Parting is a serious matter when you have thoughts like that. Freddi said: "I oughtn't to keep you from whatever you're planning to do. Put me off near a subway entrance and I'll ride to *die Palme*."

So they drove on. Lanny said: "Cheerio," English fashion, and the young Jew replied: "Thanks a million," which he knew was American. The car slowed up and he stepped out, and the great hole in the Berlin sidewalk swallowed him up. Irma had a mist in her eyes, but she winked it away and said: "I could do with some sleep." She too had learned to admire the English manner.

I V

The Reichstag met in the Kroll Opera House that afternoon and listened to Adolf Hitler's speech on foreign affairs. The speech took three-quarters of an hour and immediately afterward Göring moved approval, which was voted unanimously, and the Reichstag adjourned. Soon afterward the newsboys were crying the extra editions, and there was the full text, under banner headlines. Of course these *gleichgeschaltete* papers called it the most extraordinary piece of statesmanship.

Lanny glanced through it swiftly, and saw that it was a speech like none other in the Führer's career. It was the first time he had ever read a prepared address; as it happened, the Wilhelmstrasse, the German foreign office, had put pressure on him and persuaded him that there was real danger of overt action by France. The Fatherland had no means of resisting, and certainly it was the last thing the infant Nazi regime wanted.

So here was a new Hitler. Such a convenient thing to be able to be something new whenever you wished, unhampered by anything you had been hitherto! The Führer spoke more in sorrow than in anger of the wrongs his country had suffered, and he told the Reichstag that he was a man utterly devoted to peace and justice among the nations; all he asked of the rest of the world was that it should follow the example of Germany and disarm. There was to be no more "force" among the nations; he called this "the eruption of insanity without end," and said that it would result in "a Europe sinking into Communistic chaos."

France and Britain, which had been worried, breathed a sigh of relief. The Führer really wasn't as bad as he had been painted; his soup wasn't going to scald anybody's tongue. He would settle down and let others write his speeches for him and govern the country sanely. To the diplomats and statesmen of foreign lands it was obvious that a mere corporal and painter of picture-postcards couldn't manage a great modern state. That called for trained men, and Germany had plenty of them. In an emergency they would take control.

Lanny wasn't sure about it; but he saw that today's speech was the best possible of omens for the Robin family. Adi was singing low; he wouldn't want any family rows, any scandals going out to the world; he was in a position where he could be mildly and politely blackmailed, and Lanny had an idea how to set about it.

The telephone rang. His note to Heinrich Jung had been delivered promptly. Heinrich had attended the Reichstag meeting, and now he was taking the first opportunity to call his friend. "Oh, Lanny, the most marvelous affair! Have you read the speech?"

"Indeed I have, and I consider it a great piece of statesmanship."

"*Wundervoll!*" exclaimed Heinrich.

"*Kolossal!*" echoed Lanny. In German you sing it, with the accent on the last syllable, prolonging it like a tenor.

"*Ganz grosse Staatskunst!*"

"*Absolut!*" Another word which you accent on the last syllable; it sounds like a popgun.

"*Wirkliches Genie!*" declared the Nazi official.

So they chanted in *bel canto*, like a love duet in Italian opera. They sang the praises of Adolf, his speech, his party, his doctrine, his Fatherland. Heinrich, enraptured, exclaimed: "You really see it now!"

"I didn't think he could do it," admitted the genial visitor.

"But he *is* doing it! He will go on doing it!" Heinrich remained lyrical; he even tried to become American. "How is it that you say—*er geht damit hinweg?*"

"He is getting away with it," chuckled Lanny.

"When can I see you?" demanded the young official.

"Are you busy this evening?"

"Nothing that I can't break."

"Well, come on over. We were just about to order something to eat. We'll wait for you."

Lanny hung up, and Irma said: "Isn't that overdoing it just a little?"

Lanny put his finger to his lips. "Let's dress and dine downstairs," he said. "Your best clothes. The moral effect will be worth while."

V

There were three of them in the stately dining-room of the most fashionable hotel in Berlin; the American heiress in the showiest rig she had brought, Lanny in a "smoking," and Heinrich in the elegant dress uniform he had worn to the Kroll Opera House. *Die grosse Welt* stared at them, and the heart of Heinrich Jung, the forester's son, was bursting with pride—not for himself, of course, but for his Führer and the wonderful movement he had built. Respect for rank and station had been bred into the very bones of a lad on the estate of Stubendorf, and this was the highest he had ever climbed on the social pyramid. This smart American couple had been guests on two occasions at the Schloss; it might even happen that the General Graf would enter this room and be introduced to the son of his *Oberförster!* Lanny didn't fail to mention that he had written to Seine Hochgeboren at his Berlin palace.

The orchestra played softly, and the waiters bowed obsequiously. Lanny, most gracious of hosts, revealed his mastery of the gastronomic arts. Did Heinrich have any preference? No, Heinrich would leave it to his host, and the host said they should have something *echt berlinerisch*—how about some *Krebse*, billed as *écrevisses?* Heinrich said that these would please him greatly, and kept the dark secret that he had never before eaten them. They proved to be small crayfish served steaming hot on a large silver platter with a much embossed silver cover. The waiter exhibited the magnificence before he put some on separate plates. Heinrich had to be shown how to extract the hot pink body from the thin shell, and then dip it into a dish of hot butter. Yes, they were good!

And what would Heinrich like to drink? Heinrich left that, too, to his host, so he had Rheinwein, the color of a yellow diamond, and later he had sparkling champagne. Also he had wild strawberries with *Schlagsahne*, and tiny cakes with varicolored icing. "Shall we have the coffee in our suite?" said the heiress; they went upstairs, and on the way were observed by many, and Heinrich's uniform with its special insignia indicating party rank left no doubt that Mr. and Mrs. Irma Barnes were all right; the word would go through the hotel, and the reporters would hear of it, and the social doings of the young couple would be featured in the controlled press. The Nazis would not love them, of course; the Nazis were not sentimental. But they were ready to see people climbing onto their bandwagon, and would let them ride so far as suited the convenience of the bandwagon Führer.

VI

Up in the room they had coffee, also brandy in large but very thin goblets. Heinrich never felt better in his life, and he talked for a couple of hours about the N.S.D.A.P. and the wonders it had achieved and was going to achieve. Lanny listened intently, and explained his own position in a frank way. Twelve years ago, when the forester's son had first made known Adi Schicklgruber's movement, Lanny hadn't had the faintest idea that it could succeed, or even attain importance. But he had watched it growing, step by step, and of course couldn't help being impressed; now he had come to realize that it was what the German people wanted, and of course they had every right in the world to have it. Lanny couldn't say that he was a convert, but he was a student of the movement; he was eager to talk with the leaders and question them, so that he could take back to the outside world a true and honest account of the changes taking place in the Fatherland. "I know a great many journalists," he said, "and I may be able to exert a little influence."

"Indeed I am sure you can," responded Heinrich cordially.

Lanny took a deep breath and said a little prayer. "There's just one trouble, Heinrich. You know, of course, that my sister is married to a Jew."

"Yes. It's too bad!" responded the young official, gravely.

"It happens that he's a fine violinist; the best I know. Have you ever heard him?"

"Never."

"He played the Beethoven concerto in Paris a few weeks ago, and it was considered extraordinary."

"I don't think I'd care to hear a Jew play Beethoven," replied Heinrich. His enthusiasm had sustained a sudden chill.

"Here is my position," continued Lanny. "Hansi's father has been my father's business associate for a long time."

"They tell me he was a *Schieber.*"

"Maybe so. There were plenty of good German *Schieber;* the biggest of all was Stinnes. There's an open market, and men buy and sell, and nobody knows whom he's buying from or selling to. The point is, I have ties with the Robin family, and it makes it awkward for me."

"They ought to get out of the country, Lanny. Let them go to America, if you like them and can get along with them."

"Exactly! That is what I've been urging them to do, and they wanted to do it. But unfortunately Johannes has disappeared."

"Disappeared? How do you mean?"

"He was about to go on board his yacht in Bremerhaven when some Brownshirts seized him and carried him off, and nobody has any idea where he is."

"But that's absurd, Lanny."

"I'm sure it doesn't seem absurd to my old friend."

"What has he been doing? He must have broken some law."

"I have no idea and I doubt very much if he has."

"How do you know about it, Lanny?"

"I telephoned to the yacht and a strange voice answered. The man said he was a *Reichsbetriebszellenabteilung Gruppenführerstellvertreter.*"

"That's a part of Dr. Ley's new Labor Front. What's he got to do with a Jewish *Schieber?*"

"You may do me a great favor if you'll find out for me, Heinrich."

"Well, you know what happens in revolutions. People take things into their own hands, and regrettable incidents occur. The Führer can't know everything that's going on."

"I'm quite sure of it," said Lanny. "The moment I heard about it, I said: 'I know exactly where to go. Heinrich Jung is the person who will understand and help me.' So here I am!"

VII

The young Nazi executive wasn't a fool, not even with the Rheinwein and the champagne and the brandy. He perceived at once why he had been receiving all this hospitality. But then, he had known Lanny Budd for some twelve years, and had had other meals at his expense and no favors asked. It is injurious to one's vanity to have to suspect old friends, and Heinrich had a naturally confiding disposition. So he asked: "What do you want me to do?"

"First, I want you to understand my position in this unhappy matter. I have many friends in Germany, and I don't want to hurt them; but at the same time I can't let a member of my family rot in a concentration camp without at least trying to find out what he's accused of. Can I, Heinrich?"

"No, I suppose not," the other admitted, reluctantly.

"So far, there hasn't been any publicity that I have seen. Of course something may break loose abroad; Johannes has friends and business associates there, and when they don't hear from him they, too, may get busy on the telephone. If that happens, it will make a scandal, and I think I'm doing a favor to you and to Kurt and to Seine Hochgeboren and even to the Führer, when I come and let you know the situation. The first person I meet in Berlin is likely to ask me: 'Where is Johannes?' And what am I to say? Since he is my sister's father-in-law and my father's associate, I'd be bound to call at his home, or at least telephone and let him know of my arrival."

"It's certainly awkward," conceded Heinrich.

"Another thing: when Seine Hochgeboren gets my letter in the morning he may call up. He's a friend of Johannes—in fact, it was at Johannes's palace that I first met him. Also, Irma expects to meet the Fürstin Bismarck tomorrow—perhaps you know her, a very charming Swedish lady. What is she going to say about the matter?"

Heinrich admitted that it was *verteufelt;* and Lanny went on: "If I tell these people what has happened, I am in the position of having come here to attack the *Regierung;* and that's the last thing I want to do. But the story can't be kept down indefinitely, and it's going to make a frightful stink. So I said to Irma: 'Let's get to Heinrich quickly, and have the thing stopped before it gets started.' Johannes is absolutely a non-political person, and he has no interest in spreading scandals. I'm sure he'll gladly agree to shut up and forget that it happened."

"But the man must have done something, Lanny! They don't just grab people in Germany and drag them to jail for nothing."

"Not even Jews, Heinrich?"

"Not even Jews. You saw how orderly the boycott was. Or did the foreign press lie to you about it?"

"I have heard terrible stories; but I have refused to believe them and I don't want to have to. I want to be able to go out and tell my friends that as soon as I reported this case to the Nazi authorities, the trouble was corrected. I offer you a chance to distinguish yourself, Heinrich, because your superiors will be grateful to you for helping to avoid a scandal in the outside world."

VIII

This conversation was being carried on in German, because Heinrich's English was inadequate. Irma's German was even poorer, but she had the advantage of having been told Lanny's plan of campaign, and she could follow its progress on the young official's face. A well-chiseled Nordic face, with two sky-blue eyes looking earnestly out, and a crown of straw-colored hair shaved so that a *Pickelhaube* might fit over it—though Heinrich had never worn that decoration. The face had been pink with pleasure at the evening's start; it had become rosy with good food, wine, and friendship; now it appeared to be growing pale with anxiety and a crushing burden of thought.

"But what on earth could I do, Lanny?"

"It was my idea that you would help me to take the matter directly to the Führer."

"Oh, Lanny, I couldn't possibly do that!"

"You have access to him, don't you?"

"Not so much as I used to. Things have changed. In the old days he was just a party leader, but now he's the head of the government. You've no idea of the pressure upon him, and the swarms of people trying to get at him all the time."

"I can understand that. But here is an emergency, and surely he would thank you for coming to him."

"I simply wouldn't dare, Lanny. You must understand, I am nothing but an office-man. They give me a certain job, and I do it efficiently, and presently they give me more to do. But I have never had anything to do with politics."

"But is this politics, Heinrich?"

"You will soon find out that it is. If Dr. Ley has arrested a rich Jew, he has some reason; and he's a powerful politician, and has friends at court—I mean, near the Führer. If I go and butt in, it will be like walking into No Man's Land while the shooting is going on. What hold I have on the Führer is because I am an old admirer, who has never asked anything of him in all my life. Now, if I come to him, and he finds that I'm meddling in state affairs, he might be furious and say ' '*Raus mit dir!*' and never see me again."

"On the other hand, Heinrich, if it should ever come to his ears that you had advance knowledge of this matter and failed to give him warning, he wouldn't think it was a high sort of friendship, would he?"

The young Nazi didn't answer, but the furrows on his brow made it plain that he was facing a moral crisis. "I really don't know what to say, Lanny. They tell me he's frightfully irritable just now, and it's very easy to make him angry."

"I should think he ought to feel happy after that wonderful speech, and the praise it is bound to get from the outside world. I should think he'd be more than anxious to avoid having anything spoil the effect of such a carefully planned move."

"*Du lieber Gott!*" exclaimed the other. "I ought to have the advice of somebody who knows the state of his mind."

Lanny thought: "The bureaucrat meets an emergency, and has no orders!" Aloud he said: "Be careful whom you trust."

"Of course. That's the worst of the difficulty. In political affairs you cannot trust anybody. I have heard the Führer say it himself." Heinrich wrinkled his brows some more, and finally remarked: "It seems to me it's a question of the effect on the outside world, so it might properly come before our Reichsminister of Public Enlightenment and Propaganda."

"Do you know him?"

"I know his wife very well. She used to work in Berlin party headquarters. Would you let me take you to her?"

"Certainly, if you are sure it's the wise step. As it is a matter of politics, you ought to consider the situation between Dr. Goebbels and Dr. Ley. If they are friends, Goebbels might try to hush it up, and perhaps keep us from seeing the Führer."

"*Gott im Himmel!*" exclaimed Heinrich. "Nobody in the world can keep track of all the quarrels and jealousies and intrigues. It is dreadful."

"I know," replied Lanny. "I used to hear you and Kurt talk about it in the old days."

"It is a thousand times worse now, because there are so many more jobs. I suppose it is the same everywhere in politics. That is why I have kept out of it so carefully."

"It has caught up with you now," said Lanny; but to himself. Aloud he remarked: "We have to start somewhere, so let us see what Frau Goebbels will advise."

IX

Heinrich Jung went to the telephone and called the home of Reichsminister Doktor Joseph Goebbels. When he got the Frau Reichsminister he called her "Magda," and asked if she had ever heard of Lanny Budd and Irma Barnes. Apparently she hadn't, for he proceeded to tell her the essential facts, which were how much

money Irma had and how many guns Lanny's father had made; also
that they had visited at Schloss Stubendorf and that Lanny had once
had tea with the Führer. Now they had a matter of importance to
the party about which they wished Magda's counsel. "We are at the
Adlon," said Heinrich. "*Ja, so schnell wie möglich. Auf wieder-
sehen.*"

Lanny called for his car, and while he drove to the Reichstagplatz, Heinrich told them about the beauty, the charm, the warmth
of heart of the lady they were soon to meet. One point which should
be in their favor, she had been the adopted child of a Jewish family.
She had been married to Herr Quandt, one of the richest men in Germany, much older than herself; she had divorced him and now had
a comfortable alimony—while the man who paid it stayed in a concentration camp! She had become a convert to National Socialism
and had gone to work for the party; a short time ago she had become the bride of Dr. Goebbels, with Hitler as best man, a great
event in the Nazi world. Now she was "Frau Reichsminister," and
ran a sort of salon—for it appeared that men cannot get along without feminine influence, even while they preach the doctrine of
Küche, Kinder, Kirche to the masses.

"People accuse Magda of being ambitious," explained the young
official. "But she has brains and ability, and naturally she likes to
use them for the good of the cause."

"She will have a chance to do it tonight," replied Lanny.

They were escorted to the fashionable apartment where the lovely
Frau Quandt had once lived with the elderly manufacturer. The
"Frau Reichsminister" appeared in a cerise evening gown and a
double string of pearls that matched Irma's; both strings were genuine, but each lady would have been interested to bite the other's
to make sure. Magda had wavy fair hair, a sweet, almost childish
face, and rather melancholy eyes with the beginning of dark rings
about them. Lanny knew that she was married to one of the ugliest
men in Germany; he could believe that she had needed the spur of
ambition, and wondered if she was getting the satisfaction she craved.

It was growing late, and the visitors came to the point quickly.
Knowing that the Minister of Popular Enlightenment and Propa-

ganda was a bitter anti-Semite, Lanny said: "Whatever one's ideas
may be, it is a fact that Hansi Robin is a musician of the first rank.
The concert which he gave with the Paris Symphony this spring
brought him a tremendous ovation. He has given similar concerts
in London and in all the great cities of the United States, and that
means that thousands of people will be ready to come to his defense.
And the same thing is true about the business men who know his
father. From the purely practical point of view, Frau Reichsminister,
that is bad for your *Regierung*. I cannot see what you can possibly
gain from the incarceration of Johannes Robin that can equal the
loss of prestige you will suffer in foreign lands."

"I agree with you," said the woman, promptly. "It is one of those
irrational things which happen. You must admit, Mr. Budd, that
our revolution has been accomplished with less violence than any
in previous history; but there have been cases of needless hardship
which my husband has learned about, and he has used his influence
to correct them. He is, of course, a very hard-pressed man just now,
and it is my duty as a wife to shield him from cares rather than
to press new ones upon him. But this is a special case, as you say,
and I will bring it to his attention. What did you say was the name
of the party organization which is responsible?"

"*Die Reichsbetriebszellenabteilung.*"

"I believe that has been taken into Dr. Ley's *Arbeitsfront*. Do
you know Robert Ley?"

"I have not the honor."

"He is one of the men who came into our party from the air
service. Many of our most capable leaders are former airmen:
Gregor Strasser——"

"I have met him," said Lanny.

"Hermann Göring, Rudolph Hess—quite a long list. Airmen learn
to act, and not to have feelings. Dr. Ley, like my husband, is a
Rheinlander, and I don't know if you realize how it is in the steel
country——"

"My father is a steel man, Frau Reichsminister."

"*Ach, so!* Then you can realize what labor is in the Ruhr. The
Reds held it as their domain; it was no longer a part of Germany,

but of Russia. Robert Ley got his training by raiding their meetings and throwing the speaker off the platform. Many a time he would have the shirt torn off his back, but he would make the speech. After ten years of that sort of fighting he is not always a polite person."

"I have heard stories about him."

"Now he is head of our *Arbeitsfront*, and has broken the Marxist unions and jailed the leaders who have been exploiting our German workers and tearing the Fatherland to pieces with class war. That is a great personal triumph for Dr. Ley, and perhaps he is a little too exultant over it—he has what you Americans call a 'swelled head.' " The Frau Reichsminister smiled, and Lanny smiled in return.

"I suppose he saw a rich Jew getting out of the country in a private yacht, obtained by methods which have made the Jews so hated in our country; and perhaps it occurred to him that he would like to have that yacht for the hospitalization of National Socialist party workers who have been beaten and shot by Communist gangsters."

"*Na also*, Frau Reichsminister!" said Lanny, laughing. "Heinrich assured me that if I came to you I would get the truth about the situation. Let the *Arbeitsfront* take the yacht and give me my brother-in-law's father, and we will call it a deal. *Wir werden es als ein gutes Geschäft betrachten.*"

X

There was the sound of a door closing, and Magda Goebbels said: "I think that is the Reichsminister now." She rose, and Heinrich rose, and Irma and Lanny followed suit; for when you are in Berlin you must do as Berliners do, especially when you are suing for favors from a Cabinet Minister who is more than royalty in these modern days.

"Juppchen" Goebbels appeared in the doorway of the drawing-room. He was small indeed, but not so small as he had seemed when Lanny had seen him standing on the platform at one of those colossal meetings. He had a clubfoot and walked with a limp which could not be concealed. He had a thin face built to a point in a sharp nose. He had a wide, tightly-drawn mouth which became like a Greek comic mask when he opened it for a speech. He had prominent eyes, black hair combed back from a receding forehead, and rather wide ears slightly hanging over at the top.

Also he had a brain and a tongue. The brain was superficial, but possessed of everything that was needed to delight a hundred thousand German *Kleinbürger* packed into a swastika-bedecked stadium. The tongue was as sharp as a snake's, and unlike a snake's it exuded venom. The Goebbels mind was packed with discreditable facts concerning every person and group and nation which offered opposition to National Socialism, and his eager imagination could make up as many new facts as any poet or novelist who had ever lived. The difference between fiction and fact no longer existed for Dr. Juppchen. Inside the German realm this grotesque little man had complete and unquestioned charge of newspapers, films, and radio, the stage, literature, and the arts, all exhibitions and celebrations, parades and meetings, lectures on whatever subject, school books, advertising, and cultural relations of whatever sort that went on between Germany and the outside world, including those organizations and publications which were carrying on Nazi propaganda in several score of nations. This ugly, dark, and pitiful deformity had a budget of a hundred million dollars a year to sing the praises of the beautiful, blond, and perfect Aryan.

In private life he was genial and witty, resourceful and quick in argument, and completely cynical about his job; you could chaff him about what he was doing, and he would even chaff himself. All the world's a stage and all the men and women on it merely players; how did you like my performance tonight? Like all truly great actors, Herr Reichsminister Doktor Goebbels worked terrifically hard, driven by an iron determination to get to the top of his profession and stay there in spite of all his rivals. At the beginning of his career he had been a violent opponent of the N.S.D.A.P., but the party had offered him a higher salary and he had at once become a convert. Now, besides being Minister of Popular Enlightenment

and Propaganda, he was the party's *Gauleiter* of Berlin and director
of *Der Angriff*, the powerful Nazi newspaper of the city.

He was pleased to find two rich and influential Americans in his
home. One of his duties was to receive such persons and explain
National Socialism to them. He was quick in reading their characters and in suiting what he told them to their positions and prejudices. For the third time that evening Lanny told his story, and
the Reichsminister Doktor listened attentively. When he had heard
to the end he turned to his wife. "*Na*, Magda, there you have it!"
he said. "That pothouse brawler, that *Saalschlacht* hero, Ley! Such
a *Grobian* to represent us to the outside world and involve us in his
gangsterism!"

"*Vorsicht, Jockl!*" warned Magda.

But masterful Nazis are above heeding the warnings of their
wives. Goebbels persisted: "A drunken rowdy, who wishes to control all German labor but cannot control himself! Have you seen
that great organizer of ours, Mr. Budd?"

"Not that I know of, Herr Reichsminister."

"A pot-bellied, roaring braggart who cannot live without his
flagon at his side. He likes to tell jokes, and he explodes with laughter
and a fine spray flies over the surrounding company. You know that
he is building the new Labor Front, and it must be done with melodrama—he personally must raid the union headquarters here in
Berlin. Revolvers and hand grenades are not enough, he has to have
machine guns mounted in front of the doors—for the arresting of
cowardly fat labor parasites who find it difficult to rise out of their
swivel-chairs without assistance! That is the way it goes in our land
of *Zucht und Ordnung*—we are going to turn Berlin into another
Chicago, and have bandits and kidnapers operating freely in our
streets! I hope I do not offend you by the comparison, Mr. Budd."

"Not at all," laughed Lanny. "The home of my forefathers is a
thousand miles from Chicago—and we, too, have sometimes observed
the imperfections of human nature manifesting themselves in our
perfect political system."

"*Na!*" said the Reichsminister Doktor. Then, becoming serious:
"I leave the administration of justice to the proper authorities; but

where the matter concerns a person with international reputation, I surely have a right to be consulted. I promise you that I will look into the matter the first thing in the morning and will report to you what I find."

"Thank you very much," said Lanny. "That is all I could ask."

The little great man appeared to notice the look of worry on his wife's gentle features; he added: "You understand, I do not know what crime your Jewish friend may be accused of, nor do I know that the overzealous Dr. Ley really has anything to do with it. Let us hold our minds open until we know exactly what has happened."

"What you have said will go no further, I assure you," declared Lanny, promptly. "I am not here to make gossip but to stop it."

XI

The Reichsminister of Popular Enlightenment and Propaganda relaxed in his chair and sipped the wine which his wife poured out for him and for the guests. "*Na!*" he exclaimed. "Tell me what you think of our Führer's speech."

Lanny started to repeat what he had said to the forester's son, and the *bel canto* duet was sung over again. Juppchen proved an even more romantic tenor than Heinrich; there was no language too ardent for him to employ in praise of Hitler. Lanny realized the situation; a deputy was free to criticize his fellow deputies, the Leys and the Strassers, the Hesses and the Röhms, but the Great One was perfection, and on him the butter of flattery was laid thickly. Heinrich had informed Lanny that the Goebbels home had become Adi's favorite haunt when he was in Berlin; here Magda caused to be prepared for him the vegetable plates which he enjoyed, and afterward he relaxed, listened to music, and played with her two children. Lanny didn't have to be told that the wily intriguer would use the occasion to fill his Chief's mind with his own views of the various personalities with whom their lives were involved. So it is that sovereigns are guided and the destinies of states controlled.

The Reichsminister of Popular Enlightenment and Propaganda enjoyed every aspect of his job and worked at it day and night.

Here he had two rich and well-dressed Americans, and at least one of them appeared to be intelligent. He thought just what Heinrich had been thinking for the past twelve years—to send Lanny Budd out as a missionary to spread the faith in the lands where he was at home. Said Goebbels: "All that we National Socialists want is to be left alone, so that we can reorganize our country's industry, solve the problem of unemployment by public works, and show the world what a model state can be. We have absolutely nothing to gain by forcing our ideas upon other peoples."

Said Lanny: "Ten years ago Mussolini told me that *Fascismo* was not for export. But since then I have seen him export it to Germany."

The Reichsminister Doktor perceived that this was indeed an intelligent young man, in spite of his well-tailored clothes and rich wife. "We have learned where we could," he admitted.

"Even from Lenin," smiled the other.

"If I answered that, Mr. Budd, it would have to be, as you Americans say, off the record."

"Naturally, Herr Reichsminister. I ought to explain to you that I had the good fortune to be secretary and translator to one of the experts on the American staff at the Peace Conference. I learned there how international business is carried on, and to keep my own counsel."

"Are you older than your years, Mr. Budd—or is it that you are older than your looks?"

"I was only nineteen at the time, but I had lived all over Europe, and knew the languages better than a geographer from what we call a 'fresh-water college' in the Middle West."

"*Eine frisch-Wasser-Universität?*" translated the Minister of Enlightenment, puzzled; and when Lanny explained, "*Süsswasser,*" he said: "One thing that I envy you Americans is your amusing forms of speech."

"Other people laugh at us," responded Lanny; "they fail to realize that we are laughing at ourselves."

"I perceive that you are a philosopher, Mr. Budd. I, too, had aspirations in that direction, but the world of affairs has claimed me.

Tell me honestly, without any evasion, what will Europe and America make of the Führer's speech?"

"They will be pleased, of course, but surprised by its tone of politeness. The skeptical ones will say that he wishes to have no trouble until Germany has had time to rearm."

"Let them learn one of his sentences: 'that Germany wishes nothing but to preserve her independence and guard her borders.' "

"Yes, Herr Reichsminister; but there are sometimes uncertainties as to where borders are or should be."

The other could not fail to smile. But he insisted: "You will see that all our arming is defensive. We are completely absorbed in the problems of our own economy. We mean to make good the Socialism in our name, and show the outside world as well as our own people that the problems of unemployment can be solved. In five years—no, I dare say in three—there will not be a single man desiring work in Germany and not finding it."

"That indeed will be something to watch, Herr Reichsminister."

The great man started to explain how it could be done; and from that abnormally wide mouth there poured a torrent of words. Lanny had observed the same thing with Hitler and Mussolini and many lesser propagandists—they forgot the difference beween an audience of four and an audience of four million, and were willing to expend as much energy on the former as on the latter. Crooked Juppchen went on and on, and perhaps would have talked all night; but his tactful wife chose an opportunity when he was taking in breath, and said: "The Herr Reichsminister Doktor has a hard day's work behind him and has another before him. He ought to have some sleep."

The others started to their feet at once; and so they missed hearing about the *Autobahnen* which the new government was going to build all over Germany. They thanked both host and hostess, and took their departure quickly. After they had delivered Heinrich to his home and were safely alone in their car, Irma said: "Well, do you think you got away with it?"

"We can't tell a thing, in this world of intrigue. Goebbels will think the matter over and decide where his interests lie."

Irma had understood a little of the conversation here and there. She remarked: "At least you got the dirt on Dr. Ley!"

"Yes," replied her husband; "and if we have the fortune to meet Dr. Ley, we'll get the dirt on Dr. Goebbels!"

18

I Am a Jew

I

LANNY wasn't taking his father's suggestion of reporting to the American Embassy. The attaché who was Robbie's old friend was no longer there. The Ambassador was a Hoover appointee, a former Republican senator from Kentucky and Robbie Budd's type of man; but he was ill, and had gone to Vichy, France, from which place he had given an interview defending the Nazi regime. As for Lanny himself, he didn't expect any serious trouble, but if it came, he would put it up to the Embassy to get him out. He had agreed with Irma that when he went out alone he would set a time for his return; if anything delayed him he would telephone, and if he failed to do this, she would report him as missing.

In the morning they took things easy; had breakfast in bed and read the papers, including interviews with themselves, also full accounts of the Reichstag session and other Nazi doings. Their comments were guarded, for they had to expect some form of spying. Except when they were alone in their car, everything in Germany was to be wonderful, and only code names were to be used. Heinrich was "Aryan," Goebbels was "Mr. Mouth," and the Frau Minister "Mrs. Mouth." Disrespectful, but they were young and their manners were "smart."

There came a telephone call from Freddi; he gave no name, but Lanny, knowing his voice, said promptly: "We saw some fine Bouguereau paintings last night, and are waiting for a call telling us the price. Call later." Then he settled down and wrote a note to Mrs. Dingle, in Paris, enclosing various newspaper clippings, and saying: "The picture market appears promising and we hope to make purchases soon. The clarinet and other instruments are in good condition."

While he was writing, one of Irma's friends, the Fürstin Donnerstein, called up to invite the young couple to lunch. Lanny told Irma to accept for herself. It was a waste of time for her to sit through long interviews with officials in the German language; let her go out and spread the news about Johannes, and find out the reaction of "society" to the disappearance of a Jewish financier. Lanny himself would wait in their suite for messages.

They were dressing, when the telephone rang. The "personal secretary" to Herr Reichsminister Doktor Goebbels announced: "The Herr Reichsminister wishes you to know that he has taken entire charge of the matter which you brought to his attention, and he will report to you as soon as he has completed investigations."

Lanny returned his thanks, and remarked to his wife: "We are getting somewhere!"

Irma replied: "He was really a quite agreeable person, Lanny." He looked at her, expecting a small fraction of a wink; but apparently she meant it. He would have liked to say: "Too bad his public speeches aren't as pleasant as his private conversation." But that could be said only in the car.

He added a postscript to the note to his mother: "I have just been given reason to hope that our deal may go through quickly." He was about to offer to accompany Irma to the luncheon, when there came a tap upon the door, and a bellboy presented a card, reading: "*Herr Guenther Ludwig Furtwaengler. Amtsleiter Vierte Kammer: Untersuchungs- und Schlichtungsausschuss N.S.D.A.P.*" Lanny didn't stop to puzzle out this jet of letters, but said: "Bring the Herr up." Studying the card, he could tell something about the visitor, for the

Germans do not customarily put the title "Herr" on their cards, and this was a crudity.

The officer entered the reception room, clicked his heels, bowed from the waist, and remarked: "*Heil Hitler. Guten Morgen, Herr Budd.*" He was a clean-cut youngish man in the black and silver uniform of the S.S. with the white skull and crossbones. He said: "Herr Budd, I have the honor to inform you that I was yesterday appointed to the personal staff of the Reichsminister and Minister-Präsident of Prussia, Hauptmann Göring. I have the rank of Ober-leutnant, but have not had time to have new cards engraved. Seine Exzellenz wishes to invite you and Frau Budd to his inauguration ceremonies, which take place the day after tomorrow."

"We are greatly honored, Herr Oberleutnant," said Lanny, con-cealing his surprise.

"I present you with this card of admission. You understand it will be necessary to have it with you."

"Assuredly," said Lanny, and put the treasure safely into the inside breast pocket of his coat.

The other went on: "Seine Exzellenz the Minister-Präsident wishes you to know that he is giving immediate personal attention to the matter of Johannes Robin."

"Well, thank you, Herr Oberleutnant," said the American. This time his surprise couldn't be concealed. He explained: "Only a few minutes ago I had a call from the office of another Reichsminister, and was told that *he* had the matter in charge."

Said the officer: "I am instructed to inform you that if you will accompany me to the residence of Seine Exzellenz the Minister-Präsident, he personally will give you information about the matter."

"I am honored," replied Lanny, "and of course pleased to come. Excuse me while I inform my wife."

Irma paled when told this news, for she had heard about Göring, who had so far no rival for the title of the most brutal man in the Nazi government. "Can this be an arrest, Lanny?"

"It would be extremely bad form to suggest such an idea," he smiled. "I will phone you without fail at the Fürstin Donnerstein's by two o'clock. Wait there for me. If I do not call, it will be serious. But meantime, don't spoil your lunch by worrying." He gave her a quick kiss and went down to the big official car—a Mercédès, as big as a tank, having six wheels. It had a chauffeur and guard, both in Nazi uniforms. Lanny thought: "By heck! Johannes must be richer than I realized!"

II

A short drive up Unter den Linden and through the Branden-burger Tor to the Minister-Präsident's official residence, just across the way from the Reichstag building with its burned-out dome. Lanny had heard no end of discussion of the three-hundred-foot tunnel which ran under the street, through which the S.A. men were said to have come on the night when they filled the building with incendiary materials and touched them off with torches. All the non-Nazi world believed that Hermann Wilhelm Göring had ordered and directed that job. Certainly no one could question that it was he who had ordered and directed the hunting down and killing, the jailing and torturing, of tens of thousands of Communists and Socialists, democrats and pacifists, during the past three and a half months. In his capacity of Minister without Portfolio of the German Reich he had issued an official decree instructing the police to co-operate with the Nazi forces, and in a speech at Dortmund he had defended his decree:

"In future there will be only one man who will wield power and bear responsibility in Prussia—that is myself. A bullet fired from the barrel of a police pistol is my bullet. If you say that is murder, then I am a murderer. I know only two sorts of law because I know only two sorts of men: those who are with us and those who are against us."

With such a host anything was possible, and it was futile for Lanny to try to guess what was coming. How much would the Commandant of the Prussian Police and founder of the "Gestapo," the Secret State Police, have been able to find out about a Franco-American Pink in the course of a few hours? Lanny had been so indiscreet as to mention to Goebbels that he had met Mussolini.

Would they have phoned to Rome and learned how the son of Budd's had been expelled from that city for trying to spread news of the killing of Giacomo Matteotti? Would they have phoned to Cannes and found out about the labor school? To Paris and learned about the Red uncle, and the campaign contributions of Irma Barnes which had made him a Deputy of France? Lanny could pose as a Nazi sympathizer before Heinrich Jung—but hardly before the Führer's head triggerman!

It was all mystifying in the extreme. Lanny thought: "Has Goebbels turned the matter over to Göring, or has Göring grabbed it away from Goebbels?" Everybody knew that the pair were the bitterest of rivals; but since they had become Cabinet Ministers their two offices must be compelled to collaborate on all sorts of matters. Did they have jurisdictional disputes? Would they come to a fight over the possession of a wealthy Jew and the ransom which might be extorted from him? Göring gave orders to the Berlin police, while Goebbels, as *Gauleiter* of Berlin, commanded the party machinery, and presumably the Brownshirts. Would the cowering Johannes Robin become a cause of civil war?

And then, still more curious speculations: How had Göring managed to get wind of the Johannes Robin affair? Did he have a spy in the Goebbels household? Or in the Goebbels office? Or had Goebbels made the mistake of calling upon one of Göring's many departments for information? Lanny imagined a spiderweb of intrigue being spun about the Robin case. It doesn't take long, when the spinning is done with telephone wires.

III

Flunkies bowed the pair in, and a secretary led Lanny up a wide staircase and into a sumptuous room with a high ceiling. There was the great man, lolling in an overstuffed armchair, with a pile of papers on a small table beside him, and another table with drinks on the other side. Lanny had seen so many pictures of him that he knew what to expect: a mountain of a man, having a broad sullen face with heavy jowls, pinched-in lips, and bags of fat under the eyes. He was just forty, but had acquired a great expanse of chest and belly, now covered by a resplendent blue uniform with white lapels. Suspended around his neck with two white ribbons was a golden star having four double points.

The ex-aviator's love of power was such that he was assuming offices one after another: Minister without Portfolio of the Reich, Minister-Präsident of Prussia, Air Minister, Commander-in-Chief of the German Air Force, Chief Forester of the Reich, Reich Commissioner. For each he would have a new uniform, sky blue, cream, rose-pink. It wouldn't be long before some Berlin wit would invent the tale of Hitler attending a performance of *Lohengrin*, and falling asleep; between the acts comes the tenor in his gorgeous swanboat costume, wishing to pay his respects to the Führer; Hitler, awakened from his nap, rubs his eyes and exclaims: "*Ach, nein, Hermann! That is too much!*"

Next to his chief, Göring was the least unpopular of the Nazis. He had been an ace aviator, with a record of devil-may-care courage. He had the peculiar German ability to combine ferocity with *Gemütlichkeit*. To his cronies he was genial, full of jokes, a roaring tankardman, able to hold unlimited quantities of beer. In short, he was one of the old-time heroes of Teutonic legend, those warriors who could slaughter their foes all day and at night drink wassail with their unwashed bloody hands; if they were slain, the Valkyries would come on their galloping steeds and carry them off to Valhalla to drink wassail forever after.

IV

Lanny's first thought: "The most repulsive of men!" His second thought, close on its heels: "I admire all Nazis!" He bowed correctly and said: "*Guten Morgen, Exzellenz.*"

"*Guten Morgen, Mr. Budd,*" said the Hauptmann, in a rumbling bull voice. "*Setzen Sie sich.*"

He indicated a chair at his side and Lanny obeyed. Having met many of the great ones of the earth in his thirty-three years, Lanny had learned to treat them respectfully, but without obsequiousness.

It was the American manner, and so far had been acceptable. He knew that it was up to the host to state why he had summoned him, and meantime he submitted to an inspection in silence.

"Mr. Budd," said the great man, at last, "have you seen this morning's Paris and London newspapers?"

"I do not have the advantage of possessing an air fleet, Exzellenz." Lanny had heard that Göring possessed a sense of humor.

"Sometimes I learn about them by telephone the night before," explained the other, with a smile. "They carry a story to the effect that the Jewish moneylender, Johannes Robin, has disappeared in Germany. We do not care to have the outside world get the impression that we are adopting American customs, so I had the matter investigated at once, and have just informed the press that this *Schieber* has been legally arrested for attempting to carry a large sum of money out of the country on board his yacht. This, as you may know, is forbidden by our law."

"I am sorry to hear that news, Exzellenz."

"The prisoner is liable to a penalty of ten years at hard labor—and it will be very hard indeed, I can assure you."

"Naturally, Exzellenz, I cannot say anything about the matter until I have heard Johannes's side of the story. He has always been a law-abiding citizen, and I am sure that if he broke the law it was by oversight. He was setting out on a yachting cruise, and one cannot sail to strange lands without having cash on board to purchase food and fuel."

"It is absolutely requisite to have a permit from the Exchange Control Authority, and our records show that no such document had been issued. The law has been on the books for more than a year, and has been well advertised. We cannot afford to have our country drained of wealth, nor our currency depreciated on the world markets. At the present time, owing to the scoundrelism of the Marxist-Jews who have ruled Germany, our gold reserve is down to eight and one-half per cent, and the very life of our state is imperiled by the activities of these *Schieberschweine*. I would consider myself justified in proceeding against Johannes Robin for high treason, and may decide to do so."

"Naturally, Exzellenz, I am distressed to hear all this. Is it your intention to grant me the privilege of an interview with the prisoner?"

"There is something even more important than the protection of the Reich's currency and that is the protection of its good name. We are indignant concerning the slanders which have been broadcast by the enemies of our *Regierung*, and we intend to take all possible steps against these devils."

"So far as Johannes is concerned, Exzellenz, I can assure you positively that he has no such motives. He is an entirely non-political person, and has gone to extremes to keep friendly. He has always supposed that he had friends inside the N.S.D.A.P."

"I am taking steps to find out who they are," replied the head of the Prussian state. "When I do, I shall shoot them."

It was, in a way, as if he had shot Lanny. From behind those rolls of fat the American saw cold blue eyes staring at him, and he realized that this war-eagle was a deadly bird of prey.

"Let us get down to business, Mr. Budd. I am willing to negotiate with you, but I require your word of honor as a gentleman that whatever information I impart and whatever proposals I make will be strictly between us, now and for the future. That means exactly what it says, and the reason I am seeing you is that I have been told that you are a man who will keep his bargain."

"I do not know who has spoken that good word for me, Exzellenz, but I assure you that I have no desire in this matter except to help an old friend and connection by marriage out of the trouble into which he has stumbled. If you will enable me to do this, you may be sure that neither Johannes nor I will have any interest in making publicity out of the unfortunate affair."

"It happens that this matter was started by other persons, but now I have taken charge of it. Whatever you have heard to the contrary you are to disregard. Johannes Robin is my prisoner, and I am willing to turn him loose on certain terms. They are Nazi terms, and you won't like them, and certainly he won't. You may take them to him, and advise him to accept them or not. I put no pressure upon you, and make only the condition I have specified: the matter will be under the seal of confidence. You will agree never to reveal the facts to anyone, and Johannes will make the same agreement."

"Suppose that Johannes does not wish to accept your terms, Exzellenz?"

"You will be bound by your pledge whether he accepts or rejects. He will be bound if he accepts. If he rejects, it won't matter, because he will never speak to anyone again."

"That is clear enough, so far as regards him. But I don't understand why you have brought me in."

"You are in Berlin, and you know about the case. I am offering you an opportunity to save your friend from the worst fate which you or he can imagine. A part of the price is your silence as well as his. If you reject the offer, you will be free to go out to the world and say what you please, but you will be condemning your Jew to a death which I will make as painful as possible."

"That is clear enough, Exzellenz. It is obvious that you have me as well as Johannes. I can do nothing but accept your proposition."

V

Lanny knew that this man of *Blut und Eisen* was engaged in turning the government of Germany upside down. He was kicking out officials of all sorts, police chiefs, mayors, even professors and teachers, and replacing them with fanatical Nazis. This very day, the papers reported, the lower legislative chamber of the Prussian state was scheduled to meet and tender its collective resignation, so that Göring might replace them with his party followers. But with all this on his hands he had time to explain to a young American visitor that he, the head of the Prussian state, was not to be numbered among the anti-Jewish fanatics; his quarrel with them was the purely practical one, that they had swarmed upon the helpless body of postwar Germany to drain her white. They had been speculators in marks who had profited by the most dreadful national calamity of modern times. "You can look at our school children, Mr. Budd, and have no difficulty in picking out those who were born in the years from 1919 to 1923, because of their stunted size."

Lanny would have liked to say that he knew many Germans who had sold marks; but it would have been the worst of blunders to get into an argument. He listened politely while the head of the Prussian government employed barrack-room phrases, some of which an American esthete had never heard before.

Suddenly the heavy fat fist of the thunder-god Thor came down with a bang on the table. "*Jawohl!* To business! The Jew who has fattened himself upon our blood is going to disgorge. His yacht shall serve as a means of recreation for deserving party members. His palace shall become a public museum. I understand that it contains a well-chosen collection of old masters."

"I appreciate the compliment, Exzellenz. Or do you know that I had the pleasure of selecting them?"

"*Ach, so!* Shall I call it the Lanning Budd Museum?" The hard blue eyes twinkled between the heavy layers of fat.

"The museum should be named for the one who institutes it, Exzellenz. Johannes has often told me that he planned to leave it to the public. But now you are doing it."

"I intend to go about these matters with all proper formality," said Göring, still with the twinkle. "Our Führer is a stickler for legality. The papers will be prepared by our Staatsanwalt, and the *Schieber* will sign them before a notary. For the sum of one mark his yacht, for another his palace, and for yet other marks his shares in our leading industrial enterprises and banks. In payment for my services in the above matters, he will give me checks for the amount of his bank deposits—and be sure that I shall cash them before he gets away."

"You intend to leave him nothing, Exzellenz?"

"Each business transaction shall be for the sum of one mark, and those marks will be his inalienable personal property. For the rest— naked came he into Germany, and naked will he go out."

"Pardon me if I correct you, sir. I happen to know that Johannes was a rich man when he came into Germany. He and my father had been business associates for several years, so I know pretty well what he had."

"He made his money trading with the German government, I am informed."

"In part, yes. He sold things which the government was glad to have in wartime; magnetos which you doubtless used in the planes in which you performed such astounding feats of gallantry."

"You are a shrewd young man, Mr. Budd, and after this deal is over, you and I may be good friends and perhaps do a profitable business. But for the moment you are the devil's advocate, predestined to lose your case. I could never understand why our magnetos so often failed at the critical moment, but now I know that they were sold to us by filthy Jewish swine who probably sabotaged them so that we would have to buy more." The great man said this with a broad grin; he was a large and powerful cat playing with a lively but entirely helpless mouse. On the rug in front of his chair lay a half-grown lion-cub, which yawned and then licked his chops as he watched his master preparing for a kill. Lanny thought: "I am back among the Assyrians!"

VI

The visitor had the feeling that he ought to put up some sort of fight for his friend's fortune, but he couldn't figure out how to set about it. He had never met a man like this in all his life, and he was completely intimidated—not for himself, but for Johannes. Your money or your life!

"Exzellenz," he ventured, "aren't you being a trifle harsh on one unfortunate individual? There are many non-Jewish *Schieber*; and there are rich Jews in Germany who have so far managed to escape your displeasure."

"The *Schweine* have been careful not to break our laws. But this one has broken the eleventh commandment—he has been caught. *Man muss sich nicht kriegen lassen!* And moreover, we have use for his money."

Lanny was thinking: "It isn't as bad as it might be, because so much of Johannes's money is abroad." He decided not to risk a fight, but said: "I will transmit your message."

The head of the Prussian government continued: "I observe that you avoid mentioning the money which this *Schieber* has already shipped out and hidden in other countries. If you know the history of Europe you know that every now and then some monarch in need of funds would send one of the richest of his Hebrews to a dungeon and have him tortured until he revealed the hiding-places of his gold and jewels."

"I have read history, Exzellenz."

"Fortunately nothing of the sort will be needed here. We have all this scoundrel's bank statements, deposit slips, and what not. We have photostat copies of documents he thought were safe from all eyes. We will present checks for him to sign, so that those funds may be turned over to me; when my agents have collected the last dollar and pound and franc, then your Jew relative will have become to me a piece of rotten pork of which I dislike the smell. I will be glad to have you cart him away."

"And his family, Exzellenz?"

"They, too, will stink in our nostrils. We will take them to the border and give each of them a kick in the tail, to make certain they get across with no delay."

Lanny wanted to say: "That will be agreeable to them"; but he was afraid it might sound like irony, so he just kept smiling. The great man did the same, for he enjoyed the exercise of power; he had been fighting all his life to get it, and had succeeded beyond anything he could have dared expect. His lion-cub yawned and stretched his legs. It was time to go hunting.

"Finally," said Göring, "let me make plain what will happen to this *Dreck-Jude* if he ventures to defy my will. You know that German science has won high rank in the world. We have experts in every department of knowledge, and for years we have had them at work devising means of breaking the will of those who stand in our path. We know all about the human body, the human mind, and what you are pleased to call the human soul; we know how to handle each. We will put this pig-carcass in a specially constructed cell, of such size and shape that it will be impossible for him to stand or sit or lie without acute discomfort. A bright light will glare into his eyes day and night, and a guard will watch him and prod him if he falls asleep. The temperature of the cell will be at exactly the right degree of coldness, so that he will not die, but will become mentally a lump of putty in our hands. He will not be permitted to commit suicide. If he does not break quickly enough we will put camphor in his *Harnröhre*—you understand our medical terms?"

"I can guess, Exzellenz."

"He will writhe and scream in pain all day and night. He will wish a million times to die, but he will not even have a mark on him. There are many other methods which I will not reveal to you, because they are our secrets, gained during the past thirteen years while we were supposed to be lying helpless, having the blood drained out of our veins by filthy, stinking Jewish-Bolshevik vampires. The German people are going to get free, Mr. Budd, and the money of these parasites will help us. Are there any other questions you wish to ask me?"

"I just want to be sure that I understand you correctly. If Johannes accepts your terms and signs the papers which you put before him, you will permit me to take him and his family out of Germany without further delay?"

"That is the bargain. You, for your part agree that neither you nor the Jew nor any member of his family will say anything to anybody about this interview, or about the terms of his leaving."

"I understand, Exzellenz. I shall advise Johannes that in my opinion he has no alternative but to comply with your demands."

"Tell him this, as my last word: if you, or he, or any member of his family breaks the agreement, I shall compile a list of a hundred of his Jewish relatives and friends, seize them all and make them pay the price for him. Is that clear?"

"Quite so."

"My enemies in Germany are making the discovery that I am the master, and I break those who get in my way. When this affair has been settled and I have a little more leisure, come and see me again, and I will show you how you can make your fortune and have an amusing life."

"Thank you, sir. As it happens, what I like to do is to play the works of Beethoven on the piano."

"Come and play them for the Führer," said the second in command, with a loud laugh which somewhat startled his visitor. Lanny wondered: Did the eagle-man take a patronizing attitude toward his Führer's fondness for music? Was he perchance watching for the time when he could take control of affairs out of the hands of a sentimentalist and *Schwärmer*, an orator with a gift for rabble-rousing but no capacity to govern? Had the Minister-Präsident's Gestapo reported to him that Lanny had once had tea with the Führer? Or that he had spent part of the previous evening in the Führer's favorite haunt?

When Lanny rose to leave, the lion-cub stretched himself and growled. The great man remarked: "He is getting too big, and everybody but me is afraid of him."

VII

Four days and nights had passed since Johannes Robin had been taken captive; and Lanny wondered how he was standing it. Had they been giving him a taste of those scientific tortures which they had evolved? Or had they left him to the crude barbarities of the S.A. and S.S. such as Lanny had read about in the Manchester *Guardian* and the Pink weeklies? He hadn't thought it wise to ask the General, and he didn't ask the young Schutzstaffel Ober-leutnant who sat by his side on their way to visit the prisoner.

Furtwaengler talked about the wonderful scenes on the National Socialist First of May. His memories had not dimmed in eighteen days, nor would they in as many years, he said. He spoke with the same naïve enthusiasm as Heinrich Jung, and Lanny perceived that this was no accident of temperament, but another achievement of science. This young man was a product of the Nazi educational technique applied over a period of ten years. Lanny questioned him and learned that his father was a workingman, killed in the last fighting on the Somme—perhaps by a bullet from the rifle of Marcel Detaze. The orphan boy had been taken into a Hitler youth group at the age of fifteen, and had had military training in their camps and war experience in the street fighting of Moabit, Neuköln, Schöneberg, and other proletarian districts of Berlin. He was on his toes with eagerness to become a real officer, like those of the Reichswehr; the S.S. aspired to replace that army, considering such transfer of power as part of the proletarian revolution. Oberleutnant Furt-waengler wanted to click his heels more sharply and salute more snappily than any regular army man; but at the same time he couldn't help being a naïve workingclass youth, wondering whether he was making the right impression upon a foreigner who was obviously elegant, and must be a person of importance, or why should the Minister-Präsident of Prussia have spent half an hour with him on such a busy morning?

They were now being driven in an ordinary Hispano-Suiza, not a six-wheeled near-tank; but again they had a chauffeur in uniform and a guard. There were hundreds of such cars, of all makes, including Packards and Lincolns, parked in front of the Minister-Präsident's official residence and other public buildings near by. Such were the perquisites of office; the reasons for seizing power and the means of keeping it. Leutnant Furtwaengler was going to have a new uniform, as well as new visiting cards; it was a great day in the morning for him, and his heart was high; he needed only a little encouragement to pour out his pride to an American who must be a party sympathizer—how could anyone fail to be? Lanny did his best to be agreeable, because he wanted friends at court.

Johannes had been taken out of the Nazi barracks, the so-called Friesen Kaserne, to the main police headquarters, the Polizei-präsidium; but he was still in charge of a special group of the S.S. It was like the Swiss Guard of the French kings, or the Janissaries of the Turkish sultans—strangers to the place, having a special duty and a special trust. Johannes represented a treasure of several tens of millions of marks—Lanny didn't know how many, exactly. If he should take a notion to commit suicide, Minister-Präsident Göring would lose all chance of getting that portion of the treasure which had been stored abroad, nor could he get the part stored in Germany without violating his Führer's "legality complex."

VIII

The car stopped before a great red brick building in the Alexanderplatz, and Lanny was escorted inside. Steel doors clanged behind him—a sound which he had heard in the building of the Sûreté Générale in Paris and found intensely disagreeable. He was escorted down a bare stone-paved corridor, with more doors opening and clanging, until he found himself in a small room with one steel-barred window, a table, and three chairs. "*Bitte, setzen Sie sich,*" said the Oberleutnant. The chair which Lanny took faced the door, and he sat, wondering: "Will they have shaved his head and put him in stripes? Will he have any marks on him?"

He had none; that is, unless you counted spiritual marks. He was wearing the brown business suit in which he had set out for his yacht; but he needed a bath and a shave, and came into the room as if he might be on the way to a firing-squad. When he saw his daughter-in-law's half-brother sitting quietly in a chair, he started visibly, and then pulled himself together, pressing his lips tightly, as if he didn't want Lanny to see them trembling. In short, he was a thoroughly cowed Jew; his manner resembled that of an animal which had been mistreated—not a fighting animal, but a tame domestic one.

"*Setzen Sie sich, Herr Robin,*" ordered the Oberleutnant. On Lanny's account he would be polite, even to a *Missgeburt.* Johannes took the third chair. "*Bitte, sprechen Sie Deutsch,*" added the officer, to Lanny.

Two S.S. men had followed the prisoner into the room; they closed the door behind them and took post in front of it. As Lanny was placed he couldn't help seeing them, even while absorbed in conversation. Those two lads in shining black boots and black and silver uniforms with skull and crossbones insignia stood like two monuments of Prussian militarism; their forms rigid, their chests thrust out, their guts sucked in—Lanny had learned the phrase from his ex-sergeant friend Jerry Pendleton. Their hands did not hang by their sides, but were pressed with palms open and fingers close together, tightly against their thighs and held there as if glued. Not the faintest trace of expression on the faces, not the slightest motion of the eyes; apparently each man picked out a spot on the wall and stared at it continuously for a quarter of an hour. Did they do this because they were in the presence of an officer, or in order to impress a foreigner—or just because they had been trained to do it and not think about it?

"Johannes," said Lanny, speaking German, as requested, "Irma and I came as soon as we heard about your trouble. All the members of your family are safe and well."

"*Gott sei Dank!*" murmured the prisoner. He was holding onto the chair in which he had seated himself, and when he had spoken he pressed his lips together again. For the first time in his life Johannes Robin seemed an old man; he was sixty, but had never shown even that much.

"The situation is a serious one, Johannes, but it can be settled for money, and you and your family are to be allowed to go to France with us."

"I don't mind about the money," said the Jew, quickly. He had fixed his eyes on Lanny's face and never took them away. He seemed to be asking: "Am I to believe what you tell me?" Lanny kept nodding, as if to say: "Yes, this is real, this is not a dream."

"The charge against you is that you tried to carry money out of the country on your yacht."

"*Aber*, Lanny!" exclaimed the prisoner, starting forward in his chair. "I had a permit for every mark that I took!"

"Where did you put the permit?"

"It was in my pocket when I was arrested."

"Are you sure of that?"

"Absolutely. I would have been mad to try to carry money out of Germany without it."

Lanny was not too much surprised by this. "We have to assume that some malicious person destroyed the paper, Johannes."

"Yes, but there will be a record of it in the office of the Exchange Control Authority."

"I have been told on the best possible authority that no such record exists. I am afraid we shall have to assume that some mistake has been made, and that you had no valid permit."

Johannes's eyes darted for the fraction of a second toward the S.S. officer. Then he said, as humbly as any moneylender in a medieval dungeon: "Yes, Lanny, of course. It must be so."

"That makes a very serious offense, and the punishment, I fear, would be more than your health could stand. The only alternative is for you to part with your money. All of it."

Lanny was prepared for some anguish, some kind of Shylock scene. "Justice! the law! my ducats, and my daughter!" But Johannes sank back in his chair and resumed his dull tone. "I have been expecting that, Lanny. It is all right."

The man's aspect and manner revealed even more than his words. Lanny knew how he loved his money; how hard he had worked for it, how many plans he had for the use of it. But here he was kissing it good-by, as casually as if he had been a darling of fortune whose interest was dancing, playing the piano, and listening to parlor Pinks discussing the expropriation of the expropriators!

What had happened to him to produce such a change? Had he been worked over with rubber hose, which leaves few marks? Had he seen his fellow Jews being compelled to lash one another's faces with whips? Had he lain awake all night listening to the screams of men with camphor injected in their urinary ducts? Something of the sort must have happened.

IX

The visitor had to leave no uncertainty in his friend's mind. He had to be as implacable as Minister-Präsident Göring himself. He said: "It means everything you have, Johannes—both here and abroad."

"I understand."

"They have had a man in your office and have all the records."

"I had become aware of that."

"I have gone into the situation carefully, and I'm afraid you will have to give up."

"If they will really let me go, and my family, they may have everything."

"I have the word of Minister-Präsident Göring, and I believe that he means what he says. He has explained in the clearest language that he has no interest in you or yours, and will be glad to be rid of you."

"I am sure that Minister-Präsident Göring is a man of honor, and I accept his promise."

"He wants your money to use for the upbuilding of National Socialism. From his point of view that is, of course, a worthy purpose."

"The money would be of no use to me in this place."

"Exactly, Johannes. We can go abroad and you and Robbie can start business again. Irma will back you."

"Thank you, Lanny. I'll get along, I am sure."

"I have had to agree, and you have to agree, not to say a word about the case to anybody. We'll just get out and forget it."

"God knows I don't want to talk about it, Lanny. What good would that do me?"

"All right, then. Papers will be brought for you to sign."

"I will sign them."

"Some papers must go to New York, you know. It should take a week or two. Irma and I will wait here, and take you and the others out with us."

"I will never be able to express my gratitude, Lanny."

"Don't waste any energy on that. All we want is to have the family with us on the Riviera. We can have a good time without so much money. Are you being treated reasonably well?"

"I have no complaint."

"Is there anything I could send you—assuming I can get permission?"

"I have everything I need—everything unless perhaps some red ink."

Johannes said this without the flicker of an eyelash; and Lanny answered, without change of tone or expression: "I will see if it is possible to get some."

Rote Tinte! "Oh, the clever rascal!" Lanny thought. "His mind works like greased lightning." Johannes could sit there in the presence of a Schutzstaffel officer and two privates, and with all this pressure of terror and grief upon him—in the midst of having to make the most fateful decision of his life—he could think up a way to tell Lanny what he wished him to know, and without the slightest chance of his enemies' guessing what he had said!

For fifteen years Lanny and his old friend had been watching the experiment in the Soviet Union and arguing about it. Johannes, taking the negative, had delighted himself by collecting ironical stories, to be repeated to the credulous Lanny, and over Lanny's shoulder to Johannes's two misguided sons. One such story had to do with two German business men, one of whom was going to make a trip into the proletarian paradise, and promised his friend to write a full account of what he found there. "But," objected the friend, "you won't dare to write the truth if it's unfavorable." The other replied: "We'll fix it this way. I'll write you everything is fine, and if I write it in black ink it's true, and if in red ink the opposite is true." So he went, and in due course his friend received a letter in black ink, detailing the wonders of the proletarian paradise. "Everybody is happy, everybody is free, the markets are full of food, the shops well stocked with goods—in fact there is only one thing I cannot find, and that is red ink."

While Lanny and the Oberleutnant were driving to the hotel, the latter inquired: "What does he want red ink for?"

Lanny, who wasn't slow-minded himself, explained: "He keeps a diary, and writes it in red ink to keep it separate from his other papers."

The officer replied: "One cannot keep a diary in prison. They will surely take it away from him."

X

It was the Oberleutnant's duty to report to his superior, and meanwhile Lanny had to wait. He was deposited at his hotel a few min-

utes before two o'clock, and called his wife and told her: "I have
seen our friend and he is all right. I think matters can be arranged.
Take your time." To his mother, his father, and Rick he sent telegrams. "Have seen our friend. Believe matters arranged." He decided against using code names; if the Gestapo was interested, let
them know what he was saying, and to whom. He called Heinrich
and reported: "I think that matters are being arranged, and I am
grateful for the help of yourself and your friends. I have been asked
to keep the matter confidential, so I cannot say any more." That was
satisfactory to a perfect young bureaucrat.

The afternoon papers contained the story of the arrest of Johannes
Robin, made public by the Prussian government. Eighty million
Germans, minus the infants and a few malcontents, would learn that
a Jewish *Schieber* had been caught trying to smuggle money out of
the country on his yacht. Eighty million Germans, minus the infants and malcontents, would continue every day to believe statements issued on official authority, which statements would be carefully contrived fiction. It was a new kind of world to be living in,
and for the present Lanny had but one desire, to get out of it.

Irma came home in the middle of the afternoon and he took her
for a drive. He didn't feel in any way bound by promises made to
a bandit, so he told her the story, adding: "If you drop a hint of it
to anybody here it may cost Johannes and his family their lives."
Irma listened in wide-eyed horror. It was like the things you read
about the Borgias. He answered that there was nothing in history
to compare it to, because never before had barbarians commanded
the resources of modern science.

"Do you suppose Göring is taking that money for himself?" she
asked.

"It's all the same thing," he told her. "Göring is Germany, and
Germany will be Göring, whether it wishes to or not. The Nazis
will spend everything the Germans have."

"But the money abroad! What will he do about that?"

"They have a network of agents in other countries, and doubtless
they will have more. Also, if things should go wrong, and Göring
has to take a plane some day, it will be nice to have a nest-egg, and

be able to spend a comfortable old age in Paris or Buenos Aires."

"What perfect agony it must be to Johannes to turn all that money loose! My father would have died first!"

"Your father wouldn't have got into this position. Johannes was too trusting. He thought he could handle matters by diplomacy; but these fellows have knocked over the conference table. They have the advantage that nobody can realize how bad they are. If you and I were to go to Paris or London tomorrow and tell this story, the Nazis would call us liars and nine people out of ten would believe them."

XI

They went back to the hotel, expecting Freddi to call. But he didn't, and in the evening Colonel Emil Meissner came to dinner. He had read about the Robin case, and it did not occur to him to doubt his government's word. He said there had been a great deal of graft and favoritism under the Republic, but now, apparently, the laws were going to be enforced against rich as well as poor. This tall, severe-looking Prussian officer expressed polite regret that such misfortune should have fallen upon a relative of Lanny's. The host contented himself with replying that he had reason to hope matters would soon be straightened out, and that he had been asked to consider it confidential. Emil accepted this just as Heinrich had; all good Germans would accept it.

Emil talked freely about the new *Regierung*. He had despised the Republic, but had obeyed its orders because that was the duty of an army officer. Now Adolf Hitler had become his Commander-in-chief, and it was necessary to obey him, however one might privately dislike his manners. But Emil was sure that the stories of abuse of power had been greatly exaggerated, and for malicious purposes. There were bound to be excesses in any governmental overturn; the essential thing was that Germany had been saved from the clutches of the Reds, and every civilized person owed the new Chancellor a debt of gratitude for that. Lanny indulged in no Pink arguments, but said that he and his wife had been greatly impressed by what they had found in the country.

They waited late for a call from Freddi, but none came, and they went to bed speculating about it. Doubtless he was avoiding risks, and perhaps also afraid of bothering them; but it was too bad they couldn't give him the news which would so greatly relieve his mind. Lanny was prepared to state that he had come upon a wonderful Bouguereau!

Morning came, and the papers had editorials about the case of the Jewish *Schieber;* in Hitlerland all news stories were editorials, and were full of rancid hatred and venomous threats. At last the sneaking traitors were feeling the stern hand of the law; at last the vile Semitic parasites were being shaken from the fair body of Germania! *Der Angriff* was especially exultant. Here was proof to all the world that National Socialism meant what it said, that the stealthy influence of the Jewish plutocracy was no longer to rule the Fatherland! Lanny translated the words, which really seemed insane in their virulence. "Mr. Mouth doesn't sound so pleasant in print," he remarked.

Breakfast, and still no call from Freddi. They didn't like to go out until they had heard from him. Irma had her hair dressed and got a manicure; Lanny read a little, wrote a few notes, roamed about, and worried. They had a luncheon engagement at the Berlin home of General Graf Stubendorf, and they had to go. Irma said: "Clarinet can call again; or he can drop us a note."

Driving to the palace, they were free to discuss the various possibilities. Göring might have had Freddi arrested; or the Brownshirts might have picked him up, without Göring's knowing anything about it. Freddi was a Jew and a Socialist, and either was enough. Irma suggested: "Mightn't it be that Göring wants to keep the whole family in his hands until he's ready to put them out?"

"Anything is possible," said Lanny; "except that I can't imagine Freddi delaying this long to call us if he is free."

It rather spoiled their lunch. To tell the truth it wasn't an especially good lunch, or very good company—unless it was enough for you to know that you were the guest of a high-up Junker. The General Graf's attitude was the same as Emil's; he was a cog in the Reichswehr machine, and he obeyed orders. His special concern was get-

ting his home district out of the clutches of the Poles; he knew that
Lanny sympathized with this aim, but even so, he could talk about
it only guardedly, for the Chancellor had given the cue by a pacific
speech, so it was the duty of good Germans to let the subject of
boundary lines rest and to concentrate on the right of the Fatherland to equality of armaments. Having expressed regret over the
plight of Lanny's Jewish relative, the General Graf Stubendorf
talked about other friends, and about the condition of his crops and
the market for them, and what did Lanny's father think about the
prospects for world recovery?

Lanny answered with one part of his mind, while the other part
was thinking: "I wonder if Freddi is calling now!"

But Freddi wasn't calling.

19

No Peace in Zion

I

WHEN Mr. and Mrs. Irma Barnes had visited Berlin a year previously, they had been the darlings of the smart set, and all the important people had been glad to entertain them. But now the social
weather had changed; a thunderstorm was raging, and nobody could
be sure where the lightning might strike. The story of Johannes
Robin was known to the whole town; and who could guess what
confessions he might have made, or what might have been found in
his papers? Many persons have dealings with moneylenders which
they don't care to have become known. Many have affairs of various
sorts which they prefer not to have looked into by the Secret State

Police, and they carefully avoid anyone who might be under surveillance by that dreaded body.

Moreover, Irma and Lanny were worried, and when you are worried you are not very good company. Another day passed, and another, and they became certain that something terrible must have happened to Freddi. Of course he might have been knocked down by a truck, or slugged and robbed by one of the inmates of an *Asyl für Obdachlose* who suspected that he had money. But far more likely was the chance that a Jew and Socialist had fallen into the clutches of the Brown Terror. Their problem was, did Göring know about it, and if so was it a breach of faith, or merely a precaution against a breach of faith on their part? Would Göring be content to keep his hostage until the bargain was completed? Or was Freddi to remain in durance for a long time?

The more Lanny thought about it, the more complications he discovered. Could it be that there was a war going on between the two powerful Nazi chiefs? Had Goebbels becomes furious because Göring had taken the prisoner? Had he grabbed Freddi in order to thwart Göring and keep him from carrying out his bargain? If so, what was Lanny supposed to do? What part could a mere man play in a battle of giants—except to get his head cracked by a flying rock or uprooted tree? Lanny couldn't go to Goebbels and ask, because that would be breaking his pledge to Göring.

No, if he went to anybody it must be to Göring. But was he privileged to do this? Had it been a part of the bargain that the Minister-Präsident of Prussia and holder of six or eight other important posts was to lay aside his multifarious duties and keep track of the misfortunes of a family of Jewish *Schieber*? All Göring was obligated to do was to let them alone; and how easy for him to say: "Mr. Budd, I know nothing about the matter and have no desire to." Was Lanny to reply: "I do not believe you, Exzellenz!"?

It seemed clear that all Lanny could accomplish was to center the attention of the Gestapo upon the Robin family. If they set out to look for Freddi they would have to inquire among his friends. They might ask Lanny for a list of these friends; and what could Lanny say? "I do not trust you, *meine Herren von der Geheimen Staats-*

Polizei"? On the other hand, to give the names might condemn all these friends to concentration camps. The wife of Johannes was hiding with one of her former servants. The Gestapo would get a list of these and hunt them out—Jews, most of them, and doubtless possessing secrets of Johannes and his associates. Who could guess what they might reveal, or what anybody might invent under the new scientific forms of torture?

II

Lanny and his wife attended the very grand inauguration ceremonies of the Minister-Präsident of Prussia. They were met by Oberleutnant Furtwaengler and introduced to Ministerialdirektor Doktor X and General Ritter von Y. They were surrounded by Nazis in magnificent uniforms covered with medals and orders, behaving themselves with dignity and even with charm. Very difficult indeed to believe that they were the most dangerous miscreants in the world! Irma in her heart couldn't believe it, and when she and Lanny were driving afterward they had a bit of an argument, as married couples have been known to do.

Irma was a daughter of civilization. When she suspected a crime she went to the police. But now, it appeared, the police were the criminals! Irma had listened to Lanny's Red and Pink friends denouncing the police of all lands, and it had annoyed her more than she had cared to say; there were still traces of that annoyance in her soul, and Lanny had to exclaim: "My God, didn't Göring tell me with his own lips that he would find a hundred of Johannes's relatives and friends and torture them?"

"Yes, darling," replied the wife, with that bland manner which could be so exasperating. "But couldn't it have been that he was trying to frighten you?"

"Jesus!" he exploded. "For years I've been trying to tell the world what the Nazis are, and now it appears that I haven't convinced even my own wife!" He saw that he had offended her, and right away was sorry.

He had been through all this with his mother, starting a full decade ago. Beauty had never been able to believe that Mussolini was as bad as her son had portrayed him; she had never been able to think of an Italian refugee as other than some sort of misdoer. Beauty's own friends had come out of Italy, reporting everything improved, the streets clean, the trains running on time. Finally, she had gone and seen for herself; had she seen anybody beaten, or any signs of terror? Of course not!

And now, here was the same thing in Germany. Wherever you drove you saw perfect order. The people were clean and appeared well fed; they were polite and friendly—in short, it was a charming country, a pleasure to visit, and how was anybody to credit these horror tales? Irma was in a continual struggle between what she wanted to believe and what was being forced upon her reluctant mind. Casting about for something to do for poor Freddi, she had a bright idea. "Mightn't it be possible for me to go and talk to Göring?"

"To appeal to his better nature, you mean?"

"Well, I thought I might be able to tell him things about the Robins."

"If you went to Göring, he would want just one thing from you, and it wouldn't be stories about any Jews."

What could Irma say to that? She knew that if she refused to believe it, she would annoy her husband. But she persisted: "Would it do any harm to try?"

"It might do great harm," replied the anti-Nazi. "If you refused him, he would be enraged, and avenge the affront by punishing the Robins."

"Do you really know that he's that kind of man, Lanny?"

"I'm tired of telling you about these people," he answered. "Get the Fürstin Donnerstein off in a corner and ask her to give you the dirt!"

III

Any pleasure they might have got out of a visit to Berlin was ruined. They sat in their rooms expecting a telephone call; they waited for every mail. They could think of nothing to do that might not make matters worse; yet to do nothing seemed abominable. They thought: "Even if he's in a concentration camp, he'll find some way to smuggle out a message! Surely all the guards can't be loyal, surely some one can be bribed!"

Lanny bothered himself with the question: was he committing an act of bad faith with Johannes in not informing him of this new situation? He had assured Johannes that the family was all well. Was it now his duty to see the prisoner again and say: "Freddi has disappeared"? To do so would be equivalent to telling the Gestapo—and so there was the same round of problems to be gone over again. Even if he told Johannes, what could Johannes do? Was he going to say: "No, Exzellenz, I will not sign the papers until I know where my younger son is. Go ahead and torture me if you please." Suppose Göring should answer: "I have no idea where your son is. I have tried to find him and failed. Sign—or be tortured!"

The agonizing thing was that anywhere Lanny tried asking a question, he might be involving somebody else in the troubles of the Robin family. Friends or relatives, they would all be on the Gestapo list—or he might get them on! Was he being followed? So far he had seen no signs of it, but that didn't prove it mightn't be happening, or mightn't begin with his next step outdoors. The people he went to see, whoever they were, would know about the danger, and their first thought would be: "*Um Gottes Willen*, go somewhere else."

Rahel's parents, for example; he knew their names, and they were in the telephone book. But Freddi had said: "Don't ever call them. It would endanger them." The family were not Socialists; the father was a small lawyer, and along with all the other Jewish lawyers, had been forbidden to practice his profession, and thus was deprived of his livelihood. What would happen if a phone call were overheard and reported? Or if a rich American were to visit a third-class apartment house, where Jews were despised and spied upon, where the Nazis boasted that they had one of their followers in every building, keeping track of the tenants and reporting everything suspicious or even unusual? The Brown Terror!

Was Lanny at liberty to ignore Freddi's request, even in an effort

to save Freddi's life? Would Freddi want his life saved at the risk
of involving his wife and child? Would he even want his wife to
know about his disappearance? What could she do if she knew it,
except to fret herself ill, and perhaps refuse to let Lanny and Irma
take her out of the country? No, Freddi would surely want her to
go, and he wouldn't thank Lanny for thwarting his wishes. Possibly
he hadn't told Rahel where Lanny and Irma were staying, but she
must have learned it from the newspapers or from her parents; and
surely, if she knew where Freddi was, and if he needed help, she
would risk everything to get word to Lanny. Was she, too, in an
agony of dread, hesitating to communicate with Lanny, because
Freddi had forbidden her to do so?

IV

Lanny bethought himself of the Schultzes, the young artist couple.
Having got some of Trudi's work published in Paris, he had a legitimate reason for calling upon her. They lived in one of the industrial districts, desiring to be in touch with the workers; and this
of course made them conspicuous. He hesitated for some time, but
finally drove to the place, a vast area of six-story tenements, neater
than such buildings would have been in any other land. Almost without exception there were flower-boxes in the windows; the German
people didn't take readily to the confinements of city life, and each
wanted a bit of country.

A few months ago there had been civil war in these streets; the
Brownshirts had marched and the workers had hurled bottles and
bricks from the rooftops; meetings had been raided and party workers dragged away and slugged. But now all that was over; the promise of the *Horst Wessel Lied* had been kept and the streets were free
to the brown battalions. The whole appearance of the neighborhood
had changed; the people no longer lived on the streets, even in this
brightest spring weather; the children stayed in their rooms, and
the women with their market-baskets traveled no farther than they
had to, and watched with furtive glances as they went.

Lanny parked his car around the corner and walked to the house.

He looked for the name Schultz and did not find it, so he began knocking on doors and inquiring. He couldn't find a single person who would admit having heard of Ludi and Trudi Schultz. He was quite sure from their manner that this wasn't so; but they were afraid of him. Whether he was a Socialist or a spy, he was dangerous, and "*Weiss nichts*" was all he could get. Doubtless there were "comrades" in the building, but they had "gone underground," and you had to know where to dig in order to find them. It was no job for "parlor Pinks," and nobody wanted one to meddle with it.

V

Lanny went back to the hotel and continued his vigil. Sooner or later a note or a telephone message was bound to come, and this painful business of guessing and imagining would end. He went downstairs for a haircut, and when he came back he found his wife in a state of excitement. "Mama called!" she whispered. "She has to buy some gloves at Wertheim's, and I'm to meet her there in half an hour."

Irma had already ordered the car, so they went down, and while they were driving they planned their tactics. Irma would go in alone, because the meeting of two women would be less conspicuous. "Better not speak to her," suggested Lanny. "Let her see you and follow you out. I'll drive round the block and pick you up."

The wife of Johannes Robin didn't need any warning as to danger; she was back in old Russia, where fear had been bred into her bones. When Irma strolled down the aisle of the great department store, Mama was asking prices, a natural occupation for an elderly Jewish lady. She followed at a distance, and when Irma went out onto the street and Lanny came along they both stepped into the car. "Where is Freddi?" she whispered with her first breath.

"We have not heard from him," said Lanny, and she cried: "*Ach, Gott der Gerechte!*" and hid her face in her hands and began to sob.

Lanny hastened to say: "We have got things fixed up about Papa. He's all right, and is to be allowed to leave Germany, with you and the others." That comforted her, but only for a minute. She was like the man who has an hundred sheep, and one of them has gone astray, and he leaves the ninety and nine and goeth into the mountains, and seeketh that which is gone astray. "Oh, my poor lamb, what have they done to him?"

The mother hadn't heard a word from her son since he had called Lanny, and then written her a comforting note. She had been doing just what Lanny had been doing, waiting, numb with fear, imagining calamities. Freddi had forbidden her to call the Budds or to go near them, and she had obeyed for as long as she could stand it. "Oh, my poor darling, my poor baby!"

It was a painful hour they spent. The good soul, usually so sensible, so well adjusted to her routine of caring for those she loved, was now in a state of near distraction; her mind was as if in a nightmare, obsessed by all the horror stories which were being whispered among the Jews in the holes where they were hiding, apart from the rest of Germany. Stories of bodies found every day in the woods or dragged out of the lakes and canals of Berlin; suicides or murdered people whose fates would never be known, whose names were not mentioned in the press. Stories of the abandoned factory in the Friedrichstrasse which the Nazis had taken over, and where they now brought their victims to beat and torture them. The walls inside that building were soaked with human blood; you could walk by it and hear the screams—but you had best walk quickly! Stories of the concentration camps, where Jews, Communists, and Socialists were being made to dig their own graves in preparation for pretended executions; where they underwent every form of degradation which brutes and degenerates were able to devise—forced to roll about in the mud, to stick their faces into their own excrement, to lash and beat one another insensible, thus saving labor for the guards. "*Oi, oi!*" wailed the poor mother, and begged the *Herrgott* to let her son be dead.

Only one thing restrained her, and that was consideration for her kind friends. "I have no right to behave like this!" she would say. "It is so good of you to come and try to help us poor wretches. And of course Freddi would want us to go away, and to live the best we can without him. Do you really believe the Nazis will turn Papa loose?"

Lanny didn't tell her the story; he just said: "It will cost a lot of money"—he guessed that would help to make it real to her mind. She couldn't expect any kindness of these persecutors, but she would understand that they wanted money.

"Oh, Lanny, it was a mistake that we ever had so much! I never thought it could last. Let it all go—if only we can get out of this terrible country."

"I want to get you out, Mama, and then I'll see what can be done about Freddi. I haven't dared to try meantime, because it may make more trouble for Papa. If I can get four of you out safely, I know that is what Freddi would want."

"Of course he would," said Mama. "He thought about everybody in the world but himself. *Oi*, my darling, my little one, my *Schatz!* You know, Lanny, I would give my life in a minute if I could save him. Oh, we must save him!"

"I know, Mama; but you have to think about the others. Papa is going to have to start life over, and will need your counsel as he did in the old days. Also, don't forget that you have Freddi's son."

"I cannot believe any good thing, ever again! I cannot believe that any of us will ever get out of Germany alive. I cannot believe that God is still alive."

VI

Oberleutnant Furtwaengler telephoned, reporting that the prisoner had signed the necessary documents and that the arrangements were in process of completion. He asked what Lanny intended to do with him, and Lanny replied that he would take the family to Belgium as soon as he was at liberty to do so. The businesslike young officer jotted down the names of the persons and said he would have the exit permits and visas ready on time.

It would have been natural for Lanny to say: "Freddi Robin is missing. Please find him and put me in touch with him." But after thinking and talking it over for days and nights, he had decided that if Freddi was still alive, he could probably survive for another week or two, until the rest of his family had been got out of the country.

Lanny had no way to hold Göring to his bargain if he didn't choose to keep it, and as half a loaf is better than no bread, so four-fifths of a Jewish family would be better than none of them—unless you took the Nazi view of Jewish families!

However, it might be the part of wisdom to prepare for the future, so Lanny invited the Oberleutnant to lunch; the officer was pleased to come, and to bring his wife, a tall sturdy girl from the country, obviously very much flustered at being the guest of a fashionable pair who talked freely about Paris and London and New York, and knew all the important people. The Nazis might be ever so nationalistic, but the great world capitals still commanded prestige. Seeking to cover up his evil past, Lanny referred to his former Pinkness, and said that one outgrew such things as one grew older; what really concerned him was to find out how the problem of unemployment could be solved and the products of modern machinery distributed; he intended to come back to Germany and see if the Führer was able to carry out his promises.

A young devotee could ask no more, and the Oberleutnant warmed to his host and hostess. Afterward Irma said: "They really do believe in their doctrine with all their hearts!" Lanny saw that she found it much easier to credit the good things about the Hitler system than the evil. She accepted at face value the idea current among her leisure-class friends, that Mussolini had saved Italy from Bolshevism and that Hitler was now doing the same for Germany. "What good would it do to upset everything," she wished to know, "and get in a set of men who are just as bad as the Nazis or worse?"

One little hint Lanny had dropped to the officer: "I'm keeping away from the Robin family and all their friends, because I don't want to involve myself in any way in political affairs. I am hoping that nothing of an unhappy nature will happen to the Robins while we are waiting. If anything of the sort should come up I will count upon Seine Exzellenz to have it corrected."

"*Ja, gewiss!*" replied the officer. "Seine Exzellenz would not permit harm to come to them—in fact, I assure you that no harm is coming to any Jewish persons, unless they themselves are making some sort of trouble."

The latter half of this statement rather tended to cancel the former half; it was a part of the Nazi propaganda. That was what made it so difficult to deal with them; you had to pick every sentence apart and figure out which portions they might mean and which were bait for suckers. The Oberleutnant was cordial, and seemed to admire Lanny and his wife greatly; but would this keep him from lying blandly, if, for example, his chief was holding Freddi Robin as a hostage and wished to conceal the fact? Would it keep him from committing any other act of treachery which might appear necessary to the cause of National Socialism? Lanny had to keep reminding himself that these young men had been reared on *Mein Kampf*; he had to keep reminding his wife, who had never read that book, but instead had heard Lord Wickthorpe cite passages from Lenin, proclaiming doctrines of political cynicism which sounded embarrassingly like Hitler's.

VII

Heinrich Jung also had earned a right to hospitality, so he and his devoted little blue-eyed *Hausfrau* were invited to a dinner which was an outstanding event in her life. She had presented the Fatherland with three little Aryans, so she didn't get out very often, she confessed. She exclaimed with naïve delight over the wonders of the Hotel Adlon, and had to have Irma assure her that her home-made dress was adequate for such a grand occasion. Heinrich talked N.S.D.A.P. politics, and incidentally fished around to find out what had happened in the case of Johannes Robin, about which there was no end of curiosity in party circles, he reported. Lanny could only say that he had orders not to talk. A little later he asked: "Have you seen Frau Reichsminister Goebbels since our meeting?"

Yes, Heinrich had been invited to tea at her home; so Lanny didn't have to ask who had manifested the curiosity in party circles. Presently Heinrich said that Magda had wished to know whether Mr. and Mrs. Budd would care to be invited to one of her receptions. Irma hastened to say that she would be pleased, and Heinrich undertook to communicate this attitude. So it is that one advances in *die grosse Welt;* if one has money, plus the right clothes and manners, one can go from drawing-room to drawing-room, filling one's stomach with choice food and drink and one's ears with choice gossip.

Hugo Behr, the *Gausportführer*, had expressed his desire to meet Lanny again. Heinrich, reporting this, said: "I think I ought to warn you, Lanny. Hugo and I are still friends, but there are differences of opinion developing between us." Lanny asked questions and learned that some among the Nazis were impatient because the Führer was not carrying out the radical economic planks upon which he had founded the party. He seemed to be growing conservative, allying himself with Göring's friends, the great industrialists, and forgetting the promises he had made to the common man. Heinrich said it was easy to find fault, but it was the duty of good party members to realize what heavy burdens had been heaped upon the Führer's shoulders, and to trust him and give him time. He had to reorganize the government, and the new men he put in power had to learn their jobs before they could start on any fundamental changes. However, there were people who were naturally impatient, and perhaps jealous, unwilling to give the Führer the trust he deserved; if they could have their way, the party would be destroyed by factional strife before it got fairly started.

Heinrich talked at length, and with great seriousness, as always, and his devoted little wife listened as if it were the Führer himself speaking. From the discourse Lanny gathered that the dissension was really serious; the right wing had won all along the line, and the left was in confusion. Gregor Strasser, who had taken such a dressing down from Hitler in Lanny's presence, had resigned his high party posts and retired to the country in disgust. Ernst Röhm, Chief of Staff of the S.A. and one of Hitler's oldest friends, was active in protest and reported to be in touch with Schleicher, the "labor general," whom Hitler had ousted from the chancellorship. A most dangerous situation, and Hugo was making a tragic mistake in letting himself be drawn into it.

"But you know how it is," Heinrich explained. "Hugo was a Social-Democrat, and when the Marxist poison has once got into your veins it's hard to get it out."

Lanny said yes, he could understand; he had been in that camp a while himself; but there was no use expecting everything to be changed in a few months. "You have two elements in your party, Nationalism and Socialism, and I suppose it isn't always easy to preserve the balance between them."

"It will be easy if only they trust the Führer. He knows that our Socialism must be German and fitted to the understanding of the German people. He will give it to them as rapidly as they can adjust themselves to it."

After their guests had left, Lanny said to his wife: "If we want to collect the dirt, Hugo's the boy to give it to us."

VIII

Mama had agreed with Lanny and Irma that there was nothing to be gained by telling the family in Paris about Freddi's disappearance. They could hardly fail to talk about it, and so imperil the fate of Johannes. It might even be that Hansi or Bess would insist on coming into Germany—and the least hint of that threw poor Mama into another panic. So Lanny wrote vague letters to his mother: "Everything is being arranged. The less publicity the better. Tell our friends to go to Juan and rest; living is cheap there, and I feel sure that times are going to be hard financially." Little hints like that!

Beauty herself didn't go to Juan. Her next letter was written on stationery of the Château de Balincourt. "Do you remember Lady Caillard? She is the widow of Sir Vincent Caillard, who was one of Sir Basil's closest associates in Vickers. She is an ardent spiritualist, and has published a pamphlet of messages received from her husband in the spirit world. She is immensely impressed by Madame, and wants to borrow her for as long as Sir Basil will spare her. He invited me out here, and we have had several séances. One thing that came up worries me. Tecumseh said: 'There is a man who speaks German. Does anyone know German?' Sir Basil said: 'I know a little,' and the control said: '*Clarinet ist verstimmt.*' That was all. Madame began to moan, and when she came out of the trance she was greatly depressed and could do no more that day. I didn't get the idea for a while. Now I wonder, can there be anything the matter with *your* Clarinet? I shall say nothing to anybody else until I hear from you."

So there it was again; one of those mysterious hints out of the sub-conscious world. The word *verstimmt* can mean either "out of tune" or "out of humor." Beauty had known that "Clarinet" meant Freddi, and it was easy to imagine Tecumseh getting that out of her sub-conscious mind; but Beauty had no reason to imagine that Freddi was in trouble. Was it to be supposed that when Beauty sat in a "circle," her subconscious mind became merged with her son's, and his worries passed over into hers? Or was it easier to believe that some Socialist had been kicked or beaten or shot into the spirit world by the Nazis and was now trying to bring help to his com-rade?

Lanny sent a telegram to his mother: "Clarinet music interesting send more if possible." He decided that here was a way he could pass some time while waiting upon the convenience of Minister-Präsident Göring. Like Paris and London, Berlin was full of me-diums and fortune tellers of all varieties; it was reported that the Führer himself consulted an astrologer—oddly enough, a Jew. Here was Lanny, obliged to sit around indefinitely, and with no heart for social life, for music or books. Why not take a chance, and see if he could get any further hints from that underworld which had surprised him so many times?

Irma was interested, and they agreed to go separately to different mediums, thus doubling their chances. Maybe not all the spirits had been Nazified, and the young couple could get ahead of Göring in that shadowy realm!

IX

So there was Lanny being ushered into the fashionable apart-ment of one of the most famous of Berlin's clairvoyants, Madame Diseuse. (If she had been practicing in Paris she would have been Frau Wahrsagerin.) You had to be introduced by a friend, and sittings were by appointment, well in advance; but this was an emer-gency call, arranged by Frau Ritter von Fiebewitz, and was to cost a hundred marks. No Arabian costumes, or zodiacal charts, or other hocus-pocus, but a reception-room with the latest furniture of tubular light metal, and an elegant French lady with white hair and a St. Germain accent. She sometimes produced physical phenomena, and spoke with various voices in languages of which she claimed not to know a word. The séance was held in a tiny interior room which became utterly dark when a soft fluorescent light was turned off.

There Lanny sat in silence for perhaps twenty minutes, and had about concluded that his hundred marks had been wasted, when he heard a sort of cooing voice, like a child's, saying in English: "What is it that you want, sir?" He replied: "I want news about a young friend who may or may not be in the spirit world." After another wait the voice said: "An old gentleman comes. He says you do not want him."

Lanny had learned that you must always be polite to any spirit. He said: "I am always glad to meet an old friend. Who is he?"

So came an experience which a young philosopher would retain as a subject of speculation for the rest of his life. A deep masculine voice seemed to burst the tiny room, declaring: "Men have forgotten the Word of God." Lanny didn't have to ask: "Who are you?" for it was just as if he were sitting in the study of a rather dreary New England mansion with hundred-year-old furniture, listening to his Grandfather Samuel expounding Holy Writ. Not the feeble old man with the quavering voice who had said that he would not be there when Lanny came again, but the grim gunmaker of the World War days who had talked about sin, knowing that Lanny was a child of sin—but all of us were that in the sight of the Lord God of Sabaoth.

"All the troubles in the world are caused by men ceasing to hear the Word of God," announced this surprising voice in the darkness. "They will continue to suffer until they hear and obey. So is it, world without end, amen."

"Yes, Grandfather," said Lanny, just as he had said many times in the ancestral study. Wishing to be especially polite, he asked: "Is this really you, Grandfather?"

"All flesh is grass, and my voice is vain, except that I speak the words which God has given to men. I have been young, and now am old; yet have I not seen the righteous forsaken, nor his seed begging bread."

Either that was the late president of Budd Gunmakers, or else a highly skilled actor! Lanny waited a respectful time, and then inquired: "What is it you wish of me, Grandfather?"

"You have not heeded the Word!" exploded the voice.

Lanny could think of many Words to which this statement might apply; so he waited, and after another pause the voice went on: "Swear now therefore unto me by the Lord, that thou wilt not cut off my seed after me."

Lanny knew only too well what that meant. The old man had objected strenuously to the practice known as birth control. He had wanted grandchildren, plenty of them, because that was the Lord's command. Be fruitful and multiply and replenish the earth. It had been one of Samuel Budd's obsessions, and the first time Irma had been taken to see him he had quoted the words of old King Saul to David. But Irma had disregarded the injunction; she didn't want a lot of babies, she wanted to have a good time while she was young. The price which nature exacts for babies is far too high for fashionable ladies to pay. So now the old man had come back from the grave!

Or was it just Lanny's subconscious mind? His guilty conscience —plus that of Irma's, since she was defying not merely Lanny's grandfather in the spirit world, but her own mother in this world! A strange enough phenomenon in either case.

"I will bear your words in mind, Grandfather," said Lanny, with the tactfulness which had become his very soul. "How am I to know that this really is you?"

"I have already taken steps to make sure that you know," replied the voice. "But do not try to put me off with polite phrases."

That was convincing, and Lanny was really quite awestricken. But still, he wasn't going to forget about Freddi. "Grandfather, do you remember Bess's husband, and his young brother? Can you find out anything about him?"

But Grandfather could be just as stubborn as Grandson. "Remember the Word of the Lord," the voice commanded; and then no more. Lanny spoke two or three times, but got no answer. At last he heard a sigh in the darkness, and the soft fluorescent light was switched on, and there sat Madame Diseuse, asking in a dull, tired voice: "Did you get what you wanted?"

X

Lanny arrived at the hotel just a few minutes before Irma, who had consulted two other mediums, chosen from advertisements in the newspapers because they had English names. "Well, did you get anything?" she asked, and Lanny said: "Nothing about Clarinet. Did you?"

"I didn't get anything at all. It was pure waste of time. One of the mediums was supposed to be a Hindu woman, and she said I would get a letter from a handsome dark lover. The other was a greasy old creature with false teeth that didn't fit, and all she said was that an old man was trying to talk to me. She wouldn't tell me his name, and all he wanted was for me to learn some words."

"Did you learn them?"

"I couldn't help it; he made me repeat them three times, and he kept saying: 'You will know what they mean.' They sounded like they came from the Bible."

"Say them!" exclaimed Lanny.

"And that thou wilt not destroy my name out of my father's house."

"Oh, my God, Irma! It's a cross-correspondence!"

"What is that?"

"Don't you remember the first time you met Grandfather, he quoted a verse from the Bible, telling you to have babies, and not to interfere with the Lord's will?"

"Yes, but I don't remember the words."

"That is a part of what he said. He came to me just now and gave me the beginning of it. 'Swear now therefore unto me by the

Lord, that thou wilt not cut off my seed after me, and that thou wilt not destroy my name out of my father's house.' "

"Lanny, how perfectly amazing!" exclaimed the young wife.

"He said he had already taken steps to convince me that it was really he. He had probably already talked to you."

Irma had been living with the spirits now for nearly four years, and had got more or less used to them; but this was the first time she had come upon such an incident. Lanny explained that the literature of psychical research was full of "cross-correspondences." Sometimes one part of a sentence would be given in England and another in Australia. Sometimes there would be references by page and line to a book, and through another medium references to some other book, and when the words were put together they made sense. It seemed to prove that whatever intelligence was at work was bound by none of the limitations of time and space. The main trouble was, it was all so hard to believe—people just couldn't and wouldn't face it.

"Well," said Lanny, "do you want to have another baby?"

"What do you suppose Grandfather will do if we don't?"

"You go and ask him," chuckled Lanny.

Irma didn't. But a day or two later came a letter from Robbie, telling what the old gentleman would do if they obeyed him. He had established in his will a trust fund for Frances Barnes Budd to the amount of fifty thousand dollars, and had provided the same amount for any other child or children Irma Barnes Budd might bear within two years after his death. The old realist had taken no chances, but added: "Lanny Budd being the father."

XI

The golden-haired and blue-eyed young sports director, Hugo Behr, came to see his American friend, and was taken for a drive. Hugo didn't need any urging to induce him to "spill the dirt" about the present tendencies of his National Socialist Party; he said he had joined because he had believed it was a Socialist party and there were millions who felt as he did—they wanted it to remain Socialist and they had a right to try to keep it so, and have it carry out at least part of the program upon which it had won the faith of the German masses. Breaking up the great landed estates, socializing basic industries and department stores, abolishing interest slavery—these were the pledges which had been made, millions of times over. But now the party was hand in glove with the Ruhr magnates, and the old program was forgotten; the Führer had come under the spell of men who cared only about power, and if they could have their way, all the energies of the country would go into military preparation and none into social welfare.

"Yes," said Hugo, "many of the leaders feel as I do, and some of them are Hitler's oldest party comrades. It is no threat to his leadership, but a loyal effort to make him realize the danger and return to the true path." The young official offered to introduce Lanny to some of the men who were active in this movement; but the visitor explained the peculiar position he was in, with a Jewish relative in the toils of the law and the need of being discreet on his account.

That led to the subject of the Jews, and the apple-cheeked young Aryan proved that he was loyal to his creed by denouncing this evil people and the part they had played in corrupting German culture. But he added he did not approve the persecution of individual Jews who had broken no law, and he thought the recent one-day boycott had been silly. It represented an effort on the part of reactionary elements in the party to keep the people from remembering the radical promises which had been made to them. "It's a lot cheaper and easier to beat up a few poor Jews than to oust some of the great Junker landlords."

Lanny found this conversation promising, and ventured tactfully to give his young friend some idea of the plight in which he found himself. His brother-in-law's brother had been missing for more than a week, but he was afraid to initiate any inquiry for fear of arousing those elements about which Hugo had spoken, the fanatics who were eager to find some excuse for persecuting harmless, idealistic Jews. Lanny drew a picture of a shepherd boy out of ancient Judea, watching his flocks, playing his pipe, and dreaming of the

Lord and His angels. Freddi Robin was a Socialist in the high sense of the word; desiring justice and kindness among men, and willing to set an example by living a selfless life here and now. He was a fine musician, a devoted husband and father, and his wife and mother were in an agony of dread about him.

"*Ach, leider!*" exclaimed the sports director, and added the formula which Lanny already knew by heart, that unfortunate incidents were bound to happen in the course of any great social overturn.

"For that reason," said Lanny, "each of us has to do what he can in the cases which come to his knowledge. What I need now is some person in the party whom I can trust, and who will do me the service to try to locate Freddi and tell me what he is accused of."

"That might not be easy," replied the other. "Such information isn't given out freely—I mean, assuming that he's in the hands of the authorities."

"I thought that you, having so many contacts among the better elements of the party, might be able to make inquiries without attracting too much attention. If you would do me this favor, I would be most happy to pay you for your time——"

"Oh, I wouldn't want any pay, Herr Budd!"

"You would certainly have to have it. The work may call for a lot of time, and there is no other way I can make it up to you. My wife is here, and neither of us can enjoy anything, because of worrying about this poor fellow. I assure you, she would consider a thousand marks a small price to pay for the mental peace she would get from even knowing that Freddi is still alive. If only I can find out where he is and what he's accused of, I may be able to go to the proper authority and have the matter settled without any disagreeable scandal."

"If I could be sure that my name wouldn't be brought into the matter—" began the young official, hesitatingly.

"On that I will give you my word of honor," said Lanny. "Nothing will induce either my wife or myself to speak your name. You don't even have to give it when you call me on the phone; just tell me that you have, say, an Arnold Boecklin painting to show me, and tell me some place to meet you, and I'll come. Be so good as to accept two hundred marks for a start—on the chance that you may have to pay out sums here and there."

XII

Minister-Präsident Hermann Wilhelm Göring flew to Rome unexpectedly. He had been there once before and hadn't got along very well with his mentor, the Blessed Little Pouter Pigeon; they were quarreling bitterly over the question of which was to control Austria. But they patched it up somehow, and the newspapers of the world blazed forth a momentous event: the four great European nations had signed a peace pact, agreeing that for a period of ten years they would refrain from aggressive action against one another and would settle all problems by negotiation. Mussolini signed for Italy, Göring for Germany, and the British and French ambassadors to Vienna signed for their governments. Such a relief to the war-weary peoples of the Continent! Göring came home in triumph; and Irma said: "You see, things aren't nearly as bad as you've been thinking."

The couple went to a reception at the home of the Frau Reichsminister Goebbels, where they met many of the Nazi great ones. Lanny, who had read history, remembered the Visigoths, who had conquered ancient Rome with astonishing ease, and wandered about the splendid city, dazed by the discovery of what they had at their disposal; he remembered Clive, who had been similarly stunned by the treasures of Bengal, and had said afterward that when he considered what his opportunities had been, he was astonished at his own moderation.

So it was now with the members of the N.S.D.A.P.; not the moderation, but the opportunities. Men who a few years ago had been without the price of a meal or a place to lay their heads had suddenly come into possession of all Germany. They wore the finest uniforms that Berlin's tailors could design, and their women displayed their charms in the latest Paris models. Orders and medals, orchids and sparkling jewels—did they get all that out of party salaries, or the stipends of office in the Deutsches Reich or Preussischer Staat? Or had each one got busy on his own? They wouldn't have to rob, or even to threaten; they would only have to keep their hands out and the possessors of wealth and privilege would come running to fill them.

Here were the friends and camp followers of Juppchen Goebbels, frustrated journalist from the Rheinland, now master of his country's intellectual life. His word could make or break anyone in any profession; an invitation to his home was at once a command and the highest of opportunities. Men bowed and fawned, women smiled and flattered—and at the same time they watched warily, for it was a perilous world, in which your place was held only by sleepless vigilance. Jungle cats, all in one cage, circling one another warily, keeping a careful distance; the leopard and the jaguar would have tangled, had not both been afraid of the tiger.

But they were civilized cats, which had learned manners, and applied psychology, pretending to be gentle and harmless, even amiable. The deadliest killers wore the most cordial smiles; the most cunning were the most dignified, the most exalted. They had a great cause, an historic destiny, a patriotic duty, an inspired leader. They said: "We are building a new Germany," and at the same time they thought: "How can I cut out this fellow's guts?" They said: "Good evening, *Parteigenosse*," and thought: "*Schwarzer Lump*, I know what lies you have been whispering!" They said: "*Guten Abend, Herr Budd*," and thought: "Who is this *Emporkömmling*, and what is he doing here?" One would whisper: "The Chief thinks he can make use of him," and the other would be thinking: "The Chief must be plucking him good and plenty!"

XIII

"*Seien Sie willkommen, Herr Budd*," said the hostess, with the loveliest of her smiles. "You have been moving up in the world since we last met."

"Don't say that, Frau Reichsminister!" pleaded Lanny. "I beg you to believe that what happened was totally unforeseen by me, and unsought." Would she believe it? Of course she wouldn't—unless she happened to have inside information.

"Aren't you going to tell me about it?" A mischievous request, and therefore the way to disguise it was with the most mischievous of smiles. On the same principle that you spoke the truth only when you didn't wish to be believed.

Lanny, who had learned about intrigue when he was a tiny boy hearing his mother and father discussing the landing of a munitions contract—Lanny Budd, grandson of Budd Gunmakers, knew nothing better to do in a crisis than to be honest. "*Liebe Frau Reichsminister*," he said, "I beg you to be kind to a stranger in a strange land. I am in a painful position. I receive orders from those in authority, and I dare do nothing but obey."

"If I give you orders, will you obey, Herr Budd?" The wife of a Cabinet Minister apparently knew other ways to deal with one in a painful position. "What you call authority has a way of shifting suddenly in times like these. You had better give me an opportunity to advise you."

"Indeed, Frau Reichsminister, I will avail myself of your kindness." He had meant to say: "As soon as I am free to do so," but he decided to leave himself free to think it over.

Irma was being entertained by "Putzi" Hanfstaengl, wealthy art-publisher's son who played clown to Hitler and staff; half American and a Harvard graduate, he was tall and big and waved his arms like a windmill; for a while he was solemn, and then suddenly he danced, capered, made jokes, and laughed at them so loudly that everybody else laughed at him. The younger men were curious about the famous heiress, and she enjoyed herself as she generally did in company. Elegant, uniformed men bowed attendance and flattered her, bringing food and over-strong drink—many of them had too much of it, but that was nothing new in smart society, and Irma knew how to deal with such men.

Driving home in the small hours of the morning she was a bit fuddled and sleepy. Next morning, or rather much later that same morning, they sat in bed sipping their coffee, and Irma said what she thought of the affair. She had met agreeable people and couldn't believe they were as bad as they were painted. Lanny had to wait until they were in the car before getting in his side, which was: "I felt as if I were in a rendezvous of pirates."

Said Irma: "Listen, darling; did you ever meet a company of politicians in the United States?"

He had to admit that he lacked any basis of comparison, and his wife went on:

"They used to come to Father's house quite often, and he used to talk about them. He said they were natural-born hijackers. He said that no one of them had ever produced anything—all they did was to take it away from business men. He said they wouldn't stop till they got everything in their clutches."

"The prophecy has come true in Germany!" said Lanny.

20

Sufferance Is the Badge

I

A LONG letter from Robbie Budd, telling of the situation resulting from his father's death. The old gentleman had held on to his power up to the last moment, but had failed to decide the question of who was to be his successor. Long ago he had tried to settle the quarrel between his oldest and his youngest sons; then he had given up, and left them to fight it out—and they were doing so. Each wanted to become head of Budd's, and each was sure that the other was unfitted for the task. "I suppose," said Robbie, bitterly, "Father didn't consider either of us fitted."

Anyhow, the question was going to be settled by the stockholders. It so happened that an election of directors was due, and for the next sixty days Robbie and Lawford would be lobbying, pulling wires, trying to corral votes. They had been doing this in underground ways for years, and now the fight was in the open. Meanwhile the first vice-president was in charge—"holding the sponge," as Robbie phrased it. He was Esther Budd's brother, son of the president of the First National Bank of Newcastle. "The thing the old gentleman always dreaded," wrote Robbie; "the banks are taking us over!" Lanny knew this was said playfully, for Robbie and "Chassie" Remsen got along reasonably well, and the two couples played bridge one evening every week.

What really worried Robbie was the possibility of some Wall Street outfit "barging in." Budd's had been forced to borrow from one of the big insurance companies; it was either that or the Reconstruction Finance Corporation, which meant putting yourself at the mercy of the politicians. Robbie was in a dither over what the new administration was doing; Roosevelt had had three months in which to show his hand, and apparently the only thing he knew was to borrow money and scatter it like a drunken sailor. Of course that was just putting off the trouble, throwing the country into debt which the future would have to pay; incidentally it meant teaching everybody to come to Washington—"like hogs to the trough," said the munitions salesman, who chose the most undignified metaphors whenever he referred to his country's governmental affairs. Everything which gave power to the politicians meant debts, taxes, and troubles.

But Robbie didn't go into that subject now; he had his own immediate problems. "If only I could raise the cash to buy some Budd stock that I know of, I could settle the matter of control. Tell our friend that I want to hear from him the moment he has time to spare. I can make him a proposition which he will find advantageous." This had been written before the receipt of an unsigned note in which Lanny conveyed the news that "our friend" was being separated from every dollar he owned in the world. Poor Johannes—and poor Robbie!

The ever-discreet father didn't need any warning to be careful what he wrote about matters in Germany. His letter was a model of vagueness. He said: "There is a great deal of new business being done in Europe this year, and I ought to be there getting contracts. Once our problems at home are settled, I'll get busy." Lanny knew what this meant—the rearmament of Germany was beginning, and what the Nazis couldn't yet manufacture for themselves they would buy through intermediaries in Holland, Switzerland, Sweden. The factory chimneys of Newcastle would begin to smoke again—and it wouldn't mean a thing to Robbie Budd that he was putting power into the hands of Hitler, Göring, and Goebbels. It was the salesman's first axiom that all European nations were equally bad, and that whether the jaguar, the leopard, or the tiger came out on top was of no concern to anybody outside the jungle.

Lanny read this letter to his wife, who said: "Don't you think it might be a good idea for me to help your father?"

"You know, dear," he answered, "I have never been willing to exploit my marriage."

"Yes, but be sensible. I own a lot of stocks and bonds, and why shouldn't I exchange some of them for Budd's?"

"Your father chose those investments very shrewdly, Irma. Some of them are still paying large dividends, and Budd's isn't paying any."

"Yes, but the prices seem to find their level, according to the earnings." Irma had been putting her mind on her financial affairs ever since she had got that terrific jolt in the panic. "If we could get Budd stock at its present price, wouldn't it be safe to hold?"

"It wouldn't worry you to be financing munitions?"

"Why should it? Somebody's going to do it."

So there it was: everybody was "sensible" but Lanny. If the Nazis wanted automatics and machine guns, there were many makes on the market, and why shouldn't Budd's get the business as well as Vickers or Bofors or Skoda or Schneider-Creusot? Irma settled the matter. "When we get this business out of the way, we'll run over to New York and get Robbie and Uncle Joseph together and see what can be worked out."

Lanny said: "It's very kind of you." He knew it would have been unkind of him to say anything else.

II

A letter from Kurt, begging them to drive to Stubendorf in this very lovely season of the year. Kurt had no car, and couldn't afford the luxury of hopping about; but Seine Hochgeboren had told him that any time Irma and Lanny would come, the Schloss was at their disposal. Lanny hadn't told Kurt about Freddi. Now he was discussing whether to do it, and what to say, when the telephone rang, and he heard the voice of Oberleutnant Furtwaengler: "Herr Budd, I am happy to inform you that the government is prepared to release Johannes Robin."

Lanny's heart gave a thump. "That is certainly good news to me, Herr Oberleutnant."

"It is still your plan to drive him and his family to Belgium?"

"Whenever I am free to do so."

"You have the other members of the family with you?"

"I know where they are—at least, all but one of them. I am sorry to report that I have not heard from the son, Freddi, for a long time."

"You have no idea where he has gone?"

"Not the slightest."

"Why didn't you let me know this?"

"I have been thinking that I would surely hear from him, and I didn't want to bother you or the Minister-Präsident. I was sure that if he was a prisoner of the government, he would be released along with his father."

"I cannot say anything about it, because I do not know the circumstances. An investigation will have to be made. What do you wish to do about the others in the meantime?"

"I wish to take them out as soon as I am permitted to do so. I can come back for Freddi if you find him."

"There would be no need for you to come unless you wished. We will surely send him out if we find him."

"Very well. Shall I call at the Polizeipräsidium for Johannes?"

"That will be satisfactory."

"You understand that we wish very much to avoid newspaper

reporters, especially the foreign correspondents. For that reason it would be wise to leave as quickly as possible."

"We shall be pleased to co-operate with you to that end. We have the passports and exit permits ready."

"Does that include the visas for Belgium?"

"Everything has been foreseen. We do things that way in Germany."

"I know," said Lanny. "It is one of your great virtues."

"I bid you farewell, Herr Budd, and hope to have the pleasure of seeing you when you again visit Berlin."

"The same to you, Herr Oberleutnant. I am grateful for your many courtesies through this somewhat trying affair."

"Not at all, Herr Budd. Allow me to say that your handling of the matter has been most exemplary, and Seine Exzellenz wishes me to assure you of his sincere appreciation."

So they buttered each other, and clicked heels and bowed and scraped over the telephone; when Lanny hung up, he turned to his wife and said: "Chuck your things into the bags and we'll get going!"

He hastened to call the home of Rahel's parents, and she herself answered. "Good news," he said. "Papa is to be released at once and I am going to get him at the prison. Is Mama far from you?"

"A ten-minute drive."

"Call a taxi, take the baby and your bags, pick up Mama, and come to the Hotel Adlon as quickly as you can. Irma will be waiting for you. We are leaving at once. Is that all clear?"

"Yes; but what—" He hung up quickly, for he knew she was going to ask about Freddi, and he didn't care to impart this news. Let Mama have the painful duty!

III

Lanny drove to the great red brick building on the Alexanderplatz. Many who entered there had not come out as quickly as they had hoped; but he with his magical American passport would take a chance. He discovered that the well-known German *Ordnung* was in operation; the officer at the desk had received full instructions. *"Einen Moment, Herr Budd,"* he said, politely. *"Bitte, setzen Sie sich."*

He gave an order, and in a few minutes Johannes was brought in. Apparently he had been told what was going to happen; he had got a shave, and appeared interested in life again. The odds and ends of property which he had had upon his person were restored to him; he signed a receipt, bade a courteous *Lebewohl* to his jailers, and walked briskly out to the car.

Lanny had the painful duty of knocking this newborn happiness flat. "Painful news, my friend. Freddi has been missing for two weeks, and we have no idea what has become of him." The poor father sat in the car with tears streaming down his cheeks while Lanny told about the last meeting with Freddi, the arrangements which had been made, and the dead silence which had fallen. Lanny couldn't bear to look at him—and had a good excuse, having to drive through busy traffic.

He explained his decisions, and the heartbroken father replied: "You did what was best. I shall never be able to tell you how grateful I am."

"I'm only guessing," Lanny continued; "but I think the chances are that Göring has Freddi and intends to keep him until the scandal will no longer be news. Our only chance is to comply strictly with the terms of the understanding. It seems to me the part of wisdom for us to tell no more than we have to, even to the family. The less they know, the less trouble they will have in keeping secrets."

"You are right," agreed the other.

"I think we should say we feel certain that Freddi is a hostage, and that, since he is some day to be released, he is not apt to be mistreated. That will make it easier for them all to get over the shock."

"I will tell them that I have had an intimation to that effect," said Johannes. "Anything to get Rahel quieted down. Otherwise she might insist upon staying. We must take her at all hazards, for she can do nothing here."

When they got to the hotel they found that Mama had already

imparted the news, Irma had confirmed it, and the young wife had had her first spell of weeping. It wasn't so bad, for she had made up her mind for some days that the worst must have happened. Her father-in-law's kind "intimation" helped a little; also Lanny's promise to keep up the search. The determination of the others to get her and her child out of Naziland was not to be resisted.

It wasn't exactly a fashionable autoload which departed from under the marquee of the Adlon Hotel. The magnificent uniformed personage who opened the car doors was used to seeing independent young Americans driving themselves, but rarely had he seen three dark-eyed Jews and a child crowded into the back seat of a Mercédès limousine about to depart for foreign lands. Both Lanny and Irma were determined to finish this job, and not let their periled friends out of sight until they were safe. In the breast pocket of Lanny's tan linen suit were stowed not merely the passports of himself and wife, but a packet of documents which had been delivered by messenger from the headquarters of Minister-Präsident Göring, including four passports and four exit permits, each with a photograph of the person concerned. Lanny realized that the government had had possession of all the papers in the Robin yacht and palace. He remembered Göring's promise of a "kick in the tail," but hoped it was just the barrack-room exuberance of a *Hauptmann* of the German Air Force.

The family were not too badly crowded in that rear seat. The three adults had each lost weight during the past weeks; and as for luggage, they had the suitcases they had carried away after Johannes's arrest; that was all they owned in the world. As for Little Johannes, it was no trouble taking turns holding him in their laps; each would have been glad to hold him the entire time, until they had got him to some place where the cry of *Juda verrecke* was unknown.

I V

Irma and Lanny meant to go as they had come, straight through. Lanny would buy food ready prepared and they would eat it in the car while driving; they would take no chance of entering a restaurant, and having some Brownshirt peddling Nazi literature stop in front of them and exhibit a copy of *Der Stürmer* with an obscene cartoon showing a Jew as a hog with a bulbous nose; if they declined to purchase it, likely as not the ruffian would spit into their food and walk away jeering. Such things had happened in Berlin, and much worse; for until a few days ago these peddlers of literature had gone armed with the regulation automatic revolver and hard rubber club, and in one café where Jewish merchants had been accustomed to eat, a crowd of the S.A. men had fallen upon them and forced them to run the gantlet, kicking and clubbing them insensible.

Drive carefully, but fast, and stop only when necessary! The roads were good and the route familiar, and meantime, safe from prying ears, they had much to talk about. The Robins were informed that they owned some money which the Nazis had not been able to keep track of—those sums which Johannes had spent in entertaining Irma Barnes. They would be repaid in installments, as the family needed it, and the money was not to be considered a loan or a gift, but board and passenger fares long overdue. Irma said this with the decisiveness which she was acquiring; she had learned that her money gave her power to settle the destinies of other people, and she found it pleasant exercising this power—always for their own good, of course.

There was the estate of Bienvenu with nobody in it but Hansi and Bess and Baby Frances with her attendants. Mama and Rahel and her little one were to settle down in the Lodge and learn to count their blessings. Johannes would probably wish to go to New York with Irma and Lanny, for they had some business to transact with Robbie, and Johannes might be of help. Lanny gave him Robbie's letter to read, and the spirits of this born trader began to show faint signs of life. Yes, he might have ideas about the selling of Budd products; if Robbie should get charge of the company, Johannes would offer to take his job as European representative. Or, if Robbie preferred, he would see what he could do with the

South American trade—he had sold all sorts of goods there, including military, and had much information about revolutions, past, present, and to come.

"Sufferance is the badge of all our tribe." So Shylock had spoken, and now these three wearers of the badge confronted their future, for the most part in silence. Their long siege of fear had exhausted them, and they still found it hard to believe that they were free, that the papers which Lanny was carrying would actually have power to get them over the border. They thought about the dear one they were leaving in the Hitler hell, and the tears would steal down their cheeks; they wiped them away furtively, having no right to add to the unhappiness of friends who had done so much for them. They ate the food and drank the bottled drinks which Lanny put into their hands; a lovely dark-eyed little boy with curly black hair lay still in his mother's or his grandmother's arms and never gave a whimper of complaint. He was only three years and as many months old, but already he had learned that he was in a world full of mysterious awful powers, which for some reason beyond his comprehension meant to harm him. Sufferance was his badge.

V

They were traveling by way of Hanover and Cologne. The roads were perfect, and three or four hundred miles was nothing to Lanny; they reached Aachen before nightfall, and then came the border, and the critical moment—which proved to be anticlimactic. The examination of baggage and persons for concealed money was usually made as disagreeable as possible for Jews; but perhaps there was some special mark on their exit permits, or perhaps it was because they were traveling in an expensive car and under the chaperonage of expensive-looking Americans—anyhow the questioning was not too severe, and much sooner than anyone had expected the anxious refugees were signaled to proceed across the line. The inspection of their passports on the Belgian side was a matter that took only a minute or two; and when the last formality was com-

pleted and the car rolled on through a peaceful countryside that
wasn't Nazi, Mama broke down and wept in the arms of her spouse.
She just hadn't been able to believe that it would happen.

They spent the night in the city of Liége, where Lanny's first
duty was to send telegrams to his mother and father, to Hansi, to
Zoltan and Emily and Rick. In the morning they drove on to Paris;
and from there he telephoned to his friend Oberleutnant Furtwaengler in Berlin. What news was there about Freddi Robin? The
officer reported that the young man was nowhere in the hands of
the German authorities; unless by chance he had given a false name
when arrested, something which was often attempted but rarely
successful. Lanny said he was quite certain that Freddi would have
no motive for doing this. The Oberleutnant promised to continue
the search, and if anything came of it he would send a telegram
to Lanny at his permanent address, Juan-les-Pins, Cap d'Antibes,
Frankreich.

Lanny hung up and reported what he had heard. It meant little,
of course. Long ago Lanny had learned that diplomats lie when it
suits their country's purposes, and police and other officials do the
same; among the Nazis, lying in the interest of party and *Regierung*
was an heroic action. The statement of Göring's aide meant simply
that if Göring had Freddi he meant to keep him. If and when he
released him, he would doubtless say that an unfortunate mistake
had been made.

Beauty had gone to London with her husband, as guests of Lady
Caillard. She now wired Lanny to come and see if he could get
any hints through Madame. Since it was as easy to go to New
York from England as from France, they decided upon this plan.
But first they must run down to Juan, because Irma couldn't cross
the ocean without having at least a glimpse of her little daughter.
Also it would be "nice" for Johannes to see Hansi and Bess. In
general it was "nice" for people to dart here and there like humming-birds, sipping the honey of delight from whatever flower
caught the eye. So next morning the four Robins were again loaded
into the back seat, and in the evening they rolled through the gates
of Bienvenu amid a chorus of delighted cries in English, German,

and Yiddish; cries mostly in the treble clef, but with an undertone in the bass, because of the one sheep which had strayed and might already have been devoured by the wolves.

VI

Once again the young couple had a debauch of parental emotions; Irma hugged little Frances against all rules, talked baby-talk which interfered with the maturing of her speech, gave her foods which were unwholesome, let her stay up too late—in short disarranged all schedules and spread demoralization. She even talked about taking the whole entourage to Long Island—it would give such pleasure to the grandmother. Lanny argued against it—the child had everything that a three-year-old could really appreciate, and now was enjoying the companionship of a young Robin. Lanny and Irma were planning only a short stay, and why incur all the added expense, at a time when everything was so uncertain? Lanny was always trying to economize with the Barnes fortune—overlooking the fact that the only fun in having a fortune is if you don't economize. Just now he had the idea that they might have to buy Freddi out of Germany; and who could guess the price?

All right, Irma would stay another day, and then tear herself loose. She would lay many injunctions upon Bub Smith, the dependable bodyguard, and extract promises from Miss Severne to cable her at the smallest symptom of malaise. "Do you realize how many millions this tiny being represents?" Irma didn't say those crude words, but it was the clear implication of every command, and of the circumstances surrounding Frances Barnes Budd. "The twenty-three-million-dollar baby" was her newspaper name. The twenty-three-million-dollar baby had set out on a yachting cruise, and the twenty-three-million-dollar baby had unexpectedly returned to Bienvenu. All the expenses of maintaining the twenty-three-million-dollar baby might have been collected in admission fees from tourists who would have flocked to see her if arrangements had been made.

The men of the family had a conference in Lanny's studio.

Johannes hadn't been willing to tell the ladies what had happened to him in Germany, but he told Hansi and Lanny how he had been taken to the S.A. barracks in Bremerhaven and there subjected to a long series of indignities, obviously intended to break his spirit. They had given him strong purgatives, and amused themselves by forcing him to paddle other prisoners in the same plight, and to be paddled by them in turn, until all of them were a mess of one another's filth. While they did this they had to shout: "*Heil lieber Reichskanzler!*" As a climax they had been forced to dig a long trench, and were lined up to be shot and dumped into it—so they were told. It was only a mock execution, but they had died psychologically, and Johannes had by then become so sick with horror and pain that he had welcomed the end. He said now that he would never be the same man again; he would go on living because of his family and friends, but the game of making money would never hold the same zest. He said that, but then, being a clear-sighted man, he added: "It's a habit, and I suppose I'll go on reacting in the old way; but I can't imagine I'll ever be happy."

They talked about the problem of the missing one, and what was to be done. Lanny had promised not to name Hugo Behr, and he didn't, but said that he had a confidential agent at work, and had given him the Juan address. Hansi was to open all mail that might come from Germany, and if it contained anything significant, he was to cable it. Johannes said that Hansi and Bess would have to give up the pleasure of playing music at Red meetings, or doing anything to advertise their anti-Nazi views. They were still Göring's prisoners; and that was, no doubt, the way Göring intended it to be.

Hansi was "broke" because he and Bess had been spending all their money on refugees. That, too, would have to stop. Since it would do no good to sit around and mourn, Hansi decided to cable his New York agent to arrange a concert tour of the United States in the fall. Meantime, Irma would open an account for him at her bank in Cannes. "But remember," she said, "no more Reds and no Red talk!" Irma laying down the law!

All problems thus settled, one bright morning Irma and Lanny, with Papa in the back seat, set out amid more cries in English, Ger-

man, and Yiddish—this time not so happy. They arrived in Paris
and had dinner with Zoltan Kertezsi, and in the morning drove to
Les Forêts, and told Emily Chattersworth as much of their story as
was permitted. In the afternoon they set out for Calais, place of
bitter memories forevermore. They took the night ferry, drove
through England in the loveliest of all months, and arrived at the
Dorchester Hotel amid the gayest of all seasons.

VII

Sir Vincent Caillard, pronounced French-fashion, Ky-yahr, had
been one of Zaharoff's associates from the early days when they had
bought Vickers; in the course of the years he had become one of
the richest men in England. Also, strangely enough, he had been a
poet, and had set Blake's *Songs of Innocence* to music; he had
bequeathed these interests to his wife, along with a huge block of
Vickers shares. So it had come about that an elderly, gray-haired
lady, rather small, pale, and insignificant-looking, wielded power in
London, and concentrated upon herself the attention of a swarm of
eccentric persons, some of them genuine idealists, more of them
genuine crooks.

She had purchased a large stone church in West Halkin Street
and made it over into one of the strangest homes ever conceived
by woman. The gallery of the church had been continued all
around it and divided into bedrooms and bathrooms. The organ had
been retained, and when it was played all the partitions of the rooms
seemed to throb. On the ground floor was a grand reception room
with art treasures fit for a museum; among them was a splendid
collection of clocks; a large one struck the quarter-hours, and the
front of the clock opened and a gold and ivory bird came out and
sang lustily. Lady Caillard also collected scissors. Whoever came to
that home was at once presented with a copy of the late husband's
poems, also a copy of her ladyship's pamphlet entitled: *Sir Vincent
Caillard Speaks from the Spirit World*. If you could devise a new
kind of praise for either of these volumes it would be equivalent to

a meal-ticket for the rest of your life—or, at any rate, of Lady Caillard's life.

Mr. and Mrs. Dingle and Madame Zyszynski were comfortably ensconced in this former house of God, and Beauty had had time to collect all the delicious gossip concerning its affairs. Pausing only for a tribute of grief to Freddi, she opened up to her son a truly thrilling line of conversation. Lady Caillard had become a convert to spiritualism, and now lived as completely surrounded by angels and ministers of grace as William Blake in his most mystical hours. She maintained a troop of mediums, and one of the spirits had directed the invention of a machine called the "Communigraph," whereby Sir Vincent, called "Vinny," could send messages to his wife, called "Birdie." The machine had been set up in "The Belfry," as this home was called, and had been blessed by Archdeacon Wilberforce in a regular service; thereafter the séance room, known as the "Upper Room," was kept sacred to this one purpose, and at a regular hour every Wednesday evening Sir Vincent gave his wife a communication which he signed V.B.X., meaning "Vinnie, Birdie, and a Kiss." These messages were now being compiled into a book entitled *A New Conception of Love.*

But, alas, love did not rule unchallenged in these twice-consecrated premises. There was a new favorite among the mediums, a woman whom the others all hated. Beauty's voice fell to a whisper as she revealed what huge sums of money this woman had been getting, and how she had persuaded her ladyship to bequeath her vast fortune to the cause of spiritualism, with the spirits to control it. Lady Caillard's two children, lacking faith in the other world, wanted their father's money for themselves, and had quarreled with their mother and been ousted from her home; they had got lawyers, and had even called in Scotland Yard, which couldn't help. There was the most awful pother going on!

Into this seething caldron of jealousies and hatreds had come Mabel Blackless, alias Beauty Budd, alias Madame Detaze, alias Mrs. Dingle, herself an object of many kinds of suspicion; also her husband, teaching and practicing love for all mankind, including both adventuresses and defrauded children; also a Polish woman medium with an unspellable name. Beauty, of course, was looked upon as an interloper and intriguer, Parsifal Dingle's love was hypocrisy, and Madame's mediumship was an effort to supplant the other possessors of this mysterious gift. Beauty was as much pleased over all this as a child at a movie melodrama. Her tongue tripped over itself as she poured out the exciting details. "Really, my dears, I wouldn't be surprised if somebody tried to poison us!" Her manner gave the impression that she would find that a delightful adventure.

One of the guests in this strange ex-church was the Grand Officer of the Légion d'Honneur and Knight Commander of the Bath. He appeared to be failing; his skin had become yellowish brown, with the texture of parchment; his hands trembled so that he kept them against some part of his body, and would not attempt to write in the presence of anyone. He had grown much thinner, which accentuated the prominence of his eagle's beak. As usual, Zaharoff kept himself out of all sorts of trouble, and took no sides in this family row; his interest was in getting messages from the duquesa, and he would sit tirelessly as long as any medium would stand it. But he still hadn't made up his mind entirely; he revealed that to Lanny, not by a direct statement, but by the trend of the questions he kept putting to the younger man.

It was permissible for Lanny to mention that a young friend of his had not been heard from in Germany; whereupon this hiveful of mediums set to work secreting wax and honey for him. Most of it appeared to be synthetic; Lanny became sure that some clever trickster had guessed that the missing person was a relative of Johannes Robin, himself recently named in the newspapers as missing, and now suddenly arriving with the Budds. Since Hansi had been interviewed in Paris on the subject, it couldn't be he who was lost. Since Freddi had been in London and was known to all friends of the Budds, it really wasn't much of a detective job to get his name. Every issue of the *Manchester Guardian* was full of stories about concentration camps and the mistreatment of the Jews; so the spirits began pouring out details—the only trouble being that no two of them agreed on anything of importance.

There was only one medium whom Lanny knew and trusted,

and that was Madame; but her control, Tecumseh, was still cross with Lanny and wouldn't take any trouble for him. In New York the control had been willing to repeat French sentences, syllable by syllable, but now he refused to do the same for German. He said it was too ugly a language, with sounds that no civilized tongue could get round—this from a chieftain of the Iroquois Indians! Tecumseh said that Freddi was not in the spirit world, and that the spirits who tried to talk about Freddi didn't seem to know anything definite. Tecumseh got so that he would say to a sitter: "Are you going to ask me about that Jewish fellow?" It threatened to ruin Madame's mediumship and her career.

VIII

Marceline had been invited to spend the summer with the Pomeroy-Nielsons, as a means of making up for the yacht cruise which had been rudely snatched away. Marceline and Alfy, having the same sixteen years, were shooting up tall and what the English call "leggy." It is the age of self-consciousness and restlessness; many things were changing suddenly and confusing their young minds. With other friends of the same age they played with delicate intimations of love; they felt attraction, then shied away, took offense and made up, talked a great deal about themselves and one another, and in various ways prepared for the serious business of matrimony. Marceline exercised her impulse to tease Alfy by being interested in other boys. She had a right to, hadn't she? Did she have to fall in love the way her family expected? What sort of old-fashioned idea was that? The future baronet was proud, offended, angry, then exalted. *Himmelhoch jauchzend, zum Tode betrübt!*

Irma and Lanny motored up for a week end, to see how things were going. A lovely old place by the Thames, so restful after the storms and strains of the great world; especially after Berlin, with its enormous and for the most part tasteless public buildings, its statues, crude and cruel, celebrating military glory. Here at The Reaches everything was peaceful; the little old river seemed tame and friendly, safe to go punting on, just right for lovers and poets.

It had been here a long time and would stay while generation after generation of baronets appeared, grew up and studied at the proper schools, wore the proper comfortable clothes, established "little theaters," and wrote articles for newspapers and weeklies proving that the country was going to pot.

Here was Sir Alfred, tall, somewhat eccentric, but genial and full of humor; his hair had turned gray while his mustache remained black. Excessive taxes had completely ruined him, he declared, but he was absorbed in collecting records of twentieth-century British drama for a museum which some rich friend was financing. Here was his kind and gentle wife, the most attentive of hostesses. Here was Nina, helping to run this rambling old brick house, built onto indefinitely by one generation after another and having so many fireplaces and chimneys that in wintertime it would take one maid most of her time carrying coal-scuttles. Here were three very lovely children, eager and happy, but taught to be quieter than any you would find in America.

Finally here was the lame ex-aviator whom Lanny considered the wisest man he knew, the only one with whom he could exchange ideas with complete understanding. Rick was one who had a right to know everything about Lanny's German adventure, and they went off on the river where nobody could hear them if they talked in low tones, and Lanny told the story from beginning to end. It would be better that not even Nina should hear it, because there is a strong temptation for one woman to talk to the next, and so things get passed on and presently come to the ears of some journalist. After all, Johannes was a pretty important man, and his plundering would make a rare tale if properly dressed up.

Rick was quite shocked when he learned how Lanny had permitted the Berlin newspapers to publish that he was a sympathetic inquirer into National Socialism. He said that a thing like that would spread and might blacken Lanny forever; there would be no way to live it down, or to get himself trusted again. Lanny said he didn't mind, if he could save Freddi; but Rick insisted that a man had no right to make such a sacrifice. It wasn't just a question of saving one individual, but of a cause which was entitled to defense. Socialism had to be fought for against the monstrosity which had stolen its name and was trying to usurp its place in history. Lanny had thought of that, but not enough, apparently; he felt rather bad about it.

"Listen, Rick," he said; "there have to be spies in every war, don't there?"

"I suppose so."

"What if I were to go into Germany and become a friend of those higher-ups, and get all the dope and send it out to you?"

"They would soon get onto it, Lanny."

"Mightn't it be possible to be as clever as they?"

"A darned disagreeable job, I should think."

"I know; but Kurt did it in Paris, and got away with it."

"You're a very different man from Kurt. For one thing, you'd have to fool him; and do you think you could?"

"Beauty insists that I couldn't; but I believe that if I took enough time, and put my mind to it, I could at least keep him uncertain. I'd have to let him argue with me and convince me. You know I have a rare good excuse for going; I'm an art expert, and Germany has a lot to sell. That makes it easy for me to meet all sorts of people. I could collect evidence as to Nazi outrages, and you could make it into a book."

"That's already been done, you'll be glad to hear." Rick revealed that a group of liberal Englishmen had been busy assembling the data, and a work called *The Brown Book of the Hitler Terror* was now in press and shortly to be published. It gave the details of two or three hundred murders of prominent intellectuals and political opponents of the Nazi *Regierung*.

Lanny said: "There'll be other things worth reporting. If I go back to Germany on account of Freddi, I'll get what facts I can and it'll be up to you to figure out what use to make of them."

IX

Lanny didn't mention the name of his German agent, Hugo Behr, but he was free to tell about the left-wing movement developing inside the Nazi party. He thought it was of great importance. It was the class struggle in a new and strange form; the war between the haves and the have-nots, which apparently couldn't be kept out of any part of modern society. A leader might sell out a popular movement, but could he carry his followers along? Many people in Germany thought that Hitler could take his party wherever he chose, but Lanny saw it differently—he said that Hitler was extraordinarily sensitive to the pressure of his followers, and agile in keeping the lead wherever they were determined to go. "He got money from the biggest industrialists, and Johannes insists that he's their man; but I believe he may fool them and jump some way they have no idea of."

"Isn't there a third power," ventured Rick—"the army? Can anybody in Germany do anything without the consent of the Reichswehr?"

Lanny told of his talk with Emil and with Stubendorf, both of whom had agreed that they would obey the government loyally. Rick said: "Emil, yes; he's a subordinate. But would Stubendorf tell you his real thoughts? My guess is that he and his Junker crowd will serve Hitler so long as Hitler serves them; that is, to bring about rearmament, and get the Corridor and the lost provinces back into the Fatherland."

"Naturally," admitted Lanny, "Stubendorf thinks first about his own property. What he'd do after that I don't know."

"All Germans put their army first," insisted Rick. "The Social-Democrats brought about the revolution with the help of the common soldiers, but right away they became prisoners of the officer caste and never made any real change in the army's control. The Finance Minister of the Republic always had to be a man satisfactory to the Reichswehr, and no matter how much the politicians talked about social reforms they never made any cuts in the military budget."

Rick listened to all that his friend had to tell, and asked many questions, but refused to believe that Hitler could be pushed or dragged to the left. "No revolutionist who has become conservative ever goes back," he said, and added with a wry smile: "He learns to know the left too well, and has made too many enemies among them."

Lanny asked: "Won't he go if he sees another wave of revolt on the way?"

"He won't see it, because it won't be coming. One wave is enough for one generation. Strasser and Röhm and your friend Hugo may shout their heads off, but when Adolf tells them to shut up they will shut. And it's my belief that whatever 'socializing' Adolf does in Germany will be to make the Nazi party stronger, and enable him to smash Versailles more quickly and more surely."

X

The Conference on Limitation of Armaments was practically dead, after more than a year of futile efforts. But the nations couldn't give up trying to stop the general breakdown, and now sixty-six of them were assembled in a World Economic Conference. It was meeting in South Kensington with the usual fanfare about solving all problems. Rick, ever suspicious of what he called capitalist statesmanship, said that it was an effort of the Bank of England to get back on the gold standard, with the support of the United States, and of France, Switzerland, Holland, and the few nations still ruled by their creditor classes. While Lanny was watching this show and renewing old acquaintances among the journalists, President Roosevelt issued a manifesto refusing to be tied to this gold program. His action was called "torpedoing" the Conference, which at once proceeded to follow all the others into the graveyard of history.

Lord Wickthorpe was back at home, and desirous of repaying the hospitality which he had enjoyed in Paris; the more so when he learned that his American friends had just returned from Germany and had been meeting some of the Nazi head men. The young couple were invited to spend several days at Wickthorpe Castle, one of the landmarks of England. It was of brown sandstone, and the central structure with two great crenelated towers dated from Tudor days; two wings and a rear extension had been added in the time of Queen Anne, but the unity of style had been preserved. The ancient oaks were monuments of English permanence and solidity; the lawns were kept green by rains and fogs from several seas, and kept smooth by flocks of rolypoly sheep. Irma was fascinated by the place, and pleased her host by the naïveté of her commendations. When she heard that the estate had had to be broken up and tracts sold off to pay taxes, she counted it among the major calamities of the late war.

The Dowager Lady Wickthorpe kept house for her bachelor son. There was a younger brother whom Lanny had met at Rick's, and he had married an American girl whom Irma had known in café society; so it was like a family party, easy and informal, yet dignified and impressive. It was much easier to run an estate and a household in England, where everything was like a grandfather's clock which you wound up and it ran, not for eight days but for eight years or eight decades. There was no such thing as a servant problem, for your attendants were born, not made; the oldest son of your shepherd learned to tend your sheep and the oldest son of your butler learned to buttle. All masters were kind and all servants devoted and respectful; at least, that was how it was supposed to be, and if anything was short of perfection it was carefully hidden. Irma thought it was marvelous—until she discovered that she was expected to bathe her priceless self in a painted tin tub which was brought in by one maid, followed by two others bearing large pitchers of hot and cold water.

After the completion of this ceremony, she inquired: "Lanny, what do you suppose it would cost to put modern plumbing into a place like this?"

He answered with a grin: "In the style of Shore Acres?"—referring to his own bathroom with solid silver fixtures, and to Irma's of solid gold.

"I mean just ordinary Park Avenue."

"Are you thinking of buying this castle?"

Irma countered with another question. "Do you suppose you would be happy in England?"

"I'm afraid you couldn't get it, darling," he evaded in turn. "It's

bound to be entailed." He assured her with a grave face that everything had to be handed down intact—not merely towers and oaks
and lawns, but servants and sheep and bathing facilities.

XI

Neighbors dropped in from time to time, and Lanny listened to
upper-class Englishmen discussing the problems of their world and
his. They were not to be persuaded to take Adolf Hitler and his
party too seriously; in spite of his triumph he was still the clown,
the pasty-faced, hysterical tub-thumper, such as you could hear in
Hyde Park any Sunday afternoon; "a jumped-up house-painter,"
one of the country squires called him. They were not sorry to
have some effective opposition to France on the continent, for it
irked them greatly to see that rather shoddy republic of politicians riding on the gold standard while Britain had been ignomini-
ously thrown off. They were interested in Lanny's account of
Adolf, but even more interested in Göring, who was a kind of man
they could understand. In his capacity as Reichsminister, he had
come to Geneva and laid down the law as to Germany's claim to
arms equality. Wickthorpe had been impressed by his forceful personality, and now was amused to hear about the lion cub from
the Berlin zoo and the new gold velvet curtains in the reception
room of the Minister-Präsident's official residence.

Lanny said: "The important thing for you gentlemen to remember is that Göring is an air commander, and that rearmament for
him is going to mean fleets of planes. They will all be new and of
perfected models."

Eric Vivian Pomeroy-Nielson, ex-aviator, had laid great stress
upon this, but Lanny found it impossible to interest a representative of the British Foreign Office. To him airplanes were like Adolf
Hitler; that is to say, something "jumped-up," something cheap,
presumptuous, and altogether bad form. Britannia ruled the waves,
and did it with dignified and solid "ships of the line," weighing
thirty-five thousand tons each and costing ten or twenty million
pounds. An American admiral had written about the influence of

sea power upon history, and the British Admiralty had read it, one of the few compliments they had ever paid to their jumped-up cousins across the seas. Now their world strategy was based upon it, and when anyone tried to argue with them it was as if they all burst into song: "Britannia needs no bulwarks, no towers along the steep!"

Irma listened to the discussions, and afterward, as they drove back to London, they talked about it, and Lanny discovered that she agreed with her host rather than with her husband. She was irresistibly impressed by the dignity, stability, and self-confidence of this island nation; also by Lord Wickthorpe as the perfect type of English gentleman and statesman. Lanny didn't mind, for he was used to having people disagree with him, especially his own family. But when he happened to mention the matter to his mother, she minded it gravely, and said: "Doesn't it ever occur to you that you're taking an awful lot for granted?"

"How do you mean, old darling?"

"Take my advice and think seriously about Irma. You're making her a lot unhappier than you've any idea."

"You mean, by the company I keep?"

"By that, and by the ideas you express to your company, and to your wife's."

"Well, dear, she surely can't expect me to give up my political convictions as the price of her happiness."

"I don't know why she shouldn't—considering how we're all more or less dependent upon her bounty."

"Bless your heart!" said Lanny. "I can always go back to selling pictures again."

"Oh, Lanny, you say horrid things!"

He thought that she had started the horridness, but it would do no good to say so. "Cheer up, old dear—I'm taking my wife off to New York right away."

"Don't count on that too much. Don't ever forget that you've got a treasure, and it calls for a lot of attention and some guarding."

BOOK FIVE

This Is the Way the World Ends

21

In Friendship's Name

I

IRMA and Lanny guessed that the feelings of Fanny Barnes were going to be hurt because they weren't bringing her namesake to see her; to make up for it they had cabled that they would come first to Shore Acres. The Queen Mother was at the steamer to meet them with a big car. She wanted the news about her darling grandchild, and then, what on earth had they been doing all that time in Germany? Everybody was full of questions about Hitlerland, they discovered; at a distance of three thousand miles it sounded like Hollywood, and few could bring themselves to believe that it was real. The newspapers were determined to find out what had happened to a leading German-Jewish financier. They met him at the pier, and when he wouldn't talk they tried everyone who knew him; but in vain.

At Shore Acres, things were going along much as usual. The employees of the estate were doing the same work for no wages; but with seventeen million unemployed in the country, they were thankful to be kept alive. As for Irma's friends, they were planning the customary round of visits to seashore and mountains; those who still had dividends would play host to those who hadn't, and everybody would get along. There was general agreement that business was picking up at last, and credit for the boom was given to Roosevelt. Only a few diehards like Robbie Budd talked about the debts being incurred, and when and how were they going to be paid. Most people didn't want to pay any debts; they said that was what had got the country into trouble. The way to get out was to borrow and spend as fast as possible; and one of the things to spend for was beer. Roosevelt was letting the people buy it instead of having to make it in their bathtubs.

Robbie came into the city by appointment, and in the office of the Barnes estate, he and Irma and Lanny sat down to a conference with Uncle Joseph Barnes and the other two trustees. Robbie had a briefcase full of figures setting forth the condition of Budd Gun-makers, a list of directors pledged to him, the voting shares which he controlled, and those which he could purchase, with their prices. The trustees presented a list of their poorest-paying shares, and weighed them in the balance. Under the will the trustees had the right to say no; but they realized that this was a family matter, and that it would be a distinguished thing to have Irma's father-in-law become president of a great manufacturing concern. Also, Irma had developed into a young lady who knew what she wanted, and said it in the style of the days before parliamentary control of the purse had been established.

"There's no use going into it unless you go heavily enough to win," cautioned Uncle Joseph.

"Of course not," said Irma, promptly. "We have no idea of not winning." *L'état, c'est moi!*

"If you pay more than the market for Budd stocks, it will mean that you are reducing the principal of your estate; for we shall have to list them at market value."

"List them any way you please," said Irma. "I want Robbie to be elected."

"Of course," said Mr. Barnes, timidly, "you might make up the principal by reducing your expenditures for a while."

"All right," assented Her Majesty—"but it will be time enough to do that when you get me a bit more income."

II

Johannes went to Newcastle to visit the Robbie Budds. The firm of R and R had many problems to talk out, and when Irma and Lanny arrived the pair were deeply buried in business. Robbie considered Johannes the best salesman he had ever known, bar none, and was determined to make a place for him with Budd's. If Robbie won out, Johannes would become European representative; if Robbie lost, Johannes would become Robbie's assistant on some sort of share basis. Robbie had a contract with the company which still had nearly three years to run and entitled him to commissions on all sales made in his territory. These matters Robbie put before his friend without reserve; he did it for medico-psychological reasons as well as financial—he wanted to get Johannes out of his depression, and the way to do it was to put him to work.

Robbie added: "Of course, provided there's anything left of business." America was in the throes of an extraordinary convulsion known as "the New Deal," which Robbie described as "government by college professors and their graduate students." They were turning the country upside down under a scheme called "N.R.A." You had to put a "blue eagle" up in your window and operate under a "code," bossed by an army general who swore like a trooper and drank like the trooper's horse. New markets for goods were being provided by the simple process of borrowing money from those who had it and giving it to those who hadn't. One lot of the unemployed were put to work draining swamps to plant crops, while another lot were making new swamps for wild ducks. And so on, for as long as Robbie Budd could find anybody to listen to him.

Everybody in Newcastle was glad to see the young couple again; excepting possibly Uncle Lawford, who wasn't going to see them. The only place they had met was in church, and Irma and Lanny were going to play golf or tennis on Sunday mornings—Grandfather being out of the way. Or was he really out of the way? Apparently he could only get at them if they went to a medium! Lanny remarked: "I'd like to try the experiment of sleeping in his bed one night and see if I hear any raps." Irma said: "Oh, what a horrid thought!" She had come to believe in the spirits about half way. Subtleties about the subconscious mind didn't impress her very much, because she wasn't sure if she had one.

The usual round of pleasure trips began. They motored to Maine, and then to the Adirondacks. So many people wanted to see them; Irma's gay and bright young old friends. They had got used to her husband's eccentricities, and if he wanted to pound the piano while they played bridge, all right, they would shut the doors between. He didn't talk so "Pink" as he had, so they decided that he was getting sensible. They played games, they motored and sailed and swam, they flirted a bit, and some couples quarreled, some traded partners as in one of the old-fashioned square dances. But they all agreed in letting the older people do the worrying and the carrying of burdens. "I should worry," —meaning that I won't— and "Let George do it," —so ran the formulas. To have plenty of money was the indispensable virtue, and to have to go to work the one unthinkable calamity. "Oh, Lanny," said Irma, after a visit where an ultra-smart playwright had entertained them with brilliant conversation—"Oh, Lanny, don't you think you could get along over here at least part of the time?"

She wanted to add: "Now that you're being more sensible." She didn't really think he had changed his political convictions, but she found it so much pleasanter when he withheld them, and if he would go on doing this long enough it might become a habit. When they passed through New York he didn't visit the Rand School of Social Science, or any of those summer camps where noisy and mostly Jewish working people swarmed as thick as bees in a hive. He was afraid these "comrades" might have learned what had been published about him in the Nazi papers; also that Nazi agents in New York might report him to Göring. He stayed with his wife, and she did her best to make herself everything that a woman could be to a man.

It worked for nearly a month; until one morning in Shore Acres, just as they were getting ready for a motor-trip to a "camp" in the Thousand Islands, Lanny was called to the telephone to receive a cablegram from Cannes, signed Hansi, and reading: "Unsigned unidentifiable letter postmarked Berlin text Freddi ist in Dachau."

III

Their things were packed and stowed in the car, and the car was waiting in front of the mansion. Irma was putting the last dab of powder on her nose, and Lanny stood in front of her with a frown of thought upon his face: "Darling, I don't see how I can possibly take this drive."

She knew him well, after four years of wifehood, and tried not to show her disappointment. "Just what do you want to do?"

"I want to think about how to help Freddi."

"Do you suppose that letter is from Hugo?"

"I had a clear understanding with him that he was to sign the name Boecklin. I think the letter must be from one of Freddi's comrades, some one who has learned that we helped Johannes. Or perhaps some one who has got out of Dachau."

"You don't think it might be a hoax?"

"Who would waste a stamp to play such a trick upon us?"

She couldn't think of any answer. "You're still convinced that Freddi is Göring's prisoner?"

"Certainly, if he's in the concentration camp, Göring knows he's there, and he knew it when he had Furtwaengler tell me that he couldn't find him. He had him sent a long way from Berlin, so as to make it harder for us to find out."

"Do you think you can get him away from Göring if Göring doesn't want to let him go?"

"What I think is, there may be a thousand things to think of before we can be sure of the best course of action."

"It's an awfully nasty job to take on, Lanny."

"I know, darling—but what else can we do? We can't go and enjoy ourselves, play around, and refuse to think about our friend. Dachau is a place of horror—I doubt if there's any so dreadful in the world today, unless it's some other of the Nazi camps. It's an old dilapidated barracks, utterly unfit for habitation, and they've got two or three thousand men jammed in there. They're not just holding them prisoners—they're doing what Göring told me with his own mouth, applying modern science to destroying them, body, mind, and soul. They're the best brains and the finest spirits in Germany, and they're going to be so broken that they can never do anything against the Nazi regime."

"You really believe that, Lanny?"

"I am as certain of it as I am of anything in human affairs. I've been studying Hitler and his movement for twelve years, and I really do know something about it."

"There's such an awful lot of lying, Lanny. People go into politics, and they hate their enemies, and exaggerate and invent things."

"I didn't invent *Mein Kampf*, nor the Brownshirts, nor the murders they are committing night after night. They break into people's homes and stab them or shoot them in their beds, before the eyes of their wives and children; or they drag them off to their barracks and beat them insensible."

"I've heard those stories until I've been made sick. But there are just as many violent men of the other side, and there have been provocations over the years. The Reds did the same thing in Russia, and they tried to do it in Germany——"

"It's not only the Communists who are being tortured, darling; it's pacifists and liberals, even church people; it's gentle idealists, like Freddi—and surely you know that Freddi wouldn't have harmed any living creature."

IV

Irma had to put down her powder-puff, but was still sitting on the stool in front of her dressing-table. She had many things that she had put off saying for a long time; and now, apparently, was the time to get them off her mind. She began: "You might as well take the time to understand me, Lanny. If you intend to plunge into a thing like this, you ought to know how your wife feels about it."

"Of course, dear," he answered, gently. He could pretty well guess what was coming.

"Sit down." And when he obeyed she turned to face him. "Freddi's an idealist, and you're an idealist. It's a word you're fond of, a very nice word, and you're both lovely fellows, and you wouldn't hurt anybody or anything on earth. You believe what you want to believe about the world—which is that other people are like you, good and kind and unselfish—idealists, in short. But they're not that; they're full of jealousy and hatred and greed and longing for revenge. They want to overthrow the people who own property, and punish them for the crime of having had life too easy. That's what's in their hearts, and they're looking for chances to carry out their schemes, and when they come on you idealists, they say: 'Here's my meat!' They get round you and play you for suckers, they take your money to build what they call their 'movement.' You serve them by helping to undermine and destroy what you call capitalism. They call you comrades for as long as they can use you, but the first day you dared to stand in their way or interfere with their plans, they'd turn on you like wolves. Don't you know that's true, Lanny?"

"It's true of many, I've no doubt."

"It would be true of every last one, when it came to a show-down. You're their 'front,' their stalking horse. You tell me what you heard from Göring's mouth—and I tell you what I've heard from Uncle Jesse's mouth. Not once but a hundred times! He says it jokingly, but he means it—it's his program. The Socialists will make their peaceable revolution, and then the Communists will rise up and take it away from them. It'll be easy because the Socialists are so gentle and so kind—they're idealists! You saw it happen in Russia, and then in Hungary—didn't I hear Károlyi tell you about it?"

"Yes, dear——"

"With his own mouth he told you! But it didn't mean much to you, because it isn't what you want to believe. Károlyi is a gentleman, a noble soul—I'm not mocking—I had a long talk with him, and I'm sure he's one of the most high-minded men who ever lived. He was a nobleman and he had estates, and when he saw the ruin and misery after the war he gave them to the government. No man could do more. He became the Socialist Premier of Hungary, and tried to bring a peaceful change, and the Communists rose up against his government—and what did he do? He said to me in these very words: 'I couldn't shoot the workers.' So he let the Communist-led mob seize the government, and there was the dreadful bloody regime of that Jew—what was his name?"

"Béla Kun. Too bad he had to be a Jew!"

"Yes, I admit it's too bad. You just told me that you didn't invent *Mein Kampf* and you didn't invent the Brownshirts. Well, I didn't invent Béla Kun and I didn't invent Liebknecht and that Red Rosa Jewess who tried to do the same thing in Germany, nor Eisner who did it in Bavaria, nor Trotsky who helped to do it in Russia. I suppose the Jews have an extra hard time and that makes them revolutionary; they haven't any country and that keeps them from being patriotic. I'm not blaming them, I'm just facing the facts, as you're all the time urging me to do."

"I've long ago faced the fact that you dislike the Jews, Irma."

"I dislike some of them intensely, and I dislike some things about them all. But I love Freddi, and I'm fond of all the Robins, even though I am repelled by Hansi's ideas. I've met other Jews that I like——"

"In short," put in Lanny, "you have accepted what Hitler calls 'honorary Aryans.'" He was surprised by his own bitterness.

"That's a mean crack, Lanny, and I think we ought to talk kindly about this problem. It isn't a simple one."

"I want very much to," he replied. "But one of the facts we have to face is that the things you have been saying to me are all in *Mein Kampf*, and the arguments you have been using are the foundation stones upon which the Nazi movement is built. Hitler also likes some Jews, but he dislikes most of them because he says they are revolutionary and not patriotic. Hitler also is forced to put down the idealists and the liberals because they serve as a 'front' for the Reds. But you see, darling, the capitalist system is breaking down, it is no longer able to produce goods or to feed the people, and some other way must be found to get the job done. We want to do it peaceably if possible; but surely the way to do it cannot be for all the men who want it done peaceably to agree to shut up and say nothing, for fear of giving some benefit to the men of violence!"

V

They argued for a while, but it didn't do any good; they had said it before, many times, and neither had changed much. In the course of four years Irma had listened attentively while her husband debated with many sorts of persons, and unless they were Communists she had nearly always found herself in agreement with the other persons. It was as if the ghost of J. Paramount Barnes were standing by her side telling her what to think. Saying: "I labored hard, and it was not for nothing. I gave you a pleasant position, and surely you don't wish to throw it away!" The ghost never said, in so many words: "What would you be without your money?" It said: "Things aren't so bad as the calamity-howlers say; and anyhow, there are better remedies." When Lanny, vastly irritated, would ask: "What are the remedies?" the ghost of the utilities king would fall silent, and Irma would become vague, and talk about such things as time, education, and spiritual enlightenment.

"It's no good going on with this, dear," said the husband. "The question is, what are we going to do about Freddi?"

"If you would only tell me any definite thing that we can do!"

"But that isn't possible, dear. I have to go there and try this and that, look for new facts and draw new conclusions. The one thing I can't do, it seems to me, is to leave Freddi to his fate. It's not merely that he's a friend; he's a pupil, in a way. I helped to teach him what he believes; I sent him literature, I showed him what to do, and he did it. So I have a double obligation."

"You have an obligation to your wife and daughter, also."

"Of course, and if they were in trouble, they would come first. But my daughter is getting along all right, and as for my wife, I'm hoping she will see it as I do."

"Do you want me to come with you again?"

"Of course I want you; but I'm trying to be fair, and not put pressure upon you. I want you to do what seems right to you."

Irma was fond enough of having her own way, but wasn't entirely reconciled to Lanny's willingness to give it to her. Somehow it bore too close a resemblance to indifference. "A woman wants to be wanted," she would say.

"Don't be silly, darling," he pleaded. "Of course I want your help. I might need you badly some time. But ought I drag you there against your will, and feeling that you're being imposed on?"

"It's a horrid bore for me to be in a country where I don't understand the language."

"Well, why not learn it? If you and I would agree not to speak anything but German to each other, you'd be chattering away in a week or two."

"Is that what I do in English, Lanny?" He hastened to embrace her, and smooth her ruffled feelings. That was the way they settled their arguments; they were still very much in love, and when he couldn't bring himself to think as she did, the least he could do was to cover her with kisses and tell her that she was the dearest woman in the world.

The upshot of the discussion was that she would go with him again, but she had a right to know what he was going to do before he started doing it. "Of course, darling," he replied. "How else could I have your help?"

"I mean, if it's something I don't approve of, I have a right to say so, and to refuse to go through with it."

He said again: "Haven't you always had that right in our marriage?"

VI

Johannes had established himself in New York, where he was running errands for Robbie, and incidentally trying to "pick up a little business," something he would never fail to do while he lived. Lanny phoned to his father, who motored in, and the four had a long conference in Johannes's hotel room. They threshed out every aspect of the problem and agreed upon a code for communicating with one another. They agreed with Lanny that if Freddi was a prisoner of the government, the Minister-Präsident of Prussia knew it, and there could be no gain in approaching him, unless it was to be another money hold-up. Said Johannes: "He is doubtless informed as to how much money Irma has."

Perhaps it was up to Irma to say: "I would gladly pay it all." But she didn't.

Instead, Robbie remarked to his son: "If you let anybody connected with the government know that you are there on account of Freddi, they will almost certainly have you watched, and be prepared to block you, and make trouble for anyone who helps you."

"I have a business," replied Lanny. "My idea is to work at it seriously and use it as a cover. I'll cable Zoltan and find out if he'd be interested to give a Detaze show in Berlin this autumn. That would make a lot of publicity, and enable me to meet people; also it would tip off Freddi's friends as to where and how to get in touch with me. All this will take time, but it's the only way I can think of to work in Hitler Germany."

This was a promising idea, and it pleased Irma, because it was respectable. She had had a very good time at the London showing of Marcel's paintings. It was associated in her mind with romantic events; getting married in a hurry and keeping the secret from her friends—she had felt quite delightfully wicked, because nobody could be sure whether they were really married or not. Also the New York show had been fun—even though the Wall Street panic had punctured it like a balloon.

Lanny said that before sailing they should take some time and drum up business; if he had American dollars to pay out for German art treasures, the most fanatical Nazi could find no fault with him. Irma had so far looked upon the picture business as if it were the vending of peanuts from a pushcart; but now it became part of a melodrama—as if she were dressing up as the peanut vender's wife! But without really sacrificing her social prestige; for the richest and most fastidious persons wouldn't suspect that the daughter of J. Paramount Barnes was peddling pictures for the money. It would be for love of *les beaux arts*, a fine and dignified thing.

When Lanny telegraphed some client that he and his wife were about to leave for Germany and would like to motor out and discuss the client's tastes and wishes, the least the person could do was to invite them to tea, and often it would be to spend the night in some showplace at Bar Harbor or Newport, in the Berkshires or up the Hudson.

So, when the young couple boarded a steamer for Southampton, they really had an excellent pretext for a sojourn in Naziland. They sailed on a German liner, because Irma had set out to learn the language and wanted opportunities to "chatter." They landed in England because their car had been stored there, and because Lanny wanted a conference with Rick before taking the final plunge. Zoltan was in London, and had answered Lanny's cable with an enthusiastic assent. He was a shrewd fellow, and knowing about Freddi Robin, had no trouble in guessing what was in their heads; but he was discreet, and said not a word.

Beauty had gone back to Juan, and of course the young couple wanted to see little Frances, and also to talk things over with the Robins and make them acquainted with the code. On the way they stopped to see Emily and get her wise advice. One bright moonlit night they arrived at Bienvenu, amid the powerful scent of orange and lemon blossoms. *Kennst du das Land, wo die Zitronen blühn?* It seemed to Irma that she wanted nothing ever again but to stay in that heaven-made garden.

For three days she was in ecstasies over their darling little girl, calling Lanny's attention to every new word she had learned. Lanny, duly responsive, wondered what the little one made of these two mysterious, godlike beings called mother and father, who swooped down into her life at long intervals and then vanished in a roar of motors and clouds of dust. He observed that the child was far more interested in the new playmate whom fate permitted her to have without interruption. Baby Freddi was blooming like a dark velvet rose in the hot sunshine of the Midi, for which he had been destined many centuries ago; fear was being forgotten, along with his father. Irma withheld her thought: "I must get those two apart before they come to the falling-in-love age!"

VII

All preparations having been made as for a military campaign, at the beginning of September the young couple set out for Berlin by way of Milan and Vienna. Lanny knew of paintings in the latter city, and the art business could be made more convincing if he stopped there. He had written letters to several of his friends in Germany, telling of his intention to spend the autumn in their country; they would approve his business purpose, for he would be contributing foreign exchange to the Fatherland, and with foreign exchange the Germans got coffee and chocolate and oranges, to say nothing of Hollywood movies and Budd machine guns. To Frau Reichsminister Goebbels he wrote reminding her of her kind offer to advise him; he told of the proposed Detaze exhibit and enclosed some photographs and clippings, in case the work of this painter wasn't already known to her. Carefully wrapped and stowed in the back of the car were several of Marcel's most famous works—not the *Poilu*, not those sketches satirizing German militarism, but *Pain*, and *Sister of Mercy*, so gentle, yet moving, adapted to a nation which had just signed a pact renouncing war; also samples of the land- and sea-scapes of that romantic Riviera coast which so many Germans had visited and come to love. *Kennst du das Land!*

On the drive through Italy, safe from possible eavesdropping, they discussed the various possibilities of this campaign. Should they try to appeal to what sense of honor the Commander of the German Air Force might have? Should they try to make friends with him, and to extract a favor from him, sometime when they had him well loaded up with good liquor? Should they make him a straight-out cash proposition? Or should they try to get next to the Führer, and persuade him that they were the victims of a breach of faith? Should they play the Goebbels faction, or find somebody in power who needed cash and could pull hidden wires? Should they try for a secret contact with some of the young Socialists, and perhaps plan a jailbreak? These and many more schemes they threshed out, and would keep them in mind as they groped their way into the Nazi jungle. One thing alone was certain; whatever plan they decided upon they could carry out more safely if they were established in Berlin as socially prominent and artistically distinguished, the heirs and interpreters of a great French painter, the patrons and friends of a German Komponist, and so on through various kinds of glamour they might manage to wrap about themselves.

In Vienna it wasn't at all difficult for Lanny to resume the role of art expert. In one of those half-dead palaces on the Ringstrasse he came upon a man's head by Hobbema which filled him with enthusiasm; he cabled to a collector in Tuxedo Park, the sale was completed in two days, and thus he had earned the cost of a long stay in Berlin before he got there. Irma was impressed, and said: "Perhaps Göring might let you sell for him those paintings in the Robin palace. Johannes would be getting his son in exchange for his art works!"

VIII

A detour in order to spend a couple of days at Stubendorf; for Kurt Meissner was like a fortress which had to be reduced before an army could march beyond it. No doubt Heinrich had already written something about Lanny's becoming sympathetic to National Socialism, and it wouldn't do to have Kurt writing back: "Watch out for him, he doesn't really mean it." If Lanny was to succeed as a spy, here was where he had to begin, and the first step would be the hardest.

A strange thing to be renewing old friendships and at the same time turning them into something else! To be listening to Kurt's new piano concerto with one half your mind, and with the other half thinking: "What shall I say that will be just right, and how shall I lead up to what I want to tell him about the Robins?"

Was it because of this that Kurt's music seemed to have lost its vitality? In the old days Lanny's enthusiasm had been unrestrained; all his being had flowed along with those sweeping melodies, his feet had marched with those thundering chords, he had been absolutely certain that this was the finest music of the present day. But now he thought: "Kurt has committed himself to these political fanatics, and all his thinking is adjusted to their formulas. He is trying to pump himself up and sound impressive, but really it's old stuff. He has got to the stage where he is repeating himself."

But Lanny mustn't give the least hint of that. He was an intriguer, a double-dealer, using art and art criticism as camouflage for *his* kind of ideology, *his* set of formulas. He had to say: "Kurt, that's extraordinary; that *finale* represents the highest point you have ever attained; the *adagio* weeps with all the woe of the world." How silly these phrases of musical rapture sounded; saying them made a mockery of friendship, took all the charm out of hospitality, even spoiled the taste of the food which the *gute verständige Mutter*, Frau Meissner, prepared for her guests.

But it worked. Kurt's heart was warmed to his old friend, and he decided that political differences must not be allowed to blind one to what was fine in an opponent. Later on, Lanny went for a walk in the forest, leaving Irma to have a heart-to-heart talk with Kurt, and tackle a job which would have been difficult for Lanny. For, strangely enough, Irma was play-acting only in part. She said things to this German musician which she hadn't said to anybody else, and hadn't thought she would ever say; so she assured him, and of course it touched him. She explained that Lanny was honest, and had dealt with her fairly, telling her his political convictions before he had let her become interested in him. But she had been ignorant of the world, and hadn't realized what it would mean to be a Socialist, or one sympathetic to their ideas. It meant meeting the most dreadful people, and having them interfere in your affairs, and your being drawn into theirs. Not merely the sincere ones, but the tricksters and adventurers who had learned to parrot the phrases! Lanny could never tell the difference—indeed, how could anybody tell? It was like going out into the world with your skin off, and any insect that came along could take a bite out of you.

"And not only Socialists," said the young wife, "but Communists, all sorts of trouble-makers. You know Uncle Jesse, how bitter he is, and what terrible speeches he makes."

"We had millions like him in Germany," replied Kurt. "Thank God that danger is no more."

"I've been pleading and arguing with Lanny for more than four years. At one time I was ready to give up in despair; but now I really begin to believe I am making some headway. You know how Lanny is, he believes what people tell him; but of late he seems to be realizing the true nature of some of the people he's been helping. That's why I wanted to ask you to talk to him. He has such a deep affection for you, and you may be able to explain what is going on in Germany, and help him to see things in their true light."

"I've tried many times," said Kurt; "but I never seemed to get anywhere."

"Try once more. Lanny is impressionable, and seeing your movement going to work has given a jolt to his ideas. What he wants more than anything is to see the problem of unemployment solved. Do you think the Führer will really be able to do it?"

"I have talked with him, and I know that he has practical plans and is actually getting them under way."

"Explain that to Lanny, so that while he's here with Marcel's pictures he'll watch and understand. It may seem strange to you that I'm letting him sell pictures when I have so much money of my own; but I've made up my mind that he ought to have something to do, and not have the humiliation of living on his wife's money."

"You're absolutely right," declared the musician, much impressed by the sound judgment of this young woman, whom he had imagined to be a social butterfly. "Lanny is lucky to have a wife who understands his weaknesses so well. Make him stick at some one thing, Irma, and keep him from chasing every will-o'-the-wisp that crosses his path."

IX

So these two boyhood friends got together and renewed their confidences. Life had played strange tricks upon them, beyond any foreseeing. Back in the peaceful Saxon village of Hellerau where they had met just twenty years ago, dancing Gluck's *Orpheus*, suppose that somebody had told them about the World War, less than a year off, and five years later Kurt in Paris as a German secret agent, passing ten thousand francs at a time to Uncle Jesse to be used in stirring up revolt among the French workers! Or suppose they had been told about a pitiful artist *manqué*, earning his bread and sausage by painting picture postcards, sleeping at night among the bums and derelicts of Vienna—and destined twenty years later to become the master of all Germany! What would they have said to that?

But here was Adolf Hitler, the one and only Führer of the Fatherland, sole possessor of a solution to the social problem and at the same time of the power to put it into effect. Kurt explained what Adi was doing and intended to do, and Lanny listened with deep attention. "It sounds too good to be true," was the younger man's comment.

The Komponist replied: "You will see it, and then you will believe." To himself he said: "Poor Lanny! He's good, but he's a weakling. Like all the rest of the world, he's impressed by success." Having been Beauty's lover for eight years, Kurt knew the American language, and thought: "He is getting ready to climb onto the bandwagon."

So, when the young couple drove away to Berlin, they left everything at Stubendorf the way they wanted it. Kurt was again their friend, and ready to accept whatever good news might come concerning them. They could ask him for advice, and for introductions, if needed; they could invite him to Berlin to see the Detaze show, and exploit his musical reputation for their own purposes. Lanny didn't let this trouble his conscience; it was for Freddi Robin, not for himself. Freddi, too, was a musician, a child of Bach and Beethoven and Brahms just as much as Kurt. Many compositions those two Germans had played together, and the clarinetist had given the Komponist many practical hints about writing for that instrument.

When Lanny had mentioned to Kurt that Freddi had been missing since the month of May, Kurt had said: "Oh, poor fellow!"

—but that was all. He hadn't said: "We must look into it, Lanny, because mistakes are often made, and a harmless, gentle idealist must not be made to pay the penalties for other people's offenses." Yes, Kurt should have said that, but he wouldn't, because he had become a full-fledged Nazi, despising both Marxists and Jews, and unwilling to move a finger to help even the best of them. But Lanny was going to help Freddi—and take the liberty of making Kurt take part in the enterprise.

X

On the day that Irma and Lanny arrived at the Hotel Adlon, another guest, an elderly American, was severely beaten by a group of Brownshirts because he failed to notice that a parade was passing and to give the Nazi salute. When he went to the Polizeiwache to complain about it, the police offered to show him how to give the Nazi salute. Episodes such as this, frequently repeated, had had the effect of causing the trickle of tourists to stop; and this was fortunate for an art expert and his wife, because it made them important, and caused space to be given to Detaze and his work. Everybody desired to make it clear that the great art-loving public of Berlin was not provincial in its tastes, but open to all the winds that blew across the world.

Lanny talked about his former stepfather who had had his face burned off in the war and had done his greatest painting in a white silk mask. His work was in the Luxembourg, in the National Gallery of London, and the Metropolitan Museum of New York; now Lanny was contemplating a one-man show in Berlin, and had invited the famous authority Zoltan Kertezsi to take charge of it. Before giving out photographs or further publicity concerning the matter, he wished to consult Reichsminister Doktor Joseph Goebbels, and be sure that his plans were agreeable to the government. That was the proper way to handle matters with a controlled press; the visitor's tact was appreciated, and the interviews received more space than would have been given if he had appeared anxious to obtain it.

Lanny had already sent a telegram to Magda Goebbels, and her secretary had telephoned an appointment for the next day. While Irma stayed in her rooms and practiced her German on maids and manicurists and hair-dressers, Lanny drove to the apartment in the Reichstagplatz, and bowed and kissed the hand of the first lady of the Fatherland—such was, presumably, her position, Hitler being a bachelor and Göring a widower. Lanny had brought along two footmen from the hotel, bearing paintings, just as had been done in the days of Marie Antoinette, and those of her mother, the Empress Maria Theresa of Austria. The *Sister of Mercy* was set up in a proper light and duly admired; when the Frau Reichsminister asked who it was, Lanny did not conceal the fact that it was his mother, or that she was well known in Berlin society.

He explained his own position. He had enjoyed the advantage of having these great works explained to him by his stepfather, and so had been a lover of art since his boyhood. He had helped to select several great collections in the United States, which would some day become public property. It was pleasant to earn money, but it was even more so to be able to gratify one's taste for beautiful things; Lanny was sure the Frau Reichsminister would understand this, and she said that she did. He added that while a few of the Detazes would be sold, that was not the purpose of the exhibition, and he would not ask to take money out of the country, for he had commissions to purchase German art works for Americans, in amounts greatly exceeding what he was willing to sell. He told how he had just purchased a Hobbema in Vienna; contrary to his usual custom he named both parties to the transaction, and it was impressive.

The upshot was that Magda Goebbels declared the proposed show a worthy cultural enterprise. She said that the Führer had very decided tastes in art, he despised the eccentric modern stuff which was a symptom of pluto-democratic Jewish decadence. Lanny said he had understood that this was the case and it was one of his reasons for coming to Berlin. The work of Detaze was simple, like most great art; it was clean and noble in spirit. He would be happy to take specimens of it to show to the Führer in advance, and the Frau Reichsminister said that possibly this might be arranged. He offered to leave the paintings and photographs for the Herr Reichsminister to inspect, and the offer was accepted. He took his departure feeling hopeful that Marcel Detaze might become a popular painter among the Germans. He wondered, had Marcel heard about the Nazis in the spirit land, and what would he make of them? Lanny would have liked to go at once to consult Madame Diseuse—but who could guess what his irreverent ex-stepfather might blurt out in the séance room!

XI

Lanny's second duty was to get in touch with Oberleutnant Furtwaengler and invite him and his wife to dinner. He explained that it was his wish to show the paintings to Seine Exzellenz, the Herr Minister-Präsident General Göring. Such was now the title— for the newspapers had just made known that the Reichspräsident Feldmarschall von Hindenburg had been pleased to make the Minister-Präsident into a General of the Reichswehr. The Oberleutnant confirmed the news and showed pride in the vicarious honor; it had been somewhat awkward having his chief a mere Hauptmann while in command of several generals of the Prussian Polizei.

Lanny said he was sure that Seine Exzellenz must be a lover of art; he assumed that the new furnishings in the official residence— that great black table and the gold velvet curtains—must represent Seine Exzellenz's taste. The staff officer admitted that this was so, and promised to mention Detaze to the great man. Lanny said that during the past three months he had been in London, Paris, New York, Cannes, and Vienna; the young Nazi, who had never been outside of Germany, was impressed in spite of himself, and wanted to know what the outside world was saying about the Führer and his achievements. Lanny said he was afraid they were not getting a very fair picture; apparently the National Socialist representatives abroad were not serving their cause too efficiently. He told of things he had heard, from various persons having important titles and positions; also of efforts he had made to explain and justify—

the latter being in reality things that he had heard Lord Wick-thorpe say. Lanny added that he had some suggestions which he would be glad to make to Seine Exzellenz if this busy man could spare the time to hear them. The young staff officer replied that he was sure this would be the case.

Not once did Lanny mention the name of Robin. He wanted to see if the Oberleutnant would bring it up; for that would give him an idea whether Göring had taken the staff officer into his confidence. Near the end of the evening, while Irma was off practicing her German on the tall and rather gawky country lady who was the Frau Oberleutnant, the officer said: "By the way, Herr Budd, did you ever hear any more from your young Jewish friend?"

"Not a word, Herr Oberleutnant."

"That is certainly a strange thing."

"I had been hoping for some results from the inquiries which you were kind enough to say you would carry on."

"I have done all that I could think of, Herr Budd, but with no results."

"It was my idea that in the confusion of last spring, various groups had been acting more or less independently, and the records might be imperfect."

"I assure you we don't do things that way in Germany, Herr Budd. In the office of the Geheime Staats-Polizei is a complete card-file covering every case of any person who is under arrest for any offense or under any charge of even the remotest political nature. I don't suppose that your friend could have been arrested, say for drunk driving."

"He does not drink and he does not drive, Herr Oberleutnant. He plays delicately and graciously upon the clarinet, and is a devoted student of your classics. If you should give him the beginning of any quotation from Goethe he would complete it and tell you in what work it was to be found."

"It is really too bad, Herr Budd. If there is anything you can suggest to me——"

"It has occurred to me that the young man might be in some place of confinement outside of Prussia, and so might not appear in your police card-file. Suppose, for example, that he was in Dachau?"

Lanny was watching his dinner companion closely; but if the officer smelled the rat, he was a skillful actor. "Your friend could not be in Dachau," he declared, "unless he were a Bavarian. Being a Berliner, he would be in Oranienburg or some other place near by. However, if you wish, I will cause an inquiry to be made through the *Reichsregierung*, and see if anything can be turned up."

"That is most kind of you," declared Lanny. "It is more than I should have ventured to ask in a time when you and your associates have your hands so full. Permit me to mention that while the young man's name is actually Freddi, some official may have assumed it to be Friedrich, or they might have listed him as Fritz. Also it is conceivable that some one may have set him down as Rabinowitz, the name which his father bore in the city of Lodz."

The staff officer took out his notebook and duly set down these items. "I will promise to do my best, Herr Budd," he declared.

"Perhaps it will be better if you do not trouble Seine Exzellenz with this matter," added the visitor. "I know that he must be the busiest man in the world, and I do not want him to think that I have come to Berlin to annoy him with my personal problems."

Said the staff officer: "He is one of those great men who know how to delegate authority and not let himself be burdened with details. He has time for social life, and I am sure he will be interested to hear what you have to report from the outside world."

Said the undercover diplomat: "I got some reactions of the British Foreign Office to Seine Exzellenz's speech in Geneva. Lord Wickthorpe was really quite stunned by it. You know how it is, the British have been used to having their own way of late years— perhaps much too easily, Herr Leutnant. I doubt if it is going to be so easy for them in future!"

22

Still Get Money, Boy!

I

IT WAS Lanny's hope that as soon as his arrival was announced in the papers he would receive some sort of communication from whoever had taken the trouble to write that Freddi was in Dachau. He was careful in his newspaper interviews to declare himself a non-political person, hoping that some of his former acquaintances among the Social-Democrats would take the hint. But the days passed, and no letter or telephone call was received. Lanny had got from Rahel a list of Freddi's former comrades; most of them would probably be under arrest, or in hiding, "sleeping out," as it was called, never two nights in the same place. Before trying to meet any of them, it seemed wiser for Lanny to try out his Nazi contacts. It would be difficult to combine the two sorts of connections.

He went to call on Heinrich Jung, who burst into his customary excited account of his activities. He had recently come back from the *Parteitag* in Nürnberg; the most marvelous of all *Parteitage*—it had been five days instead of one, and every one of the hundred and twenty hours had been a new climax, a fresh revelation of *das Wunder, die Schönheit, der Sieg* hidden in the soul of National Socialism. "Honestly, Lanny, the most cynical persons were moved to tears by what they saw there!" Lanny couldn't summon any tears, but he was able to bring smiles to his lips and perhaps a glow to his cheeks.

"Do you know Nürnberg?" asked Heinrich. Lanny had visited that old city, with a moat around it and houses having innumerable sharp gables, crowded into narrow streets which seldom ran straight for two successive blocks. An unpromising place for the convention of a great political party, but the Nazis had chosen it because of its historic associations, the memories of the old Germany they meant to bring back to life. Practical difficulties were merely a challenge to their powers of organization; they would show the world how to take care of a million visitors to a city whose population was less than half that. Suburbs of tents had been erected on the outskirts, and the Stormtroopers and Hitler Youth had slept on straw, six hundred to each great tent, two blankets to each person. There had been rows of field kitchens with aluminum spouts from which had poured endless streams of goulash or coffee. Heinrich declared that sixty thousand Hitler Youth had been fed in half an hour—three half-hours per day for five days!

These were specially selected youth, who had labored diligently all year to earn this reward. They had been brought by special trains and by trucks, and had marched in with their bands, shaking the air with songs and the great Zeppelin Meadow with the tramp of boots. For five days and most of five nights they had shouted and sung themselves hoarse, making up in their fervor for all the other forty-four political parties which they had wiped out of existence in Germany. Only one party now, one law, one faith, one baptism! A temporary hall had been built, accommodating a small part of the hundred and sixty thousand official delegates; the others listened to loud-speakers all over the fields, and that served just as well, because there didn't have to be any voting. Everything was settled by the Führer, and the million others had only to hear the speeches and shout their approval.

Heinrich, now a high official in the Hitler Youth, had been among those admitted to the opening ceremonies. He lacked language to describe the wonders, he had to wave his arms and raise his voice. The frenzied acclaim when the Führer marched in to the strains of the *Badenweiler Marsch*—did Lanny know it? Yes, Lanny did, but Heinrich hummed a few bars even so. After Hitler had reached the platform the standards were borne in, the flags consecrated by being touched with the Blood Flag, which had been borne in the Munich civil struggle. Heinrich, telling about it, was like a good Catholic witnessing the sacred mystery of the Host. He told how Ernst Röhm had called the roll of those eighteen martyrs, and of all the two or three hundred others who had died during the party's long struggle for power. Muffled drums beat softly, and at the end the S.A. Chief of Staff declared: "*Sie marschieren mit uns im Geist, in unseren Reihen.*"

Five days of speechmaking and cheering, marching and singing by a million of the most active and capable men in Germany, nearly all of them young. Heinrich said: "If you had seen it, Lanny, you would know that our movement has won, and that the Fatherland is going to be what we make it."

"I had a long talk with Kurt," said Lanny. "He convinced me that you and he have been right." The young official was so delighted that he clasped his friend's hand and wrung it. Another Hitler victory. *Sieg Heil!*

II

Most of Irma's fashionable acquaintances had not yet returned to the city, so she employed her spare time accustoming her ears to the German language. She struck up an acquaintance with the hotel's manicurist, a natural blonde improved by art, sophisticated as her profession required, but underneath it naïve, as all Germans seemed to Irma. An heiress's idea of how to acquire knowledge was to hire somebody to put it painlessly into her mind; and who could be a more agreeable injector than a young woman who had held the hands of assorted millionaires and celebrities from all parts of the world, chattering to them and encouraging them to chatter back? Fräulein Elsa Borg was delighted to sell her spare hours to Frau Budd, *geborene* Barnes, and to teach her the most gossipy and idiomatic Berlinese. Irma practiced laboriously those coughing and sneezing sounds which Tecumseh had found too barbarous. To her husband she said: "Really the craziest way to put words together! I will the blue bag with the white trimmings to the hotel room immediately bring let. I will the eggs without the shells to be broken have. It makes me feel all the time as if children were making it up."

But no one could question the right of Germans by the children their sentences to be shaped let, and Irma was determined to speak properly if at all; never would she consent to sound to anybody the way Mama Robin sounded to her. So she and the manicurist talked for hours about the events of the day, and when Irma mentioned the *Parteitag*, Elsa said yes, her beloved *Schatz* had been there. This "treasure" was the block leader for his neighborhood and an ardent party worker, so he had received a badge and transportation and a permit to leave his work, also his straw and two blankets and goulash and coffee—all free. Irma put many questions, and ascertained what the duties of a block leader were, and how he had a subordinate in every apartment building, and received immediate reports of any new person who appeared in it, and of any whose actions were suspicious, or who failed to contribute to the various party funds, the *Büchsen*, and so on. All this would be of interest to Lanny, who might use a block leader, perhaps to give him information so that he could outwit some other block leader in an emergency.

Elsa's "treasure" afforded an opportunity to check on the claims of Heinrich and to test the efficiency of the Nazi machine. One of a hundred clerks in a great insurance office, Elsa's Karl worked for wretched wages, and if it had not been for his "little treasure" would have had to live in a lodging-house room. Yet he was marching on air because of his pride in the party and its achievements. He worked nights and Sundays at a variety of voluntary tasks, and had never received a penny of compensation—unless you counted the various party festivals, and the fact that the party had power to force his employers to grant him a week's holiday to attend the *Parteitag*. Both he and Elsa swelled with pride over this power, and a word of approval from his party superior would keep Karl happy for months. He thought of the Führer as close to God, and was proud of having been within a few feet of him, even though he had not seen him. The "treasure" had been one of many thousands of Brownshirts who had been lined up on the street in Nürnberg through which the Führer made his triumphal entrance. It had been Karl's duty to hold the crowds back, and he had faced the crowds, keeping watch lest some fanatic should attempt to harm the holy one.

Elsa told how Karl had seen the Minister-Präsident General Göring riding in an open car with a magnificent green sash across his brown party uniform. He had heard the solemn words of Rudolf Hess, Deputy of the Führer: "I open the Congress of Victory!" He had heard Hitler's own proud announcement: "We shall meet here a year from now, we shall meet here ten years from now, and a hundred, and even a thousand!" And Reichsminister Goebbels's excoriation of the foreign Jews, the busy vilifiers of the Fatherland. "Not one hair of any Jewish head was disturbed without reason," Frau Magda's husband had declared. When Irma told Lanny about this, he thought of poor Freddi's hairs and hoped it might be true. He wondered if this orgy of party fervor had been paid for out of the funds which Johannes Robin had furnished. Doubtless that had been "reason" enough for disturbing the hairs of Johannes's head!

III

Lanny took Hugo Behr for a drive, that being the only way they could talk freely. Lanny didn't say: "Did you write me that letter?" No, he was learning the spy business, and letting the other fellow do the talking.

Right away the sports director opened up. "I'm terribly embarrassed not to have been of any use to you, Lanny."

"You haven't been able to learn anything?"

"I would have written if I had. I paid out more than half the money to persons who agreed to make inquiries in the prisons in Berlin, and also in Oranienburg and Sonnenburg and Spandau. They all reported there was no such prisoner. I can't be sure if they did what they promised, but I believe they did. I want to return the rest of the money."

"Nonsense," replied the other. "You gave your time and thought and that is all I asked. Do you suppose there is any chance that Freddi might be in some camp outside of Prussia?"

"There would have to be some special reason for it."

"Well, somebody might have expected me to be making this inquiry. Suppose they had removed him to Dachau, would you have any way of finding out?"

"I have friends in Munich, but I would have to go there and talk to them. I couldn't write."

"Of course not. Do you suppose you could get leave to go?"

"I might be able to think up some party matter."

"I would be very glad to pay your expenses, and another thousand marks for your trouble. Everything that I told you about the case applies even more now. The longer Freddi is missing, the more unhappy the father grows, and the more pressure on me to do something. If the Detaze show should prove a success in Berlin, I may take it to Munich; meantime, if you could get the information, I could be making plans."

"Have you any reason to think about Dachau, especially?"

"I'll tell you frankly. It may sound foolish, but during the World War I had an English friend who was a flyer in France, and I was at my father's home in Connecticut, and just at dawn I was awakened by a strange feeling and saw my friend standing at the foot of the bed, a shadowy figure with a gash across his forehead. It turned out that this was just after the man had crashed and was lying wounded in a field."

"One hears such stories," commented the other, "but one never knows whether to believe them."

"Naturally, I believed this. I've never had another such experience until the other night. I was awakened, I don't know how, and lying in the dark I distinctly heard a voice saying: 'Freddi is in Dachau.' I waited a long time, thinking he might appear, or that I might hear more, but nothing happened. I had no reason to think of Dachau—it seems a very unlikely place—so naturally I am interested to follow it up and see if I am what they call 'psychic.' "

Hugo agreed that he, too, would be interested; his interest increased when Lanny slipped several hundred-mark notes into his pocket, saying, with a laugh: "My mother and stepfather have paid much more than this to spiritualist mediums to see if they could get any news of our friend."

IV

Hugo also had been to the *Parteitag*. To him it was not merely a marvelous demonstration of loyalty, but a call to every *Parteigenosse* to see that the loyalty was not wasted. Those million devoted workers gave their services without pay, because they had been promised a great collective reward, the betterment of the lot of the common man in Germany. But so far they had got nothing; not one of the promised economic reforms had been carried out, and indeed many of the measures which had been taken were reactionary, making the reforms more remote and difficult. The big employers had got a commanding voice in the control of the new shop councils—which meant simply that wages would be frozen where they were, and the workers deprived of all means of influencing them. The same was true of the peasants, because prices were being fixed. "If this continues," said Hugo, "it will mean a slave system, just that and nothing else."

To Lanny it appeared that the young sports director talked exactly like a Social-Democrat; he had changed nothing but his label. He insisted that the rank and file were of his way of thinking, and that what he called the "Second Revolution" could not be more than a few weeks off. He pinned his hopes upon Ernst Röhm, Chief of Staff and highest commander of the S.A., who had been one of the ten men tried for treason and imprisoned after the Beerhall Putsch; a soldier and fighter all his life, he had become the hero of those who wanted the N.S.D.A.P. to remain what it had been and to do what it had promised to do. The Führer must be persuaded, if necessary he must be pushed; that was the way it was in politics—it was no drawing-room affair, but a war of words and ideas, and if need be of street demonstrations, marching, threats. None knew this better than Hitler himself.

Lanny thought: "Hugo is fooling himself with the Chief of Staff, as earlier he fooled himself with the Führer." Ernst Röhm was a homosexual who had publicly admitted his habits; an ignorant rough fellow who rarely even pretended to social idealism. When he denounced the reactionaries who were still in the Cabinet, it was

because he wanted more power for his Brownshirts and their commander. But it wasn't Lanny's business to hint at this; he must find
out who the malcontents were—and especially whether any of them
were in power at Dachau. Such men want money for their pleasures, and if they are carrying on a struggle for power they want
money for that. There might be a good chance of finding one who
could be paid to let a prisoner slip through the bars.

Their conference was a long one, and their drive took them into
the country; beautiful level country, every square foot of it tended
like somebody's parlor. No room for a weed in the whole of the
Fatherland, and the forests planted in rows like orchards and tended
the same way. It happened to be Saturday afternoon, and the innumerable lakes around Berlin were gay with tiny sailboats, the shores
lined with cottages and bathhouses. The tree-lined paths by the
roads were full of *Wandervögel*, young people hiking—but it was
all military now, they wore S.A. uniforms and their songs were of
defiance. Drill-grounds everywhere, and the air full of sharp cries
of command and dust of tramping feet. Germany was getting ready
for something. If you asked what, they would say "defense," but
they were never clear as to who wished to attack them—right after
signing a solemn pact against the use of force in Europe.

Another way in which Hugo resembled the Social-Democrats
rather than the Nazis—he hated militarism. He said: "There are two
ways the Führer can solve the problem of unemployment; one is
to put the idle to work and make plenty for all, including themselves; the other is to turn them over to the army, to be drilled and
sent out to take the land and resources of other peoples. That is the
question which is being decided in the inner circles right now."

"Too bad you can't be there!" remarked Lanny; and his young
friend revealed what was in the depths of his mind. "Maybe I will
be some day."

V

Seine Exzellenz, Minister-Präsident General Göring, was pleased
to invite Mr. and Mrs. Lanny Budd to lunch at his official residence.
He didn't ask them to bring their paintings, and Lanny wasn't sorry

about it, for somehow he couldn't see the *Sister of Mercy* in company with a lion cub. He doubted very much if Seine Exzellenz was being deceived as to the real reason for Lanny's coming to Berlin; and anyhow, the Commander of the German Air Force was having his own art made to his own order—a nude statue of his deceased wife, made from photographs and cast in solid gold!

At least that was what the Fürstin Donnerstein had told Irma. There was no stopping the tongues of these fashionable ladies; the Fürstin had poured out the "dirt," and Irma had collected it and brought it home. The good-looking blond aviator named Göring, after being wounded in the Beerhall Putsch, had fled abroad and married a Swedish baroness; the lady was an epileptic and her spouse a morphia addict. There could be no doubt about either of these facts, for they had been proved in court when the baroness was refused custody of her son by a former marriage. Later on, the lady had died of tuberculosis, and Göring, returning to Germany, had chosen Thyssen and the former Crown Prince for his cronies, and the steel king's sister for his "secretary"; the quotation marks were indicated by the Fürstin's tone as she said the last word. It had been assumed that he would marry this Anita Thyssen, but it hadn't come off; perhaps he had become too great—or too fat! At the moment Anita was "out," and the "in" was Emmy Sonnemann, a blond Nordic Valkyrie who acted at the State Theater and could have any role she chose. "But that doesn't exclude other *Damen*," added the serpent's tongue of Fürstin Donnerstein. "*Vorsicht, Frau Budd!*"

So Irma learned a new German word.

VI

The utility king's daughter had lived most of her life in marble halls, and wasn't going to be awed by the livery of Göring's lackeys or the uniforms of his staff and self. The lion cub was not for ladies, it appeared—and she didn't miss him. The great ebony table with gold curtains behind it was really quite stunning; they made Irma think of Dick Oxnard's panels, and she couldn't see why Lanny had made fun of them. Pink jackets and white silk pumps and stockings for footmen—yes, but hardly in the daytime; and the General's medals seemed more suited to a state dinner than a private luncheon.

However, the ex-aviator was very good company; he spoke English well, and perhaps wanted to prove it. He did most of the talking, and laughed gaily at his own jokes. There was nobody else present but Furtwaengler and another staff officer, and needless to say they laughed at the jokes and didn't tell any of their own. Apparently it was a purely social affair; not a word about ransoms or hostages, Jews or concentration camps. No need for Lanny to say: "I hope you have noticed, Exzellenz, that I have kept my agreement." The fact that he was here, being served cold-storage plovers' eggs and a fat squab was proof enough that he had kept it and that his host had made note of the fact.

The assumption was that the holder of eight or ten of the most responsible positions in the "Third Reich" enjoyed nothing so much as sipping brandy and chatting with two idle rich Americans; it was up to Lanny to play his role, and let it come up quite by accident that he and his wife had visited Lausanne in the early days of the Conference on Arms Limitation, and could tell inside stories about the prominent personalities there, including the German. This led to the mention that Lanny had been on the American staff at Paris, and had met many of the men, and had helped a German agent to escape to Spain. He knew leading members of several of the French parties, including Daladier, the Premier, and he had visited in the homes of some of the British Foreign Office set—yes, there could be no doubt that he was a young man of exceptional opportunities, and could be very useful to a Reichsminister without Portfolio if he happened to be well disposed! Not a word was spoken, but always there was floating in the air the thought: "Why not take a chance, Exzellenz, and turn loose my Jewish *Schiebersohn?*"

VII

Herr Reichsminister Joseph Goebbels was so gracious as to indicate his opinion that the work of Marcel Detaze was suitable for showing in Germany; quite harmless, although not especially distinguished. Lanny understood that he could expect no more for a painter from a nation which the Führer had described as "Negroid." It was enough, and he wired Zoltan to come to Berlin.

What did one do to obtain publicity with a *gleichgeschaltete Presse?* Lanny found out, even before his friend arrived. A youngish, very businesslike gentleman called; one of those Berliners who wear a derby hat, and on a hot day a vest-clip on which they may hang the hat, thus preserving comfort and respectability at the same time. His card made him known as Herr Privatdozent Doktor der Philosophie Aloysius Winckler zu Sturmschatten. In a polite philosophical voice he informed Lanny that he was in position to promote the reputation of Detaze—or otherwise. The Privatdozent spoke as one having both authority and determination; he didn't evade or drop his eyes, but said: *"Sie sind ein Weltmann, Herr Budd.* You know that a great deal of money can be made from the sale of these paintings if properly presented; and it happens that I am a *Parteigenosse* from the early days, the intimate friend of persons of great influence. In past times I have rendered them services and they have done the same for me. You understand how such things go."

Lanny said that he understood; but that this was not entirely a commercial undertaking, he was interested in making known the work of a man whom he had loved in life and admired still.

"Yes, yes, of course," said the stranger, his voice as smooth and purring as that of a high-priced motor-car. "I understand what you want, and I am in position to give it to you. For the sum of twenty thousand marks I can make Marcel Detaze a celebrated painter, and for the sum of fifty thousand marks I can make him the initiator of a new era in representational art."

"Well, that would be fine," said Lanny. "But how can I know that you are able to do these things?"

"For the sum of two thousand marks I will cause the publication of an excellent critical account of Detaze, with reproductions of a couple of his works, in any daily newspaper of Berlin which you may select. This, you understand, will be a test, and you do not have to pay until the article appears. But it must be part of the understanding that if I produce such an article, you agree to go ahead on one of the larger projects I have suggested. I am not a cheap person, and am not interested in what you Americans call *kleine Kartoffeln.* You may write the article yourself, but it would be wiser for you to provide me with the material and let me prepare it, for, knowing the Berlin public, I can produce something which will serve your purposes more surely."

So it came about that the morning on which Zoltan Kertezsi arrived at the hotel, Lanny put into his hands a fresh newspaper containing an account of Detaze at once critically competent and journalistically lively. Zoltan ran his eyes over it and exclaimed: "How on earth did you do that?"

"Oh, I found a competent press agent," said the other. He knew that Zoltan had scruples, whereas Zoltan's partner had left his in the Austrian town whence he had crossed into Naziland.

Later that morning the Herr Privatdozent called and took Lanny for a drive. The stepson of Detaze said that he wanted his stepfather to become the initiator of a new era in representational painting, and offered to pay the sum of ten thousand marks per week for one week preceding the show and two weeks during it, conditioned upon the producing of publicity in abundant quantities and of a standard up to that of the sample. The Herr Privatdozent accepted, and they came back to the hotel, where Zoltan, possibly not so innocent as he appeared, sat down with them to map out a plan of campaign.

VIII

Suitable showrooms were engaged, and the ever dependable Jerry Pendleton saw to the packing of the pictures at Bienvenu. He hired a *camion,* and took turns with the driver, sleeping inside and coming straight through with that precious cargo. Beauty and her husband came by train—there could have been no keeping her away, and anyhow, she was worth the expenses of the journey as an auxiliary show. She was in her middle fifties, and with Lanny at her side couldn't deny it, but she was still a blooming rose, and if you questioned what she had once been, there were two most beautiful paintings to prove it. Nothing intrigued the crowd more than to have her standing near so that they could make comparisons. The widow of this initiator of a new era, and her son—but not the painter's son —no, these Negroid races run to promiscuity, and as for the Americans, their divorces are a joke, they have a special town in the wild and woolly West where the broken-hearted ladies of fashion stay for a few weeks in order to get them, and meantime are consoled by cowboys and Indians.

For the "professional beauty" it was a sort of public reception, afternoons and evenings for two weeks, and she did not miss a minute of it. A delightfully distinguished thing to be able to invite your friends to an exhibition of which you were so unique a part: hostess, biographer, and historian, counselor and guide—and in case of need assistant saleslady! Always she was genial and gracious, an intimate of the great, yet not spurning one lowly lover of *die schönen Künste*. Zoltan paid her a memorable compliment, saying: "My dear Beauty Budd, I should have asked you to marry me and travel about the world promoting pictures." Beauty, with her best dimpled smile, replied: "Why didn't you?" (Mr. Dingle was off visiting one of his mediums, trying to get something about Freddi, but instead getting long messages from his father, who was so happy in the spirit world, and morally much improved over what he had been—so he assured his son.)

There were still rich men in Germany. The steelmasters of the Ruhr, the makers of electrical power, the owners of plants which could turn out the means of defense—all these were sitting on the top of the Fatherland. Having wiped out the labor unions, they could pay low wages without fear of strikes, and thus count upon profits in ever-increasing floods. They looked about them for sound investments, and had learned ten years ago that one inflation-proof material was diamonds and another was old masters. As a rule the moneylords didn't possess much culture, but they knew how to read, and when they saw in one newspaper after another that a new school of representational art had come to the front, they decided that they ought to have at least one sample of this style in their collections. If they were elderly and retired they came to the show;

if they were middle-aged and busy they sent their wives or daughters. Twenty or thirty thousand marks for a landscape did not shock them, on the contrary it made a Detaze something to brag about.

So it was that the profits of Lanny, his mother, and his half-sister —less the ten per cent commission of Zoltan—covered twenty times over what they had paid to the efficient Herr Privatdozent, and Zoltan suggested that they should pay this able promoter and continue the splurge of glory for another week. Even Irma was impressed, and began to look at the familiar paintings with a new eye. She wondered if it mightn't be better to save them all for the palace with modern plumbing which she meant some day to have in England or France. To her husband she remarked: "You see how much better everything goes when you settle down and stop talking like a Red!"

IX

The Detaze show coincided in time with one of the strangest public spectacles ever staged in history. The Nazis had laid the attempt to burn the Reichstag upon the Communists, while the enemies of Nazism were charging that the fire had been a plot of the Hitlerites to enable them to seize power. The controversy was brought to a head by the publication in London of the *Brown Book of the Hitler Terror*, which charged that the Nazi Chief of Police of Breslau, one of the worst of their terrorists, had led a group of S.A. men through the tunnel from Göring's residence into the Reichstag building; they had scattered loads of incendiary materials all over the place, while another group had brought a half-witted Dutch tramp into the building by a window and put him to work starting fires with a domestic gas-lighter. This was what the whole world was coming to believe, and the Nazis couldn't very well dodge the issue. For six or seven months they had been preparing evidence, and in September they began a great public trial. They charged the Dutchman with the crime, and three Bulgarian Communists and a German with being his accessories. The issue thus became a three-months' propaganda battle, not merely in Germany but wherever news was read and public questions discussed. Ten

thousand pages of testimony were taken, and seven thousand electrical transcriptions made of portions of the testimony for broad-
casting.

The trial body was the Fourth Criminal Senate of the German
Supreme Court in Leipzig; oddly enough, the same tribunal before
which, three years previously, Adolf Hitler had proclaimed that
"heads will roll in the sand." Now he was going to make good his
threat. Unfortunately he had neglected to "co-ordinate" all five of
the court judges; perhaps he didn't dare, because of world opinion.
There was some conformity to established legal procedure, and the
result was such a fiasco that the Nazis learned a lesson, and never
again would political suspects have a chance to appear in public and
cross-question their accusers.

In October and November the court came to Berlin, and it was a
free show for persons who had leisure; particularly for those who
in their secret hearts were pleased to see the Nazis humiliated. The
five defendants had been kept in chains for seven months and wore
chains in the courtroom during the entire trial. The tragedy of the
show was provided by the Dutchman, van der Lubbe, half-blind as
well as half-witted; mucus drooled from his mouth and nose, he
giggled and grinned, made vague answers, sat in a stupor when let
alone. The melodrama was supplied by the Bulgarian Dimitroff, who
"stole the show"; a scholar as well as a man of the world, witty,
alert, and with the courage of a lion, he turned the trial into anti-
Nazi propaganda; defying his persecutors, mocking them, driving
them into frenzies of rage. Three times they put him out of the
room, but they had to bring him back, and again there was sarcasm,
defiance, and exposition of revolutionary aims.

It soon became clear that neither Dimitroff nor the other defendants had ever known van der Lubbe or had anything to do with
the Reichstag fire. The mistake had arisen because there was a parliamentary archivist in the Reichstag building who happened to resemble the half-witted Dutchman, and it was with him that the
Communist Torgler had been seen in conversation. The proceedings
gradually turned into a trial of the *Brown Book*, with the unseen
British committee as prosecutors and the Nazis as defendants.

Goebbels appeared and denounced the volume, and Dimitroff mocked him and made him into a spectacle. Then came the corpulent head of the Prussian state; it was a serious matter for him, because the incendiaries had operated from his residence and it was difficult indeed to imagine that he hadn't known what was going on. Under the Bulgarian's stinging accusations Göring lost his temper completely and had to be saved by the presiding judge, who ordered Dimitroff dragged out, while Göring screamed after him: "I am not afraid of you, you scoundrel. I am not here to be questioned by you . . . You crook, you belong to the gallows! You'll be sorry yet, if I catch you when you come out of prison!" Not very dignified conduct for a Minister-Präsident of Prussia and Reichsminister of all Germany!

X

During these entertaining events two communications came to Lanny Budd at his hotel. The first was painful indeed; a cablegram from his father, saying that the newly elected directors of Budd Gunmakers had met, and that both Robbie and his brother had been cheated of their hopes. Seeing the younger on the verge of victory, Lawford had gone over to a Wall Street group which had unexpectedly appeared on the scene, backed by the insurance company which held the Budd bonds. The thing which Grandfather Samuel had dreaded and warned against all his life—Budd's had been taken out of the hands of the family!

"Oh, Lanny, how terrible!" exclaimed Irma. "We should have been there to attend to it."

"I doubt if we could have done anything," he replied. "If Robbie had thought so, he would surely have cabled us."

"What Uncle Lawford did was an act of treason to the family!"

"He is that kind of man; one of those dark souls who commit crimes. I have often had the thought that he might shoot Robbie rather than let him get the prize which both have been craving all their lives."

"What does he get out of the present arrangement?"

"The satisfaction of keeping Robbie out; and, of course, the Wall Street crowd may have paid him. Anyhow, Robbie has his contract, so they can't fire him."

"I bought all that stock for nothing!" exclaimed the young wife.

"Not for nothing, but for a high price, I fear. You had best cable Uncle Joseph to look into the matter thoroughly and advise you whether to sell it or hold on. Robbie, no doubt, will be writing us the details."

The other communication was very different; a letter addressed to Lanny in his own handwriting, and his heart gave a thump when he saw it, for he had given that envelope to Hugo Behr. It was postmarked Munich and Lanny tore it open quickly, and saw that Hugo had cut six letters out of a newspaper and pasted them onto a sheet of paper—a method of avoiding identification well known to kidnapers and other conspirators. "*Jawohl*" can be one word or two. With space after the first two letters, as Hugo had pasted them, it told Lanny that Freddi Robin was in Dachau and that he was well.

So the American playboy forgot about his father's lost hopes and his own lost heritage. A heavy load was lifted from his mind, and he sent two cablegrams, one to Mrs. Dingle in Juan—the arrangement being that the Robins were to open such messages—and the other to Robbie in Newcastle: "Clarinet music excellent," that being the code. To the latter message the dutiful son added: "Sincere sympathy don't take it too hard we still love you." Robbie would take this with a grin.

Irma and Lanny tore Hugo's message into small pieces and sent it on its way to the capacious sewers of Berlin. They still had hope of some favor to be gained from the head of the Prussian government. At any moment Leutnant Furtwaengler might show up and announce: "We have found your Yiddisher friend." Until then, Lanny could only wait; for when you are cultivating acquaintances in *die grosse Welt*, you don't say to these persons: "I have made certain that you are lying to me, and propose that we now proceed to negotiate upon that basis." No, Lanny couldn't even say: "I have doubts." For right away the Oberleutnant would look sur-

prised and ask: "What is the basis of them?" Lanny couldn't even
say: "I urge you to try harder"; for important persons must be
assumed to have their hands full.

XI

The sum of more than four hundred thousand marks which had
been paid for Detaze pictures had been deposited in Berlin banks.
It would be up to Lanny and Zoltan to use those marks in purchasing art works for their American clients, who would make their
payments in New York; thus the pair would have to ask no favors
of the Nazis. Lanny had obtained information from a list of clients
in America, and Zoltan had a list which he had been accumulating
over a period of many years; so there would be no difficulty in
doing a sufficient amount of business. They had agreed to go fifty-
fifty on all transactions.

Lanny had suggested taking the show to Munich for a week, and
his friend had approved. Here was a great art-loving public, and
sales were certain; moreover, Beauty got fun out of it, and Lanny
knew of pictures which might be bought there. Jerry Pendleton,
who had been waiting in Berlin to take the unsold Detazes back to
France, would see to packing and transporting them to Munich.
The Herr Privatdozent assured them that he enjoyed even more
influence in the Bavarian city, the cradle of National Socialism. He
would be paid another fifteen thousand marks for his services, plus
his expenses for two weeks. He was planning to live high.

Hugo Behr returned to Berlin, reporting that he had made contact with an old party acquaintance who was now one of the S.A.
guards in the camp of Dachau. To this man Hugo had explained
that he had a friend who was owed money by a young Jew, and
wondered if the debtor was still alive and if there was any prospect
of his coming out. The report had been that Freddi Robin had been
in the camp for four or five months; had been pretty roughly
treated before he came there, and now was kept by himself, for
what reason the S.A. man didn't know. What he had meant by
reporting Freddi as "well" was that he was alive and not being

abused, so far as the informant had heard. Nobody was happy in Dachau, and least of all any Jew.

Hugo added: "We might be able to trust that fellow, because I had a long talk with him and he feels about events pretty much as I do. He's sick of his job, which isn't at all what he bargained for. He says there are plenty of others who feel the same, though they don't always talk. You know, Lanny, the Germans aren't naturally a cruel people, and they don't like having the most brutal and rowdyish fellows among them picked out and put in charge."

"Did he say that?" inquired Lanny.

"He said even more. He said he'd like to see every Jew put out of Germany, but he didn't see any sense in locking them up and kicking them around, just for being what they were born. I told him my idea that the party is being led astray and that it's up to the rank and file to set it straight. He was interested, and maybe we'll have an organized group in Dachau."

"That's fine," commented the American; "and I'm ever so much obliged to you. I'm going to Munich pretty soon and perhaps you can come again, and I'll have some other message for your friend." At the same time he took a little roll of hundred-mark notes out of his pocket and slipped them into his friend's—a matter of only a few inches as they sat side by side in the car.

XII

To his wife Lanny said: "There might be a possibility of getting Freddi out without waiting forever on the fat General."

"Oh, do be careful!" exclaimed Irma. "That would be a fearful risk to take!"

"Only as a last resort. But I really think Göring has had time enough to peer into all the concentration camps in the Reich."

He made up his mind to call up Oberleutnant Furtwaengler and inquire concerning the promised investigation. But he put it off till the next morning, and before he got round to it the young staff officer was announced and ushered up to the suite. "Herr Budd," he said, "are you free for the next two or three days?"

"I could get free."

"Seine Exzellenz has earned a holiday after the strain of his court appearances." The serious young officer said this without the least trace of a smile, and Lanny assented with the gravest of nods. "Seine Exzellenz is taking a shooting trip to the estate of Prinz von Schwarzerober in the Schorfheide, and would be pleased if you would accompany him."

"That is very kind indeed," replied the American, with a carefully measured amount of cordiality. "I appreciate the honor and will enjoy the opportunity to know the General better."

"Unfortunately," added the other, "this is what you Americans, I believe, call a 'stag' affair."

"A stag affair in two senses of the word," smiled Lanny, who knew about shooting in the German forests. "My wife won't object to staying here, for she has friends who keep her entertained."

"Very well, then," replied the Oberleutnant. "The car will call for you at fifteen o'clock tomorrow."

Later, the young couple went driving and talked over the situation. "He wants something," declared the husband. "I suppose I'm going to find out about it now."

"Let him do the talking," cautioned Irma. "You saw that he expects it." She was nine years younger than her husband, and had met the General only once, but she knew all about his *Prunksucht*, his delight in self-display, both physical and mental. "He has to prove that he's the greatest man in the company, the greatest in the government, perhaps the greatest in the world. He will do anything for you if you convince him you believe that."

Lanny's mother had been supplying him with that sort of instruction all through his life. He wondered: had Irma got it from Beauty —or from the Great Mother of them all?

23

All the Kingdoms of the World

I

LANNY in his boyhood had observed the feudal system operating in Stubendorf, and had found it paternal and pleasant; so he could understand how the Nazis had made the same discovery. The party was bound for the hunting preserve of one of those great landlords who had been the friends of Hauptmann Göring in the days when he was an ace aviator, successor to von Richthofen in command of that famous squadron. These wealthy Junkers had allied themselves with the Hitler party upon Göring's assurance that they would be properly cared for, and Göring now was seeing that the pledge was kept. There wasn't going to be any "Second Revolution" in Prussia if the head of the government could prevent it, and he thought that he could.

The party traveled in that six-wheeled Mercédès which Lanny had come to call "the tank." The chauffeur and the guard who rode beside him were black-uniformed Schutzstaffel men, both well armed. The very large General lolled in the back seat, with Lanny in the place of honor beside him. In two retractable seats rode Oberst Siemans, a Reichswehr officer who was a World War buddy of the General's, and Hauptmann Einstoss, an S.A. man who had accompanied Göring in his flight to Switzerland after the Beerhall Putsch. A second car followed with Furtwaengler and another staff officer, a secretary, a telephone operator, and a valet.

The party in the "tank" talked about the trial. Lanny wished he might hear what they would have said if he hadn't been along, but there was no way to arrange that. They talked on the assumption that the five prisoners were the spawn of Satan, and that the

General had completely annihilated Dimitroff. When they asked
Lanny what would be the opinion of the outside world, he replied
that all people were inclined to believe what it was in their interest
to believe, and the outside world was afraid of the Nazis because it
suspected that they meant to rearm Germany. Thus, if one was
cautious, it was possible to avoid lying and at the same time avoid
giving offense.

They drove at high speed, with a powerful horn giving notice
to all the world to clear the way. Toward dusk they left the highway and entered a heavy forest; they drove many miles on a private
road before coming to a hunting lodge, well lighted for their reception. A spacious hall, with bearskins on the floor and trophies
on the walls; a glass-cased rack of guns at one end, a banquet-table
at the other, and a great stone fireplace with logs blazing. There was
no host—the place had been turned over to the General. Servants in
green foresters' uniforms brought drinks, and when Seine Exzellenz
called for supper there came a procession of men, each bearing a
silver platter: the first containing a huge roasted boar's head, steaming hot, the second a haunch of venison, the third several caper-
cailzie, a kind of grouse bigger than any chicken, and the fourth
some fricasseed hares. Lanny, dining under the feudal system, could
only laugh and beg for mercy. His host, proud of his prowess as
a trencherman, was not displeased to have others take an attitude
of inferiority.

It was the same with the drinking. Hot punch and cold Moselle,
burning brandy sauces, cocktails, beer—there was apparently no
ordained sequence; the valiant air commander took everything that
he saw and called for more. The way Lanny saved himself was by
music; when they started singing he took his glass of punch to the
piano and played and sang: "Show me the way to go home, boys,"
and other "college songs" which he had learned as a boy from his
father. The General was amused, and Lanny kept him entertained
with various kinds of American humor: "Yankee Doodle" and
"Down Went McGinty" and "There'll be a Hot Time in the Old
Town Tonight." Whether they all knew the language didn't matter,
for pretty soon they didn't know what they knew. He played "My

Old Kentucky Home" and they wept; he played "The Arkansas Traveler" and "Turkey in the Straw" and they tried to dance. Lanny cut his capers on the keyboard, and the head of the Prussian state approved of him so ardently that he wouldn't let his own valet help him upstairs, but insisted upon having the young American on one side and a blue-eyed Wendish damsel on the other.

This was another aspect of the feudal system about which Lanny had heard talk and which he now saw in action. The men servants who had brought in the heavy dishes had disappeared, and desserts and coffee and various drinks were served by young women in peasant costumes with flaxen hair in heavy braids down their backs. They were not prostitutes, but daughters of the servants and retainers; they curtsied to these high-born great gentlemen in uniforms, danced with them when invited, and were prepared to be honored by their further attentions. Not much flirtation or cajoling was called for; they obeyed commands. Fortunately for Lanny there were not enough to go around, and his renunciation was appreciated.

The party arose late next day. There was no hurry, for this kind of shooting proceeds according to the convenience of the shooters and not of the game. After a "fork breakfast" they set out to stands in the forests, and beaters drove stags and buffalo and boar out of the thickets into the open ranges. Lanny had the honor of being posted with the General, and he waited respectfully while the great man shot, and when he was told that it was his turn he upheld the reputation of Budd Gunmakers. It was worth while for him to do so, for he guessed it wouldn't be long before Robbie would be making use of these valuable connections.

II

Having obtained recreation and exercise by pulling the trigger of a rifle, Seine Exzellenz returned to the hunting lodge and took up the reins of government. Apparently he had had a private wire run into the estate, and for a couple of hours he listened to reports and gave orders. He sounded angry most of the time—or was that just his way of governing? It was almost as if he were trying to communicate with Berlin by the medium of the air instead of by a copper wire. His bellowing echoed through the house, and Lanny, anxious not to overhear, went into the billiard room and watched the two junior officers winning small sums from each other. Now and then, when the tones rose especially loud, they would grin at Lanny and he would grin back—this being a privilege of subordinates.

The guest would have liked to walk in that lovely deep forest, but had the idea that he should hold himself at the disposal of his host; and sure enough, after the State of Prussia had received its marching orders for the morrow, Lanny was summoned to the Presence, and found out why he had been taken on a shooting trip. Reclining at ease in a sky-blue silk dressing gown with ermine trimmings, the portly Kommandant of the German Air Force led the conversation into international channels, and began explaining the difficulties of getting real information as to the attitude of ruling circles in other European capitals. He had agents aplenty, paid them generous salaries, and allowed them to pad their expense accounts; but those who were the most loyal had the fewest connections, while those who really had the connections were just as apt to be working for the other side.

"Understand me, Budd"—he had got to that stage of intimacy— "I am not so foolish as to imagine that I could employ you. I know you have a well-paying profession, not to mention a rich wife. I also had one, and discovered that such a spouse expects attentions and does not leave one altogether free. But it happens that you go about and gather facts; and no doubt you realize when they are important."

"I suppose that has happened now and then," said Lanny, showing a coming-on disposition, but not too much.

"What I should like to have is, not an agent, but a friend; a gentleman, whose sense of honor I could trust, and who would not be indifferent to the importance of our task in putting down the Red menace in Germany, and perhaps later wiping out the nest where those vipers are being incubated. Surely one does not have to be a German in order to approve such an aim."

"I agree with you, Exzellenz."

"Call me Göring," commanded the great one. "Perhaps you can understand how tired one gets of dealing with lackeys and flatterers. You are a man who says what he thinks, and when I box with you I get some competition."

"Thank you, Ex—Göring."

"I am sure you understand that we Nazis are playing for no small stakes. You are one of the few who possess imagination enough to know that if you become my friend you will be able to have anything you care to ask for. I am going to become one of the richest men in the world—not because I am greedy for money, but because I have a job to do, and that is one of the tools. We are going to build a colossal industry, which will become the heritage of the future, and most certainly we are not going to leave it in the hands of Jews or other Bolshevist agencies. Sooner or later we shall take over the industry of Russia and bring it into line with modern practices. For all that we need brains and ability. I personally need men who see eye to eye with me, and I am prepared to pay on a royal scale. There is no limit to what I would do for a man who would be a real associate and partner."

"I appreciate the compliment, my dear Göring, but I doubt my own qualifications for any such role. Surely you must have among your own Germans men with special training——"

"No German can do what I am suggesting to you—an American, who is assumed to be above the battle. You can go into France or England and meet anybody you wish, and execute commissions of the most delicate sort without waste of time or sacrifice of your own or your wife's enjoyment. Be assured that I would never ask you to do anything dishonorable, or to betray any trust. If, for example, you were to meet certain persons in those countries and talk politics with them, and report on their true attitudes, so that I could know which of them really want to have the Reds put down and which would rather see those devils entrench themselves than to see Germany get upon her feet—that would be information almost priceless to me, and believe me, you would have to do no more than hint your desires. If you would come now and then on an art-buying expedition to Berlin and visit me in some quiet retreat like this, the information would be used without any label upon it, and I would pledge you my word never to name you to anyone."

III

Lanny perceived that he was receiving a really distinguished offer, and for a moment he was sorry that he didn't like the Nazis. He had a feeling that Irma would be willing for him to say yes, and would enjoy helping on such international errands. Doubtless the General had invited her to lunch in order that he might size her up from that point of view.

"My dear Göring," said Irma's husband, "you are paying me a compliment, and I wish I could believe that I deserve it. To be sure, I sometimes meet important persons and hear their talk when they are off their guard; I suppose I could have more such opportunities if I sought them. Also I find Berlin an agreeable city to visit, and if I should run over now and then to watch your interesting work, it would be natural for you to ask me questions and for me to tell you what I had heard. But when you offer to pay me, that is another matter. Then I should feel that I was under obligations; and I have always been a *Taugenichts*—even before I happened to acquire a rich wife I liked to flit from one place to another, look at pictures, listen to good music or play it not so well, chat with my friends, and amuse myself watching the human spectacle. It happens that I have made some money, but I have never felt that I was earning it, and I would hate to feel that I had to."

It was the sort of answer a man would make if he wished to raise his price; and how was a would-be employer to know? "My dear Budd," said the General, in the same cautious style, "the last thing in the world I desired was to put you under any sense of obligation, or to interfere with your enjoyments. It is just because of that way of life that you could be of help to me."

"It would be pleasant indeed, Exzellenz, to discover that my weaknesses have become my virtues."

The great man smiled, but went on trying to get what he wanted.

"Suppose you were to render me such services as happened to amuse you, and which required no greater sacrifice on your part than to motor to Berlin two or three times a year; and suppose that some day, purely out of friendship, I should be moved to present you with a shooting preserve such as this, a matter of one or two hundred square kilometers—surely that wouldn't have to be taken as a humiliation or indignity."

"*Gott behüte!*" exclaimed the playboy. "If I owned such a property, I would have to pay taxes and upkeep, and right away I should be under moral pressure to get some use out of it."

"Can you think of nothing I might do for you?"

Lanny perceived that he was being handled with masterly diplomacy. The General wasn't saying: "You know I have a hold on you, and this is the way you might induce me to release it!" He wasn't compelling Lanny to say: "You know that you are holding out on me and not keeping your promise!" He was making things easy for both of them; and Lanny was surely not going to miss his chance! "Yes, Göring," he said, quickly, "there is one thing—to have your wonderful governmental machine make some special effort and find that young son of Johannes Robin."

"You are still worried about that Yiddisher?"

"How can I help it? He is a sort of relative—my half-sister is married to his brother, and naturally the family is distressed. When I started out for Berlin to show my Detaze paintings, I had to promise to do everything in my power to find him. I have hesitated to trouble you again, knowing the enormous responsibilities you are carrying——"

"But I have already told you, my dear Budd, that I have tried to find the man without success."

"Yes, but I know how great the confusion of the past few months has been; I know of cases where individuals and groups have assumed authority which they did not legally possess. If you want to do me a favor I shall never forget, have one of your staff make a thorough investigation, not merely in Berlin but throughout the Reich, and enable me to get this utterly harmless young fellow off my conscience."

"All right," said the Minister-Präsident; "if that is your heart's desire, I will try to grant it. But remember, it may be beyond my power. I cannot bring back the dead."

IV

Back in Berlin, Lanny and his wife went for a drive and talked out this new development. "Either he doesn't trust me," said Lanny, "or else I ought to hear from him very soon."

"He must pretend to make an investigation," put in Irma.

"It needn't take long to discover a blunder. He can say: 'I am embarrassed to discover that my supposed-to-be-efficient organization has slipped up. Your friend was in Dachau all along and I have ordered him brought to Berlin.' If he doesn't do that, it's because he's not satisfied with my promises."

"Maybe he knows too much about you, Lanny."

"That is possible; but he hasn't given any hint of it."

"Would he, unless it suited his convenience? Freddi is his only hold on you, and he knows that. Probably he thinks you'd go straight out of Germany and spill the story of Johannes."

"That story is pretty old stuff by now. Johannes is a poor down-and-out, and I doubt if anybody could be got to take much interest in him. The *Brown Book* is published and he isn't in it."

"Listen," said the wife; "this is a question which has been troubling my mind. Can it be that Freddi has been doing something serious, and that Göring knows it, and assumes that you know it?"

"That depends on what you mean by serious. Freddi helped to finance and run a Socialist school; he tried to teach the workers a set of theories which are democratic and liberal. That's a crime to this *Regierung*, and people who are guilty of it are luckier if they are dead."

"I don't mean that, Lanny. I mean some sort of plot or conspiracy, an attempt to overthrow the government."

"You know that Freddi didn't believe in anything of the sort. I've heard him say a thousand times that he believed in government by popular consent, such as we have in America, and such as the Weimar Republic tried to be—or anyhow, was supposed to be."

"But isn't it conceivable that Freddi might have changed after the Reichstag fire, and after seeing what was done to his comrades? It wouldn't have been the Weimar Republic he was trying to overthrow, but Hitler. Isn't it likely that he and many of his friends changed their minds?"

"Many did, no doubt; but hardly Freddi. What good would he have been? He shuts his eyes when he aims a gun!"

"There are plenty of others who would do the shooting. What Freddi had was money—scads of it that he could have got from his father. There were the months of March and April—and how do you know what he was doing, or what his comrades were planning and drawing him into?"

"I think he would have told us about it, Irma. He would have felt in honor bound."

"He might have been in honor bound the other way; he couldn't talk about those comrades. It might even be that he didn't know what was going on, but that others were using him. Some of those fellows I met at the school—they were men who would have fought back, I know. Ludi Schultz, for example—do you imagine he'd lie down and let the Nazi machine roll over him? Wouldn't he have tried to arouse the workers to what they call 'mass action'? And wouldn't his wife have helped him? Then again, suppose there was some Nazi agent among them, trying to lure them into a trap, to catch them in some act of violence so that they could be arrested?"

"The Nazis don't have to have any excuses, Irma; they arrest people wholesale."

"I'm talking about the possibility that there might be some real guilt, or at any rate a charge against Freddi. Some reason why Göring would consider him dangerous and hold onto him."

"The people who are in the concentration camps aren't those against whom they have criminal charges. The latter are in the prisons, and the Nazis torture them to make them betray their associates; then they shoot them in the back of the neck and cremate them. The men who are in Dachau are Socialist politicians and editors and labor leaders—intellectuals of all the groups that stand for freedom and justice and peace."

"You mean they're there without any charge against them?"

"Exactly that. They've had no trial, and they don't know what they're there for or how long they're going to stay. Two or three thousand of the finest persons in Bavaria—and my guess is that Freddi has done no more than any of the others."

Irma didn't say any more, and her husband knew the reason—she couldn't believe what he said. It was too terrible to be true. All over the world people were saying that, and would go on saying it, to Lanny's great exasperation.

V

The days passed, and it was time for the Munich opening, and still nobody had called to admit a blunder on the part of an infallible governmental machine. Lanny brooded over the problem continually. Did the fat General expect him to go ahead delivering the goods on credit, and without ever presenting any bill? Lanny thought: "He can go to hell! And let it be soon!"

In his annoyance, the Socialist in disguise began thinking about those comrades whom he had met at the school receptions. Rahel had given him addresses, and in his spare hours he had dropped in at place after place, always taking the precaution to park his car some distance away and to make sure that he was not followed. In no single case had he been able to find the persons, or to find anyone who would admit knowing their whereabouts. In most cases people wouldn't even admit having heard of them. They had vanished off the face of the Fatherland. Was he to assume that they were all in prisons or concentration camps? Or had some of them "gone underground"? Once more he debated how he might find his way to that nether region—always being able to get back to the Hotel Adlon in time to receive a message from the second in command of the Nazi government!

Irma went to a *thé dansant* at the American Embassy, and Lanny went to look at some paintings in a near-by palace. But he didn't find anything he cared to recommend to his clients, and the prices seemed high; he didn't feel like dancing, and could be sure that his wife had other partners. His thoughts turned to a serious-minded young "commercial artist" who wore large horn-rimmed spectacles and hated his work—the making of drawings of abnormally slender Aryan ladies wearing lingerie, hosiery, and eccentric millinery. Also Lanny thought about the young man's wife, a consecrated soul, and an art student with a genuine talent. Ludwig and Gertrude Schultz —there was nothing striking about these names, but Ludi and Trudi sounded like a vaudeville team or a comic strip.

Lanny had phoned to the advertising concern and been informed that the young man was no longer employed there. He had called the art school and learned that the former student was no longer studying. In neither place did he hear any tone of cordiality or have any information volunteered. He guessed that if the young people had fled abroad they would surely have sent a message to Bienvenu. If they were "sleeping out" in Germany, what would they be doing? Would they go about only at night, or would they be wearing some sort of disguise? He could be fairly sure they would be living among the workers; for they had never had much money, and without jobs would probably be dependent upon worker comrades.

VI

How to get underground! Lanny could park his car, but he couldn't park his accent and manners and fashionable little brown mustache. And above all, his clothes! He had no old ones; and if he bought some in a secondhand place, how would he look going into a de luxe hotel? For him to become a slum-dweller would be almost as hard as for a slum-dweller to become a millionaire playboy.

He drove past the building where the workers' school had been. There was now a big swastika banner hanging from a pole over the door; the Nazis had taken it for a district headquarters. No information to be got there! So Lanny drove on to the neighborhood where the Schultzes had lived. Six-story tenements, the least "slummy" workingclass quarter he had seen in Europe. The people still stayed indoors as much as they could. Frost had come, and the window-boxes with the flowers had been taken inside.

He drove past the house in which he had visited the Schultzes. Nothing to distinguish it from any other house, except the number. He drove round the block and came again, and on a sudden impulse stopped his car and got out and rang the *Pförtner's* bell. He had already made one attempt to get something here, but perhaps he hadn't tried hard enough.

This time he begged permission to come in and talk to the janitor's wife, and it was grudgingly granted. Seated on a wooden stool in a kitchen very clean, but with a strong smell of pork and cabbage, he laid himself out to make friends with a suspicious woman of the people. He explained that he was an American art dealer who had met an artist of talent and had taken some of her work and sold it, and now he owed her money and was troubled because he was unable to find her. He knew that Trudi Schultz had been an active Socialist, and perhaps for that reason did not wish to be known; but he was an entirely non-political person, and neither Trudi nor her friends had anything to fear from him. He applied what psychology he possessed in an effort to win the woman's confidence, but it was in vain. She didn't know where the Schultzes had gone; she didn't know anybody who might know. The apartment was now occupied by a laborer with a family of several children. "*Nein*," and then again "*Nein, mein Herr.*"

Lanny gave up, and heard the door of the *Pförtnerin* close behind him. Then he saw coming down the stairway of the tenement a girl of eight or ten, in a much patched dress and a black woolen shawl about her head and shoulders. On an impulse he said, quickly: "*Bitte, wo wohnt Frau Trudi Schultz?*"

The child halted and stared. She had large dark eyes and a pale undernourished face; he thought she was Jewish, and perhaps that accounted for her startled look. Or perhaps it was because she had never seen his kind of person in or near her home. "I am an old friend of Frau Schultz," he continued, following up his attack.

"I don't know where she lives," murmured the child.

"Can you think of anybody who would know? I owe her some money and she would be glad to have it." He added, on an inspiration: "I am a comrade."

"I know where she goes," replied the little one. "It is the tailorshop of Aronson, down that way, in the next block."

"*Danke schön*," said Lanny, and put a small coin into the frail hand of the hungry-looking little one.

He left his car where it stood and found the tailorshop, which had a sign in Yiddish as well as German. He walked by on the other side of the street, and again regretted his clothes, so conspicuous in this neighborhood. "Aronson" would probably be a Socialist; but maybe he wasn't, and for Lanny to stroll in and ask for Trudi might set going some train of events which he could not imagine. On the other hand, he couldn't walk up and down in front of the place without being noticed—and those inside the shop no doubt had reasons for keeping watch.

What he did was to walk down to the corner and buy a *Bonbon-Tüte* and come back and sit on a step across the street from the shop but farther on so that he was partly hidden by a railing. Sitting down made him less tall, and holding a bag of candy and nibbling it certainly made him less fashionable. Also it made him interesting to three children of the tenement; when he shared his treasure, which they called *Bom-bom*, they were glad to have him there, and when he asked their names, where they went to school, what games they played, they made shy answers. Meanwhile he kept his eyes on the door of Aronson's tailorshop.

Presently he ventured to ask his three proletarian friends if they knew Trudi Schultz. They had never heard of her, and he wondered if he was on a wild-goose chase. Perhaps it would be more sensible to go away and write a note; not giving his name, just a hint: "The friend who sold your drawings in Paris." He would add: "Take a walk in front of the enormous white marble Karl der Dicke (the Stout), in the Siegesallée at twenty-two o'clock Sunday." With one-third of his mind he debated this program, with another he distributed *Leckereien* to a growing throng, and with the remaining third he watched the door of *"Aronson: Schneiderei, Reparatur."*

VII

The door opened suddenly, and there stepped forth a young woman carrying a large paper bundle. Lanny's heart gave a jump, and he handed the almost empty *Tüte* to one of his little friends, and started in the same direction as the woman. She was slender, not so tall as Lanny, and dressed in a poor-looking, badly-faded brown coat, with a shawl over her head and shoulders. He couldn't see her hair, and being somewhat behind her he couldn't see her face, but he thought he knew her walk. He followed for a block or so, then crossed over and came up behind her and to her side. Her face was paler and thinner than when he had last seen her; she appeared an older woman; but there was no mistaking the finely chiseled, sensitive features, which had so impressed him as revealing intelligence and character. *"Wie geht's, Trudi?"* he said.

She started violently, then glanced at him; one glance, and she turned her face to the front and walked steadily on. "I am sorry, *mein Herr*. You are making a mistake."

"But Trudi!" he exclaimed. "I am Lanny Budd."

"My name is not Trudi and I do not know you, sir."

If Lanny had had any doubt as to her face, he would have been sure of her voice. It had rather deep tones, and gave an impression of intense feelings which the calm features seemed trying to repress. Of course it was Trudi Schultz. But she didn't want to know him, or be known.

It was the first time Lanny had met a Socialist since he set out to save the Robin family. He had kept away from them on purpose; Rick had warned him what he might be doing to his own reputation, and now here he saw it! He walked by this devoted comrade's side, and spoke quickly—for she might come to her destination and slam a door in his face, or turn away and forbid him to follow her. "Trudi, please hear what I have to say. I came to Germany to try to save the Robins. First I got Johannes out of jail, and I took him and his wife with Rahel and the baby, out to France. Now I have come back to try to find Freddi and get him free."

"You are mistaken, sir," repeated the young woman. "I am not the person you think."

"You must understand that I have had to deal with people in authority here, and I couldn't do it unless I took an attitude acceptable to them. I have no right to speak of that, but I know I can trust you, and you ought to trust me, because I may need your help—I am a long way from succeeding with poor Freddi. I have tried my best to find some of his old friends, but I can't get a contact anywhere. Surely you must realize that I wouldn't be dropping my own affairs and coming here unless I was loyal to him and to his cause. I have to trust somebody, and I put you on your honor not to mention what I am telling you. I have just learned that Freddi is in Dachau——"

She stopped in her tracks and gasped: "In *Dachau!*"

"He has been there for several months."

"How do you know it?"

"I am not free to say. But I am fairly certain."

She started to walk again, but he thought she was unsteady on her feet. "It means so much to me," she said, "because Ludi and Freddi were arrested together."

"I didn't know that Ludi had been arrested. What has happened to him?"

"I have heard nothing from him or concerning him since the Nazis came and dragged them both away from our home."

"What was Freddi doing there?"

"He came because he had been taken ill, and had to have some place to lie down. I knew it was dangerous for him, but I couldn't send him away."

"The Nazis were looking for Ludi?"

"We had gone into hiding and were doing illegal work. I happened to be away from home at the time and a neighbor warned me. The Nazis tore everything in the place to pieces, as if they were maniacs. Why do you suppose they took Freddi to Dachau?"

"It's a long story. Freddi is a special case, on account of being a Jew, and a rich man's son."

It seemed to Lanny that the young woman was weak, perhaps from this shock, perhaps from worry and fear, and not getting enough to eat. He couldn't suggest that they sit on some step, because it would make them conspicuous. He said: "Let me carry that bundle."

"No, no," she replied. "It's all right."

But he knew that it wasn't, and in the land of his forefathers men did not let women carry the loads. He said: "I insist," and thought that he was being polite when he took it out of her arms.

Then right away he saw why she hadn't wanted him to have it. It was wrapped like a bundle of clothing, and was soft like such a bundle, but its weight was beyond that of any clothing ever made. He tried to guess: did the bundle contain arms of some sort, or was it what the comrades called "literature"? The latter was more in accord with Trudi's nature, but Irma had pointed out that one couldn't count upon that. A small quantity of weapons might weigh the same as a larger quantity of printed matter. Both would be equally dangerous in these times; and here was Lanny with an armful of either or both!

VIII

They must keep on walking and keep on talking. He asked: "How far do you have to go?"

"Many blocks."

"I have a car, and I could get it and drive you."

"A car must not stop there, nor can I let you go to the place."

"But we ought to have a talk. Will you let Irma and me meet you somewhere and take you for a drive? That way we can talk safely."

She walked for a space without speaking. Then she said: "Your wife is not sympathetic to our ideas, Genosse Budd."

"She does not agree with us altogether," he admitted; "but she is loyal to me and to the Robins."

"Nobody will be loyal in a time like this except those who believe in the class struggle." They walked again in silence; then the young artist continued: "It is hard for me to say, but it is not only my life that is at stake, but that of others to whom I am pledged. I would be bound to tell them the situation, and I know they would not consent for me to meet your wife, or to let her know about our affairs."

He was a bit shocked to discover what the comrades had been thinking about his marriage; but he couldn't deny Trudi's right to decide this matter. "All right," he said. "I won't mention you, and don't you mention me. There might be a spy among your group, I suppose."

"It's not very likely, because our enemies don't wait long when they get information. They are efficient, and take no chances. It is dangerous for you to be walking with me.'"

"I doubt if it could make serious trouble for an American; but it might cost me my chance to save Freddi if it became known that I was in touch with Socialists."

"It is certainly unwise for us to meet."

"It depends upon what may happen. How can we find each other in case of need?"

"It would not do for you to come where I am. If I need to see you, I'll send you an unsigned note. I read in the papers that you were staying at the Adlon."

"Yes, but I'm leaving tomorrow or the next day for Munich, where I'll be at the Vier Jahreszeiten. Letters will be forwarded, however."

"Tell me, Genosse Lanny," she exclaimed, in a tense voice; "do you suppose there could be any chance for you to find if Ludi is in Dachau?"

"I can't think of any way now; but something might turn up. I must have some way to get word to you."

"Notice this corner ahead of us; remember it, and if you have any news for me, walk by here on Sunday, exactly at noon. I'll be watching for you, and I'll follow you to your car. But don't come unless you have something urgent."

"You mean that you will come to this corner every Sunday?"

"So long as there's any chance of your coming. When you leave Germany, I can write you to Juan-les-Pins."

"All right," he said; and then, as a sudden thought came to him: "Do you need money?"

"I'm getting along all right."

But he knew that propagandists can always use money. He didn't take out his billfold, that being a conspicuous action; he reached under his coat, and worked several bills into a roll, and slipped them into the pocket of that well-worn brown coat. He was becoming expert in the art of distributing illicit funds. What he gave her would be a fortune for Social-Democrats, underground or above. He would leave it for her to explain how she had got it.

When he returned to the hotel, Irma said: "Well! You must have found some paintings that interested you!"

He answered: "A couple of Menzels that I think are worth Zoltan's looking at. But the works by the Maris brothers were rather a disappointment."

IX

The period of the Detaze show in Berlin corresponded with an election campaign throughout the German Reich; assuredly the strangest election campaign since that contrivance had been born of the human brain. Hitler had wiped out all other political parties, and all the legislative bodies of the twenty-two German states; by his methods of murder and imprisonment he had destroyed democracy and representative government, religious toleration and all civil rights; but being still the victim of a "legality complex," he insisted upon having the German people endorse what he had done. A vote to say that votes had no meaning! A Reichstag to declare that a Reichstag was without power! A completely democratic repudiation of democracy! Lanny thought: "Has there ever been such a madman since the world began? Has it ever before happened that a whole nation has gone mad?"

Living in the midst of this enormous institute of lunacy, Lanny Budd tried to keep his balance and not be permanently stood upon his head. If there was anything he couldn't comprehend, his Nazi friends were eager to explain it, but there wasn't a single German from whom he could hear a sane word. Even Hugo Behr and his friends who were planning the "Second Revolution" were all loyal Hitlerites, co-operating in what they considered a sublime demonstration of patriotic fervor. Even the members of smart society dared give no greater sign of rationality than a slight smile, or the flicker of an eyelash so faint that you couldn't be sure if you had seen it. The danger was real, even to important persons. Only a few days later they would see Herzog Philip Albert of Württemberg imprisoned for failing to cast his vote in this sublime national referendum.

Hitler had raised the issue in the middle of October when the British at Geneva had dared to propose a four years' "trial period" before permitting Germany to rearm. The Führer's reply was to withdraw the German delegates from both the League of Nations and the Conference for Arms Limitation. In so doing he issued to the German people one of those eloquent manifestoes which he delighted to compose; he told them how much he loved peace and how eager he was to disarm when the other nations would do the same. He talked to them about "honor"—he, the author of *Mein Kampf*—and they believed him, thus proving that they were exactly what he had said they were. He proclaimed that what the German people wanted was "equal rights"; and, having just deprived them of all rights, he put to them in the name of the government this solemn question:

"Does the German people accept the policy of its National Cabinet as enunciated here and is it willing to declare this to be the expression of its own view and its own will and to give it holy support?"

Such was the "referendum" to be voted on a month later. In addition, there was to be a new Reichstag election, with only one slate of candidates, 686 of them, all selected by the Führer, and headed by the leading Nazis: Hitler, Göring, Goebbels, Hess, Röhm, and so on. One party, one list—and one circle in which you could mark your cross to indicate "yes." There was no place for you to vote "no," and blank ballots were declared invalid.

For that sort of "election" the Fatherland was kept in a turmoil for four weeks, and more money was spent than had ever been spent by all the forty-five parties in any previous Reichstag election. The shows and spectacles, the marching and singing, the carrying of the "blood banners," the ceremonies in honor of the Nazi martyrs; the posters and proclamations, the torchlight processions, the standing at attention and saluting, the radio orations with the people assembled in the public squares to listen to loud-speakers—and a few sent to concentration camps for failing to listen. Hitherto the business of standing silent had been reserved as an honor for the war dead; but now all over Germany the traffic came to a halt and people stood in silence with bared heads; all the factories ceased work and thirty million workers stood to listen to the voice of Adolf Hitler, speaking in the dynamo hall of the enormous Siemens-Schuckert Electrical Works in Berlin. Afterward they stayed and worked an hour overtime, so that they and not their employers might have the honor and glory of making a sacrifice for the Fatherland!

X

On a bright and pleasant Sunday in mid-November, great masses of the German *Volk* lined up in front of polling-places all over the land, and even in foreign lands, and in ships upon the high seas. They voted in prisons and even in concentration camps. Late in the day the Stormtroopers rounded up the lazy and careless ones; and so more than forty-three million ballots were cast, and more than ninety-five per cent voted for the Hitler Reichstag and for the solemn referendum in favor of their own peace and freedom. Irma read about it, the next day and the days thereafter, and was tremendously impressed. She said: "You see, Lanny, the Germans really believe in Hitler. He is what they want." When she read that the internees of Dachau had voted twenty to one for the man who had shut them up there, she said: "That seems to show that things can't be so very bad."

The husband replied: "It seems to me to show that they are a lot worse."

But he knew there was no use trying to explain that. It would only mean an argument. He was learning to keep his unhappiness locked up in his soul. His wife was having a very good time in Berlin, meeting brilliant and distinguished personalities; and Lanny was going about tormenting himself over the activities and the probable fates of a little group of secret conspirators in a Berlin slum!

He could guess pretty well what they were doing; he imagined a small hand-press in the back of the tailor shop, and they were printing leaflets, perhaps about the *Brown Book* and its revelations concerning the Reichstag fire, perhaps quoting opinions of the outside world, so as to keep up the courage of the comrades in a time of dreadful anguish. Probably Trudi was carrying some of this "literature" to others who would see to its distribution. All of them were working in hourly peril of their lives; and Lanny thought: "I ought to be helping them; I am the one who could really accomplish something, because I could get money, and bring them information from outside, and carry messages to their comrades in France and England."

But then he would think: "If I did that, I'd ruin the happiness of my mother and my wife and most of my friends. In the end I'd probably wreck my marriage."

24

Die Juden Sind Schuld

I

A PLEASANT thing to leave the flat windy plain of Prussia at the beginning of winter and motor into the forests and snug valleys of South Germany. Pleasant to arrive in a beautiful and comparatively modern city and to find a warm welcome awaiting you in an establishment called the "Four Seasons of the Year" so as to let you know that it was always ready. Munich was a "Four Seasons of the Year" city; its life was a series of festivals, and the drinking of beer out of *Masskrügen* was a civic duty.

The devoted Zoltan had come in advance and made all arrangements for the show. The Herr Privatdozent Doktor der Philosophie Aloysius Winckler zu Sturmschatten had applied his arts, and the intellectuals of Munich were informed as to the merits of the new school of representational painting; also the social brilliance of the young couple who were conferring this bounty upon them.

In the morning came the reporters by appointment. They had been provided with extracts from what the Berlin press had said about Detaze, and with information as to the Barnes fortune and the importance of Budd Gunmakers; also the fact that Lanny had been on a shooting trip with General Göring and had once had tea with the Führer. The young couple exhibited that affability which is expected from the land of cowboys and movies. Lanny said yes, he knew Munich very well; he had purchased several old masters here— he named them, and told in what new world collections they had found havens. He had happened to be in the city on a certain historic day ten years ago and had witnessed scenes which would make the name of Munich forever famous. Flashlight bulbs went off while he talked, reminding him of those scenes on the Marienplatz when the Nazi martyrs had been shot down.

The interviews appeared in due course, and when the exhibition opened on the following afternoon the crowds came. An old story now, but the people were new, and those who love greatness and glory never tire of meeting Herzog und Herzogin Überall und Prinz und Prinzessin Undsoweiter. A great thing for art when ladies of the highest social position take their stand in a public gallery to pay tribute to genius, even though dead. While Parsifal Dingle went off to ask the spirit of the dead painter if he was pleased with the show, and while Lanny went to inspect older masters and dicker over prices, Beauty Budd and her incomparable daughter-in-law were introduced to important personages, accepted invitations to

lunches and dinners, and collected anecdotes which they would retail to their spouses and later to their relatives and friends.

There was only one thing wrong between this pair; the fact that
Marcel Detaze had died when Irma was a child and had never had
an opportunity to paint a picture of her. Thus Beauty got more
than her proper share of glory, and there was no way to redistribute
it. The mother-in-law would be humble, and try not to talk about
herself and her portraits while Irma was standing by; but others
would insist upon doing so, and it was a dangerous situation. Beauty
said to her son: "Who is the best portrait painter living?"

"Why?" he asked, surprised.

"Because, you ought to have him do Irma right away. It would
be a sensation, and help to keep her interested in art."

"Too bad that Sargent is gone!" chuckled Lanny.

"Don't make a joke of it," insisted the mother. "It's quite inex-
cusable that the crowds should come and look at pictures of a faded
old woman who doesn't matter, instead of one in the prime of her
beauty."

"Art is long and complexions are fleeting," said the incorrigible
one.

II

A far greater event than the Detaze exhibition came to Munich,
causing the city to break out with flags. The Reichskanzler, the
Führer of the N.S.D.A.P., had been motoring and flying all over his
land making campaign speeches. After his overwhelming triumph
he had sought his mountain retreat, to brood and ponder new policies; and now, refreshed and reinspired, he came to his favorite city,
the one in which his movement had been built and his crown of mar-
tyrdom won. Here he had been a poor *Schlawiner*, as they called a
man whose means of subsistence they did not know, a *Wand- und
Landstreicher*, who made wild, half-crazy speeches, and people went
to hear him because it was a *Gaudi*, or what you would call in English a "lark." Munich had seen him wandering about town looking
very depressed, uncouth in his rusty worn raincoat, carrying an

oversize dogwhip because of his fear of enemies, who, however, paid no attention to him.

But now he had triumphed over them all. Now he was the master of Germany, and Munich celebrated his arrival with banners. Here in the Braune Haus he had the main headquarters of the party; a splendid building which Adolf himself had remodeled and decorated according to his own taste. He, the frustrated architect, had made something so fine that his followers were exalted when they entered the place, and took fresh vows of loyalty to their leader and his all-conquering dream.

Mabel Blackless, alias Beauty Budd, alias Madame Detaze, had done some conquering in her time, and was still capable of dreams. "Oh, Lanny!" she exclaimed. "Do you suppose you could get him to come to the exhibition? It would be worth a million dollars to us!"

"It's certainly worth thinking about," conceded the son.

"Don't delay! Telephone Heinrich Jung and ask him to come. Pay him whatever he wants, and we'll all stand our share."

"He won't want much. He's not a greedy person."

The young Nazi official was staggered by the proposal. He feared it was something far, far beyond his powers. But Lanny urged him to rise to a great occasion. He had worked hard through the electoral campaign and surely was entitled to a few days' vacation. What better way to spend it than to pay his compliments to his Führer, and take him to see some paintings of the special sort which he approved?

"You can bring them to him if he prefers," said Lanny. "We'll close the show for a day and pick out the best and take them wherever he wishes." He spoke with eagerness, having another scheme up his sleeve; he wasn't thinking merely about enhancing the prices of his family property. "If you can get off right away, take a plane. There's no time to be lost."

"*Herrgott!*" exclaimed the ex-forester. He was in heaven.

Then Lanny put in a long distance call to Kurt Meissner in Stubendorf. Kurt had refused an invitation to Berlin because he couldn't afford the luxury and wasn't willing to be put under obligations. But now Lanny could say: "This is a business matter. You will be doing us a service, and also one for the Führer. You can play your new compositions for him, and that will surely be important for your career. Heinrich is coming, and we'll paint the town brown." He supposed that was the proper National Socialist formula!

Irma took the phone and added: "Come on, Kurt. It will be so good for Lanny. I want him to understand your movement and learn to behave himself." Impossible for an apostle and propagandist to resist such a call. Irma added: "Take a plane from Breslau if that's quicker. We'll have a room reserved for you."

III

Somewhat of an adventure for Beauty Budd. Six years had passed since Kurt had departed from Bienvenu and had failed to return. He had found himself a wife, and she a husband, and now they would meet as old friends, glad to see each other, but with carefully measured cordiality; their memories would be like Marcel's paintings hanging on the walls—but not for public showing.

Parsifal Dingle was here, and he had heard much talk about the wonderful German composer who had lived for so long with the Budds. He hadn't been told that Kurt had been Beauty's lover for eight years, but he couldn't very well have failed to guess. He never asked questions, that being contrary to his philosophy. A wise and discreet gentleman with graying hair, he had found himself an exceptionally comfortable nest and fitted himself into it carefully, taking up no more than his proper share of room. He cultivated his own soul, enjoyed the process, and asked nothing more of life. If a German musician who had read Hegel, Fichte, and others of his country's philosophers wished to ask questions about the inner life, Parsifal would be glad to answer; otherwise he would listen to Kurt play the piano in their suite and give his own meanings to the music.

Friendship to Lanny Budd had always been one of life's precious gifts. Now he was happy to be with Kurt and Heinrich again; yet he was torn in half, because he wasn't really with them, he was lying to them. How strange to be using affection as a camouflage; feeling sympathy and oneness, yet not really feeling it, working against it all the time! Lanny's friendship was for Freddi, and Freddi and these two were enemies. With a strange sort of split personality, Lanny loved all three; his friendship for Kurt and Heinrich was still a living thing, and in his feelings he went back to the old days in Stubendorf, twelve years ago, when he had first met the Oberförster's son. To be sure, Heinrich had been a Nazi even then, but Lanny hadn't realized what a Nazi was, nor for that matter had Heinrich realized it. It had been a vision of German progress, a spiritual thing, constructive and not destructive, a gain for the German *Volk* without any loss for Jews or Socialists or democrats or pacifists—all those whom the Nazis now had in their places of torture.

The three talked about old times and were at one. They talked about Kurt's music, and were still at one. But then Heinrich fell to talking about his work, and recent developments in party and national affairs, and at once Lanny had to start lying. It wasn't enough just to keep still, as he had done earlier; no, when the young party official went into ecstasies over that marvelous electoral victory, Lanny had to echo: *"Herrlich!"* When Kurt declared that the Führer's stand for peace and equality among the nations was a great act of statesmanship, Lanny had to say: *"Es hat was heroisches."* And all the time in his soul he wondered: "Which of us is crazy?"

No easy matter to stick to the conviction that your point of view is right and that all the people about you are wrong. That is the way not merely with pioneers of thought, with heroes, saints, and martyrs, but also with lunatics and "nuts," of whom there are millions in the world. When one of these "nuts" succeeds in persuading the greater part of a great nation that he is right, the five per cent have to stop and ask themselves: "How come?" Particularly is this true of one like Lanny Budd, who was no pioneer, hero, or saint, and surely didn't want to be a martyr. All he wanted was that his friends shouldn't quarrel and make it necessary for him to choose between them. Kurt and Rick had been quarreling since July 1914, and Lanny had been trying to make peace. Never had he seemed less successful than now, while trying to act as a secret agent for Rick, Freddi, and General Göring all at the same time!

They talked over the problem of approaching the Chancellor of Germany, and agreed that Kurt was the one to do it, he being the elder, and the only one with a claim to greatness. Kurt called the Führer's secretary at the Braune Haus, and said that he wished not merely to play the piano for his beloved leader, but to bring the Führer's old friend, Heinrich Jung, and the young American, Lanny Budd, who had visited the Führer in Berlin several years ago. Lanny would bring a sample of the paintings of Marcel Detaze, who was then having a one-man exhibition and had been highly praised in the press. The secretary promised to put the matter before the Chancellor in person, and the Komponist stated where he could be reached. Needless to say, it added to his importance that he was staying at the most fashionable of Munich's hotels, with its fancy name, "The Four Seasons."

IV

Irma invited Kurt into her boudoir for a private chat. She was in a conspiracy with him against her husband—for her husband's own good, of course; and Kurt, who had had professional training in intrigue, was amused by this situation. A sensible young wife, and it might be the saving of Lanny if he could be persuaded to follow her advice. Irma explained that Lanny had been behaving rationally on this trip, and was doing very well with his picture business, which seemed to interest him more than anything else; but he still had Freddi on his conscience, and was convinced that Freddi was innocent of any offense. "I can't get him to talk about it," said Irma, "but I think somebody has told him that Freddi is a prisoner in a concentration camp. It has become a sort of obsession with him."

"He is loyal to his friends," said the Komponist, "and that's a fine quality. He has, of course, no real understanding of what the Jews have done to Germany, the corrupting influence they have been in our national life."

"What I'm afraid of," explained Irma, "is that he might be tempted to bring up the subject to the Führer. Do you think that would be bad?"

"It might be very unfortunate for me. If the Führer thought that I had brought Lanny for that purpose, it might make it impossible for me ever to see him again."

"That's what I feared; and perhaps it would be wise if you talked to Lanny about it and warned him not to do it. Of course don't tell him that I spoke to you on the subject."

"Naturally not. You may always rely on my discretion. It will be easy for me to bring up the subject, because Lanny spoke to me about Freddi in Stubendorf."

So it came about that Lanny had a talk with Kurt without being under the necessity of starting it and having Kurt think that that was why he had been invited to Munich. Lanny assured his old friend that he had no idea of approaching the Führer about the matter; he realized that it would be a grave breach of propriety. But Lanny couldn't help being worried about his Jewish friend, and Kurt ought to be worried too, having played so many duets with him and knowing what a fine and sensitive musician he was. Lanny said: "I have met one of Freddi's old associates, and I know that he is under arrest. I could never respect myself if I didn't try to do something to aid him."

Thus the two resumed their old intimacy; Kurt, one year or so the elder, still acting as mentor, and Lanny, the humble and diffident, taking the role of pupil. Kurt explained the depraved and antisocial nature of *Juda*, and Lanny let himself be convinced. Kurt explained the basic fallacies of Social-Democracy, one of the Jewish perversions of thought, and how it had let itself be used as a front for Bolshevism—even when, as in the case of Freddi, its devotees were ignorant of what base purposes they were serving. Lanny listened attentively, and became more and more acquiescent, and Kurt became correspondingly affectionate in his mood. At the end of the conversation Kurt promised that if they had the good fortune to be received by the Führer, he would study the great man's moods, and if it could be done without giving offense, he would bring up the subject of Lanny's near-relative and ask the Führer to do the favor of ordering his release, upon Lanny's promise to take him out of Germany and see to it that he didn't write or speak against the Fatherland.

"But don't you bring up the subject," warned Kurt. Lanny promised solemnly that he wouldn't dream of committing such a breach of propriety.

V

They waited in the hotel until the message came. The Führer would be pleased to see them at the Braune Haus next morning; and be sure they would be on hand!

It proved to be one of those early winter days when the sun is bright and the air intoxicating, and they would have liked to walk to the appointment; but they were taking the picture, *Sister of Mercy*, so Lanny would drive them. Heinrich, who had learned as a youth to labor with his hands, offered to carry the burden into the Braune Haus, but Beauty insisted that things had to be done with propriety, by a uniformed attendant from the hotel. She herself called up the management to arrange matters, and they fell over themselves to oblige. No charge, Frau Budd, and a separate car if you wish—what hotel in all Germany would not be honored to transport a picture to the Führer? The word spread like wildfire through the establishment, and the three young men were the cynosure of all eyes. The Führer, they learned, had been a familiar figure in this fashionable hotel; for many years he had been entertained here by two of his wealthy supporters, one of them a piano manufacturer and the other a Prussian *Graf* whose wife was conspicuous because of her extreme friendliness with the bellhops. Irma knew all about this, for the reason that she was practicing her German on one of the women employees of the establishment. One would never lack for gossip in a *grand hôtel* of Europe!

The Braune Haus is on the Briennerstrasse, celebrated as one of the most beautiful streets in Germany; a neighborhood reserved for millionaires, princes, and great dignitaries of state and church. In fact, the palace of the Papal Nuncio was directly across the street, and so the representatives of the two rival faiths of Munich could keep watch upon each other from their windows. The princely delegate of the lowly Jewish carpenter looked across to a square-fronted three-story building set far back from the street and protected by high fences; on top of it a large swastika flag waved in the breeze which blew from the snow-clad Alps; in front of its handsome doorway stood day and night two armed Stormtroopers. If the Catholic prelate happened to be on watch that morning he saw a luxurious Mercédès car stop in front of the Nazi building and from it descend a blond and blue-eyed young Nazi official in uniform, a tall Prussian ex-artillery captain with a long and somewhat severe face, and a fashionably attired young American with brown hair and closely trimmed mustache; also a hotel attendant in a gray uniform with brass buttons, carrying a large framed picture wrapped in a cloth.

These four strode up the walk, and all but the burden-bearer gave the Nazi salute. Heinrich's uniform carried authority, and they came into an entrance hall with swastikas, large and small, on the ceiling, the windows, the doorknobs, the lamp-brackets, the grillework. They were a little ahead of time, so Heinrich led them up the imposing stairway and showed them the Senatorensaal, with memorial tablets for the Nazi martyrs outside the doors. Inside were forty standards having bronze eagles, and handsome red leather armchairs for the "senators," whoever they were—they couldn't have met very often, for the Führer gave all the orders. "*Prachtvoll!*" was the comment of Heinrich and Kurt. Lanny had the traitor thought: "This came out of the deal with Thyssen and the other steel kings!"

The offices of Hitler and his staff were on the same floor, and promptly at the appointed hour they were ushered into the simply decorated study of the head Nazi. They gave the salute, and he rose and greeted them cordially. He remembered Lanny and shook hands with him. "*Willkommen, Herr Budd*. How long has it been since we met—more than three years? How time does fly! I don't have a chance to notice it, to say nothing of enjoying it."

Once more Lanny felt that soft moist hand, once more he looked into those gray-blue eyes set in a pale, pasty face, rather pudgy now, for Adi was gaining weight, in spite of or possibly because of his gall-bladder trouble. Looking at him, Lanny thought once more that here was the world's greatest mystery. You might have searched all Europe and not found a more commonplace-appearing man; this Führer of the Fatherland had everything it took to make mediocrity. He was smaller than any of his three guests, and as he was now in a plain business suit with a white collar and black tie, he might have been a grocery assistant or traveling salesman for a hair tonic. He took no exercise, and his figure was soft, his shoulders narrow and hips wide like a woman's. The exponent of Aryan purity was a mongrel if ever there was one; he had straight thick dark hair and wore one lock of it long, as Lanny had done when a boy. Apparently the only thing he tended carefully was that absurd little Charlie Chaplin mustache.

Watching him in his Berlin apartment, Lanny had thought: "It is a dream, and the German people will wake up from it." But now they were more deeply bemused than ever, and Lanny, trying to solve the riddle, decided that here was the *Kleinbürgertum* incarnate, the average German, the little man, the "man in the street." Thwarted and suppressed, millions of such men found their image in Adi Schicklgruber, understood him and believed his promises. The ways in which he differed from them—as in not eating meat and not getting drunk when he could—these made him romantic and inspiring, a great soul.

VI

The hotel attendant was standing in the doorway, with the picture resting on the floor; he steadied it with his left hand while keeping his right arm and hand extended outward and upward in a permanent salute. The Führer noticed him and asked: "What is this you have brought me?"

Lanny told him, and they stood the picture on a chair, with the attendant behind it, out of sight, holding it firmly. Hitler placed himself at a proper distance, and Lanny ceremoniously removed the cover. Then everybody stood motionless and silent while the great man did his looking.

"A beautiful thing!" he exclaimed. "That is my idea of a work of art. A Frenchman, you say? You may be sure that he had German forefathers. Who is the woman?"

"She is my mother," replied Lanny. He had made that statement hundreds of times in his life—Munich being the fifth great city in which he had assisted at an exhibition.

"A beautiful woman. You should be proud of her."

"I am," said Lanny, and added: "It is called *Sister of Mercy*. The painter was badly wounded in the war, and later killed. You can see that he felt what he was painting."

"Ah, yes!" exclaimed Adi. "I too, have been wounded, and know how a soldier feels about the women who nurse him. It would appear that great art comes only by suffering."

"So your Goethe has told us, Herr Reichskanzler."

A silence, while Hitler studied the painting some more. "A pure Aryan type," he commented; "the spiritual type which lends itself to idealization." He looked a while longer, and said: "Pity is one of the Aryan virtues. I doubt if the lesser races are capable of feeling it very deeply."

This went on for quite a while. The Führer looked, and then made a remark, and no one else ventured to speak unless it was a question. "This sort of art tells us that life is full of suffering. It should be the great task of mankind to diminish it as far as possible. You agree with that, Herr Budd?"

"Indeed I do; and I know that it was the leading idea of Marcel's life."

"It is the task of the master race. They alone can fulfill it, because they have both the intelligence and the good will." Lanny was afraid he was going to repeat the question: "You agree with that?" and was trying to figure how to reply without starting an argument. But instead the Führer went on to inform him: "That should be our guiding thought in life. Here in this room we have three of the world's great nationalities represented: the German, the French, the American. What a gain if these nations would unite to guard their Aryan purity and guarantee the reign of law throughout the world! Do you see any hope for that in our time?"

"It is a goal to aim at, Herr Reichskanzler. Each must do what he can."

"You may be sure that I will, Herr Budd. Tell it to everyone you know."

The master of Germany returned to the seat at his desk. "I am obliged to you for bringing me this portrait. I understand that you are having an exhibition?"

"Yes, Herr Reichskanzler; we should be honored if you would attend; or if you prefer, I will bring other samples of the work."

"I wish I could arrange it. Also"—turning to Kurt—"I was hoping to have you come to my apartment, where I have a piano. But I'm afraid I have to leave for Berlin. I was a happier man when I had only a political party to direct; now, alas, I have a government as well, and therefore a lover of music and art is compelled to give all his time and attention to the jealousies and rivalries of small men."

The picture-viewing was over, and the attendant carried it out, backing away and bowing at every step. The Führer turned to Kurt and asked about his music, and lifted a Komponist to the skies by saying that Kurt had rendered a real service to the cause. "We have to show the world that we National Socialists can produce talent and even genius, equal to the best of the past. Science must be brought to reinforce inspiration so that the *Herrenvolk* may ascend to new heights, and, if possible, raise the lesser tribes after them."

He turned to Heinrich. He wanted to hear all that a young official could tell him concerning the Hitler Jugend and its progress. The efficient head of a great organization was getting data about personalities and procedures over which he had control. He asked probing questions, watching the respondent through half-closed eyes. He could be sure that this official was telling him the truth, but it would be colored by the young man's enthusiastic nature. Heinrich was hardly the one to report upon backstairs intrigue and treachery. "I wish I had more young men like you," remarked the Reichskanzler, wistfully.

"You have thousands of them, mein Führer," replied the enraptured ex-forester; "men whom you have never had an opportunity to meet."

"My staff try to shut me up as though I were an oriental despot," said Adi. "They talk to me about physical danger—but I know that it is my destiny to live and complete my work."

VII

It was quite an interview, and Lanny was on pins and needles for fear the great man might rise and say: "I am sorry, but my time is limited." Nobody could imagine anyone in a better humor; and Lanny looked at Kurt, and would have winked at him, only Kurt was keeping his eyes fixed upon his master and guide. Lanny tried telepathy, thinking as hard as he could: "Now! *Now!*"

"Mein Führer," said Kurt, "before we leave there is something which my friend Budd thinks I ought to tell you."

"What is it?"

"A great misfortune, but not his fault. It happens that his half-sister is married into a Jewish family."

"*Donnerwetter!*" exclaimed Adolf. "A shocking piece of news!"

"I should add that the husband is a fine concert violinist."

"We have plenty of Aryan artists, and no need to seek anything from that polluted race. What is the man's name?"

"Hansi Robin."

"Robin? Robin?" repeated Hitler. "Isn't he the son of that notorious *Schieber*, Johannes?"

"Yes, mein Führer."

"She should divorce him." The great man turned upon Lanny. "My young friend, you should not permit such a thing to continue. You should use your authority, you and your father and the other men of the family."

"It happens that the couple are devoted to each other, Herr Reichskanzler; also, she is his accompanist, and is now playing with him in a tour of the United States."

"But, Herr Budd, it is sordid and shameful to admit considerations of worldly convenience in such a matter. Your sister is a Nordic blond like yourself?"

"Even more so."

"Yet she gets upon public platforms and advertises her ignominy! And think of what she is doing to the future, the crime she commits against her children!"

"They have no children, Herr Reichskanzler. They are devoting their lives to art."

"It is none the less an act of racial pollution. Whether she has children or not, she is defiling her own body. Are you not aware that the male seminal fluid is absorbed by the female, and thus her bloodstream is poisoned by the vile Jewish emanations? It is a dreadful thing to contemplate, and if it were a sister of mine, I would rather see her dead before my eyes; in fact, I would strike her dead if I knew she intended to commit such an act of treason to her race."

"I am sorry, Herr Reichskanzler; but in America we leave young women to choose their own mates."

"And what is the result? You have a mongrel race, where every vile and debasing influence operates freely, and every form of degradation, physical, intellectual, and moral, flourishes unhindered. Travel that highway into hell, if you please, but be sure that we Germans are going to preserve our purity of blood, and we are not going to let ourselves be seduced by tricky words about freedom and toleration and humanitarianism and brotherly love and the rest. No Jew-monster is a brother of mine, and if I find one of them attempting to cohabit with an Aryan woman I will crush his skull, even as our Stormtrooper song demands: 'Crush the skulls of the Jewish pack!' Pardon me if I speak plainly, but that has been my life's habit, it is the duty which I have been sent to perform in this world. Have you read *Mein Kampf?*"

"Yes, Herr Reichskanzler."

"You know what I have taught in it: 'The Jew is the great instigator of the destruction of Germany.' They are, as I have called them, 'true devils, with the brain of a monster and not that of a man.' They are the veritable *Untermenschen*. There is a textbook of Hermann Gauch, called *Neue Grundlage der Rassenforschung*, which is now standard in our schools and universities, and which tells with scientific authority the truths about this odious race. Our eminent scientist classifies the mammals into two groups, first the Aryans, and second, non-Aryans, including the rest of the animal kingdom. You have seen that book, by chance?"

"I have heard it discussed, Herr Reichskanzler."

"You do not accept its authority?"

"I am not a scientist, and my acceptance or rejection would carry no weight. I have heard the point raised that Jews must be human beings because they can mate with Aryans and Nordics, but not with non-human animals."

"Dr. Gauch says it has by no means been proved that Jews cannot mate with apes and other simian creatures. I suggest this as an important contribution which German science can make—to mate both male and female Jews with apes, and so demonstrate to the world the facts which we National Socialists have been proclaiming for so many years."

VIII

The master of all Germany had got started on one of his two favorite topics, the other being Bolshevism. Again Lanny observed the phenomenon that an audience of three was as good as three million. The sleepy look went out of the speaker's eyes and they became fixed upon the unfortunate transgressor in a hypnotic stare. The quiet voice rose to a shrill falsetto. Something new appeared in the man, demonic and truly terrifying; the thrust-out finger struck as it were hammer blows upon Lanny's mind. A young American playboy must be made to realize the monstrous nature of the treason he was committing in condoning his sister's defilement of the sacred Aryan blood. Somehow, at once, the evil must be averted; the man who had been commissioned by destiny to save the world must prove his power here and now, by bringing this strayed sheep back into the Nordic fold. "*Gift!*" cried the Führer of the Nazis. "Poison! *Poison!*"

Back in New England, Lanny's Great-Great-Uncle Eli Budd had told him the story of the witch-hunt in early Massachusetts. "Fanaticism is a destroyer of mind," he had said. Here it was in another form—the terrors, the fantasies born of soul torment, the vision of supernatural evil powers plotting the downfall of all that was good and fair in human life. Adi really loved the Germans: their *Gemüt-lichkeit*, their *Treue und Ehre*, their beautiful songs and noble symphonies, their science and art, their culture in its thousand forms. But here was this satanic power, plotting, scheming day and night to destroy it all. *Die Juden sind schuld!*

Yes, literally, the Jews were to blame for everything; Hitler called the roll of their crimes for the ten thousandth time. They had taught revolt to Germany, they had undermined her patriotism and discipline, and in her hour of greatest peril they had stabbed her in the back. The Jews had helped to shackle her by the cruel *Diktat* of Versailles, and then had proceeded to rivet the chains of poverty upon her limbs. They had made the inflation, they had contrived the Dawes Plan, the Young Plan, the systems of interest and reparations slavery; the Jewish bankers in alliance with the Jewish Bolsheviks! They had seduced all German culture—theater, literature, music, journalism. They had sneaked into the professions, the sciences, the schools, and universities—and, as always, they had defiled and degraded whatever they touched. *Die Juden sind unser Unglück!*

This went on for at least half an hour; and never once did anybody else get in a word. The man's tirade poured out so fast that his sentences stumbled over one another; he forgot to finish them, he forgot his grammar, he forgot common decency and used the words of the gutters of Vienna, where he had picked up his ideas. The perspiration stood out on his forehead and his clean white collar began to wilt. In short, he gave the same performance which Lanny had witnessed in the Bürgerbräukeller of Munich more than a decade ago. But that had been a huge beerhall with two or three thousand people, while here it was like being shut up in a small chamber with a hundred-piece orchestra including eight trombones and four bass tubas playing the overture to *The Flying Dutchman*.

Suddenly the orator stopped. He didn't say: "Have I convinced you?" That would have been expressing a doubt, which no heaven-sent evangelist ever admits. He said: "Now, Herr Budd, go and

do your duty. Make one simple rule that I have maintained ever
since I founded this movement—never to speak to a Jew, even over
the telephone." Then, abruptly: "I have other engagements and
have to be excused."

The three quickly said their adieus; and when they were outside,
Lanny, in his role of secret agent, remarked: "No one can wonder
that he stirs his audiences."

When he was back in the hotel with his wife and mother, he exclaimed: "Well, I know now why Göring is keeping Freddi."

"Why?" they asked, with much excitement.

Lanny answered, in a cold fury: "He is going to breed him with
a female ape!"

IX

Lanny had to play out the game according to the rules. He must
not let either of these friends discover that he had brought them
here solely in the hope of persuading Hitler to release a Jewish
prisoner. It was for friendship, for sociability, for music and art.
Lanny and Kurt must play piano duets as in the old days. Zoltan
must take them through the two Pinakotheks and give them the
benefit of his art knowledge. Beauty and Irma must put on their
best togs and accompany them to the Hof-und-National Theater
for *Die Meistersinger*, and to the Prinz-Regenten Theater for
Goethe's *Egmont*. There must be a dinner at which distinguished
personalities in the musical world were invited to meet a leading
Komponist. After a symphony concert in the Tonhalle, Lanny
listened to Kurt's highly technical comments on the conductor
and the sounds produced. The tone was hard, cold, and brilliant;
it lacked "body," by which Kurt explained that he meant a just
proportion of low and middle to high registers. He accused the
too-ardent Kapellmeister of exaggerating his nuances, of expanding
and contracting his volume unduly, fussing over his orchestra like
an old hen with a too-large brood of chicks—certainly an undignified procedure, and by no means suitable to the rendition of Beethoven's *Eroica*.

But to Lanny it seemed more important to try to understand what the composer of that noble symphony was trying to tell him than to worry about details of somebody's rendition. The last time Lanny had heard this work had been with the Robin family in Berlin, and he recalled Freddi's gentle raptures. Freddi wasn't one of those musicians who have heard so much music that they have got tired of it, and can think about nothing but technicalities and personalities and other extraneous matters. Freddi loved Beethoven as if he had been the composer's son; but now father and son had been torn apart. Freddi wasn't fit to play Beethoven, by Heinrich's decree, because he was a Jew; and certainly he wasn't having any chance to hear Beethoven in Dachau. Lanny could think of little else, and the symphony became an appeal to the great master for a verdict against those who were usurping his influence and his name.

In Beethoven's works there is generally a forceful theme that tramples and thunders, and a gentle theme that lilts and pleads. You may take it as pleading for mercy and love against the cruelties and oppressions of the world. You may take it that the grim, dominating theme represents these cruelties, or perhaps it represents that which rises in your own soul to oppose them. Anyhow, to Lanny the opening melody of the *Eroica* became the "Freddi theme," and Beethoven was defending it against the hateful Nazis. The great democrat of old Vienna came into the Tonhalle of Munich and laid his hand on Lanny's burning forehead, and told him that he was right, and that he and his Jewish friend were free to march with Beethoven on the battlefields of the soul and to dance with him on the happy meadows.

Was it conceivable that Beethoven would have failed to despise the Nazis, and to defy them? He had dedicated his symphony to Napoleon because he believed that Napoleon represented the liberating forces of the French revolution, and he had torn up the title page of his score when he learned that Napoleon had got himself crowned Emperor of France. He had adopted Schiller's *Hymn to Joy*, sending a kiss to the whole world and proclaiming that all men became brothers where the gentle wing of joy came to rest. Very certainly he had not meant to exclude the Jews from the human race, and would have spurned those who built their movement out of hate.

That was what this urgent music was about; that was what gave it drive and intensity. The soul of Beethoven was defending itself, it was defending all things German from those who would defile them. The "Freddi theme" pleaded, it stormed and raged, heaving itself in mighty efforts as the kettledrums thundered. The young idealist had told his friends that he wasn't sure if he had within him the moral strength to withstand his foes; but here in this symphony he was finding it; here he would prevail, and rejoice— but then would come the rushing hordes and bowl him over and trample him. When the first movement came to its tremendous climax Lanny's hands were tightly clenched and perspiration stood on his forehead.

The poignant, majestic march was Beethoven walking through the Nazi concentration camps—as Lanny had walked so many times in imagination. It was the grief and suffering of fifty or a hundred thousand of the finest and best-trained minds of Germany. It was Beethoven mourning with them, telling them that the blackest tragedy can be turned to beauty by the infinite powers of the soul. The *finale* of the symphony was a victory—but that was a long way off, and Lanny couldn't imagine how it would come; he could only cling to the hand of the great master like a little child to its father.

After hearing this concert Lanny had to face the fact that his love for Kurt and Heinrich had come to an end. He found it hard to be polite to his old friends; and he decided that being a spy, or secret agent, or whatever you chose to call it, was first and foremost a damnable bore. The greatest of all privileges in this life is saying what you think; and your friends have to be people who can at least give decent consideration to your ideas. Lanny was glad when he got Kurt and Heinrich on their separate trains for home. He thanked them for what they had done, assured them that it had been worth while, and thought: "I am going to get Freddi out of this hell, and then get myself out and stay out."

X

For a week Lanny had been living in close proximity to that mass of human misery known as Dachau; he had pretended to be indifferent to it, and had spoken of it only when he and Irma were alone in their car. Dachau is a small market-town nine miles northwest of the city, and a well-paved highway leads to it. Inevitably their thoughts had turned there, and the car had taken them at the first opportunity. They didn't, like most tourists, inspect the castle on the height; they looked for the concentration camp, which wasn't hard to find, as it occupied a square mile of ground. It had been a World War barracks and training camp, disused since the peace. A concrete wall seven feet high ran around it, having on top a tangle of barbed wire, no doubt electrically charged. Lanny thought about somebody trying to climb that wall; it seemed less possible when he came at night, and saw a blaze of white searchlights mounted in towers, moving continually along the walls.

The report, published in the newspapers, that the Führer had seen the *Sister of Mercy*, filled thousands of Bavarians with a desire to see it, and accordingly it was decided to continue the exhibition another week. But Lanny was tired of telling people about it, and tired of what they said; in fact, he was tired of what everybody said in Nazi Germany. If they said it because they wanted to, he hated them; if they said it because they had to, he was sorry for them; but in neither case could he be interested.

Deciding to take the bull by the horns, he picked out a sunshiny morning when the inmates of Dachau might be outdoors—those who were allowed out. He put in his pocket a newspaper clipping about the Führer having viewed and approved the Detaze painting; also a few of the interviews with himself and Irma, containing his portrait, and mention of his having been a guest of Göring. These ought to be equivalent to a ticket of admission to any place in Naziland. Leaving Irma to do some shopping, he drove out the Dachau road, and instead of parking his car like a humble nobody, drove to the main gates and announced his desire to see the Kommandant.

They looked at his car, they looked at his clothes and his Aryan face, and at the engraved card which he gave them. "Mr. Lanning Prescott Budd" might be somebody so important that he didn't bother to put his titles and honors on his card, as was the German custom. They let him through the steel gates, and two Storm-troopers stood guard while a third took his card to the office. In front of him was a drill ground, and at one side a clatter of hammers; they were putting up new buildings, doubtless with the labor of prisoners. Stormtroopers were everywhere, all with their rubber truncheons and automatics; there were now half a million of these fighting men for whom jobs had to be provided.

XI

The Kommandant consented to see Herr Budd, and he was escorted to the private office of a tough young Süddeutscher with a scarred face and a round head with black hair close cropped. Having met Göring, Lanny thought he had no more to learn about toughness. He sat down and came straight to the point:

"Herr Kommandant, I am an American sympathizer who happens to be in Munich because I am interested in an art exhibition. You may have read about it, and possibly about me. I had the honor of spending a morning with the Führer at the Braune Haus a few days ago. I am a friend of Minister-Präsident General Göring, and had the pleasure of accompanying him on a shooting trip last month. I live in France and visit frequently in England and America, where I hear a great deal of propaganda against your *Regierung*—you no doubt know of the charges of cruelty and torturing which are being widely published. I thought it might be a good thing if I could say: 'I have visited one of the large concentration camps and seen conditions with my own eyes.' I appreciate that this is a request you would hardly grant to a stranger; but it happens that I have some clippings from Munich newspapers which will show you who I am—and incidentally they contain pictures of myself, so that you can see I'm not anybody else."

The smiling visitor handed over the clippings; the tough Nazi studied them, and his toughness evaporated like early morning frost in sunshine. This elegant rich foreigner had actually enjoyed the highest privilege which any good Stormtrooper could imagine—of walking into the Führer's private study and discussing art with him! "Certainly, Herr Budd; we are always pleased to show our camp to properly accredited persons. We have taken several foreign journalists through in the past month or two." The Kommandant arose, prepared to do the honors himself—perhaps he could find the secret of how to make friends with the Führer!

So Lanny strolled about and saw what was inside those concrete walls with heavily electrified barbed wire. The officer explained the routine of the camp, and led his visitor over to the corner where the barracks were situated, fenced off from the rest of the grounds with barbed-wire entanglements. They were dismal, unpainted, and half-rotted buildings which had been erected of flimsy materials in wartime and had been neglected ever since. There were numerous cracks in the board walls and some of the windows had missing glass. There were thirteen one-story buildings, each with five connecting rooms, and in each room were fifty or more berths, arranged in three tiers like shelves. The floors were of concrete, and the mattresses were straw sacks. There was one washstand in each room.

Many of the inmates were outside the camp, working on the roads under heavy guard. Others were in the workshops, or building the new barracks, or in the offices. The old and the sick were getting the advantage of the sunshine, the only gift of nature which was still free to them. They sat leaning against the sides of the buildings, or strolling slowly. Apparently they were forbidden to converse; at any rate they weren't doing it. They looked dully at Lanny, and he was ashamed to meet their eyes. Fortunately he had no acquaintances among the Reds and Pinks of Bavaria, so he gave no soul-wounds.

A drab and distressing spectacle the prisoners presented. They had close-cropped heads. They wore the clothes in which they had been arrested; but that had been months ago, in many cases nearly a year, and doubtless they were sleeping in their clothes on these near-winter nights. The intellectuals of Bavaria had evidently not been fond of outdoor sports; some were lean and stoop-shouldered, others were paunched and flabby. Many had white hair, and might have been the grandfathers of their guards, but that earned them no consideration. Ill health and depression were written all over them. They did not know what they were here for, or how long they would have to stay—they who had been free men, free thinkers, the best of the land's intellectuals. They had dreamed of a happier and more ordered world, and this was the punishment which fitted their crime. "We are not running a health resort," remarked the Kommandant.

Lanny kept walking, as long as there was anything to be seen: sixty-five bunk-rooms, several mess-halls, a dozen workshops, and various outdoor constructions. Everywhere he scanned the faces, looking for that of his brother-in-law's brother or that of Trudi Schultz's husband. He saw neither; and after he had covered all the ground he could find out about, he ventured the question: "Don't you have any Jews?"

"Oh, yes," replied the host, "about forty; but we keep them apart, out of consideration for the others."

"They work, I suppose?"

"They work good and hard, you may be sure."

"Could I see them?"

"That, I am sorry to say, is contrary to the regulations."

The man volunteered no more; and Lanny, having asked as many questions as he dared, let himself be led back to his car. "I thank you, Herr Kommandant," he said. "I will be able to tell newspaper reporters that I didn't see any bruised or bloody inmates, or any wire whips or rubber hose for beatings."

"You might have looked still farther and not seen any," replied the tough Nazi. The remark was open to more than one interpretation, and Lanny thought: "Maybe he is like me, and prefers not to lie if he can help it!"

XII

The amateur investigator drove back to the city, wondering how Freddi was standing it. Freddi himself had wondered, did he have the needed courage, could he find in himself the spiritual resources?

Lanny, being of an imaginative temperament, asked the same questions of himself; he lived in those dingy and squalid sheds and felt on his back the lash of those whips which he had not seen.

Then his busy mind began inventing a little story. He went to see the tough Nazi Kommandant, and invited him to see the show, and after that to take a ride. When they were well out in the country Lanny addressed him as follows:

"Herr Kommandant, one of the Jews whom you are providing with plenty of hard work happens to be a sort of relative of mine. He is a harmless young fellow, and if I should take him to my home in France he would be content to play the clarinet for the rest of his life and never do any harm to your glorious movement. It happens that I have just sold some paintings and have cash in a Munich bank. Suppose I were to pay you, say twenty-five thousand marks, in any form and by any method you direct, and you in turn would find some way to let me pick up that prisoner in my car and whisk him up into the mountains and across the Austrian border—would that appeal to you as a good night's work?"

Lanny's fancy created several dénouements for that story. He knew that the Nazi machine was pretty well riddled with graft; Johannes Robin had told many tales of pure Aryan business men who were getting what they wanted by such methods, old as the first despotism. On the other hand, this particular toughie might be a sincere fanatic—it was impossible to tell them apart. Lanny was sure that if Hugo Behr had been in charge of the camp, he would have taken the money; on the other hand, Heinrich Jung would probably have reported him to the grim Gestapo.

And what would happen then? They couldn't very well do worse than escort him to the frontier, as Generalissimo Balbo's men had done in Rome nearly ten years ago. But here was the thing to give Lanny pause: if the Kommandant was a really virtuous Nazi, he might go back to his camp and make it impossible for Lanny to corrupt any weakling among his men, by the simple method of taking Freddi Robin and beating him to death and cremating the body.

"I must think of something better," said the grown-up playboy.

BOOK SIX

Blood Hath Been Shed

25

Grasping at Air

I

CHRISTMAS was coming; and Irma had been away from her darling for more than three months. It was unthinkable to stay longer. What was Lanny accomplishing? What was he hoping to accomplish? Göring was just playing with him. He was trying to get something out of them, and for nothing. He was keeping them quiet, sealing their lips. Not that Irma minded so very much having her husband's lips sealed. If only he wouldn't worry, and fill his mind with horrors so that he started in his sleep!

The Detaze show was over, and a happy development had come. One of the great museums in Dresden had asked to have the paintings for a while; they would treat them in a distinguished way, putting them in a separate room. The art lovers of that *Luxusstadt* would come and admire them, inquiries would be made, and it would be a good thing both from the point of view of art and of money. Zoltan would be coming and going, and inquiring purchasers could be referred to him. Much better than having the pictures stuck away in a storeroom on a private estate!

Beauty and Parsifal were going to London, on account of the strangest development you could imagine. Lady Caillard had sent a dear friend of hers all the way to Munich to persuade the American couple to come again as her guests, on account of a presentiment which had seized her; she was going very soon to rejoin her beloved "Vinnie" in the spirit world, and she wanted Beauty's dear man of love to be in her home at that time to close her eyes and take charge of her funeral which was to be like none other in modern times, a thing of joy and not of mourning. The guests were to wear white, and there would be happy music and feasting, all under the sign of "V.B.X"—Vinnie, Birdie, and a Kiss. "Perhaps she will send us some word about Freddi," said Beauty; and then—a horrid thought: "Perhaps she will leave us some of her money."

The museum in Dresden was attending to the pictures, so Jerry Pendleton was free. Irma and Lanny took him with them through a pass in those snow-covered mountains which make for Munich a setting like a drop curtain. They crossed the narrow belt which the Versailles *Diktat* had left to Austria, and through the Brenner pass which had been included in Italy's share of the loot. There Mussolini's Blackshirts were busily engaged in making Aryans into Mediterraneans by the agency of rubber truncheons and dogwhips. It made bad blood between *Fascismo* and its newborn offspring in the north. Dr. Goebbels's well-subsidized agitators were working everywhere in Austria, and not a few of them were in Italian dungeons. Optimistic young Pinks looked forward to seeing the Fascists and the Nazis devour each other like the two Kilkenny cats.

Home sweet home seemed ever so humble when you had been dwelling and visiting in palaces; but roses were in bloom beside its gates, and down the drive came racing a treasure without price, a tiny creature in a little blue dress, with dark brown hair streaming and dark brown eyes shining—she had been told two days ago that mother and father were on the way, and had been prattling about them and asking questions ever since. She was more than halfway through her fourth year, and it is astounding how fast they grow; you come back after three or four months and a new being confronts you; you cannot restrain your cries of delight, and a watchful expert has to check your ardors, lest you promote the evil quality of self-consciousness. Irma Barnes, who had been brought up in a play-world herself, had a hard time realizing that a child is more than a plaything for two delighted parents. Irma Barnes, who had always had her own way, had to learn to submit to discipline in the name of that very dogmatic new science of "child study."

Yes, indeed; for even a twenty-three-million-dollar baby has to learn to use her hands, and how shall she learn if someone does everything for her and never lets her make any effort? How will she learn discipline if she always has her own way, and if she gets the idea that she is the center of attention, more important than any of those with whom she has to deal? The severe Miss Severne persisted in the notion that her professional authority must be respected; and likewise the conscientious Miss Addington, no longer needed as Marceline's governess, but staying on as half-pensioner, half-friend of the family until she would take charge of Frances. Those two Church-of-England ladies had been conspiring together, and enlisted Lanny's help against a doting mother, two rival grandmothers, and a Provençal cook and major domo—to say nothing of Santa Claus.

II

A merry Christmas, yet not too much so, for over the household hangs the shadow of sorrow; nobody can forget those two bereaved Jewish women and the grief that is in their hearts. Rahel and Mama try their best to restrain themselves, and not to inflict their suffering upon their friends; but everybody knows what they are thinking about. Really, it would be less sad if Freddi were dead and buried, for then at least they would be sure he wasn't suffering. But this way the worst is possible, and it haunts them; they stay by themselves in the Lodge, their lost one always in the back of their minds and most of the time in the front. They are touchingly grateful for everything that has been done for them, but there is one thing more they have to ask; their looks ask it even when their lips are silent. Oh, Lanny, oh, Irma, *can't* you think of *something* to do for poor Freddi?

Hansi and Bess are in the Middle West, giving concerts several times every week. They have cabled money after the first concert, so Mama and Rahel no longer have to use Irma's money to buy their food. They have offered to rent a little place for themselves, but Beauty has said No, why should they—it would be very unkind. Irma says the same; but in her heart she cannot stifle the thought that she would like it better if they did. She feels a thunder-cloud hanging over the place, and wants so much to get Lanny from under it. She is worried about what is going on in his mind, and doesn't see why she should give up all social life because of a tragedy they are powerless to avert. Irma wants to give parties, real parties, of the sort which make a social impression; she will put up the money and Beauty and Feathers will do the work—both of them happy to do so, because they believe in parties, because parties are what set you apart from the common herd which cannot give them, at least not with elegance and *chic*.

Then, too, there is the question of two little tots. They are together nearly all the time, and this cannot be prevented; they clamor for it, take it for granted, and the science of child study is on their side. Impossible to bring up any child properly alone, because the child is a gregarious creature; so the textbooks agree. If little Johannes were not available it would be necessary to go out and get some fisherboy, Provençal, or Ligurian or what not. There isn't the slightest fault that Irma can find with the tiny Robin; he is a dream of brunette loveliness, he is gentle and sweet like his father, but he is a Jew, and Irma cannot be reconciled to the idea that her darling Frances should be more interested in him than in any other human being, not excepting herself. Of course, they are such tiny things, it seems absurd to worry; but the books and the experts agree that this is the age when indelible impressions are made, and is it wise to let an Aryan girl-child get fixed in her mind that the Semitic type is the most romantic, the most fascinating in the world? Irma imagines some blind and tragic compulsion developing out of that, later on in life.

Also, it means that the spirit of Freddi Robin possesses the whole of Bienvenu. The frail little fellow looks like his father, acts like him, and keeps him in everybody's thoughts; even the visitors, the guests. Everybody has heard rumors that Johannes Robin has been deprived of his fortune by the Nazis, and that his grandchild is here, a refugee and pensioner; everybody is interested in him, asks questions, and starts talking about the father—where is he, and what do you think, and what are you doing about it? The fate of Freddi Robin overshadows even the Barnes fortune, even the twenty-three-million-dollar baby! Bienvenu becomes as it were a haunted house, a somber and serious place where people fall to talking about politics, and where the frivolous ones do not feel at home. Irma Barnes certainly never meant to choose that kind of atmosphere!

III

There wasn't anything definite the matter with Lady Caillard, so far as any doctor could find out; but she had got her mind thoroughly made up that she was going to join her "Vinnie" in the spirit world, and sure enough, in the month of January she "passed on." The funeral was held, and then her will was read. She had left to her friend Mrs. Parsifal Dingle her large clock with the gold and ivory bird that sang; a pleasant memento of "Birdie," and one about which there would be no controversy. The medium to whom the Vickers stock had been promised got nothing but a headache out of it, for the directors of the huge concern were determined to protect Sir Vincent's son and daughter, and they worked some sort of hocus-pocus with the stock; they "called" it, and since the estate didn't have the cash to put up, the company took possession of the stock and ultimately the legitimate heirs got it. There was a lot of fuss about it in the papers, and Lanny was glad his mother and his stepfather were not mixed up in it.

With the proceeds of their dramatic success Nina and Rick had got a small car. Rick couldn't drive, on account of his knee, but his wife drove, and now they brought the Dingles to the Riviera, and stayed for a while as guests in the villa. Rick used Kurt's old studio to work on an anti-Nazi play, based on the *Brown Book*, the stories Lanny had told him, and the literature Kurt and Heinrich had been sending him through the years. It would be called a melodrama, Rick said—because the average Englishman refused to believe that there could be such people as the Nazis, or that such things could be happening in Europe in the beginning of the year 1934. Rick said furthermore that when the play was produced, Lanny would no longer be able to pose as a fellow-traveler of the Hitlerites, for they would certainly find out where the play had been written.

Lanny was glad to have this old friend near, the one person to

whom he could talk out his heart. Brooding over the problem of
Freddi Robin day and night, Lanny had about made up his mind
to go to Berlin, ask for another interview with General Göring, and
put his cards on the table, saying: "Exzellenz, I have learned that
my brother-in-law's brother is a prisoner in Dachau, and I would
like very much to take him out of Germany. I have about two
hundred thousand marks in a Berlin bank which I got from sales
of my stepfather's paintings, and I have an equal amount in a New
York bank which I earned as commissions on old masters purchased
in your country. I would be glad to turn these sums over to you to
use in your propaganda, in return for the freedom of my friend."

Rick said: "But you can't do such a thing, Lanny! It would be
monstrous."

"You mean he wouldn't take the money?"

"I haven't any doubt that he'd take it. But you'd be aiding the
Nazi cause."

"I don't think he'd use the money for that. I'm just saying so to
make it sound respectable. He'd salt the New York funds away, and
spend the German part on his latest girl friend."

"You say that to make it sound respectable to yourself," countered Rick. "You don't know what he'd spend the money for, and
you can't get away from the fact that you'd be strengthening the
Nazi propaganda. It's just as preposterous as your idea of giving
Göring information about British and French public men."

"I wouldn't give him any real information, Rick. I would only
tell him things that are known to our sort."

"Göring is no fool and you can't make him one. Either you'd
give him something he wants, or you wouldn't get what you want.
He has made that perfectly plain to you, and that's why Freddi is
still in Dachau—if he is."

"You think I have to leave him there?"

"You do, unless you can work out some kind of jailbreak."

"I'd have to pay somebody, Rick—even if it was only a jailer."

"There'd be no great harm in paying a jailer, because the amount
would be small, and you'd be undermining the Nazi discipline.
Every prisoner who escapes helps to do that."

"You think I did wrong to help Johannes out?"

"I don't think that made much difference, because Johannes would have given up anyhow; he's that sort of man. He thinks about himself and not about a cause."

"You wouldn't have done it in his place?"

"It's hard to say, because I've never been tortured and I can't be sure how I'd stand it. But what I should have done is plain enough—hang myself in my cell, or open my veins, rather than let Göring get hold of any foreign exchange to use in keeping his spies and thugs at work."

I V

Rick talked along the same line to Mama and Rahel; he was the only one who had the courage to do it. He spoke gently, and with pity for their tears, but he told them that the only way he knew of helping Freddi was by writing an anti-Nazi play. He bade them ask themselves what Freddi would want them to do. There could be no doubt about the answer, for Freddi was a devoted Socialist, and would rather die than give help to the enemies of his cause. Rahel could see that, and said so. Mama could see it, also—but couldn't bring herself to say it.

"Consider this," persisted Rick. "Suppose that what Göring wanted of Freddi was to betray some of his comrades. It's quite possible that that may be happening; and would he pay that price for his freedom?"

"Of course he wouldn't," admitted the young wife.

"Well, money's the same thing. The Nazis want foreign exchange so they can buy weapons and the means to make weapons. They want it so they can pay their agents and carry on their propaganda in foreign lands. And in the end it adds up to more power for Nazism, and more suffering for Jews and Socialists. These Hitlerites aren't through; they never can be through so long as they live, because theirs is a predatory system; it thrives on violence, and would perish otherwise. It has to have more and more victims, and if it gets money from you it uses the money to get more money from the next lot. So whatever resources we have or can get, have to go to fighting them, to making other people understand what Nazism is, what a menace it represents to everything that you and I and Freddi stand for."

Rick spoke with eloquence, more than he usually permitted himself. The reason was that it was a scene from his play. He was writing about people confronted with just such a cruel decision. He didn't say: "Let's all put our money and our labors into getting an anti-Nazi play produced, and use the proceeds to start a paper to oppose the Nazis." But that was what he had in mind, and Rahel knew that if her husband could speak to her, he would say: "Rick is right."

But poor Mama! She was no Socialist, and couldn't make real to herself the task of saving all the Jews in Germany. She kept silence, for she saw that Rick had convinced Rahel and Lanny; but what gave her hope was a letter from Johannes, about to sail for Rio de Janeiro to try to work up business for Budd Gunmakers. "I'm going to get some money again, and then I'll find a way to get Freddi out." That was the sort of talk for a sensible Jewish mother!

V

The Riviera was full of refugees from Germany; all France was the same. Many of these unfortunates tried to get hold of Lanny Budd, but he was afraid even to answer their letters. He was still clinging to the idea that Göring might release Freddi; if not, Lanny was going back to make some sort of effort. Therefore he had to be circumspect. Trying to play the spy makes one spy-conscious. How could he be sure that any refugee who appealed to him for aid might not have come from Göring, to find out how he was behaving, and whether he was a person to be dealt with?

All this suited Irma completely. She didn't care what was the reason, so long as her husband kept away from Reds and trouble-makers. She and Beauty and Emily and Sophie consulted and conspired to keep him busy and contented; to provide him with music and dancing and sports, with interesting people to talk to, with

Jerry Pendleton and the faithful Bub Smith to go fishing. Best of all for the purpose was little Frances; Irma got a book on child psychology and actually read every word of it, so as to be able to make intelligent remarks, and keep Lanny interested in what his home had to offer. She made love to him assiduously; and of course he knew what she was doing, and was touched by it. But he took Dachau with him everywhere; at one of Emily's *soirées musicales* a strain of sad music brought tears to his eyes, and then a pro-Nazi remark by one of the ladies of the *haut monde* made the blood rush to his head and ruined his appetite for the delicate viands.

Early in February Robbie Budd arrived in Paris on a business trip. Irma thought that change of scene would help, and she knew that the father would back her point of view; so they put their bags into the car and arrived at the Crillon the evening before Robbie was due. Always a pleasant thing to see that man of affairs, sound and solid, if a little too rotund and rosy. He was taking his loss of the presidency of the company as just one of those things; what can't be cured must be endured, and Robbie was getting along with the new head. A self-made man, well informed on financial conditions, he had won everyone's respect; he didn't try to tell Robbie how to sell goods in Europe, and had taken Robbie's word as to the capabilities of Johannes Robin. Things were going on much as in the old days.

Robbie wanted to hear every detail of what had happened in Germany. It was important for him to understand the Nazis, for they were trying to get credit from Budd's and from the banking group which now had Budd's under its wing. Morals had nothing to do with it—except as they bore on the question whether the Third Reich would meet its notes on time.

Robbie and the two young people discussed the problem of Freddi from every point of view, and Robbie gave his approval of what had been done. He said no more in his son's presence, but when he was alone with Irma he confirmed her idea that the Reds and Pinks of Germany had brought their troubles upon themselves. Nor was he worried about Hitler; he said that all Britain and France had to do was to stand together firmly, and let the Nazis devote their energies to putting down the Red menace throughout eastern and central Europe.

Of course it was unfortunate that one of the victims of this conflict had to be a young Jewish idealist. They must try to help the poor fellow, if only for the family's peace of mind. Robbie, who usually thought of money first, made the guess that if Freddi really was in Dachau it was because of Irma's stocks and bonds. Rumor invariably multiplied a rich person's holdings by three or four, and sometimes by ten or twenty; the fat General doubtless was expecting to get many millions in ransom. Robbie said that he himself would offer to go in and see what could be done; but he didn't propose to see Irma plundered, so the best thing was to wait and let Göring show his hand if he would. Irma appreciated this attitude, and wondered why Lanny couldn't be as sensible.

One thing Robbie said he was unable to understand: the fact that they had never received a single line of writing from Freddi in more than eight months. Surely any prisoner would be permitted to communicate with his relatives at some time! Lanny told what he had learned from the Kommandant of Dachau, that the inmates were permitted to write a few lines once a week to their nearest relatives; but this privilege was withheld in certain cases. Robbie said: "Even so, there are ways of smuggling out letters; and certainly there must be prisoners released now and then. You'd think some one of them would have your address, and drop a note to report the situation. It suggests to me that Freddi may be dead; but I don't say it to the Robins."

VI

Hard times were producing in France the same effects they had produced in Germany; and now the political pot boiled over, making a nasty mess. It was the "Stavisky case," centering about a swindler of Russian-Jewish descent. "Too bad he had to be a Jew!" said Irma, and Lanny wasn't sure whether she was being sympathetic or sarcastic. "Handsome Alex," as he was called, had been engaged in one piece of financial jugglery after another, culminating

in a *tour de force* which sounded like comic opera—he had promoted an extensive issue of bonds for the pawnshops of the town
of Bayonne! Altogether he had robbed the French public of something like a billion francs; and it was discovered that he had been
indicted for a swindle eight or nine years previously, and had succeeded in having his trial postponed no less than nineteen times.
Obviously this meant collusion with police and politicians; either he
was paying them money or was in position to blackmail them. When
Robbie read the details he said it sounded exactly like Chicago or
Philadelphia.

Stavisky had gone into hiding with his mistress, and when the
police came for him he shot himself; at least, so the police said, but
evidence began to indicate that the police had hushed him up. The
Paris newspapers, the most corrupt in the world, printed everything
they could find out and twenty times as much. Two groups were
interested in exploiting the scandals: the parties of the extreme
right, the Royalists and Fascists, who wanted to overthrow the
Republic and set up their kind of dictatorship; and the Communists,
who wanted a different kind. The two extremes met, and while
vowing the deadliest hatred, they made war on the same parliamentary system.

Lanny couldn't afford to visit his Red uncle, but he invited Denis
de Bruyne to dinner, and the three Budds listened to the story from
the point of view of a French Nationalist. The situation in the de
Bruyne family bore an odd resemblance to that between Robbie and
his son. Denis belonged to a respectable law-and-order party, and
was distressed because his younger son had joined the Croix de Feu,
most active of the French Fascist groups. Now Charlot was off
somewhere with his fellows, conspiring to overpower the police and
seize control of the country's affairs. At any moment he and his
organization might come out on the streets, and there would be
shooting; the unhappy father couldn't enjoy his dinner, and wanted
Lanny to find the crazy boy and try to bring him to his senses.
Such were the duties you got in for when you chose a lovely French
lady for your *amie!*

Lanny said no; he had tried to influence both boys, and had failed, and now he was out of politics; he had made a promise to his wife. He listened to the innermost secrets of *la république française*, derived from first-hand observation. He learned about Daladier, the baker's son, who had just become Premier, the fourth within a year; what interests had subsidized his career, and what noble lady had become his mistress. He learned about Chiappe, chief of the Paris police, a Corsican known as "the little Napoleon"—he was five feet three inches, and had just been "fired" for being too intimate with Stavisky. He had known all the wholesale crooks, the black-mailers and Jewish *métèques* of France, and had whispered their secrets to his son-in-law, publisher of one of the great gutter-journals of Paris.

Lanny observed that the individuals who awakened the anger and disgust of Denis de Bruyne were the climbers, those struggling for wealth and power to which they had no valid claim. He rarely had any serious fault to find with the *mur d'argent*, the members of the "two hundred families" who had had wealth and power for a long time. They had to pay large sums of money in these evil days, and the basis of Denis's complaint was not the corruption but the increasing cost. The politicians demanded larger campaign funds, and at the same time kept increasing taxes; their idea of economy was to cut the salaries of civil servants—which Denis had discovered was bad for the taxicab business. To make matters worse, the taxicab drivers were on strike! Robbie listened sympathetically, and when his friend got through scolding Daladier, Robbie took a turn at Roosevelt.

VII

Next day Lanny escorted his wife to the Summer Fashion Show. This wasn't a public affair, but one for the trade; an exhibition of the new styles which the manufacturers intended soon to release. Irma was invited as a special honor by the fashion artist to whom she entrusted her social destiny. Lanny went along because, if she endeavored to take an interest in his things, it was only fair that he should do the same for hers. They sat in a hall with many potted palms, gazing at a long ramp with dark blue curtains behind it;

along the ramp paraded beautiful and *chic* young women wearing summer costumes with a strong Japanese flavor, or note, or atmosphere—the journalists groped about for a metaphor. There were bamboo buttons and coolie hats; the ladies' gowns had fan-tails like Japanese goldfish, the afternoon costumes had cut sleeves like kimonos, and the evening wraps had designs resembling Japanese flower prints.

Among the favored guests at this show was an old friend of Lanny's; Olivie Hellstein, now Madame de Broussailles, very lovely daughter of Jerusalem whom Emily had picked out as a proper match for Lanny. That had been some eight years ago, and now Olivie had three or four children, and had become what you called "maternal," a kinder word than "plump." Words which have an unpleasant connotation change frequently in the best society, where people try so hard not to wound one another's feelings.

Olivie was a woman of Irma's type, a brunette with deep coloring, in temperament rather placid, in manner sedate. They had entertained each other, exchanged visits, and satisfied their curiosity. Now they talked about having to wear summer clothing with a strong Japanese flavor, or note, or atmosphere; they would have to wear it, of course—it would never occur to them to rebel against what the fashion creators decided was the fashion.

Lanny, wishing to be polite, remarked: "We were talking about your family last night. My father is having a meeting with your father."

"A business matter?" inquired Olivie.

"Mine is trying to persuade yours that he can deliver certain railroad equipment at Brest at a lower price than it can be manufactured in France."

"It will be pleasant if they become associated," replied the young matron. "My father has a great admiration for American production methods, and wishes they might be imported into France."

Pierre Hellstein was a director in the Chemin de Fer du Nord, and controlled one of the biggest banks in Paris. Robbie had asked Denis about him, and they had discussed this wealthy Jewish family spread widely over Europe; also the position of the railroad, reputed to be run down and overloaded with bonds. The Hellsteins didn't have to worry, because the government covered its deficits; there had been criticism in the Chamber—the French Republic was going broke in order to protect the railroad bondholders. Denis de Bruyne, who owned some of the bonds, resented these criticisms as irresponsible and demagogic. As for Olivie, beautiful, serene, magnificent in a long sable coat, she was perfect evidence of the wisdom of guaranteeing large incomes to a few chosen individuals, in order that they may be free to attend fashion shows and constitute themselves models of elegance and refinement.

VIII

"Oh, by the way," said the daughter of Jerusalem, all at once; "I understand that you were in Germany not long ago."

"Just before Christmas," replied Lanny.

"I do wish you would tell me about it. It must be dreadful."

"In some ways, and for some people. Others hardly notice it."

"Oh, Monsieur Budd," said Olivie, lowering her voice, "may I tell you something without its going any farther? I'm really not supposed to talk, but we are all so worried."

"You may be sure that my wife and I will respect your confidence, Madame."

"We have just learned that the Nazis have arrested my· Uncle Solomon. You know him, possibly?"

"I had the pleasure of meeting him at the home of Johannes Robin. Also, I am one of his depositors in Berlin."

"They have trumped up some charge against him, of sending money out of Germany. You know, of course, that a banker cannot help doing that; especially a family like ours, doing business in Austria and Czechoslovakia and Rumania, and so many other countries."

"Of course, Madame."

"We Jews hear the most dreadful stories—really, it makes you quite sick."

"I am sorry to say that many of them are true. They tell you

that such things happen in violent social overturns. But I doubt if
the Nazis would do physical harm to a man like your uncle. They
would be more likely to assess him a very large fine."

"It is all so bewildering, Monsieur Budd. Really, my father cannot
be sure whether it would be safe for him to go into Germany to
see about it."

"I will make a suggestion, Madame, if you don't mind."

"That is just what I was hoping you might do."

"I ask you to consider it confidential, just as you have asked me.
Tell your mother and father, but nobody else."

"Certainly, Monsieur Budd."

"I suggest their sending somebody to interview General Göring.
He has a great deal of influence and seems to understand these
matters."

"Oh, thank you!" exclaimed Olivie Hellstein. "I am so glad I
thought to ask you about it."

Irma put in: "Send somebody who is dignified and impressive-
looking, and tell him to be dressed exactly right, and not forget any
of the Minister-Präsident General's titles."

IX

Out of duty to the memory of Marie de Bruyne, Lanny made
an effort to see her younger son, but found it impossible. Charlot
was meeting somewhere with the leaders of his society, and the
inquiries of strangers were not welcomed. This Tuesday, the sixth
of February, was to be the great night in which all the organizations of the Right in France would "demonstrate" against the government. Marching orders had been published in all the opposition papers, under the slogan: "*À bas les voleurs!* Down with
the thieves!" At twilight Charlot would emerge from his hiding
place, wearing his tricolor armband with the letters F.C.F., which
meant that he was a Son of the Cross of Fire. He would be singing
the *Marseillaise;* an odd phenomenon, the battle-song of one revolution becoming the anti-song of the next! In between singing, Charlot
and his troop of patriotic youths would be yelling the word

"*Démission!*"—which meant the turning out of the Daladier government. Less politely they would cry: "*Daladier au poteau!*" meaning that they wished to burn him alive.

Lanny drove his wife to the Chamber, going by a circuitous route because the Pont de la Concorde was blocked by gendarmes. For an hour the couple sat in the public gallery and listened to an uproar which reminded Lanny of what he had heard on the floor of the New York Stock Exchange at the height of the panic. Daladier couldn't make his speech; his political enemies hurled at him every abusive name in the extensive French vocabulary, while at the same time the Communists sang the *Internationale*.

When this became monotonous, the Americans went out to have a look at the streets. They couldn't see much from a car, for fear of being caught in fighting, and decided that the best place from which to witness a Paris *démonstration* was from the windows of their hotel suite. Robbie, sensible fellow, was in his rooms, talking business with the head of a French building concern which sometimes bought *ascenseurs*. The two younger people stood on the balcony of their drawing-room, which looked over the great Place de la Concorde, brilliantly lighted, and with an obelisk in the center having floodlights on it. Directly across the Place was the bridge over the Seine to the Palais-Bourbon, where the deputies met; a building in Roman style with many tall pillars brightly shining.

There must have been a hundred thousand people in the Place, and more pouring in by every street. They were trying to get across the bridge, but the police and troops had blocked it with patrol-wagons. The mob started throwing things, and soon there was a pitched battle, with charges and counter-charges going on most of the night. The Fascists hurled whatever they could lay hands on. They pried up stones from the pavement, and tore off the scaffolding from the American Embassy, which was under repair. The railings of the Tuileries gardens provided them with an iron missile, shaped like a boomerang and impossible to see in the dark. When the mounted *gardes républicaines* tried to drive them off the bridge, charging and striking with the flat of their sabers, the mob countered with walking-sticks having razor-blades fastened to the ends, to slash the bellies of the horses. In one attack after another they crippled so many of the police and *gardes* that they came very near getting across the bridge and into the Chamber.

So at last shooting began. The street-lights were smashed, and the floodlights on the obelisk were turned off, so you couldn't see much. An omnibus had been overturned and set afire near the bridge, but that gave more smoke than light, and it soon burned out. The last sight that Lanny saw was a troop of the Spahis, African cavalrymen in white desert robes looking like the Ku Kluxers, galloping up the Champs Élysées and trampling the mob. There came screams directly under where Irma and Lanny were standing; a chambermaid of the hotel had been shot and killed on the balcony. So the guests scrambled in quickly, deciding that they had seen enough of the class war in France.

"Do you think they will raid the hotel?" asked Irma; but Lanny assured her that this was a respectable kind of mob, and was after the politicians only. So they went to bed.

X

"Bloody Tuesday," it was called, and the Fascist newspapers set out to make it into the French "Beerhall Putsch." From that time on they would have only one name for Daladier: "*Assassin!*" They clamored for his resignation, and before the end of the next day they got it; there were whispers that he could no longer depend upon the police and the *gardes*. More than two hundred of these were in the hospitals, and it looked like a revolution on the way. There was wreckage all over Paris, and the Ministry of Marine partly burned. Charlot had got a slash across the forehead, and for the rest of his life would wear a scar with pride. "*La Concorde*," he would say, referring to the bridge; it would become a slogan, perhaps some day a password to power.

On Wednesday night matters were worse, for the police were demoralized, and the hoodlums, the *apaches*, went on the warpath. They smashed the windows of the shops in the Rue de Rivoli and other fashionable streets and looted everything in sight. It wasn't a pleasant time for visitors in Paris; Robbie was going to Amsterdam on business, so Irma and Lanny stepped into their car and sped home.

But you couldn't get away from the class war in France. The various reactionary groups had been organized all over the Midi, and they, too, had received their marching orders. They had the sympathy of many in the various foreign colonies; anything to put down the Reds. Rick, after hearing Lanny's story, said that *la patrie* was awaiting only one thing, a leader who would have the shrewdness to win the "little man." So far, all the Fascist groups were avowedly reactionary, and it would take a leftish program to win. Lanny expressed the opinion that the French man in the street was much shrewder than the German; it wouldn't be so easy to hoodwink him.

Life was resumed at Bienvenu. Rick worked on his play and Lanny read the manuscript, encouraged him, and supplied local color. In the privacy of their chamber Irma said: "Really, you are a collaborator, and ought to be named." She wondered why Lanny never wrote a play of his own. She decided that what he lacked was the impulse of self-assertion, the strong ego which takes up the conviction that it has something necessary to the welfare of mankind. Uncle Jesse had it, Kurt had it, Rick had it. Beauty had tried in vain to awaken it in her son, and now Irma tried with no more success. "Rick can do it a lot better"—that was all she could get.

Irma was becoming a little cross with this lame Englishman. She had got Lanny pretty well cured of his Pinkness, but now Rick kept poking up the fires. There came a series of terrible events in Austria—apparently Fascism was going to spread from country to country until it had covered all Europe. Austria had got a Catholic Chancellor named Dollfuss, and a Catholic army, the Heimwehr, composed mainly of peasant lads and led by a dissipated young prince. This government was jailing or deporting Hitlerites, but with the help of Mussolini was getting its own brand of Fascism, and now it set out to destroy the Socialist movement in the city of Vienna. Those beautiful workers' homes, huge apartment blocks which Lanny had inspected with such joy—the Heimwehr brought up its motorized artillery and blasted them to ruins, killing about a thousand men, women, and children. Worse yet, they killed the workers' movement, which had been two generations building.

A terrible time to be alive in. Lanny and Rick could hardly eat or sleep; they could only grieve and brood over the tragedy of the time into which they had been born. Truly it seemed futile to work for anything good; to dream of peace and order, justice or even mercy. This wholesale slaughter of working people was committed in the name of the gentle and lowly Jesus, the carpenter's son, the social rebel who had been executed because he stirred up the people! A devout Catholic Premier ordering the crime, and devout Catholic officers attending mass before and after committing it! And not for the first time or the last in unhappy Europe. Rick reminded his friend of that cardinal in France who had ordered the St. Bartholomew massacre, saying: "Kill them all; God will be able to pick out His Christians."

XI

Hot weather came to the Riviera, and the people whom Irma considered important went away. Those who were poor, like the Dingles and the Robins, would stick it out and learn to take a siesta. But Nina and Rick went back to England, and Emily Chattersworth moved her servants to Les Forêts and invited Irma and Lanny to visit her and see the spring Salon and the new plays. It was Irma's idea, to keep her husband's mind off the troubles of the world. They went, and after they had played around for a couple of weeks, Irma had a letter from her mother, begging them to come to Shore Acres and bring Baby Frances for the summer. Really it was a crime to have that magnificent place and never use it; also it was grossly unfair that one grandmother should have her heart's desire all the time and the other not at all. "I don't believe that Beauty cares for the child anything like as much as I do," wrote the Queen Mother; a sentence which Irma skipped when she read the letter aloud.

The couple talked over the problem. Irma was reluctant to take her precious darling on board a steamer; she hadn't got over her memories of the Lindbergh kidnaping, and thought that an ocean liner was an ideal place for a band of criminals to study a twenty-three-million-dollar baby, her habits and entourage. No, it would be better to spend the summer in England's green and pleasant land, where kidnapers were unknown. Let Mother be the one to brave the ocean waves! Irma hadn't spent any money to speak of during the past year, and now interest on bonds was being paid and dividends were hoped for. She said: "Let's drive about England, the way we did on our honeymoon, and see if we can find some suitable place to rent."

Nothing is more fun than doing over again what you did on your honeymoon; that is, if you have managed to keep any of the honeymoon feeling alive after five years. "There are so many nice people there," argued the young wife. Lanny agreed, even though he might not have named the same persons.

He knew that Rick's play was nearly done, and he wanted to make suggestions for the last act. Then there would be the job of submitting it to managers, and Lanny would want to hear the news. Perhaps it might be necessary to raise the money, and that wouldn't be so easy, for it was a grim and violent play, bitter as gall, and would shock the fashionable ladies. But Lanny meant to put up the money which he had earned in Germany—all of it, if necessary, and he didn't want Irma to be upset about it. They were following their plan of keeping the peace by making concessions, each to the other and in equal proportions.

They crossed the Channel and put up at the Dorchester. When their arrival was announced in the papers, as it always would be, one of the first persons who telephoned was Wickthorpe, saying: "Won't you come out and spend the week end?"

Lanny replied: "Sure thing. We're looking for a little place to rent this summer. Maybe you can give us some advice." He said "little" because he knew that was good form; but of course it wouldn't really be little.

"I have a place near by," responded his lordship. "I'll show it to you, if you don't mind."

"Righto!" said Lanny, who knew how to talk English to Englishmen.

When he told Irma about it, she talked American. "Oh, heck! Do you suppose it'll have tin bathtubs?"

XII

But it didn't. It was a modern villa with three baths, plenty of light and air, and one of those English lawns, smooth as a billiard table, used for playing games. There was a high hedge around the place, and everything lovely. It was occupied by Wickthorpe's aunt, who was leaving for a summer cruise with some friends. There was a staff of well-trained servants who would stay on if requested. "Oh, I think it will be ducky!" exclaimed the heiress. She paid the price to his lordship's agent that very day, and the aunt agreed to move out and have everything in order by the next week end. Irma cabled her mother, and wrote Bub Smith and Feathers to get everything ready and bring Baby and Miss Severne and the maid on a specified date. Jerry Pendleton would see to the tickets, and Bub would be in charge of the traveling, Feathers being such a featherbrain.

So there was a new ménage, with everything comfortable, and no trouble but the writing of a few checks and the giving of a few orders. A delightful climate and many delightful people; a tennis court and somebody always to play; a good piano and people who loved music; only a few minutes' drive to the old castle, where Lanny and his wife were treated as members of the family, called up and urged to meet this one and that. Again Lanny heard statesmen discussing the problems of the world; again they listened to what he had to tell about the strange and terrifying new movement in Germany, and its efforts to spread itself in all the neighboring countries. Englishmen of rank and authority talked freely of their empire's affairs, telling what they would do in this or that contingency; now and then Lanny would find himself thinking: "What wouldn't Göring pay for *this!*"

Zoltan had been in Paris, and now came to London. It was the "season," and there were exhibitions, and chances to make sales. An art expert, like the member of any other profession, has to hear the gossip of his *monde;* new men are coming in and old ones going out, and prices fluctuating exactly as on the stock market. Lanny and his partner still had money in Naziland, and lists of pictures available in that country, by means of which they expected to get their money out. Also, there was the London stage, and Rick to go with them to plays and tell the news of that world. There was the fashion rout, with no end of dances and parties. Dressmakers and others clamored to provide Irma with costumes suited to her station; they would bring them out into the country to show her at any hour of the day or night.

Good old Margy Petries, Dowager Lady Eversham-Watson, had opened her town house, and begged the young couple to make it their headquarters whenever they came to town; she telegraphed Beauty and Sophie to bring their husbands and come and have a good old-fashioned spree. When Mrs. Barnes arrived, she, too, was "put up"; that was the custom in Kentucky, and Margy still called herself a blue-grass-country girl, even at the age of fifty-five.

So it was just like Bienvenu at the height of midwinter; so many things going on that really you had a hard time choosing, and would rush from one event to the next with scarcely time to catch your breath. It was extremely difficult for Lanny to find time to brood over the fate of the world; and that was what his wife had planned. She saw that she was winning out, and was happy, and proud of her acumen. Until one Saturday noon, arriving at their villa for a week end, Lanny found a telegram from Bienvenu, signed "Rahel" and reading:

"Letter from Clarinet in place you visited most distressing circumstances he implores help am airmailing letter."

26

Out of This Nettle, Danger

I

THE argument started as soon as Irma read the telegram and got its meaning clear. She knew exactly what would be in her husband's mind; she had been thinking about it for more than a year, watching him, anticipating this moment, living through this scene. And she knew that he had been doing the same. They had talked about it a great deal, but she hadn't uttered all of her thoughts, nor he of his; they had dreaded the ordeal, shrinking from the things that would be said. She knew that was true about herself, and guessed it was true about him; she guessed that he guessed it about her—and so on through a complication such as develops when two human souls, tied together by passionate love, discover a basic and fundamental clash of temperaments, and try to conceal it from each other and even from themselves.

Irma said: "Lanny, you can't do it! You can't, you can't!" And he replied: "Darling, I have to! If I didn't I couldn't bear to live!"

So much had been said already that there was nothing to gain by going over it. But that is the way with lovers' quarrels; each thinks that if he says it one time more, the idea will penetrate, it will make the impression which it so obviously ought to make, which it has somehow incomprehensibly failed to make on previous occasions.

Irma protested: "Your wife and child mean nothing to you?"

Lanny answered: "You know they do, dear. I have tried honestly to be a good husband and father. I have given up many things that I thought were right for me, when I found they were wrong for you. But I can't give up Freddi to the Nazis."

"A man is free to take up a notion like that—and then all his family duties become nothing?"

"A man takes up a notion like that when there's a cause involved; something that is more precious to him than his own life."

"You're going to sacrifice Frances and me for Freddi!"

"That's rather exaggerated, darling. You and Frances can stay quite comfortably here while I go and do what I can."

"You're not asking me to go with you?"

"It's a job for someone who believes in it, and certainly not for anyone who feels as you do. I have no right to ask it of you, and that's why I don't."

"What do you suppose will be my state of mind while you are in there risking your life with those dreadful men?"

"It will be a mistake to exaggerate the danger. I don't think they'll do serious harm to an American."

"You know they have done shocking things to Americans. You have talked about it often."

"What happened in those cases was accidental; they were mix-ups in street crowds and public places. You and I have connections in Germany, and I don't think the authorities will do me any harm on purpose."

"Even if they catch you breaking their laws?"

"I think they'll give me a good scare and put me out."

"You know you don't believe that, Lanny! You're only trying to quiet me down. You will be in perfectly frightful danger, and I will be in torment."

She broke down and began to weep. It was the first time he had seen her do that, and he was a soft-hearted man. But he had been thinking it over for a year, and had made up his mind that this would be the test of his soul. "If I funk this, I'm no good; I'm the waster and parasite I've always been called."

There was no way to end the argument. He couldn't make her realize the importance of the matter to him; the duty he owed to what he called "the cause." He had made Freddi Robin into a Socialist; had taught him the ideal of human brotherhood and equality, what he called "social justice." But Irma hated all these

high-sounding words; she had heard them spoken by so many disagreeable persons, mostly trying to get money, that the words had
become poison to her. She didn't believe in this "cause"; she believed that brotherhood was rather repulsive, that equality was
another name for envy, and social justice an excuse for outrageous
income and inheritance taxes. So her tears dried quickly, and she
grew angry with herself for having shed them, and with him for
making her shed them.

She said: "Lanny, I warn you; you are ruining our love. You
are doing something I shall never be able to forgive you for."

All he could answer was: "I am sorry, darling; but if you made
me give up what I believe is my duty, I should never be able to
forgive either you or myself."

II

The airmail letter from Juan arrived. Freddi's message had been
written in pencil on a small piece of flimsy paper, crumpled up as
if someone had hidden it in his mouth or other bodily orifice. It
was faded, but Rahel had smoothed it out and pasted the corners
to a sheet of white paper so that it could be read. It was addressed
to Lanny and written in English. "I am in a bad way. I have written
to you but had no reply. They are trying to make me tell about
other people and I will not. But I cannot stand any more. Do one
thing for me, try to get some poison to me. Do not believe anything
they say about me. Tell our friends I have been true."

There was no signature; Freddi knew that Lanny would know
his handwriting, shaky and uncertain as it was. The envelope was
plain, and had been mailed in Munich; the handwriting of the address was not known to Lanny, and Rahel in her letter said that
she didn't know it either.

So there it was. Irma broke down again; it was worse than she
had imagined, and she knew now that she couldn't keep Lanny
from going. She stopped arguing with him about political questions, and tried only to convince him of the futility of whatever
efforts he might make. The Nazis owned Germany, and it was

madness to imagine that he could thwart their will inside their own country. She offered to put up money, any amount of money, even if she had to withdraw from social life. "Go and see Göring," she pleaded. "Offer him cash, straight out."

But Rick—oh, how she hated him all of a sudden!—Rick had persuaded Lanny that this was not to be done. Lanny wouldn't go near Göring, or any of the other Nazis, not even Kurt, not even Heinrich. They wouldn't help, and might report him and have him watched. Göring or Goebbels would be sure to take such measures. Lanny said flatly: "I'm going to help Freddi to escape from Dachau."

"Fly over the walls, I suppose?" inquired Irma, with bitterness.

"There are many different ways of getting out of prison. There are people in France right now who have managed to do it. Sometimes they dig under the walls; sometimes they hide in delivery wagons, or are carried out in coffins. I'll find somebody to help me for a price."

"Just walk up to somebody on the street and say: 'How much will you charge to help me get a friend out of Dachau?'"

"It's no good quarreling, dear. I have to put my mind on what I mean to do. I don't want to delay, because if I do, Freddi may be dead, and then I'd blame myself until I was dead, too."

So Irma had to give up. She had told him what was in her heart, and even though she would break down and weep, she wouldn't change; on the contrary, she would hold it against him that he had made her behave in that undignified fashion. In her heart she knew that she hated the Robin family, all of them; they were alien to her, strangers to her soul. If she could have had her way she would never have been intimate with them; she would have had her own yacht and her own palace and the right sort of friends in it. But this Socialism business had made Lanny promiscuous, willing to meet anybody, an easy victim for any sort of pretender, any slick, canting "idealist"—how she loathed that word! She had been forced to make pretenses and be polite; but now this false "cause" was going to deprive her of her husband and her happiness, and she knew that she heartily despised it.

It wasn't just love of herself. It was love of Lanny, too. She wanted to help him, she wanted to take care of him; but this "class struggle" stepped in between and made it impossible; tore him away from her, and sent him to face danger, mutilation, death. Things that Irma and her class were supposed to be immune from! That was what your money meant; it kept you safe, it gave you privilege and security. But Lanny wanted to throw it all away. He had got the crazy notion that you had no right to money; that having got it, you must look down upon it, spurn it, and thwart the very purposes for which it existed, the reasons why your forefathers had worked so hard! If that was not madness, who could find anything that deserved the name?

III

All social engagements were called off while this duel was fought out. Irma said that she had a bad headache; but as this affliction had not been known to trouble her hitherto, the rumor spread that the Irma Barneses were having a quarrel; everybody tried to guess what it could be about, but nobody succeeded. Only three persons were taken into the secret; Rick, and the mothers of the two quarrelers. Rick said: "I wish I could help you, old chap; but you know I'm a marked man in Germany; I have written articles." Lanny said: "Of course."

As for Fanny Barnes, she considered it her duty to give Lanny a lecture on the wrongness of deserting his family on account of any Jew or all of them. Lanny, in turn, considered it his duty to hear politely all that his mother-in-law had to say. He knew it wasn't any good talking to her about "causes"; he just said: "I'm sorry, Mother, but I feel that I have incurred obligations, and I have to repay them. Do what you can to keep Irma cheerful until I get back." It was a rather solemn occasion; he might not come back, and he had a feeling that his mother-in-law would find that a not altogether intolerable solution of the problem.

As for Beauty, she wasn't much good in this crisis; the sheer horridness of it seemed to paralyze her will. She knew her boy's feeling for the Robin boys, and that it couldn't be overcome. She knew also that he suspected her concern about Irma's happiness as being not altogether disinterested. The mother dared not say what was in the deeps of her heart, her fear that Lanny might lose his ultra-precious wife if he neglected her and opposed her so recklessly. And of all places to leave her—on the doorstep of Lord Wickthorpe! Beauty developed a *crise des nerfs*, with a real headache, and this didn't diminish the gossip and speculation.

Meanwhile, Lanny went ahead with his preparations. He wrote Rahel to have a photograph of Freddi reduced to that small size which is used on passports, and to airmail it to him at once; he had a reason for that, which she was at liberty to guess. He wrote Jerry Pendleton to hold himself in readiness for a call to bring a *camion* to Germany and return the Detaze paintings to their home. That would be no hardship, because the tourist season was over and Cerise could run the office.

Lanny gave his friend Zoltan a check covering a good part of the money he had in the Hellstein banks in Berlin and Munich; Zoltan would transfer the money to his own account, and thus the Nazis wouldn't be able to confiscate it. In case Lanny needed the money, he could telegraph and Zoltan could airmail him a check. The ever discreet friend asked no questions, and thus would be able to say that he knew nothing about the matter. Lanny talked about a picture deal which he thought he could put through in Munich, and Zoltan gave him advice on this. Having been pondering all these matters for more than a year, Lanny was thoroughly prepared.

When it came to the parting, Lanny's young wife and Lanny's would-be-young mother both broke down. Both offered to go with him; but he said No. Neither approved his mission, and neither's heart would be in the disagreeable task. He didn't tell the plain truth, which was that he was sick of arguments and excitements; it is one of the painful facts about marital disputes that they cause each of the disputants to grow weary of the sound of the other's voice, and to count quiet and the freedom to have one's own way as the greatest of life's blessings. Lanny believed that he could do this job himself, and could think better if he didn't have opposition. He said: "No, dear," and "No, darling; I'm going to be very careful, and it won't take long."

IV

So, bright and early one morning, Margy Petries's servants deposited his bags in his car, and not without some moisture in his eyes and some sinkings in his inside, he set out for the ferry to Calais, whose name Queen Mary had said was written on her heart, and which surely existed as some sort of scar on Lanny's. He went by way of Metz and Strasbourg, for the fewer countries one entered in unhappy Europe, the less bother with visas and customs declarations. How glorious the country seemed in the last days of June; and how pitiful by contrast that *Missgeburt* of nature which had developed the frontal lobes of its brain so enormously, in order to create new and more dreadful ways of destroying millions of other members of its own species! "Nature's insurgent son" had cast off chain-mail and dropped lances and battle-axes, only to take up bombing-planes and Nazi propaganda.

The blood of millions of Frenchmen and Germans had fertilized this soil and made it so green and pleasant to Lanny's eyes. He knew that in all these copses and valleys were hidden the direful secrets of the Maginot Line, that series of complicated and enormously expensive fortifications by which France was counting upon preventing another German invasion. Safe behind this barricade, Frenchmen could use their leisure to maim and mangle other Frenchmen with iron railings torn from a beautiful park. Where Lanny crossed the Rhine was where the child Marie Antoinette had come with her train of two or three hundred vehicles, on her long journey from Vienna to marry the Dauphin of France. All sorts of history around here, but the traveler had no time to think about it; his mind was occupied with the history he was going to make.

Skirting the edge of the Alps, with snow-clad peaks always in view, he came to the city of Munich on its little river Isar. He put up at a second-class hotel, for he didn't want newspaper reporters after him, and wanted to be able to put on the suit of old clothes which he had brought, and be able to walk about the city, and perhaps the town of Dachau, without attracting any special attention. At the Polizeiwache he reported himself as coming for the purpose of purchasing works of art; his first act after that was to call upon a certain Baron von Zinszollern whom he had met at the Detaze show and who had many paintings in his home. This gentleman was an avowed Nazi sympathizer, and Lanny planned to use him as his "brown herring," so to speak. In case of exposure this might sow doubts and confusion in Nazi minds, which would be so much to the good.

Lanny went to this art patron's fine home and looked at his collection, and brought up in his tactful way whether any of the works could be bought; he intimated that the prices asked were rather high, but promised to cable abroad and see what he could do. He did cable to Zoltan, and to a couple of customers in America, and these messages would be a part of his defense in case of trouble. All through his stay in Munich he would be stimulating the hopes of a somewhat impoverished German aristocrat, and diminishing the prices of his good paintings.

V

Upon entering Germany the conspirator had telephoned to Hugo Behr in Berlin, inviting that young Nazi to take the night train to Munich. Lanny was here on account of pictures, he said, and would show his friend some fine specimens. Hugo had understood, and it hadn't been necessary to add, "expenses paid." The young sports director had doubtless found some use for the money which Lanny had paid him, and would be pleased to render further services.

He arrived next morning, going to a different hotel, as Lanny had directed. He telephoned, and Lanny drove and picked him up on the street. A handsome young Pomeranian, alert and with springy step, apple-cheeked and with wavy golden hair, Hugo was a walk-

ing advertisement of the pure Nordic ideal. In his trim Brownshirt
uniform, with insignia indicating his important function, he received a salute from all other Nazis, and from many civilians wishing to keep on the safe side. It was extremely reassuring to be with
such a man in Germany—although the "Heil Hitlers" became a bit
monotonous after a while.

Lanny drove his guest out into the country, where they could
be quiet and talk freely. He encouraged the guest to assume that
the invitation was purely out of friendship; rich men can indulge
their whims like that, and they do so. Lanny was deeply interested
to know how Hugo's movement for the reforming of the Nazi
party was coming along, and as the reformer wanted to talk about
nothing else, they drove for a long time through the valleys of the
Alpine foothills. The trees were in full splendor, as yet untouched
by any signs of wear. A beautiful land, and Lanny's head was full
of poetry about it. *Die Fenster auf, die Herzen auf! Geschwinde,
geschwinde!*

But Hugo's thoughts had no trace of poetic cheerfulness. His
figure of a young Hermes was slumped in the car seat, and his
tone was bitter as he said: "Our Nazi revolution is *kaput*. We
haven't accomplished a thing. The Führer has put himself completely into the hands of the reactionaries. They tell him what to
do—it's no longer certain that he could carry out his own program,
even if he wanted to. He doesn't see his old friends any more, he
doesn't trust them. The Reichswehr crowd are plotting to get rid
of the Stormtroopers altogether."

"You don't really mean all that, Hugo!" Lanny was much distressed.

"Haven't you heard about our vacation?"

"I only entered Germany yesterday."

"All the S.A. have been ordered to take a vacation during the
month of July. They say we've been overworked and have earned
a rest. That sounds fine; but we're not permitted to wear our uniforms, or to carry our arms. And what are they going to do while
we're disarmed? What are we going to find when we come back?"

"That looks serious, I admit."

"It seems to me the meaning is plain. We, the rank and file, have done our job and they're through with us. We have all been hoping to be taken into the Reichswehr; but no, we're not good enough for that. Those officers are Junkers, they're real gentlemen, while we're common trash; we're too many, two million of us, and they can't afford to feed us or to train us, so we have to be turned off—and go to begging on the streets, perhaps."

"You know, Hugo, Germany is supposed to have only a hundred thousand in its regular army. Mayn't it be that the Führer doesn't feel strong enough to challenge France and Britain on that issue?"

"What was our revolution for, but to set us free from their control? And how can we ever become strong, if we reject the services of the very men who have made National Socialism? *We* put these leaders in power—and now they're getting themselves expensive villas and big motor-cars, and they're afraid to let us of the rank and file even wear our uniforms! They talk of disbanding us, because the Reich can't afford our magnificent salaries of forty-two pfennigs a day."

"Is that what you get?"

"That is what the rank and file get. What is that in your money?"

"About ten cents."

"Does that sound so very extravagant?"

"The men in our American army get about ten times that. Of course both groups get food and lodgings free."

"Pretty poor food for the S.A.; and besides, there are all the levies, which take half what anybody earns. Our lads were made to expect so much, but now all the talk is that the Reich is so poor. The propaganda line has changed; Herr Doktor Goebbels travels over the land denouncing the *Kritikaster* and the *Miessmacher* and the *Nörgler* and the *Besserwisser*—" Hugo gave a long list of the depraved groups who dared to suggest that the Nazi *Regierung* was anything short of perfect. "In the old days we were told there would be plenty, because we were going to take the machinery away from the *Schieber* and set it to work for the benefit of the common folk. But now the peasants have been made into serfs, and the workingman who asks for higher pay or tries to change his job is treated as a criminal. Prices are going up and wages falling, and what are the people to do?"

"Somebody ought to point these things out to the Führer," suggested Lanny.

"Nobody can get near the Führer. Göring has taken charge of his mind—Göring, the aristocrat, the friend of the princes and the Junker landlords and the gentlemen of the steel *Kartell*. They are piling up bigger fortunes than ever; I'm told that Göring is doing the same—and sending the money abroad where it will be safe."

"I've heard talk about that in Paris and London," admitted Lanny; "and on pretty good authority. The money people know what's going on."

VI

They were high up in the foothills, close to the Austrian border. *Auf die Berge will ich steigen, wo die dunkeln Tannen ragen!* The air was crystal clear and delightfully cool, but it wasn't for the air that Lanny had come, nor yet on account of Heine's *Harzreise*. They sat on an outdoor platform of a little inn looking up a valley to a mountain that was Austria; Lanny saw that the slopes about him were not too precipitous, nor the stream in the valley too deep. He remarked to his companion: "There's probably a lot of illegal traffic over these mountain paths."

"Not so much as you might think," was the reply. "You don't see the sentries, but they're watching, and they shoot first and ask questions afterward."

"But they can't do much shooting on a stormy night."

"They know where the paths are, and they guard them pretty closely. But I've no doubt some of the mountaineers take bribes and share with them. The Jews are running money out of Germany by every device they can think of. They want to bleed the country to death."

That didn't sound so promising; but Lanny had to take a chance somewhere. When they were back in the car, safe from prying ears, he said: "You know, Hugo, you're so irritated with the Jews,

and yet, when I hear you talk about the ideals of National Socialism, it sounds exactly like the talk of my friend Freddi Robin whom
I've told you about."

"I don't deny that there are good Jews; many of them, no doubt;
and certainly they have plenty of brains."

"Freddi is one of the finest characters I have ever known. He is
sensitive, delicate, considerate, and I'm sure he never had a vice.
He was giving all his time and thought to the cause of social justice,
exactly as you believe in it and have explained it today."

"Is he still in Dachau?"

"I want to talk to you about him, Hugo. It's so important to
me; I can't have any peace of mind while the situation stands as
it is, and neither can anybody who knows Freddi. I'd like to take
you into my confidence, and have your word that you won't
mention it to anybody else, except by agreement with me."

"I don't think it'll be possible to get me to take an interest in the
affairs of any Jew, Lanny. I don't even care to know about him,
unless I can have your word that you won't tell anybody that you
have told me."

"You certainly can have that, Hugo. I have never mentioned
your name to anyone except my wife, and this time I didn't even
tell her that I was planning to meet you. I've told everybody I was
coming for the purpose of buying some pictures from Baron von
Zinszollern."

On that basis the young Aryan athlete consented to risk having
his mind sullied, and Lanny told him he had positive information
that Freddi was being tortured in Dachau. Lanny intimated that
this news had come to him from high Nazi sources; Hugo accepted
this, knowing well that the rich American had such contacts.
Lanny drew a horrifying picture, using the details which Göring
had furnished him; Hugo, a fundamentally decent fellow, said it
was a shame, and what did they expect to accomplish by such proceedings? Lanny answered that some of the big Nazis had learned
that Lanny's wife had a great deal of money, and were hoping to
get a chunk of it—money they could hide in New York, and have
in case they ever had to take a plane and get out of Germany. Irma

had been on the verge of paying; but Lanny's English friend, Rick, had said No, those men were betraying the Socialist movement of the world, and nobody should furnish them with funds. It had occurred to Lanny that he would rather pay money to some of the honest men in the movement, those who took seriously the second half of the party's name, and would really try to promote the interests of the common man.

In short, if Hugo Behr would spend his vacation helping to get Freddi out of Dachau, Lanny would pay him five thousand marks at the outset, and if he succeeded would pay him another five thousand, in any form and any manner he might desire. Hugo might use the money for the movement he was building, and thus his conscience would be clear. Lanny would be glad to put up whatever additional sums Hugo might find it necessary to expend in order to interest some of the proletarian S.A. men in Dachau in bringing about the escape of a comrade who had the misfortune to have been born a Jew. They, too, might use the money to save National Socialism.

"Oh, Lanny!" exclaimed the young sports director. "That's an awfully serious thing to be trying!"

"I know that well. I've been hesitating and figuring it for a year. But this news about the torturing decided me—I just can't stand it, and I'm willing to run whatever risk I have to. It's something that ought to be stopped, Hugo, and every decent Nazi ought to help me, for the good name of the party. Is that guard you told me about still there?"

"I'd have to make sure."

"I don't ask you to tell me anything you're doing, or thinking of doing. I have complete confidence in your judgment. It'll be up to you to make some friends in the camp and decide who are the right ones to trust. Don't mention me to them, and I won't mention you to anybody, now or later. We'll carry this secret to our graves."

"There'll be the question of getting your man over the border."

"You don't have to bother about that part of it. All I ask is for you to deliver Freddi to me on some dark night at a place agreed

upon, and without anybody to stop me or follow me. I don't want
to rush you into it—take your time, think it over, and ask me all
the questions you want to. Let's have a complete understanding,
so that you'll know exactly what you're getting in for, and each
of us will know exactly what we're promising."

VII

Hugo did his thinking right there in the car. He said it was a
deal; but when Lanny asked him how he wanted his first payment,
he was afraid to take the money. He said he wouldn't dare to
carry such a sum on his person, and he had no place to hide it;
he was a poor man, and had no right to have money, but Lanny,
a rich man, did, so keep it for him until the job was done and the
danger was over. Lanny said: "I am touched by your confidence."

They worked out their arrangements in detail. Neither would
ever visit the other's hotel. When Hugo wanted Lanny he would
telephone, and always use the code name of "Boecklin." They
agreed upon a certain spot on a well-frequented street, and whenever they were to meet, Lanny would stop at that spot and Hugo
would step into the car. They would do all their talking in the
car, so there could never be any eavesdropping. All this having
been agreed upon, Lanny drove his fellow conspirator to Dachau
and left him near the concentration camp, so that he might start
getting in touch with his friend.

The art expert telephoned the American consul in Munich. He
had taken the precaution to meet that gentleman on his previous
visit and to invite him to the Detaze show. Now he took him to
dinner, and over a bottle of good wine they chatted about the
affairs of Germany and the outside world. Lanny contributed an
account of the riots in Paris, and the consul said that this kind of
thing proved the need of a strong government, such as Hitler was
now furnishing to the German people. The official was sure that
the excesses of the *Regierung* had no great significance; National
Socialism would soon settle down and get itself on a living basis

with the rest of Europe. Lanny found this a sensible point of view, and his conversation showed no faintest trace of Pinkness.

Incidentally he mentioned that he was in Munich to arrange for a picture deal with Baron von Zinszollern. He wondered if the consul knew anything about this gentleman, and his reputation in the community. The reply was that the baron bore an excellent reputation, but of course the consul couldn't say as to his financial situation. Lanny smiled and said: "He is selling, not buying." He knew that the consul would take this inquiry as the purpose for which he had been invited to dine; it was a proper purpose, it being the duty of consuls to assist their fellow countrymen with information. They parted friends, and the official was satisfied that Lanny Budd was in Munich for legitimate reasons, and if later on Lanny should get into any sort of trouble, the representative of his country would have every reason to assist him and vouch for him.

Lanny stayed in his room the rest of the evening and read the *Münchner Neueste Nachrichten* from page one to the end. He learned a little of what was happening in Germany, and still more of what the Nazis wanted the Germans to believe was happening. The Reichsführer was in the Rheinland, attending the wedding of one of his Gauleiter. He was stopping at the Rhein Hotel in Essen, and had visited the Krupp works and conferred with several of the steel magnates. That was in accord with what Hugo had said; and so was the fact that Minister-Präsident General Göring was accompanying him. Flying in the rear cabin in a plane was the best of occasions for one man to whisper into another man's ear; and what was Göring telling Adi about plots against him, and the urgent need to disband the S.A. and avert the "Second Revolution"? Lanny put his imagination to work; for it was a part of his job to point out these things to Hugo and have Hugo pass them on to discontented members of the S.A. in Dachau. From the leading editorial in the newspaper Lanny followed the campaign now going on against those evil persons who were described by the German equivalents of grouches, knockers, and smart Alecks, soreheads, muckrakers, and wet blankets.

VIII

Late at night Lanny was summoned to the telephone. There being none in his room, he went downstairs, and there was the voice of "Boecklin," saying: "Can I see you?" Lanny replied, *"Ja, gewiss,"* which in American would have been "Sure thing!"

He went to his car and picked up his friend at the place agreed upon. "Well," said Hugo, "I believe it can be arranged."

"Oh, good!" exclaimed the other.

"I promised not to name any names, and there's no need of your knowing the details, I suppose."

"None in the world. I just want to know that I can come to a certain place and pick up my friend."

"There's only one trouble: I'm afraid it will cost a lot of money. You see, it can't be done by a common guard. Somebody higher up has to consent."

"What do you think it will cost?"

"About twenty thousand marks. I can't be sure what will be demanded; it might be twenty-five or thirty thousand before we get through."

"That's all right, Hugo; I can afford it. I'll get the cash and give it to you whenever you say."

"The job ought to be put through as soon as it's agreed upon. The longer we wait, the more chance of somebody's talking."

"Absolutely. I have certain arrangements to make, and it's hard for me to know exactly how long it will take, but I'm pretty sure I can be ready by Friday night. Would that be all right?"

"So far as I can guess."

"If something went wrong with my plans I might have to put it off till Saturday. Whenever you are ready for the money, you have to let me know before the bank closes."

All this was assented to; and after dropping his friend on a quiet street Lanny went to one of the large hotels where he would find a telephone booth, and there put in a call for Jerry Pendleton, Pension Flavin, Cannes. It takes time to achieve such a feat in

Europe, but he waited patiently, and at last heard his old pal's sleepy voice.

Lanny said: "The Detazes are ready, and I'm waiting in Munich for you. I am buying some others, and want to close the deal and move them on Friday. Do you think you can get here then?"

"By heck!" said Jerry. It was Wednesday midnight, and his voice came suddenly awake. "I can't get visas until morning."

"You can hunt up the consul tonight and pay him extra."

"I'll have to go and make sure about Cyprien first." That was a nephew of Leese, who did truck-driving for Bienvenu.

"All right, get him or somebody else. Make note of my address, and phone me at noon tomorrow and again late in the evening, letting me know where you are. Come by way of Verona and the Brenner, and don't let anything keep you from being here. If you should have a breakdown, let Cyprien come with the truck, and you take a train, or a plane if you have to. I have somebody here I want you to meet on Friday."

"O.K." said the ex-tutor and ex-soldier; he sort of sang it, with the accent on the first syllable, and it was like a signature over the telephone.

IX

Baron von Zinszollern possessed an Anton Mauve, a large and generous work portraying a shepherd leading home his flock in a pearly gray and green twilight. It seemed to Lanny a fine example of that painter's poetical and serious feeling, and he had got the price down to thirty thousand marks. He had telegraphed Zoltan that he was disposed to buy it as a gamble, and did his friend care to go halves? His friend replied Yes, so he went that morning and bought the work, paying two thousand marks down and agreeing to pay the balance within a week. This involved signing papers, which Lanny would have on his person; also, an influential Nazi sympathizer would have an interest in testifying that he was really an art expert. Incidentally it gave Lanny a pretext for going to the Munich branch of the Hellstein Bank, and having them pay him thirty thousand marks in Nazi paper.

At noon the dependable Jerry telephoned. He and Cyprien and the *camion* were past Genoa. They would eat and sleep on board, and keep moving. Lanny told him to telephone about ten in the evening wherever they were. Jerry sang: "O.K."

A little later came a call from "Boecklin," and Lanny took him for a drive. He said: "It's all fixed. You're to pay twenty-three thousand marks, and your man will be delivered to you anywhere in Dachau at twenty-two o'clock tomorrow evening. Will you be ready?"

"I'm pretty sure to. Here's your money." Lanny took out his wallet, and handed it to his friend beside him. "Help yourself."

It was improbable that Hugo Behr, son of a shipping clerk, had ever had so much money in his hands before. The hands trembled slightly as he took out the bundle of crisp new banknotes, each for one thousand marks; he counted out twenty-three of them, while Lanny went on driving and didn't seem to be especially interested. Hugo counted them a second time, both times out loud.

"You'd better take your own, also," suggested the lordly one. "You know I might get into some trouble."

"If you do, I'd rather be able to say you hadn't paid me anything. I'm doing it purely for friendship's sake, and because you're a friend of Heinrich and Kurt."

"Lay all the emphasis you can on them!" chuckled Lanny. "Mention that Heinrich told you how he had taken Kurt and me to visit the Führer last winter; and also that I told you about taking a hunting trip with Göring. So you were sure I must be all right."

Hugo had got some news about Freddi which the other heard gladly. Apparently Lanny had been right in what he had said about the Jewish prisoner; he had won the respect even of those who were trying to crush him. Unfortunately he was in the hands of the Gestapo, which kept him apart from the regular run of inmates. A prison inside the prison, it appeared! The rumor was that they had been trying to force Freddi to reveal the names of certain

Social-Democrats who were operating an illegal press in Berlin; but he insisted that he knew nothing about it.

"He wouldn't be apt to know," said Lanny. To himself he added: "Trudi Schultz!"

It had been his intention to make a casual remark to his friend: "Oh, by the way, I wonder if you could find out if there's a man in Dachau by the name of Ludwig Schultz." But now he realized that it was not so simple as he had thought. To tell Hugo that he was trying to help another of the dreaded "Marxists" might sour him on the whole deal. And for Hugo to tell his friends in the concentration camp might have the same effect upon them. Lanny could do nothing for poor Trudi—at least not this trip.

X

He drove the car to Dachau, and they rolled about its streets, to decide upon a spot which would be dark and quiet. They learned the exact description of this place, so that Hugo could tell it to the men who were going to bring Freddi. Hugo said he had an appointment to pay the money to a man in Munich at twenty o'clock, or 8:00 p.m. according to the American way of stating it. Hugo was nervous about wandering around with such an unthinkable sum in his pocket, so Lanny drove him up into the hills, where they looked at beautiful scenery. The American quoted: "Where every prospect pleases and only man is vile." He didn't translate it for his German friend.

Hugo had been talking to some of his party comrades in Munich, the birthplace of their movement, and had picked up news which didn't get into the *gleichgeschaltete Presse*. There was a terrible state of tension in the party; everybody appeared to be quarreling with everybody else. Göring and Goebbels were at daggers drawn over the question of controlling policy—which, Lanny understood, meant controlling Hitler's mind. Goebbels had announced a program of compelling industry to share profits with the workers, and this, of course, was criminal to Göring and his friends the industrialists. Just recently von Papen, still a Reichsminister, had made

a speech demanding freedom of the press to discuss all public questions, and Göring had intervened and forbidden the publication of
this speech. A day or two ago the man who was said to have written the speech for the "gentleman jockey" had been arrested in
Munich, and the town was buzzing with gossip about the quarrel. It
was rumored that a hundred and fifty of Goebbels's personal guards
had mutinied and been sent to a concentration camp. All sorts of
wild tales like this, and who knew what to believe?

They had come to the Tegernsee, a lovely mountain lake, and
there was a road-sign, reading: "Bad Wiessee, 7 km." Hugo said:
"The papers report that Röhm is having his vacation there. I hear
he's had several conferences with the Führer in the past week or
two, and they've had terrible rows."

"What's the trouble between them?" inquired the gossip-hungry
visitor.

"The same old story. Röhm and his friends want the original
party program carried out. Now, of course, he's wild over the
idea of having his Stormtroopers disbanded."

Lanny could credit the latter motive, if not the former. He had
heard the red-headed Chief of Staff speak at one of the Nazi *Ver-
sammlungen*, and had got the impression of an exceedingly tough
military adventurer, untroubled by social ideals. Perhaps that was
due in part to his battle-scars, the upper part of his nose having
been shot away! Röhm wanted the powers of his Brownshirts increased, and naturally would fight desperately against having them
wiped out.

Seven kilometers was nothing, so Lanny turned his car in the
direction indicated by the sign. A lovely little village with tree-
shaded streets, and cottages on the lakefront. In front of one of
the largest, and also of the Gasthaus Heinzlbauer, were parked a
great many fancy cars. Hugo said: "They must be having a conference. Only our leaders can afford cars like those." The note of
bitterness indicated that he didn't trust his new Führer much more
than his old.

"Do you know him?" asked Lanny.

"I know one of the staff members in Berlin, and he has told the Chief that I am working on his behalf."

"Would you like to go in and meet him?"

"Do *you* know him?" countered Hugo, startled.

"No; but I thought he might be interested to meet an American art expert."

"*Aber*, Lanny!" exclaimed the young sports director, whose sense of humor was not his strongest suit. "I really don't think he has much time to think about art right now!"

"He might take a fancy to a magnificent young athlete like yourself, Hugo."

"*Gott behüte!*" was the reply.

It seemed almost blasphemy to talk about this subject while under the shadow of Röhm and his entourage; but when the American put the question point blank, Hugo admitted that he had heard about the habits of the Sturmabteilung Chief of Staff. Everybody in Germany knew about them, for Hauptmann Röhm, while acting as a military instructor in Bolivia, had written a series of letters home admitting his abnormal tastes, and these letters had been published in the German press. Now, said Hugo, his enemies gave that as the reason for not taking him and his staff into the regular army. "As if the Reichswehr officers were lily-white saints!" exclaimed the S.A. man.

XI

Back in the city, Lanny took a long walk in the Englischer Garten, going over his plans and trying to make all possible mistakes in advance. Then he went back and read the co-ordinated newspapers, and picked up hints of the struggle going on—you could find them if you were an insider. It looked very much as if the N.S.D.A.P. was going to split itself to pieces. Lanny was tempted by the idea that if he waited a few days, Freddi Robin might come out from Dachau with a brass band leading the way!

At the appointed hour Jerry Pendleton called; he was rolling on, and all was well. It was slow on the mountain roads, but he thought he could make it by noon the next day. "What is the deadline?" he asked, and Lanny replied: "Two o'clock." Jerry sang: "O.K." and Lanny lay down and tried to sleep, but found it difficult, because he kept imagining himself in the hands of the Gestapo, who had prisons inside of prisons. What would he say? And more important yet, what would they do?

Next morning the conspirator received a telephone call from "Herr Boecklin," and drove to meet his friend and receive some bad news; one of the men concerned was demanding more money, because the thing was so very dangerous. Lanny asked how much, and the answer was, another five thousand marks. Lanny said all right, he would get it at once; but Hugo wanted to change the arrangement. He hadn't paid out the money, and wanted to refuse to pay more than half until the prisoner was actually delivered. His idea now was to drive to Dachau with Lanny at the appointed time, and to keep watch near by. If Freddi was produced and everything seemed all right, he would emerge and pay the rest of the money.

Lanny said: "That's a lot more dangerous for you, Hugo."

"Not so very," was the reply. "I'm sure it's not a trap; but if it were, they could get me anyhow. What I want to do is to keep you from paying the money and then not getting your man."

XII

Lanny went back to his hotel and waited until early afternoon, on pins and needles. At last came a telephone call; Jerry Pendleton was at the hotel in Munich to which Lanny had told him to come. "Everything hunkydory, not a scratch."

Lanny said: "Be out on the street; I'll pick you up."

"Give me ten minutes to shave and change my shirt," countered the ex-lieutenant from Kansas.

Delightful indeed to set eyes on somebody from home; somebody who could be trusted, and who didn't say "Heil Hitler!" The ex-lieutenant was over forty, his red hair was losing its sheen and he had put on some weight; but to Lanny he was still America, prompt, efficient, and full of what it called "pep," "zip," and "ginger." A lady's man all his life, Lanny was still impressed by the masculine type, with hair on its chest. Though he would have died before admitting it, he was both lonely and scared in Naziland.

Driving in the traffic of the Ludwigstrasse, he couldn't look at his ex-tutor, but he said: "Gee whiz, Jerry, you're a sight for sore eyes!"

"The same to you, kid!"

"You won't be so glad of my company when you hear what I'm in this town for."

"Why, what's the matter? I thought you were buying pictures."

"I am buying Freddi Robin out of the Dachau concentration camp."

"Jesus Christ!" exclaimed Jerry.

"He's to be delivered to me at ten o'clock tonight, and you've got to help me smuggle him out of this goddam Nazi country!"

27

A Deed of Dreadful Note

I

JERRY had known that Freddi Robin was a prisoner in Germany, but hadn't known where or why or how. Now, in the car, safe from eavesdroppers, Lanny told the story and expounded his plan. He was proposing to take his own photograph from his passport and substitute that of Freddi Robin which he had brought with him. Then he would pick up Freddi in Dachau, drive to some other part of the town and get Jerry, and let Jerry drive Freddi out of Germany under the name of Lanning Prescott Budd. Such was the genial scheme.

"At first," Lanny explained, "I had the idea of fixing up your passport for Freddi to use, and I would drive him out. But I realized, there's very little danger in the driving part—the passports will be all right, and once you get clear of Dachau everything will be O.K. But the fellow who's left behind without a passport may have a bit of trouble; so that's why I'm offering you the driving part."

"But, my God!" cried the bewildered Kansan. "Just what do you expect to do about getting out?"

"I'll go to the American consul and tell him my passport has been stolen. I have made friends with him and he'll probably give me some sort of duplicate. If he won't, it'll be up to me to find a way to sneak out by some of the mountain passes."

"But, Lanny, you're out of your mind! In the first place, the moment Freddi's escape is discovered they'll know he's heading for the Austrian border, and they'll block the passes."

"It'll take you only an hour or two to get to the border from Dachau, and you'll be over and gone. You're to drive my car, understand, not the *camion*."

"But there will be the record of the Lanny Budd passport and of mine at the border."

"What then? They'll draw the conclusion that you are the man who stole my passport. But it's not an extraditable offense."

"They'll know it was a put-up job! You're the brother-in-law of Freddi's brother and you've been trying to get him released. It'll be obvious that you gave me your papers."

"They won't have a particle of evidence to prove it."

"They'll sweat it out of you, Lanny. I tell you, it's a bum steer! I could never look your mother or your father or your wife in the face if I let you put your foot into such a trap." As ex-tutor, Jerry spoke for the family.

"But I have to get Freddi out of Germany!" insisted the ex-pupil. "I've been a year making up my mind to that."

"All right, kid; but go back to your original idea. *You* steal *my* passport and drive Freddi out."

"And leave you in the hole?"

"That's not nearly so bad, because I'm not related to the prisoner and I'm not known. I'm a fellow you hired to get your paintings, and you played a dirty trick on me and left me stuck. I can put up a howl about it and stick to my story."

"They'd sweat you instead of me, Jerry."

So the two argued back and forth; an "Alphonse and Gaston" scene, but deadly serious. Meanwhile the precious time was passing in which exit permits and visas had to be got. There appeared to be a deadlock—until suddenly an inspiration came to the ex-tutor. "Let's both go out with Freddi, and leave Cyprien to face the music. I'll steal *his* passport in earnest."

"That would be a rotten deal, Jerry."

"Not so bad as it seems. Cyprien's a French peasant, who obviously wouldn't have the brains to think up anything. He'll be in a rage with us, and put on a fine act. I'll get him loaded up with good Munich beer and he'll be smelling of it when the police come for him. When we get to France you can telegraph some money to the French consul here and tell him to look after his own. When Cyprien gets home with his truck you can give him a few thousand francs and he'll think it was the great adventure of his life."

Lanny didn't like that plan, but his friend settled it with an argument which Lanny hadn't thought of. "Believe me, Freddi Robin looks a lot more like the name Cyprien Santoze than like the name Lanning Prescott Budd!" Then, seeing Lanny weakening: "Come on! Let's get going!"

II

Jerry took the truckman to get their exit permits and to have their passports "visaed" for Switzerland—he thought it better not to trust themselves in Mussolini's land. Lanny went separately and did the same, while Jerry treated Cyprien to a square meal, including plenty of good Munich beer. The Frenchman, who hadn't grown up as saintly as his mother had named him, drank everything that was put before him, and then wanted to go out and inspect the girls of thirteen years and up who were offering themselves in such numbers on the streets of Munich. His escort said: "Those girls sometimes pick your pockets, so you'd better give me your papers to keep." The other accepted this as a reasonable precaution.

Lanny drove his friend out to Dachau to study the lay of the land. He pointed out the spot where the prisoner was to be delivered, and made certain that Jerry knew the street names and landmarks. It was the Kansan's intention to "scout around," so he said; he would find a place from which he could watch the spot and see that everything went off according to schedule. Hugo would be doing the same thing, and Lanny wasn't at liberty to tell Jerry about Hugo or Hugo about Jerry. It sufficed to warn his friend that there would be a Nazi officer watching, and Jerry said: "I'll watch *him*, too!"

One serious difficulty, so far as concerned the ex-tutor, and that was, he knew only a few words of German. He said: "Tell me, how do you say: 'Hands up!'?"

Lanny answered: "What are you thinking about, idiot? Have you got a gun?"

"Who? Me? Who ever heard of me carrying a gun?" This from one who had been all through the Meuse-Argonne in the autumn of 1918!

"You mustn't try any rough stuff, Jerry. Remember, murder is an extraditable offense."

"Sure, I know," responded the other. "They extradited a couple of million of us. You remember, the A.E.F., the American Extraditable Force!" It was the old doughboy spirit.

Lanny knew that Jerry owned a Budd automatic, and it was likely he had brought it along with him in the truck. But he wouldn't say any more about it; he just wanted to learn to say: "*Hände hoch!*"

They studied the map. They would drive north out of Dachau,

then make a circle and head south, skirt the city of Munich and streak for the border. When they had got the maps fixed in mind, they went over the streets of Dachau, noting the landmarks, so as to make no mistake in the dark. All this done, they drove back to Munich and had a late supper in a quiet tavern, and then Jerry went to his hotel. There were a few things he didn't want to leave behind, and one or two letters he wanted to destroy. "I didn't know I was embarking upon a criminal career," he said, with a grin.

At the proper hour he met his pal on the street and was motored out to Dachau and dropped there. It was dark by then, a lovely summer evening, and the people of this workingclass district were sitting in front of their homes. Lanny said: "You'll have to keep moving so as not to attract attention. See you later, old scout!" He spoke with assurance, but didn't feel it inside!

III

Back in Munich, the playboy drove past the spot where he was accustomed to meet Hugo, in front of a tobacco shop on a well-frequented street. Darkness had fallen, but the street was lighted. Lanny didn't see his friend, and knowing that he was ahead of time, drove slowly around the block. When he turned the corner again, he saw his friend not far ahead of him, walking toward the appointed spot.

There was a taxicab proceeding in the same direction, some thirty or forty feet behind Hugo, going slowly and without lights. Lanny waited for it to pass on; but the driver appeared to be looking for a street number. So Lanny went ahead of it and drew up by the curb, where Hugo saw him and started to join him. Lanny leaned over to open the door on the right side of the car; and at the same moment the taxicab stopped alongside Lanny's car. Three men sprang out, wearing the black shirts and trousers and steel helmets of the Schutzstaffel. One of them stood staring at Lanny, while the other two darted behind Lanny's car and confronted the young sports director in the act of putting his hand on the car door.

"Are you Hugo Behr?" demanded one of the men.

"I am," was the reply.

Lanny turned to look at the questioner; but the man's next action was faster than any eye could follow. He must have had a gun in his hand behind his back; he swung it up and fired straight into the face in front of him, and not more than a foot away. Pieces of the blue eye of Hugo Behr and a fine spray of his Aryan blood flew out, and some hit Lanny in the face. The rest of Hugo Behr crumpled and dropped to the sidewalk; whereupon the man turned his gun into the horrified face of the driver.

"*Hände hoch!*" he commanded; and that was certainly turning the tables upon Lanny. He put them high.

"*Wer sind Sie?*" demanded the S.S. man.

It was a time for the quickest possible answers, and Lanny was fortunate in having thought up the best possible. "I am an American art expert, and a friend of the Führer."

"Oh! So you're a friend of the Führer!"

"I have visited him several times. I spent a morning with him in the Braune Haus a few months ago."

"How do you come to know Hugo Behr?"

"I was introduced to him in the home of Heinrich Jung, a high official of the Hitler Jugend in Berlin. Heinrich is one of the Führer's oldest friends and visited him many times when he was in the Landsberg fortress. It was Heinrich who introduced me to the Führer." Lanny rattled this off as if it were a school exercise; and indeed it was something like that, for he had imagined interrogations and had learned his *Rolle* in the very best German. Since the S.S. man didn't tell him to stop, he went on, as fast as ever: "Also on the visit to the Reichsführer in the Braune Haus went Kurt Meissner of Schloss Stubendorf, who is a Komponist and author of several part-songs which you sing at your assemblies. He has known me since we were boys at Hellerau, and will tell you that I am a friend of the National Socialist movement."

That was the end of the speech, so far as Lanny had planned it. But even as he said the last words a horrible doubt smote him: Perhaps this was some sort of anti-Nazi revolution, and he was sealing his own doom! He saw that the point of the gun had come down, and the muzzle was looking into his navel instead of into his face; but that wasn't enough to satisfy him. He stared at the S.S. man, who had black eyebrows that met over his nose. It seemed to Lanny the hardest face he had ever examined.

"What were you doing with this man?"—nodding downward toward what lay on the pavement.

"I am in Munich buying a painting from Baron von Zinszollern. I saw Hugo Behr walking on the street and I stopped to say *Grüss Gott* to him." Lanny was speaking impromptu now.

"Get out of the car," commanded the S.S. man.

Lanny's heart was hitting hard blows underneath his throat; his knees were trembling so violently he wasn't sure they would hold him up. It appeared that he was being ordered out so that his blood and brains might not spoil a good car. "I tell you, you will regret it if you shoot me. I am an intimate friend of Minister-Präsident General Göring. I was on a hunting trip with him last fall. You can ask Oberleutnant Furtwaengler of Seine Exzellenz's staff. You can ask Reichsminister Goebbels about me—or his wife, Frau Magda Goebbels—I have visited their home. You can read articles about me in the Munich newspapers of last November when I conducted an exhibition of paintings here and took one of them to the Führer. My picture was in all the papers——"

"I am not going to shoot you," announced the S.S. man. His tone indicated abysmal contempt of anybody who objected to being shot.

"What are you going to do?"

"Take you to Stadelheim until your story is investigated. Get out of the car."

Stadelheim was a name of terror; one of those dreadful prisons about which the refugees talked. But it was better than being shot on the sidewalk, so Lanny managed to control his nerves, and obeyed. The other man passed his hands over him to see if he was armed. Then the leader commanded him to search the body of Hugo, and he collected a capful of belongings including a wad of bills which Lanny knew amounted to some fifteen thousand marks.

Apparently they meant to leave the corpse right there, and Lanny wondered, did they have a corpse-collecting authority, or did they leave it to the neighborhood?

However, he didn't have much time for speculation. "Get into the back seat," commanded the leader and climbed in beside him, still holding the gun on him. The man who had got out on Lanny's side of the car now slipped into the driver's seat, and the car sprang to life and sped down the street.

· I V

Lanny had seen Stadelheim from the outside; a great mass of buildings on a tree-lined avenue, the Tegernsee road upon which he had driven Hugo Behr. Now the walls of the place loomed enormous and forbidding in the darkness. Lanny was ordered out of the car, and two of his captors escorted him through the doorway, straight past the reception room, and down a stone corridor into a small room. He had expected to be "booked" and fingerprinted; but apparently this was to be dispensed with. They ordered him to take off his coat, trousers, and shoes, and proceeded to search him. "There is considerable money in that wallet," he said, and the leader replied, grimly: "We will take care of it." They took his watch, keys, fountain-pen, necktie, everything but his handkerchief. They searched the linings of his clothing, and looked carefully to see if there were any signs that the heels of his shoes might be removable.

Finally they told him to put his clothes on again. Lanny said: "Would you mind telling me what I am suspected of?" The reply of the leader was: "*Maul halten!*" Apparently they didn't believe his wonder-tales about being the intimate friend of the three leading Nazis. Not wishing to get a knock over the head with a revolver butt, Lanny held his mouth, as ordered, and was escorted out of the room and down the corridor to a guarded steel door.

The head S.S. man appeared to have the run of the place; all he had to do was to salute and say: "*Heil Hitler!*" and all doors were swung open for him. He led the prisoner down a narrow flight of stone stairs, into a passage dimly lighted and lined with steel doors.

Old prisons have such places of darkness and silence, where deeds without a name have been done. A warder who accompanied the trio opened one of these doors, and Lanny was shoved in without a word. The door clanged behind him; and that, as he had learned to say in the land of his fathers, was that.

V

In the darkness he could only explore the place by groping. The cell was narrow and had an iron cot built into the stone wall. On the cot were two sacks of straw and a blanket. In the far corner was a stinking pail without a cover; and that was all. There was a vile, age-old odor, and no window; ventilation was provided by two openings in the solid door, one high and one low; they could be closed by sliding covers on the outside, but perhaps this would be done only if Lanny misbehaved. He didn't.

He was permitted to sit on the straw sacks and think, and he did his best to quiet the tumult of his heart and use his reasoning powers. What had happened? It seemed obvious that his plot had been discovered. Had the would-be conspirators been caught, or had they taken the money and then reported the plot to their superiors? And if so, would they shoot Freddi? No use worrying about that now. Lanny couldn't be of any use to Freddi unless he himself got out, so he had to put his mind on his own plight, and prepare for the examination which was bound sooner or later to come.

Hugo's part in the jailbreak had evidently been betrayed; but Hugo had never named Lanny, so he had said. Of course this might or might not have been true. They had found a bunch of thousand-mark notes on Hugo, and they had found some on Lanny; suddenly the prisoner realized, with a near collapse of his insides, what a stupid thing he had done. The clue which a criminal always leaves! He had gone to the bank and got thirty new thousand-mark bills, doubtless having consecutive serial numbers, and had given some of these to Hugo and kept some in his own wallet!

So they would be sure that he had tried to buy a prisoner out of Dachau. What would the penalty be for that crime? What it would have been under the old regime was one thing, and under the Nazis something else again. As if to answer his question there came terrifying sounds, muffled yet unmistakable; first, a roll of drums, and then shooting somewhere in those dungeon depths or else outside the walls. Not a single shot, not a series of shots, but a volley, a closely-packed bunch of shots. They were executing somebody, or perhaps several bodies. Lanny, who had started to his feet, had to sit down again because his legs were giving way.

Who would that be? The S.A. man in Dachau with whom Hugo had been dealing? The man higher up who had demanded more money? The plot must have been betrayed early, for it couldn't be much after ten o'clock, and there had hardly been time for the jailbreak to have been attempted and the guilty parties brought from Dachau to this prison. Of course it might be that this was some execution that had nothing to do with Dachau. Shootings were frequent in Nazi prisons, all refugees agreed. Perhaps they shot people every night at twenty-two o'clock, German time!

After the most careful thought, Lanny decided that the Nazis had him nailed down; no chance of wriggling out. He had come to Germany to get Freddi Robin, and the picture-dealing had been only a blind. He had had a truck brought from France—they would be sure he had meant to take Freddi out in that truck! And there was Jerry—with two one-thousand-mark bills which Lanny had handed him! Also with the passport of Cyprien Santoze, having the picture of Freddi Robin substituted! Would they catch the meaning of that?

Or would Jerry perhaps get away? He would be walking about, passing the appointed spot, waiting for the prisoner and for Lanny to appear. Would the Nazis be watching and arrest anybody who passed? It was an important question, for if Jerry escaped he'd surely go to the American consul and report Lanny as missing. Would he tell the consul the whole truth? He might or he might not; but anyhow the consul would be making inquiries as to the son of Budd Gunmakers.

VI

More drum-rolls and more shooting! Good God, were they killing people all night in German prisons? Apparently so; for that was the way Lanny spent the night, listening to volleys, long or short, loud or dim. He couldn't tell whether they were inside or out. Did they have a special execution chamber, or did they just shoot you anywhere you happened to be? And what did they do with all the blood? Lanny imagined that he smelled it, and the fumes of gunpowder; but maybe he was mistaken, for the stink of a rusty old slop-pail can be extremely pungent in a small cell. An art expert had seen many pictures of executions, ancient and modern, so he knew what to imagine. Sometimes they blindfolded the victims, sometimes they made them turn their backs, sometimes they just put an automatic to the base of their skulls, the medulla; that was said to be merciful, and certainly it was quick. The Nazis cared nothing about mercy, but they surely did about speed.

Every now and then a door clanged, and Lanny thought: "They are taking somebody to his doom." Now and then he heard footsteps, and thought: "Are they coming or going?" He wondered about the bodies. Did they have stretchers? Or did they just drag them? He imagined that he heard dragging. Several times there were screams; and once a man going by his door, arguing, shouting protests. What was the matter with them? He was as good a Nazi as anyone in Germany. They were making a mistake. It was *eine gottverdammte Schande*—and so on. That gave Lanny something new to think about, and he sat for a long time motionless on his straw pallet, with his brain in a whirl.

Maybe all this hadn't anything to do with Freddi and a jailbreak! Maybe nothing had been discovered at all! It was that "Second Revolution" that Hugo had been so freely predicting! Hugo had been shot, not because he had tried to bribe a Dachau guard, but because he was on the list of those who were actively working on behalf of Ernst Röhm and the other malcontents of the Sturmabteilung! In that case the shootings might be part of the putting down of that movement. It was significant that Lanny's captors had

been men of the Schutzstaffel, the "élite guard," Hitler's own chosen
ones. They were putting their rivals out of business; "liquidating"
those who had been demanding more power for the S.A. Chief of
Staff!

But then, a still more startling possibility—the executions might
mean the success of the rebels. The fact that Hugo Behr had been
killed didn't mean that the S.S. had had their way everywhere.
Perhaps the S.A. were defending themselves successfully! Perhaps
Stadelheim had been taken, as the Bastille had been taken in the
French revolution, and the persons now being shot were those who
had put Lanny in here! At any moment the doors of his cell might
be thrown open and he might be welcomed with comradely rejoicing!

Delirious imaginings; but then the whole thing was a delirium.
To lie there in the darkness with no way to count the hours and
nothing to do but speculate about a world full of maniacal mur-
derers. Somebody was killing somebody, that alone was certain, and
it went on at intervals without any sign of ending. Lanny remembered the French revolution, and the unhappy aristocrats who had
lain in their cells awaiting their turn to be loaded into the tumbrils
and carted to the guillotine. This kind of thing was said to turn
people's hair gray over night; Lanny wondered if it was happening
to him. Every time he heard footsteps he hoped it was somebody
coming to let him out; but then he was afraid to have the footsteps
halt, because it might be a summons to the execution chamber!

He tried to comfort himself. He had had no part in any conspiracy of the S.A. and surely they wouldn't shoot him just because
he had met a friend on the street. But then he thought: "Those
banknotes!" They would attach a still more sinister meaning to
them now. They would say: "What were you paying Hugo Behr
to do?" And what should he answer? He had said that he hadn't
known what Hugo wanted of him. They would know that was a
lie. They would say: "You were helping to promote a revolution
against the N.S.D.A.P." And that was surely a shooting offense—
even though you had come from the sweet land of liberty to do it!

Lanny thought up the best way to meet this very bad situation.

When he was questioned, he would talk about his friendship with the great and powerful, and wait to pick up any hint that the questioner had made note of the bills, or had found out about Freddi Robin. If these discoveries had been made, Lanny would laugh—at least he would try to laugh—and say: "Yes, of course I lied to those S.S. men on the street. I thought they were crazy and were going to shoot me. The truth is that Hugo Behr came to me and asked for money and offered to use his influence with the S.A. in Dachau to get my friend released. There was no question of any bribe, he said he would put the money into the party funds and it would go for the winter relief." One thing Lanny could be sure of in this matter—nothing that he said about Hugo could do the slightest harm to the young sports director.

VII

Footsteps in the corridor; a slot at the bottom of Lanny's door was widened, and something was set inside. He said, quickly: "Will you please tell me how long I am to be kept here?" When there was no reply, he said: "I am an American citizen and I demand the right to communicate with my consul." The slot was made smaller again and the footsteps went on.

Lanny felt with his hands and found a metal pitcher of water, a cup of warm liquid, presumably coffee, and a chunk of rather stale bread. He wasn't hungry, but drank some of the water. Presumably that was breakfast, and it was morning. He lay and listened to more shooting off and on; and after what seemed a very long time the slot was opened and more food put in. Out of curiosity he investigated, and found that he had a plate of what appeared to be cold potatoes mashed up with some sort of grease. The grease must have been rancid, for the smell was revolting, and Lanny came near to vomiting at the thought of eating it. He had been near to vomiting several times at the thought of people being shot in this dungeon of horrors.

A bowl of cabbage soup and more bread were brought in what he assumed was the evening; and this time the warder spoke. He said:

"Pass out your slop-pail." Lanny did so, and it was emptied and passed back to him without washing. This sign of humanity caused him to make a little speech about his troubles. He said that he had done nothing, that he had no idea what he was accused of, that it was very inhuman to keep a man in a dark hole, that he had always been a lover of Germany and a sympathizer with its struggle against the Versailles *Diktat*. Finally, he was an American citizen, and had a right to notify his consul of his arrest.

This time he managed to get one sentence of reply: "*Sprechen verboten, mein Herr*." It sounded like a kind voice, and Lanny recalled what he had heard, that many of the permanent staff of these prisons were men of the former regime, well disciplined and humane. He took a chance and ventured in a low voice: "I am a rich man, and if you will telephone the American consul for me, I will pay you well when I get out."

"*Sprechen verboten, mein Herr*," replied the voice; and then, much lower: "*Sprechen Sie leise*." Speaking is forbidden, sir; speak softly! So the prisoner whispered: "My name is Lanny Budd." He repeated it several times: "Lanny Budd, Lanny Budd." It became a little song. Would that it might have wings, and fly to the American consulate!

VIII

For three days and four nights Lanny Budd stayed in that narrow cell. He could estimate the number of cubic feet of air inside, but he didn't know what percentage of that air was oxygen, or how much he needed per hour in order to maintain his life. His scientific education had been neglected, but it seemed a wise precaution to put his straw sacks on the floor and lie on them with his mouth near the breathing hole.

Saturday, Sunday, Monday—he could tell them by the meal hours —and during a total of some eighty-two hours there were not a dozen without sounds of shooting. He never got over his dismay. God Almighty, did they do this all the time? Had this been going on ever since the National Socialist revolution, one year and five months ago? Did they bring all the political suspects of Bavaria to this one place? Or was this some special occasion, a Nazi St. Bartholomew's Eve? "Kill them all; God will be able to pick out His Christians!"

Lanny, having nothing to do but think, had many and varied ideas. One was: "Well, they are all Nazis, and if they exterminate one another, that will save the world a lot of trouble." But then: "Suppose they should open the wrong cell door?" An embarrassing thought indeed! What would he say? How would he convince them? As time passed he decided: "They have forgotten me. Those fellows didn't book me, and maybe they just went off without a word." And then, a still more confusing possibility: "Suppose they get shot somewhere and nobody remembers me!" He had a vague memory of having read about a forgotten prisoner in the Bastille; when the place was opened up, nobody knew why he had been put there. He had had a long gray beard. Lanny felt the beginnings of his beard and wondered if it was gray.

He gave serious study to his jailers and their probable psychology. It seemed difficult to believe that men who had followed such an occupation for many years could have any human kindness left in their systems; but it could do no harm to make sure. So at every meal hour he was lying on the floor close to the hole, delivering a carefully planned speech in a quiet, friendly tone, explaining who he was, and how much he loved the German people, and why he had come to Munich, and by what evil accident he had fallen under suspicion. All he wanted was a chance to explain himself to somebody. He figured that if he didn't touch the heart of any of the keepers, he might at least get them to gossiping, and the gossip might spread.

IX

He didn't know how long a person could live without food. It wasn't until the second day that he began to suffer from hunger, and he gnawed some of the soggy dark bread, wondering what was in it. He couldn't bring himself to eat the foul-smelling mash or the lukewarm boiled cabbage with grease on top. As for the bitter-tasting drink that passed for coffee, he had been told that they put sal soda into it in order to reduce the sexual cravings of the prisoners. He didn't feel any craving except to get out of this black hole. He whispered to his keepers: "I had about six thousand marks on me when I was brought in here, and I would be glad to pay for some decent food." The second time he said this he heard the kind voice, which he imagined coming from an elderly man with a wrinkled face and gray mustaches. "*Alles geht d'runter und d'rüber, mein Herr.*" . . . "Everything topsy-turvy, sir; and you will be safer if you stay quiet."

It was a tip; and Lanny thought it over and decided that he had better take it. There was a civil war going on. Was the "Second Revolution" succeeding, or was it being put down? In either case, an American art lover, trapped between the firing lines, was lucky to have found a shell-hole in which to hide! Had the warder been a Cockney, he would have said: "If you knows of a better 'ole, go to it!"

So Lanny lay still and occupied himself with the subject of psychology, which so far in his life he had rather neglected. The world had been too much with him; getting and spending he had laid waste his powers. But now the world had been reduced to a few hundred cubic feet, and all he had was the clothes on his back and what ideas he had stored in his head. He began to recall Parsifal Dingle, and to appreciate his point of view. Parsifal wouldn't have minded being here; he would have taken it as a rare opportunity to meditate. Lanny thought: "What would Parsifal meditate about?" Surely not the shooting, or the fate of a hypothetical revolution! No, he would say that God was in this cell; that God was the same indoors as out, the same yesterday, today, and forever.

Then Lanny thought about Freddi Robin. Freddi had been in places like this, and had had the same sort of food put before him, not for three days but for more than a year. What had he said to himself all that time? What had he found inside himself? What had he done and thought, to pass the time, to enable him to endure what came and the anticipation of what might come? It seemed time for Lanny to investigate his store of moral forces.

X

On Tuesday morning two jailers came to his cell and opened the door. " *'Raus, 'raus!*" they said, and he obeyed to the best of his ability; he was weak from lack of food and exercise—not having dared to use up the air in that cell. Also his heart was pounding, because all the psychology exercises had failed to remove his disinclination to be shot, or the idea that this might be his death march. Outside the cell he went dizzy, and had to lean against the wall; one of the jailers helped him up the flight of stone stairs.

They were taking him toward an outside door. They were going to turn him loose!—so he thought, for one moment. But then he saw, below the steps, a prison van—what in America is called "Black Maria," and in Germany "Grüne Minna." The sunlight smote Lanny's eyes like a blow, and he had to shut them tight. The jailers evidently were familiar with this phenomenon; they led him as if he were a blind man and helped him as if he were a cripple. They put him into the van, and he stumbled over the feet of several other men.

The doors were closed, and then it was mercifully dim. Lanny opened his eyes; since they had been brought to the condition of an owl's, he could see a stoutish, melancholy-looking gentleman who might be a businessman, sitting directly across the aisle. At Lanny's side was an eager little Jew with eyeglasses, who might be a journalist out of luck. Lanny, never failing in courtesy, remarked: "*Guten Morgen*"; but the man across the way put his finger to his lips and nodded toward the guard who had entered the van and taken his seat by the door. Evidently "*Sprechen verboten*" was still the rule.

But some men have keen wits, and do not hand them over when they enter a jail. The little Jew laid his hand on Lanny's where it rested on the seat between them. He gave a sharp tap with his finger, and at the same time, turning his head toward Lanny and from the guard, he opened his mouth and whispered softly: "*Ah!*" just as if he were beginning a singing lesson, or having his throat examined for follicular tonsillitis. Then he gave two quick taps, and

whispered: *"Bay!"* which is the second letter of the German alpha-
bet. Then three taps: *"Tsay!"*—the third letter; and so on, until the
other nodded his head. Lanny had heard tapping in his dungeon,
but hadn't been sure whether it was the water-pipes or some code
which he didn't know.

This was the simplest of codes, and the Jew proceeded to tap
eighteen times, and then waited until Lanny had calculated that this
was the letter R. Thus slowly and carefully, he spelled out the
name "R-O-E-H-M." Lanny assumed that the little man was giving
his own name, and was prepared to tap "B-U-D-D," and be glad
that it was short. But no, his new friend was going on; Lanny
counted through letter after letter: "E-R-S-C-H-O-S—." By that
time the little Jew must have felt Lanny's hand come alive beneath
his gentle taps, and realized that Lanny had got his meaning. But
he finished the word to make sure. It took twice as long as it would
have taken in English: *"Röhm shot!"*

XI

That simple statement bore a tremendous weight of meaning for
Lanny. It enabled him to begin choosing among the variety of tales
which he had constructed for himself in the past three days and four
nights. If Ernst Röhm, Chief of Staff of the Sturmabteilung, had
been shot, it must mean that the much-talked-of "Second Revolution" had failed. And especially when the tapping continued, and
Lanny counted out, letter by letter, the words "in Stadelheim."
That was a flash of lightning on a black night; it told Lanny what
all the shooting had been about. The S.A. Chief of Staff and his
many lieutenants who had been gathered for a conference! They
must have been seized, carried from Wiessee, and shot somewhere
in the grim old prison! The quick finger tapped on, and spelled the
name of Heines, followed again by the dread word *"erschossen."*
Lanny knew that this was the police chief of Breslau, who had led
the gang which had burned the Reichstag; he was one of the most
notorious of the Nazi killers, and Hugo had named him as one of
Röhm's fellow-perverts, and a guest at the Wiessee villa.

And then the name of Strasser! Lanny put his hand on top of the little Jew's and spelled the name "Otto"; but the other wiggled away and spelled "Gr——" so Lanny understood that it was Gregor Strasser, whom he had heard getting a tongue-lashing from the Führer, and whom he and Irma had heard speaking at a *Versamm-lung* in Stuttgart. Otto Strasser was the founder of the hated "Black Front," and was an exile with a price on his head; but his elder brother Gregor had retired from politics and become director of a chemical works. Lanny had been surprised when Hugo had mentioned him as having had conferences with Röhm.

The little Jewish intellectual was having a delightful time breaking the rules and gossiping with a fellow-prisoner, telling him the meaning of the terrific events of the past three days. Even into a prison, news penetrates and is spread; and never in modern times had there been news such as this! The eager finger tapped the name of Schleicher; the one-time Chancellor, the self-styled "social general" who had tried so hard to keep Hitler out of power; who had thwarted von Papen, and then been thwarted in turn. Of late he had been dickering with the malcontents, hankering to taste the sweets of power again. "*Schleicher erschossen!*" A high officer of the Reichswehr, a leading Junker, one of the sacred ruling caste! Lanny looked at the face of the stoutish gentleman across the aisle, and understood why his eyes were wide and frightened. Could he see the little Jew's finger resting on Lanny's hand, and was he perhaps counting the taps? Or was he just horrified to be alive in such a world?

Lanny had heard enough names, and began tapping vigorously in his turn. "*Wohin gehen wir?*" The answer was: "Munich Police Prison." When he asked: "What for?" the little Jew didn't have to do any tapping. He just shrugged his shoulders and spread his two hands, the Jewish way of saying in all languages: "Who knows?"

28

Bloody Instructions

I

IN THE city jail of Munich Lanny was treated like anybody else; which was a great relief to him. He was duly "booked": his name, age, nationality, residence, and occupation—he gave the latter as *Kunstsachverständiger*, which puzzled the man at the desk, as if he didn't get many of that kind; with a four days' growth of brown beard Lanny looked more like a bandit, or felt that he did. He was, it appeared, under "protective arrest"; there was grave danger that somebody might hurt him, so the kindly Gestapo was guarding him from danger. By this device a Führer with a "legality complex" was holding a hundred thousand men and women in confinement without trial or charge. The American demanded to be allowed to notify his consul, and was told he might make that request of the "inspector"; but he wasn't told when or how he was to see that personage. Instead he was taken to be fingerprinted, and then to be photographed.

All things are relative; after a "black cell" in Stadelheim, this city jail in the Ettstrasse seemed homelike and friendly, *echt süddeutschgemütlich*. In the first place, he was put in a cell with two other men, and never had human companionship been so welcome to Lanny Budd. In the next place, the cell had a window, and while it was caked with dust, it was permitted to be open at times, and for several hours the sun came through the bars. Furthermore, Lanny's money had been credited to his account, and he could order food; for sixty pfennigs, about fifteen cents, he could have a plate of cold meat and cheese; for forty pfennigs he could have a shave by the prison barber. For half an hour in the morning while his cell was being cleaned he was permitted to walk up and down in the corridor, and for an hour at midday he was taken out into the exercise court and allowed to tramp round and round in a large circle, while from the windows of the four-story building other inmates looked down upon him. Truly a *gemütlich* place of confinement!

One of his cell-mates was the large business man who had been his fellow-passenger in the *Grüne Minna*. It turned out that he was the director of a manufacturing concern, accused of having violated some regulation regarding the payment of his employees; the real reason, he declared, was that he had discharged an incompetent and dishonest Nazi, and now they were going to force him out and put that Nazi in charge. He would stay in prison until he had made up his mind to sign certain papers which had been put before him. The other victim was a Hungarian count, who was a sort of Nazi, but not the right sort, and he, too, had made a personal enemy, in this case his mistress. Lanny was astonished to find how large a percentage of prisoners in this place were or thought they were loyal followers of the Führer. Apparently all you had to do in order to get yourself into jail was to have a quarrel with someone who had more influence than yourself, then you would be accused of any sort of offense, and you stayed because in Naziland to be accused or even suspected was worse than being convicted.

Lanny discovered that having been in a "black cell" of Stadelheim for three days and four nights had made him something of a distinguished person, a sort of Edmond Dantès, Count of Monte Cristo. His cell-mates fell upon him and plied him with questions about what he had seen and heard in those dreadful underground dungeons. Apparently they knew all about the killings; they could even tell him about the courtyard with a wall against which the shooting was done, and the hydrant for washing away the blood. Lanny could add nothing except the story of how he had lain and listened; how many drum-rolls and volleys he had heard, and about the man who had argued and protested, and Lanny's own frightful sensations. It was a relief to describe them, he found; his Anglo-Saxon reticence broke down in these close quarters, where human companionship was all that anybody had, and he must furnish his share of entertainment if he expected others to furnish it to him.

II

Newspapers had been forbidden in the prison during this crisis; but you could get all sorts of things if you had the price, and the Hungarian had managed to secure the *Münchner Zeitung* of Monday. He permitted Lanny to have a look at it, standing against the wall alongside the door, so as to be out of sight of any warder who might happen to peer through the square opening in the door; if he started to unlock the door Lanny would hear him and slip the paper under the mattress or stuff it into his trousers. Under these romantic circumstances he read the flaming headlines of a radio talk in which his friend Joseph Goebbels had told the German people the story of that dreadful Saturday of blood and terror. Juppchen had been traveling about the Rheinland with the Führer, dutifully inspecting labor-camps, and he now went into details, in that spirit of melodrama combined with religious adoration which it was his job to instill into the German people. Said crooked little Juppchen:

"I still see the picture of our Führer standing at midnight on Friday evening on the terrace of the Rhein Hotel in Godesberg and in the open square a band of the Western German Labor Service playing. The Führer looks seriously and meditatively into the dark sky that has followed a refreshing thunderstorm. With raised hand he returns the enthusiastic greetings of the people of the Rheinland . . . In this hour he is more than ever admired by us. Not a quiver in his face reveals the slightest sign of what is going on within him. Yet we few people who stand by him in all difficult hours know how deeply he is grieved and also how determined to deal mercilessly in stamping out the reactionary rebels who are trying to plunge the country into chaos, and breaking their oath of loyalty to him under the slogan of carrying out a 'Second Revolution.' "

Dispatches come from Berlin and Munich which convince the Führer that it is necessary to act instantly; he telephones orders for the putting down of the rebels, and so: "Half an hour later a heavy tri-motored Junkers plane leaves the aviation field near Bonn and disappears into the foggy night. The clock has just struck two. The Führer sits silently in the front seat of the cabin and gazes fixedly into the great expanse of darkness."

Arriving in Munich at four in the morning they find that the traitorous leaders have already been apprehended. "In two brisk sentences of indignation and contempt Herr Hitler throws their whole shame into their fearful and perplexed faces. He then steps to one of them and rips the insignia of rank from his uniform. A very hard but deserved fate awaits them in the afternoon."

The center of the conspiracy is known to be in the mountains, and so a troop of loyal S.S. men have been assembled, and, narrates Dr. Juppchen, "at a terrific rate the trip to Wiessee is begun." He gives a thrilling account of the wild night ride, by which, at six in the morning "without any resistance we are able to enter the house and surprise the conspirators, who are still sleeping, and we arouse them immediately. The Führer himself makes the arrest with a courage that has no equal . . . I may be spared a description of the disgusting scene that lay before us. A simple S.S. man, with an air of indignation, expresses our thoughts, saying: 'I only wish that the walls would fall down now, so that the whole German people could be a witness to this act.'"

The radio orator went on to tell what had been happening in Berlin. "Our party comrade, General Göring, has not hesitated. With a firm hand he has cleared up a nest of reactionaries and their incorrigible supporters. He has taken steps that were hard but necessary in order to save the country from immeasurable disaster."

There followed two newspaper columns of denunciation in which the Reichsminister of Popular Enlightenment and Propaganda used many adjectives to praise the nobility and heroism of his Führer, "who has again shown in this critical situation that he is a Real Man." A quite different set of adjectives was required for the "small clique of professional saboteurs," the "boils, seats of corruption, the symptoms of disease and moral deterioration that show themselves in public life," and that now have been "burned out to the flesh."

"The Reich is there," concluded Juppchen, "and above all our Führer."

III

Such was the story told to the German people. Lanny noticed the curious fact that not once did the little dwarf name one of the victims of the purge; he didn't even say directly that anybody had been killed! As a specimen of popular fiction there was something to be said for his effusion, but as history it wouldn't rank high. Lanny could nail one falsehood, for he knew that Hugo Behr had been shot at a few minutes after nine on Friday evening, which was at least three hours before the Führer had given his orders, according to the Goebbels account. The jail buzzed with stories of other persons who had been killed or arrested before midnight; in fact some had been brought to this very place. Evidently somebody had given the fatal order while the Führer was still inspecting labor camps.

It was well known that Göring had flown to the Rheinland with his master, and had then flown back to Berlin. Hermann was the killer, the man of action, who took the "steps that were hard but necessary," while Adi was still hesitating and arguing, screaming at his followers, threatening to commit suicide if they didn't obey him, falling down on the floor and biting the carpet in a hysteria of bewilderment or rage. Lanny became clear in his mind that this was the true story of the "Blood Purge." Göring had sat at Hitler's ear in the plane and terrified him with stories of what the Gestapo had uncovered; then, from Berlin, he had given the orders, and when it was too late to reverse them he had phoned the Führer, and the latter had flown to Munich to display "a courage that has no equal," to show himself to the credulous German people as "a Real Man."

The official statement was that not more than fifty persons had been killed in the three days and nights of terror; but the gossip in the Ettstrasse was that there had been several hundred victims in Munich alone, and it turned out that the total in Germany was close to twelve hundred. This and other official falsehoods were freely discussed, and the jail buzzed like a beehive. Human curiosity broke down the barriers between jailers and jailed; they whispered news to one another, and an item once put into circulation was borne by busy tongues to every corner of the institution. In the corridors you were supposed to walk alone and not to talk; but every time you passed other prisoners you whispered something, and if it was a tidbit you might share it with one of the keepers. Down in the exercise court the inmates were supposed to walk in silence, but the man behind you mouthed the news and you passed it on to the man in front of you.

And when you were in your cell, there were sounds of tapping; tapping on wood, on stone, and on metal; tapping by day and most of the night; quick tapping for the experts and slow tapping for the new arrivals. In the cell directly under Lanny was a certain Herr Doktor Obermeier, a former Ministerialdirektor of the Bavarian state, well known to Herr Klaussen. He shared the same water-pipes as those above him, and was a tireless tapper. Lanny learned the code, and heard the story of Herr Doktor Willi Schmitt, music critic of the *Neueste Nachrichten* and chairman of the Beethoven-Vereinigung; the most amiable of persons, so Herr Klaussen declared, with body, mind, and soul made wholly of music. Lanny had read his review of the *Eroica* performance, and other articles from his pen. The S.S. men came for him, and when he learned that they thought he was Gruppenführer Willi Schmitt, a quite different man, he was amused, and told his wife and children not to worry. He went with the Nazis, but did not return; and when his frantic wife persisted in her clamors she received from Police Headquarters a death certificate signed by the Bürgermeister of the town of Dachau; there had been "a very regrettable mistake," and they would see that it did not happen again.

Story after story, the most sensational, the most horrible! Truly, it was something fabulous, Byzantine! Ex-Chancellor Franz von Papen, still a member of the Cabinet, had been attacked in his office and had some of his teeth knocked out; now he was under "house arrest," his life threatened, and the aged von Hindenburg, sick and near to death, trying to save his "dear comrade." Edgar Jung, Papen's

friend who had written his offending speech demanding freedom
of the press, had been shot here in Munich. Gregor Strasser had
been kidnaped from his home and beaten to death by S.S. men in
Grunewald. General von Schleicher and his wife had been riddled
with bullets on the steps of their villa. Karl Ernst, leader of the
Berlin S.A., had been slugged unconscious and taken to the city.
His staff leader had decided that Göring had gone crazy, and had
flown to Munich to appeal to Hitler about it. He had been taken
back to Berlin and shot with seven of his adjutants. At Lichterfelde,
in the courtyard of the old military cadet school, tribunals under
the direction of Göring were still holding "trials" averaging seven
minutes each; the victims were stood against a wall and shot while
crying: *"Heil Hitler!"*

IV

About half the warders in this jail were men of the old regime and
the other half S.A. men, and there was much jealousy between them.
The latter group had no way of knowing when the lightning might
strike them, so for the first time they had a fellow-feeling for their
prisoners. If one of the latter had a visitor and got some fresh information, everybody wanted to share it, and a warder would find
a pretext to come to the cell and hear what he had to report. Really,
the old Munich police prison became a delightfully sociable and
exciting place! Lanny decided that he wouldn't have missed it for
anything. His own fears had diminished; he decided that when the
storm blew over, somebody in authority would have time to hear
his statement and realize that a blunder had been made. Possibly his
three captors had put Hugo's money into their own pockets, and
if so, there was no evidence against Lanny himself. He had only to
crouch in his "better 'ole"—and meantime learn about human and
especially Nazi nature.

The population of the jail was in part common criminals—thieves,
burglars, and sex offenders—while the other part comprised political
suspects, or those who had got in the way of some powerful official.
A curious situation, in which one prisoner might be a blackmailer
and another the victim of a blackmailer—both in the same jail and

supposedly under the same law! One man guilty of killing, another guilty of refusing to kill, or of protesting against killing! Lanny could have compiled a whole *dossier* of such antinomies. But he didn't dare to make notes, and was careful not to say anything that would give offense to anybody. The place was bound to be full of spies, and while the men in his own cell appeared to be genuine, either or both might have been selected because they appeared to be that.

The Hungarian count was a gay companion, and told diverting stories of his *liaisons;* he had a passion for playing the game of Halma, and Lanny learned it in order to oblige him. The business man, Herr Klaussen, told stories illustrating the impossibility of conducting any honest business under present conditions; then he would say: "Do you have things thus in America?" Lanny would reply: "My father complains a great deal about politicians." He would tell some of Robbie's stories, feeling certain that these wouldn't do him any harm in Germany.

Incidentally Herr Klaussen expressed the conviction that the talk about a plot against Hitler was all *Quatsch;* there had been nothing but protest and discussion. Also, the talk about the Führer's being shocked by what he had discovered in the villa at Wiessee was *Dummheit*, because everybody in Germany had known about Röhm and his boys, and the Führer had laughed about it. This worthy *Bürger* of Munich cherished a hearty dislike of those whom he called *die Preiss'n*—the Prussians—regarding them as invaders and source of all corruptions. These, of course, were frightfully dangerous utterances, and this was either a bold man or a foolish one. Lanny said: "I have no basis to form an opinion, and in view of my position I'd rather not try." He went back to playing Halma with the Hungarian, and collecting anecdotes and local color which Eric Vivian Pomeroy-Nielson might some day use in a play.

V

Lanny had spent three days as a guest of the state of Bavaria, and now he spent ten as a guest of the city of Munich. Then, just at the end of one day, a friendly warder came and said: "*Bitte, kommen Sie, Herr Budd.*"

It would do no good to ask questions, for the warders didn't know. When you left a cell, you said *Adé*, having no way to tell if you would come back. Some went to freedom, others to be beaten insensible, others to Dachau or some other camp. Lanny was led downstairs to an office where he found two young S.S. men, dapper and correct, awaiting him. He was pleased to observe that they were not the same who had arrested him. They came up, and almost before he realized what was happening, one had taken his wrist and snapped a handcuff onto it. The other cuff was on the young Nazi's wrist, and Lanny knew it was useless to offer objections. They led him out to a courtyard, where he saw his own car, with another uniformed S.S. man in the driver's seat. The rear door was opened. "*Bitte einsteigen.*"

"May I ask where I'm being taken?" he ventured.

"It is not permitted to talk," was the reply. He got in, and the car rolled out into the tree-lined avenue, and into the city of Munich. They drove straight through, and down the valley of the Isar, northeastward.

On a dark night the landscape becomes a mystery; the car lights illumine a far-stretching road, but it is possible to imagine any sort of thing to the right and left. Unless you are doing the driving, you will even become uncertain whether the car is going uphill or down. But there were the stars in their appointed places, and so Lanny could know they were headed north. Having driven over this route, he knew the signposts; and when it was Regensburg and they were still speeding rapidly, he made a guess that he was being taken to Berlin.

"There's where I get my examination," he thought. He would have one more night to do his thinking, and then he would confront that colossal power known as the Geheime Staats-Polizei, more dark than any night, more to be dreaded than anything that night contained.

The prisoner had had plenty of sleep in the jail, so he used this time to choose his *Ausrede*, his "alibi." But the more he tried, the worse his confusion became. They were bound to have found out that he had drawn thirty thousand marks from the Hellstein bank in Munich; they were bound to know that he had paid most of it to Hugo; they were bound to know that some sort of effort had been made to take Freddi out of Dachau. All these spelled guilt on Lanny's part; and the only course that seemed to hold hope was to be frank and naïve; to laugh and say: "Well, General Göring charged Johannes Robin his whole fortune to get out, and used me as his agent, so naturally I thought that was the way it was done. When Hugo offered to do it for only twenty-eight thousand marks, I thought I had a bargain."

In the early dawn, when nobody was about except the milkman and the machine-gun detachments of the Berlin police, Lanny's car swept into the city, and in a workingclass quarter which he took to be Moabit, drew up in front of a large brick building. He hadn't been able to see the street signs, and nobody took the trouble to inform him. Was it the dreaded Nazi barracks in Hedemannstrasse, about which the refugees talked with shudders? Was it the notorious Columbus-Haus? Or perhaps the headquarters of the Feldpolizei, the most feared group of all?

"*Bitte aussteigen,*" said the leader. They had been perfectly polite, but hadn't spoken one unnecessary word, either to him or to one another. They were machines; and if somewhere inside them was a soul, they would have been deeply ashamed of it. They were trying to get into the Reichswehr, and this was the way.

They went into the building. Once more they did not stop to "book" the prisoner, but marched him with military steps along a corridor, and then down a flight of stone stairs into a cellar. This time Lanny couldn't be mistaken; there was a smell of blood, and there were cries somewhere in the distance. Once more he ventured a demand as to what he was being held for, what was to be done to him? This time the young leader condescended to reply: "*Sie sind ein Schutzhäftling.*"

They were telling him that he was one of those hundred thousand persons, Germans and foreigners, who were being held for their own good, to keep harm from being done to them. "*Aber,*" insisted

Lanny, with his best society manner, "I haven't asked to be a *Schutzhäftling*—I'm perfectly willing to take my chances outside."

If any of them had a sense of humor, this was not the place to show it. There was a row of steel doors, and one was opened. For the first time since these men had confronted Lanny in the Munich jail the handcuff was taken from his wrist, and he was pushed into a "black cell" and heard the door clang behind him.

VI

The same story as at Stadelheim; only it was more serious now, because that had been an accident, whereas this was deliberate, this was after two weeks of investigation. Impossible to doubt that his plight was as serious as could be. Fear took complete possession of him, and turned his bones to some sort of pulp. Putting his ear to the opening in the door, he could have no doubt that he heard screaming and crying; putting his nose to the opening, he made sure that he smelled that odor which he had heretofore associated with slaughter-houses. He was in one of those dreadful places about which he had been reading and hearing, where the Nazis systematically broke the bodies and souls of men—yes, and of women, too. In the *Brown Book* he had seen a photograph of the naked rear of an elderly stout woman, a city councilor of the Social-Democratic party, from her shoulders to her knees one mass of stripes from a scientific beating.

They weren't going to trouble to question him, or give him any chance to tell his story. They were taking it for granted that he would lie, and so they would punish him first, and then he would be more apt to tell the truth. Or were they just meaning to frighten him? To put him where he could hear the sounds and smell the smells, and see if that would "soften him up"? It had that effect; he decided that it would be futile to try to conceal anything, to tell a single lie. He saw his whole past lying like an open book before some *Kriminalkommissar*, and it was a very bad past indeed from the Nazi point of view; every bit as bad as that which had brought Freddi Robin some fourteen months of torture.

Whatever it was, it was coming now. Steps in the corridor, and they stopped in front of his door; the door was opened, and there were two S.S. men. New ones—they had an unlimited supply, and all with the same set faces, all with the same code of *Blut und Eisen.* Black shirts, black trousers, shiny black boots, and in their belts an automatic and a hard rubber truncheon—an unlimited supply of these, also, it appeared.

They took him by the arms and led him down the corridor. Their whole manner, the whole atmosphere, told him that his time had come. No use to resist; at least not physically; they would drag him, and would make his punishment worse. He was conscious of a sudden surge of anger; he loathed these subhuman creatures, and still more he loathed the hellish system which had made them. He would walk straight, in spite of his trembling knees; he would hold himself erect, and not give them the satisfaction of seeing him weaken. He dug his nails into the palms of his hands, he gritted his teeth, and walked to whatever was beyond that door at the end of the corridor.

VII

The sounds had died away as Lanny came nearer, and when the door was opened he heard only low moans. Two men were in the act of leading a beaten man through a doorway at the far side of the room. In the semi-darkness he saw only the dim forms, and saw one thrown into the room beyond. Apparently there were many people there, victims of the torturing; moans and cries came as from a section of Dante's inferno; the sounds made a sort of *basso continuo* to all the infernal events which Lanny witnessed in that chamber of horrors.

A room about fifteen feet square, with a concrete floor and walls of stone; no windows, and no light except half a dozen candles; only one article of furniture, a heavy wooden bench about eight feet long and two feet broad, in the middle of the room. From end to end the bench was smeared and dripping with blood, and there was blood all over the floor, and a stench of dried blood, most sickening. Also there was the pungent odor of human sweat, strong, am-

moniacal; there were four Nazis standing near the bench, stripped
to the waist, and evidently they had been working hard and fast,
for their smooth bodies shone with sweat and grease, even in the
feeble light. Several other Nazis stood by, and one man in civilian
clothes, wearing spectacles.

Lanny had read all about this; every anti-Nazi had learned it by
heart during the past year and a half. He took it in at a glance,
even to the flexible thin steel rods with handles, made for the purpose of inflicting as much pain as possible and doing as little permanent damage. If you did too much damage you lost the pleasure
of inflicting more pain—and also you might lose important evidence.
Lanny had read about it, heard about it, brooded over it, wondered
how he would take it—and now here it was, here he was going to
find out.

What happened was that a wave of fury swept over him; rage at
these scientifically-trained devils, drowning out all other emotion
whatsoever. He hated them so that he lost all thought about himself, he forgot all fear and the possibility of pain. They wanted to
break him; all right, he would show them that he was as strong
as they; he would deny them the pleasure of seeing him weaken,
of hearing him cry out. He had read that the American Indians had
made it a matter of pride never to groan under torture. All right,
what an American Indian could do, any American could do; it was
something in the climate, in the soil. Lanny's father had hammered
that pride into him in boyhood, and Bub Smith and Jerry had
helped. Lanny resolved that the Nazis could kill him, but they
wouldn't get one word out of him, not one sound. Neither now nor
later. Go to hell, and stay there!

It was hot in this underground hole, and perhaps that was why
the sweat gathered on Lanny's forehead and ran down into his eyes.
But he didn't wipe it away; that might be taken for a gesture of
fright or agitation; he preferred to stand rigid, like a soldier, as he
had seen the Nazis do. He realized now what they meant. All right,
he would learn their technique; he would become a fanatic, as they.
Not a muscle must move; his face must be hard, turned to stone
with defiance. It could be done. He had told himself all his life

that he was soft; he had been dissatisfied with himself in a hundred ways. Here was where he would reform himself.

He was expecting to be told to strip, and he was ready to do it. His muscles were aching to begin. But no, apparently they knew that; their science had discovered this very reaction, and knew a subtler form of torture. They would keep him waiting a while, until his mood of rage had worn off; until his imagination had had a chance to work on his nerves; until energy of the soul, or whatever it was, had spent itself. The two men who led him by the arms took him to one side of the room, against the wall, and there they stood, one on each side of him, two statues, and he a third.

VIII

The door was opened again, and another trio entered; two S.S. men, leading an elderly civilian, rather stout, plump, with gray mustaches, a gray imperial neatly trimmed; a Jew by his features, a business man by his clothes—and suddenly Lanny gave a start, in spite of all his resolutions. He had talked to that man, and had joked about him, the rather comical resemblance of his hirsute adornments to those of an eminent and much-portrayed citizen of France, the Emperor Napoleon the Third. Before Lanny's eyes loomed the resplendent drawing-room of Johannes Robin's Berlin palace, with Beauty and Irma doing the honors so graciously, and this genial old gentleman chatting, correct in his white tie and tails, diamond shirt-studs no longer in fashion in America, and a tiny square of red ribbon in his buttonhole—some order that Lanny didn't recognize. But he was sure about the man—Solomon Hellstein, the banker.

Such a different man now: tears in his eyes and terror in his face; weeping, pleading, cowering, having to be half dragged. "I didn't do it, I tell you! I know nothing about it! My God, my God, I would tell you if I could! Pity! Have pity!"

They dragged him to the bench. They pulled his clothes off, since he was incapable of doing it himself. Still pleading, still protesting, screaming, begging for mercy, he was told to lie down on the bench. His failure to obey annoyed them and they threw him down on his belly, with his bare back and buttocks and thighs looming rather grotesque, his flabby white arms hanging down to the floor. The four shirtless Nazis took their places, two on each side, and the officer in command raised his hand in signal.

The thin steel rods whistled as they came down through the air; they made four clean cuts across the naked body, followed by four quick spurts of blood. The old man started up with a frightful scream of pain. They grabbed him and threw him down, and the officer cried: "Lie still, *Juden-Schwein!* For that you get ten more blows!"

The poor victim lay shuddering and moaning, and Lanny, tense and sick with horror, waited for the next strokes. He imagined the mental anguish of the victim because they did not fall at once. The officer waited, and finally demanded: "You like that?"

"*Nein, nein! Um Himmel's Willen!*"

"Then tell us who took that gold out!"

"I have said a thousand times—if I knew, I would tell you. What more can I say? Have mercy on me! I am a helpless old man!"

The leader raised his hand again, and the four rods whistled and fell as one. The man shuddered; each time the anguish shook him, he shrieked like a madman. He knew nothing about it, he would tell anything he knew, it had been done by somebody who had told him nothing. His tones grew more piercing; then gradually they began to die, they became a confused babble, the raving of a man in delirium. His words tripped over one another, his sobs choked his cries.

Of the four beaters, the one who was working on the victim's shoulders apparently held the post of honor, and it was his duty to keep count. Each time he struck he called aloud, and when he said "*Zehn*" they all stopped. Forty strokes had been ordered, and the leader signed to the civilian in spectacles, who proved to be a doctor; the high scientific function of this disciple of Hippocrates was to make sure how much the victim could stand. He put a stethoscope to the raw flesh of the old Jew's back, and listened. Then he nodded and said: "*Noch eins.*"

The leader was in the act of moving his finger to give the signal when there came an interruption to the proceedings; a voice speaking loud and clear: "You dirty dogs!" It rushed on: "*Ihr dreckigen Schweinehunde, Ihr seid eine Schandfleck der Menschheit!*"

For a moment everybody in the room seemed to be paralyzed. It was utterly unprecedented, unprovided for in any military regulations. But not for long. The officer shouted: "*'Rrraus mit ihm!*" and the two statues besides Lanny came suddenly to life and led him away. But not until he had repeated loudly and clearly: "I say that you dishonor the form of men!"

IX

Back in his cell, Lanny thought: "Now I've cooked my goose!" He thought: "They'll invent something special for me." He discovered that his frenzy, his inspiration, whatever it was, had passed quickly; in darkness and silence he realized that he had done something very foolish, something that could do no good to the poor old banker and could do great harm to himself. But there was no undoing it, and no good lamenting, no good letting his bones turn to pulp again. He had to get back that mood of rage and determination, and learn to hold it, no matter what might come. It was a psychological exercise, a highly difficult one. Sometimes he thought he was succeeding, but then he would hear with his mind's ears the whistle of those terrible steel rods, and he would find that a disgraceful trembling seized him.

Waiting was the worst of all; he actually thought he would feel relief when his cell door was opened. But when he heard the steps coming, he found that he was frightened again, and had to start work all over. He must not let them think that they could cow an American. He clenched his hands tightly, set his teeth, and looked out into the corridor. There in the dim light was the S.S. man to whom he had been handcuffed for a whole night—and behind that man, looking over his shoulder, the deeply concerned face of Oberleutnant Furtwaengler!

"Well, well, Herr Budd!" said the young staff officer. "What have they been doing to you?"

Lanny had to change his mood with lightning speed. He was busily hating all the Nazis; but he didn't hate this naïve and worshipful young social climber. "Herr Oberleutnant!" he exclaimed, with relief that was like a prayer.

"Come out," said the other, and looked his friend over as if to see if he showed any signs of damage. "What have they done to you?"

"They have made me rather uncomfortable," replied the prisoner, resuming the Anglo-Saxon manner.

"It is most unfortunate!" exclaimed the officer. "Seine Exzellenz will be distressed."

"So was I," admitted the prisoner.

"Why did you not let us know?"

"I did my best to let somebody know; but I was not successful."

"This is a disgraceful incident!" exclaimed the other, turning to the S.S. man. "Some one will be severely disciplined."

"*Zu Befehl, Herr Oberleutnant!*" replied the man. It conveyed the impression: "Tell me to shoot myself and I am ready."

"Really, Herr Budd, I don't know how to apologize."

"Your presence is apology enough, Herr Oberleutnant. You are, as we say in America, a sight for sore eyes."

"I am sorry indeed if your eyes are sore," declared the staff officer, gravely.

It was like waking up suddenly from a nightmare, and discovering that all those dreadful things had never happened. Lanny followed his friend up the narrow stone stairway, and discovered that there were no more formalities required for his release than had been required for his arrest. Doubtless the officer's uniform bore insignia which gave him authority. He said: "I assume responsibility for this gentleman," and the S.S. man repeated: "At command, Herr Oberleutnant."

They went out to the official car which was waiting. Rain was falling, but never had a day seemed more lovely. Lanny had to shut his eyes from the light, but he managed to get inside unassisted. Sinking back in the soft seat he had to struggle to make up his mind which was real—these cushions or that dungeon! Surely both couldn't exist in the same city, in the same world!

29

Too Deep for Tears

I

LANNY was living in a kaleidoscope; one of those tubes you look into and observe a pattern, and then you give it a slight jar, and the pattern is gone, and there is an utterly different one. He was prepared for anything, literally anything. But when he heard his friend give the order: "Seine Exzellenz's residence," he came to with a start, and became what he had been all his life, a member of the *beau monde*, to whom the proprieties were instinctive and inescapable. "Surely," he protested, "you're not taking me to Seine Exzellenz in this condition! Look at my clothes! And my beard!" Lanny ran his hand over it, wondering again if it was gray.

"Where are your clothes, Herr Budd?"

"When last heard from they were in a hotel in Munich."

"A most preposterous affair! I will telephone for them this morning."

"And my money?" added the other. "That was taken from me in Stadelheim. But if you will drive me to the Adlon, I am sure they will cash my check."

The orders were changed, and the young staff officer entered with amusement into the enterprise of making his friend presentable by the magic of modern hotel service. While the guest bathed himself, a valet whisked his clothes away to sponge and press them, and a bellboy sped to the nearest haberdashers for a shirt, tie, and hand-kerchief. A barber came and shaved him—and collected no gray hairs. In half an hour by the Oberleutnant's watch—Lanny had none—he was again the picture of a young man of fashion, ready to meet all the world and his wife.

It was truly comical, when they were motored to the official residence of the Minister-Präsident of Prussia and escorted up to his private apartments. This mighty personage had all the sartorial appurtenances of his office: blue trousers with a broad white stripe; a coat of lighter blue with a white belt and broad white sash from one shoulder crossing his chest; numerous gold cords and stars, epaulets and insignia of his rank—but it was a blazing hot day in mid-July, and all this honorificabilitudinitatibus had become intolerable to a fat man. He had it hung on a chair near-by, and was sitting at his desk in his shorts and that large amount of soft white skin with which nature had endowed him. Beads of perspiration stood out on the skin, and before Lanny's mind flashed the vision of a Jewish banker. Impossible to keep from imagining this still larger mass of flesh and fat laid out on a blood-soaked and slimy bench, bottom up!

II

It was the General's intention to take Lanny Budd's misadventure as a comic opera *divertissement* in the midst of very grave business; and it was up to Lanny to be a good sport and do the same. "*Ja aber, mein lieber Herr Budd!*" cried Seine Exzellenz, and caught Lanny's hand in a grip that showed he was by no means all fat. "*Was ist Ihnen denn passiert?*"—he insisted upon hearing all about a playboy's misadventures. "Were you afraid?" he wanted to know; and Lanny said: "Wait until your turn comes, Exzellenz, and see if you're not afraid."

That wasn't so funny. The great man replied: "You had the misfortune to get caught in the traffic at a very busy hour. We have some wild fellows in our party, and it was necessary to teach them a lesson. I think they have learned it thoroughly."

Lanny had done a bit of thinking while he was in the bathtub at the hotel. He would never trust any Nazi again. It seemed unlikely that the head of the Prussian state had no information as to what had been happening to one who claimed to be his friend; almost incredible that his efficient secret police had failed to send him any report during the past two weeks. A thousand times more likely that there had been some purpose in what had befallen an American visitor; also in this sudden change of front, this explosion of friendliness and familiarity. Last-minute rescues belong in melodramas, where they are no accidents, but have been carefully contrived. Lanny had begun to suspect this particularly hair-raising dénouement.

The Minister-Präsident of Prussia didn't keep him long in suspense. There was a large stack of papers on his desk and he was obviously a busy fat man. "*Jawohl, Herr Budd!*" he said. "You had the opportunity of studying our penal institutions at first hand; also our methods of dealing with Jew *Schieber!* You can testify that they are effective."

"I had no opportunity to observe the outcome, Exzellenz."

"I will see that you are informed about it, if you so desire. Do you have any idea who that Jew was?"

"It so happens that I had met him in Berlin society."

"Indeed? Who was he?"

"His name is Solomon Hellstein."

"*Ach!* Our *weltberühmter* Shylock! You will indeed have an interesting story to tell the outside world."

Lanny thought he saw a hint. "You will remember, Exzellenz, that you asked me to say nothing to the outside world about the case of Johannes Robin. Fourteen months have passed, and still I have not done so."

"I have made a note of the fact, Herr Budd, and appreciate your good judgment. But now there is a quite different set of circumstances. We have a saying in German: *Es hängt ganz davon ab.*"

Lanny supplied the English: "It all depends."

"*Also, Herr Budd!* Would you be greatly embarrassed if I should suggest that you narrate the story of what you saw this morning?"

"I should be somewhat puzzled, Exzellenz."

"It is a bright idea which occurs to me. Are you still interested in that *Jude Itzig* of yours?" This is a German name of jeering derived from the Hebrew word for Isaac, which is Yitzchock.

"If you mean the son of Johannes Robin, I am still deeply interested, Exzellenz."

"I have recently learned that he is in the *Lager* at Dachau. Would you like to have him turned loose?"

"*Aber natürlich, Exzellenz.*"

"*Na, also!* I offer him to you in exchange for a small service which you may render me. Go to Paris and tell the members of the Hellstein family what you have seen happening to their Berlin representative. You know them, possibly?"

"It happens that I know them rather well."

"I will explain to you: This *Dreck-Jude* has succeeded in shipping a fortune out of Germany, and we were not so fortunate as in the case of Robin, we do not know where the money is. The family is scattered all over Europe, as you know. We have no claim to their money, but we intend to have Solomon's, every mark of it— if we have to flay him alive."

"You wish me to tell them that?"

"They know it already. All you have to tell is what you saw with your own eyes. Make it as realistic as you know how."

"Am I to mention that you have asked me to tell them?"

"If you do that, they may suspect your good faith. It will be better not to refer to me. Simply tell what happened to you and what you saw."

"And then, Exzellenz?"

"Then I will release your pet Jew."

"How am I to let you know that I have done my part?"

"I have my agents, and they will report to me. The story will be all over Paris in a few hours. It will be a good thing, because our rich *Schieber* have got the idea that we dare not touch them, and they think they can bleed Germany to death."

"I get your point, Exzellenz. How will I know where I am to get Freddi Robin?"

"Leave your Paris address with Furtwaengler, and within a day

or two after you have talked with the Hellsteins he will telephone
you and arrange to ship your precious *Itzig* to the French border.
Is that according to your wishes?"

"Quite so, Exzellenz. I can see no reason why I shouldn't comply
with your request."

"*Abgemacht!* It is a deal. It has been a pleasure to meet you, Herr
Budd; and if, after you think it over, you wish to do more business
with me, come and see me at any time."

"*Danke schön, Exzellenz.* I will bear your suggestion in mind and
perhaps avail myself of the opportunity."

"*Dem mutigen ist das Glück hold!*" The fat commander had
risen from his chair to speed his parting guest, and now favored
him with a staggering slap upon the back, and a burst of merriment
which left the visitor uncertain whether he was being laughed with
or at.

III

So Lanny went out from the presence of this half-naked freebooter, and was courteously driven back to his hotel by the young
staff officer. Evidently Lanny's papers had been brought along on
the trip from Munich, for Furtwaengler put his passport and his six
thousand marks into his hands; also an exit permit. He promised to
have Lanny's clothes and other belongings forwarded to Juan. The
American didn't lay any claim to the money which had been found
on the body of Hugo Behr!

His car had been delivered to the hotel, and the Oberleutnant assured him that it had been properly serviced and supplied with a
tank full of petrol. They parted warm friends; and Lanny stayed in
Berlin only long enough to pay his hotel bill and send telegrams to
Rahel in Juan, to his father in Newcastle, to his mother and his wife
in England: "Leaving for Crillon Paris hopeful of success notify
friends all well." He dared say no more, except to ask Irma to meet
him in Paris. He knew that they must have been in an agony of
dread about him, but he wouldn't make any explanations until he
was out of Germany and had got Freddi out. There would be a

chance that an old-style Teutonic freebooter might get some additional information and change his mind. The Hellstein family in Paris might "come across," or the Gestapo in Munich might unearth the story of the attempted jailbreak.

Or had they already done so, and had the Minister-Präsident of Prussia tactfully refrained from mentioning the subject? No chance to fathom the mind of that master of intrigue, that wholesale killer of men! At some time in the course of the past two weeks of madness and murder he had found time to take note that he had an American playboy in his clutches, and to figure out a way to make use of him. Lanny shook with horror every time he recalled those minutes in the torture-chamber; nor was the experience a particle less dreadful because he now perceived that it had been a piece of stageplay, designed to get his help in extorting some millions of marks, possibly some scores of millions of marks, from a family of Jewish bankers.

IV

Lanny didn't feel very much like driving, but he didn't want to leave his car to the Nazis, so he stuck it out, and drove steadily, with a mind full of horrors, not much relieved by hope. The Nazi General, who had cheated him several times, might do it again; and anyhow, Lanny had come to a state of mind where he wasn't satisfied to get one Jewish friend out of the clutches of the terror. He wanted to save all the Jews; he wanted to wake up Europe to the meaning of this moral insanity which had broken out in its midst. The *gemütliche* German *Volk* had fallen into the hands of gangsters, the most terrible in all history because they were armed with modern science. Lanny echoed the feelings of the "simple S.A. man" of whom Goebbels had told, who had wanted the walls of Röhm's bedroom to fall down, so that the German people might see. Lanny wanted the walls of that torture chamber to fall down, so that all the world might see.

He crossed the border into Belgium in the small hours of the morning and went to a hotel and had a sleep, full of tormenting dreams. But when he awakened and had some breakfast, he felt better, and went to the telephone. There was one person he simply couldn't wait to hear from, and that was Jerry Pendleton in Cannes —if he *was* in Cannes. Lanny's guess proved correct, and his friend's voice was the most welcome of sounds.

"I am in Belgium," said the younger man. "I'm all right, and I just want a few questions answered—with no names."

"O.K.," sang Jerry.

"Did you see our friend that evening?"

"I saw him brought out; but nobody came for him."

"What happened then?"

"I suppose he was taken back; I had no way to make sure. There was nothing I could do about it. I was tempted to try, but I didn't see how I could get away without a car."

"I was afraid you might have tried. It's all right. I have a promise and have some hopes."

"I was worried to death about you. I went to the American authority and reported your absence. I went again and again, and I think he did everything he could, but he was put off with evasions."

"It was serious, but it's all right now. What did you do then?"

"I couldn't think of anything to do for you, so I came out to report to the family. They told me to come home and wait for orders, and I did that. Gee, kid, but I'm glad to hear your voice! Are you sure you're all right?"

"Not a scratch on me. I'm leaving for Paris."

"I just had a wire from your wife; she's on the way to meet you at the Crillon. She's been scared half out of her wits. There's been a lot in the papers, you know."

"Thanks, old sport, for what you did."

"I didn't do a damn thing. I never felt so helpless."

"It's quite possible you saved me. Anyhow, you've got an interesting story coming to you. So long!"

V

The traveler reached Paris about sunset, and surprised Irma in the suite she had taken. She looked at him as if he were a ghost; she seemed afraid to touch him, and stood staring, as if expecting to find him scarred or maimed. He said: "I'm all here, darling," and took her in his arms.

She burst into tears. "Oh, Lanny, I've been living in hell for two weeks!" When he started to kiss her, she held off, gazing at him with the most intense look he had ever seen on her usually calm face. "Lanny, promise me—you *must* promise me—you will never put me through a thing like this again!"

That was the way it was between them; their argument was resumed even before their love. It was going to be that way from now on. He didn't want to make any promises; he didn't want to talk about that aspect of the matter—and she didn't want to talk about anything else. For two weeks she had been imagining him dead, or even worse, being mutilated by those gangsters. She had had every right to imagine it, of course; he couldn't tell her that she had been foolish or unreasonable; in fact he couldn't answer her at all. She wanted to hear his story, yet she didn't want to hear it, or anything else, until her mind had been put at rest by a pledge from him that never, never would he go into Germany, never, never would he have anything to do with that hateful, wicked thing called the class struggle, which drove men and women to madness and crime and turned civilized life into a nightmare.

He tried his best to soothe her, and to make her happy, but it couldn't be done. She had been thinking, and had made up her mind. And he had to make up his mind quickly. For one thing, he wouldn't tell her the whole story of what happened to him in Hitlerland. That would be for men only. He would have to tell the Hellstein ladies about the torturing; but only Robbie and Rick would ever know about his deal with Göring. Rumors of that sort get twisted as they spread, and Lanny might get himself a name that would make him helpless to serve the movement he loved.

Now he said: "Control yourself, darling; I'm here, and I'm none the worse for an adventure. There's something urgent that I have to do, so excuse me if I telephone."

Her feelings were hurt, and at the same time her curiosity was aroused. She heard him call Olivie Hellstein, Madame de Broussailles, and tell her that he had just come out of Germany, and had seen her Uncle Solomon, and had some grave news for her; he thought her mother and father also ought to hear it. Olivie agreed to cancel a dinner engagement, and he was to come to her home in the evening.

He didn't want to take Irma, and had a hard time not offending her. What was the use of subjecting her to an ordeal, the witnessing of a tragic family scene? He had to tell them that the Nazis were cruelly beating the brother of Pierre Hellstein to get his money; and of course they would weep, and perhaps become hysterical. Jews, like most other people, love their money; also they love their relatives, and between the two the Hellstein family would suffer as if they themselves were being beaten.

Then, of course, Irma wanted to know, how had he been in position to see such things? He had a hard time evading her; he didn't want to say: "Göring had me taken there on purpose, so that I might go and tell the Hellsteins; that is the price of his letting Freddi go." In fact, there wasn't any use mentioning Freddi at all, it was clear that Irma didn't care about him, hadn't asked a single question. What she wanted to know was that she was going to have a husband without having to be driven mad with fear; she looked at Lanny now as if he were a stranger—as indeed he was, at least a part of him, a new part, hard and determined, insistent upon having its own way and not talking much about it.

"I owe Olivie Hellstein the courtesy to tell her what I know; and I think it's common humanity to try to save that poor old gentleman in Berlin if I can."

There it was! He was going on saving people! One after another —and people about whom Irma didn't especially care. He was more interested in saving Solomon Hellstein than in saving his wife's peace of mind, and their love, which also had been put in a torture chamber!

VI

The scene which took place in the very elegant and sumptuous home of Madame de Broussailles was fully as painful as Lanny had foreseen. There was that large and stately mother of Jerusalem who had once inspected him through a diamond-studded lorgnette to consider whether he was worthy to become a progenitor of the Hellstein line. There was Pierre Hellstein, father of the family, stoutish like the brother in Berlin, but younger, smarter, and with his mustaches dyed. There was Olivie, an oriental beauty now in full ripeness; she had found Lanny a romantic figure as a girl, and in her secret heart this idea still lurked. She was married to a French aristocrat, a gentile who had not thought it his duty to be present. Instead there were two brothers, busy young men of affairs, deeply concerned.

Lanny told the story of the dreadful scene he had witnessed, sparing them nothing; and they for their part spared him none of their weeping, moaning, and wringing of hands. They were the children of people who had set up a Wailing Wall in their capital city, for the public demonstration of grief; so presumably they found relief through loud expression. Lanny found that it didn't repel him; on the contrary, it seemed to be the way he himself felt; the tears started down his cheeks and he had difficulty in talking. After all, he was the brother-in-law of a Jew, and a sort of relative to a whole family, well known to the Hellsteins. He had gone into Germany to try to save a member of their race, and had risked his life in the effort, so he couldn't have had better credentials. He told them that he had expected to be the next victim laid on the whipping-bench, and had been saved only by the good luck that an officer friend had got word about his plight and had arrived in time to snatch him away. They did not find this story incredible.

Lanny didn't wait to hear their decision as to the payment of ransom to the Nazis. He guessed it might require some telephoning to other capitals, and it was none of his affair. They asked if the story he had told them was confidential, and he said not at all; he thought the public ought to know what was happening in Naziland, but he doubted if publicity would have any effect upon the extortioners. Olivie, in between outbursts of weeping, thanked him several times for coming to them; she thought he was the bravest and kindest man she had ever known—being deeply moved, she told him so. Lanny was tempted to wish she had said it in the presence of his wife, but on second thought he decided that it wouldn't really have helped. Nothing would help except for him to conduct himself like a proper man of fashion, and that seemed to be becoming more and more difficult.

VII

Lanny's duty was done, and he had time to woo his wife and try to restore her peace of mind. When she found that he was trying not to tell her his story, her curiosity became intensified; he made up a mild version, based upon his effort to buy Freddi out of Dachau, which Irma knew had been his plan. He said that he and Hugo had been arrested, and he had been confined in the very *gemütlich* city jail of Munich. He could go into details about that place and make a completely convincing story; his only trouble had been that they wouldn't let him communicate with the outside world. It was on account of the confusion of the Blood Purge; Irma said the papers in England had been full of that, and she had become convinced that she was a widow.

"You'd have made a charming one," he said; but he couldn't get a smile out of her.

"What are you waiting for now?" she wanted to know. He told her he had had a conference with Furtwaengler, and had a real hope of getting Freddi out in the next few days. He couldn't think of any way to make that sound plausible, and Irma was quite impatient, wanting to be taken to England. But no, he must stay in this hotel all day—the old business of waiting for a telephone call that didn't come! She wanted to get away from every reminder of those days and nights of misery; and this included Freddi and Rahel and all the Robin family. It made her seem rather hard; but Lanny realized that it was her class and racial feeling; she wanted to give her time and attention to those persons whom she considered important. Her mother was in England, and so was Frances; she had new stories to tell about the latter, and it was something they could talk about and keep the peace. It was almost the only subject.

There being more than one telephone at the Crillon, Lanny was able to indulge himself in the luxury of long-distance calls without a chance of delaying the all-important one from Berlin. He called his mother, who shed a lot of tears which unfortunately could not be transmitted by wire. He called Rick, and told him in guarded language what were his hopes. He called Emily Chattersworth and invited her to come in and have lunch, knowing that this would please Irma. Emily came, full of curiosity; she accepted his synthetic story, the same that he had told his wife. The episode of Solomon Hellstein was all over Paris, just as Göring had predicted; Emily had heard it, and wanted to verify it. Lanny explained how he had been under detention in Berlin, and there had got the facts about what was being done to the eldest of the half dozen banking brothers.

Also Lanny wrote a long letter to his father, telling him the real story; a shorter letter to Hansi and Bess, who had gone to South America, along with Hansi's father—the one to sell beautiful sounds and the other to sell hardware, including guns. The young Reds hadn't wanted to go, but the two fathers had combined their authority. The mere presence in Europe of two notorious Reds would be an incitement to the Nazis, and might serve to tip the scales and defeat Lanny's efforts to help Freddi. The young pair didn't like the argument, but had no answer to it.

VIII

Early in the morning, a phone call from Berlin! The cheerful voice of Oberleutnant Furtwaengler announcing: *"Gute Nachrichten, Herr Budd!* I am authorized to tell you that we are prepared to release your friend."

The man at the Paris end of the wire had a hard time preserving his steadiness of voice. "Whereabouts, Herr Oberleutnant?"

"That is for you to say."

"Where is he now?"

"In Munich."

"You would prefer some place near there?"

"My instructions are that you shall name the place."

Lanny remembered the bridge by which he had crossed the river

Rhein on his way to Munich; the place at which the child Marie Antoinette had entered France. "Would the bridge between Kehl and Strasbourg be acceptable to you?"

"Entirely so."

"I will be on that bridge whenever you wish."

"We can get there more quickly than you. So you set the time."

"Say ten o'clock tomorrow morning."

"It is a date. I won't be there personally, so this is to thank you for your many courtesies and wish you all happiness."

"My wife is in the room, and desires to send her regards to you and your wife."

"Give her my greetings and thanks. I am certain that my wife will join in these sentiments. *Adieu*." Such were the formulas; and oh, why couldn't people really live like that?

IX

"Now, dear," said Lanny to his wife, "I think we can soon go home and have a rest."

Her amazement was great, and she wanted to know, how on earth he had done it? He told her: "They were trying to find the whereabouts of some of Freddi's friends and comrades. My guess is, they've got them by now, so he's of no use to them. Also, it might be that Göring thinks he can make some use of me in future."

"Are you going to do anything for him?"

"Not if I can help it. But all that's between you and me. You must not breathe a word of it to anybody else, not even to your mother, nor to mine." It pleased her to feel that she stood first in his confidence, and she promised.

He went to the telephone and put in a call for his faithful friend in Cannes. "Jerry," he said, "I think I'm to get Freddi out, and here's another job. Call Rahel at Bienvenu and tell her to get ready; then get her, and motor her to Strasbourg. Don't delay, because I have no idea what condition Freddi will be in, and she's the one who has to handle him and make the decisions. You know the sort of people we're dealing with; and I can't give any guarantees, but I believe

Freddi will be there at ten tomorrow, and it's worthwhile for Rahel to take the chance. Get Beauty's car from Bienvenu, if you like. I advise you to come by way of the Rhone valley, Besançon and Mulhouse. Drive all night if you can stand it and let Rahel sleep in the back seat. I will be at the Hotel de la Ville-de-Paris in Strasbourg."

Lanny had another problem, a delicate one. He didn't want to take Irma on this trip, and at the same time he didn't want to hurt her feelings. "Come if you want to," he said, "but I'm telling you it may be a painful experience, and there won't be much you can do."

"Why did you ask me to Paris, Lanny, if you didn't want my help?"

"I asked you because I love you, and wanted to see you, and I thought you would want to see me. I want your help in everything that interests you, but I don't want to drag you into something that you have no heart for. I haven't seen Freddi, and I'm just guessing: he may look like an old man; he may be ill, even dying; he may be mutilated in some shocking way; he may be entirely out of his mind. It's his wife's job to take care of him and nurse him back to life; it's not your job, and I'm giving you the chance to keep out of another wearing experience."

"We'll all be in it, if they're going to live at Bienvenu."

"In the first place, Rahel may have to take him to a hospital. And anyhow, we aren't going back until fall. Hansi and Bess are making money, and so is Johannes, I have no doubt, and they'll want to have a place of their own. All that's in the future, and a lot of it depends on Freddi's condition. I suggest leaving you at Emily's until I come back. I'm having Jerry bring Rahel in a car, so he can take her wherever she wants to go, and then you and I will be free. There's a *maison de santé* here in Paris, and a surgeon who took care of Marcel when he was crippled and burned; they're still in business, and I phoned that I might be sending them a patient."

"Oh, Lanny!" she exclaimed. "How I would enjoy it if we could give just a little time to our own affairs!"

"Yes, darling," he said. "It's a grand idea, and England will seem delightful after I get this job off my hands. I'm eager to see what

Rick has done with his last act, and maybe I can give him some hints."

It wasn't until he saw Irma's *moue* that he realized what a slip he had made. Poor Lanny, he would have a hard time learning to think about himself!

X

Irma was duly deposited at the Château les Forêts, an agreeable place of sojourn in mid-July. In fifteen years the noble beech forests had done their own work of repair, and the summer breezes carried no report of the thousands of buried French and German soldiers. Since Emily had been a sort of fostermother to Irma's husband, and had had a lot to do with making the match, they had an inexhaustible subject of conversation, and the older woman tried tactfully to persuade a darling of fortune that every man has what the French call *les défauts de ses qualités*, and that there might be worse faults in a husband than excess of solicitude and generosity. She managed to make Irma a bit ashamed of her lack of appreciation of a sweet and gentle Jewish clarinetist.

Meanwhile Lanny was speeding over a fine highway, due eastward toward the river Rhein. It was in part the route over which the fleeing king and queen had driven in their heavy "berlin"; not far to the south lay Varennes, where they had been captured and driven back to Paris to have their heads cut off. Human beings suffer agonies, and their sad fates become legends; poets write verses about them and playwrights compose dramas, and the remembrance of past grief becomes a source of present pleasure—such is the strange alchemy of the spirit.

The traveler had supper on the way, and reached his destination after midnight. There was no use looking at an empty bridge, and he wasn't in the mood for cathedrals, even one of the oldest. He went to bed and slept; in the morning he had a breakfast with fruit, and a telegram from Jerry saying that they were at Besançon and coming straight on. No use going to the place of appointment ahead of time, so Lanny read the morning papers in this town which had changed hands many times, but for the present was French. He read that Adolf Hitler had called an assembly of his tame Reichstag in the Kroll Opera House, and had made them a speech of an hour and a half, telling how he had suffered in soul over having to kill so many of his old friends and supporters. When he was through, he sat with head bowed, completely overcome, while Göring told the world how Hitler was the ordained Führer who was incapable of making a mistake; to all of which they voted their unanimous assent.

With thoughts induced by this reading Lanny drove three or four miles to the Pont de Kehl, parked his car, and walked halfway across. He was ahead of time, and standing by the railings he gazed up and down that grand old river. No use getting himself into a state of excitement over his own mission; if it was going to succeed it would succeed, and if it didn't, he would go to the nearest telephone and get hold of the Oberleutnant and ask why. No use tormenting himself with fears about what he was going to see; whatever Freddi was would still be Freddi, and they would patch it up and make the best of it.

Meantime, look down into the depths of that fast-sliding water and remember, here was where the Rheinmaidens had swum and teased the dwarf Alberich. Perhaps they were still swimming; the *motif* of the Rheingold rang clear as a trumpet call in Lanny's ears. Somewhere on the heights along this stream the Lorelei had sat and combed her golden hair with a golden comb, and sung a song that had a wonderfully powerful melody, so that the boatman in the little boat had been seized with a wild woe, and didn't see the rocky reef, but kept gazing up to the heights, and so in the end the waves had swallowed boatman and boat; and that with her singing the Lorelei had done. Another of those tragic events which the alchemy of the spirit had turned into pleasure!

Every minute or two Lanny would look at his watch. They might be early; but no, that would be as bad as being late. "*Pünktlich!*" was the German word, and it was their pride. Just as the minute hand of Lanny's watch was in the act of passing the topmost mark of the dial, a large official car would approach the center line of the bridge, where a bar was stretched across, the east side of the bar being German and the west side French. If it didn't happen exactly so, it would be the watch that was wrong, and not *deutsche Zucht und Ordnung*. As a boy Lanny had heard a story from old Mr. Hackabury, the soapman, about a farmer who had ordered a new watch by mail-order catalogue, and had gone out in his field with watch and almanac, announcing: "If that sun don't get up over that hill in three minutes, she's late!"

XI

Sure enough, here came the car! A Mercédès-Benz, with a little swastika flag over the radiator-cap, and a chauffeur in S.S. uniform, including steel helmet. They came right up to the barrier and stopped, while Lanny stood on the last foot of France, with his heart in his mouth. Two S.S. men in the back seat got out and began helping a passenger, and Lanny got one glimpse after another; the glimpses added up to a gray-haired, elderly man, feeble and bowed, with hands that were deformed into claws, and that trembled and shook as if each of them separately had gone mad. Apparently he couldn't walk, for they were half-carrying him, and it wasn't certain that he could hold his head up—at any rate, it was hanging.

"*Heil Hitler!*" said one of the men, saluting. "Herr Budd?"

"*Ja*," said Lanny, in a voice that wasn't quite steady.

"*Wohin mit ihm?*" It was a problem, for you couldn't take such a package and just walk off with it. Lanny had to ask the indulgence of the French police and customs men, who let the unfortunate victim be carried into their office and laid on a seat. He couldn't sit up, and winced when he was touched. "They have kicked my kidneys loose," he murmured, without opening his eyes. Lanny ran and got his car, and the Frenchmen held up the traffic while he turned it around on the bridge. They helped to carry the sufferer and lay him on the back seat. Then, slowly, Lanny drove to the Hotel de la Ville-de-Paris, where they brought a stretcher and carried Freddi Robin to a room and laid him on a bed.

Apparently he hadn't wanted to be freed; or perhaps he didn't realize that he was free; perhaps he didn't recognize his old friend.

He didn't seem to want to talk, or even to look about him. Lanny waited until they were alone, and then started the kind of mental cure which he had seen his mother practice on the broken and burned Marcel Detaze. "You're in France, Freddi, and now everything is going to be all right."

The poor fellow's voice behaved as if it was difficult for him to frame sounds into words. "You should have sent me poison!" That was all he could think of.

"We're going to take you to a good hospital and have you fixed up in no time." A cheerful "spiel," practiced for several days.

Freddi held up his trembling claws; they waved in the air, seemingly of their own independent will. "They broke them with an iron bar," he whispered; "one by one."

"Rahel is coming, Freddi. She will be here in a few hours."

"No, no, no!" They were the loudest sounds he could make. "She must not see me." He kept that up for some time, as long as his strength lasted. He was not fit to see anybody. He wanted to go to sleep and not wake up. "Some powders!" he kept whispering.

Lanny saw that the sick man was weakening himself by trying to argue, so he said, all right. He had already called for a doctor, and when the man came he whispered the story. Here on the border they knew a great deal about the Nazis, and the doctor needed no details. He gave a sleeping powder which quieted the patient for a while. The doctor wanted to examine him, but Lanny said no, he would wait until the patient's wife had arrived to take charge. Lanny didn't reveal that he had in mind to get an ambulance and take the victim to Paris; he could see that here was a case that called for a lot of work and he wanted it done by people whom he knew and trusted. He was sure that Rahel would agree with this.

XII

A moment not soon to be forgotten when the two travelers arrived, and Freddi's wife came running into the hotel suite, an agony of suspense in her whole aspect; her face, gestures, voice. "He's here? He's alive? He's ill? Oh, God, where is he?"

"In the next room," replied Lanny. "He's asleep, and we'd better not disturb him."

"How is he?"

"He needs to be gone over by a good surgeon and patched up; but we can have it done. Keep yourself together, and don't let him see that you're afraid or shocked."

She had to set her eyes upon him right away; she had to steal into the room, and make it real to herself that after so many long months he was actually here, in France, not Germany. Lanny warned her: "Be quiet, don't lose your nerve." He went with her, and Jerry on the other side, for fear she might faint. And she nearly did so; she stood for a long while, breathing hard, staring at that gray-haired, elderly man, who, a little more than a year ago, had been young, beautiful and happy. They felt her shuddering, and when she started to sob, they led her out and softly closed the door.

To Lanny it was like living over something a second time, as happens in a dream. "Listen, Rahel," he said: "You have to do just what my mother did with Marcel. You have to make him want to live again. You have to give him hope and courage. You must never let him see the least trace of fear or suffering on your face. You must be calm and assured, and just keep telling him that you love him, and that he is going to get well."

"Does he know what you say to him?"

"I think he only half realizes where he is; and perhaps it's better so. Don't force anything on him. Just whisper love, and tell him he is needed, and must live for your sake and the child's."

The young wife sat there with her whole soul in her eyes. She had always been a serious, intellectual woman, but having her share of vigor and blooming. Now she was pale and thin; she had forgotten to eat most of the time; she had dined on grief and supped on fear. It was clear that she wanted only one thing in the world, to take this adored man and devote her life to nursing him and restoring him to health. She wouldn't rebel against her fate, as Beauty Budd, the worldling, had done; she wouldn't have to beat and drive herself to the role of Sister of Mercy. Nor would she have herself painted in that role, and exhibit herself to smart crowds; no, she would just go wherever Freddi went, try to find out what Freddi needed and give it to him, with that consecrated love which the saints feel for the Godhead.

Lanny told her what he had in mind. They would take him in an ambulance to Paris, quickly but carefully, so as not to jar him. Rahel could ride with him, and talk to him, feed him doses of courage and hope, even more necessary than physical food. Jerry and Lanny would follow, each in his own car; Jerry would stay in Paris for a while, to help her in whatever way he could. Lanny would instruct the surgeon to do everything needed, and would pay the bill. He told Jerry to go and get some sleep—his aspect showed that he needed it, for he had driven five or six hundred miles with only a few minutes' respite at intervals.

XIII

Lanny had food and wine and milk brought to the room, and persuaded Rahel to take some; she would need her strength. She should give Freddi whatever he would take—he probably had had no decent food for more than a year. Preparing her for her long ordeal, he told more of the story of Marcel, the miracle which had been wrought by love and unfailing devotion. Lanny talked as if he were Parsifal Dingle; incidentally he said: "Parsifal will come to Paris and help you, if you wish." Rahel sat weeping softly. With half her mind she took in Lanny's words, while the other half was with the broken body and soul in the next room.

Presently they heard him moaning. She dried her eyes hastily, and said. "I can never thank you. I will do my best to save Freddi so that he can thank you."

She stole into the other room, and Lanny sat alone for a long while. Tears began to steal down his cheeks, and he leaned his arms upon the table in front of him. It was a reaction from the strain he had been under for more than a year. Tears because he hadn't been able to accomplish more; because what he had done might be too late. Tears not only for his wrecked and tormented friend, not only for that unhappy family, but for all the Jews of Europe, and for their tormentors, just as much to be pitied. Tears for the unhappy people of Germany, who were being lured into such a deadly trap, and would pay for it with frightful sufferings. Tears for this unhappy continent on which he had been born and had lived most of his life. He had traveled here and there over its surface, and everywhere had seen men diligently plowing the soil and sowing dragon's teeth—from which, as in the old legend, armed men would some day spring. He had raised his feeble voice, warning and pleading; he had sacrificed time and money and happiness, but all in vain. He wept, despairing, as another man of gentleness and mercy had wept, in another time of oppression and misery, crying:

"O Jerusalem, Jerusalem, thou that killest the prophets, and stonest them which are sent unto thee, how often would I have gathered thy children together, even as a hen gathereth her chickens under her wings, and ye would not! Behold, your house is left unto you desolate."

BOOKS BY UPTON SINCLAIR

BETWEEN TWO WORLDS
WORLD'S END
EXPECT NO PEACE
YOUR MILLION DOLLARS
LITTLE STEEL
OUR LADY
THE FLIVVER KING
NO PASARAN!
THE GNOMOBILE
CO-OP: A NOVEL OF LIVING TOGETHER
WHAT GOD MEANS TO ME: AN ATTEMPT
  AT A WORKING RELIGION
I, CANDIDATE FOR GOVERNOR AND HOW
  I GOT LICKED
THE EPIC PLAN FOR CALIFORNIA
I, GOVERNOR OF CALIFORNIA
THE WAY OUT: WHAT LIES AHEAD FOR
  AMERICA
UPTON SINCLAIR PRESENTS WILLIAM FOX
AMERICAN OUTPOST: AUTOBIOGRAPHY
THE WET PARADE
ROMAN HOLIDAY
MENTAL RADIO
MOUNTAIN CITY
BOSTON
MONEY WRITES!
OIL!
THE SPOKESMAN'S SECRETARY

LETTERS TO JUDD
MAMMONART
THE GOSLINGS—A STUDY OF THE AMERI-
  CAN SCHOOLS
THE GOOSE-STEP—A STUDY OF AMERICAN
  EDUCATION
THE BOOK OF LIFE
THEY CALL ME CARPENTER
100%—THE STORY OF A PATRIOT
THE BRASS CHECK
JIMMIE HIGGINS
KING COAL, A NOVEL OF THE COLORADO
  STRIKE
THE PROFITS OF RELIGION
THE CRY FOR JUSTICE
DAMAGED GOODS
SYLVIA'S MARRIAGE
SYLVIA
LOVE'S PILGRIMAGE
THE FASTING CURE
SAMUEL, THE SEEKER
THE MONEYCHANGERS
THE METROPOLIS
THE MILLENNIUM
THE OVERMAN
THE JUNGLE
MANASSAS, A NOVEL OF THE CIVIL WAR
THE JOURNAL OF ARTHUR STIRLING

Plays

PRINCE HAGEN
THE NATUREWOMAN
THE SECOND STORY MAN
THE MACHINE
THE POT-BOILER
HELL

SINGING JAILBIRDS
BILL PORTER
OIL! (DRAMATIZATION)
DEPRESSION ISLAND
MARIE ANTOINETTE